Title: Timber

Series: Steel Archangel's MC, SAFC2 (Book 2)

Copyright 2024 R. Knight Publications LLC

Paperback Copyright 2025 R. Knight Publications LLC

Cover by: Belle Ames Designs

Original Chapter Headers & Formatting by: Whitnay Edes

Updated Ebook & Paperback Formatting by: Becky Hodges

Edited by: Franklin Beck

Contents

Dedication

To MY LOVING HUSBAND and children. Thank you for believing in me and supporting me <3

To my alpha's and the Steel Archangel's men they licked before I wrote their stories. This one's for you Pam <3

Acknowledgements

To my readers, thank you for joining me as we learn more about the men and women who make up the Steel Archangel's MC, where the men are possessive, protective alpha's who will do anything to protect their woman and partners. Women who are kickass and strong in their own way, whether they realize it or not.

To my PA, Becky Hodges, I don't know what I'd do without you! You're a lifesaver and the Goddess of PA's! I look forward to working with you for a long time <3 You are the credit for Mae's curse word, futtenfarter, and I love hearing your stories from growing up <3

To my Alpha Team, I can't thank you enough! You all have been a tremendous help when I've hit roadblocks, you've been there when I needed to bounce ideas around, character inspiration, and so much more. Thank you for your support and keeping me going <3

To my editor, formatter, and cover designer, thank you all for everything you did to help make Timber into the book that it is. I loved working with all of you <3

Reading Order & Other Works by R. Knight

Steel Archangel's MC

Thor & Dragon (SAFC1)

Timber (SAFC2)

Patch (SAFC3)

Patch & Mary: A SAMC Christmas to Remember (SAFC3.5)

Reaper (SAJC1—coming soon)

Smoke (SAFC4—TBD)

Cannon & Atlas (SAJC2—TBD)

Children of Prophecy

Hell's Lost Princess, Book 1

Book 2 (coming soon)

Shifter Royalty

Mates, Book 1
Spirits, Book
Book 3 (coming soon)

Standalones

New Beginnings
*This is in the process of being rewritten
and rebranded. The link will be coming soon*

Content & Trigger Warning

THIS BOOK IS INTENDED for a mature audience aged 18+. It contains foul language, violence (including beatings, torture and murder), adult situations, kidnapping, human trafficking, sexual assault, rape (does not go into detail), and grooming.

There is no cheating and there is a HEA. Each book can be read as a standalone, but it is best read in order as the story builds on the members and their women/partners in the Steel Archangel's MC.

Steel Archangel's MC Members

Forest Creek Chapter (SAFC)

Ryan Gilbert (Thor)—President

Reed Thomson (Phoenix)—Vice President

Nick Gilbert (Dragon)—Enforcer

Alexander 'Alex' Carter (Ryder)—Sergeant at Arms

Elijah Anderson (Tripp)—Secretary

Liam Caldwell (Timber)—Treasurer

Noah Banks (Judge)—Road Captain

Levi Wallace* (First Lady)—Unofficial 2nd Enforcer

Jaxon 'Jax' Witlock (Smoke)

Luke Morgan (Patch)

Malcolm Hart (Bones)

Michael Adams (Gunner)

Aiden Hunt (Axe)

Owen Burke (Bear)

Troy Simpson (Colt)—Prospect

Drae Black—Prospect

Alexei Petrov—Prospect

Sasha Petrov—Prospect

Ethan Mills—Prospect

Old Lady / Girlfriend

Levi Gilbert*—Old Lady to Thor & Dragon
Jane Wright—Girlfriend to Drae Black

Children

Lindsey Joy Black—Daughter to Drae Black

Steel Archangel's MC Members

Junction Creek Chapter (SAJC)

Anthony 'Tony' Leyton (Reaper)—President

Isaac Lopez (Devil)—Vice President

Kai Miller (Punisher)—Enforcer

Leon Foster (Razor)—Sergeant at Arms

Tyson Manning (Smithy)—Treasurer

Grant McGee (Beast)—Secretary

Adam Collins (Loki)—Road Captain

Cole Thornton (Python)

Hunter Beck (Doc)

Ragnar Miller (Odin)

Duncan Goodwin (Atlas)

Theodore 'Theo' Harris (Cannon)

Drake Olsen—Prospect

Nathan Flynn—Prospect

Old Lady

Astrid Miller—Old Lady to Odin

Steel Archangel's MC Series Song Inspiration

Man of Steel by Brantley Gilbert
Tough Town by Brantley Gilbert
Who Hurt You by David Morris
Warriors by Imagine Dragons
Simple Man by Lynyrd Skynyrd
Ride the Wind by Poison
Miracle by Shinedown
Monsters by Shinedown

Timber Song Inspiration

I Cross My Heart by George Strait

Another One Bites the Dust by Queen

45 by Shinedown

Cut the Cord by Shinedown

Get Up by Shinedown

Born to Be Wild by Steppenwolf

Your Guardian Angel by The Red Jumpsuit Apparatus

Get Out Alive by Three Days Grace

Painkiller by Three Days Grace

The Keeper Of The Stars by Tracy Byrd

Synopsis

Mae

MY LIFE IS NOT all roses and sunshine. An abusive deadbeat of a stepfather has made my life a living hell since I was eight. At fifteen, I started taking care of myself. My stepfather keeps my mom so strung out on drugs so that she won't fight him on anything.

Everything I thought I knew about my family is in question after I discover secrets that rock me to my core.

The name I've gone by my entire life is not my real name. In fact, I'm not even supposed to be alive.

Just when I find out that my birth father has been tricked into thinking I'm dead, my stepfather decides I'm the perfect currency to pay off his drug dealer. I only have one choice.

Run.

While I know it's a risk, my only chance at protection is finding my dad and the motorcycle club that has become his family.

Just when I think things might be going my way, fate seems to think my life isn't hard enough. The curve ball I'm thrown is a huge one. One I don't know if I'll ever be able to overcome.

Timber

I never thought I'd find a woman I'd want to settle down with. Until she showed up. My Sunshine Goddess. Finding out what her "family" has put her through has me wanting to go hunting. But first, I have to help my woman get over a different hurdle.

Convincing her father that the information he's been given about Mae is all a lie.

Even with her father's stubbornness causing issues, Mae has discovered a found family and brothers from two different clubs.

Danger lurks around every corner. Her stepfather is hellbent on getting her back in his clutches, no matter what. Through hell or high water, I'll fight for my woman, because there's no way I'll be able to survive without her. My Sunshine Goddess.

Chapter 1
Mae

I PULL MY MOM's rusty old beater to a stop outside our trailer and groan. Even with the engine still running, I can hear my mom and stepdad, Preston, yelling from inside. I can't even turn on the radio to drown them out until they're done. That old thing died years ago. Also, there's no sense in buying a new radio when it'd probably be stolen within a week, since I can't even lock the car doors anymore. The thing has more rust on it than metal these days. Besides, I have better uses for my money.

Louder yelling draws my gaze back to our trailer. Knowing them, they're arguing about money, drugs, booze, food, or me. And it's usually in that order. A glance at the clock shows it's just before midnight. If they keep up their yelling, the neighbors are going to call the cops.

Again.

With a grunt, I heave the car door open, grab my backpack, and carefully shut the door. It's not that I'm trying to be quiet. It's worrying that one of these days, the rusty old hinge is going to break and then I won't have a usable driver side door. If that happens, the door will have to be secured permanently in place, which means I'd have to pull a *Dukes of Hazzard* stunt to get in. Or use the passenger door and crawl over the console to get into the driver's seat.

Slipping the strap of my backpack over my shoulder, I try to ignore the rundown state of our home, but it's hard, and I can't help but pause as I take in what used to be a nice home for Mom and me.

Preston's oldest piece of junk car rests on blocks under a tree that's half dead. He says he's going to restore it someday, but it's really not worth it. That car has more rust on it than Mom's car does. His other car, an old *Bronco* that barely runs, is parked in front of it.

A shed sits at the back of our property and I'm surprised it hasn't collapsed in on itself since almost all the boards are rotten. The grass is almost knee high again, but I always save that chore for when I know Preston will be gone at work. Unfortunately, he's barely left the trailer the last couple of months, so I don't even know if he has a job anymore. If I were to mow the yard tomorrow when he's home, I'd probably earn a beating for causing a ruckus and interrupting his TV shows.

Our trailer is covered in so much grime and dirt that you can barely tell the siding used to be white and the shutters blue. My chest tightens when my gaze roams over the spots near the siding trim where Mom and I used to paint our handprints every year on my birthday. They're no longer visible, but I know they're still there under all that dirt.

That tradition unfortunately stopped when Preston saw us painting our hands on my tenth birthday. We had just placed that year's handprints when he asked Mom why she was allowing me to continue such a childish act. Then he demanded that we paint over all of them so it wouldn't be an eyesore. That's one of the few things I remember her fighting back on and actually winning. While we couldn't do anymore handprints, a compromise she said, those ten sets remained untouched. Well, at least until they started getting covered by the dirt and grime.

When Mom first introduced Preston to me shortly after my eighth birthday, I had doubts, especially because of what she'd previously told me about him. I think I was six when she first told me about when she and Preston were married before I was born. That he had convinced her that my father, who was in a motorcycle club, was cheating on her with every skirt that walked into the club. That being with him instead of her boyfriend would provide a stable environment for me.

It wasn't until after I was born that she realized he'd tricked her, but it was too late. She was already married to Preston when she found out that my dad had never cheated on her. In fact, it was actually Preston who'd been cheating on her all along. I'm not sure if that's the reason why they annulled their marriage a month later or not. Whenever I asked, Mom would never tell me the reason or would change the subject.

So when she said they had started dating again, I was worried that he'd try and trick her again. Whenever I'd talk to her about it, she said that he seemed to have changed and matured since they were together last.

Still, I could tell she was cautious around him. At least whenever he was around me, that is. However, I'm guessing either she still loved him or thought she wouldn't do any better than him, because they were married again, not even a year after they started dating.

The first couple of years after they got married were rocky before it all went to heck in a handbasket. I didn't know it at the time, but looking back, his nagging and nitpicking every little thing Mom did eventually broke her down, making her a shell of her former self.

It was then, when she'd hit that low point, that his physical abuse started. And it's only gotten worse throughout the years.

With a sigh, I push those memories back and carefully make my way up our rickety stairs, trying to avoid the worst of the rotten spots. My hand pauses on the door handle when I hear Preston talking again.

"When she's eighteen, she's gone, Lillian. That'll settle everything and then we won't have to worry about things for a while."

What is he talking about? What does he mean I'll be gone?

"You can't, Preston! She's my baby. Please! There has to be another way."

A loud smack rings through the air, followed by the sound of something heavy falling.

Crap.

It sounds like Preston hasn't kept Mom pumped full of drugs like he usually does.

Another cry from my mom has me shaking off my thoughts, and I turn, quietly walking back down the steps. Since it isn't used as often, I head to the rear passenger door, open it, and then slam it shut. Instantly, the yelling stops and I walk back up the steps, making sure they creak and groan with each step.

Opening the trailer door, my gaze instantly latches on Preston, who's sitting on our beat-up couch watching TV and drinking a beer. No surprise there. A quick glance around the living room and tiny kitchen shows only him and the dilapidated state of our once nice trailer. Everything is practically falling apart, held together with duct tape and bungee cords. Since Mom's nowhere to be found, she must be hiding in their bedroom. I'm sure she'll be sporting another bruise tomorrow that her makeup won't be able to hide.

Shutting the front door, I flip the flimsy lock. Not that it'll stop anyone from trying to get in. That thing is so weak it would break as soon as someone tugs hard enough on it. Keeping my head down, I let my long, blonde hair fall so that it hides him from my view as I cross the dingy living room, hoping I'll be able to escape to my bedroom without him taking notice of me. I hear couch springs squeak as he shifts before he grunts. Crap.

"You've got a birthday coming up, don't you? Eighteen, is it?" Preston asks.

I stop in my tracks, fear crawling through me. I learned long ago that if I didn't answer him or at least act like I was paying attention when he spoke, his beatings would be worse than usual.

"Y-yes. In a few days." *Please let me just go to my room.*

He grunts again and goes back to watching his show. Thank you, universe!

Chapter 2

Mae

Releasing an internal sigh of relief that I got off easier than usual, I head toward the hallway trying not to rush too much. Rushing would only result in another beating, as he'd see it as me disrespecting him.

When I get to my room, I quietly shut the door. Grabbing the chair from my desk, I wedge it under the doorknob to keep anyone from entering. Preston has long since changed out all the interior doorknobs for ones that don't lock. The only exception being our bathroom door. That was another battle that Mom, thankfully, won.

Frowning, I look back down at the chair. It won't stop someone if they really want to force their way in here, but it might buy me enough time to escape through the window. Breathing another sigh of relief at having gotten off easy tonight, I carefully set my backpack down beside my rickety nightstand.

Even though they don't do much, I close my threadbare curtains, hoping they at least make it a little harder for someone if they are watching what I'm doing. Walking the few steps across the room to my closet, I quietly move a stack of boxes on the floor to reveal the boards along the back wall that I had pried loose years ago. My little hidey-hole is the only way to make sure Preston or Mom doesn't find stuff I want to keep hidden.

Mainly my money.

I learned that the hard way years ago when I'd realized Preston had stolen my birthday money from my grandparents. He, of course, denied it, but I never made the mistake again. Any money I received since then was always painstakingly hidden around my room in various places until I realized I could pry these boards loose.

Kneeling, I carefully move the boards and grab my coffee tin where I keep my stash of wages and tips until it's a decent amount to deposit at the bank. Stashing today's tips inside, I put the tin back in my hidey-hole but freeze when my hand brushes up against something.

Panic gnaws at my chest.

Did Mom or Preston remove any boards in the back of their closet? I've checked here hundreds of times and have never found anything of theirs in here before. What could it be? I freeze again.

Fiddlesticks.

Did they take any of my money?

Pulling the coffee tin back out, I double check. I'm shocked to see there's almost three hundred dollars more than there should be, and that's including what I just put in there. Where did the extra money come from?

Shaking my head, I set the tin down next to me. Maybe I just put money in one or two nights and didn't count it. I've been working a lot of late shifts lately on top of helping open the diner. I usually prefer not to have more than five hundred in the tin in case Preston finds it. Tomorrow I'll have to see if Peggy will let me take a longer lunch break than usual so that I can run to the bank.

Reaching back into the closet, I try to be as quiet as I can as I blindly pat around, hoping I don't cut myself on anything rusty. A second later, my hand brushes up against a stack of what feels like books. Taking the one on top, I pull it out and realize it's a notebook. What's a notebook doing in here and whose is it?

Frowning, I sit down. Leaning against my dresser, I open it and suck in a breath when I see Mom's handwriting. It's a journal she started a couple of weeks ago. Flipping through the pages, I find the latest entry which is for today.

Preston's gone too far this time. He owes his dealer a couple thousand dollars, and his dealer isn't falling for his usual tricks to get out of paying. He won't take anything but cash and Preston has until the 9th, which is next weekend, to square up what he owes.

Preston's already taken the remaining money from my monthly checks, but somehow, it isn't enough to cover the amount. He must owe more than he's telling me, or he has more than one dealer he owes.

I overheard him on the phone a few weeks ago. He's arranged for someone to buy my baby girl after she turns 'eighteen'. I've tried talking him out of it, but each time, he beats me and then drugs me to shut me up.

I don't know what to do. I have no family or friends anymore. The only other person I could go to is Jax, and I know he won't talk to me. I hate that I listened to Preston back then, but he convinced me it would be best for Mae.

How wrong I was.

I wish I could take it all back.

My chest is in knots as fear runs through me. He's going to sell me to someone? Is that what he meant earlier when he said I'd be gone after my birthday? Who is this Jax person?

Then I freeze as my gaze goes back to the notebook.

Cheese and crackers!

Is she sober enough to remember how old I really am? Wait, is sober the right word for when someone isn't strung out on drugs? Shaking my head, I refocus. If she tells Preston how old I really am, or if he beats it out of her, I'm screwed.

With a shaky hand, I set the journal down. Reaching back into the closet, I pull out the rest of the journals. There are six in total as well as a few papers tucked in between them. I poke my cheap phone through the gap and open my camera to see if there's anything else hidden in here, but it's too dark.

Knowing it's a risk but needing to see if there's anything else in here that might help me, I turn on the flashlight feature and see a few more papers and letters.

Quickly, I pull them out and turn the flashlight off. Picking everything up, I bring it over to my bed so that I can somewhat sit comfortably as I look through everything.

After arranging the notebooks from oldest to newest, my focus turns to the loose papers and envelopes. Picking up the first few, I freeze.

What the fudge nuggets?

My name is on two birth certificates as well as a death certificate. The only thing that's different is the father, last name, and birthdates. Everything else matches.

The first birth certificate is one I've seen before. *Mae Rose Cole. Born: September 2nd, 2002. Father: Unknown.*

The second birth certificate has a tear rolling down my cheek. *Mae Rose Witlock. Born: September 1st, 2002. Father: Jaxon Witlock.*

My death certificate also has the last name of Witlock, and that I had died that same day.

Holy cannoli!

Hope blossoms in my chest. I finally know my father's name. I can finally see if what Preston said years ago was true or not. To see if my real dad is alive. Also, my twenty-first birthday isn't in two days. It's tomorrow.

Wait, no.

Twisting my neck, I glance at my clock. It's after midnight. Friday the 1st. Today's my real birthday.

Scrambling to my feet, I almost trip as I rush over to my bookcase. I flip through everything until I find what I'm looking for—a clear plastic folder that zips shut, something left over from high school. Why I hung onto it, I don't know, but I'm glad I did now.

Sitting back down on the bed, I slip all three documents inside the folder, facing them together so no one can read what's on them. The rest of the loose papers are things I don't know anything about, but I still put them in the folder. They must be important if someone saved them.

My mind freezes as I wonder if Mom put them there, knowing I'd find everything. If she knows I've been using that spot as a hidey-hole, how long has she known about it? Shaking my head, I refocus—I can't go down the rabbit hole of playing the 'what if' game.

Picking up one of the envelopes, I pull out the papers inside and my jaw drops as I read the contents. Mom and Preston took out a life insurance policy for me after they were married for fifty thousand dollars. A few months after I 'died', the insurance paid it out in full.

Angrily, I wipe away a few tears that escape. Was I just a scam for them to get money from the government? Was my dad in on it, too?

The other envelopes are from some guy named Jack who got my new identity set up. Stuffing all the envelopes into the folder, I zip it closed before picking up the oldest journal and start reading. I need to know more about what happened, even if it is only from Mom's point of view.

I'm not sure how long I'm reading for when I hear Preston's voice coming from their bedroom, startling me so much I nearly scream. It takes me a bit to realize that his voice is clearer than usual because I haven't put the boards back in place yet. I can even hear mom's soft snores. Quietly, I creep closer so I can hear him better.

"I'll have the money next weekend, X. I have something already set up and you'll be paid in full."

He's silent for a little while and then he curses. His breathing becomes harder, sort of like he's panicking. After a few moments, I hear him dialing someone.

"Bruce—any chance you want her sooner? I'll even shave a little off the price if you pick her up on the 2nd."

There's silence from the bedroom for a few moments, and then Preston grunts.

"Perfect. Come to the trailer and we'll get it all settled. Soon you'll have your young bride and will be set."

Holy shit, that fucking asshole!

He's really going to sell me? Tomorrow? Knowing him, he's probably trying to sell me off to one of his dealers. Then my mental words come back to me, making me wince, but at least I didn't say them out loud. Not only would I have potentially given away the fact that I now know Preston's plans, but I've always tried really hard not to curse. My dream job is to own and run my own daycare someday, and no one wants to hire a childcare provider that cusses up a storm around their children.

Preston's words tumble around my brain and bile rises in my throat, but I push it down.

I need to pack.

Quickly, but quietly, I put the boards back in place, followed by the boxes. Standing, I grab my biggest duffle bag down off the top shelf and set it on my bed. Picking my backpack up off the floor, I empty its contents onto my bed. After topping off my wallet, I put the coffee tin in my backpack, followed by the folder, notebooks, my laptop, and its charger.

My gaze frantically sweeps around my room, looking for things I'll need. All the while, my mind tries to figure out the best way to pack them so I'm not carrying a bunch of bags.

Clothes.

Need to pack those first since they'll take up the most space. A week's worth should get me by long enough. Once I find a place to stay, I'll buy some better clothing. I've always purposely stuck to thrift stores for all of my clothes and shoes. If I suddenly came home with better things, I would have been busted for working so much and then the lie about my age would have come to light.

On top of my piles of clothes, I put in a couple of my favorite pairs of shoes and my makeup bag. Our bathroom is tiny, so I've usually done my hair in there, since the outlets in here don't always work the greatest, and then do my makeup in my room.

Looking around my small room, I spot a couple of pictures from when I was a kid and pick them up, rubbing my thumb along the edges. They're from back when it was just Mom and me. Back when, for the most part, we were both happy. I carefully slide them in between my clothes and hope that's enough padding to protect them. Quickly, I gather a few other items that have sentimental value and pack them as well.

Once I think I have everything packed, I look around one more time and in all my drawers to make sure I have everything I need or want. My gaze snags on the rest of the money envelopes for groceries for this month and next month.

Screw it.

They're going to sell me, so I might as well get something out of it. There's a few hundred in each envelope, so it'll definitely help. Grabbing them, I slip them into my backpack and zip it up before storing both bags in my closet.

My clothes for tomorrow are already set aside in my dresser. If, for some reason either of them gets in here tonight, I don't want anything looking amiss that could tip them off that I know what Preston's up to. Even though my room is small and dingy, I've always kept it as clean and tidy as I can.

Slipping into my threadbare pajamas, I carefully pull down another duffle bag from my closet and pull out my rolled up sleeping bag. Tucking it under my covers, I crawl into bed, snuggling deep into the sleeping bag, and pull my thin comforter over the top of it.

My boss, Peggy, and her husband, Glen, gave me this sleeping bag one year for Christmas. It's a camping one that's rated down to zero degrees. If I didn't keep it hidden or make sure my covers are always wrapped tight around me and the bag, I'm sure Preston would have taken it from me a long time ago. I wish I could take it with me tomorrow since it's a good sleeping bag, but then I'd be traveling with a lot of bags and I'm not sure how much room I'll have on the bus. Hopefully, I'll be able to find a place to stay in whatever town my dad lives in.

Sighing, I set my alarm for 5 am and will myself to sleep. I'll only get a few hours of sleep, but it is what it is. I need to be gone before Preston wakes up and realizes my ruse.

Something vibrating on my bed wakes me and it takes a few moments before I realize it's the alarm on my phone. Yawning, I rub the sleep from my eyes, shut off the alarm and get out of bed. A shiver racks through me as I walk across the room. The insulation is terrible in this trailer. If there even is any left in between the walls, that is. I'm sure most of it's been stolen by mice or other vermin for their nests by now.

Quietly, I slip the chair out from under the doorknob and listen. Relief fills me when I still hear Preston's loud snores coming from their bedroom. Turning the doorknob, I tiptoe out of my room and head to the bathroom with another small travel bag in hand. I hadn't wanted to try to get anything from the bathroom last night when Preston was still awake for fear that he'd ask what the bag was for.

Shutting the door and quietly locking it, I open the cabinet and pull out new bottles of my shower gel, shampoo, conditioner, a couple of disposable razors, deodorant, perfume, toothpaste, a new toothbrush, comb, and a few hair ties. Spying the tampons, I grab a box. When I get to wherever my dad lives, I can buy anything else I've forgotten. I put everything into the travel bag and since I can feel a headache brewing, I also grab a bottle of ibuprofen as well as a couple of other items in the medicine cabinet. Everything else of mine I leave as is, not wanting to raise any alarm bells sooner than necessary.

After doing my business, I pull out some baby wipes Mom keeps stashed in here in case our water gets turned off, or a pipe freezes, and take a poor man's shower. I don't want to run the risk of waking Preston up by taking a real shower and then having him asking about my bags. Putting the baby wipes back in the cupboard, I pause, and then drop them into my travel bag instead. I don't know where my dad lives, if he's even still alive that is, but it might take me a couple of days to get there. Who knows if I might need them in the meantime?

Zipping up my bag, I open the bathroom door and my shoulders relax slightly when I can still hear Preston snoring. Making my way to my room, I get dressed and pack my frayed phone charger, praying it'll last a little longer. Slipping on my coat and tennis shoes, I grab my bags and tiptoe out to the living room.

Playing up the lie, I leave Mom a note saying I got called into the diner before school because someone's sick. Neither one of them will think anything of it because I get called in a lot to fill in for people. I don't get very many extra shifts at the grocery store, but everyone at the diner knows I'll take any extra shifts I can get.

Quietly stepping out the front door, I look longingly at Mom's rusty old beater, but then shake my head. I can't chance waking them if I want to get as far away as I can before they realize I've lied. Mom's and Preston's bedroom window is right by where the car is parked so they'd hear it right away. If they see it out here when they get up, they'll probably assume it wouldn't start. Wouldn't be the first time that happened.

With a sigh, I pull my jacket tighter and start my trek into town.

Chapter 3

Mae

IT'S A LITTLE BEFORE 6 am by the time I make it to the diner. I know Peggy will already be here because we get a breakfast rush around 7 am.

Checking the front door, I breathe a sigh of relief that it hasn't been unlocked yet. We open at 6 am, so I'm thankful there aren't any customers here yet. Unlocking the door, I step inside and relock it. I have no idea if anyone else is here yet besides Peggy, but I hope not.

Speak of the devil, well not really because Peggy's the sweetest person I'd ever met, her head pokes out of the pass through and a smile lights up her face until she notices my bags. She waves a hand and I follow her back to her office. Once inside, I shut the door behind me.

"Don't worry, no one else is here yet. What happened? Did the asshole finally figure out your ruse?"

I can't help the small smile that tugs at my lips before I sober again. "No, but something happened, and I need to get out of town as soon as possible. I'm sorry, Peggy, but I can't give you two weeks' notice."

She takes the keys I hold out and says nothing as she studies my face. A few moments later, she gives me a curt nod and turns toward the picture that I know hides her safe since I help her open and close so much. Once the door is open, she shuffles something around in there, but I can't see what she's doing. When she closes it, she's holding two envelopes, one small, and another that looks the size of regular printer paper and is bulky.

"It's probably best that you don't tell me where you're going in case that asshole comes here asking for you. That said, I want you to let me know you're safe when you're able to. You know Glen and I will be worried sick until we hear from you.

Here's the money for what you would have earned from last week and the couple of days this week that you worked."

She passes me both envelopes.

Hesitantly, I look up at her. "What's in the other one?"

Her eyes turn misty, and she takes a shuddery breath as a tear escapes. "I always knew that asshole would do something to send you running. Not that I blame you in the least. It's something Glen and I started squirreling away the day you came through that door looking for a job all those years ago. We want you to have it, Sweetie. I know you saved as much as possible over the years, but both of us want to help provide you with a bit more of a buffer. You know we love you like our own. Always have."

Now it's my turn to cry. Peggy pulls me in for a hug and I cling to her as my tears fall harder. I've always wished they could have been my parents. They were never able to have children of their own. Said the diner and their employees are who they consider their children.

After a few minutes, I pull back, wipe the tears from my face, and then tuck both envelopes in my backpack. "Thank you. Once I'm safe, I'll give you a call. I need to look something up on my computer and then I'll head out of town. Can I use the Wi-Fi here?"

That's one thing Preston cut out a couple of years ago, saying the internet wasn't really a necessary expense for us. My phone was never much help either because it's very old. The thing takes forever to pull anything up, especially on the internet. Honestly, I think Preston tries to do anything he can to prevent us from communicating with people outside our little slice of hell.

Twatwaffle.

Peggy nods as she wipes away another tear. "Of course, Sweetie. Stay strong and keep your wits about you. Never leave your bags alone until you get where you're going. If you run into any problems, give us a call. We'll help you as best as we can."

"Thank you, Peggy. Thank you for everything you, Glen, and the others have done for me over the years."

She waves off my thanks. "Let me at least get you a hot biscuit sandwich, so you have some food in ya before you leave. I'll wrap one of them to go, so you have something for later, along with a tall cup of coffee."

Nodding, we hug one more time before I pull away. She skirts around me and heads to the kitchen while I walk out into the dining area to wait.

Thankfully, no other employees have come in yet, which means I can take my time looking over the place as I try to burn everything into my memory without them questioning me as to what I'm doing. The diner has been like a second home to me these past six years. I'm going to miss it, but I can't risk staying in town. Preston would be able to easily track me down and then he'd force me to marry that Bruce guy so he can pay off his debts.

With a heavy sigh, I grab a coffee mug and help myself to the coffee so Peggy doesn't have to get it. Coffee in hand, I walk over to a far booth that's kind of hidden from view, slide in, and pull out my old laptop.

An old friend of mine had to get a new one when this one crashed back in high school, and I asked if I could buy it off her. She gave it to me for free since her parents were going to buy her a new one. It didn't take long to fix it after doing a little research online at the library. Plus, I cleared out a couple of viruses that she had somehow gotten. The only thing that needed fixing on the inside was the fan, but after cleaning it, it worked fine since I'm usually not on it for very long periods of time anymore.

Accessing the Wi-Fi, I bring up an internet browser and search for 'Steel Archangel's MC, Forest Creek'. According to Mom's journal, that's the club my dad used to belong to.

Whenever I would ask about my dad over the years, Mom and Preston would never tell me his name or the name of the motorcycle club he was in. Just that he wasn't a good man and that he was in an MC. That his club was into drugs and human trafficking. Mom never corrected him, but the looks she gave him when he would go on his drunken rants about the MC always had me wondering if he was lying. Preston said my dad was killed in a drug bust not too long after I was born, but once again, the way Mom acted made me think it was also a lie. With the way he was talking, it almost seemed like he was jealous of my dad for some reason.

A few minutes later, Peggy comes back with a plate of sausage and egg biscuit, a couple pieces of bacon, some fruit, and a wrapped-up sandwich to go. Setting them down, she heads back to the counter and pulls a thermos off the sale rack before heading back into the kitchen. I shake my head at her but won't turn down the coffee or the thermos. I'm sure whatever they'll have at the bus stop will be absolutely terrible.

Turning my attention back to my laptop, my fingers freeze, poised over the keys as I stare at the club's logo at the top of their webpage. Instead of reading about the club right away, I open a new tab and do a search for Jaxon Witlock.

I breathe out a sigh of relief when I find out he's still alive and that he still lives in Forest Creek, Wisconsin. Well... as long as it isn't a different Jaxon Witlock, that is. Relief once again flows through me that he isn't that far away, just a little over an hour away, but I know it'll take longer by bus.

Then my chest starts to burn as my anger grows. My dad didn't die, and he's been close this entire time. Why did Preston lie to me? What's the reason behind his hate and anger toward my dad? Is there bad blood between them? Why didn't Mom tell me the truth? Or is she hiding something, too?

Pushing down my anger, I dig into my breakfast, go back to the other tab, and start reading about the club, soaking up all the information I can find. My brow creases the more I read. The club owns a lot of businesses in town, and they do a lot of poker and rally runs to help out the community. Though, I know the club could still be into illegal things. However, the more I read about them, the more I get the impression that they most likely aren't into anything illegal.

My anger rises once again as proof of Preston's lies is right in front of me in black and white. My chest tightens even more as the hurt of Mom's betrayal hits even deeper. She never refuted what Preston said, but she could have at least told me my dad was still alive instead of letting me believe I had no one else. My only other family were Mom's parents, and they died back when I was twelve. Then again, I overheard Preston threatening her many times. Maybe my dad was one of the things he threatened her about. That he'd beat her or something worse if she told me about him. Wouldn't be the first time he's threatened her to get his way.

Shaking my head, I refocus back on the webpage. They don't have their members listed by picture, but I can at least confirm my dad's still in the club according to the roster. There are a few pictures that show some of the members during rallies or on poker runs, but none of the men look like my carbon copy. Thanks to a few pictures Mom had stuffed in her journals, I know I'm the spitting image of my dad. One even had a picture of him in his vest and his road name, as Mom called it, was stitched on the front. As long as he hasn't left the club, then I should be able to find him there.

That is, if he'll even talk to me. Preston said my dad didn't want me—that he wanted Mom to get an abortion. When Mom told him she was pregnant, he kicked her out of his place and out of his life.

Futtenfarter...

It could just be another one of Preston's lies, but if it's true and he won't talk to me, then I'll move on to another town and start fresh there. I'm not sure if I'll be able to find some place that will pay me in cash again. I know I'll have to get an apartment, so there will most likely be no hiding my name if Preston or this Bruce guy comes looking. If they do, then I'll stay on the move.

Doing a quick google search of the town, I snap a few pictures of where the club is, so I'll have a reference for later. My old, cheap phone won't bring up maps very well anymore, so I'd rather be prepared just in case. I don't want to bring too much attention to myself if I have to ask for directions. If I'm not going to stay in Forest Creek, the fewer people that can recognize me, the better.

Finishing my breakfast, I shut down my laptop and stow it, as well as my to-go sandwich, before grabbing my bags and ducking into the bathroom. After doing my business, I pick up my dirty dishes from the booth and take them back into the kitchen.

"Thanks for breakfast, Peggy. I'll ring myself up at the register."

She waves me off as she thrusts one of the store thermos' in my hands. "Don't even think of paying for breakfast or that thermos. Consider it my 'goodbye for now' present. Top yourself off with coffee before you go. Travel safe, Sweetie. Love you."

After another hug and tearful goodbye, I fill the thermos with coffee and step out into the parking lot. With one more look at the diner, I head toward the bus station.

Thankfully, there's a stop in Forest Creek, but the station is about three or so miles from the club. It'll be a trek, but I don't really have much of a choice. I'm not sure if I should trust an uber driver or not. I guess I'll just see how things feel when I get there.

Twenty-five minutes later, I have my ticket for the 9 am bus to Forest Creek. Since I have some time to kill, I set my alarm for 8:30 am before pulling out a journal and pick up where I last left off.

My alarm startles me and my phone slides off my lap, falling on the tile floor. A curse slips past my lips before I can stop it. A little old lady sitting nearby gives me a disapproving look and I roll my eyes internally. Lady, even though I try not to, I can cuss if I want to. It's my life.

Looking down at my phone, I wince as I bend down to pick it up, praying it isn't broken worse than it already is. A breath of relief escapes when there's no new cracks in the screen and it doesn't act slower than usual.

Slipping my phone in my pocket, I look around the terminal. There's a fair amount of people here already. Nerves start to swirl in my belly as I try not to think about how full the bus might be. I've never been good with big crowds—I'm more of a loner than a social butterfly. Sliding my backpack over my shoulder, I pick up my duffle bag and head to the bathroom. I know there's one on the bus, but I'd like to not have to use it right away, if at all possible.

As I step back out into the terminal after doing my business, I double check the board. My anxiety starts to increase for a few reasons when it says we'll start loading in five minutes.

One reason being, is that I really hope I don't get stuck sitting next to a chatterbox. Or the type of person you sometimes hear about that eats so many onions that their sweat practically reeks of onions. Two, is that I'm this much closer to meeting my dad for the first time. And three, I'm worried that he'll shut me out after finding out who I am and refuse to help me, all because of what

Mom did to him years ago. If he'd spend five minutes with me, he'd see I'm hardly anything like her and I don't take after her look-wise except for my dark blue, almost sapphire eyes.

Taking a deep breath, I sit back down to wait. My fingers fidget with the zipper on my bag as I look around. There are a few families in the waiting area, but most look to be couples or people traveling alone.

Something bumps my shoe, and I jump, startled. Looking down, I realize it's just a little ball. Jeez, my nerves really are wrecked. Picking it up, I scan the crowd again, wondering whose it is. I get my answer a moment later when a little boy with adorable brown curls skids to a halt in front of me, and I can't help the smile that pulls at my lips.

"Is this yours?"

He grins and nods. "I dropped it on accident."

My smile widens at how cute he is as I hand him the ball back.

"Thank you!"

"You're welcome."

He returns my smile before he runs back to a woman sitting not too far from me, most likely his mother. She waves at me, and I return it.

The speaker crackles above me. "Now boarding for Forest Creek, Wisconsin."

Taking a deep breath, I stand and get in line.

Chapter 4
Mae

SHAKING BRINGS ME OUT of my reading and I look around, wondering what's going on. Then I feel it again. A feeling I've felt far too many times in my mom's old beater.

There's something wrong with the bus.

Panic instantly claws at my chest. Are we going to be stuck on the side of the road? For how long? Looking around, I notice we're in between towns without a house in sight.

A child's whine to my left catches my attention and I realize it's the little boy who had dropped his ball at the station. Apparently, he and his mother sat across from me. Luckily, no one chose to sit next to me, so I'm in the aisle seat and my bags are in the seat by the window.

"But Mom, I'm bored," the boy cries as he throws his hands in the air.

I bite my lip to keep from laughing and turn, digging in my bag for some pens. There are only a few pages left to read in Mom's last journal, but there are a lot of empty pages in it. I have an idea that might help the little boy, and me for that matter, keep our minds off our predicament. As long as his mom is okay with it, that is.

Unlike how I am around adults, I'm hardly ever nervous around kids. Since I was little, I've always wanted to run a daycare. To find creative ways to get them to learn, and of course, to have fun. Also, to help build some of their foundation blocks that they'll build on over the years as they grow into adults.

Turning back to the mom and boy, I can see the tiredness and exasperation on her face, which makes me wonder how long he's been bored while I'd been reading.

"Um, excuse me."

They both turn toward me, and the mom eyes me warily.

"My name is Mae, and I couldn't help but overhear that you're bored. I happen to have some paper." I pause again as I show them, and then lean in a little closer. "Do you like playing tic-tac-toe?"

His eyes light up and he quickly turns to his mom. "Mom, can I? Please?" he begs.

She gives him a hesitant nod and I hold out the journal, thankful its wire bound, as that will make this easier. "Do you want to start first?"

He happily takes the notebook from me and starts drawing the grid. His mom mouths 'thank you' to me and I smile, waving her off. Turning sideways in the chair, I cross my legs and settle in to play tic-tac-toe and who knows what else while we wait for an update on the bus.

Three hours later, the repair truck finally makes its way out to us, along with another bus. Our bus driver stands up and whistles to get everyone's attention.

"I'm very sorry for the wait, everyone, but another bus just arrived that will take you the rest of the way into Forest Creek."

"Mae, will you sit by us again?" Jordan, the little boy, asks as he bounces on his toes.

"Absolutely, Little Man. Do you want to go back to hangman or play some more tic-tac-toe?"

He scrunches up his face as he thinks. "Hangman! I think I have one that will stump you."

The smile that lights up his face is absolutely blinding, and I can't help but smile in return. Shifting in my seat, I grab my bags and wait for them to gather their things. When they're ready, Jordan leads the way, skipping up the aisle.

"I can't thank you enough, Mae. From now on, I think I'll always carry around some extra notebooks and pens on future trips just in case this ever happens again," Susie says as she laughs, and I join in.

"It's not a problem. I love kids. Besides, playing games with him and talking to both of you helped pass the time."

She bumps my shoulder. "Are you nervous?"

Biting my lip, I nod. When Susie asked what my plans were in Forest Creek, I'd told her I was going to meet my dad for the first time and that he didn't know about me. I left out the other stuff. I didn't want everyone on the bus to know exactly who I was going to see, and I didn't want them to hear about my backstory or how rough it was growing up either.

"Yeah. I have no idea if he'll even talk to me, but I want to try at least. Find out his side of what happened if I can."

"I'm sure he'll talk to you. It might be a little bumpy at first, but I think it'll work out. Besides, you're a nice person. He'd be an idiot to cut you out of his life."

My chest tightens, hoping she's right. Jordan tugs on my hand, and I look down at him.

"Where do you want to sit, Mae?"

I smile, thankful to have met him and his mom. I would have been bored out of my mind and trapped in my thoughts all this time if I hadn't.

"How about you pick our seats? Just make sure the seats across from yours are empty, too."

He grins and bounds up the stairs. I follow after Susie and we both settle into our seats while Jordan bounces in his. When everyone on board has taken their seats, the driver stands up and everyone quiets down.

"Once again, we sincerely apologize for the delay. When we get to the Forest Creek station, one of the attendants will give you all a couple of vouchers for some restaurants around town, so please make sure you get them before you head to your final destinations."

I perk up at that. If things go south with my dad, I might be able to at least get a semi-decent meal before finding a cheap place to stay for the night.

For the rest of the ride, Jordan, Susie, and I switch between playing hangman and tic-tac-toe as we continue to talk. She's going to Forest Creek to see her parents and brother. They're also attending their friend's baby shower and wedding. I'm surprised when I find out her brother is in the same MC as my dad.

"What does your brother do?" I ask, hoping my face doesn't give away the real reason behind asking about the club.

The proud smile that lights up Susie's face eases some of my nerves. From the little I know about her; she wouldn't approve of her brother doing anything illegal.

"He runs their tattoo parlor, Steel's Ink. His road name is Axe."

"That's awesome. So, it is true what I've heard about them? That they own a bunch of businesses around town?"

"Oh, yeah. Let's see," she says as she pauses and nibbles on her lip. "Besides Steel's Ink, there's a body shop, a bar they partially own, and a construction business. They own a couple of apartment buildings and a few houses that they rent out. Oh, and they have a security business. I know they're looking into a few other businesses, but I don't think they've finalized anything on them. They're the best group of guys I know. They do a lot of things to help out the community there, too. Every time we go back home after visiting, I miss Forest Creek so much. The small town where we live in Illinois is pretty boring in comparison and it doesn't have the sense of community that there is in Forest Creek."

I look down as Jordan hands me back the notebook and after marking 'x', I look up as Susie gasps.

"Is your dad part of the club? Is that why you were curious about what they do?"

I nod sheepishly. "Guess I must have been pretty obvious, but yeah, he is. At least from what I could find online, that is. They didn't list his real name, so I don't know if it's him or if someone else joined with that same road name or not."

"Which one is he? Wait, let me guess." Her forehead scrunches up, no doubt running everyone through everyone in the club.

"I think it's Uncle Smoke. He always looks so sad, but he gives me awesome puzzle books whenever I see him," Jordan says.

My heart breaks a little at his words. I don't want him to be sad.

Hearing another gasp, I look up to find Susie holding both hands over her mouth as she stares at me in shock. "It's him, isn't it?"

At my hesitant nod, she does a little happy dance in her seat. "I can't wait for him to meet you and find out he's got a daughter!"

I panic a little at her excitement. "Please don't say anything to Axe or any of the others! If he finds out ahead of time, he could have them prevent me from entering and even talking to him altogether."

She gives me a sympathetic look. "I won't say anything, but even if they somehow did find out ahead of time, I doubt they'd prevent you from talking to him. They really are a good group of guys. Two of them even settled down recently and found an Old Lady. Their wedding is the one we're going to next week and tonight is her baby shower."

My nose scrunches. "Old Lady? Aren't they mad at being called 'old'?"

Susie laughs at my confusion. "In the biker world, Old Lady is what bikers call their woman or wife. Though bikers view Old Ladies as being even higher than being married."

She goes on, telling me a few things about club life and the women they call 'club bunnies'. I shake my head at the thought of the bunnies. How someone is okay with having sex with multiple people each night is beyond me. I've always felt it should be between you and your partner, but I'm not gonna toss stones about it.

We keep chatting and playing games for the next half hour until the bus pulls into the station in Forest Creek. As we exit the bus, a lady hands each of us a couple vouchers for some restaurants in town. One is for a bar and grill, Wallace's B&G, and another is Mama's Kitchen, which looks like it's a small diner. Maybe if I stick around, I can look them up and see if either one needs any extra help.

Susie gives me a hug and points to my backpack. "I jotted down my number in your notebook. Give me a call and maybe we can get together sometime while we're still in town?"

I blush and nod. Other than Peggy and Glen, I've never really had friends. Those that I thought were my friends, ended up backstabbing me. "I will. Thank you and hopefully I'll see you again soon."

Jordan gives me a hug and then runs off toward an older man and woman. With a wave, I turn toward where my map had pointed me to go.

A little over an hour later, I'm getting even more nervous by how much cinderblock wall I've already passed. It's even topped with barbwire. Is all of this land part of their club? Why do they need such a big place? Why do they need such protective measures?

Up ahead, I spot a gate and my nerves skyrocket even more. Looking through the gate, there's an enormous three-story building that must be their clubhouse. Off to the left of it, I can see some houses in the distance. It almost looks like a small community.

Please don't let them be like a cult.

"Can I help you?" a voice calls from my right, and I jump, startled. Stepping out of a booth is a guy that looks a few years older than me, and his vest says he's a Prospect.

"I-I'm looking for Smoke. Is he here?"

He shakes his head. "Not right now. Is there something I can help you with?"

My cheeks flame as he looks me over closer. He's a good-looking guy, but nope, not going down that road.

"Please, I just need to talk to Smoke. Can I come inside until he comes back?"

He frowns. "I'm sorry, but my orders are to not let anyone in right now that doesn't live here."

I groan and rub my temples.

"Why are you so hung up on Smoke? If you're looking to score, he won't touch you. Not that I'm saying you aren't good looking, it's just that he doesn't hook up with anyone."

Groaning again, I slip my bag off my shoulder but freeze when the man pulls a gun.

"I was going to get some papers and a notebook out of my bag. I don't have a weapon. Not even a pocketknife."

Please don't shoot me. That's all I need. To bleed out before I can even meet my dad for the first time.

"With what's been going on, I'd rather be on the safe side. I'll lower it once you have your stuff out of your bag and it's back on your shoulders."

Rolling my eyes, I pull out the folder, but as I'm digging for the right notebook, my bag slips and the guy steps forward a bit more. Immediately, I drop the folder and backpack, putting my hands back up in the air.

"It slipped while I was trying to get the right notebook. I'll open the bag up further so you can see I have a lot of them in here. Give me a break. I've been on the road all day and it was a little over an hour's trek from the bus station in town."

He lifts his chin at me, but still steps even closer as he watches me intently. Picking up my bag and the spilled contents, I set it on the ground and fully open it so he can see what I'm doing. Flipping through them, I find the one I want before finding the entry that I was looking for. Opening the folder, I grab a couple of pictures and hesitate for a moment, but then decide against grabbing both of my birth certificates and death certificate.

Jeez, that's weird to say.

If things don't go well, I don't want to risk those documents being ruined even though I know I could request a new birth certificate. However, there's no way they'd give me replacements of my certificates with my dad's name on them since I 'died'. Dusting off the folder, I put it back in my bag before zipping it up and slowly standing up. I don't want to startle the Prospect and end up with a hole in me.

"Here. It's from one of my mom's journals. Smoke is my dad, but because of her stupid actions, he thought I died."

I hand him the notebook and pictures through the metal bars of the gate. He holsters his gun and I feel my shoulders sag in relief. He must not consider me a threat anymore.

His gaze lingers on my face a little more before he looks down at what I gave him. Seconds later, shock registers on his face. He scoffs before he shakes his head and looks back up at me.

"Damn. No offense, but your mom sounds like a fucking bitch to pull a stunt like this."

I can't help but snort at that and raise my hands to lift my long hair off my neck as the breeze picks up again. Instantly, my flushed skin starts to cool. I knew I should have bought another water bottle at the bus station instead of just filling up my thermos at the bubbler. It was a long walk to their clubhouse, and I'm not even sure if they'll let me in. The trip may end up being a bust and I'll have walked here for nothing. If that happens, I wonder if they'd let me refill my thermos with water before leaving?

"Yeah, she is, and my stepdad's even worse."

He hands me back everything just as I hear the rumble of motorcycles coming down the road and I turn in the direction of the sound. Half of them are leading the group, and the other half are at the tail end with an SUV and a car in the middle. It almost looks like the men on the bikes are escorting whoever's in the SUV and car.

Holy cannoli... there's a lot of them. And that's not even counting all the bikes I saw parked in front of the clubhouse. Is my dad one of these guys since the Prospect said he wasn't here?

As they get closer, my whole body trembles slightly and I fight the urge back away, but I force myself not to move a muscle, even though they're intimidating as heck.

The five in front come to a stop just outside the gate before turning off their bikes and removing their helmets. However, it doesn't escape my notice that the SUV stays on the street along with the car and rest of the bikes. The SUV looks like there are a bunch of women in it and a couple of them have vests similar to the bikers' vests.

A tall man with black hair approaches me along with another man. The second man also has black hair but has streaks of gray and white running throughout his hair, even though he doesn't really look old enough to have gray or white hair. Both men look lethal and could probably break me in half if they wanted to. The first man's vest says his name is Thor, and that he's the President. The other is Phoenix, the Vice President.

Oh, fiddlesticks...

Do not panic, Mae. Do not faint. I need to be able to stay conscious long enough to talk to my dad without embarrassing myself.

"Can we help you?" Thor asks.

I wet my parched lips and repeat what I told the Prospect. When I'm done, both men look surprised before angry looks cross their faces. I thought they were intimidating before, but it's nothing compared to when they look angry. These men look downright terrifying when they're mad, and I don't ever want to be the reason behind their anger.

A small whimper slips out before I can stop it and I take a couple of steps backward, but make sure I'm still close enough to be able to grab my things out of his hands if need be.

Thor's face instantly softens. "Didn't mean to scare you. People pulling shit like this pisses us the fuck off."

He turns to Phoenix, and they seem to have some sort of silent communication going on. After a few moments, they both face me again.

"When the gate opens, step inside near the booth so everyone can get in and you don't get hurt," Thor says as he hands me back my things. He then gives the Prospect a chin lift. "Open the gate, Ethan."

As I'm waiting for the gate to open, I look over the other three men that are in the first group of bikes. One looks just like Thor. Maybe they're twins? Another has dark brown wavy hair and piercing green eyes. He studies me but doesn't react positive or negative to me.

The last guy freezes me in place. His light brown hair is cut short on the sides and is longer on top. His eyes are the palest blue I've ever seen. He's got a five o'clock shadow covering his strong jaw and his skin is tan, like he spends a lot of time outdoors. His arms are covered in tattoos, both color and black and white. My gaze cuts to his vest, which says his name is Timber.

My brain immediately thinks of lumberjacks yelling out the word as they fell trees the old school way using axes. Judging by how tight his shirt is pulled over his muscles and how his jeans fit his tree-trunk muscular thighs, Timber would have no problem passing as a lumberjack.

When I lift my gaze, I can't help but blush at the smirk playing on his lips. Butterflies instantly swirl in my belly.

Oh, crap! He saw me ogling him.

He tilts his head toward the gate, and I nod as I break out of my haze and hastily pick up my bags.

Oh, dear lord, I should not be having these intense feelings just from one look. I quickly step inside the gate once it opens fully and try to get a handle on these new emotions. No one has ever made me feel this way before.

Chapter 5
Timber

HOLY SHIT...

The woman standing in front of me is fucking gorgeous and looks like a fucking ray of sunshine. The sight of her knocks the wind out of me while also sending a jolt through me. A jolt that's unlike anything I've ever felt before.

Her long blonde hair almost seems to glow in the sunlight and her eyes are dark blue, like sapphires. She looks like she's in her early twenties and maybe five foot five or a little shorter. She seems thin, though. Not in the 'have to keep my figure' thin sense, but more like she hasn't had much food growing up. While her clothes are clean, they are baggy. Almost like she's trying to hide or blend into the background. Unfortunately, both are something I'm familiar with.

A surge of protectiveness shoots through me at that. The need to protect her and keep her from harm intensifies even further after hearing her tell Thor and Phoenix why she's here. Personally, I hope I meet her bitch of a mother. I can't hurt her cause she's a woman, but I'll definitely be having words with her and make sure she stays away from my Sunshine.

My Sunshine?

Fuck, it's crazy as shit to be feeling this way about her already when I haven't even spoken to her yet. I'm already half gone and honestly, I wouldn't change a fucking thing about it.

For a while, I've been feeling like something's been missing in my life, but just didn't know what. I stopped using the bunnies a long time ago and just stuck with using my hand. Having meaningless sex wasn't what I wanted anymore. Not to mention I didn't want to deal with all the cattiness and backstabbing the bunnies were doing to each other. I haven't even hooked up with anyone in town, though there have been many that have tried.

Then seeing Levi come live on the compound and settling down with my President and Enforcer made me realize what I was missing. And I definitely wasn't going to find that with the bunnies.

Something's telling me that my Sunshine is what I've been missing. Even though she's a few feet away, it feels right having her near me. She settles something inside of me. Something that I haven't felt since I was a kid. A feeling of being home when I'm near her.

Fuck, now I'm going all sappy and shit, but it's still true. It's what I see with Levi, Thor, and Dragon.

And it's what I want with *her*.

I can't help my smirk when I realize she's been checking me out and I love the blush that stains her cheeks and runs down her slender neck. At least the attraction doesn't appear to be one-sided. Nodding toward the gate, she snaps out of her trance and hastily grabs her bags.

As Ethan opens the gate, I notice him checking her out and when his gaze reaches back to me; he flinches slightly from my glare.

He needs to back the fuck off.

She's mine.

And while I can already tell it'll take a bit for her to warm up to me, I'll do what it takes to tie her to me in every way.

Ethan gives me a startled look after a few seconds, but then grins and gives me a chin lift. Thank fuck he's not going to fight me for her. However, if it came down to it, I would.

When she's clear of the gate, I restart my bike, once again thankful she's closer to me so I can get a better look at her. As I drive past, I can't help but notice the sheen of sweat on her forehead.

Shit.

Did she walk all the way out here? At first when I saw her by the gate, I figured she had an Uber drop her off or something. Even though it's early September, it's a warm, sunny day.

As soon as I park, I grab a water bottle from my saddlebag and then drop it back inside.

She'll probably appreciate a colder one more.

Digging out my phone, I text Drae to have him bring me out a cold bottle of water for her. Pocketing my phone, I take quick strides to where Thor's standing over by the gate.

A few moments later, I hear someone hurry over to me and I'm relieved it's Drae with not one but two water bottles for which I'm thankful for. Her face is turning a little redder as she eyes us warily and I'm not sure if it's from fear, the heat, sunburn, or any combination of the three.

Stepping forward, I make sure Thor sees me before I offer her them. Normally, he'd lead the questioning of someone showing up out of the blue like this at our compound. He looks her over quickly and gives me a chin lift. Even if he hadn't, I still would have offered them to her, but unless they were an enemy, I doubt he'd deny someone a drink of water.

"They're still sealed, and you look like you could use them. Did you walk here?"

She takes them both and lowers her bags to the ground after stowing one of the water bottles in her duffle bag. Tucking her papers under her arm, she quickly breaks the seal and downs about half the bottle before tucking the bottle into the pouch next to her other one.

Once she turns back to me, she gives me a hesitant smile. "Thank you for the water. I ran out a while ago. To answer your question, yes, I walked here from the bus station in town."

"Why are you here?" Thor asks again, since the others didn't hear what she said before. She hesitates as she bites her lip and looks at all of us. She seems startled when Levi steps up next to Thor.

"A-Are you Thor? The President of Forest Creek Steel Archangel's MC?" she asks nervously, which is odd since I saw her eyeing his patches earlier. The tremor in her voice makes my chest tighten and I hate that she seems nervous or scared of us.

"Yes. Now answer me. Why are you here?"

"I need help and I'm looking for my dad. I have information that says he's a member here."

"Why do you need help?"

"I think my stepdad, and maybe my mom, are trying to sell me to someone."

I curse and hear more curses ring out behind me. Thor looks at Levi hesitantly, a worried look crossing his face.

Fuck. What is it with people and trying to sell those close to them?

He turns back to the woman. "Who's your dad?"

"Jax. Jaxon Witlock."

Turning, I look at Smoke and wince at the anger radiating off him.

"I've only had one daughter, and she died the day she was born twenty-one years ago to the day. I haven't touched a woman since that day when I broke up with my girlfriend. There's no way you're my daughter," he says in a hard voice.

Fuck, he went twenty-one years without having sex? That's some fucking monk-like restraint. And here I was thinking my streak was a long one. While none of us know what happened years ago, some say he was burned pretty badly by his pregnant girlfriend. From what we just heard, it sounds like that's true.

I turn back to the woman, along with most everyone else, and I'm surprised that she has a sad look on her face and her eyes are misting up as she shakes her head.

Smoke steps up in between me and Thor and she holds out some pictures to him. He takes them, and instead of looking over his shoulder at the pictures, I keep an eye on him to make sure he doesn't freak out and possibly hurt her. I know he'd never do it intentionally, but the anger rolling off him is making me cautious.

After a few moments, his hands start to shake. He looks back up at her and she hands him some papers and a notebook before pointing to a passage.

"I never died, but they made it look that way. I have more information to show you if you want, but after reading Mom's journals, I figured this would be the best place to start."

Jax reads the page and then the next couple. While he reads, my attention turns back to her. She's nibbling on her lip as she toys with the hem of her shirt. As the silence wears on, she starts to shuffle on her feet and her face seems a bit paler than before.

After a few more moments, Jax closes the notebook and looks back up at her. "What's your name?

"Mae. Mae Rose Cole."

I hear Levi gasp and my gaze snaps to hers in confusion, but she's watching Smoke with concern. I switch my focus to him and the look on his face is fucking murderous.

Mae whimpers and instinctively, I step in front of her, shielding her in case Smoke flips the fuck out. One of her small hands clutches the back of my cut and I feel her other hand land on my arm.

Shocks shoot down my arm and I inhale sharply. She inhales sharply as well, and some part of me settles when I realize it wasn't just me that felt that. Also, the need to protect her skyrockets even further.

"I get you're pissed as fuck, Smoke, and I don't fucking blame you, but scaring her until she faints isn't the answer. How about we go inside so she can sit down, and we can talk more? She's got to be tired as fuck after walking all the way out here under the hot sun and who knows what else to get here."

Out of the corner of my eye, I notice Levi walking toward Smoke and she hugs him, whispering something in his ear. After a few minutes, his breathing returns to normal and the scowl that's been a memory since Levi came here is now fully back in place. He gives her a curt nod and thrusts the papers toward Mae. The abrupt action causes her to jump back behind me and she whimpers again. I look over my shoulder at her in shock.

Fuck, did her stepdad beat her?

Turning back toward Smoke, I'm guessing he's thinking the same thing based on the look on his face. I hold out my hand for the papers and after hesitating for a moment; he thrusts them into my hand before stalking inside.

I quickly tuck the papers and pictures inside the notebook without looking at them and turn toward her so she's more at my side. She switches her grip to the front of my cut as she watches his retreating back with a scared and nervous expression on her face. I place a hand on her lower back, resisting the urge to wrap her tight against me. She's mine, but I'm even more certain that she'll be hesitant to agree to be mine, which makes my chest ache.

"None of us will hurt you as long as you aren't trying to bring harm to the club. We don't hurt women or children," I say as I look down at her. What I don't say is that sometimes we do have to take care of women depending on the situation, but Levi and Sasha have handled those instances in the past.

Her face screws up in confusion as she looks up at me. "Why the heck would I intentionally bring harm to the club? All I wanted to do was to meet my dad. Find out his side of the story because I now know my mom and stepdad have been lying to me my whole life. If he's willing, I was wondering if he'd be able to help me figure out a way to stay safe from my stepdad and Bruce."

Well, at least she still has a bit of sass and, for some reason, I'm finding her lack of actual cussing adorable as fuck.

Her face pales at the mention of them. "Oh, coconuts. Am I going to be in trouble or hurt if I stay here and Bruce or my stepdad bring their mess to your doors?"

I curse and wrap my arm around her trembling shoulders, pulling her closer to me. "If they come here looking for you, they'll have a fight on their hands."

In more way than one.

Levi looks up at me, a question in her eyes and I fucking pray she doesn't say anything right now. With how scared Mae was before and feeling her trembling increase, I'm afraid she might bolt or faint.

She winks and smirks at me. I return it, and then she turns toward Thor, patting his chest. "I'm going to check on Jax. Be nice, Hun."

He grunts and then smacks her ass as she walks past. She mock glares at him and then shrieks and laughs when Dragon picks her up bridal style, he laughs along with her.

"Dragon, put me down! I may be pregnant, but I can still walk, you jackass!"

Their laughter breaks the tension and has the rest of us laughing. Shaking my head, I look down at Mae, who's staring after them in confusion.

I lean down, whispering to fill her in. "That's Levi, Thor and Dragon's Old Lady. They're getting married next week."

Shock fills her face before she slightly tilts her head and nods. "Oh, they must have been who Susie and Jordan were talking about."

Someone abruptly stops next to me and when I look up, I'm surprised to see Axe's face tight with anger. Thor's looking between her and Axe, his face tight with concern.

"What'd you say?" Axe asks.

Mae shrinks back a little at his tone and presses closer into me. While I'm glad she's stepped closer in my arms and is seeking safety with me, I wish she were pressing against me for a different reason. I glare at Axe for scaring her again.

"I'm guessing you're Axe? Susie's older brother? I rode the bus from Rixen to here, and met Susie and her son, Jordan. They sat across the aisle from me. I was reading Mom's journals when the bus broke down. That's when I heard Jordan complaining that he was bored. Since I didn't know how long it would take to get fixed, I pulled out some paper."

Mae twists as she bends down to get something out of her bag. I have to bite my tongue to silence my groan at seeing her cute heart-shaped ass sticking out at me. When she stands back up, she has a notebook and flips to the back before handing it to Axe. She steps closer to me again, and I put my hand back on her hip, relieved when she leans into me further.

"Jordan and I played tic-tac-toe and hangman for about three hours while we waited for a new bus, and then again for almost another half-hour till we arrived in town on the second bus. We talked, and I found out the stuff I read online about the club was true, which is the complete opposite of what Preston told me throughout the years. Susie said they were coming to town to visit you, her parents, and to attend a baby shower as well as a wedding. I assume she means theirs. Or is someone else also getting married and having a baby?"

"Nah, it's just Levi, Thor, and Dragon for both events. Well, she's actually marrying just Thor, but her and Dragon will also say the vows." I pause and clear my throat as jealousy swirls in my gut. "Who's Preston, Sunshine?"

She blushes when my nickname for her slips and fuck do I love the pink that tinges her cheeks and neck. She winces, and my gut clenches tighter.

"Sorry that I didn't say that earlier. Preston is my stepdad. Preston Cole. The guy that I think they are going to sell me to is Bruce. My mom's name is Lillian Cole."

Instantly my body relaxes, and I release the breath I hadn't realized I'd been holding. Fuck, this woman already has me all twisted up over her.

Axe sighs and hands Mae back her notebook. "Sorry if I scared you, but it always freaks me the fuck out that her and Jordan take multiple buses to get here when they visit. Not to mention the return trip. I tried to get her a car, but she turned that down. Since then, I've offered multiple times to come get her, but she says she doesn't want to take me away from my appointments," he says, his voice heavy with irritation.

"While I was worried about the trip as well, I was more worried about them when she said they take four buses to get here. She seems really stubborn and the type of person not to take a handout from anyone," Mae says with a small smile.

Laughter rings out across the yard from the guys still out here and a few more clap Axe on the shoulder before heading inside. Axe shakes his head, smiling.

"You nailed that one, Sunshine. Both Axe and Susie are as stubborn as a mule."

"You keep it up, brother, and I'll make sure to tell Susie you called her a mule," Axe teases me as he winks at Mae.

I try to bite back my growl at him winking at Sunshine. She's mine and I won't stand for anyone flirting with my woman. Then what he says sinks in, and the growl comes out anyway.

"That's not what I said. If you get me cut off from my enchiladas with that bullshit, I'll beat your ass, Axe. Brother or not."

Susie's enchiladas are the best that I've ever had. She learned how to make them from their aunt and whenever Susie visits, she always brings me a bunch. They're fucking drool worthy.

Mae's laughter rings out and before long, me and the others join in. When I look down at her, I feel like the wind's been knocked out of me once again. The smile that lights up her face as she laughs makes her even more gorgeous.

As everyone's laughter dies down, I notice Thor eyeing both of us. Instinctively, I tighten my grip on her waist. The fucker just smirks at me.

"Mae, in a few hours, we're having a gender reveal party and sort of a baby shower all in one. You're welcome to join us. We can talk later about your situation. For now, why don't you rest and grab something to eat? While there will be food catered in for the party, feel free to grab something from the kitchen if you want it before then. You must be starving after walking here from town."

She looks at him, surprised, and then nods. "Congratulations and thank you for the invite. I accept. Also, thank you for letting me talk to Smoke and all of you."

He smiles and gives her a chin lift before heading inside, the rest of the guys following him.

Chapter 6
Timber

WITH EVERYONE HEADING TOWARD the clubhouse, I bend down and pick up Mae's bags off the ground. She whirls around almost instantly and tries to grab her backpack, but I sling it over my shoulder. She's been carrying them for who knows how long. It's the least I can do.

"It's okay, Sunshine. I'll carry them for you. Let's head inside, and you can sit down. Are you hungry?"

She eyes the backpack hesitantly and her fingers fidget at her sides, as if she wants to reach out and snag it from me. Remembering my own youth of always having to keep anything valuable with me or well-hidden lest my father sell it, I hand her back her backpack. Her body sags visibly in relief as she clutches it to her chest. Then she slips the notebook back inside and slides the strap over her shoulder.

"Thank you, it's just... My purse and a gift from my old bosses are in here," she whispers as her hand clutches the strap so hard that her knuckles turn white, which confirms my suspicions.

Taking a chance, and from my own personal experience, I bend down closer so only she can hear. "If you want someplace to lock up your purse and valuables while we're at the party, I have a safe bolted to the floor in my room in the clubhouse. That way, you won't have to carry your bag around all the time. You can use it and unless it's an emergency, I won't open it. I keep a couple of guns and some ammo in there."

She eyes me warily, almost like she's trying to decide if she can trust me. Fuck, I hope she does and that she'll let me help her. Plus, it'll give me an excuse to be able to talk to her more and get to know her better. Finally, she nods, and my body relaxes.

"Thank you, I'd appreciate it. Is there somewhere where I can get cleaned up before the party? I've been on the road all day and feel gross from being on that bus for so long. I don't have many clothes with me. Hopefully something that I brought will be acceptable enough for the party," she says as she nibbles her lip, her gaze lowering to the duffle bag hanging off my shoulder.

"Yeah. You can use the shower that's in my room here at the clubhouse. Though, while you're here, staying at the clubhouse might not be the best place long term for you. It can get loud and kind of crazy here. However, it'd be safer staying here in the compound rather than in town. We'd be able to protect you better against Preston and that Bruce guy," I say, spitting out their names before forcing myself to calm down.

"I've got lots of guest rooms in my house if you want to stay with me. Each room also has a safe bolted in the closet to store your stuff. It's the blue one with white trim over there," I say as I point at my house. "To the left of mine is Bear's, then it's Levi, Thor and Dragon's house, and finally, Phoenix's. He's our VP. Currently, we're the only ones with houses, but a few of my brothers are in the planning stages of building their own house. If you aren't comfortable staying with me, I bet Levi, Thor and Dragon would be okay to let you stay at their house. If you want to go into town to get anything, just let me know. I'll drive you."

Her gaze roams over the houses as she nibbles her lip. Fuck, I hope she takes my offer. Then she turns to me as she tilts her head slightly, a question in her eyes.

"Why are you offering to help me so much? You don't even know me."

Fuck. Might as well put some of it out there and hope she doesn't run. "How about we walk while we talk? Or would you prefer to go inside to sit down as we talk?"

She nods. "Let's walk. The breeze has picked up again, so it doesn't feel as hot anymore."

I lead her over to the road that winds through the compound to our houses. Taking a chance, I reach out and snag her hand, threading my fingers through hers. Thankfully, she doesn't pull away, but I can tell she's on edge from the tension I can feel running through her.

"I'll be completely honest with you. I'm offering because the instant I saw you, I wanted to know more about you. Your likes and dislikes. Favorite foods, movies, hobbies, everything. I want to spend more time with you. I like you. A lot. You're gorgeous, kind, and loving. I want to protect you and make sure no one will hurt you. And just to be clear, cause I'm sure Levi or Sasha would kick my ass if I don't clarify this. I'm not undermining you or assuming you can't protect yourself by that statement. It's just that I want to add my layer of protection to yours. Everything will go at your pace, but I'm hoping you'll let me get to know you better, just as you'll get to know me better."

I leave off the part that I'm almost positive she's the one for me and that I'm already half in love with her.

Her steps falter, and she turns to look at me in surprise. Her lips are slightly parted and it takes everything in me not to run my thumb across her plump lower lip. A second later, her eyes turn misty and my stomach bottoms out.

Shit.

Did I come on too strong?

"No one has ever said anything like that to me before. Or wanted to know that much about me. Ever," she whispers.

A tear escapes, and I find myself wiping it away before I even realize what I'm doing. A small gasp escapes her as my skin touches hers. When she slightly leans into my touch, it takes all my restraint not to lean down and kiss her.

After a few moments, I lower my hand and once again, take her hand in mine. A slight blush colors her cheeks again as she licks her lips. Even though I can tell she's nervous, she straightens her posture as her gaze locks with mine.

"I must be crazy, but I feel safe with you even though we only just met. Something tells me I can trust you and I've only been able to trust two other people after my grandparent's died – my old boss, Peggy, and her husband, Glen. Everyone else... Everyone else in my life has shown me that I can only depend on myself. I couldn't even rely on my mom. Preston was even worse. If it weren't for Peggy and the food banks, I probably would have died of starvation or the elements years ago. I've been mostly supporting myself since I was fifteen. I've seen and been through things no child should ever have to see or endure."

She pauses and licks her lips again as a variety of emotions flit across her face. My chest tightens and I want to know more, but the fear of pushing too much too soon has me biting my tongue.

"That said, I would like to get to know you better. You protected me, even from my dad and your friends, when they startled or scared me. My past doesn't help with those types of situations, either. You all are an intimidating bunch. However, there is something I need to know before we go any further. Are you seeing anyone? I won't be a side piece to anyone and if we do decide to take this further, I won't share you. If you cheat, I'm gone."

The tightness in my chest loosens at hearing she's willing to get to know me, and I can't stop my smile. "It may be hard to believe, especially with me being a biker, but I haven't been with anyone for almost nine months. Not even the bunnies. Shit, I should tell you about the bunnies."

I groan and wipe my hand over my face, but when I look back down at her, I have to bite my lip to keep my groan in at how sexy she looks right now. Her jaw is dropped in shock, and fuck, I really shouldn't be thinking about how good her lips would look around my dick.

At that thought, my dick twitches and strains against my jeans even harder. Fuck, I can already tell this is going to be a major test of restraint. I've never gotten this aroused by anyone before. She closes and opens her mouth a few times before eventually nodding. I tug a little on her hand and we start walking again.

"Okay. Not going to lie, but yeah, that is surprising for a biker to go that long without sex, even though we just heard how long it's been for my dad. I would have thought that you'd still be using the bunnies even if you weren't seeing someone. And Susie did tell me a little about them. Well, as much as she could since we were around Jordan and neither one of us wanted him to hear all that. I don't understand the appeal of being a bunny, but I'm not one to throw stones. She did mention there were two that usually stir up trouble, but there are four that seem pretty nice."

I groan again because that's putting it lightly for those two. Very lightly. "Yeah, there's two new bunnies, Crystal and Gigi. Even though they know Thor, Dragon, and Colt are taken, they still try to tempt them to stray from their women. None of them ever would, though. Thor and Dragon are crazy in love with Levi. Same for Colt and Sasha.

"As soon as Crystal and Gigi hear about you, they'll probably try to feed you a bunch of lies, so I'll just tell you now. I haven't been with either of them, though not for lack of trying on their part. The other bunnies, Roxy, CJ, Ashley, Ginger, Sarah, and Amy, have been here for a long time and yes, I've been with all of them except for Roxy. Roxy works here, but she isn't here for sex with any of us. CJ no longer has sex with my brothers, but she does still work here. We don't really consider Roxy or CJ bunnies anymore, even though that's what their job titles are on our books."

Her face scrunches up a little. "What made CJ change her mind? Sorry! I shouldn't have asked. It's not my business, so I shouldn't dig. Ignore me," she says as she winces and waves her free hand.

A chuckle escapes as I grin. "I'd never be able to ignore you, Sunshine." Pausing, I take in the slight blush that colors her cheeks. I fucking love seeing her flushed.

"It's alright in this case since everyone knows. CJ found out her brother, Drae, was Prospecting for our club. Long story short, she'd been taken, and neither had seen each other for about five years. CJ was injured, pretty badly, and had to have a bunch of plastic surgery done on her face. Drae was a teenager when CJ was taken and, from what they said, he was pretty scrawny at the time. Neither one recognized each other when CJ came here to be a club bunny. Both were also wearing colored contacts, so that didn't help either. When CJ found out about Drae, she asked if she could just work here, like Roxy, and not be here for the guys. Thor and Levi obviously didn't have any issue with it."

"They didn't..." she trails off as her cheeks heat.

I bite back a groan at how innocent she is and I wonder exactly *how* innocent she really is? Fuck, I need to stop thinking like this or I'll make her run for sure. Shaking my head, I continue.

"No, they didn't. Our Prospects aren't allowed to be with the bunnies—sexually or orally. They aren't allowed to drink, either, when they're Prospecting. They need to make sure they're ready for whenever one of us needs them to do something. Though, on very rare occasions, they will be allowed to drink, but they can't get drunk. For example, Sasha, Alexei, and Ethan have a pass today because they are Levi's family and it's a big celebration for them."

She nods. "That's a relief that they didn't do that. I bet that would have messed with their heads if they had."

We walk in silence as we loop around and start our way back toward the clubhouse. The closer we get, the more nervous I get since she hasn't said where she wants to stay while she's here. Or even said she wants to stay here to begin with.

Turning toward her, I notice she's nibbling on her bottom lip. She stops walking and I can't help but reach up and lightly tug her lip free of her teeth. Rubbing my thumb across her lip, I bite back another groan as her breath hitches and her cheeks tinge pink.

"What's got you nervous, Sunshine?"

The pink on her cheeks darkens. "I must be crazy, but if we're going to get to know each other better, I think I'd like to take you up on your offer to stay with you. Though, I'd like to take one of the spare rooms if that's okay? I'm not the type of woman to just fall into bed with someone."

She looks up at me shyly and I have to fight not to lean down and kiss her. I smile and she returns it.

"I'd love to have you stay with me and, of course, taking a spare room is alright. How about we head inside and you can freshen up? Do you need to run into town for anything before the party?" I leave out the part about falling in bed with someone, because the thought of her doing that with another man has my anger rising. Though I would have liked her in my bed tonight and in my arms, I know she's nowhere near ready for that.

She nibbles her lip again as she looks down at her duffel bag that I'm still carrying for her. "I have a sundress in there that I'm hoping will be okay enough for the party. I'm not even sure why I grabbed it since I've always tried not to wear anything that would draw attention to me."

Doesn't she know how beautiful she is? She could wear a burlap sack and still be sexy as fuck. My brain freezes as the rest of her words register. The last part of what she said has me instantly on edge. "Can I ask why you didn't want to draw attention to yourself?"

"Is," she pauses as she clears her throat as she looks at me hesitantly. "Is it okay to save that story for another time? It's kind of a long story, and I'm not sure what time the party starts."

Nodding, I squeeze her hand. While I know it's a delay tactic, I let it go. I'll get her history soon and show her she can rely on me.

"Of course, Sunshine. And we've got a little over an hour before the party starts. There will be some people from town coming and I think even Susie and Jordan are coming. Smoke's sister, Nikki, is here with her daughter, Sadie, too. Let's get you up to my room and I'll show you the safe you can use. Then you can freshen up. Later tonight, we'll get your things from my room before we go to my house."

I wince as I realize we never asked her something and we should have. Her brow furrows in confusion when she catches it.

"Sorry, we should have asked you before, but do you have any weapons on you? We're not saying you can't have them depending on what they are, but if you do, we just need to know about them. Also, we don't allow drugs anywhere inside the compound. Though if you did have any, I'm sure Bastion, Levi's dog, would have been over here already warning us."

She shakes her head, but I don't miss how her eyes light up at the mention of a dog on the compound. "I don't have any weapons, not even a pocketknife, and I told your Prospect that earlier as well. I've never done drugs, but don't know if Bastion will be able to smell them on my stuff or not. Preston does a lot of drugs and he keeps my mom strung out on them as a way to control her. His words, not mine. That's why I stuck around so long. I was saving up for us both to leave. If I could talk her into it, that is. Also, to get her into rehab if she agrees. She was a pretty good mom before Preston came back into our lives."

My chest aches at the helpless look on her face. Fuck, if Preston is doing that to her mom, she's lucky as shit that he didn't try anything with her.

"So, how is it that Bastion is able to detect drugs?"

"He used to be a police force dog. Him being able to sniff out drugs has helped us a few times when we'd have parties here. Some people came here from town and had some on them. I'm not sure if they were trying to deal once they got here or if it was for personal use, but the drugs were trashed, and they were banned from ever coming back."

"So, it's true then? You guys aren't into anything illegal?"

"No, we aren't into anything illegal. We make our money from the businesses we own or have a stake in around town. Those of us that manage a business get a larger cut of the profits than those that don't." I don't tell her that sometimes we have to take out the trash. I'm sure it will come up at some point, especially if Preston or Bruce cause a lot of trouble.

"What do you do? I'm guessing something outdoors since you're so tan," she says as she runs her hand along my arm. A shiver runs through me at her touch. Fuck, I've never responded like this to a woman before.

Clearing my throat, I answer her question. "Well, you're half right. I run our construction business, Steel Construction. I spend a lot of time in the office, but I also like to be out on the construction sites, getting my hands dirty so to speak. Besides, it helps me to get a closeup view on how the projects are going."

"Wait," she says as she looks over her shoulder and gestures to the houses behind us. "Did your crews build these houses?"

I can't stop the grin that pulls at my lips. "Yes, we did. We also did the expansion on the club house years ago when we added the second and third floors as well as going further back into the property."

"Holy cannoli," she whispers as she looks around again with her jaw dropped. "You guys do amazing work. Now I'm really curious about what your house looks like on the inside."

My chest swells at her praise and her cheeks flush once again when her gaze returns back to me. "Later tonight, I'll give you the tour when you're ready to head home. I hope you'll like it."

Fuck, I really hope she likes my house, but if there is something she doesn't like, I'll rip it out if need be and redo it to her tastes.

Chapter 7

Mae

As we near the clubhouse, all of the motorcycles parked outside start to make me nervous again. I hadn't realized there were that many before, but my attention had mainly been focused on the bikers on the road rather than on the bikes at the clubhouse.

"Is your club really big? There are a lot of bikes here."

Timber shakes his head. "Our club has twelve chapters across six states. Some of these bikes belong to my brothers in the Junction Creek chapter. They're almost four hours away. We've always been close to them, but ever since Reaper, who is the President of the Junction Creek chapter, adopted Levi as his sister, we've become even closer."

A haunted look crosses his face before he masks it. I'm curious what that look was about, but now isn't the right time. Especially since I just put off a pretty big topic myself. Well, big in the fact that there's a lot of information packed into the whole 'why I try to hide and blend in' thing.

When we walk up the porch steps of the clubhouse, my nerves return full force. Timber must be able to sense it, because he gives my hand a squeeze.

"Everything's going to be okay, but if the bunnies give you any shit, just let me know."

How can he say everything's going to be okay? And right now, the bunnies are the furthest thing from my mind. I'm almost positive that a certain someone doesn't like me and doesn't want anything to do with me.

Though to be fair, Mom really did do a number on him by lying to him and saying I died. I know I said that I was trying to get Mom away from Preston and into rehab, which is true, but I'm not sure if I can ever forgive her for keeping my dad from me. Even if he does hate me, wants nothing to do with me, and I never see him again after this. It's not like I asked for any of this to happen.

Taking a deep breath, I follow Timber into the clubhouse. As we walk through what looks to be the main room, I can't keep myself from blushing at the looks the other men and a few women give us when they notice Timber is still holding my hand. I try to pull away, but his grip tightens, which makes them grin even wider.

Feeling a heavy gaze on me, I look around, and almost trip over my feet when I see my dad over in a corner, taking a long pull off of whatever's in the bottle in his hand. He's practically fuming as he tracks my every move, and it increases when his gaze locks onto our joined hands.

As my dad continues to stare at me, or maybe us, I can feel myself wilting under his heavy, hateful gaze. Maybe I shouldn't have come here. Maybe he really didn't want me and loathes me even more now that he knows I'm alive. Tears prick my eyes, and I barely notice when Timber opens a door and leads me inside before shutting it and locking it.

Instead of letting my emotions out in front of Timber, I force myself to look around his room. I'm slightly surprised that he's kept it clean and tidy. I don't know if that's his doing though or the bunnies that work here.

A shiver runs up my spine, and I wonder how many women he's had in here. Even though he said he hasn't been with anyone for a long time, they were still in here. Is it right to trust Timber so much? Especially since we literally just met? Am I making a fool of myself? I wish I had someone I could talk to about this, but there's no one except Peggy. If I call her to talk about him, then she'll know where I am. There's no way I'd put her in harm's way if Preston comes asking around about where I went.

My hands tighten on my backpack and I wish I had my duffel bag. Maybe I should just leave after freshening up. If my dad doesn't want me or won't help me, his brothers as Timber calls them, would side with him over me any day. Though the thought of leaving makes my chest ache.

Crap.

I should probably stop calling him Dad, even in my head, and just refer to him as Smoke, since it's pretty obvious he doesn't want me. Maybe the shower will help settle my thoughts so I can think straight.

"I-is it okay to shower first?"

Timber pauses at his closet, his hand on the doorknob as he looks at me curiously. Instead of asking me the questions he seems to want an answer to, he just nods and crosses the room. He opens another door and I realize there's a bathroom adjoined to his room. After he sets my duffle bag on the counter, he steps back into the bedroom.

"The towels are clean. Let me know if there's anything else you need. If we don't have it here, we can send a Prospect in to get it unless you need to go yourself. If that's the case, I'll take you into town."

I shake myself internally. There's no way a guy like him hasn't been with anyone for as long as he says he has. Besides being unbelievably handsome, he's too nice, too considerate, and too helpful. There's no way he'd want to be with someone like me. At that thought, all the comments about me from the past bombard me, making it hard to breathe.

Keeping my eyes downcast, I nod, not able to trust my voice right now. I need to get away from him and his incredibly good smelling cologne so I can think straight.

Out of the corner of my eye, I notice him frowning and my chest aches even more at the sight, but I can't let myself get closer to him. Even if I said I would, and I do want to, it's just that I'd most likely end up being hurt even more. There's no way I'll be able to be with Timber since he's in the same club as Smoke.

Stepping into the bathroom, I continue to keep my gaze down and go to shut the door. I gasp in shock as Timber's arm lashes out, his hand landing with a thud on the door, making it bang against the wall.

"I want you to get rid of those thoughts about running away, Sunshine."

My eyes widen and I finally look up at him, only to shrink back a little at the hard look on his face. How did he know what I was thinking about? For a few moments, neither of us says anything. Then his face softens.

"Smoke's been given a shock of a lifetime. Give him a little time to adjust to the news. To you. And in case you're also questioning me, I meant every word. We'll talk more after your shower, but please don't run without talking to him or me. Please."

Tears prick my eyes again, and I swallow thickly. Licking my dry lips, I nod as I take a shuddery breath. "Okay, but he isn't the only one that's been given a shock of a lifetime and hasn't had much time to process things. He doesn't know everything that I found out between last night and now. I darn near fainted when I found a birth certificate and death certificate for me under a different last name and birthdate."

Shaking my head, I ignore the increasing tension in the room. Crap, maybe I shouldn't have said that. Sighing, I clear my throat. "However, if he makes it clear that he doesn't want anything to do with me or won't help me, then I'll have to leave. Preston will most likely assume I've found out about Smoke somehow and will come here at some point. If he won't help me, I'll need to get in as much distance as I can from here before Preston or Bruce find me. I refuse to allow myself to be sold to settle Preston's drug debt."

"If Smoke won't help you, I will. Don't go running, Sunshine. Please."

A tear escapes at the intense look on his face, even though I try to stop it. I duck my head and turn away before he can see me. However, his large hand encircles my wrist before I get very far, and I can't hold in my squeak of shock when I'm abruptly pulled into his arms.

My hands land on his chest and I push away slightly, even though we can both tell I don't want to since I barely put any effort into the motion. Sighing, I rest my forehead against his chest as I try to calm my racing heart. It shocks me how much my body starts to relax the longer he holds me.

When he kisses my hair, that seems to be the thing that triggers my tears, and I cling to his vest as I sob. His arms tighten around me, which only makes me cry harder. Aside from Peggy, I can't even remember a time when someone comforted me like this.

I'm not sure how long I stand in his arms crying before my body sags. I feel even more dehydrated than before, thanks to how much crying I've done. Timber kisses my hair again before pulling back slightly and then kissing my forehead as his hands settle on my waist.

"Feel a little better, Sunshine?"

Taking a deep breath, I nod. Surprisingly, I do feel better even though I'm still anxious as hell. He kisses my forehead again, and I'm shocked when I find myself leaning into his kiss. What the hell is happening to me?

"How about you freshen up? We can talk more when you're done."

"Okay, thank you, Timber." My voice is practically a whisper but judging by how his hands tighten around my hips, I'm positive he heard me.

"When it's just us, call me Liam. If we're around the clubhouse or out in public, that's where you'll need to call me Timber. It's my road name."

I look at him in confusion. Why is it so important that I not call him Liam when we're around others? Before I can ask, he places a finger to my lips.

"We'll talk more later. Now, scoot that pretty ass of yours into the bathroom before I take matters into my own hands and clean you myself."

My eyes widen and my lips part in surprise at how forward he is. I lick my dry lips without thinking as I feel myself flushing. His eyes darken and he moans when my tongue brushes against his finger. He lowers his head, his mouth hovering over mine for a second, and when I don't pull away, he leans in further and kisses me.

Sweet mother of Jesus.

I've never kissed anyone before, but even in my wildest dreams, I never expected it to feel like this. My lips move tentatively at first as I try to mimic the way his lips move. His tongue teases the crease of my lips as his hands move lower from my waist until they cup my ass. He pulls me closer to him, and I gasp when I feel the bulge in his jeans against my belly. The second my lips part, he thrusts his tongue inside my mouth. I moan when the kiss turns more passionate and heated. My thighs clench as his hands tighten around me.

I'm not sure how long we stand there kissing, but when he pulls back, both of us are breathing heavily and his lips are red and swollen. Mine are most likely the same.

"Need you to go in the bathroom, Sunshine, and shut the door before I do something I know you aren't ready for." His voice is lower and huskier than usual. My thighs clench once again and his blue eyes darken even further at the action.

Chapter 8

Mae

A SQUEAK ESCAPES ME at Liam's hungry look, and I hurry to do as he says. Even though I don't think he'd enter, I still find myself locking the door. A habit from living with Preston.

I pause with my hand still on the doorknob as the other goes to my lips. *I can't believe I just had my first kiss!*

That thought has my body freezing as I realize I have absolutely no experience and I have a feeling Liam has way more than me. Will he be satisfied being with someone who isn't experienced? Or will he get bored with me eventually and kick me out?

Shaking my head, I push those thoughts out of my head as I strip and turn on the water. Rummaging through my bag, I pull out my shower supplies and step into the shower once the water's warm. I can't contain my moan at feeling the warm water pounding down on me. When was the last time I felt true warm water? Maybe earlier this spring, so early May? Was that when the water heater finally crapped out? Preston always said he'd get around to it, but so far, he hasn't. Regardless, I'm going to take advantage of the warm water while I have it.

I lather up my hair and shampoo it a couple of times before finally conditioning it. Next, I shave my legs and do some way overdue grooming. With the onset of fall, the water temperature started to cool dramatically. I never lingered for very long under the cold water to keep everything groomed how I normally like it, even if I am the only one that sees it.

Once that's done, I grab my lavender body wash and lather up, making sure to really scrub myself clean. I've always felt like there was a layer of grime covering me whenever I was in our trailer or around Preston when he was drinking or using drugs. The thought has me scrubbing even harder to completely wash him and that place off me.

When I feel like I'm finally clean, I rinse off one more time, shut the water off and dry off. Digging through my clothes, I get dressed and pray my sundress will look good enough for the party. I may be a little chilly later on if the party goes into the evening since I don't have a jacket that will look good with it, but I'll deal with that later. It's my nicest outfit, so it'll have to do.

Pulling out my makeup, I quickly apply it. My skin is pretty fair and clear, so I don't need much. A little blush, eyeshadow, mascara, and some lip gloss. Grabbing my brush, I start combing my hair and a groan escapes when I realize I didn't grab my blow dryer and straightener. Darnit. Now my hair will be frizzy.

With a sigh, I look at my reflection. The blue fabric makes my dark blue eyes pop even more than usual. My long blond hair hangs down to the middle of my back. The dress hugs my ample chest before tapering in some at the waist and then flaring a little at my hips before ending a few inches above my knees. Even though I'm skinny due to how I've grown up, my hips have always been a bit wider than the other skinny girls in school or at the diner. I've always hated that because they make my already weird body size even weirder. Not to mention they made clothes shopping even harder. I probably wouldn't have minded them if I had grown up in a normal household and had always had as much food as I needed growing up.

A frown pulls at my lips when I realize this dress showcases exactly how skinny I really am due to lack of consistent meals. Although Peggy gave me as many shifts as she could, it wasn't every day. Even with offering to take extra shifts if someone had something come up, it wasn't enough. For the past few years, the only good, filling meals I had were when I worked at the diner. While I also worked at the grocery store, my shifts there were less than my normal shifts at the diner, unfortunately.

On the days that I didn't work at the grocery store or diner, I'd spend a few dollars at the store to get me enough food to fill my belly. However, since I couldn't go home to eat, that meant I had no means to cook anything or store refrigerables. The food I usually got on those days were a few granola bars and maybe an apple or banana.

Over the years, I'd grown accustomed to only having one small meal a day. I barely get any food when I'm at home anymore, so there was no point in trying to eat more than once a day while I was still living there. Preston would have been jumping on me like white on rice about where I was getting money for food and then taking what money I had on me for himself. However, once I find a job here, or wherever I'm going if I end up leaving, I'll be able to buy whatever the heck I want for groceries.

A knock on the door startles me out of my thoughts and I look down at myself, doing one last look over to make sure I'm presentable. With a sigh, I realize I look as good as it'll get with the clothes and supplies I currently have. I need to go shopping at some point.

Opening the door, Liam's on the other side and is looking down at his phone. It takes me a moment to realize that he has a couple of bags in his hand. He looks up and I can feel myself blushing under the weight of his heat-filled gaze as it travels up and down my body.

"You look gorgeous, Sunshine."

"Thank you," I whisper as I shift anxiously. No one has ever described me as good looking, let alone gorgeous.

I was always bullied while growing up because we lived in a trailer park, and the bullying got even worse after Preston moved in with us. Even though my weight hardly ever fluctuated, he'd frequently tell me I was too fat, and then the next day he'd tell me I was so skinny no one would ever want me because I was all skin and bones. Who'd want to feel up a skeleton?

At school, it was no better. On top of being trailer park trash, I'd been told more times than I could count that I was ugly and no one would ever want me. That my mom and stepdad would have to pay someone to be with me. A pang hits me as the memory of Preston's phone conversation with Bruce bombards me. Shaking myself internally, I push those memories aside for now.

Timber... I mean, Liam, shakes his head and clears his throat, before holding up the bags. "Sasha, one of our Prospects, ran to the store to get you a few things. She saw you didn't have much with you, so she wanted to grab you some stuff just in case you needed anything."

"Thank you," I say as I take the bags, which are surprisingly heavy. As his words sink in, I pause and look back up at him, tilting my head slightly. "Wait, you guys allow women to Prospect? I thought only men could be in MC's."

He grins and damn do I have to fight not to clench my thighs in response. Holy heck, this man is sex on a stick.

"Yeah, we recently voted to allow women to put their name in to join the club. We currently have one woman, Levi, who is fully patched into the club. Sasha is our only woman Prospect so far."

Wow, that's surprising. Though the little I know about motorcycle clubs comes from movies and a few books, which I always figured weren't a true portrayal. Not to mention everything Preston had told me about the club throughout the years. Though, I now realize I need to take his words with a grain of salt. While, yes, I'm sure there are clubs out there that do everything he said, it doesn't seem like the Steel Archangel's are into that stuff.

Then the rest of his words sink in and I shake my head, confused. "Wait, the same Levi that's getting married to two guys?"

"Yeah, that's her," he says, his grin getting wider and my curiosity increases about this Levi woman. She must have done something to impress these guys to vote to allow women to patch in. They don't look like the kind of guys that would vote in a woman just because she's engaged to someone in the club. Er, two someones I guess.

"Later you'll have to tell me more about MC life. I'm afraid I don't know much and what I do know is probably inaccurate to some degree."

Liam smiles fully at that, and my breath hitches at how his smile lights up his handsome face, even more so than usual.

"I'll hold you to that, Sunshine." He leans in to place a chaste kiss on my lips, and then playfully swats my thigh. "Now get that sexy ass in there and finish getting ready. The party starts soon."

My cheeks heat as I watch him walk away. Holy cow, he's got a nice ass! My cheeks heat as I chastise myself for cursing. He turns to sit down on his bed, and when he sees me staring at him, he cocks an eyebrow at me as he smirks.

Crap, he caught me ogling him again!

My cheeks flame even hotter as I pivot on my heel and rush back into the bathroom, shutting the door again. Even through the door, I can hear the deep rumble of his laughter, the sound sending tingles down my spine.

Shaking my head, I sift through the bags and feel my cheeks heating yet again when I realize Sasha got me some sexy lingerie and underwear. Holy frick... Who the heck would I wear this for? It's not like anyone's going to see my pajamas while I'm staying here. And while, yes, Liam kissed me a couple of times, it doesn't mean I'm just going to hop into his bed.

Taking a deep breath, I pull out the lingerie and take stock of what else she got me. A sigh of relief escapes when I see some normal underwear as well. There are also some skinny jeans, leggings, t-shirts, socks, and flip-flops in the first bag. The other bags have some makeup, shower supplies, hygiene and hair products. I almost do a happy dance when I see a hair dryer, straightener, and a curling iron among them. Quickly, I unbox the hair dryer and straightener before getting to work taming my frizzy hair.

Thirty minutes later, I finish straightening the last portion of my hair and I rummage through my makeup bag until I find my sculpting mud. Opening it, I frown as I see how little I have left—enough for today and maybe one or two more days. I'll need to run into town tomorrow so I don't run out. I should probably get some more clothes, too.

And more regular undergarments.

I don't need a lot of frilly things and I'm not sure my skin would like the lacy bras and underwear Sasha picked out for me. Shaking off my thoughts, I apply the sculpting mud and smooth down my little fly aways.

Taking in my reflection, I hardly recognize myself. My cheeks and neck are still a little pink, and not from the makeup. For once, a real smile tugs at my lips.

I look happy, and for the most part, I am.

Though, that is in part thanks to the man on the other side of the door. Quickly, I put away my things and tidy up so that I'm not leaving a mess behind for Liam.

Grabbing the bags, I inhale deeply and turn the doorknob. Liam looks up from his phone as I walk back into his room and set the bags down on a chair. His eyes darken as his gaze roams over me as he sits up on the bed.

As the silence drags on, I shift in place, feeling uncomfortable under the weight of his gaze. Seeing me shift, he shakes his head and clears his throat as he gets up and walks over to me. His large, rough hand cups my jaw as he tilts my head up as he runs this thumb across my bottom lip.

"Make sure you stick by me tonight, Sunshine. Don't want my brothers getting any ideas."

I frown in confusion about what he could be talking about, but then my mind blanks as he lowers his head and kisses me. His other hand moves to the back of my head as he angles me before deepening the kiss.

Shakily, I raise my arms and wrap them around his neck, my hands automatically going to his hair. As my fingers play with his hair, I feel his chest rumble before one of his hands snakes down my side. He grips my hip and pulls me against him. A whimper escapes me as I feel a hard bulge in his pants. My core heats as his grip tightens on my waist.

A knock sounds at the door, breaking the spell. Liam pulls back, breathing heavily. "Let me see who it is, and then we'll lock up your stuff before heading down."

All I can do is nod, and when he steps away, my body instantly feels cold. Something that I'm surprised to find I really don't like.

Chapter 9

Mae

ONCE MY THINGS ARE locked up, Timber leads me downstairs after giving me a key to his room. As we pass people, he introduces me. By the tenth person, I'm extremely thankful that almost everyone has on a vest, I mean a cut as Timber calls them, since they have their names sewn onto them.

When we make it to the bar, Timber grabs a beer. "What would you like, Sunshine?"

"C-can I have a bottle of water? I still feel a little dehydrated after today."

Timber nods and I'm thankful he doesn't pry. I really don't want to get into the fact that I've never had an alcoholic drink in my life. Mainly because my view on alcohol has been severely tainted due to what I've seen Preston do when he was drunk.

The Prospect, who I find out is called Drae, hands me my water and Timber takes my hand before leading me down a hallway. He points out the kitchen and I practically drool at the commercial grade appliances. While I mainly waitressed at the diner, I also helped in the kitchen. My fingers itch to cook something, and at some point, I'll have to make my enchiladas since Timber says he loves them. I'm not sure if they'll measure up to Susie's, but there's only one way to find out.

Timber's chuckle pulls me out of my thoughts and I feel my face heat. "Sorry—I love to cook, and that kitchen is flippin' gorgeous! I wonder if they'd let me help cook meals? Or bake!"

"I bet they would. Later we can ask Levi. She oversees all of the meal planning. I'm sure Thor and Dragon would appreciate your help because Levi doesn't rest as much as they'd like, what with her being pregnant with twins and all that."

My eyes widen at the news. She's involved with two men and is now pregnant with twins? The woman must have the patience of a saint.

Timber laughs as he winks at me. "Yeah, she definitely deserves a medal for putting up with them, as well as the rest of us assholes."

I wince as I realize I must have said that out loud. Crap, I hope I didn't insult anyone. I try to shake off my nerves when Timber tugs slightly on my hand, pulling me back out into the hallway and then outside.

There are several tables set up around the backyard and they've already lit all four of the firepits. In the distance, there's a large wooden stage that has a large wood backdrop on it.

Wait.

Are those targets painted on them? I frown as I stare at them. They aren't like normal targets because there are three bullseyes in a vertical line instead of the usual one bullseye that you'd see. Plus, there's two other blue dots that I'm not sure what they're for. Does someone have a bow and arrow they practice with?

I'm pulled out of my thoughts when Timber squeezes my hand. He pauses as he looks around before leading me through the sea of people, but he doesn't introduce me like before. When he comes to a stop, I realize why. In front of us are some women and the one that I remember being called Levi.

"Pregnancy looks good on you, Levi. Any chance you can give me a hint as to if I picked the right team?" he asks as he gives her puppy dog eyes, which makes me laugh along with the rest of the women.

"You know as well as I do that the genders were sealed and only Reaper and Ethan know the results since they're doing the reveal. What was your pick again?"

He smiles widely. "Team girl—all the way."

Levi winks at him and two other women pump their fists in the air before reaching out to high five Timber. "Team girl!" one of them whisper shouts.

I look between them all, confused. Seeing my confusion, Levi leans toward me.

"Don't tell my fiancés but there's a bet going around as to what the babies' genders will be," she whispers.

Shock fills me at that. "Is everyone else in on it?"

She nods as she laughs. "Everyone in our chapter and even my brother, Reaper's chapter, are in on it. I'm not sure how everyone has kept their big mouths shut around my men, but I don't think they suspect anything." She pauses as she looks over at her men, a smirk forming. "It'll be interesting to see how they react when Timber and Smithy dole out everyone's winnings."

Why would Timber be handing out everyone's winnings? At my confused look, Levi glares at Timber.

"I see someone hasn't told you much about us, has he?"

"No, he said we'd talk later about it. I wanted to freshen up before the party since I was traveling all day."

Timber winces. "I promise we'll talk more about the club, but Smithy and I are the Treasurers for our respective chapters. I—... I mean, would you ladies like me to bring you over some cupcakes?"

I look up at him, confused once again. When he sees me looking at him, he subtly nods to my right and when I turn, Thor and someone who looks exactly like him are walking toward us. Oh, right. They don't know about the bet.

"Yes, if you could please," one of the women says as she bats her eyes at Timber.

My stomach tightens at the gesture until I see that she's wearing a Prospect cut. She must be Sasha and if memory serves, she's with another guy in the club. Colt, I think it was.

Looking over my shoulder, I see Thor and his twin got sidetracked on their way here and are now talking with some other guys from Junction Creek according to the back of their cuts. Turning around, I have to bite my cheek to keep from giggling as Sasha continues to give Timber a puppy dog look.

Timber scowls at her. "I should make you go and get them, Prospect."

Sasha feigns shock. "I'm one of the twins' godmothers! Also, you know Thor gave the okay for me to not work during the party, so you aren't allowed to pull that tonight."

Timber grumbles, but I can tell it's just an act. He turns toward me, his hand tightening on my waist and he kisses my forehead. Out of the corner of my eye I can see Levi and Sasha sharing a look and my cheeks heat. Crap, if everyone keeps this up, I'll be in a permanent state of redness.

"Stay here with Levi and the ladies. I'll be back with some food in a few." Then he turns and weaves back into the crowd.

I look around, suddenly unsure, but then relax slightly when Levi smiles widely at me.

"Sit with us, Mae," she says as she pats the chair next to her. Once I sit, she squeezes my hand. "Now, let me introduce you. These are my sisters, Sasha and Nikki, respectively. On Nikki's lap is my adorable niece, Sadie," she says, confirming that the Prospect is in fact Sasha. "Then it's my friends, Roxy, Allison, and Erin. Ladies, this is Mae."

Shyly, I give a small wave. "Hello."

"Is it true?" Nikki asks hesitantly as she looks between Levi and me.

Then Levi's and Timber's words from earlier sink in and I swallow nervously. Holy cow, I'm meeting with my aunts and cousin for the first time. Please don't let me screw this up.

"Y-yes. I didn't know until last night when I found my real birth certificate. I had no idea what my dad's name was until then because neither my mom nor my stepdad, Preston, would tell me his name. Just that he died not too long after I was born. That the club he was in did a lot of illegal things, like running drugs, weapons, and was involved with human trafficking. I know that's not true now, but that's what I've been told since I was little."

All the women scowl, almost in unison, but it's the looks on Levi's and Sasha's faces that really have me nervous. They're almost as intimidating as the men are when they're angry. No wonder they fit in well with the guys.

"That bitch and asshole are in for a rude awakening if they ever show their faces here," Levi hisses.

That sets me immediately on edge, darn near panicking. "Please don't hurt my mom. Well, unless she is also in on this or if she does something else to deserve it in the future. Aside from what she pulled on my dad when I was born, she was a good mom back before Preston came back into our lives when I was eight. Ever since I started working, I've been saving up so that I can get her away from Preston and into rehab if she'll accept it. He keeps her pumped full of drugs as a way to control her.

"I don't think I'll ever be able to forgive her for not telling me the truth about my dad. I have no idea if I'll ever be able to be close to her again, but I don't want her hurt. She's been through enough pain because of the car accident and then Preston's abuse on top of that. Please don't let anyone hurt her," I beg her.

A growl comes from behind me as cupcakes are plopped down unceremoni-ously on the table. Large hands lift me up before I find myself sitting on Timber's lap, one of his hands holding my hand and the other wrapped tightly around my waist. Despite not even knowing him for a day, my body starts to relax as his rough hands rub soothingly against my hand and waist. Leaning forward, he kisses my temple before leveling Levi with a hard look.

"Why is my Sunshine damn near crying?"

Oh, sugar honey ice tea.

Chapter 10
Mae

HOW MUCH DID HE hear? Though I also don't miss the fact that several eyebrows go up at his statement. Wow, I am totally not ready to unpack all that right now. Instead, I ignore him as I continue to stare at Levi.

"Please?"

Levi sighs. "I'll do what I can, but it would help if I knew more about what happened. How about we get together later? Or I can come over tomorrow morning so we can talk more? For the time being though, you might want to steer clear of Jax. Nikki and I were barely able to get him to calm down and have him not shut himself up in his room. The only thing that is keeping him slightly sane and grounded right now is finding out if he's getting more nieces, nephews, or one of each."

I nod, and then tilt my head in confusion as I look over Levi, Sasha, and Nikki again. Levi said all three of them are sisters, but none of them look alike. Plus, Sasha has a bit of a Russian accent. Or maybe they're adopted?? The three of them grin as they share a look before turning to me.

"You're trying to figure out if we're related by blood, aren't you?" Nikki asks.

My cheeks heat as I wince and nod. "Sorry, but yes, since none of you look alike."

Everyone laughs at my confusion, and I fight against my body's instincts, trying not to shrink in on myself. They aren't laughing *at* me. Relax, girl.

"Jax adopted me as his sister a few of weeks after I came here. And I mean that in a club way, not legally. I have no biological siblings, but I do have a large chosen family. Aside from Jax, that includes Sasha and her twin brother Alexei, Ethan, Jax, and Reaper or Andre as I call him, as my siblings. As well as my Uncle Bear. My dad, Roy, is somewhere around here, but he's not part of the club.

"Since Jax adopted me, he also got my entire family. Plus, both Nikki and Sadie have welcomed me into their family, just like mine has welcomed both of them. I see everyone from both our club and Andre's club as my family, which does include a few bunnies. Also, if you really are Jax's daughter, then that means you are family as well," Levi says as she grins at me.

"I'm Jax's only sibling by blood, so aside from Levi's family, there are no other blood aunts or uncles. That is, unless you end up staying here after everything is settled. Then you will earn a whole slew of uncles from the club since you're Jax's daughter and a true princess of the club," Nikki says as she winks at me.

Timber's grip tightens around me, and I find myself squeezing his hand back, even though I'm extremely nervous about everything between us. That doesn't even include my anxiety about if Smoke will accept me or not. I don't want to cause any problems with the club if Smoke and I continue to have issues, plus any additional tension if I keep seeing Timber. And I don't even want to unpack the whole princess thing right now, whatever that means.

We fall into conversation and the ladies fill me in on club life and good places to go around town to shop. When the conversation turns to today's party, I'm surprised to find out there's going to be a knife throwing competition. Turns out, Levi used to compete professionally.

"How will the competition work?" I ask.

"There will be two teams of eight people. It was decided months ago that we'd go club against club so there will be two people at a time, one from each club, that will compete against each other per the WKTL rules. We'll go over the rules and scoring before the competition for everyone watching, but those that are competing are aware of them already."

"What's the WKTL?"

"World Knife Throwing League. That's the league I used to compete in," Levi says. "For our club, it will be Timber, Tripp, Gunner, Bones, Sasha, Alexei, Dragon, and myself competing. For the Junction Creek club, it will be Reaper, Punisher, Beast, Razor, Loki, Python, Drake, and Nathan. Thor will draw who will compete against who."

I look up at Timber in shock. "You're going to participate?"

He grins back at me as his thumb rubs against my waist again. "Yeah, Sunshine, I'm going to throw. Will you cheer for me?" he asks and wiggles his eyebrows at me, causing me to laugh.

"Of course, I'll cheer for you."

The look he gives me makes me blush and shift nervously on his lap, only to freeze when I feel his hard length underneath me, which causes my blush to deepen. His shoulders shake with silent laughter and his eyes are bright with amusement and something else I can't recognize.

"Stop it," I hiss quietly, which only makes him laugh harder.

Shaking my head, I think back to who all Levi said was going to be competing. Wait...

"Is that fair if you used to compete and your brothers and sister have also trained for years? Doesn't that weigh the odds too much in your club's favor?"

Laughter once again rings out at my question.

"A little bit, but when Reaper stayed here a few months back, Levi worked with him a lot and then he passed on her training to his club. Plus, there were a few times we went to Reaper's clubhouse, and same for them coming here. Each time, Levi, Alexei, and I worked with everyone as well," Sasha replies.

Dark looks cross both her and Levi's faces for a moment before they're masked. Wonder what that was about?

Levi shakes her head as she clears her throat. "Doing the competition by club was what was voted for the most by everyone, so that's what we're doing. We'll keep going until there's one person left. The guys all want to make this a reoccurring thing, so there's a main trophy that will get passed from winner to winner each time. The winner will also get a blade engraved with the Steel Archangel's logo and today's date that they'll get to keep as a souvenir.

We're interrupted by a child's squeal and when I turn to see who it is, I can't stop my smile.

"Mae!" Jordan yells as he runs toward me.

I slide off Timber's lap, much to his unhappiness, and kneel down on the ground, opening my arms to catch Jordan. Giving him a tight hug, I go to release him, but his arms stay wrapped around me. Repositioning my arms around him, I pick him up as I stand, and he wraps his legs around my waist.

"I was hoping we'd see you here," Jordan says as he buries his head in my neck.

"I missed you too, Little Man." Giving him a squeeze, I look up, smiling at Susie. "Good to see you again, Susie."

"Same," she says as she steps closer. "How did it go?" she whispers, and immediately I feel my body sag.

"Not the best. I'll tell you later," I whisper back, and she nods, offering me a small smile. Jordan pulls away and makes a funny face at me, which has me laughing despite my nerves. Making a funny face of my own, we both laugh and I lower him down to the ground. He's immediately by Sadie's side in an instant and soon the pair dissolves into talk about bikes and showing each other their boots.

Smiling, I turn toward Susie just as Timber comes back with another chair for her.

"Good to see you again, Susie," Timber says as he sets her chair down and a squeak escapes me when he tugs me back into his lap.

"Timber!"

"What? I like you in my arms, Sunshine."

My cheeks heat at his words and Susie winks at me. I think I really am going to be a tomato for the rest of the afternoon.

"Seems like you've snagged yourself a biker, Mae." She grins at me, and I can't help the butterflies in my stomach.

"We're taking it slow. We only just met today, and I don't want to rush into anything." I keep off the part that I'd never been with anyone before or that I had my first kiss today. They don't need to know that.

"You never know. I heard that Levi came here one day and the next, both Thor and Dragon claimed her as their woman," she says.

My eyes bug out at that, and I look at Levi in surprise, who's just smiling as if she's remembering it.

"Yeah, I had some reservations about being tied to a club because of my history, but even after hearing the things that I went through, they still wanted to be with me. Similar to you, I decided to just try and I am so grateful that I did, because I love both of them. And now, they've given me these twin babies, who I can't wait to meet!"

Her hands caress her baby bump, and I can't help but smile, hoping that someday, I'll get to be a mother as well.

We're interrupted again, but this time by an ear-piercing whistle. I look around, trying to find the person behind the sound. I don't have to look too hard to see Thor and his twin, Dragon, standing close together, their gazes trained on Levi. Without a word, Levi rises and walks over to them, giving them both a kiss.

"Is everyone ready to find out what we're having?" Thor asks and the crowd cheers in response.

The trio turns to two men who are sitting nearby on dirt bikes.

"Alright, Ethan. Show us if baby A is a girl or a boy!" Thor shouts.

Ethan, the Prospect who I talked to at the gate earlier, nods at him and fires up his dirt bike. Pink smoke plumes out of the exhaust pipe and everyone erupts in cheers. Levi and Sasha share a look as they give each other thumbs up. I'm surprised to see Timber doing the same.

"Please let it be another girl," Timber whispers, crossing his fingers as he peeks around me to gesture to Sasha and Nikki, who also raise their crossed fingers.

That's right—all of them were for team girl for both babies. Though I am curious as to why Timber wants both babies to be girls. You would think he'd be for boys so they could join the club when they're older. No—wait. They just voted to allow women to patch in, so it can't be that. Maybe it's tormenting the fathers? To be able to tease them about all the future boys that will want to date their daughters. On second thought, that's probably the reason.

"Show us if baby B is a girl or a boy, Reaper!" shouts Dragon.

Reaper gives Dragon a wicked smile before he starts up his bike and another plume of pink smoke appears.

Cheers erupt, even louder than before, and I can't help but laugh at the stricken looks on both Thor and Dragon's faces before they change into huge grins as they take turns hugging and kissing Levi.

Behind me, I can hear whispering and turn to see Timber talking to another man, but I can't see his patch to know his name. He passes Timber a pile of envelopes and he nods before patting my hip.

"Can you get up, Sunshine? I need to hand out the winnings."

A laugh escapes as he wiggles his eyebrows. His eyes sparkle with mischief as he looks over at Thor and Dragon.

I stand and he leans down, placing a quick kiss on my lips before walking with the man he was talking to over to Thor and Dragon. When the man turns and lets loose another ear-piercing whistle, I can see from his cut that his name is Smithy.

"Quiet down, assholes and ladies," Smithy says, his voice growly and booming so loud he'd make a perfect school principal. He'd definitely be able to quickly set straight any students that are causing trouble in school.

Rather than saying anything out loud, both Smithy and Timber pull envelopes out of their cuts and get to work handing out everyone's earnings and ending with Levi.

"Here you go, my Queen," Timber says as he hands Levi two envelopes and Smithy also hands her an envelope.

That's not the first time I've heard Levi being called a Queen, and if it were only Timber saying that, then I think I'd have an issue about it, but I've heard four different people calling her that over the last few hours. I'll have to ask him later about what they mean by her being a Queen.

"This is from our club. One envelope is your share, and the other is a gift for the babies from everyone who placed a bet."

Levi looks like she's going to start crying any minute as she takes the envelopes and hugs Timber before shouting her thanks to everyone. Shock fills Thor's and Dragon's faces before their eyes narrow on Timber. They go to speak, but Smithy cuts them off.

"My Queen, this is a gift from us Junction Creek guys for you and the babies."

Levi hugs Smithy right as Dragon growls. I kid you not—he freaking growls.

"You all bet on our kids?" Dragon roars, which has everyone laughing. Even Levi.

"You too, Wildcat?" Thor asks, his annoyance evident on his face and in his body posture.

"Of course. It's just a little good-hearted fun. However, I have no idea how everyone kept it from you two for the last couple of months," Levi says with a smirk as she tucks the envelopes inside her cut.

Both Thor and Dragon level everyone with a hard look that promises retribution. I have a feeling the next time someone's woman gets pregnant, those two will be causing all types of havoc for the lucky couple.

Stepping slightly away from her men, Levi claps her hands and everyone quiets down.

"Alright, everyone! First, I would like to say thank you again for the gifts and helping us celebrate. Now, before I start bawling from these hormones, it's time for our much anticipated knife throwing contest! Everyone, grab yourselves a drink and possibly a snack. We'll get started when everyone's settled in!"

Chapter 11
Timber

AFTER GETTING MYSELF ANOTHER beer and Mae a water, I wait for her at the table with the rest of the women. They all decided to move to a closer table so they could see better. Scanning the crowd, I start to get nervous when I realize Mae left for the bathroom five minutes ago and has yet to return. Worry gnaws at my gut as my gaze once again cuts through the crowd, looking for Smoke, but he's nowhere to be found.

Fuck. He better not be messing with her. I haven't told Sunshine yet, but I heard everything she said about her mother earlier, even though she told me a little about the drug part before. I need to talk to her later about her stepdad and that asshole Bruce or convince her to let me be there when she talks to Levi tomorrow morning. It'd be easier to help and protect her if I know what happened.

The memory of her saying she'd leave if Smoke or the club won't help her has my stomach twisting in knots. I've seen the hateful glares Smoke has been sending her ever since she got here. I'm not positive if she's seen them or not but judging by the number of times I've felt her body tense up and shrink in on herself, I think she has.

If the club sides with Smoke, I'll protect her myself. Though I don't think the guys would turn away a woman in need of help. While I don't know much about her, what I have seen and heard leads me to believe she'd never pull a stunt like that just to weasel something out of Smoke, the club, or me. She doesn't seem like the person who'd manipulate you into doing whatever she wants, but she could also be just that good at it.

As soon as that thought pops into my head, I immediately push it aside. No, the way she talked about Preston the few times he was brought up this afternoon makes me believe she'd never do that to anyone after seeing him manipulate her mom all these years.

I'm about to go check on her when she suddenly steps out of the clubhouse. However, her posture and body language have me instantly on guard. She's curled in on herself, trying to blend in and hide as she carefully weaves through the crowd.

What the fuck?

When she gets to me, she doesn't step into me like before. Instead, she stops a few feet away and won't make eye contact with me. Her eyes are misty, and I can tell she's trying to keep her bottom lip from trembling.

What'd that asshole do or say to her?

Taking her hand, I pull her away from the crowd and over by the trees. "What happened, Sunshine? Did Smoke say or do something? Or someone else?"

She shakes her head vehemently. "It's nothing, Timber. I'm okay."

I ignore the fact that she called me Timber instead of Liam, since we're not within earshot of the others. Instead, I focus on her. "You're not okay. You're shaking like a leaf and you're really pale. What happened?"

She bites her lip as she shakes her head again, looking down. "I don't want to talk about it. Not here when we're supposed to all be happy and celebrating the twins," she whispers as a tear finally escapes and the knots in my gut get tighter.

She wipes the tear away angrily and then uses her fingers to wipe away other tears at her lash line. The fact that she still won't look at me is bugging the shit out of me.

"We'll talk later then, but I do expect you to tell me what happened. I can't help if I don't know what's going on. Whenever you want to go, I'll take you back to the house where you can get settled in and we can talk with it just being us or we can just relax for a while. I'll skip the competition if you feel like you need to leave the party now. Someone can fill in for me or they can skip straight to round two with me being eliminated first. Do you want to leave or stay for a while?"

Emotions flit across her face before she lowers her head. "Stay. I want to see the competition. I've never seen one before and it intrigues me," she whispers.

Pulling her into my arms, I hate how her body remains stiff. Kissing the crown of her head, I hope I'm not right, but it seems like I might be. If that fucker scares her off and she leaves the safety of the compound, I'll kill him myself. Especially if her stepdad or Bruce get their fucking hands on her because of his fucking issues.

Pulling back slightly, I lift her chin so that she's forced to look at me. "If whatever happened scared you, please don't run, Sunshine. We'll talk and go from there. If you still feel like you want to leave after that, then I'll pack a bag and we'll go together. You're not getting away from me that easily now that I've finally found you, Sunshine."

Her lips part as her brow furrows. Later I'll make her see she's it for me. My Old Lady. My wife. She's my everything now.

She frowns and another tear escapes. "What if he won't ever accept me? That me staying here and being with you causes a rift between all of you in the club. If we live here at the compound in your house, I'd have to always walk around on eggshells because of him. Not knowing who's truly my friend or who's looking for a way to stab me in the back the first chance they get so they can throw me out. I refuse to keep living my life like that. I also refuse to be the person that causes that kind of rift. A club that's divided will crumble at some point since you never know if your brothers will have your back or not if things turn ugly. I won't be the reason why people get hurt or if the club disbands."

Swallowing, I realize this can't wait until later. At least not this part. "Sunshine, I fully intend to make you my Old Lady. I'm already more than half-way in love with you, even though we just met. And if the club won't accept or support us, then I'll leave with you. As much as I'd miss them, I could never forgive myself if I let you go. You're my everything, Sunshine, and I hope you'll see me as your man, your everything, soon too."

Her eyes once again turn misty as her lips part further in surprise. Not being able to take it anymore. I lean down and kiss her, trying to push all of my emotions into the kiss so she realizes I'm not joking about any of this.

She kisses me back, hesitantly at first, before she melts against me, kissing me harder. When I pull back, we're both breathing heavily. Out of the corner of my eye, I see Smoke come out of the clubhouse and his gaze zeroes in on her instantly. His scowl deepens when he sees her in my arms. I'll wait till later to kick his ass so I don't ruin Levi's party. Plus, I don't want to scare Mae.

"Come on," I say as I take her hand and lead her over to the other ladies. Once she's settled, I lean down and wiggle my eyebrows. "How about a kiss for good luck?"

She laughs, though I can tell it's still strained and not as bright and bubbly as earlier. She leans forward and gives me a quick kiss, then laughs harder when I pout.

"Nope. Now, go kick butt and maybe you'll get another one later."

I go to protest, but her gaze quickly cuts to my right before landing back on me. It's then that I notice Sadie's watching us, so I bite back my reply and instead kiss her forehead.

"You got it, Sunshine. Make sure you cheer for me." I wink at her and she smiles, but then I see her start to wilt in on herself. Looking around quickly, I almost instantly spot the reason why her mood's changed, even though he isn't in her line of sight. *God damn mother fucker.*

"Try not to let him get to you," I whisper and with another quick kiss, I go to pull back but stop when she whispers back in reply.

"Easier said than done," she says as her eyes turn misty again. It takes everything in me not to pick her up and just take her home, but she said she wanted to stay.

"Let me know whenever you want to go home, okay?"

"Okay."

I steal one more quick kiss before leveling Smoke with a glare of my own as I stand. He holds my gaze for a few moments before he looks away. However, he doesn't look away because of how pissed I am at him and whatever the hell he said to Sunshine. No, he looks away to grab another bottle of beer on the table next to him. He's been guzzling drinks left and right tonight.

Turning, I walk toward the targets, even though everything in me is screaming at me to turn around and take care of my woman. When I get to the table set in between both groups, I pick up a pack of three blades. Pulling them out, I get a feel for their weight again and check the tips before we start.

While the rest of us wait for the others to show up, I notice Sasha frequently looking over toward where Sunshine and the other women are sitting. Levi walks over to her and soon they're talking quietly in Russian. My worry increases, but before I can head over to talk to them, a heavy hand lands on my shoulder.

"That's quite some girl you got there, Timber," Reaper says with a smirk right as Dragon walks over by us.

"Yeah, she's definitely something, so you better make sure you and your guys back the fuck off, Reap. She's mine." His eyebrows raise at the warning in my voice before his smirk deepens.

"Well, hot damn. Looks like another one caught the bug."

Dragon looks between me and the direction Sunshine's sitting and I narrow my eyes at him, not liking where this could go. He sighs when his gaze returns to mine.

"All I was going to say was to be careful, Timber. We don't know anything about her other than what she told us out front. Besides, we haven't even confirmed what little she told us yet. How do we know she isn't lying?"

"Sunshine's not lying, Dragon. While I've heard a bit more about her story over the last few hours, she doesn't strike me as someone who'd lie about this. And I fucking hope you aren't going to have Smoke run a check on her cause that's fucked up. With how he's been all afternoon, I wouldn't put it past him to put some asinine bullshit in there just to get everyone else to not help her. That is, if he can even type straight. The asshole's fucking wasted already."

Reaper looks between us, confused, but on alert. "What happened? Is she in trouble? Why's Smoke against helping her?"

Dragon hesitates, and I narrow my gaze on him again before answering Reaper myself.

"Yes, she's in trouble. Her name's Mae and she's Smoke's long-lost daughter, who he thought had died when she was a baby. She found out her stepdad's trying to sell her off to someone, so she came here looking for him, hoping he'd help her."

Turning to Dragon, I decide to address this shit. I don't want her hearing any of this shit, especially after whatever the fuck Smoke just pulled.

"Until I find evidence that says otherwise, I'm going to believe my woman, Dragon. I don't want to hear one more person fucking badmouthing her and judging her about something she only just discovered last night after finding her real birth certificate as well as her own fucking death certificate. And if the club fucking fights us on it, then I'll fucking leave and protect her from those bastards myself. I'll be taking my business back, too, if that happens."

Chapter 12
Timber

REAPER'S EYEBROWS DAMN NEAR shoot up to his hairline when I'm done. My uncle left me the construction business when he retired. After I patched in, I offered the club a percentage of the business. I've got more than enough to buy them out of the contract if need be.

"We don't know anything—," Dragon tries again, but I cut him off.

"How long was it after meeting Levi that you knew she was going to be your woman?"

His eyes harden when I bring Levi into this, but I need to. It's the same fucking thing—I just need him to realize it, too.

"Why the fuck are you bringing my Old Lady into this? I ought to beat your ass for pulling this shit," he growls as he shifts his stance.

"Just answer the fucking question, Dragon. How long was it before you knew she was the one for you?"

"Almost instantly, but Thor and I knew her beforehand. You haven't—you only met her today. You don't know anything about her. She could be lying or trying to pull a fast one over on us, but you're thinking with your dick, not your head."

A humorless chuckle escapes me, and it doesn't escape my notice that Reaper's giving Dragon the side eye. I'm glad he isn't butting in on this, but I'm also relieved someone else is witnessing this fucking bullshit. Especially since Dragon can't fault me for falling fast when he did the same.

"Oh, I'm sorry. Are all of us only supposed to find Old Lady's that we've known for years? Is there some fine print in the bylaws that only you know about? That if we meet someone new, and we like them, that we can't pursue anything with them because we don't know everything about their history upfront? Because if that is the case, it's complete and fucking bullshit. If that's what's expected of us, then I'll turn in my cut right now because there's no fucking way I'm letting Mae go. You fell hard and fast for Levi, but when someone else does the same thing, you want to suddenly put the brakes on and want to fight about it? To not help someone in need?"

"Levi's case was different. We don't know anything about Mae. She could be just as manipulative as the fucking bunnies and hang-arounds who would do anything to bag themselves a biker. She could be a plant that could destroy us from the inside out. You need to stop thinking with your fucking dick and you'd see that you need to keep your fucking distance from her." He pauses as he looks down at me with a sneer on his face. "Or have you met her before and she's already pregnant? That this is just a ploy to get us to kill off someone she's pissed at? An ex-boyfriend, her dealer, or even her pimp?"

It takes everything in me not to punch him for what he's implying Mae is and what she's doing.

"Mae's not a fucking slut and doesn't do drugs! Why are you treating her like she's out to stab us in the back? And I can't believe you'd think that of me or that I'd stoop to doing something like that. You've known me for ten years, Dragon. For fuck's sake, you asked me to even be one of your groomsmen! Do you really think I'd do the shit you just spewed? One would think you'd know me well enough by now to know that isn't the case. Then again, I never thought you'd turn away someone who needed help, especially a woman. That you'd turn on a brother like this. Is this what you're going to think and act like anytime a brother brings a woman here? That you're instantly going to suspect them of being the enemy and anything they say is a lie?"

He remains silent as he fumes at me, but he doesn't respond or disagree with anything I just said. That only makes my anger rise further and I'm really questioning if I should stay in the club if the others are thinking along the same lines as Dragon.

"Yes, I only just met Mae, but I'm already halfway in love with her. I want her as my Old Lady, my wife. Despite what you might think, I am thinking clearly about this. None of us were against helping Levi with her stalkers, so why is Mae different? Why are you so against helping her? While her scenario is slightly different from Levi's, her stepdad's trying to fucking sell her to settle his fucking drug debt. Why are you so against protecting Mae when she's in just as much danger as Levi was? Are you going to just throw her out without protection despite the danger she's facing?" I should stop, but this is making me question a lot of things about the club.

"What if another brother brings home a woman who also has problems? Are you going to pull this same shit with them? Cause that's fucking bullshit and extremely hypocritical of you. Maybe we need to get Thor and everyone else over here to hash a few things out now instead of having this fucking competition." I pause as I make sure he sees the fury coursing through me. I'm so fucking pissed I'd rather spar or throw every single knife here at the targets because of his bullshit attitude against my Sunshine.

"Let me make one thing clear, Dragon. I will be staying by Mae's side, with or without the club's protection. You can take your fucking self-righteousness and shove it up your fucking hypocritical ass if you keep saying that bullshit about her. You don't know her story," I grit out through clenched teeth. And while I don't know her full story, I know enough. I will protect her by myself if it comes down to it.

My body tenses further when I hear a pair of feminine gasps from behind me, but I don't turn around. Though I am wondering how much of that they heard. I'm also pretty sure who's behind me because there are the only two women participating in the competition. I hope like fuck I don't end up with a blade in my back because of how I'm talking to her Old Man, but right now, I'm really fucking pissed off at how he's talking about Mae.

"Dragon, I cannot believe that horseshit just came out of your mouth," Levi hisses as she comes round me and stands in front of Dragon, poking his chest angrily. "I hope like fuck Mae hasn't overheard anything you just said. She's been through more than enough in her life to have to put up with your bullshit as well. I can't believe you'd think that of someone! I've heard the same things as Timber this afternoon and I'm with him for saying we can trust her. My gut says we can trust her. I don't think she's lying or trying to manipulate us. The next time I hear anything like that bullshit coming out of your mouth, you'll have a blade sticking out of you. And you can bet your fucking ass that you'll be sleeping on the couch for the foreseeable future."

Dragon's icy glare cuts to me as if it's my fault he's getting kicked out of his woman's bed.

"If I weren't Prospect, he'd already have blade sticking out of him," Sasha growls, her voice thick with her Russian accent and she's slipped into a bit of broken English since she's pissed.

Dragon's face hardens even further before Reaper's large hands land with a thud on both Dragon's and my shoulders, and fuck do I have to fight not to wince in pain. Judging by the tight pinch around Dragon's eyes, he's in the same boat.

"We all need to relax. If you all need to verify anything that you learn from Mae, then I'll volunteer Python to look into it. That way, there's no conflict of interest. That said, I will put my two cents in. Until proven otherwise, I'd suggest believing Mae. When are you guys going to talk to her? Tomorrow or tonight still?"

"I talked to Thor, and he suggested tomorrow since Mae's traveled all day to get here and she's barely eaten anything. But when he hears about this, he may end up moving it up to tonight," Levi says, her arms crossed as she glares at Dragon. The way she's scowling at Dragon makes me believe she might have heard our whole argument.

Sighing, I think back to how little Sunshine nibbled on her food today. "Too much sugar gives her migraines, so that's why she'd never eat the sweets you ladies would bring back to the table. Besides, she said she's used to eating only once a day and she had, in her words, a good-sized breakfast at the diner she used to work at this morning. Sometimes she'd have a small snack later in the day, but that's rare." I growl, pissed again at what that fucker put her through for his own fucking greed. Seeing Dragon and Reaper's confused faces makes me scowl at Dragon again.

"It's her story to tell, but yeah, her asshole stepdad really did a number on her, and her own fucking mother didn't even stand up for her. Until you hear Mae's story, maybe you should stop judging her and give her the benefit of the fucking doubt in the meantime. And you better not fucking spew any of the bullshit you just said to her or we will be throwing down because of it," I hiss out at him. At least he has the decency to look sort of guilty.

Sasha clears her throat, and it takes a lot of fucking willpower to turn my attention from Dragon to her.

"I was just telling Levi this, but I wanted to let you know as well, Timber. Might as well let the asshole know too, even though he was probably there based on what he just said," she says as she sneers at Dragon. When she turns toward me, her face instantly switches to one of worry.

"When Mae went to the bathroom just a few minutes ago, I followed her in case anyone messed with her. Like Levi, my gut says we can trust her, but I was worried about her because of the looks Smoke's been giving her all afternoon. I don't think she knows it was me in there with her. I was about to step out from my stall when I heard her give a startled squeak after opening the door to the hallway. I couldn't see much between the gaps in the stall, but it was enough of a gap to see Smoke standing there looming over her. The things he said to her," she pauses as she winces.

"The things he said to her were pretty bad, Timber. Like really fucked up, especially since he's her dad. I don't know how much of what he said is from how he really feels or how much is from the beer he's been practically chugging since finding out about her. She stood up to him, but I could tell every word hit her hard. She's rattled and she's probably gonna need you later, but I don't know if she'll tell you what he said right away or not. The only reason why I'm not going to tell you the rest of what he said is because if the roles were reversed, I'd want to tell Colt myself rather than have him find out from someone else. I didn't even tell Levi what Smoke said."

A groan escapes as I tilt my head up to the sky and close my eyes. I hate that she wouldn't tell me what he said earlier, but I get it. Sunshine's had enough choices taken from her, and unless her safety's in question, I don't want to take any more from her. Shaking my head, I look over at Sasha but she's looking over her shoulder again at Mae, who is thankfully being preoccupied by Susie who's sitting next to her.

"Thanks for keeping an eye on her, Sasha. I appreciate it."

"Anytime, Timber. She's a sweet girl. Has to be if she won't even swear because she wants to run a daycare someday when she's certified."

I chuckle and nod at that because that is some next level dedication in my opinion. Dragon's eyebrows furrow in confusion and I hope like fuck he's gonna start changing his tune when it comes to Sunshine. And for that matter, anyone a brother brings back here.

"Well, how about we get started so you can get back to your woman? My guys and I have been practicing, so who knows, you might get to go sit with her before long," Reaper says as he winks at me and claps my shoulder again. At least it isn't as hard as last time.

The others walk off, but it doesn't escape my notice that Levi's keeping her space from Dragon, choosing to walk on the other side of Sasha so that she's in between them.

Reaper squeezes my shoulder as he leans in close, so only I can hear him. "If you need any help with anything regarding Mae, you call me. You hear? Brothers help brothers out, but I can understand if she doesn't want to stay here because of this shit with Smoke and Dragon. Especially if either of them gets worse about that shit. I doubt Thor would turn her away if she really does need help, but it could get awkward around here really quick. You hear me?"

A weight that was sitting on my shoulders lessens when I read between the lines. If my brothers won't help or if Smoke puts up enough of a fight, the Junction Creek chapter will have our backs.

"Thanks, Reaper. I hear you and I appreciate it. I'll keep you posted."

Chapter 13
Timber

To start us off, Levi steps up in front of the targets on our mini stage that I built for us to use. The guys had tried to go simple in the beginning when we were planning this. That is, until Roy brought in a few tapes he had from when Levi competed when she was younger. After watching them, everyone decided to do things like they did in the league.

I've seen most of hers and Gray Miller's competitions throughout the years. They became friends while they were competing and now, he's the guy who makes her blades. I stumbled across one of their competitions on television when I was a kid and was instantly hooked. Not that I could afford my own set of blades though, with my worthless, good-for-nothing parents. So, I settled on watching the competitions whenever I could and practiced throwing sticks in my spare time.

The thought of them deepens my scowl, but Levi's voice pulls me back to the present and out of my memories.

"Okay, everyone! For the sake of those who aren't participating and may not be familiar with knife throwing competitions, I'll give a brief overview of the rules. We are playing to the WKTL rules, which stands for the World Knife Throwing League. You'll see that these are not your normal targets as we have three bullseyes in a vertical row instead of just one bullseye in the center. That's right, there is a chance that the participant can score three bullseyes in a turn, or two depending on the round." She pauses as she gestures to the targets.

These targets are different from normal ones in that instead of just one bullseye in the center, there's two more, all in a vertical line and evenly spaced out. In the very outer ring, there are two blue dots, known as the killshots, that are the same size as the red of the bullseye. They are positioned a little higher than the top bullseye. Kind of like a wide 'v'.

Levi clears her throat and continues. "Points will be scored only if the knife tip or edge is inside the black scoring lines. From the outer circle in, they are worth one point, two, three and then four points. If the knife lands in the white area surrounding one the bullseyes, it's five points. If the red of the bullseye is hit, it's six points. And those two blue dots up at the top, which are called the killshots, those are eight points.

"Two people, one from each club, will compete at a time and take turns throwing. They will throw three single rotation throws from ten feet and then scoring will take place before the blades are retrieved. If a blade drops because of another throw or it doesn't stick, tough shit. You don't get points for that throw.

"After the blades are retrieved, the competitors will throw two more single rotation throws. Once again, scoring will take place before the blades are retrieved. Then the competitors will switch sides and we'll do it all over again, but this time from the fifteen-foot line. The person who wins the best two out of three will proceed to the next round.

"We'll continue until there's one person left who will win a specially made knife by Gray Miller as well as a trophy. The winner will get to keep the knife, but the trophy will be passed onto to the next winner when we have another competition. The winner's knife looks similar to the blade that's won at a WKTL competition, except ours isn't gold. Also, the winner's knife has other specifications that are unique to us. The Steel Archangel's club logo is etched onto it as well as today's date. Now, I'll turn it over to Thor, who will be deciding who is pitted against who."

Levi steps down from the stage, but before she can get far, Thor's at her side talking quietly with her. And I'll bet it has nothing to do with the competition but about how tense she was on stage and that she wouldn't look at Dragon at all while she was talking. I'm sure he's noticed how on edge Dragon and I are, but I don't know if he was close enough to hear any of our little 'talk'. Or if Reaper talked to him already.

Thor's body goes rigid and the look he gives Dragon would make a weaker man piss his pants in fear. His gaze finds mine and when he inclines his head toward me, the knot in my chest loosens a little at his support. He kisses Levi's temple and steps up on stage. Smithy and Patch step up to the side of the stage as well.

"All right. As Wildcat said, I'll be drawing to see who is pitted against who for the first round. Patch and I will be judging the scores. Smithy will keep a tally as we go. So, let's see which of you fuckers and ladies will be going first!"

Cheers erupt as Thor makes a show of dumping all the popsicle sticks into the bowls, one for each club, and mixing them up.

"All right, settle down," Thor shouts as he raises a hand. One by one, he pulls out names as he pairs us up and Smithy arranges the magnets with our names on them on a nearby board so we can all see the order if need be.

SAFC VS SAJC

Gunner ~ Razor
Tripp ~ Punisher
Levi ~ Drake
Alexei ~ Python
Sasha ~ Nathan
Bones ~ Beast

Thankfully, I'm throwing fifth for our team because I need some time to get my emotions in check after my spat with Dragon. Unfortunately, that fucker's right behind me as the sixth thrower for our team. He better not say anything about her while we're waiting for our turns.

While I wish I could go over and sit with my Sunshine until my turn, we had all previously decided that the participants would stay near the stage and in throwing order if possible. Unless we needed to grab a beer or take a piss, that is. Though if we don't show within a couple minutes of our names being called, we end up forfeiting. There are also chairs scattered nearby if we want, but I'm too anxious and pissed to sit down right now.

Cheers erupt once again when both Gunner and Razor step up to throw first for both teams. My gaze locks with Sunshine and my shoulders relax slightly at seeing her smile, even though I can tell it's strained as fuck. She gives me a thumbs up, which has me grinning like a madman despite how I'm feeling.

As I try to ignore Dragon, who's still standing behind me, my attention wanders over to the Junction Creek guys since I'm pretty familiar with how well everyone on our team throws. Based on the last time I saw them throw, which was almost a month ago, they've improved a lot going off of how much better Razor's doing.

With what I saw before for the Junction Creek guys, I'm guessing Punisher for sure will be in the end mix. I've also seen enough of his knife work throughout the years to know he's damn good with a blade. Then probably Reaper and Razor, unless some of the others have improved more since last time. Once Reaper healed enough from the wounds he sustained when he and Levi were kidnapped a few months ago, he put his all into training. I think it gave his mind something to focus on besides what they both had gone through together.

For our team, in all honesty, I'm almost positive it'll come down to Levi, Sasha, and Alexei since they were all trained the longest by Levi's grandfather. He was, well still is, a fucking legend in the knife throwing community. And me? I'll be lucky if I make it to the second round. While I love the sport, I'm definitely not even close to being as good as them.

Glancing back over at Sunshine, I smile when I see both Jordan and Sadie sitting on her lap as they cheer for everyone. My smile grows when I see Sunshine laughing and smiling with only a hint of the dark cloud hanging over her. The sight has me wishing for something I've never really thought I'd have. To have my own children sitting on her lap as she plays, reads, or just talks with them. A family. My family.

Fuck.

My body freezes at that thought since I've never considered having children in the past after witnessing my parents fuck it all up with my siblings and me. Whenever I was with a woman before, and yes, there were a lot of them, I never pictured having a family with them. And I haven't even been with Sunshine in that sense yet. Still, the thought of her belly round with my child has my cock straining against my jeans even harder than it already was.

Thor's voice calls out my name and I'm surprised so much time has passed already. Fuck, was I really in my head for that long?

Climbing the steps, I do my best to breathe deep to try and steel my nerves. When I hear Sunshine, Jordan, and Sadie cheering for me, I look over my shoulder and can't help the smile that pulls at my lips. Giving her a wink, I turn back toward the targets and get in position, letting out another deep breath in the process. Loki throws his first blade and I follow suit, just barely missing a bullseye.

A chuckle escapes me when I hear a loud 'whoop!' from Sunshine and my shoulders relax even further with her support, which is a strange feeling for me.

We each take turns throwing our blades at the ten-foot line and then the fifteen-foot line before switching sides and doing it again. Round one ends with a score of 25—20, with me in the lead.

Loki ends up winning round two at 20—18. Round three goes to me at 28—15, though his blade did drop a couple of times, which moves me onto the next round.

"Congrats, man," Loki says as he clasps my shoulder and follows me down the stairs.

"Thanks."

Normally I'd bullshit with him, but my mind's too preoccupied right now.

As I make my way through my team, they each give me a shoulder slap of congratulations. Even Dragon congrats me as he climbs the stairs, which surprises the fuck out of me. He pauses as he gets to the ten-foot line, his gaze fixed out at the crowd before it lands on me. His head tilts toward the crowd before he turns to face his target.

Murmurs have me turning around to find Susie and Sunshine carrying a cooler between them toward us. Both Jordan and Sadie are trailing behind them, each with water bottles in their arms. I rush forward, along with Tripp.

"Let us carry that, Sunshine."

She gives me a small smile as she stops and lets me take the handle from her while Susie lets Tripp do the same. The kids wander through the crowd, passing out water to whoever wants one.

"The kids wanted to make sure all of you had something to drink. We weren't sure of the rules for if you'd be able to leave the stage area or not, so we figured it wouldn't hurt."

She steps closer to me, and it takes everything in me not to pull her flush against me. "The kids picked out the drinks saying you guys need to stay hydrated since you're all out here under the sun." She pauses as she tries to keep from laughing. "There's also no beer in there for the same reason. Well, that, and I quote, 'beer and weapons don't mix'."

Both of us start chuckling at that. "Fuck, that sounds just like something Jordan would say."

Her grin widens as she shakes her head. "They both said that in almost unison. Though I happen to agree with them, but I doubt any of you guys would get wasted while doing this," she says as she gestures to the stage.

Tripp and I set the cooler down and I take a water from Sadie. "Thanks, Munchkin."

"You're welcome, Uncle Timber."

It's still a little odd to hear Sadie calling us 'Uncle' instead of 'Unca'. Apparently, she had a hard time saying that word when she was younger, and even when she grew out of it, she still called us all 'Unca'. Then, suddenly, she started saying the correct word. I'm not sure what triggered the change, but I fucking hope she wasn't getting bullied at school or by other kids because of it.

Shaking my head, I look back down at her and can't help but smile as she darts off, handing out waters along with Jordan. Turning back to Sunshine, I can tell she's trying her damnedest not to show her nerves. Pulling her into my side, I kiss her forehead and she settles further into me.

For a few minutes, we stand there like that till Susie, Jordan, and Sadie come back. She looks up at me and sighs.

"I better get back to our table, so we don't distract any of you," she says. She goes to pull away from me, but I tighten my grip, tilt her chin up and drop my lips to hers. Cheers erupt around us. I flip off my brothers. Sunshine pulls away, her cheeks and neck turning pink. A chuckle escapes me, and I give her another quick kiss before lightly smacking her thigh.

She walks back to the table with the others, but the grin that spreads across her face when she looks over her shoulder at me makes me feel like I'm ten feet tall.

As she settles in her chair, I notice a shadow crossing her face, and my gaze immediately shoots to Smoke's. He's still sitting where he was, fuming with a beer bottle in his hand. When I get a chance, I need to talk with the fucker. I won't stand for his treatment to continue.

A hand clasps my shoulder, and I turn. Sasha's grip tightens, and I read her message as she nods, her gaze going to Sunshine. She'll continue to help keep an eye out for my woman. The tightness in my chest loosens and I give her a chin lift that she returns before heading to the back of the line.

Once everyone's been through once, Smithy updates the board for the next round.

SAFC VS SAJC

Sasha ~ Punisher
Timber ~ Reaper
Levi ~ Razor
Alexei ~ Beast

Those that lost go and mingle with the others watching the competition. I grimace when I see who I'm up against next.

Reaper.

Yeah, there's no way I'm heading to the next round. Though I am curious to see who will come out ahead between Sasha and Punisher.

They both get set up. First round goes to Sasha at 23—21. Second round goes to Punisher, 20—22. The crowd erupts when Smithy announces that they are both tied at 43 points overall. Everyone's eyes, even Smoke's, are on Sasha and Punisher, who somehow end up tying again with a score of 24—24 in the third round.

Levi steps up onto the stage and waits until both Sasha and Punisher acknowl-edge her, then she comes to stand at the center.

"All right, settle down, everyone!" She pauses while the cheers die down. "We've got a Sudden Death situation here as both Sasha and Punisher are tied at a total of sixty-seven points. For Sudden Death, the rules are different. Only killshots are valid points. If you hit anywhere else, you get nothing. Sasha and Punisher will be throwing from the fifteen-foot line. We'll go until someone doesn't hit a killshot. If neither person ends up hitting a killshot, we'll take a measurement and see whose blade is the closest to a killshot. The closest person is the winner. Good luck to both of you!" Levi calls out and everyone cheers again. She hugs both of them before heading back down the stairs and taking her place in line behind me.

Everyone seems to wait with bated breath.

Sasha scores a killshot.

Punisher scores a killshot.

The crowd cheers again and I smile when I hear Sunshine cheering for Sasha.

They both retrieve their blades and set up again.

Sasha misses.

Punisher misses.

Thor pulls out a measuring tape and both he and Patch talk quietly as they see who's closest.

Thor turns around and waits for a few moments.

"Spit it out already," Ryder yells, which has some of us chuckling.

The glare Thor gives Ryder could cut ice before he turns back to me and the others competing. He holds out his hand. "Punisher is the winner by an eighth of an inch!"

Cheers erupt out of everyone, and even though Sasha looks bummed, she cheers and hugs Punisher.

Taking a deep breath, I walk up the stage and fist bump Reaper.

My inexperience shows, even though I trained whenever I could. Reaper wins two of the three rounds with a total score of 63—51.

Giving him another fist bump, I jog down the steps and stalk toward Sunshine.

Chapter 14

Mae

EVEN THOUGH I'M BUMMED Timber didn't win, I still cheer my heart out for him.

"Good job, Uncle Timber," Jordan shouts and Sadie cheers next to him, both of them sitting on my lap.

After fist bumping Reaper, Timber jogs down the stairs and stalks toward me. A pool of desire curls in my belly at the heated look he's giving me. I'm vaguely aware of Jordan and Sadie sliding off my lap and going over to Susie. I shift nervously in my seat, but I can't tear my gaze from him.

When he reaches me, he picks me up as though I weigh no more than a small child and sets me down on his lap so that my shoulder is to his chest. His rough hand pushes my chin up and his lips claim mine.

As our lips connect, I sink into his arms and as he holds me, the world falls away. All my worries about my dad... I mean Smoke, fade away. About Bruce. About Preston. About X, Preston's dealer. For a moment, I feel like I'm where I'm supposed to be. In Timber's arms. Safe, protected, and cared for. It's too soon to be love, but it's not far off. I'm already half gone for him.

Whistles and cheers break me from my thoughts, and I feel my cheeks heating as Timber's chest shakes with laughter. His rough thumbs caress my cheeks and it's only then that I realize I had been crying.

"You okay, Sunshine? I didn't push too much too fast?" His voice is tight with worry and as I open my eyes to look up at him, his worry shows even more with the tightness around his pale blue eyes.

Swallowing the lump in my throat, I nod. "They're happy tears, L—I mean, Timber."

His face immediately lights up with his smile. He leans forward and kisses my forehead. Thankfully, he doesn't say anything about my near slip up with his name.

"You were amazing up there. It must have taken a lot of practice."

He nods, his gaze going back to the competition. "I trained a lot with Levi, Lex or Alexei as you may hear him called, and Sasha. It's also a lot of fun and another way to blow off steam. Even though the others aren't competing, almost all of my brothers have taken to it."

Timber pulls me closer, tucking my head under his chin as we watch Levi and Razor finish their rounds.

Not surprisingly, Levi wins. I still can't believe how her knives sink into the wood of the targets so much. They went deeper than any of the others' knives. Each time she retrieved them, it seemed like she actually had to work to get them out of the wood.

In the last round, Alexei tromps Beast, much like Levi did in the previous round. It's obvious that Levi, Sasha, and Alexei are even more skilled than I realized. Almost every time they hit the bullseye, or if they missed, it was by a hair.

"Quiet down," Thor bellows out. After a few moments, he nods and then gestures to the board where Smithy has just finished rearranging the names for the order they'll go in.

SAFC VS SAJC

Levi ~ Punisher
Alexei ~ Reaper

"We've got two more rounds and then we'll go into the finals. First up is Wildcat and Punisher. Then Alexei will go against Reaper. Good luck."

As Levi steps up to her spot, Thor pulls her flush against her and kisses her passionately. My cheeks heat at watching them so in love. When he pulls back, he bends down and kisses her stomach twice before stepping back near Patch.

My gaze goes to Dragon and I frown at how strained his face is. I wonder how much he heard of Smoke's hateful words earlier in the bathroom. Judging by how hard his face was in that hallway compared to when I saw him earlier in the afternoon, I'm afraid he heard all of it. Will he vote against helping me because of what

Smoke said, even though everything he said was a lie?

I shake my head, pushing those thoughts out of my mind for now. If I let myself focus on that, I'll spiral, and I don't want to break down here in front of everyone. Plus, there's still a few more pages in Mom's journal that I need to read through.

I stiffen, remembering my promise to Peggy.

Crap.

My phone's upstairs.

"What's wrong, Sunshine?"

Nibbling my lip, I debate asking him. His thumb captures my lip and pulls it slightly, so I'm no longer nibbling on it. "I forgot to text Peggy to let her know I made it here safely."

Understanding dawns in his eyes. He must remember she's one of the few people that I'm close to. Then something else flashes in his eyes that I can't identify before it's gone. Is it because I said I was safe?

He reaches into his cut and pulls out his phone, unlocking it before handing it to me. "Use mine and text her. If she can't reach you on your phone, she can always reach out to me. Besides, I'd like to meet her and her husband sometime to thank them for everything they did for you."

Tears prick my eyes, but I blink them away as warmth spreads throughout my chest. I've never had someone care about me this much.

Nodding, since I don't trust my voice, I lean back against his chest and pull up a new text thread.

> Mae: Hi Peggy, it's Mae. I'm using my friend's phone, Timber. I just wanted to let you and Glen know that I made it safely to where my dad lives.

I pause, nibbling my lip as I contemplate how much to tell her.

> Peggy: Thank God, you made it alright! Glen and I were worried sick. How'd he take the news?

Sighing, I figure I'll let her know but not give too many details away in case Preston asks her where I am.

> Mae: He didn't take the news well. I hope we can work things out eventually, but even if we don't, Timber said he'd help protect me from Preston.

Her reply is almost immediate, and it has my cheeks heating. I can almost see her cocking her eyebrow at me as I read her words.

> Peggy: Already found a male friend, huh? You're an adult, so I won't smother you with my worries and such, but I will say be careful and not to take things too fast. We love you, Mae, and don't want your heart broken.

Her next text has my body tensing, which has Timber tightening his arms around me.

> Peggy: Also, keep your wits about you. Preston's been going around town trying to find out where you are. He was in here earlier today but didn't get anything out of me since I didn't know where you went. I didn't tell him you put in your notice either, but he forced his way into every back room in the diner and the apartment above, making sure you weren't here.

> Mae: Did he hurt you?

> Peggy: Nothing serious—just a few bruises, but they'll heal. Theresa phoned Glen as soon as Preston showed up and immediately started yelling for you. Glen got here just as Preston was about to leave. When he saw what Preston had done to me, he threatened him that he better stay away from the diner and that he was banned for life for putting his hands on me.

My chest tightens as my fears come to light. Peggy got hurt because of me.

Timber takes the phone out of my trembling hands. His eyes scan the messages, his lip kicking up a bit, but then he scowls before his fingers quickly fly over the screen. After a few moments, he hands me back the phone.

> Timber: Peggy, this is Timber. If that dickhead ever shows his face again, call me and we'll be on our way. I'm with the Steel Archangel's MC in Forest Creek, so we aren't that far away. And as for my Sunshine, I never intend to break her heart.

Peggy: You don't know how much hearing that you're a Steel Archangel helps calm my worries about Mae's safety. My niece lives in Forest Creek and has told us many good things about your club. Thank you for taking care of our Mae. I'll keep you posted if anything else happens. Is it okay if I give your number to my husband, Glen?

Timber: Not a problem. Anyone Mae considers as part of her true family, blood or chosen, is family of mine.

Peggy: I'm glad she found you, Timber. Mae's been dealt a shit hand at life, but like you said, she is a ray of sunshine, and we don't want to see that light dimmed. Take care of her. We'll be in touch.

Timber: Of course—she's quickly becoming my everything.

My breath hitches and my fingers tighten around his phone. My gaze flies to his, and the intensity and heat in his eyes shoots straight through me. I wrap my arms around his neck and pull his head down closer to me, instantly capturing his lips. His hands tighten around me and he pulls me closer. I can feel the bulge in his jeans lengthening which sends tingles throughout me. The feelings he's drawing out of me are intense, and if this keeps up, I'm not sure how long I'll be able to resist him before giving him my virginity.

He pulls back, resting his forehead on mine. Both of us breathing heavily.

"Woman, you're making it hard to take this slow."

My cheeks heat and he chuckles before placing a quick kiss on my lips. He reaches between us, adjusting himself, and then he pulls me back against his chest.

My gaze goes back to the competition just in time for Thor to declare Reaper the winner against Alexei.

"Alright, everyone, now for the final round. Wildcat versus Reaper!" Cheers erupt as Levi and Reaper both hug. Reaper whispers something in Levi's ear which has her throwing her head back in laughter. Even Thor's grinning like mad at the two of them. You can really tell that they care a lot about each other.

My gaze snags on Levi's thigh, and I lean forward, squinting. She has a beautiful tattoo that looks like it goes from her knee all the way up under her shorts. I'm surprised I didn't notice it before. But... wait. There's something else there. Scarring of some kind?

Timber's hand tightens on my thigh and he pulls me back closer to him. "That's a story for a different time," he whispers.

When I turn to look at him, a shadow crosses over his face, but he's not looking at me. He's looking at Levi and Reaper. Reaper then turns and I notice scarring on his neck and arms. I'd only noticed the one on his face before. Now that I'm looking for them, I can see some faint scars on Levi's arms as well.

My heart constricts as I wonder what they've gone through to get those scars. And for that matter, is it really safe that I'm here? In the books I've read about motorcycle clubs, life is sometimes dangerous. Then again, I could get gunned down or die in a car accident at any point. A shudder runs through me. Or if Preston gets his way, I'll be sold to Bruce and who knows what my fate would be like in his hands.

Shaking off those thoughts, I turn my focus back to the competition. Levi and Reaper take their positions and I'm surprised they're so closely matched. Then again, Sasha said Reaper trained a lot with Levi when he was staying here earlier this year for a few months.

My jaw drops as Levi hits her second bullseye. I don't think Reaper's hit one, but it seems like he just barely missed them.

"Whoop! Get it girl," Sasha cries out, which has everyone's cheers increasing, and not just the volume, as they root for both Levi and Reaper. Caught up in the excitement, I can't help but cheer for them as well.

"Sunshine," Timber groans, and I pivot looking back at him. His face is tight and pinched. Instantly, I'm alarmed.

"What? What's wrong? Did I hurt you? Am I too heavy?"

He leans forward and nips my ear. Shivers wrack down my spine and he groans again.

"You're definitely not too heavy. But if you keep bouncing on me like that, I'm gonna blow my load in my pants like a fucking teenager. You're sexy as fuck, and I'm trying hard to keep from throwing you over my shoulder and taking you to my room, because I know you aren't ready for that."

I feel my face turning beet red. Looking down, I can see he's even larger than before.

Holy cannoli...

He's got a monster in his pants.

How is it even possible that he's bigger than before when I felt his hard bulge? How in the world will that even fit in me?

His laughter has me turning even redder, and he nips my ear again. "Don't worry your pretty little head, Sunshine. When you decide you're ready, I'll make sure your pussy's ready to take me. I'd never hurt you." His voice is a whisper, but it still has me shivering with anticipation.

Looking into his pale blue eyes, I see the sincerity in there. As well as a promise. Taking a deep breath, I lean forward and kiss him. I know I can trust him whenever I feel ready, but he's right. I'm not there yet.

He pulls back, kisses my forehead, and turns back to the competition.

As Levi wins the first round, they switch places and start again.

Reaper throws, just barely missing the bullseye. As soon as the blade leaves Reaper's hand, Levi's hands fly to her stomach, and she takes a few steps back. Oh, no. Are the babies okay?

Reaper's head whips toward her, and in an instant, Reaper and Thor are at her side. Dragon jumps up on the stage to join them.

"What's wrong? Do we need to take you to the Doc?" Thor demands, his hand cupping her cheek, the other on her stomach.

Levi reaches up and wipes tears away as she shakes her head. "I felt the babies kick for the first time."

She reaches out to move their hands to her side and moments later, all of their faces light up with huge smiles.

"Well, I think it's official, Half-pint. My future nieces will be excellent knife throwers, just like their mama."

Sasha shrieks and launches herself out of her chair, running toward the group. "Move your asses, Godmother coming through!"

Laughter rings out as she quickly scales the stage and she pushes Reaper's hands aside. I'm sure if she would have done that to Thor and Dragon, they would have had words with her, but Reaper takes it in stride. Seconds later, Sasha's face lights up and she wraps Levi in a fierce hug that has her rocking back on her heels. Thor steadies her.

As they pull apart, Levi's face hardens as she talks quietly to Dragon. The atmosphere changes drastically on the stage, and Dragon nods glumly as he looks over at me and then back to her.

Oh no. Does Levi know what Smoke said, too? Oh God. I just want to crawl into a hole and die. How many people heard his lies and hateful words? Do they believe them?

I need to get out of here to gather my thoughts.

Chapter 15

Mae

As I slide off Timber's lap, I avoid looking at him. "I'll be back. Just gotta go to the bathroom."

I go to step away, but his hand snaps out to grab my wrist. Not being able to help it anymore, my gaze locks with his worried one.

"What's wrong, Sunshine?"

Oh God, this man is going to be the death of me. Shaking my head slightly, I nibble my lip. "I just need a few moments. And I really do need to go to the bathroom."

"Perfect timing. I've got to go, too, so I'll walk with you," Sasha says as she slips her arm through mine.

When did she get over here? I just saw her on the stage.

Nodding weakly, I catch her winking at Timber, and he finally releases my wrist. What was that wink for?

"Okay, come get me if there's any trouble."

"I'll keep your woman safe. Don't worry, big guy." With that, she pulls me toward the clubhouse and I numbly follow her.

Right before we head inside, I hear Thor declaring Levi the winner, and everyone cheers loudly. I wish I could join in, but I'm desperately trying to rein in my panic attack.

When we're in the bathroom, she guides me to a stall and I close the door behind me before leaning my head against the cool metal. Closing my eyes, I force myself to take a few deep breaths and then go about doing my business.

Opening the stall door, I find Sasha leaning her hip against the counter. I quickly wash my hands, dry them off, and lean against the counter as I watch her through the mirror.

"Were you the one that was in the stall earlier?"

She grimaces slightly and nods. "With how Smoke was acting, I wanted to keep an eye on you in case he did anything stupid." She sighs, running a hand through her hair. "Granted, I haven't known him that long, but in that time, I've never seen him pounding drinks this hard. Or acting like this, for that matter." She shakes her head, looking down at the ground.

Nibbling my lip, I decide to ask what's on the tip of my tongue. "Does Levi and Dragon know what he said? Timber?"

This time she full on grimaces. "I gave a very high overview to Levi. I figured two sets of eyes watching out for you is better than just me. While I was telling her, I heard Dragon spewing a bunch of shit at Timber and some of it was what Smoke had said. So yeah, I think Dragon heard him. I didn't tell anyone what else Smoke said, even though I could tell it killed Timber not knowing. But if the roles were reversed, I'd prefer to be the one to tell Colt first rather than him learning about it secondhand."

My shoulders slump.

So it's true. He did hear it. Shaking my head, I sigh. "Great. Now he'll probably vote against helping me, even though nothing Smoke said is true."

"I know Smoke's going to regret everything he said when he's sober and looks at the camera feed tomorrow. I have a feeling Timber, not to mention Thor, will be chewing his ass out tomorrow as well. Then Levi and I will be taking our turns and chewing his ass out."

The fierceness of her words has me turning and looking at her in surprise. "But you didn't know what he was saying wasn't true earlier. It's his word against mine. Everyone's known Smoke for a long time and I'm new. They'll believe him over me."

She tilts her head as she studies me. "I've always been a good judge of character and have been able to read people well. Levi too. My gut and my instincts are both saying I can trust you. That we can trust you. I have a feeling what Smoke was saying was his feelings that have been festering all these years. In his anger and hurt over your mom's betrayal, I bet he thinks that you've grown up to be just like her since you've spent so much time around her. And he's so drunk that he can't see that that's not true at all. In the short amount of time I've been around you, I know that you'd never intentionally manipulate anyone. Not after what Preston's done to your mom. Hell, I bet you've never even had a drink, smoked, or did any drugs after what you saw."

My cheeks heat, and she laughs.

"Nailed it!"

Giving her a small smile, I nod. "Yeah, it's true. I've never done any of that, and I'm not sure if I ever will. Drink alcohol, I mean." Nibbling my lip, I fidget. "Will that be a problem here? That I don't drink?"

Sasha immediately shakes her head. "Not at all. I'm sure you'll get razzed by a couple of bunnies, though, if they notice it. Then again, they'll find anything possible to razz you, including telling you a bunch of horseshit or bragging about being with Timber at some point."

Sighing, I nod. I kind of guessed it'd be like that. "Timber already told me Crystal and Gigi would cause problems, but the others most likely wouldn't. Though he did say he'd...," I pause, licking my lips and decide to just put it out there. Sasha seems like someone I can trust and she just said she trusts me.

Taking a deep breath, I continue. "He said that he'd been with all of them except for Roxy, Crystal, and Gigi. I know he hasn't been a saint, and I, well, I have been, but not intentionally. I'm also worried that he'll get bored with me since I don't have any experience."

Blinking rapidly, I try to keep my tears at bay. Sasha pushes off the counter and walks over to me before wrapping me in a hug.

"I'll let you in on a little secret." She pauses and blushes when I step back and look up at her. "When I got together with Colt, I had never been with anyone before him. And since I know she won't care that I tell you, same goes for Levi. I think us being virgins actually excites them more since they get to be the ones that expand our horizons, so to speak. What I'm trying to say is, don't say no to being Timber's woman because you're scared. Yes, it can be dangerous from time to time. But these men truly do protect the innocent and that protectiveness increases when a guy claims a woman as his Old Lady."

"Are you an Old Lady? Are there any others besides Levi?"

She blushes again. "She's the only one so far. I think Colt was planning to ask me after he patches in, but then they voted to allow women in the club. After seeing how the club was, I wanted to help protect my family, so I put my name in to Prospect. If I do patch in, then I'd be like Levi and wear an actual cut with the full-on club logo on the back, even if I do become Colt's Old Lady."

Sasha pauses as she pulls out her phone before fiddling with it. When she flips it around, it's of Levi, but her cut is different than the one she's currently wearing. On the cut in the picture, her road name is Enchantress and in the next photo, on the bottom, it says 'Property of Thor & Dragon'.

"If you were to become Timber's Old Lady and didn't want to become a full club member, this is what the back of your cut would look like. This is how Levi's was before she was patched in."

"What did she do that convinced the club to allow women to patch in?"

Sasha nibbles her lip and shakes her head. "I think you should ask Levi that question. And maybe even Thor and Dragon. It's hers and Reaper's story to tell, and I'm not sure how much they want to share. What I can say is that some major shit went down and both Levi and Reaper were injured because of it. I think the club will protect you regardless of if you choose to be with Timber, but that protection will increase if you do become his Old Lady, and I'm not saying that to push you towards Timber. The club will do anything to keep their women and children safe."

Nodding, I look down at my hands as I take in her words. Though part of my nervousness is because my emotions seem to be at war right now. Between finding out about Preston's deal to sell me, about Smoke, him acting like this, and then add on top of that my developing feelings for Timber, I'm a complete mess.

Tonight or tomorrow, I think I'll need to talk to Timber about everything. Maybe even Levi, too. They need to know what happened in case Smoke continues to act like this.

"Will you... Can you be there when I talk to Levi tomorrow? Maybe I can see if Nikki will, too? If Smoke won't talk to me, I'd at least like you guys to know since you all are my family now. Timber, too. I'm assuming Thor should probably know since he's the President of the club."

Out of the corner of my eye, I see her face soften and she once again steps forward to wrap me in a hug. After a few moments, she pulls back and we both wipe a few stray tears away.

"If Smoke doesn't come around after he sobers up, I'm so gonna beat his ass for putting you through this. And yes, I'll be there. I heard Timber saying you said you'd like to stay at his house. I'll talk to the others and we can all meet over at Timber's house tomorrow morning so that you won't have to come to the clubhouse. You'll have more privacy there as well."

Nodding, we both move to the door and since I'm closer, I open it only to stagger back in surprise.

Not again...

Smoke is at the door and his face is contorted in anger and rage.

Suddenly, Sasha pulls me behind her and she brandishes a blade in each hand, both of them pointed at Smoke. Wait, where did the blades come from? I shake my head to clear away my shock.

"Please don't hurt him!" Even though he's been acting like a son of a monkey, he's still my dad.

Unfortunately, my insistence that he not be hurt only makes him angrier. "Move, Sasha. I don't know what lies she's told all of you to have you all wrapped around her finger, but this ends now. I'm tossing her out of here like the whoring, junkie, trailer park piece of trash that she is!" he snarls.

Sasha's hands tighten around the hilts of her blades.

"Smoke, you're drunk off your ass. For fuck's sake, you're so drunk a stiff breeze would blow you over. You need to go upstairs and sleep this all off."

"Move, Sasha. Before I make you move."

He starts reaching for her but Sasha doesn't get to reply or act because suddenly Smoke is pulled away from us and thrown up against the other wall of the hallway. Timber's broad back is facing me and he's holding Smoke up by the neck of his shirt.

"Sasha, get Sunshine upstairs to my room so she can get her things and then take her to my house. I'll be there shortly after I set a few things straight with my brother here."

The coldness of his voice sends ice down my spine. Sasha nods and puts one of her blades away... somewhere on her body. She grabs the keys Timber holds out and then tugs my arm, making sure she stays between Smoke and me as we sidestep out of the bathroom and start down the hall.

I pause behind Timber and touch my hand to the small of his back and then rest my forehead against his back.

"Please, don't hurt him. I know he's drunk and angry, but he's still my dad and I don't want him to get hurt."

The muscles in Timber's back tense, and for a moment, I think he's going to deny me, but then they relax.

"So long as he doesn't lay a finger on you and he stops this fucking nonsense and listens to reason like a normal fucking adult from here on out, then no, I won't hurt him. But if he does any of that after our talk..."

His voice trails off, and I hear the underlying threat. Nodding, I place a kiss on his back and Sasha tugs on my arm again. She doesn't take her eyes off Smoke as we cross the main room to the stairs. Rushing up the stairs in front of her, I darn near run to Timber's room. My shaky hands are barely able to unlock his door, but somehow, I manage. I need to get to Timber's house before the dam holding my emotions back gives way entirely.

Sasha grabs the bags she bought for me earlier, and I kneel next to the safe after opening my backpack. Taking a quick peek behind me, I notice Sasha's checking the windows while also keeping an eye on the door. I don't know what training she's had before, but I can tell she knows how to fight.

Quickly, I enter the passcode and retrieve my documents, money, and my pictures before stuffing them into my backpack. Rezipping it, I stand and sling the duffle bag over my shoulder.

"I'm ready," I tell her, though even I can hear the waver in my voice.

Nodding, she strides to the door but then pauses as if she's listening for something. Peeking her head out, she gives me a chin lift and I follow her.

"This feels so weird. Having to watch my back in our own clubhouse," she mutters under her breath.

I shrink in on her words. This is all my fault. By coming here, I've created such a mess in their clubhouse.

"Get those thoughts out of your head, Mae. This is his fuckup, not yours."

I startle at Sasha's voice. While I may not agree with her, I nod anyway and follow her to the house Timber pointed out was his earlier. As we walk up to it, I take in the blue and white two-story craftsman style house with a wrap-around porch. Off to the side is a three-stall garage with the same color scheme. It must be Timber's as well.

Looking back at the house, it's absolutely gorgeous. If I ever had the means to be able to pick a house to build from scratch, it would have been a craftsman style house like his. I've always loved the columns, hand-crafted wood features and exposed beams in a house. There's been numerous times I flipped through house magazines at the library, dreaming of what my future would look like if I had the means to better myself. Each time, I came back to the craftsman style as my favorite.

Shaking off my thoughts, I climb the steps and follow Sasha inside after she unlocks the door.

Chapter 16
Timber

THANK FUCK I FOLLOWED not too long after Sunshine and Sasha. When I hear Sunshine damn near running to my room and shutting the door loudly, I tighten my grip on Smoke's shirt. Lifting him a little higher, I shake him and slam him against the wall. Not hard enough to get a concussion, but enough to rattle him and know I mean business.

"Get the fuck off me, Timber," he growls as he claws at my hand.

"Why? So you can go and do fuck knows what to my woman? Your daughter?"

He scowls as he continues to try and get free. "She is no daughter of mine. My daughter died twenty-one years ago. All she is, is a carbon copy of Lillian. A deceitful and manipulative fucking junkie whore."

I see red and a second later, my fist collides with his jaw.

"Office! Now!" Thor bellows.

Releasing my hold on Smoke's shirt, I immediately clamp down on his shoulder and half frog-march, half drag him with me into Thor's office.

Dragon follows me in.

Just fucking peachy. Is he going to start in on Sunshine, too?

Shoving Smoke toward the couch, I pace as I run a hand over my face. A grunt draws my attention back to Smoke. He's so fucking drunk that he stumbles and damn near falls onto the floor, but I don't help him. I'm so fucking pissed at him.

Quiet talking draws my gaze to the door. Thor's talking to Levi in hushed tones, and I have a feeling it's about Sunshine. Levi nods at him, and then does the same to me before leaving. Thor turns around and gives me a chin lift. My shoulders relax. They'll watch after my Sunshine for me and will make sure she's alright until I can get to her.

Thor shuts the door and as he walks to his desk, he transitions from loving husband to that of an MC President in the blink of an eye. He looks down at Smoke, his lip curling slightly as he sits behind his desk.

"Care to explain why you two were going at each other in the hallway?"

"I'm sick and fucking tired of how this asshole's been treating Mae all afternoon. This is the second time he's got up in her face and at least this time I was there to stop most of it. Good thing too, cause he was about to try and force Sasha out of the way to get to Mae. Who knows what he would have tried to do to get to her."

I scowl at that thought. I never thought he would have been one to put a hand on a woman, but I honestly think he's too drunk to even make heads or tails of anything.

Thor roars and slams his fist down on the table. "Smoke, you're confined to your room to sleep off whatever the fuck you've been drinking. The only reason why you're getting this slight leniency is I know your backstory. Tomorrow when you're sober, we'll be having a long chat, you and I. We do not put our hands on a woman like that."

Thankfully, Smoke just nods instead of putting up a fight, but I don't know if he actually heard Thor or if he's about to pass out. Thor gives Dragon a chin lift and he opens the door. Ethan and Drae enter.

"Escort Smoke to his room and make sure he stays there."

They both give him a chin lift and hoist Smoke up off the couch. When they're gone, Dragon shuts the door again.

Thor keeps his attention on Dragon, his scowl still in place. "And as for you, I never want to hear you spewing the shit you said earlier. It's true we don't know much about Mae, but you don't go judging people based on someone's drunken rant and not knowing if what was said was true or not. I expect you to make things right with Mae and Timber. Not to mention our Old Lady."

Dragon's eyes darken at mentioning Levi. He gives him and me a curt nod, but otherwise doesn't say anything.

"Now, get out of here. I need to talk to Timber."

Once again, Dragon gives him a chin lift. His gaze hesitates on me, indecision warring on his face. My scowl deepens, still not able to believe that he trusted the shit that came out of Smoke's mouth and for accusing me of what he did. Especially after knowing me for so long. His shoulders slump a bit and he leaves, slamming the door on the way out.

Thor stares at the door for a bit before shaking his head and turning to me. "Wildcat told me a little about what happened before the competition, but I'd like to hear it from you."

I fill him in on everything that was said. His face darkens the more I talk, his hands fisting repeatedly. The thunderclouds brewing in his eyes mean he's probably going to be having a little 'chat' with Dragon later.

And by chat, I mean his fists will be doing the talking.

There are a couple reasons why he's named Thor. One, his weapon of choice during interrogations, is a fucking hammer that looks a lot like what you'd imagine the old God Thor wielding. The other being the man's fists are almost as strong as the fucking hammer. If he lets loose on you, you'll be sporting bruises for weeks.

I debate about telling him about Reaper's offer, but if we do decide to take him up on it, I'll have to tell him anyway. That and I need to stress that my threat was real.

Clearing my throat, I shake my head. "Reaper also offered his help. That Python could look into things regarding Mae's history or background, so there's no conflict of interest. Also, for if things get too tense and strained here with Smoke and Dragon, that we'd have a place in his club until things calmed down. If they calm down, that is." I pause, licking my lips. "I meant what I said about my business. If the club won't help protect her, I'll turn in my cut and leave. Buy out the club's percentage. Nothing's more important than Mae's safety."

His face softens, and he nods. "You claiming her?"

"Yeah, I'm claiming her as my Old Lady, even though I know she won't get a unanimous vote because of Smoke. Told her earlier that I want her as my woman, my Old Lady, my wife. She's not there yet, but she's getting there. If only things weren't so fucked up with Smoke, she might get there sooner."

Thor nods. "You'll have protection and backing one way or another from the club. I'm glad Reaper offered you a place if need be. In fact, it might not be a bad idea depending on how things go with Smoke tomorrow. It's going to be rough. Lillian burned him in more than one way."

I pause, more things clicking in place. "You were there, weren't you? You know what went down that day."

Thor nods. "Me and Patch were there. I can't believe that bitch did something so fucking vile. With Mae showing up out of the blue, I get that the man's been thrown a clusterfuck, but that's no excuse for what he's done or said. That said, it may take time to come to terms with the fact that his daughter didn't die. A little space might be good for both of them."

He shakes his head and continues. "Apparently, Mae's asked that the ladies, you, and I meet with her tomorrow and she'll tell us what's all happened so far. Depending on Smoke's... condition, both physical and mental, he might be there as well, but that is ultimately up to Mae. If Mae doesn't want anyone else there, then those of us that are there will relay the information to the rest of the brothers at Church."

Nodding, I run my hand through my hair. God fuck damn. This is such a fucking mess.

"After talking to Mae, I'll have a sit down with Smoke. Make him watch the feed of what he did and said. Then share anything Mae wants me to with him, unless she wants to sit in on that part to tell him herself."

I start to object, but he raises his hand.

"It's ultimately up to her. If she chooses to take that path, I'll make sure nothing happens to her, but if she requests you there, I'll allow it. Mainly because I think after all this mess, she'll need your support when she tells him."

Sighing, I give him a chin lift. He's right. It's up to her how she wants to tell Smoke. And probably show him whatever was in the rest of her notebooks and folder.

"Now, get out of here and go to your woman. I bet she's about to crack from what I saw earlier. She'll need you. Text me if anything else comes up. I'll let you know when we're heading over in the morning."

Giving him another chin lift, I leave the office and stalk out of the clubhouse, ignoring my brothers on the way out. I need to see my woman.

Firing up my bike, I make my way down the winding road to my house. Thank fuck Thor and the others listened back when we first started planning to build houses here. Having a paved lot and road instead of gravel helps with a number of things, but especially when we need to get out of here quickly. None of us have to worry about kicking up a bunch of rocks in the process and scuffing someone's paint job.

Within minutes, I'm pulling up to my house and turn off my bike. Some of the tension in my shoulders lessens a bit when I hear laughter coming from behind the house.

Making my way up the porch steps, I walk around the porch toward the back of my property. It butts up along the tree line, which is something I love. I've always preferred being outside, and having this space helps calm my nerves.

Leaning against the house, I watch the women. They've lit a fire, and Levi, Sasha, Nikki, Susie, and Sunshine are all sitting around it. Sunshine and Levi have water, but the others have beer. Does Mae not drink? Not that it would matter if she didn't.

As if feeling my gaze on her, Sunshine looks up at me and the smile that lights up her face is fucking beautiful. How the fuck did I get lucky enough to have her in my life?

The others finally take notice of me, and Susie raises her beer. "Hope you don't mind that we grabbed a few beers."

Pushing off the corner, I grab myself a beer out of my outside refrigerator before making my way to them. Reaching Sunshine's chair, I pick her up, sit down and settle her in my lap.

Shaking my head, I shrug. "Don't worry about it." I pause, nodding at Sasha. "Thanks for helping Sunshine earlier." Taking a drink, I set the beer down in the cupholder built into the chair.

She waves me off. "We're family. That's what we do."

Sunshine squirms on my lap. Her cheeks heat a little, and she dips her head to try to hide it. I wonder if the family comment got to her? From what little I know, she really only includes Peggy and Glen as her family. I'm not even sure if she has any friends.

"How are you doing, Sunshine?" I whisper in her ear as I brush a lock of hair behind her shoulder.

Her gaze meets mine and my chest tightens at seeing the whirlwind of emotions in her eyes. "Barely holding together," she whispers back.

"What do you want to happen tonight? Watch a movie? Talk? Or head upstairs to go to bed? Whatever you want to do, we'll do it."

She nibbles her lip as she thinks. A slight blush creeps across her face again. "Can you just hold me for a bit? I feel safe when I'm in your arms. That everything isn't falling apart around me."

Fuck, if that doesn't hit me hard. "Of course, Sunshine."

I pull her closer to me and she leans her head against my shoulder as we listen to the women talk. She takes one of my hands and threads her fingers through mine. With my other hand, I run my fingers up and down her back. She sighs and snuggles deeper into me.

We sit there like that for about an hour, talking, when a yawn escapes her.

"Tired, Sunshine?"

She nods and another yawn escapes.

"That's our cue. We'll see you in the morning, Mae," Levi says, and the others get up. I stand and sit Mae back down, praying she'll let us take care of this last part. Thankfully, she nods as she leans back against the chair. She's so tired she's about to conk out. If her mind will let her, that is. We put the fire out and they toss their empty bottles, saying good night.

Picking Mae back up, I head in through the back door.

"Your house is gorgeous, Liam. I looked around downstairs earlier. I'm absolutely in love with your kitchen," she says, and then another yawn escapes her.

Pride runs through me that she loves the house so far. Though if there's anything she doesn't like, I'll change it, no matter what it is.

Entering the living room, I spot her bags on the sofa, and I set her down. I pick up the shopping bags and when she takes her other bags, I lead her to the stairs.

"I've got four other bedrooms up here besides the master. You can take your pick of where you want to sleep."

I wish like fuck she'll choose to be in my arms tonight, even if I can only hold her. I know she isn't ready to go further right now. Especially if she is as innocent as I think she is.

She peeks into each room and chooses the room next to mine. Setting the shopping bags on the bed, I pull her into my arms.

"Let me know if you need anything, Sunshine. Sleep well." Leaning down, I give her delectable lips a kiss. She melts into me, and it takes everything in me to pull away. Resting my forehead on hers, I take a deep breath.

"Goodnight, Sunshine."

Something flickers in her eyes that I can't read, but I'm loving how pink her cheeks are.

"Goodnight, Liam."

Chapter 17
Mae

As I watch Liam leave my room to head to his, it's surprising how much I want to ask him to stay or to ask if I can stay in his room. Not to have sex, but just to keep feeling his arms around me. Is it weird that I feel so safe and comfortable around him in such a short amount of time?

I think back to what I asked the ladies before Liam came home. Both Levi and Sasha said that they fell quickly for their men, and it was the same for the guys. Quick as in the same day they met them, they agreed to be with them. Though I guess that's what I've done. I said I wanted to get to know Liam better, and he's already told me he wants me as his Old Lady.

Even though I didn't ask them about it, and I had no intentions to, the ladies confirmed what Liam said earlier about not being with the bunnies for a long time. Every time one of the bunnies would try to have sex with him or offer to suck his... um, member... he would push them off him.

Shaking my head, I walk over to the bed and start going through the bags. As I do, I look around the room a bit more. This room is gorgeous. But what am I saying? His whole house is gorgeous.

The walls are painted a pale blue color. There's a queen bed with a fluffy white bedspread and a couple of pillows in various shades of blue. The nightstands and dresser are stained a light shade of oak. The closet doors are open and I'm surprised that it's a walk-in closet. And just like Liam said, there's a safe bolted to the floor.

There's a full bathroom attached as well, and I'm seriously eyeing that claw-foot tub. If I weren't so tired, I'd take a bath. Last time I was able to do enjoy a bath was when I was staying at my grandparent's house about a month before they died. Our trailer only has a small shower stall. There was absolutely no way a tub would have fit into that tiny bathroom.

The other three bedrooms are similar in size, but they all have twin beds. Two of the bedrooms share a Jack-and-Jill bathroom and the third has its own full bathroom. They are all similarly decorated, too.

As for downstairs, it has an open floor plan that I absolutely love. Liam's office is downstairs and there is another spare bedroom down there as well with its own full-sized bathroom. In the living room, a couple of leather couches and a leather recliner surround a large TV that's mounted on the wall, which I wasn't surprised by. I mean, he is a single guy and even I know how much most guys love big TV's.

The kitchen is huge with double ovens, a gas stove, a large island with a farmer's sink, and a large pantry. There's a dining room off to the side that would be perfect for holiday dinners. But what I really love is that you can see into the living room from the kitchen, which would be nice for whenever I'm cooking and the kids are watching TV.

Whoa.

I freeze, the clothing in my hands falling to the bed.

Kids? I mean, I've always wanted them someday. But who am I kidding? It's way too soon to be thinking about kids... Isn't it? I mean, I have no idea if Liam even wants kids. Or if he wants them with me.

Sighing, I turn my attention back to my clothes. Thankfully, Sasha bought me some decent pajamas so that I won't have to wear the ones I brought with me. I'll need to ask Liam or the girls if they can take me shopping tomorrow. I'm more than ready to get rid of my baggy clothes and get things that actually fit my body.

Removing the tags, I put the clothes in the dresser. I'll wash them tomorrow, but I don't want to leave them all out.

Emptying my backpack, I take Mom's notebooks, the folder, and my money over to the closet and set them down by the safe. Remembering that I only have a few pages left to read, I pull out the last journal and quickly read the entries.

A few minutes later, I set the journal down. While I'm happy that I've read all of Mom's journals, I'm still confused by everything. Sighing, I turn my attention to the safe. It's open, but there's a piece of paper inside that says how to change the passcode. I change it and secure my items inside.

Gathering my bathroom supplies, I take them into the bathroom along with my new pajamas. After putting my things away in the cupboards and drawers, I wash my face and teeth before brushing and loosely braiding my hair. Slipping into the silk pajama shirt and shorts, I pick up my sundress off the floor.

As I stand, my gaze catches in the mirror and my jaw drops. Both the top and shorts hug my body like a glove. I'm a little self-conscious of how much cleavage the shirt shows, but then again, I can't deny how good the pj's make me feel. The image of Liam seeing me in this has me blushing and my thighs clench remembering how he felt against me earlier.

Knowing I'm not ready to go further yet, I push those thoughts out of my head. Heading back into the bedroom, I put my clothes in the hamper.

Crawling under the covers, a sigh escapes when I feel how comfortable the mattress is. Soft enough where my body slightly sinks in, but also firm enough to support my body as well. I no longer have to sleep on that old twin mattress where the springs poke me all over. Snuggling deeper into the covers, I try to will myself to sleep.

Waking up the next morning, I groan and bury my face in my pillow. I don't want to get up. I hardly got any sleep last night. My brain wouldn't shut off and scenario after scenario kept running through my head about talking to Smoke and the others today.

Hearing Liam's shower turn on, I groan again and look at the clock. It's 7 am. I'm surprised I didn't wake up earlier since I'm normally out of the trailer by 6 am at the latest to try and avoid Preston.

With a sigh, I fling the covers off me and walk over to the dresser. From my new clothes, I pick out a t-shirt, jeans, underwear, bra, and socks before heading into the bathroom.

After doing my business, I turn on the water and strip while I wait for it to warm up. Snagging a hair tie, I put my long hair up in a messy bun on top of my head so it won't get wet. I normally only wash my hair every two to three days. Since my hair is so long and thick, it takes forever to dry it.

Stepping under the spray, I snag my body wash.

As I'm lathering up, I can hear a groan coming from another room and I realize my bathroom must be next to Liam's. Then I hear another groan. And then my name.

Holy moly.

It's then that my foggy brain puts things together.

Liam is in the shower that's next to my bathroom.

Naked.

And he's thinking about *me.*

That thought has my thighs clenching and for the first time ever, I contemplate actually acting on my desires myself. I've never touched myself that way before because the walls in our trailer are paper thin and I know most of the insulation is gone between the walls with how cold it gets in there. There's no way I was going to do that when Preston could hear what I'm doing. I always feared that if I would do that, that he'd think I've had sex before. That he'd make me do things in exchange for his drugs, much like he makes Mom do.

A shudder runs through me at the mental images of Mom strewn out on the couch or coffee table as one of Preston's dealers has his way with her. Each time, her eyes were dazed and I knew Preston had pumped her full of drugs to make her comply.

Those thoughts have my mood instantly souring. With the desire to bring myself to my first orgasm gone, I finish cleaning off and shut off the water. Drying off, I turn on my straightener before using lotion all over my body and slipping on my clothes.

Glancing in the mirror as I dress, my mood instantly lifts. I definitely need to go shopping with Sasha, as this outfit is further proof of how good her tastes are and her ability to know my size even through my baggy clothes. Especially since I could never find pants that fit me, but she did.

The bra lifts and supports my ample chest better than the cheap cotton bras I had before. While I don't put on any of the sexier underwear, I did snag some soft boy shorts that make my butt look cute. The t-shirt is fitted and shows off a little cleavage and the skinny jeans hug my body like a second skin. I wish I had some boots or something, but I'll have to make do with my old tennis shoes for now.

Undoing my bun, I brush out my hair. With the straightener, I touch up a few areas. Pulling out my make-up, I apply a little blush, eyeshadow, mascara and lip gloss. I tuck my lip gloss into my pocket and take a look at myself in the mirror.

Despite everything with Smoke hanging over me, I'm happy with how I look. Since being here, I've started feeling more like myself than ever before. Probably because I'm not constantly looking over my shoulder, worrying about what Preston will do next.

Now, there's a lightness to my shoulders and overall, I feel lighter, too. Part of that is because of Liam. He's slowly starting to dispel some of the things people have said to me in the past about my appearance. Smiling, my body further relaxes when I remember how good it felt to have his arms around me last night in his backyard as we chatted. For the most part, it was the girls and me talking, but every now and then Liam would speak up.

The smell of bacon coming from downstairs has my stomach growling and I quickly put my things away. Heading into my bedroom, I pick up my tennis shoes and slip my phone into my pocket. Grinning, I remember the text I had waiting for me from Peggy that I saw last night after getting to Liam's house. She sent it after I had talked to her using Liam's phone.

Needless to say, I need to find some time today and call her as she wants to know more about him. Now that she knows he's in the club, I don't feel like I need to hide as much about Smoke as I had originally thought. She knows I'm here and I'm guessing she put two and two together that Smoke is part of the club as well.

Heading downstairs, I put my shoes in the entryway and walk into the kitchen only to stop and stare. Liam's at the stove in nothing but basketball shorts that hang low on his hips. His muscles and tattoos are on full display, and suddenly, I'm itching to trace them all with my fingers and tongue.

My gaze lowers and I have to bite my tongue at how good his butt looks. Oh my lordy, do I need a fan, and maybe a napkin to wipe my drool off, because Liam is hot as heck. If he keeps this up, I don't know how long I'll be able to hold out.

"Morning, Sunshine."

His voice snaps me out of my thoughts and I look up at him, only to see he's turned his head and is smirking at me. I swear I turn even redder than I already was when his gaze slowly takes in what I'm wearing. When his gaze meets mine again, my thighs clench at seeing the heat in his eyes.

Clearing his throat, he turns back to the stove. "I know you said you mainly eat only one meal a day, but I thought if you had multiple small meals throughout the day, that they might help you get used to eating more than once." He reaches over to the counter and snags a plate before putting a small helping of eggs and a few pieces of bacon on it. He then loads up another plate for himself and shuts the stove off.

"Thank you. That's actually what I was planning to start doing now that I'm away from him."

Rather than focus on Preston, I walk around the island and wrap my arms around his waist. Placing a quick kiss on his back, I step around him, intent on heading to the coffee pot when he snags my waist and pulls me flush against him. Seconds later, his lips crash down on mine as his hands tighten on my waist.

Moaning, I sink into him and wrap my arms around his neck. My fingers go up to his hair, and when he nibbles on my lip, I can't help but tug slightly on his hair.

In an instant, he hoists me up onto the island and he steps in between my parted legs. His hard length is at my core and I can't help but moan and tilt my hips, needing to ease the ache. At the action, he groans and pulls me tighter against him.

"That's it, Sunshine. Grind your pussy against my cock. Take what you need."

My cheeks heat as I realize I'm out of my depth here. "I... I don't know..." I pause as I lick my lips, not sure how to say what I need to say.

Liam groans as his hips thrust against me. "Are you saying you've never touched yourself, Sunshine? That you've never had an orgasm?"

My cheeks heat and I duck my head to try to hide my embarrassment instead of answering him. God, I hope he doesn't push me away now that he knows.

This time, an almost feral groan leaves Liam's lips as his hands grip my hips tighter. "Let me take care of you, Sunshine."

His lips recapture mine as he brings me closer to the edge of the counter before he starts to rock himself against my center again. The tingling feeling that had been there before, starts up again, and the more he rubs against me, the bigger the feeling gets.

One of his hands slides up my side, and he cups my breast, squeezing it slightly. Through the material, he plays with my nipple. My hips roll on their own as I try to chase that heady feeling. His other hand moves to my butt and he squeezes the cheek at the same time as he pinches my nipple. I cry out as my body shudders. Liam keeps grinding against me, prolonging that feeling.

My chest heaving, I finally open my eyes to see him staring down at me. The heat in his eyes is a promise that I know will come sooner rather than later, but I'm thankful that he isn't pushing me to do more right now.

Not sure how to show my thanks, I lean up and kiss him again.

"God, you're so beautiful when you come, Sunshine. I can't wait to see that look on you again."

My cheeks heat, but this time I don't look away. I nibble my lip, wondering what he would look like when he comes, but I don't say that out loud. On that thought, did he come, too?

My hands go to his waistband, wanting to make him feel just as good, but he stops me.

"Stop looking at me like that, Sunshine. I know you're not ready to go further. And if you're wondering about me, I came in my shorts like a teenager as I got you off."

"But what if I want to make you feel good?"

He groans and his hands tighten on my hips. "Fuck, Sunshine, I definitely want more with you. Later, we can explore that if you want, but now isn't the time. Thor texted right before you came downstairs and said they'll be over here in about twenty minutes." He hoists me in his arms and sets me down on a stool at the island. "Here, eat this, and I'll be right back. If you want more, steal off my plate. Gonna clean up and change before they get her e."

Liam gives me a quick kiss and then he heads upstairs.

As I watch him disappear upstairs, I rub my chest. The feelings that I have for Liam have grown even more with everything he's done for me. And while what we just did was beyond phenomenal, that's not what's driving my decision. I know everything's happened so fast between us, but is it too soon to be feeling this way? I'm a hair's breadth away from jumping all in and seeing where this goes.

Sighing, I refocus on breakfast and my stomach growls at the heavenly aroma. I pull the plate toward me and realize I never got my coffee earlier. Sliding down off the stool, I head over to the coffeepot and start looking in the cupboards for a mug. Finding one, I pour myself a cup and sit down. As I sit, I realize now that I'm no longer forced to drink black coffee.

I had never wanted to splurge to get creamer before because of Preston. I know that if I started bringing home specialty stuff like that, he'd be demanding where the extra money came from and then taking any that I had on me. It's happened a few times over the years and I'm glad I no longer have to live under his thumb. Maybe I can test out some creamers to see if there are any that I like? For that matter, I can really expand my horizons and see if there's anything else I might like food-wise, too.

Halfway through my eggs, Liam comes back downstairs just as there's a knock on the door.

"Hey, ladies, Thor, come on in," he says as he opens it and stands back.

I turn, slide off my chair, and smile as I see my aunts coming in along with Susie. She walks straight toward me and wraps me in a hug.

"I hope you don't mind that I'm crashing this party. I came back this morning to check on you and I heard you had a rough night."

Sighing, I nod. "You can say that again."

"Sit girl, we can chat while you're finishing up your breakfast before we get into the heavy stuff," Levi says as she sits down at the kitchen table. Grabbing my plate and coffee, I move to sit down with them.

We chat about little stuff and they all agree to go shopping with me later. Sasha was thrilled when I said I loved what she had gotten me before. But since I'm not as familiar with them, and the fact that Thor and Liam aren't too far away, I say nothing about the sexy lingerie. She winks at me, as if she knows what I'm thinking about, which has me blushing.

I'd just finished the last of my bacon when Thor curses. Looking over at him, he's showing something to Liam on his phone, and both of them look extremely angry.

"Is... is something wrong?" I ask, afraid that Smoke's done something else.

Both Thor and Liam share a look, which seems to make Liam even madder.

"Sorry ladies, but we need to get to Church. Mae, I'm going to need you to come with us," Thor says instead of answering my question.

My stomach sinks. Oh, God. This is it. Time to see if they'll side with Smoke or if they'll help me. My gaze goes to Liam. God, I hope they help me. I don't want to leave him.

Chapter 18
Timber

I'm fucking pissed. Smoke's destroying the common room with this new news and I'm worried like fuck about how Sunshine's going to take it. Phoenix texted some of the things Smoke's ranting about and I already have my suspicions that they're false. Then there are others that I for sure know are false.

I've seen Mae's arms and there are no needle tracks. Granted, I know that's not the only way to take drugs, but I honestly don't think she has. No, I think someone is messing with us to get us to deny Mae protection.

Looking over at Sunshine, she's white as a ghost and her hands are trembling. Fuck, I really don't want her to have to share everything like this, but it looks like we have no choice. Walking over to her, I squat down in front of her and take her hands, kissing the backs of them before looking up at her.

"Sunshine, can you grab all the documents you wanted to show Smoke? I think we're going to need them."

Her worry visibly increases at my words. "With how he's been, though, I don't want him to have the originals. Especially my real birth certificate and my 'death' certificate. There's no way I'll be able to replace those. If I bring everything there, I risk him destroying them and then there goes some of my proof against what he said yesterday."

"Mae, I'll give you my word that he won't be able to destroy your stuff, but I gotta know before we head in there. What all did Smoke accuse you of yesterday?" Thor asks.

I didn't think it was possible, but Sunshine's face pales even more as she licks her lips nervously. The trembling in her hands increases.

"He called me a whore and implied I'd have sex in exchange for drugs so I can get my next fix. He accused me of also being a dealer for Preston and that I ran drugs for him and my mom. That I use my body to bring in more customers for him. That I allow him to pimp me out. He said that there probably isn't a man in town that I haven't slept with. That I'd take a man in every hole and sometimes two men in my whoo-ha at the same time. He said I was trying to get cozy with the club to try and get an ex-boyfriend taken out. That I was probably already pregnant with some crack-head's baby. And the one that really confused me was that I probably helped Preston with bringing in women. I don't know what he meant by that."

I have to fight to keep from launching off my feet and going after Smoke. His ass is mine for what he's said and what he's put her through already. And that's not even counting what's gonna go on in Church in a bit.

She pauses and licks her lips nervously again. "None of what he said is true. I've never done drugs, smoked or drank alcohol. I've never even been in a relationship with anyone, let alone a sexual one. Heck, my first kiss was from Timber yesterday." Her cheeks heat and I know she's remembering what we just did, judging by how she's squirming in her seat a little.

Taking her hands, I pull her to her feet and kiss her forehead. "How about you go get everything you need, Sunshine? Then we'll head over to the clubhouse."

Nodding weakly, she heads upstairs without another word.

Once she's out of sight, I turn back to Thor. "This is fucked up and you know it."

His jaw clenches but he nods in agreement.

"I agree. There's no way she did any of what he said. Not after the little she told us yesterday as well as our little chat one-on-one in the bathroom before Smoke tried to corner her that second time. I mean, I know I said this before, but for fuck's sake, the woman tries her damnedest not to swear because she wants to own and run her own daycare once she gets certified. That's some next level dedication shit, in my opinion. Besides, someone who wants to own her own daycare wouldn't be pumping themselves full of drugs or spreading their legs for any and every asshole that crosses her path." Sasha fumes as she crosses her arms over her chest.

Levi nods in agreement as she stares down at her phone. "Something smells fishy here. I think someone's messing with us to keep us from protecting Mae. They want us out of the way so they can get to her easier."

Thor must have sent her a screenshot of the messages Phoenix sent him.

"But who would have found out where she was already? Other than texting her friend Peggy yesterday, she said she didn't tell anyone where she was going. And from what Mae told me, there is no way Peggy would tell her stepfather where she was," Susie says.

"I'm betting that asshole Preston guessed that she somehow found out about Smoke and came here. Mae told me yesterday before the party that she was worried that he'd guess she came straight to Smoke. We'll just have to see what's all in the envelope that was sent to Smoke when we get to Church," I say, trying to contain my anger and not go after Smoke right now.

As we wait for Mae to come downstairs, I continue to fume. It's going to be hard to not launch myself at Smoke the moment I see him. "Is Smoke at least sober now?"

Thor gives me a chin lift. "He is. Made sure Phoenix saw to that since we were coming here. I had planned to talk to Smoke after speaking with Mae, but that's now gone to shit with this new clusterfuck."

"I'm sorry. I-I didn't mean to cause problems for the club by coming here. M-maybe I should just leave," Mae says softly from behind me.

Spinning on my heel, I see her standing at the base of the stairs. I hadn't even heard her coming down the stairs.

Her arms are wrapped around her waist, and she's sunk in on herself as she stares at her feet. Her eyes are shiny with unshed tears and fuck does that twist my gut. I hate seeing my Sunshine cry.

"Get that leaving shit out of your head, Sunshine. I don't give a fuck what Smoke says. I want you as my Old Lady, wife, and mother of my children. You aren't ever leaving me, Baby," I say as I quickly cross the room to her and wrap her in my arms.

Fuck, she can't leave. Not when I just found her.

"But I don't want to be the reason the club's divided. I know how much you love being part of the club. I could never ask you to leave them. As much as I'm in love with you, I can't ask you to leave the club. I just can't."

Tears streak down her face, but I barely notice them.

She said she loved me.

"Fucking love you, too, Sunshine." I slam my lips to hers, trying to put all my emotions into the kiss so she knows it's true. I'd fucking die for this woman.

Pulling back, I dry her cheeks. "If need be, I'll put in a transfer. Reaper already said that we could stay at their clubhouse if things got too tense here. Doubt he'd be against it."

"You can't transfer. Your business. You said your uncle left it to you when he retired," she argues, and I shake my head.

"I can always look into opening a branch and putting someone else in charge of this location. Stop trying to think up excuses, Sunshine, cause I'm not letting you go. Not after finally finding you."

Fresh tears stream down her face and she finally nods. A sniffling sound comes from behind me and I turn, only to find Levi, Nikki, and Susie dabbing at their eyes whereas Sasha's grinning like a loon, a pen twirling in her fingers.

"Don't mind me, hormones are running crazy today," Levi says as she wipes her eyes and Thor passes her some tissues.

"How about we head over to the clubhouse?" Thor asks, as he watches Sunshine.

Mae nods, and she moves to the kitchen as the rest of the women get up from their seats. Picking up her plate, she downs the rest of her coffee and puts her dishes in the sink. Turning to the counter, she picks up my plate, still piled high with food, and sets it in the fridge.

I almost tell her not to worry about the food or the dishes, but seeing the faraway look in her eyes, I bite my tongue. She must be doing this out of habit. Mae shakes her head slightly, as if she's trying to silence whatever the fuck is going on in her mind and grabs a water bottle from the fridge. Coming over by me, she slips on her shoes she left by the front door earlier. When she stands, I wrap my arm around her, pulling her into my side. Giving Thor a chin lift, we head out and I lock up the house.

We're silent as we make the short walk up to the clubhouse. Thor opens the door, and the ladies all gasp when we step inside. Colt, Ethan, and Alexei all pause with cleaning up when they hear us enter. I don't see Drae, so he must be at the gate.

The room is trashed even worse than I thought.

Tables are upturned. Chairs are thrown about, and a few are broken. There's also a few broken bottles or glasses scattered across the floor. Turning toward the pool table area, a few cues are broken, but otherwise the tables are intact.

Colt's the first to snap out of it and starts sweeping a path into Church, getting the broken glass out of the way. Alexei does the same but over to the couches where Sadie and Jordan are watching a movie.

Mae darts from my side over to the kids with the other women hot on her heels. "Are you two okay?" She squats down in front of them, frantically looking both of them over and both kids instantly throw themselves at her.

"MaeMae! You can't leave! Don't let Uncle Smoke make you leave," Sadie cries as she buries her head in Sunshine's neck.

The look on Sunshine's face is like a sucker punch to my gut. I'm going to ream Smoke's ass for doing this in front of the kids. They could have been hurt.

Thor steps closer, and Mae nods at him. He's pissed as fuck, but thankfully, he's keeping a lid on it in front of the kids and ladies.

She hugs both kids tight, then pulls back, drying their tears. "It'll be okay. We're going to go into Church and get everything sorted out. How about when I'm done in there, we go over to Timber's house and we can watch a movie?"

Her gaze finds mine over the kids' shoulders, and I give her a chin lift. I'd rather have the kids over there than around all the broken glass and wood. And who knows how Smoke will be after we get done with Church?

Relief fills her and she kisses both of their foreheads before standing and walking back over to me. Susie and Nikki are quick to take her place as they check over their children and hug them tight.

"Timber, is it okay if we head over to your house right away? Don't really want the kids to get hurt and who knows what the asshole will do when he gets out of Church." Sasha whispers as she steps closer to me.

"Yeah, it's fine with me. There should be some popcorn in the pantry. Go all out and get them comfortable. Hate that they had to see this."

"Same, brother," Thor bites out. He turns and gives the Prospects a chin lift. "Colt, when you're done in here, go over and watch the perimeter of Timber's house. Alexei and Ethan, when we're done, I'll have some stuff I need you to scan as quick as possible."

"You got it, Prez. I already hooked up a laptop and portable scanner by Timber's usual spot in case Mae wanted to show something to everyone on the big screen. Ethan said she had a bunch of papers with her," Alexei says with a nod toward Ethan before he starts cleaning again.

I give him a chin lift and lead Mae over to Church. Before I go in, I put my phone in the basket on the bar and ask for Mae's as well. She looks up at me, confused.

"Only Thor and Phoenix are allowed phones in Church unless there's a special circumstance. Everyone else puts theirs in the basket."

Her mouth drops in an 'o' and she puts her phone in the basket before tucking herself into my side. Placing my hand at the small of her back, I lead her into Church, though I don't miss the fact that I can still feel her body trembling.

Once inside, I have to bite my cheek from smirking. Phoenix and Bear are standing on either side of Smoke with their hands resting on his shoulders. Smoke's already sporting a bruise along his jaw, so they must have had to use force to get him to calm down. Either that, or it's from my punch last night. His face turns thunderous when he sees Mae, but thankfully, he doesn't say anything. Though, that could be because Bear's hand visibly tightens on his shoulder. It also doesn't escape my notice the Junction Creek guys are in here, too.

Sitting down, I pull Mae down to sit on my lap so that her back is to my chest. I could have had her sit next to me, but I have a feeling she's going to need my support during this.

Thor bangs his hammer on the table.

"All right, before we get to the clusterfuck of this morning, Mae, why don't you fill us in on what you found out and what led you to come here yesterday?" Thor asks and Mae nods.

She picks up her backpack and pulls out a bunch of notebooks, a folder, and some pictures before setting the bag back down on the ground.

Taking a look around, all of my brothers are pissed and shooting Smoke glares, however, Levi's glare is the deadliest. Now I'm wondering what all was said and done this morning. After Church, maybe I can talk Lex into showing me the video feed.

Resting one hand on Sunshine's hip and the other on her thigh, I give her hip a little squeeze of encouragement. I have a feeling she'll be needing a lot of it.

Chapter 19

Mae

Taking a deep breath, I nod at Thor and begin.

"For those that don't know, my stepdad's name is Preston Cole and my mom is Lillian Cole." Pausing, I lick my lips and take another deep breath. God, I hope I can get through all of this without breaking down or fainting. I can feel the tension in the room, and while I'm sure it's because of the state of the main room, everyone's masking their anger.

For now, at least.

Out of the corner of my eye, I can feel Smoke's hate-filled gaze boring into me. My gaze lands on Levi across the room, and she gives me a slight nod and a small smile. Keeping my focus on her, I continue.

"I had gotten home from a late shift at the grocery store two nights ago when I heard Preston and Mom yelling from outside the trailer. It was a little before midnight. Preston said something about when I'm eighteen, I would be gone and then they wouldn't have to worry about things for a while."

I pause, shuddering as the memories wash over me.

"The thing is though, a few years ago, I had to lie about my age to get out of a sticky situation. I said I was sixteen instead of nineteen, when his dealers tried to come after me for their drug 'payment' like they were already doing with Mom. Lying about my age was the only thing I could think of since I knew I wasn't strong enough to fight them off. I've always looked a little young for my age, but wasn't sure if I looked that young anymore.

"Thankfully, the lie worked, and it saved me from sharing the same fate as Mom that night. Though it didn't stop them from leering at me or trying to 'accidentally' bump into me or pushing past me in the hallway. At least they didn't come around very often at the time.

"A bonus out of the lie about my age was that Preston remembered the next day and asked me how my classes were going. I fumbled awkwardly through his questions and then bolted afterward, saying I needed to get to school on time when, in reality, I was going to work."

"Wait a minute. Preston actually believes you're eighteen? Cause you sure as fuck don't look eighteen, Sweetheart," Ryder says.

His nickname has Timber growling at him and I squeeze his hand that's on my thigh. I'm his. He doesn't have to worry about me going anywhere. Not anymore. Not after what we just talked about at his house.

Nodding, I grimace. "Yeah, he's not the brightest and most of the time, he's either drunk or high. Or both, which makes it even worse. I still can't believe he remembered my 'age' the next day, but I've been living up the lie ever since then. I spent almost all my time working so that I could get Mom out of there and into rehab. Before Preston came into our lives, the second time around, she was a fairly good mom."

At this, Smoke snorts, but I ignore him. Taking a chance, I decide to describe what it was like before he came into our lives.

"A little backstory. I don't know everything that happened that first time around, but Mom married Preston before I was born. A month or so after I was born, they got a divorce. Again, I don't know the details about why they divorced, but I have my suspicions it's because Preston cheated on her the whole time.

"Mom worked two jobs to make sure I had everything I needed. Clothes that fit, as much food as I wanted, the utilities stayed on, and our trailer was never cold in the winter or too hot in the summer. Not to mention I had everything I needed for school when the time came.

"Even though she worked a lot, she always made sure to take time out of her day to spend with me. She worked at Peggy's diner most of the time as well as doing the paper route for Rixen, the town we lived in. Whenever I got out of school, I would get dropped off at the diner until Mom got off work. One of Mom's friends was a teacher at the school I went to and since the diner was on the way to her house, she offered to drop me off at the diner whenever Mom was working. I'd do my homework, if I had any, or I'd hang out in Peggy's office where they had set up a TV for me.

"When Mom married Preston the second time around, things were okay for a while."

I go on to explain everything he did to Mom since then. How he'd slowly start knocking her down until she became the shell of the person she once was. That he keeps her strung out on drugs to do whatever he wants her to. That he frequently uses her body in exchange for drugs, or as a toy for his associates that came around. How he has her to the point where the only times she's able to fight back is when he doesn't have enough drugs to keep her strung out.

Timber's grip on my thigh and waist tightens, and I squeeze his hand on my thigh again, thankful that he's here for me. It doesn't escape my notice that the tension in the room has increased and there's been a few times where I've noticed Smoke looking confused, but I don't acknowledge noticing his reaction.

Running my finger along the spine of the journals, I continue. "Back to two nights ago. After getting into my room, I went to stash my tips. Years ago, I had pried the boards loose on the back wall of my closet. I'd learned the hard way that if I had any money in my room, or anything of value, that Preston would find it when I was gone and take it. When I was putting my tin of money back into the hole, my fingers brushed against Mom's journals." I pause, flipping open the most recent entry. "This is what started me down the rabbit hole of everything."

Taking the scanner that Alexei set up, I scan the most recent entry and then bring it up so that everyone can read it on the big screen.

> *Preston's gone too far this time. He owes his dealer a couple thousand dollars, and his dealer isn't falling for his usual tricks to get out of paying. He won't take anything but cash and Preston has until the 9th, which is next weekend, to square up what he owes.*
>
> *Preston's already taken the remaining money from my monthly checks, but somehow, it isn't enough to cover the amount. He must owe more than he's telling me, or he has more than one dealer he owes.*
>
> *I overheard him on the phone a few weeks ago. He's arranged for someone to buy my baby girl after she turns 'eighteen'. I've tried talking him out of it, but each time, he beats me and then drugs me to shut me up.*
>
> *I don't know what to do. I have no family or friends anymore. The only other person I could go to is Jax, and I know he won't talk to me. I hate that I listened to Preston back then, but he convinced me it would be best for Mae.*
>
> *How wrong I was.*
> *I wish I could take it all back.*

I wait while they all read the entry. When they're done, I push the stack of journals aside slightly.

"While I was reading Mom's journals, I overheard a couple of phone calls of Preston's. The first was that he told his dealer, X, that he'd have the money he owed him next weekend. That he'd be paid in full. I couldn't hear whatever X said, but soon Preston was cursing and he immediately called Bruce. I don't know what his last name is and I've never even heard Preston talking about him before. Preston asked if Bruce was willing to pick me up today, and if he did, he'd shave off some of the price. He was going sell me so that he'd be able to pay off his drug debts."

Curses ring out through the room.

"They're not getting their hands on you," Tripp grunts, and the look he gives me makes me believe him.

"They're all fucking dead men walking," Bear growls.

All of these men look lethal, but Bear especially so. He's a mountain of a man and I'd hate to be the one that comes across him in a dark alley.

Licking my lips, I give them all a small smile, even though I'm trying my hardest not to shake like a leaf. My gaze goes back to Levi and she gives me another encouraging nod. Taking a deep breath, I go to continue, but Timber cuts me off.

"So that's why Preston had his shorts in a twist when Peggy told you how he was at her diner yesterday. He's got till sometime today to produce you. If not, he won't be able to pay off his debt to his dealer," Timber says.

Nodding, I frown. "Yes."

I hate that Preston hurt Peggy. If I get my hands on him, I'm going to make him pay for what he did to her.

Seeing confused looks, I tell them about our texts with Peggy yesterday.

Shaking my head, my gaze goes back to the journals and then to Thor. "You can read the journals once Alexei has them all scanned. The summary version of the journals is that somehow Preston and Mom were able to trick Smoke into thinking I was stillborn. I don't know how—she didn't go into that in any of her journals. Preston had apparently convinced her it was the right thing to do for me. With what was in the journals and everything that Preston ranted about over the years, I get the feeling that he's jealous of Smoke and angry at him for some reason. However, I don't know why."

"Probably because he's a stupid little fucker who couldn't even keep any of his business ventures afloat for more than a few years, max. His last one was the car dealership he owned, but that went up in smoke years ago," Smoke says with a smirk.

Suddenly, things click into place. "You were the one that blew up the dealership. That's why he wasn't able to launder his money anymore."

"Wait, what?" Smoke says as he scowls and sits up straighter, or at least tries to since Phoenix and Bear still have a hold of his shoulders. "I scoured over all of his information. There weren't any clues about him laundering money, even though we suspected him to be doing it." Inwardly, I smirk at the fact that he didn't deny blowing up Preston's car dealership.

Instead of answering him right away, I pull the stack of journals closer and start flipping through them until I find the right entry. Scanning it, I put it up on the screen.

> *I can't believe what I heard tonight. Preston thinks I was passed out, but he doesn't know that I pretend to be so that him and his cronies will tire of me sooner.*
>
> *Somehow, they all got onto the topic of the car dealership Preston used to own years ago when we were first together. He was bitching about it going up in flames and that it was a waste of a good cover. The explosion happened about a month after Mae was born. At the time, he'd apparently been using the car dealership to launder money into an account under my daughter's 'dead' name. I don't think he's still using her name, but you never know with that asshole.*
>
> *Jax would be able to find out in a heartbeat, but I know I can't go to him. He'll never talk to me again after what I stupidly did to him. If I could talk to him again, I'd tell him everything. Everything about what Preston said and did to convince me to marry him. What happened that brought about my decision to divorce him. I'd give him all the information I know about Preston's 'dealings' so that they could be shut down. But I know it'll never happen. This is my punishment for what I did all those years ago, and as long as I can keep their attention off of my daughter, then everything I endure will be worth it.*

Smoke goes to stand but he's pushed back down in his seat by Phoenix and Bear.

"If you won't let me up, then someone grab my laptop for me," he growls.

Ryder gets up, grabs his laptop and gives it to Smoke, who immediately starts typing away.

Putting the journals back in order, I turn to the folder. "Among the papers, I found my real birth certificate and my 'death' certificate," I say using quotation marks. "That's how I finally found out my dad's name."

Pulling them out, I scan them so everyone can see all three. I start with my fake one, and then go onto the others. As I'm scanning, I keep filling them in on what I'd been told over the years.

"Whenever I'd ask about my dad, they'd never tell me his name. Just that he was in an MC that did a lot of illegal things. Drugs, dealing weapons, human trafficking. Preston also said he had died not too long after I was born in a drug bust. Mom never corrected him about anything, but I overheard him more than once threatening to beat her. Maybe one of those threats was for if she ever told me anything about him."

Out of the corner of my eye, I can see Smoke's face getting thunderous again and he's clenching his fists repeatedly, but I don't know if it's from what I'm saying or what he's found on the computer.

Deciding to keep going, I pull out the next couple of documents. My throat tightens at my mom's betrayal once again as I open the first envelope and start scanning.

"Apparently, Mom and Preston bought a life insurance policy for me about a month before I was born. Then, about a month after I 'died', the insurance was paid out in full. Fifty thousand dollars."

Curses ring out through the room again.

Timber kisses my shoulder before burying his head in the crook of my neck. "He's a fucking dead man."

I know it shouldn't, but that statement from him warms my heart. Reaching up, I wrap my arm around his neck and lean into him for a few moments while I wait for the guys to finish reading the document. After a bit, I lean forward and start scanning the next document.

"This one is from some guy called Jack. He was the one that helped them get my new birth certificate that states my last name is Cole and that I was born on September 2nd, 2002 instead of on the 1st."

I pull out the remaining papers and scan them. "These are the confusing ones. I don't know what any of these are for, but they were tucked in with and between the journals, so I'm guessing they're important. Maybe they mean something to you guys."

Instantly, the air in the room is even thicker with tension, and I start to worry. They know what it means, and whatever it is, it isn't good.

"I'm going to take a stab that you all know what this means," I say quietly and Timber's grip on me tightens even more. The worry that was spreading through me increases, and I sink further into Timber's embrace, needing his strength.

"Yeah, Sunshine, we do," Timber growls.

Looking over my shoulder, I find Timber's gaze is locked on Thor. Turning, I look at Thor as well, who's standing with his arms crossed over his chest as he stares at the screen.

Chapter 20

Mae

THOR FROWNS AND TURNS away from the screen. "Before we get to into this, Smoke, care to explain what the fuck happened and why our main room is trashed?" His gaze zeroes in on Smoke and holy crap... I'd have fainted if that look was directed at me.

Smoke's eyes and face turn murderous as he glares at me. Bear passes an envelope to Thor. I'm guessing that whatever's in the envelope, Smoke thinks it has to do with me.

Thor pulls out a small piece of paper and then a bunch of pictures. He curses but when he looks at me, it's with sympathy.

"W-what is it?" I try to keep my nerves under control, but my voice cracks anyway.

Thor walks over to me and hands me the note and pictures.

My stomach sinks as I get a glimpse of the pictures and my hands start trembling, but I force myself to look at the note first.

> *Thought you'd like to know that that cunt you're protecting isn't the innocent little girl you think she is. Return her before midnight tonight or else.*

Setting the note down, I turn my attention to the pictures, fanning them out in front of me, and checking the backs of them. Even without seeing the date I would have known the pictures were old. One from the slight yellowing on the edges and the other is that they weigh more than the printouts you get today. These are from back when cameras needed film to take pictures.

However, the pictures aren't of me.

I look up at Thor and then Smoke. "This isn't me in the pictures."

Smoke scoffs. "Of course you'd say that so that you'd get our protection."

"Smoke, man, you really should have looked at these pictures closer before going on your rant earlier," Axe says from beside me.

Looking over my shoulder, I realize he's leaned closer without me realizing it and has been looking at the pictures as well.

Picking them up, I go to stand, but Timber doesn't let go. Turning toward him, I give him a small smile. "Please, I need to do this."

"Fine," he grumbles as he lets me up and I'm not surprised when he stands up as well. He's been protective since the moment we met. I walk around the table and Timber follows me.

The room is set up so that three large tables make up a 'u' in the room where the brothers all sit at. Then there's another table near the front of the room where Thor stands, but it's not as long as the other tables, so there's a gap on either end where someone can walk to the center, which I do, and come to a stop on the other side of the table from Smoke.

Flipping through the pictures, I find the one that I want to address first and hold it out for Smoke to look at. "Look at my arms," I say as I hold them out to him, showing him the insides of my arms. "There's no track marks on either of my arms, unlike the woman in the picture."

Setting down that picture in front of him, I find the next one. "The woman in this picture has a birthmark on her left side, above her hip that's sort of in the shape of a heart." I set the picture down, and then lift up my shirt, showing him that there's no such birthmark on me.

"Could have had it lasered off," he bites out.

"That would have left some sort of a scar, jackass," Axe says and I can tell he's getting angrier the longer Smoke's refusing to see the truth.

"You can see every single, very pronounced rib on the woman." I pause as I pull my shirt higher until it's right below my bra. "While yes, you can also see my ribs because Preston darn near starved me, they aren't as pronounced as the woman's in the picture.

"I was only allowed one very small meal at home, and the only other meal I got was when I was in school and that was the free lunches. Sadly, those lunches consisted of a cheese sandwich, milk, and a little fruit. Sometimes, it'd be a bologna sandwich, but that was rare. Since then, I've lived off one meal a day when Preston fully got his hooks in Mom and that meal was usually when I was working at the diner. It's been going on for about thirteen years now. Another thing is that my hair is naturally blond, like yours. You can tell the woman in the photos has had her hair dyed because of her brown roots, that are about an inch long."

"You could have been sneaking extra meals as of late and not telling anyone. You also could be lying about having natural blond hair," he sneers.

I don't miss the glares everyone's giving him, especially Levi, who is twirling a pen in her fingers. Judging by the look on her face, I bet she wishes it was a blade.

Ignoring the curses from the others, I lower my shirt. Even though I want to shrink into a ball at the look Smoke is giving me, I give into my feelings and make them known.

"Holy mother of all flying monkeys in the sky! You cannot be this blind or pigheaded! I know how smart you are from the journals. How can you not realize or accept that it is not me in these pictures?"

Laughter rings out at my words, but I don't break eye contact with Smoke. I cannot believe he's being this dense.

"God, I love you, woman. If you weren't my niece, I'd be adopting you as a sister," Levi says as she laughs, though I can tell it's strained. However, her words have my chest warming at her considering me family even though Smoke won't have anything to do with me.

"God fuck damn, I love your version of cursing, Sunshine," Timber rasps out as his laughter dies down.

"Yeah, well, with me trying not to swear, I had to get creative in expressing myself," I mumble as I run a hand through my hair.

"Why do you try not to cuss?" Tripp asks as he looks at me in confusion.

It's then that I realize only a few people know what I want to do with my life. "Because once I'm certified, I want to own and run my own daycare. No one wants someone watching their kids that cusses all the time," I snap without meaning to.

My anger is rising at how Smoke continues to glare at me as if I was the person behind all of this. I never asked for any of this to happen.

Turning my attention back on him, I return his glare. "What more do I have to do to prove that I'm not the woman in the photos? That I am who I say I am. That everything I've said is true. That nothing of what you ranted about at me yesterday is true."

I pause, but he doesn't say anything. "I'll take a drug test to prove I've never done any type of drug. I've never smoked. I've never had a sip of alcohol. After seeing how badly things got when Preston was drunk, I've never had the urge. I've never even been in a relationship with anyone, let alone a sexual one. Reason being is that I feared what Preston would do if he found out I was seeing anyone. Or make me do. I'll even go to an OB-GYN so you can verify that my barrier is still intact. I know there's no way to test that I've taken someone in my rear or mouth, but I haven't done either of those things. Heck, my first kiss was from Timber yesterday." My cheeks heat at admitting to everyone that I'm a virgin and Timber was my first kiss, but they need to know the truth.

"Also, to top it off, maybe you should have looked at the pictures even closer, because if you had, you'd have noticed the ducking time stamps on the backs! I was twelve and thirteen when these were taken. You and I both know *exactly* who it is in these pictures. It's just for some reason, you have it in your head that it's me and it's not."

I throw the rest of the pictures down on the table in front of him. I'm breathing hard after my rant, and I'm so angry that it hurts that he continues to not see the truth. He's so blinded by his rage and his own hurt, that I'm not sure if he'll ever see the truth.

That realization shatters something deep inside me.

Something that I don't think will ever be repaired.

Chapter 21
Timber

MAE IS FUCKING PISSED at Smoke, and she has every right to be. If he had just calmed down and looked at the pictures with a clear head, this part of the fucking fiasco could have been avoided.

I pull her into my arms, but her body remains tense, and she doesn't break eye contact with Smoke. Looks like she inherited his stubbornness.

Turning to Thor, I raise an eyebrow in question. He shakes his head. Good, cause I think she needs to get out of here.

"Mae, why don't you take everything you didn't scan and give it to Alexei? He can finish up the rest and then return everything to you," Thor says. His voice is gentle, but I can hear the underlying anger in his words. He's also fucking pissed and I think once Mae's out of the clubhouse, shit's gonna hit the fan. Or he'll save it for their talk later.

"Come on, Sunshine," I say and turn her around.

Thankfully, Axe already put her things back in her backpack. He hands it to me along with the scanner and laptop, and I lead Mae out into the common room where she grabs her phone out of the basket on the bar. Looking around, I'm surprised that the Prospects have gotten everything back in order already.

Alexei and Ethan immediately stand when they see us. I set everything down on the table they're at.

"She's already scanned a few things, but here's everything. When you're done, bring it to my house. Ethan, in a minute, will you walk Mae to my house? Afterward, come back and finish helping Lex."

"You got it, Timber."

"No problem, Timber. Just call when she's ready to go."

Walking over to the door so we have a little privacy, I pull Sunshine into my arms again. This time, she melts into me. "Want you to go with Ethan to my house and relax with the ladies. You got me, Sunshine?"

"Okay," she says quietly as she buries her head in my chest.

"I'll be back as soon as we're done, and then we'll go from there."

She nods but doesn't reply.

Pulling back slightly, I lift her chin so she has to look at me. Her eyes are swimming with unshed tears, but she's trying to be strong.

Leaning down, I give her a kiss that ends far too quickly, but there's no way in hell anyone's hearing her moans but me.

Resting my forehead against hers, I try to keep a lid on my emotions for a few more moments. "Ethan," I call out. Seconds later, he's at my side.

"See you soon, Sunshine. If there's any problems, have Sasha get ahold of Thor or Phoenix. Like I said before, they're the only ones allowed to have phones while we're in Church. In fact, have her give you all the guys' numbers, so you have them as well."

"Okay," she says quietly and then she gives me a quick kiss. Ethan gives me a chin lift, and they leave the clubhouse.

Turning, I stalk back into Church and march right up in front of Smoke, purposefully keeping the table between us. I made a promise to Sunshine that I wouldn't hurt him unless he did anything else to her, and I intend to keep that promise, even if I did sort of break it last night by punching the fucker. Though, I don't miss that Levi is standing and her chest is heaving as she glares at him.

Fuck, I missed whatever the hell she ranted at Smoke about.

"What the fuck is wrong with you? Why can't you see that Mae is innocent in all of this?" I damn near roar.

"You're too busy thinking with your dick instead of your head. She's a carbon copy of Lillian and therefore can't be trusted. She's already manipulated you and played you like a fiddle, just like she planned," he growls.

Judging by the white fingertips of Phoenix and Bear, he's been trying to get out of his seat, or maybe even succeeded a moment ago.

"You're a fucking idiot," Phoenix mutters as he sneers down at Smoke. "You're too blinded by your own anger and hurt that Lillian's caused to see the fucking truth. If you don't pull your head out of your ass, you're going to lose the one thing you've been hoping for, for all these years. On top of that, you blew your top this morning in front of your niece and Jordan. You're lucky as fuck that Alexei and Colt got them out of the room right away or we'd be having a *very* different conversation," Phoenix growls and visibly tightens his grip on Smoke's shoulder.

Oh fuck.

If either kid had gotten hurt, Phoenix would have beaten his ass to a bloody pulp. His drunk ass father killed his kid sister when she was six during a drunken rage. He's very protective of those two kids as a result.

"Enough!" Thor's voice rings out. "Timber, take your seat. We need to talk about the rest of the shit Mae gave to us."

Reluctantly, I retake my seat.

For the next twenty minutes, we go over the codes Mae brought. They're drop-off points and schedules for weapon shipments, drug hand-offs, loan collections, and of course, trafficking women and kids.

"Smoke, do some digging to see if you can find anything out about this X guy. We can't move forward unless we know who we're going up against."

Smoke curls his lip but gives a curt nod.

"Good, now everyone get out of here except for Phoenix and Smoke."

We all get up, but Levi stays in her seat. Thor gives her a look, but she shakes her head.

"I want to say something else to my dear brother and then I'll leave."

Thor gives her a chin lift before his gaze goes back to Smoke.

Giving Smoke one more scathing look, I head to the door and collect my phone.

Axe slaps me on the shoulder. "Give me a few minutes and I'll head over with you."

Giving him a chin lift, I'm tempted to grab a beer from the Prospect, but I don't since I'll be driving soon.

After a few minutes my phone dings and I open it up to see a picture Sasha sent me. Mae's laying on the couch asleep with both Sadie and Jordan snuggled up in her arms, also asleep.

"Awwww, that's cute. Send it to me, too," Levi says, having come up behind m e.

Guess whatever she said was quick, but I don't miss the grip she has on the pen in her hands. I'm honestly surprised she didn't pull out a blade and was twirling it instead.

"You okay?" I ask her and she sighs.

"I will be once he pulls his head out of his ass."

Nodding, I frown but then my phone dings again with another picture from Sasha. This one must have been from earlier because the kids are still snuggled deep in Sunshine's arms, but all three of them are talking in this picture.

"What's got you grinning?" Axe asks as he comes over and slaps my back. I turn my phone around and he grins as well, then I show him the other picture.

"Send me those, brother. Now, come on. Susie mentioned Mae wanted to go shopping for some stuff. I'll tag along and help keep an eye out with you."

Without saying a word, Tripp and Gunner join us as well. The five of us exit the clubhouse and walk to my house in silence.

Quietly, I open the door. Levi pushes past me and makes a beeline straight toward Mae, who is now awake. She hugs her, careful not to wake the kids.

"I've got your back, Babe," I hear Levi saying quietly to her.

Tears fill Mae's eyes as she says thank you.

Sunshine turns toward me, and I can't help but grin. Walking over to her, I kiss her. "Ready to go shopping, Sunshine?"

"Yeah, but who's going to watch the kids? The ladies all want to go with me."

"I wanna go with MaeMae, too," Sadie says as she sits up and rubs her eyes.

"Me, too. I want to keep you safe from the bad guys. Don't worry, Auntie MaeMae, Uncle Smoke will soon realize that he's wrong, and then he'll help protect you from the bad guys, too," Jordan says.

All of us go still at his words.

Fuck, what all did Smoke go on a rant about in front of them? Axe looks at me and gives me a slight chin lift, though I see the muscle in his jaw tick from clenching. He'll fill me in about what all was said in a bit. My gaze snags to Sunshine, who's doing her damnedest not to cry. She pulls both kids in close and kisses their temples.

Tripp squats down in front of Jordan and gently squeezes his knee. "You're right. Smoke will come around eventually, and when he does, I'm sure Mae here will put him through the wringer, making him grovel like crazy." His words instantly cut through the tension and a few of us chuckle while the kids laugh.

Sunshine's cheeks heat, but she doesn't deny his words as she shakes her head.

Jordan sits up straighter. "Wait. That means Auntie MaeMae's the club princess. She's the firstborn girl to the club."

Holy shit, he's right. I didn't think about it before, but shit. She's going to have even more protection than I realized.

"That's right, Little Man. Sunshine won't be lacking protection, especially with us being the original club chapter." My gaze cuts to Sunshine and I say these next words for her since the others know already. "What I mean by that is Thor's the President of *all* the Steel Archangel's chapters. You already would have had protection due to being Smoke's daughter, but with Smoke adopting Levi, that makes you Thor's niece. And while we're on that topic, I'm sure you've all heard us call Levi, Queen. That's because she's the Queen of all the Steel Archangel's Old Ladies, since she's Thor's Old Lady."

Mae looks at Levi, and at Levi's nod, understanding seems to dawn on Sunshine.

A thought pops into my head, and as much as I try, I can't push it away. I know she said she loved me, but if she just wants protection, she'll get it because of who she is. She doesn't have to stay with me to get it.

Sunshine gently lifts the kids off her lap, gets up, and walks over to me, wrapping her arms around my waist. Tilting her head up, I cup one of her cheeks while the other rests on her waist.

"I'm not leaving, Timber. I want to be with you and only you," she whispers before placing a kiss on my chest.

Leaning down, I give her a quick kiss and push the thought from my head. I don't know how she knew what I was worried about, but she quickly dispelled it.

Tripp quirks an eyebrow at me and I smirk, giving him a chin lift. I need to get it on order for her ASAP. I know that I won't get a unanimous vote unless Smoke miraculously pulls his head out of his ass, but I don't want to wait. He pulls out his phone and texts our contact.

Tapping her thigh, I pull back slightly and she looks up at me. "Why don't you get your purse? Then we'll all go shopping to get whatever else you need."

She nods, pivots, but then turns back toward me. "Can we stop and get a new phone, too? Mine is second hand from a friend and I'm afraid that it'll soon crap out on me," she says as she pulls out a *really* old phone that has a lot of cracks in the screen.

Fuck, I'm surprised that model even still works. Previously, I only saw the back of her case, and I'm betting that was on purpose.

My anger rises again at what Lillian and her stepdad have put her through and what they've denied her. I can't wait to get my hands on those fuckers.

Clearing my throat, I nod. "Yeah, Sunshine, we'll stop by a phone place today."

The smile she gives me has me wishing no one else was here so I could kiss the fuck out of her, but that'll have to wait. "Go get your shit, Baby."

Nodding, she quickly heads upstairs, and I turn my attention to the others, then down to Sadie and Jordan.

"Are you sure you both want to go with us? We're probably going to be doing a lot of walking today and going to a lot of stores," Susie asks and both kids nod eagerly, and Susie nods in return. "Okay then, I don't want to hear any complaining later on. Both of you go to the bathroom and we'll head out in a few minutes."

Both kids race to the downstairs bathroom, and I can't help but laugh. With how close those two are, I bet when they're older, they'll end up together.

"Did Mae by chance say what all she was wanting to get today beside the phone she just mentioned?" I ask Levi, who nods.

"Yes. Clothes, shoes, and bathroom supplies to start with. Later on, she said she wants to go to a bookstore and she wants to look into getting a used car. If she's going to be on the back of your bike eventually, we'll need to get her proper gear for that as well."

I grind my teeth at that. She doesn't need a used car. I'd rather have her have a new one, so we don't have to worry about what the fuck the previous owner did or didn't do to the car. There's no way I'm letting her pay for the car, either.

"Since I can guess as to what you're grinding your teeth about over there, let me make a suggestion. Tell her why you want to do what you're thinking about and list everything out for her regarding your concerns. She'll probably fight you on money, but you gotta remember where she's coming from. She's used to buying everything she needs for herself and relying only on herself. It'll take some time to get used to having someone there to help her out," Levi says quietly but gently.

Gunner grunts in agreement. "She mentioned wanting to pay for her mom to get into rehab. Maybe you can say she should keep more of her money for that, even though I'm guessing you were already planning to do that if we find out the bitch isn't working with that fucker in selling her."

I grunt. "You're right. If she's innocent in that, I was going to offer my help in getting Lillian the help she needs. If she wants it. But based on how she'd act when Preston couldn't keep her strung out, I'm guessing she'll take the help. No one should be pumped full of drugs against their will," I grind out.

God, I can't wait to get my hands on that fucker. I'll make him pay for not only what he put Mae through, but also her mom.

Footsteps on the stairs have me turning and at the same time, both Jordan and Sadie come running back into the living room. Realizing how many people are going on this outing, I turn to Levi.

"Can we take your SUV? That's the only vehicle that'll fit everyone and have room for whatever Mae gets."

"Yup, I was going to offer to drive, anyway. I'd also rather only have one vehicle today, as that'd be easier to watch with only four of you," she replies.

"Colt offered to come with us if you want him to. Said he could help with the kids if they want to go with us or run bags back and forth to the car," Sasha says. I give her a chin lift and she pulls out her phone to text him.

Though I'm sure Colt's offer to help Mae is real, I now get the need to also want to keep eyes on your woman when out and about. In a couple of months,

Colt will be up to earn his patch. While I know he wishes Sasha didn't want to join the club, it was only because he wanted to ask her to be his Old Lady when he patches in. Now, he'll have to wait till she patches in. And I have no doubt in my mind that she'll earn her patches. Especially for all the help she's already done for the club.

Pulling out my own phone, I shoot a text off to Thor, letting him know who all is going with us. His reply is almost immediate, saying to make sure we watch our backs and no one goes off alone.

Stepping up to Mae, I wrap my hand around her waist and look from her to the kids. "No one wonders off alone, okay? We have to assume Preston's the one who sent Smoke the information earlier, so he knows where she is. You hear me?"

"Yes, Uncle Timber," both kids say in unison and Mae agrees as well.

I look up at my brothers and sisters. "Thor said that goes for us as well." They all give me a chin lift.

We all head to the door, but Levi calls out to Mae.

"Wait, Mae, before we go, I want to give you these." She holds out a familiar bag and I mouth 'thank you' to her.

Mae takes the bag from her and pulls out two bracelets. "Thank you."

"They aren't ordinary bracelets. Let me show you what they do." Levi twists where the ends connect and she shows her the hidden blades.

Sunshine's eyes widen in surprise. "Um... I'm kind of scared to ask why I would need hidden blades in a bracelet?"

Levi swallows hard as a dark look crosses her face before she masks it. "Later, when we have more time, I'll tell you my story, but just know, these will cut through ropes if those assholes do get a hold of you and tie your hands behind your back. There's also a tracker embedded into each bracelet. It's not monitored unless it needs to be."

Sunshine's gaze goes to everyone, and she sees us all wearing them, including Sadie and Jordan, before back to Levi. Her eyes mist with tears as she nods. Taking a deep breath, she steps forward and hugs Levi. "Thank you."

Levi helps her put them on. Later I'll help her get familiar with them, so she's able to easily get them off and on.

We all head outside and the women and kids veer off to head to Levi's house. When we're up by our bikes, Tripp steps closer to me and I give him the information he needs for our contact. Surprisingly, Dragon comes out and straddles his bike as he gives me a chin lift. I hope like fuck he's starting to realize how wrong he was yesterday.

A few minutes later, Levi pulls up and we split up—three in front of the vehicle and three behind it. Levi already told me where we're going first, and while I don't like it, I understand why they picked the mall. It'll be easier to go there first and get everything she needs while not driving to a bunch of different stores all day.

Chapter 22
Thor

"Good, now everyone get out of here except for Phoenix and Smoke."

They all get up, but Wildcat stays in her seat. I level her a look for not listening, but she shakes her head.

"I want to say something else to my dear brother and then I'll leave."

I give her a chin lift because I know how much she needs to do this. Her and Mae have become really close already, and Smoke needs a wake-up call. One I'm hoping Wildcat can give him.

Everyone can see the truth except for him. I get that Lillian screwed him over years ago, but he's taking things too far with Mae. My gaze goes to Smoke, and he swallows thickly when he sees how pissed I am. On the way out, Reaper steps up close to me.

"My offer still stands to have Python look into anything regarding Mae, so there's no conflict of interest. My other offer regarding those two also still stands if she needs to get away from this," he tells me quietly, his gaze going to Smoke before coming back to me.

"Thanks, and I'll take you up on having him verify and look into things on her. I'll talk to Mae and Timber about your other offer," I reply with a chin lift. Without even asking, and especially after what just happened, I'm pretty sure I know what they're going to do, but the decision is ultimately Mae's.

I'd already intended to ask him about Python before Timber told me he'd offered yesterday. Having already seen the papers in her hand, I knew Smoke would flip the fuck out as soon as she said he was her dad. I just didn't realize how bad it would turn out.

Bear's the last one out and he closes the door behind him. Instantly, Levi's out of her seat and in front of Smoke, brandishing a blade at him.

"I cannot fucking believe the bullshit that you've been spewing to that sweet girl. I get that you're pissed as fuck at what Lillian did to you, but Mae never asked for any of this to happen. She's innocent in all of this. How can you say such hateful things to your own daughter? The daughter you've been mourning all this time. The daughter that you thought you'd lost forever and had contemplated I don't know how many times in joining her. The daughter that's so much like you, that if you looked close enough, you'd see it. She's practically your carbon copy, not Lillian's. Did you notice she didn't need any help with the computer? While I know what she did were pretty simple tasks, the fact of the matter is, she didn't even bat an eye at it."

I'm tempted to step in, but I know my Wildcat needs to get this all off her chest. I just hope she doesn't work herself up too much. Stress isn't good for her or the babies.

"I want you to watch everything on the feeds that you did and said to her yesterday when you were drunk. Then I want you to read through everything in those journals and papers once they are scanned. And I know for a fact that what she told us in Church was only a fraction of what that fucker did to her over the years.

"She told us ladies last night that in the beginning, she tried to get Preston to stop hurting her mom or giving her drugs. That he ended up beating them both whenever she tried to intervene. She only stopped interfering when her mom left her a note telling her to stop. That it was better that only she be hurt. That didn't save Mae from all of his beatings, though. He'd regularly beat her and tried to break her down like he did Lillian, but it didn't work." She pauses, her chest heaving.

If it weren't that I need to set Smoke straight, I'd be dragging her out of here and sinking into her wet pussy. Fuck, I love when she's feisty like this. So long as those blades and blazing eyes aren't pointed in my direction, that is.

"You need to think long and hard about what you've done to that poor girl. And even though I'm pissed as fuck at you, I'm also here for you. I get this is a major cluster-mind-fuck. Not only for you, but also for Mae. If you need to talk to someone, I'll be there for you. Now, I'll leave so Thor can do his thing."

She pulls back, sheaths her knife, and walks over to me. Pulling her close, I give her a kiss that ends far too fucking quick. "You going with Mae today?"

"Yeah, I'll help her get what she needs, but also be there for her. Smoke's world isn't the only one that's been blown apart. So has hers since she only found out the truth of things a little over a day ago."

"Take the club card. She's family, so get her riding gear on us."

"Alright. Just so you know, I also plan to pay for some things today as well. Last night, when Nikki mentioned we should have a party for Mae's birthday, Mae immediately said she didn't want us to fuss over her birthday. That she didn't need a party or anything." Wildcat pauses and judging by the emotions flitting across her face, there was more to that conversation that she isn't telling me.

She takes a deep breath and shakes her head. "Mae's gone far too many years without anyone giving a shit about her. That ends today. We won't do a party, but we are going to take care of her and get her a few things."

Giving her hip a squeeze, I let go and wait for her to shut the door. Only then do I let Smoke see exactly how fucking pissed I am. I already know without looking that Phoenix is giving Smoke his own icy glare. Smoke's face pales slightly as his gaze bounces between us and he swallows thickly.

"Speaking as a friend, you are a fucking asshole for what you've done and said to that poor girl. I get that your mind is in a fucked-up place right now, but you need to get your head on straight because I will not allow your behavior to continue. She doesn't deserve to be treated the way you're treating her.

"As your President, you're lucky I'm not stripping you of your patch for what you've done, especially this morning. You do not flip your shit in front of children. When you watch the video feed, I want you to make sure you take into account how scared they both were."

I pause and it's only then that a sliver of guilt flashes on his face. Fucking asshole. He should have been feeling guilty far before now.

"I know Mae's asked that you not be hurt for what you've done to her, but you're still going to take a beating once everyone's back. You're lucky that's all I'm making you go through and that's only because I was there that day and know just how much that fucked you up. But if you do anything else toward Mae, your ass will be out of here. We don't treat women like that. Right now, you're acting no better than Preston is with Lillian."

Smoke blanches at that and thank fuck he's starting to realize just how much of an asshole he really was. He gives me a chin lift.

"When Alexei and Ethan are done scanning everything, I'll have them send it over to you. I agree with everything Levi said and was already planning to have you do the same. You will watch what you did yesterday when you were drunk, then read through everything she brought with her. That's an order. That said, like Levi stated a few minutes ago, I'll be here if you need someone to talk to, but don't you fucking dare pull out your 45 again like you did all those years ago."

He winces, but nods. He didn't know it at the time, but I had cameras of my own snuck into his room and had a trigger for whenever he opened his gun case or his nightstand drawer where he always kept a gun. The trigger would send a notification to Phoenix and me. We knew every time he pulled that fucking gun out. Both of us would be on alert, and ready to step in if he pointed that gun at himself, but each time, he put the gun away. Thank fuck.

"Now, after you've seen the video feeds and are waiting on Alexei and Ethan to finish scanning everything, I want you looking into this X fellow along with that Bruce fucker. Work with Python on Preston, too. I'll be having Python verify what Mae sent so that there's no conflict of interest. I'll give him the heads up to let you know what he finds out about Mae as well, after it's confirmed. Let me know if you find anything out about Preston using Mae's dead name as well."

Smoke clenches his jaw but gives me a chin lift. I don't give a flying fuck if he's pissed I'm bringing in Python, but there's no way I'm letting him verify what Mae said when he's like this. I'd always be questioning if he was telling me the truth.

"Alright, get the fuck out and you'd best not fuck shit up anymore."

Without a word, he grabs his laptop and leaves. When the door shuts, my gaze goes to Phoenix, my best friend. We grew up together and went to school together. Hell, we even Prospected together. For many years, we even lived together after my parents took him in because what his asshole parents did to him and his little sister, Ember. His fucking asshole father killed Ember in a drunken rage and got forty years in jail for it. Then his bitch of a mom sided with that fucker and laid all the blame on Phoenix as well as taking out her frustrations on him, too.

"This is fucked up and you know it, man," he says as he rubs at his temple. I nod as I shake off those memories.

"I can't wait to get my hands on that fucking weasel. For Mae's sake, I hope Lillian isn't involved in any of this shit with Bruce. If she is, Levi will have a field day."

Phoenix snorts. "Not just her. I'm sure Sasha will be itching to sink a blade into her as well. If Mae weren't Smoke's daughter, I'm sure the two of them would have adopted Mae as their sister."

Grunting in agreement, I slap him on the shoulder. "Come on, let's grab a beer. Hopefully, someone will have news for us soon and then we can start planning."

Chapter 23
Mae

WHEN WE PULL UP to the mall, my nerves go into overdrive. Well, even worse than what they were after Church and hearing more of Smoke's hateful words. Part of those nerves are because Dragon joined us at the last minute. The other part is because I hate big crowds, always have. I'm also thankful that I put some extra money into my purse because I have a feeling that I'm going to be coming home with a lot of things from what the women are saying.

"Mae, I'm not trying to scare you or anything, but we aren't going thrift store shopping. We're going to get you good quality clothes and shoes that will last for a while, okay?" Levi says as she looks at me in the rear-view mirror.

Nodding, I clench my hands in my lap as I try to calm my nerves.

"So, you said you liked the style of clothes I grabbed for you yesterday, right?" Sasha asks and I nod as I lick my lips.

"The clothes, yes. Though some of the undergarments were a bit much."

My cheeks heat as I remember the lacy and silk lingerie that she got me as well as the thongs. The ladies chuckle and my cheeks heat even more.

"Good, then we'll go to those stores and you can pick out more. We'll also make sure you have a few things for when you want to take that next step with Timber," Sasha says with a wink.

Butterflies swirl in my stomach as my gaze goes to Timber, who's riding point in front of us. I want to take that next step, but I'm nervous. I really don't know what I'm doing.

Deciding to just trust her, I nod again, and she smiles widely.

Levi parks but doesn't get out. Her gaze locks with mine in the rear-view mirror. "Never get out of a car until Timber or another brother comes up to your door. Let them do their thing and check the surrounding area to make sure it's safe for us to get out."

Confused, I nod. I need to talk to Timber about MC life. I'm completely out of my element here.

After a few moments, Timber comes up to my door and opens it. Unbuckling, I step out and he wraps an arm around my waist as we wait for the others to get out of Levi's SUV.

"Where are we heading first, Sunshine?"

"Um, I'm not sure. Sasha said she'd take me to the stores that she went to yesterday since I like the style," I reply as I look down at my clothes.

I really do love what she's picked out for me. Looking up at Timber, my thighs clench as his heated gaze travels up and down my body. He's about to say something when we're interrupted as Sadie runs over and grabs my hand.

"Come on, MaeMae. Time to do some shopping!"

I can't help but laugh at her excitement. I would never have guessed that she loves to shop as much as she does. And she's only seven.

Looking up at Nikki, I grin. "Looks like you're going to have a shopaholic when she grows up."

Nikki groans and shakes her head. "I'm not looking forward to it."

All the ladies laugh and even a couple of the guys before we head into the mall.

As soon as we step into the first store, the ladies pull me toward the racks and I try my best not to look at the price tags. I knew I was going to have to get new clothes when we got here, but I wasn't planning to go to the mall. Levi had called it earlier. I was planning to go to the thrift stores first to see what I could get for cheap.

Browsing through the racks, I pick out a few shirts and tank tops, getting the size Sasha had grabbed for my other shirts. Walking over to the jeans, I feel a little lost. There're so many styles of jeans that I'm not sure which to go with. Feeling overwhelmed, I decide to just stick with skinny jeans for now since that's what Sasha got me. I can always get different styles of jeans later when things settle down.

Grabbing three pairs in the size Sasha got me, I turn and feel the blood drain from my face.

All five of the women, and yes I'm also including Sadie, have clothes in their arms.

"Um... I hope that means you all are getting clothes for yourselves, too. Right?" I lick my lips nervously. I cannot spend *that* much money on clothes. While I'd avoided looking at the prices on the shirts, it couldn't be ignored on the pants. They're $70 a piece.

Levi shakes her head. "I've already talked to the saleslady, and she has a dressing room set up for you. Try on your things first and we'll give you a few more to try on. But you have to come out and show us everything."

Taking a deep breath, I decide not to fight her on this. Just because I try them on doesn't mean I'll be buying them. Looking over my shoulder, I chew on my lip as my gaze finds Timber. He nods in encouragement, and I slowly nod in return.

I can't believe I'm doing this.

Following the ladies further toward the back of the store, I stop at the entrance of the fitting rooms, my eyes wide.

Off to one side, there's a changing area, but there's also a few seats around a small table. There's also mirrors out here where I can get a better look at the outfits. Ducking my head, I make a beeline for the dressing room door.

Once it's shut and locked, I strip out of my shoes, shirt, and jeans before trying on the first outfit. Turning in the mirror, I love how I feel wearing it. The jeans fit me like a glove. The shirt is a fitted short-sleeved shirt, dark purple with a v-neck that shows a fair amount of cleavage.

My worries come back as I stare at my revealed skin. I could always wear a tank-top under it to reduce the peep show. I've never liked to draw attention to myself and I feel like I would if I don't cover up a bit more with this shirt. That and I don't know what Timber would think about me showing so much skin. Not that I'd let him dictate what I wear or what my wardrobe will be like, but I want to take his opinions into account. Quickly, I take the shirt off, slip on a white tank top and put the shirt back on.

That's better.

"Get out here, girl! We want to see everything!" Nikki shouts.

Shaking my head, I open the door and instantly their faces light as they smile.

"That's a keeper!" Susie says.

"You should wear that without the tank top. Timber would be all over you in an instant," Sasha says as she wiggles her eyebrows at me.

My cheeks heat and I turn around and flee back into the dressing room, the ladies laughing behind me.

Oh, my lanta. I think I may be in trouble if they're going to be like this all day.

Somehow, I get through everything that the ladies had picked out for me. I've got everything from tank tops, t-shirts, a couple of blouses, a few nice sweaters, and jeans picked out.

I'll need to make sure we stop somewhere where I can get some hoodies and a decent fall jacket. Mine barely keeps the wind out.

Grabbing my clothes, I make my way out of the dressing room to find the room empty. I shrug. Guess the ladies all went out front already.

As I approach the cash register, I freeze. The guys are all carrying a bunch of bags. My cheeks heat, but this time, it's in embarrassment.

Timber's instantly by my side, and I realize I've back pedaled in my shock. "What's going on in that pretty head, Sunshine?"

Shaking my head, I can't tear my gaze from the bags. "When I asked to go shopping, I wasn't expecting charity. I don't want charity. I was, *am*, going to pay for my own things. This is too much. They need to return them. It's too much."

My breath is coming faster and I'm sure I'm bright red from embarrassment. I didn't want their pity. I'm not a charity case. I refuse to be. I just wanted help to pick out clothes that would fit and to hang out with them.

"Sunshine, no one pities you and you aren't a charity case."

Crap, I must have said that out loud.

"Yes, Sunshine, you said both of those things out loud." He sets down his bags and cups my cheeks, making me look at him.

Pure love is shining out through his pale blue eyes and I inhale sharply from the intensity of it. I barely register someone taking the clothes from my arms and I immediately wrap them around Timber's waist.

"If you take a look out there, that's your family, Sunshine. Your blood family, chosen family, and club family. None of us pity you. You aren't a charity case. You said you needed a new wardrobe, and Baby, you're getting it. They all want to help because you are *family*.

"You've had years of practically being on your own and providing for yourself, but that stops now. You've got me now and you've got all of them. Let us help you. You don't have to do everything by yourself. Not everything is solely on your shoulders anymore. Everyone wanted to pitch in and help to make up for years of not being able to care for you. Please, let us in. Let us help."

Tears well in my eyes and his calloused thumbs dry them as they fall. My gaze goes over his shoulders and despite the war going on inside me, a giggle escapes when I see Sasha holding Sadie, both of them making puppy dog eyes at me. Sadie's even holding up her hands together to amp up the pleading look. Timber looks over his shoulder and chuckles at them.

Sighing, I nod. I have a feeling I'm not going to win this argument, but when we're alone, I'm going to talk to him about this.

"No going much more overboard though, okay? I still need to get some hoodies, a fall jacket, some underclothes, socks, and shoes. Plus, some toiletry things. Oh, and a phone."

"While you were shopping, I went and got you a phone, Sunshine." He pauses as he pulls it out and hands it to me. "Everything was transferred and I made sure you have everyone's number in there. Once you have everything you need, there's going to be one more stop. I want you on the back of my bike, but first you need the right gear. That means helmet, jacket, and boots."

Shyly, I nod as I bite my lip. I've never been on a motorcycle before, but it looks fun. "Okay." Going up on my toes, I give him a quick kiss.

He grabs my hand and leads me out of the store. I look around for the clothes that I'd had in my hands before. Not finding them, I turn to the ladies in question and Nikki holds up a couple of bags.

"Wanted to treat my niece since I have years of birthdays and Christmas presents to make up for."

"We also snagged some jewelry that you were looking at before," Susie says with a wink.

"You guys are going to spoil me rotten, aren't you?" I sigh heavily as I run a hand through my hair.

While it's going to take a bit to get used to the fact that I now have a support group, a small part of me is drinking up the fact that I *do* have a support group as it does a little happy dance in my mind. And they are also giving me presents in the form of what I need.

I haven't received a present in years.

Surprisingly, it's Sadie that answers my earlier question.

"You know it, MaeMae." She wraps her arms around my waist and gives me a hug before pulling back and tugging on my hand. Bending down, she whispers in my ear. "I also picked out a few pieces of jewelry for you. I hope you like them."

She holds up a little bag, and I take it, peaking inside. There's a cute gold necklace with a sun charm hanging in the center, along with some gold hoop earrings and a ring with blue gemstones in them.

"They're gorgeous. I love them, thank you."

And I really do. I'd been looking at all of them earlier but had decided to wait. Pulling out the jewelry, I take the tags off and put them on. I'm surprised the ring fits. She must have seen me trying them on. When I have everything on, she claps her hands in excitement.

Tucking the now empty bag into another bag, I look to Sasha, deciding to just go with the flow for right now. "Where to next?"

She loops her arm through mine, smiling mischievously, and takes me into the shop next door.

Victoria's Secret.

Oh my.

My cheeks heat at all of the scanty material. I wonder if I'll be able to find something that covers all of my rear. I'm not exactly wanting to try on a thong. Who would want a piece of floss between their butt cheeks? Though a good bra does sound nice. Maybe even a couple of them. I've heard that this store has good quality stuff. I just hope what I heard was right.

"Hello, ladies. Do you need any help with anything?" A sales lady says as she walks up to us. Though I notice, she keeps sending seductive looks to the guys.

"Yes, we need a bra fitting."

I cut a glance over at Levi and note she's all business. Gone is the playful smile from a moment ago, and I'm going to take a stab that it's because this woman is trying to flirt with the guys.

"Of course. For all of you, or just a few of you?"

I step forward. "I need it, please."

Knowing Sasha and Levi will prefer to stay out here to keep that woman from flirting with their men, I grab Susie's hand and make her come back with me. I doubt this woman would do anything to me, but I really don't want to be alone, either.

After a few minutes, I have my correct bra size. For years I thought I was a 34C but I'm really a 36D. Then again, I always bought the cheapest I could get in the past.

With my fitting done, Susie and I make our way back onto the floor and she helps me look through all the different types of bras. I end up getting two types and grab one in white as well as black in both styles. Having already talked about what type of underwear I want; she suggests going with boyshorts. Surprisingly that's what I'm currently wearing, so I don't have to try any on since I know the size. I grab a few cute colors, making sure I have a little over a week's worth.

"Hey, Mae, come over here," Sasha calls out and I head over toward her. I fight my blush when I see she's looking at some cute panty and bra sets.

"You should get a couple of matching sets, too." She pauses and leans in close so only I can hear her. "I've always found wearing something sexy boosts my confidence, even if you're the only one that will be seeing it."

This time I can't fight my blush, but she's got a point. I know what I'm currently wearing isn't really that sexy, but I feel better because they are sexier than what I had. That, combined with the cute clothes she's already picked out for me, has really boosted my confidence.

"Nothing too lacy, though. I've never been one to like the feeling of lace on my bare skin." Her face lights up that I'm going to get some and I can't help but smile in return.

As we're picking out more things, my mood instantly sours when I hear a couple of women talking behind us.

"God what I wouldn't give to have a night with that one called Timber. Fuck, he's sex on a stick."

"Mmm, definitely. They're all sex on a stick. Fuck, I wouldn't mind a night with anyone of them, but yeah. That Timber guy's hot."

"Guys, lay off it. I overheard he's here with his girlfriend. Almost all of them are with these ladies."

"Shut up, Ivy. No one asked you. Now cover for us. We're going to see if one of them will be making our night tonight."

Grabbing the few sets, as well as a few pajamas I picked out, I turn around, noticing their nametags—Stacy and Jade. There's no way I'm going to let this continue. Normally I don't like confrontation, but I'm not about to listen to them talk about Timber like that or have to watch them try to corner him if I don't speak up.

I walk over to the one called Ivy and hand her my bag holding my items. "Can you please ring me up?" I turn and face the other ladies. "And Ivy's right. Timber's my man and I'd appreciate it if you'd stop talking about him like he's a piece of meat."

The two of them curl their lips as they eye me up and down. I know I'm skinny, but I've got a fairly decent sized chest and butt.

"There's no way he's with a plain Jane like you. God, I bet you can't even please him right. You look like you'd break in half just with one thrust."

Sasha huffs. "And what makes you think that you have the right to decide who they want to make their woman? If any of them heard you guys trying to pick which one to spend the night with like one would pick a meal at a fast-food place, they wouldn't touch your asses."

"And how would you know? You probably started Prospecting there just to be a whore for them and spread your legs. Hell, maybe we should Prospect, Stacy."

"Like hell would they ever let you Prospect. They'd maybe accept you as a club bunny, but that's it. And as for me, my man is Colt. I'm not a bunny that spreads her legs for the single brothers."

"You got everything you need, Sunshine?"

Feeling his heat at my back, my body melts into him as he places his hands on my hips. I'm glad he's here, one for me, and two for Sasha. She looks like she's about ready to come to blows with these women.

I turn partially and tilt my head up. He leans down and gives me a toe-curling kiss. When he pulls back, I have to fight to not reach up and kiss him again.

Licking my lips, I answer him. "Just putting these Johnson Chasers in their place. They were going to try to hook up with you and maybe a few others."

His chest shakes with laughter and he leans down to kiss me again. When he straightens, I immediately feel the shift in him and look toward the two women. I can't help but smirk when I see their shocked faces.

"I can guarantee I won't be tapping either of you. As she said, Sunshine here is my woman and most of the other men are taken, too. And for the record, the men in Steel Archangel's don't cheat on their women. Though, I doubt the single guys will want either of you, since you both seem like you are clingy bitches out to trap a biker." He pauses and I feel him tense up even more. "And don't even think about coming around the club. Sasha here earned the right to Prospect and she's right. No brother would take an Old Lady that has spread her legs for all the brothers. None of us will tap someone that's as clingy as your asses. Come on, Sunshine, let's get you settled."

Walking over to the cash register, I don't put up a fight when Timber squeezes my hip and pulls out his wallet. I get that he's making a statement to those two women by providing for me right now.

Taking my bag, I lace my fingers through his and walk out of the store. Dragon has his arm wrapped around Levi's waist and Sasha's in Colt's arms. Both Sasha and Colt are glaring at the two women in the store who, by the looks of things, could cause some problems down the road.

Despite the warnings, they're still eyeing our men like they have a chance with them. Even the ones that are taken.

If these items work out, I'll just order more online when the time comes. I don't really want to step into this store again if they're working here.

Wanting to break the tension, I give Timber a quick kiss and go over to snag Sasha's arm. I can tell she's madder than a pack of wild dogs on a three-legged cat from the tension running through her.

"We are not letting them ruin today. Come on. Where to next?"

Chapter 24
Timber

IT TAKES EVERYTHING COLT has to keep Sasha from going back into the store and setting those two bitches straight. She doesn't take kindly to people threatening the club, her family, or treating any of us like meat. But those bitches went even further and practically called her a whore. I don't blame her for getting pissed, but we also can't cause a scene. I know she would have preferred to have pulled out her knives, but thank fuck, she didn't.

Dragon even went as far as taking their pictures and sending them to Thor, saying Stacy and Jade aren't allowed on clubhouse grounds. If they create any issues at our businesses, then they'll be banned from all Steel Archangel's establishments.

Thank fuck Sunshine was able to redirect Sasha and break the tension, though the rest of my brothers are on higher alert. If it weren't for Susie coming out to get us, we might not have realized there was a problem.

Shaking my head, I watch as the women bounce from store to store, getting the last of Sunshine's things.

Well, most of them.

We'll still have two more stops after we leave the mall.

Earlier, it took all of my restraint when the ladies went into a shoe store. Sasha picked out some sexy as fuck boots for my woman and when she's ready, she'll definitely be wearing them when I sink into her tight pussy. The thought has my cock straining even more against the zipper of my jeans.

With the last of the shopping done at the mall, we all decide to hit the food court while we're here.

I walk over to Sunshine, who looks like she's lost. I wonder if she's ever eaten at any of these restaurants before.

"Hey, Sunshine, what would you like to have?"

She licks her lips nervously as her gaze bounces around. "Um... I've never eaten at any of these places before. I don't want much, but since we're out and about, I don't want to have anything that might possibly make me sick."

"In that case, how about we get you a sub sandwich?" I pause as I point over at one of them. "All you have to tell them is if you want a half or a whole sub. The half is about six inches long. Then you pick the type of bread, what type of sandwich you want and then pick what toppings and dressing you want on it. How's that sound?"

She nods. "Yeah, that sounds like it would be easy for my first to-go meal like this."

That pulls me up short. "You've never eaten fast-food before?"

She shakes her head. "Ever since I got out of high school, the only hot meal I'd get would be at Peggy's diner. Her and Glen would always give me a little extra protein and veggies than would normally come with the dish. Or if I was working in the kitchen, I'd make it myself.

"At the grocery store, they have a hot bar, but it's disgusting. I ate there once when I started working there while in high school, but got sick. I never ate from it again. If I wasn't working at the diner, I'd get something easy at the grocery store, like granola bars and a few pieces of fruit. On the rare occasions that I'm home, I only got the discarded items from what was left of the groceries or from the food bank. It was usually cans of beans, stale bread, and if I was lucky, some peanut b utter."

I grit my teeth at how bad she's had it. Out of the corner of my eye, both Axe and Dragon's jaws tense and I'm guessing they both heard that as well. Clearing my throat, I try to keep my anger out of my voice. "Then let's get you a sub. Later, I'll introduce you to some of the other restaurants and fast-food places."

Stepping up in line, I go first so she can see how the process goes. We get our subs, drinks, and I grab us some chips as well before leading Sunshine over to a set of tables the others are sitting at. They kept two spots open for us, so she sits down across from me.

Half-way through her sub, Sunshine freezes and her face pales as she stares at something over my shoulder.

"What's wrong, Sunshine?"

She licks her lips and lowers her sub. "Preston's here," she whispers.

Her gaze meets mine and I can see how freaked out and scared she is. Then her gaze bounces back over my left shoulder. I know my brothers and sisters heard her because they all tense as well.

"Describe him, Sis," Axe says quietly.

He's sitting to Sunshine's right, so he'll be able to spot him. It takes everything in me not to turn around, but I don't want to give away that we're onto him.

"He's balding, but has a bad, greasy comb-over. He has a mustache and beard, both poorly maintained and equally as greasy. Black shirt with a blue jacket and dirty, stained blue jeans. He's very portly. If he were a woman, I'd guess she'd go into labor with multiples at any minute. He's your stereotypical, sleezy, slimeball car salesman. What's funny is that's what I always thought he looked like before coming here. Now knowing that he used to be a car salesman, it just makes it even funnier."

Despite the seriousness of the situation, all of us chuckle at her description of him being a sleezy car salesman, even Sunshine. Axe pulls out his phone, acting normal, but I know he's taking the guy's picture and notifying the others.

"Sunshine, do you have enough of your stuff to last a couple of days? We really should get back to the clubhouse with him showing up here."

"Yeah. The only thing I'm short on is some sculpting mud. I used the last of mine up today."

What the fuck is sculpting mud?

"I got you covered on that end, Babe. You can have my spare one and I'll get another the next time I'm at the store. I always keep an extra one on hand," Sasha says.

"God, I swear you ladies and gents are like my very own fairy biker godmothers and godfathers with everything you're doing for me and helping me with."

The guys all sit up a bit straighter, their chests puffed out slightly at her words. The ladies all grin widely at her in response and Sadie giggles. Knowing her, I bet she's picturing us guys all wearing fairy wings like Tinkerbell. However, I can tell Sunshine really means it by how she's looking at each one of them.

Jordan, who's sitting next to me, tugs on my cut and I lean down. "We should get Auntie MaeMae back to the clubhouse. I don't want the bad man to get her," he whispers. I give him a chin lift and ruffle his hair.

Little Man's been a champ today. He watched how we were keeping an eye on the women but also keeping an eye out for any potential problems, and then he started doing the same thing. The kid's going to be one hell of a Prospect when he's old enough.

"Let's wrap up and head back to the clubhouse," I say quietly. Most everyone's done, but Sunshine wraps the rest of her sub and chips in her bag. While I'm happy she had about half of her 6-inch sub, I bet her nerves are going into overdrive and she's not able to eat anymore.

We all stand up and dump our trays. My neck prickles like someone's watching us, which means the assholes spotted Mae already. After dumping my tray, I turn and casually glance around, easily spotting the prick. There's two men with him, but I don't recognize them. I'll have to talk to Smoke to see if he can hack into the security cameras here. At least I hope he'll do it. If not, I'll ask Python.

Wrapping an arm around Sunshine's waist, we head toward the opposite end of the food court. Though it doesn't escape my notice that Axe is holding Jordan and Gunner is holding Sadie. If shit goes south in here, they'll be able to protect the kids better this way. Jordan looks over Axe's shoulder and when he turns back around, whispers something to Axe and he nods. Axe's gaze finds mine and he gives me a subtle nod. The fuckers are following us.

We make it out of the mall without incident, and when we get to Levi's SUV and our bikes, I see that more of our brothers are waiting for us. Thor gets off his bike and walks over toward us. His gaze goes over my shoulder and judging by the tightening of his jaw, he's spotted the assholes.

"Got them," he says quietly, then turns to me. "Python and Smoke are both working on the cameras trying to see what the assholes do as we leave. Lex is running a program to try to find information on the other two with him."

I know Lex works in our tattoo shop, but fuck, does the kid have a knack for computers and shit. However, it is a relief to have two tech guys in our club. Bones can do it in a pinch, but it isn't his strong-suit. It's helped on more than one occasion.

Quickly, we get the women and kids loaded up. Once Sunshine's buckled in, I lean in and give her a kiss.

"Be safe," she whispers, and fuck does the fear in her voice have my stomach twisting in knots.

"Always. I'll always come back to you, Sunshine. You're my heart." I give her another quick kiss. "If anything happens, listen to Levi and Sasha. This isn't our first rodeo, and I know it won't be our last."

When she nods, I shut the door, walk over to my bike, put my skull cap on and start her up. Pulling out, half of us lead the way back and the other half trail behind the SUV.

About midway to the clubhouse, I spot them.

We've got two black cars on our tail. I give a quick hand signal to the others and a call comes through on my Bluetooth.

"Got two tails. Watch yourselves and keep the line open," Thor's voice comes through the line.

I bob my head slightly so he can see me in his mirrors. None of us talk unless we have to in these types of situations so that, hopefully, no one talks over each other.

Minutes later, I catch sight of a car coming in fast from my left. *"Got a third coming in hot from the left. Speed up or break off."*

Immediately I punch it and know Levi's hot on our tail since she's in on the call. My gut knots further when I see the blacked out car just barely miss the tail end of the SUV and I pray that fucker didn't hit any of my brothers.

Chapter 25

Levi

THE CALL COMES THROUGH the SUV's bluetooth from Thor and immediately everyone stops talking. You could cut the tension in the car with a knife. My gaze flicks to Mae in the middle behind me and she's freaking the fuck out, but thankfully, she's staying quiet.

"Sasha. Call Ethan. Have him go to my house, and as soon as he sees the gates open, he's to open my garage door. We're going straight in and staying there till the guys give us the all clear. Have him pass on the message to Phoenix and Andre that we have two tails. Also, have them get the girls and bunnies in their rooms. No one comes out until they're told it's clear."

I kept my voice quiet, but when I see Thor's head bob in front of me and he gives me a hand signal, I know he heard me. Next to me, Sasha's quietly giving my orders to Ethan.

When Timber's voice comes over the other line, I speed up immediately as I keep an eye on the car to my left. I'm vaguely aware of Sasha updating the rest of the club and I'm grateful I had her call them.

The guys behind me split off to avoid the incoming car, and I breathe a sigh of relief when none of them are hit or go down. Three of them immediately are behind us again, but the others break off to follow the other cars.

A few minutes later, I see the gate and it instantly opens. I barely slow down and the guys in front of me break off quickly. It's only as we're approaching my house that I start slowing down. As soon as the car is in the garage, Ethan closes the door again. Putting the car in park and turning it off, I let out a breath I hadn't realized I'd been holding.

"Leave everything in the car for now. Everyone out and head into the house."

Once inside, I see Andre, Punisher, Doc, Judge and Uncle Bear already patrolling around the inside of my house. Breathing another sigh of relief, I know no one else got in here and all the windows and doors are secure.

Turning back toward Mae, I notice she's shaking like a leaf and I pull her into the living room with Doc hot on my heels. Pulling her down to the couch next to me, I shift so I'm facing her and take her hands in mine.

"Mae, I need you to take some big, deep breaths. The guys know what they're doing, and they won't let Preston, Bruce, or that X guy, or any of their cronies get you."

She doesn't answer me or acknowledge me. Fuck, she's stuck in her head. Scooting forward slightly, I cup her cheeks and make her look at me.

"Mae, you're safe. Do you hear me?"

She blinks a couple of times and takes a shaky breath before nodding. "S-sorry."

"You have nothing to be sorry for, Mae, but I need you to get control of your breathing. I'd hate for you to faint," Doc says, and I notice he's got his fingers pressed against her wrist, checking her pulse.

Nodding again, she takes some deep breaths, and slowly, her body stops shaking. After a few moments, she looks around at everyone before settling her gaze on me.

"None of the guys behind us got hurt, did they?"

I shake my head. "Thanks to Timber's warning, they all broke off in time. A few are following all three cars to see what they can find out. Aside from that, I don't know anything more."

And while that is true, even if I did know more, I wouldn't be able to tell her since it's now club business.

Shit, that reminds me, I should tell her about that.

"Did Timber talk to you more about how the club works?"

She shakes her head. "No, he said he'd tell me more later today after we were done shopping, but then this happened." She bites her lip nervously.

"Okay. I'm going to tell you a little about it because at first, there was one thing that really rubbed me raw. However, after a bit, I understood it even if I didn't like it. When Thor and Dragon couldn't tell me more about something, even if it affected me, they would say the dreaded phrase I hated. That it was 'club business'. Has he mentioned that at all to you yet?"

"No. So you mean, I'll be left out of some things even though it's regarding my safety?" she asks and her brow furrows in confusion.

Sighing, I nod. "Yes, but you should still talk to Timber. He can tell you some things, but not all the details. I almost left my guys because they wouldn't tell me *anything* at first, but Uncle Bear convinced them that I'd be safer even if I only knew tidbits of information. It's better to be aware that there's danger and maybe they'll be able to tell you some things to watch out for. But that's a big maybe. When it gets to the in-depth details and specifics, that's where they won't be able to tell you anything. What I mean by that is how they're going to protect you or any of us women and kids. Does that make sense?"

Her brow furrows further as she thinks, and I hope she's going to be okay with this because she'll have to deal with it for the rest of her life if she stays with Timber. I doubt she'll want to Prospect to be a full club member based on what I know about her so far.

"Do you mean like plausible deniability? That they won't tell me something as a way to protect me for if something goes wrong and cops are called in or something? Though from the little I've read, and I could be wrong, it sounds like clubs usually try to take care of their problems themselves rather than involving the cops."

"Holy fuck, I hope when I find a woman that she understands this like you do," Andre says from behind me, which has all of us laughing, but I notice his skin tightening around his eyes and I wonder if he already has his eye on someone.

Mae looks around, confused. "Wait, what?" she asks, getting more even confused.

Punisher plops down next to her and puts an arm around her shoulders. "Don't you worry your pretty little head there, Sis. You didn't say anything wrong. We're all just surprised by how well you understand what Levi's saying.

"She's right, though. We're not going to be able to tell you the deets, but Timber should be able to give you the cliff note version. Especially if they already did that with Levi when her shit went down. If they did that for her, then I'm guessing Thor's also going to be okay with Timber giving you a little information.

If you don't know you should be looking out for something, then that just puts you in even more danger and makes our job harder as well."

He hugs her close and starts talking to her quietly. It's surprising to see her relaxing as much as she does while he continues to talk to her.

My heart clenches at Punisher's words and seeing him take care of Mae like a little sister right now. I know this must be hitting him hard. He wasn't able to protect his own sister, and she died by her abusive boyfriend's hand. Thank fuck the club tracked the asshole down and delt with him.

My cell phone dings twice and I pull it out of my cut to see one's from Thor and the other's from Timber. Then, I hear my brothers' phones ding as well.

> Thor: We're calling Church, Wildcat, so we'll need you all to come over to the clubhouse. Prospects will watch over the ladies and kids in the main room. We're on semi-lock-down.

> Timber: How is she? She okay?

I smile at Timber's text and my gaze goes back to Mae and Punisher. I quickly snap a picture of them together before sending it to him.

> Levi: She's calmed down since I talked with her, but she's doing even better now that Punisher is talking to her. I think he may be adopting Mae as his little sister before long, if he hasn't already.

> Timber: As long as his relationship stays that way since she's my woman. Fuck, I bet this is dredging up a shit ton of memories for him.

I bite my lip to suppress a giggle at the first part of Timber's text. Then my mood instantly sours because he's right. I can see the tightness around Punisher's eyes and I bet he's reliving some awful memories.

Pushing those thoughts away, I pull up the message from Thor and respond to him.

> Levi: We'll be there in a few minutes, Hun.

Standing, I clear my throat to get everyone's attention, even though the guys are already ready to head out having read Thor's message already. "We all need to head to the clubhouse. Thor's called Church and said we're on semi-lockdown."

Quickly, we all gather our things as I explain to Mae what semi-lockdown means, and the guys surround us as we walk to the clubhouse.

Chapter 26

Mae

WHEN WE GET TO the clubhouse, Timber visibly relaxes when he sees me, though his eyes narrow at the sight of Punisher's arm slung over my shoulder. At Levi's house, he declared me his sister as he quietly talked to me and helped calm me down, but I'm not sure how Timber's going to feel about that. I've always wanted a brother, and now I have one.

Axe even comes over and gives me a hug before heading into Church, which is really sweet. He's sort of taken on a protector role for me as well, especially with how close Susie, Jordan, and I have been getting. Then I remember him calling me 'Sis' at the mall. Did he claim me as a sister, too?

Timber pulls me out of Axe's arms and my body relaxes even further. I tilt my head back and he gives me another toe-curling kiss.

God, I wish we were back in his house. I don't want to stop kissing him, but I know he needs to go to his meeting, and I don't want Thor to get mad at me for keeping him waiting.

Pulling back, I giggle at the little pout he gives me. "Later," I whisper, and my thighs clench at the heated look he gives me.

"Stay in the clubhouse, don't leave. Not even for a breath of fresh air. You got me, Sunshine?"

"I'll stay here with the ladies. Don't worry. You go do your thing."

After they all go into Church, we get the kids settled in front of the TV with a movie.

Walking over to the bar, I ask Drae for a bottle of water, which he gets for me right away. Water in hand, I make my way over to the ladies and note that even though Sasha is over here, she's standing and her eyes keep darting around.

After talking for about twenty minutes or so, Roxy and a woman I haven't met yet come over to join us.

"So, you're Timber's woman and Smoke's daughter. Nice to meet you. I'm CJ. Drae's my brother," she says as she sits down and holds out a hand.

Tentatively, I shake it. I hope like heck she isn't going to be telling me what it was like being with Timber sexually.

"Um, hi. I'm Mae."

"Glad you're here. I know he's upset right now, but Smoke really is an awesome guy. I'm sure that whenever he calms down, he'll see things straight," Roxy says, and just like that, my nerves ramp up even more than they were.

God, with the shopping trip, I'd been able to push my worries about Smoke to the back of my mind for a while, which was a relief.

Then with Preston showing up, being back here and now Roxy's words, they all bring everything right back to the front of my mind.

I'm kind of thankful that I didn't see Smoke when I came in. Either that or the guys are making sure there's room between us. God, maybe I should take Reaper up on the offer Timber mentioned earlier. To stay at his club until Smoke calms down.

If he calms down, that is.

I'm brought out of my thoughts by heels clicking on the wood floor. Looking up, I really wish I hadn't. I'm going to take a guess that these women are some of the bunnies because their skirts barely cover their va-jay-jays and their shirts barely cover their obviously fake boobs. Though only two are barely dressed—the other four are in t-shirts and blue jeans. Those four must be the bunnies that Susie said usually don't cause problems.

Suddenly, my insecurities come back full force. All of these women are beautiful and have curves in all the right places. Plus, they aren't skin and bones like me.

"Those women got nothing on you, Mae. Remember that. Timber chose you to be his woman, not those bunnies. The bunnies are just here as a release for the guys. Nothing more," Susie says quietly as she squeezes my hand. I smile up at her in thanks.

Sasha swears in a foreign language and I look up in confusion. Her gaze is trained across the room, and I turn, following her gaze.

Two women are glaring at me and but then one scowls and turns her gaze to the kids. She marches up to them, steals the remote, shuts off the movie and knocks over their popcorn bowls.

"This is a clubhouse, not a daycare. Scram, you little brats." She sneers at them as she takes a step forward.

Jordan gets up and pulls Sadie behind him, protecting her. Dang, that boy is just like his uncle.

The woman then turns her sneer toward us. "Get your worthless spawn out of here. Unless you want them to get an up-close lesson about the birds and the bees tonight."

I shake off my shock at how she's acting and jump up and out of my seat. Rushing across the room, I step in front of the kids, shielding them from this vile woman. Both Susie and Nikki step up behind me after checking that their kids are okay.

"Keep your skanky hands away from Sadie and Jordan!"

The woman scoffs and curls her lip as her gaze roams over my body. "Ah, you must be the fresh meat. You might as well scram because you'll break in half before one of these guys even finds their release. These guys like to fuck long and hard. They have all they want in us and you aren't fit to join the ranks of club bunny. They don't need you, and certainly not Timber. He's mine." Her eyes flash in anger as she stares at me.

"Gigi, shut the fuck up. We're on semi-lockdown, which means if you're going to be out here, you sure as hell are not supposed to be dressed like that," Sasha scowls. Out of the corner of my eye, I catch something metal and realize Sasha's twirling a blade in her hands.

So, this is Gigi.

Her words, as well as Timber's from yesterday, have my spine straightening like steel. There's no way I'm going to let her talk to me like this.

"Well, apparently I am what Timber wants because I'm his woman and he's mine. And we were all asked to come to the clubhouse, kids included. So why don't you go back to your room and see if you have any clothes that actually fit.

There's no need for you dressing like a skank around the kids. They're family of the club, so you might as well get used to them being here."

She waves a well-manicured hand in my direction as she looks down her nose at me. "Oh, please. He'll tire of your ass eventually and then he'll be back in my bed. And as for the brats, if their tawdry ass mothers want to come here, then they should get a sitter."

"They don't have to get a sitter—the kids deserve the right to be around their uncles. As for Timber, he won't be leaving my bed. And there was never going to be a 'back in your bed' scenario because I know for a fact that he's never been with you. He hasn't been with any of the bunnies for months. Maybe if you weren't spreading your legs for all the single brothers, one of them might have taken a chance on you, but I doubt it would have lasted. Your vile personality would have them running in an instant."

The next thing I know, Gigi's hand smacks across my cheek, and from the burn, I'm guessing her gaudy ring cut my cheek.

While I know I'm not the best, Glen did teach me some moves to defend myself in case Preston or his goons ever tried anything. Though, I'd never win if a few of his guys came at me at once.

Gigi goes to strike me again but I swing my leg out, knocking her off her feet, and she falls hard on the ground, crying out as she lands on her tailbone. Jumping on her, I grab her wrists with one hand and pound my fist into her face with the other for what she said about Sadie and Jordan. After a couple of hits, the sound of boots fill the air.

"What the fuck is going on?" Thor bellows.

Knowing I've done nothing wrong, and having already heard of what Levi's had to deal with with the bunnies in the past, I smile sweetly up at him, but don't release Gigi.

"Just dealing with the trash. I'm going to assume you have cameras around for surveillance. Alexei, since you have your computer out here, can you replay what this skank said? Then there's no way for Gigi to twist anything that was said. Sadie, Jordan, earmuffs please. You don't need to hear what she said about you twice."

At that last bit, I get mad again. No one talks about my chosen family like that and gets away with it. Gigi squirms underneath me and I tighten my hand around her wrists and my thighs around her sides, preventing her from pushing me off her.

A lot of the guys' faces grow dark with anger at me saying the kids shouldn't be hearing what she said again. I purposefully keep my gaze on Thor, though I don't miss Timber's angry face next to him. I just don't know if he's angry at me or Gigi.

"Thor, this bitch went crazy on me for no reason. Kick her ass out of here!"

"Shut your mouth, bitch. We all heard and saw what you did. You're just lucky Mae got to you first, because I wouldn't have been as nice," Sasha sneers as a she twirls a blade and then flips it in the air.

Gigi jumps as much as she can with me still pinning her down. Her face pales and I bet she's probably worried that Sasha's going to throw it at her. Thankfully, Gigi doesn't say anything else or struggles to get free. She just continues to glare at me. I stay seated on her, not wanting to let her get away in case she goes after me or the kids again.

Alexei does as I ask and pulls up the video feed on the big TV since both chapters have filed out into the common room. Both Nikki and Susie help muffle the kids' ears as well.

After the video's done, Thor turns back to us, his eyes fill with thunder as they land on Gigi.

"This is your second strike. One more and you're banned from all of the Steel Archangel's establishments. And that includes Levi's place, Wallace's B&G, since the club owns a percentage. Get the fuck out of here. You're banned for the night, and I don't mean banned to your room here. I want you out of my sight. You're also on bathroom duty for a month on top of your other cleaning duties."

Timber moves toward me, but I hold out my hand to stop him.

"Give me a minute. I'm just going to continue taking out the trash."

He looks at me, confused, but nods before stepping back.

Getting a grip on Gigi's hair, I stand and start dragging her across the floor. Laughter rings out as I continue toward the door. Her nails scratch my arm and hand a couple of times, but I ignore it.

"You heard the man. Your cooperation in leaving is, obviously, not required right now. If you have any complaints or suggestions, you can submit them to the brick wall. Feel free to make several. In fact, I encourage it."

Sasha and Levi open the doors for me with smirks on their faces. I continue down the porch steps, letting her butt hit each stair before grabbing under her arms, lifting, and tossing her down onto the ground.

"Now, stay away from my man."

The look Gigi gives me would have made me curl in on myself in the past, but not anymore. Being here with Timber and the ladies, and now my chosen family, has given me back some of the confidence I used to have.

Ethan grabs her by her arm and drags her toward the gate, all while she's screaming that I'm in the wrong, not her.

Dusting my hands off, I turn and freeze. Everyone's staring and smirking at me.

Susie and Sasha are the first to break from the group and rush at me, hugging me.

"That was epic, girl! And thank you for standing up for Jordan."

I squeeze her tighter at that last part.

"Girl, that was fantastic! Though, we will be working on your form and start training you with knives so you can defend yourself better."

Grinning, I nod and let go of them, only to be swooped up into Timber's arms. Wrapping my arm around his neck to steady myself, I rest my head on his shoulder as he carries me inside.

Setting me down on a chair, he kneels in front of me as he cups my hand and cheek. I wince when his finger grazes over one of my knuckles and he frowns. Before he can get up, Patch hands him an ice pack as he sits down next to me.

First, Patch looks at my knuckles. He must not see anything worrying because he gives Timber a chin lift and then the icepack is gently placed on them. Even though he's gentle, I bite my lip to keep from wincing again. Patch then looks at the cut on my cheek.

"I'm just going to disinfect this for you quick, Mae, so it doesn't get infected. You won't need stitches, thankfully, so it shouldn't scar. You should take some ibuprofen as well to help with any swelling with your hand." He sets a little packet of pills on my lap and opens the alcohol wipe packet. I do my best not to wince at the sting, but I don't think I'm successful judging by Timber looking even more concerned than he was before.

"Baby Sis, that was fucking phenomenal to watch. And kudos for taking out the trash yourself," Axe says as he wraps an arm around my shoulder when Patch steps back. Seconds later, Punisher also wraps an arm around my other shoulder.

"Sasha's right though, Sis. We need to work on your form and the fact that knowing how to handle knives, as well as how to shoot a gun, would be an extra layer of protection."

I nibble my lip as I look from them to Timber and back. "I've never shot a gun or even used a knife for anything other than cooking. Glen, my old boss' husband, taught me a little, but I would appreciate more lessons, nonetheless. Can never be too careful."

As I turn back to Timber, my gaze snags on Smoke. He's at the bar, getting a beer from Drae, but when he turns around, he purposefully doesn't look at me.

The fact that he won't acknowledge me guts me like no other. Guess I'll just have to learn to live with the fact that he'll never be part of my life.

At that, I feel myself starting to wilt inward, and the next thing I know, I'm being lifted up into Timber's arms. Not wanting to fight him, I rest my head on his shoulder as he heads upstairs. Somehow, he gets his door unlocked and opened without putting me down.

Shutting and locking the door behind him, he crosses the room and lays me down on the bed. Crawling up the bed, my legs part automatically for him. He hovers over me for a second before slamming his lips down on mine. Dropping the ice pack, I wrap my arms around his neck and run my fingers through his hair.

He moans into my mouth before leaning on me more. Feeling him hard at my center through our clothes has me moaning, and I can't stop from rolling my hips against him.

He pulls back and starts peppering kisses along my jaw and down my throat.

"Liam," I gasp as he bites down on the spot where my neck connects to my shoulder.

"You were so fucking hot taking care of that bitch. As much as I need you, I know you aren't ready for that, but I'm still going to make you feel good."

"Yes, please," I gasp out.

I definitely want more of what we did this morning. One of his hands skims down my side before going under my shirt. When I don't stop him, he pulls back enough to pull the shirt off me.

"Fuck, you're gorgeous, Sunshine," he moans as he stairs down at me in the satin padded bra that Sasha had gotten me.

Feeling sexy as he stares at me, I decide to take the next step.

Undoing the front clasp of the bra, I let the material fall to my sides. Groaning again, his mouth latches onto a nipple while his other hand massages the other breast and tweaks the nipple. His teeth gently bite down on my nipple and my core heats even more.

"Liam!" My hands fly to his head.

Oh, my lanta!

I press harder on his head, wanting more as I rock my hips against him.

He chuckles lightly as he switches breasts, paying it just as much attention with his tongue and teeth as he did the other one. His other hand snakes lower, and I moan when I feel him undoing the button on my jeans and reaching into my panties.

"Fuck, Baby. You're drenched for me."

I cry out when he runs a finger through my slit. The pressure building inside of me is almost at the tipping point. Frantically, I try to press myself harder against his hand, needing him to bring me over the ledge.

"Mmmm, does my Sunshine want to come?" he growls as he kisses down my stomach.

"Yes, please, Liam."

He hums in appreciation and the sound has my thighs clenching around his hand as he continues to tease my slit with his finger.

Looking up at me in question, I nod at him, needing more of what he's giving me. He quickly takes off my shoes, socks, jeans, and panties.

"Fuck, your pussy is fucking drenched for me. Give me that cream, Sunshine."

He buries his face at my core and I cry out as his tongue slides through my slit. My hands fly to his head, pushing him harder against me.

More, I need more.

Liam moans and the vibrations send a shiver through me. His mouth latches onto my clit, his teeth gently scraping against it. He slips a finger inside me and when he curls it, I detonate. My thighs clamp around his head, holding him in place as my orgasm rips through me.

He continues to pump his fingers into me as his tongue to tease my clit. Just as my orgasm subsides, another one quickly builds. His fingers shift and they curl, rubbing some magical spot and I detonate once again around him.

After a few moments, I start to feel too sensitive and try to pull away from him, but his hand bands across my stomach, keeping me in place. He increases the speed of his fingers.

"Please, Liam. It's too much."

"Give me one more, Sunshine," he growls. His voice combined with the vibrations has another orgasm starting to build. He adds another finger, rubbing that same spot as he gently bites down on my clit.

Holy fudge nuggets! I go from zero to toppling over the ledge almost instantaneously.

"Liam!"

This time, he takes his fingers out but still teases me with his tongue as my orgasm washes through me.

When my thighs stop shaking, he lifts his head and I see my release coating his chin and short beard. He raises his hand and my core clenches when he licks his fingers clean.

Licking my lips, I sit up and push him up. I want to take care of him. My hands go to his belt, but he stops me.

"Sunshine, you don't have to. This was about you."

"But I want to take care of you, too, Liam. This is twice now that you've brought me pleasure and I want to do this. Show me what you like, Liam. How you like it."

He curses but quickly undoes his belt, shoving his jeans and boxers down his thighs. I darn near feel my eyes pop out when his cock bobs up to hit his stomach. He is long and thick. I hope it'll fit when I'm ready to go all the way with him.

Kneeling in front of him, I notice a bead of precum on his tip and run my tongue over it. Liam breathes in sharply and moans.

Feeling more confident, I brace one hand on his thigh and wrap my other hand around him. Pumping a bit, I take him into my mouth before bobbing my head. Liam groans, and if I weren't feeling it myself, I wouldn't believe that he'd gotten harder and longer than he already was.

His fingers run through my hair, and I moan, loving the feel.

"You can squeeze harder, Baby. It won't hurt."

Looking up at him, I do just that, and he groans as he starts thrusting his hips into my mouth. Sensing that he wants to take over that part, I still.

"Fuck, Sunshine. You're fucking beautiful, taking my cock like you are. Tap my leg or pull back if it gets to be too much."

I nod as best as I can and tighten my grip again. With the other hand, I move to massage his balls and Liam curses again before pumping his hips faster. I tilt my head slightly, hoping to take more of him.

His grip tightens on my head and I can feel his thighs clench. He's getting close.

I moan again, wondering if the vibrations feel the same for him as it does when he moaned while making me come.

"I'm gonna cum, Sunshine. If you don't want me to cum in that pretty mouth, then you need to pull back now."

Wanting to see what he tastes like, I tighten my grip.

His curses are the only notice I get before I feel ropes of his cum sliding down my throat. I swallow, trying to take everything he gives me.

When he pulls from my mouth, I lean forward, running my tongue across his length, making sure to get everything off him.

Liam grabs under my arms and he hoists me up to my feet before slamming his mouth down on mine. His lips tease across mine and I open for him immediately.

God, I can't get enough of this man's kisses.

Chapter 27

Mae

LIAM BREAKS THE KISS, and I groan, not wanting to stop. He chuckles at my pout and kisses me again.

"Sunshine, as much as I love kissing you, having my mouth on you and yours on me, we need to talk."

Instantly, the bliss he'd given me fades away as if someone had dumped a bucket of ice water over me, and I sigh. "Are you mad about what I did to Gigi?"

"Fuck no, Sunshine. That bitch had it coming for going after Sadie, Jordan and you like that. I only wish it was her third strike, so she'd be out of here."

Sighing again, I rest my forehead against his chest. "Me, too. I have a sneaky suspicion that she's going to be a rabble-rouser."

Liam chuckles again and kisses the top of my head. "Fuck, I love your version of swearing, Sunshine."

Smiling, I pull back and start getting dressed again. When Liam tucks himself back into his jeans, I immediately wish I could have seen him naked. Actually.

"Next time we do this, you're getting undressed. I want to see you and those beautiful tattoos. It's not fair that I was the only one to get naked."

"I'll hold you to that, Sunshine." The huskiness in his tone has me shivering in anticipation. My gaze roams his body, wondering what he looks like under all those clothes.

Liam groans. "Sunshine, as much as I love that look on you, if you keep looking at me like that, we'll be going a lot further than oral and heavy petting. We gotta talk, Baby."

This time it's my turn to groan and I sit down on his bed. Liam sits down next to me but lifts me up and sets me down on his lap so I'm straddling him.

"Okay. What do you want to talk about?"

"First is, I know I told you I want you as my Old Lady, but I never asked. Will you be?"

Wrapping my arms around his neck, I kiss him. "Of course, I'll be your Old Lady. I'm surprised at how quickly I fell in love with you, but I'm not going to fight it."

He grins and gives me another kiss. "Good, because I had Tripp order your cut earlier this morning. It should be done right before Levi, Thor, and Dragon's wedding. The other thing I wanted to talk to you about was Smoke."

Immediately, my body tenses and my heart clenches.

God, it hurts so much to remember how he reacted and treated me yesterday and this morning. Fudge nuggets on a stick... I really didn't want to think about that right now.

Liam sighs and his hands tighten on my waist. "Based on that look, I think I already know the answer to my question, but I'm gonna ask anyway. Reaper's offer still stands for if we'd like to stay at his clubhouse for a while. We can drive back before the wedding and see how things are then. Not to mention, Punisher said he'd like to introduce you to his parents. Axe does too."

Nibbling my lip, I debate my options. My shoulders slump and I sigh. "I don't want it to look like I'm running away, but space may be what we need. Plus, with Preston showing up today at the mall, that means he was probably following us earlier. Getting out of town might help, but I don't know if he'll just follow us there."

"That was one of our concerns, too. We'll know he's keeping tabs on you if he shows up in Junction Creek. In case he had a tracker on your old phone, we tossed it after making sure everything was transferred onto your new one. We actually have a few devices that can tell if something's bugged. If you want, we can check what you brought with you as a precaution. We found out the stalker that was after Levi had tagged a bunch of her shit and clothes. Fuck, I heard he had a listening device in every one of her bras."

My eyes widen at that, and I lick my lips nervously. "Can we check my stuff? I doubt Preston would do that. He's not the brightest, but then again, Bruce or that X guy could have done something when I wasn't home. Even Phillip."

"Yeah, Sunshine. We'll get the devices in a bit. So, should I tell Reaper yes?"

My heart clenches again, but I nod. "Yes, I'd like to take him up on his offer. Plus, I really would like to meet Punisher's parents. I'd like to introduce you to Peggy and Glen, too. Maybe I could see if they'd come over sometime around the wedding so I can introduce Axe and Punisher to them as well."

"I bet if you ask Levi, she'd let you invite them to the wedding. Since she's your aunt now, she most likely wants to meet the people who helped her niece all those years."

"I will. Might as well ask when we get to her house since I need to get my stuff out of Levi's car. Oh, and borrow some sculpting mud from Sasha."

He looks at me in confusion and I can't help but giggle. "It's a sticky cream that you use on your hair to help with little fly-aways, or if you have your hair up in a ponytail, it helps keep everything in place."

Smiling, he shakes his head as he reaches into his pocket and pulls out his phone before texting someone. After a few moments, he puts his phone back in his pocket.

"Guess we better go visit Sasha. While you're talking with her, I'll get with Smoke to get the scanners. Then we'll head on over to Levi's to get your stuff so we can get you packed. Sasha's gonna drive you in the club SUV. She's already got her bike trailered on it and will ride back with Colt and a few others from our club tomorrow morning. With not having any riding gear for you and having never ridden before, I'm not going to have you start on a four-hour drive. When we come back for the wedding, one of Reaper's Prospects will bring back the SUV. Reaper wants to leave in an hour, so we get back before dark."

"But I'll be able to ride with you soon?"

He grins. "You bet your ass. Tomorrow, after Sasha, Colt, and whoever else from Forest Creek leaves, I'll take you to the Harley dealership to get everything. Punisher will probably go with us since he runs it."

Excited to be on the back of his bike soon, I get up and grab my new phone. Gosh, I can't believe I have a new phone. I've never had a new... well, anything of value before.

> Mae: Is it still okay if I borrow your sculpting mud?

> Sasha: Girl, you can have it. Actually, I have it in the SUV with me already. I'm headed over to Levi's now to grab your stuff from her SUV. Oh, and I also have all of your information that Alexei and Ethan scanned today. The only things you need are whatever you have in Timber's house or his room at the clubhouse. When I'm done at Levi's, I'll park outside of Timber's house so you can load it whenever you're ready.

> Mae: Okay. I'll see you soon.

As I put back on my shoes, I tell Liam what Sasha said.

"Okay. Wait for me in the main room while I get the scanners. Then we'll head to the house so we can both pack."

Four hours later, we arrive in Junction Creek, though we did stop halfway at a fast-food drive through place. The burgers and fries were so good. However, I was a little embarrassed when Timber asked me how my first time was having actual fast food because everyone heard it and quite a few of the guys cursed. Regardless, I loved it and can't wait to see what else I can have in the future. Today's also the first day in forever that I ate three meals. I know each one was small, but it's still progress.

My thoughts turn back to Junction Creek and I smile. It's a cute little town and almost has the same feel as Forest Creek. There are a couple of little waterfalls in the creek that runs through town, and there are a lot of trees throughout town and around it. Not as many as Forest Creek, but still quite a few.

As we head out of town, I start to get curious about what their clubhouse will look like. Do they also have houses on clubhouse grounds?

I'm about to ask Sasha when I see a chain link fence. Huh. I wonder why they don't have cinderblock like Timber's club? I mean, I know a cinderblock wall is more expensive than a chain link fence, but someone could cut through the fence and get on club grounds pretty easily.

"The fence is monitored by a bunch of cameras and sensors. If need be, Python can electrify the fence," Sasha says.

I turn to her, surprised that she knew what I was thinking about. She laughs.

"I kind of figured you were comparing the two clubs and with how intent you were staring at the fence kind of cinched it. Not all of their fencing is chain link. It's cinderblock around the main part of the clubhouse and by the gate."

"Did they always have cinderblock?"

She shakes her head. "No. From what I understand, there were problems for both clubs about eight years back or so. They both just had chain link fences at the time and I don't think they had gates yet, but Prospects were stationed at the entrances. Back then, everyone lived in the clubhouses, so there weren't any houses on the club grounds yet. A shared enemy of the club was able to sneak onto club grounds at both sites and attacked. I don't think any of our guys died, but a few were injured."

"So it was after the attack that they put in the cinderblock and gates?"

"Yup. It's just that Forest Creek took it a bit further and, except for where the forest is, there's cinderblock all around the clubhouse. For the section of the property line going through the forest, they have a chain link fence like this one that's heavily monitored and can be electrified as well. There's a gate back there, too, but you need a code to get through.

"And FYI, I'm only telling you about that back gate right now because you're an Old Lady and Thor said I could tell you about it. Only club members and their Old Ladies are allowed to know about the gate. I don't know if you'll be given the access code or not though. Levi did when she first became an Old Lady, but she's also the Old Lady to the President, so I'm not sure how all that works out. I only found out about the gate when I started Prospecting. We have to do rounds to check the fence."

Nodding, I take in everything she's told me. I wonder if the club has a lot of problems they have to deal with on a regular basis or if it's just every now and then that things go down the crapper?

Seeing the gate, I push those thoughts out of my mind for right now. I can ask Timber about it later.

As we pull through, I notice four houses are set back from the clubhouse as well as a few of town houses. The guys park their bikes, but Sasha turns toward the road leading to the houses and comes to a stop. A few members come out on the porch along with an older couple. Timber walks up to one of the guys on the porch who hands him something and then Timber turns, walking toward us. He opens my door and helps me out, even though I'm perfectly capable of getting out on my own, but I like that he offers.

He tosses some keys to Sasha and she catches them. "Reaper said we can take the first one. Can you put our stuff in the bedroom?"

"You got it, Timber. I'll be up when I'm done."

Giving her a chin lift, he shuts the door and she drives toward the townhouses.

"They built those for when they have a lot of guests or if a couple comes up to visit, like someone's parents. Now that there's three of us with Old Ladies, we get first pick of them. Then again, Thor will always get first pick since he's the President."

Turning to him, I nibble my lip. "Is there anything in the plans to do something like this back home? There were a lot of people there the past couple days. It might help to have some townhouses or even a row of condos where there's two or three bedrooms in each for couples or if you have a couple of clubs coming in to visit for an extended time."

"I've thought about that before, but never brought it up to the club. At the time, we all lived in the clubhouse and had just expanded, adding some more rooms for guests or if the club got more members. Next time we have Church, I'll bring it up if it's not an emergency session."

"They could also be temporary housing. For example, take us but in this scenario, you don't have a house—you live in the clubhouse. Since you claimed me as your Old Lady, we could stay in the townhouse until our house was built."

Timber leans down and kisses me. "That's a good idea. I know a few brothers are hoping to settle down soon but are hesitant to start building a house because they want their woman's input on it. That would be a good in-between idea."

Wrapping an arm around my waist, he leads me over to the porch where Punisher walks over and wraps an arm around my shoulders.

"Ma, Pops, you already know Timber, but let me introduce Mae, his Old Lady. She's the one Axe and I claimed as our sister."

The older woman hurries down the steps toward us.

She has Punisher's blond hair that's done up in long intricate braids and she has the same beads in her hair like he does. Her blue eyes are bright as she smiles and wraps me in a tight hug, pulling me out of Timber's and Punisher's arms.

After a few moments, she pulls back. "I'm Astrid. The guys all call me Mama Astrid and you're welcome to do the same. Welcome to the family, Dear." She pauses as she steps off to my side, gesturing to the man next to her. "And this is my husband and Old Man, Odin."

Odin wraps me in a hug, and instantly, I feel safe. My body relaxes in his arms and when he places a kiss at my temple, I have to blink away tears. I had hoped that Smoke would accept me like this when I showed up at the club. Obviously, that didn't happen.

"What Ma said, welcome to the family. You can call me Ragnar if you want, Sweetheart. Odin's my road name."

"Thank you."

When he pulls back, I have to blink rapidly to keep the tears at bay. With the way my emotions are being flung around, I feel like I have whiplash and am on the brink of breaking down again.

Arms wrap around my waist and I sink back into Timber.

"Well, let's get inside and have a drink to unwind after the trip," Reaper says. We all file in, but I stop when I reach Reaper.

"Thank you for letting me stay here with you guys for a bit."

"No need to thank me, Lil' Bit. I would have done this for anyone in that sort of situation. I have a feeling Smoke will be beating himself up pretty bad about the way he treated you and what he said to you within the next day or so. And besides, I wasn't gonna leave my niece out high and dry. Plus, this will also allow us to get to know each other as well. Same for Punisher and his folks."

Instead of answering, I just nod as I blink to keep more tears from falling at his kind words. I'm not so sure about what he said regarding Smoke, but I guess time will tell.

Chapter 28
Timber

WALKING THROUGH THE CLUBHOUSE doors, Atlas steps up close to me. He didn't come out for Levi's baby shower, instead; he stayed behind with a couple others to keep watch over the clubhouse. We never leave our clubhouses completely unmanned.

"Just to give you a heads up, Timber, Luscious has been on a tear since she found out you were coming to stay for a bit." His voice is quiet, but I know Sunshine hears him since her body instantly tenses at his words.

"Who's Luscious? Is she another one of the Johnson Chasers?" she whispers as she looks around. Atlas roars at her description of the bunnies and I can't help but laugh along with him.

"Yeah, she is, Sunshine. Not gonna lie, I've been with her and the other two bunnies that are here, but it's been well over a year. Whenever I visit, they all try to get into my bed. Especially Luscious. Fuck, one time the bitch even picked the lock and crawled into bed with me," I say, scowling at the m emory.

"Well, what does she look like so I know which one she is? If she tries to pull anything though, I'll be taking out the trash again."

"You won't be able to miss her. She's got bright blue hair that's shoulder-length, and her clothes barely cover the important bits," Atlas replies. Honestly, I'm surprised he's talking and interacting with Mae, since he usually avoids most women for some reason. Then again, maybe something's changed recently. Or someone's caught his eye to make him rethink his stance.

"Well then, if she does try anything, maybe part of her punishment could be being fully dressed. I bet she'd hate that," Sunshine says with a smirk as she leans into me more.

A few guys around us bust out laughing and I kiss the top of her head. Sasha comes in and makes a beeline for us.

"What'd I miss?" she asks as she takes the water Colt holds out for her. With both of them Prospecting, neither of them can drink unless it's a special occasion, like the other day at the baby shower. We fill her in and she busts out laughing as well.

"Fuck, you're made from the same cloth Half-pint is," Reaper says as he grabs a beer Nathan, one of their Prospects, brings over for him. "Half-pint pulled that card a few times when a bunny over in your chapter pulled some shit a while back. Crystal couldn't have sex for a month either, including oral. She was pissed, especially when it overlapped when both of our clubs got together. She went on a tear saying how unfair it was. Which was stupid of the bitch because she did it in front of everyone. Half-pint just smirked at Crystal and added on another two weeks to both of her punishments."

Sunshine laughs and fuck am I glad that she's getting along with everyone so far. I lead her over to the bar, asking for a beer for me and water for her. I'll have to find out what else she likes to drink so it can be stocked in both clubs. I don't want her to feel like she has to always have water.

"Here, Sunshine." Passing her the water, she smiles up at me. I hope she doesn't think I'll judge her for not wanting to have an alcoholic drink. I get her reasoning behind her decision and I'll always support her in that.

"Thanks, Babe."

We've been talking with the guys for a while when I feel Sunshine tensing slightly in my arms before relaxing again. Following her line of sight, I notice the bunnies are glaring daggers at her, Luscious in particular. Atlas was right. She's barely wearing any clothing. She's got some sort of wrap going across her breasts, which are fake, and her stomach is bare. Her skirt has slits on both sides and barely covers her ass cheeks.

Sunshine turns in my arms and wraps her arms around my neck. Knowing what she's doing, and I'm fucking happy to oblige, I crash my lips onto hers. Fuck, I can't get enough of her lips. After a few moments, she pulls back and hands me her water.

"I'm going to go to the restroom. Be right back, Babe."

Nodding, I take her water and watch her cute ass until it disappears around the corner. Turning back to the guys, I quirk an eyebrow in question at them all smiling like loons.

"What?"

"Just never thought you'd be one to settle down, Timber," Beast replies.

"You're lucky I like you, you little fucker, since she's now my sister," Punisher says as he clasps my shoulder.

"She was my Old Lady first." She may not have said it until earlier today, but I knew she was it for me the moment I saw her.

Fucker grins at me and then suddenly he scowls, but he's no longer looking at me.

Arms snake around me and before I can react, Luscious is pressed up against me as one of her hands rubs my cock, the other working to undo my belt.

Suddenly, she's pulled off me and thrown to the floor. Sunshine stands between the two of us, her hands on her hips as she stares down at her.

"What in hell's bells do you think you're doin' pawing at my man and trying to get into his pants?"

Seconds later, Luscious gets to her feet. "Ha! There's no way he's really with you. No one would want your bony ass. It'd be like feeling up a skeleton."

Oh fuck.

Mae's body goes rigid, and I know it's not going to be good.

"Is that so? Well, I'm sure if you were nearly starved for thirteen years, you'd look much the same. Whether you like it or not, Timber is no longer on the market. He's with me, so you'll have to make do with having sex with the other single brothers."

Luscious sneers at Mae and steps forward. "You're not cut out for biker life. When Timber tires of your ass, he'll be back in my bed where he belonged all along."

Mae laughs dryly. "Wow, all of you Johnson Chasers must compare notes because you all say the same things. Or maybe you're related to Gigi and that's how you were raised. Either way, you need to listen and listen good, Missy. You are nothing but a pizza burn on the roof of the world's mouth. Somewhere out there, a tree is tirelessly producing oxygen for you, and you should really apologize to it.

"While you're at it, you need to get over yourself. Just because you wear the bare minimum amount of clothing that you think is seductive, have a crap ton of makeup caked onto your face, bought a Winnebago upgrade for your boobs, and that you take a man in any hole as often as you can get it does not mean you get to have any man you want. Timber will never be coming back to your bed because he will be in mine. He doesn't want your cum bucket of a snatch or any other loose as heck hole of yours."

The room erupts in laughter and I step up behind Sunshine, resting my hands on her hips when really, all I want to do is hoist her over my shoulder and take us back to the house.

"There is nothing wrong with the way I look or dress," Luscious huffs, as she crosses her arms, which puts her fake tits even more on display.

"Sure, keep thinking that. I bet people clap when you're out in public. And I don't mean that in a good way—they're clapping their hands over their kids' eyes to keep them from seeing your skanky snatch or tits. I sure hope you don't catch pneumonia cause that skirt sure is breezy."

Laughter rings out again and Reaper steps forward.

"Luscious, get back to your room for the night and don't come out. Consider this your first strike. You know you're not supposed to mess with an Old Lady and whether you like it or not, Mae is Timber's Old Lady. Not to mention, she's legacy. Now scram before Lil' Bit here decides her fists are hungry again and takes you out like she did with Gigi earlier today," Reaper growls.

Luscious' face transforms into shock, most likely at the legacy bit, not knowing she's the daughter of an original member. When the club was just starting, Smoke's old man, Ice, had suggested that his son Prospect. Instead, he was brought on and got a patch right away.

Smoke was a wiz even back then with computers. He'd skipped a few grades in school because he was so smart and finished high school. He was sixteen at the time.

Back then, the bylaws just stated that you had to have graduated high school, so Smoke and Ice were part of the original members of the club along with Thor and Dragon's old man, Poseidon, who passed away earlier this year.

The only other remaining original members in our chapter besides Smoke are Bear, Gunner, Bones, and Tripp. There are a few more, but they moved to start some of our other chapters. Here in Junction Creek, it's Odin, Doc, Smithy and Razor for original members.

Luscious' face turns even redder as she continues to stare at Mae.

"You keep standing there, and I will take you out like the trash you are. Reaper wasn't lying." Mae flexes her hand, and Luscious' face suddenly pales slightly. She must have caught sight of her raw and swollen knuckles.

With a huff, Luscious flicks her hair over her shoulder and struts out of the room.

Spinning Mae around, I slam my mouth down on hers and she moans as she melts into me. I only stop when my brothers start catcalling us. Sunshine shocks the shit out of me when she flips them off and kisses me again. This starts a whole 'nother round of laughter. Fuck, I'm seeing more and more that Reaper is right. She really is cut from the same cloth Levi is.

When I pull back, Sasha and Mama Astrid both pull Mae over to a table in the corner that's away from the bunnies. Thank fuck both of them are here. Mae needs all the strong women in her life that she can get.

"Well, fuck. Does she have a sister?" Razor asks, and I shake my head.

"She's an only child."

My gut tightens as my mind goes back to Smoke. Fuck, I hope he gets his head on straight. I saw Sunshine fighting tears when Odin hugged her and I'm willing to bet that she'd hoped Smoke would have been like that from the get-go.

Smithy claps my shoulder. "He'll come round and pull his head out of his ass. Until then, we'll all help your woman come out of her shell more. She needs a proper family and the Steel Archangel's will give her that."

My chest warms as each of my brothers give me chin lifts, agreeing with Smithy. "Thanks, brothers."

"Now, before we all grow vaginas and start braiding each other's hair, how about you fill us in on what's going on with your Old Lady," Devil says. He's Reaper's VP and was one of the guys to stay behind for this trip.

Odin gives him a look to which Devil just grins. Apparently, Odin's known Reaper and Devil since they were kids seeing as they were all friends with Punisher. Also, Odin used to be the club's Enforcer before he passed down the reins to Punisher and stepped back a bit. In his words, it was time to pass the torch to the next generation.

Odin and Mama Astrid both have Viking heritage even though you wouldn't guess it from their last name, Miller. They also wear their hair with lots of braids. Punisher doesn't take his hair to the extreme his parents do with all their braids, but then again, his head is partially shaved and he wears it much shorter. Also, surprisingly, they didn't give Punisher a Viking name, but they did keep with tradition of naming him after an ancestor, which is how he ended up being named Kai.

"Let's take this to Church then," Reaper says and I give him a chin lift before heading over to Mae.

"Sunshine, we're going to go into Church for a bit so we can get the rest of Reaper's men up to date. Stay in the clubhouse, alright?"

"No problem. Wait, did Thor email you and Reaper a copy of the documents?"

"Yeah, he did. Besides us two, the only other ones that got copies are Smoke, Phoenix and, of course, Thor has one as well. The email came through as we were riding, so Reaper hasn't sent it to Devil yet since he's Reaper's VP. We weren't sure who all you wanted reading your mom's stuff."

Her shoulders slump in relief. "I'm glad not everyone's going to read them. I guess it'd be okay for Odin, Punisher, and Axe to read them since they're all family now. But is it okay if it's only those other three? That not everyone reads them?"

She looks up at me hesitantly as she bites her lip. Reaching forward, I trace my thumb along her bottom lip and gently pull it free of her teeth. Her pupils dilate and fuck does that action have my cock straining harder against my jeans. Even more so when I realize I'm also partially gripping her neck. Fuck, I can't wait till I'm able to sink into her.

"Yeah, it's okay that not everyone reads the journals. We are showing the other documents though because they all have information they need to know about." Bending down, I give her a kiss that ends far too fucking quickly.

"If you get tired, you can always crash in my room until we're done. Ma has keys to it and everything's clean. I only sleep here when I'm drunk off my ass," Punisher says as he leans down and kisses both Mama Astrid's and Mae's foreheads. It's kind of weird seeing him act like this to anyone other than his mom, even though it's not the first time I've seen it. Before though, it was Mama Astrid and his late sister, Frida. To anyone else, he's a cold ass 'I'll break your neck' biker.

"Thanks, Punisher."

He tugs on her hair, making her head tilt back so she's looking up at him. "What'd I tell you before, Mae?"

Sunshine rolls her eyes at him, but smiles. "Thanks, Kai."

Holy shit.

It's a good thing I know he's not trying to worm in on my woman, otherwise, I'd be having words with him.

Fists too.

Then again, his mom always calls him Kai even though his dad still calls him Punisher, but he's still in the club so that part makes sense. Though, his brothers, Erik and Dom, also call him Punisher.

He grins. "That's better. Don't do anything I wouldn't do," he says with a wink, which has us all laughing.

Grabbing another beer from the bar, I put my phone in the basket and head into Church, shutting the door behind me.

"Python, pull up the documents I sent you. Devil, I just sent you a few other documents as well for you to read over later."

"Reaper, can you forward that email to Odin and Punisher? Mae just said that they could read the journals since they're now family. I'll forward them to Axe after we're done here."

"I'll just tag Axe onto the email then." He pulls out his phone and quickly sends a message while Python pulls up Mae's birth certificates side by side.

"Timber, since you're her Old Man, you want to take the lead on this?" Reaper asks and I give him a chin lift.

For the next twenty minutes, I give those that weren't at Forest Creek a run-down of everything that happened yesterday and today. To say Odin is pissed is putting it lightly. I'm sure if Smoke were here, he'd be feeling Odin's fists.

"I can't believe Smoke is letting his own anger and hurt blind him so badly that he hurt that sweet girl like that and is still hurting her," Odin seethes as he clenches and unclenches his fists. His gaze snaps to me. "I didn't miss how her body tensed when she was putting Luscious in her place. I bet that asshole stepfather of hers said something similar to her in the past."

Sighing, I nod. "I had the same thought. It'll take time, but eventually, I'll get her to see that whatever she's been told in the past isn't true."

"Alright, that's basically all we know right now. Python and Smoke are both looking into things with Preston, Bruce and trying to find a lead on whoever the fuck this X guy is. Not to mention checking to see if that asshole's still laundering under Mae's dead name. When we know more, I'll call Church again." With that, Reaper bangs his gavel and we all get up. Filing out to the main room, I'm relieved to see Sunshine still out here, but she looks dead on her feet.

Placing my empty beer bottle on the bar, I grab my phone, head over to her and pull her up to her feet. "How about we head to the house, Sunshine? You look like you're about ready to pass out."

She nods and leans into me. "I'd like that." She steps over and hugs both women good night. "If you leave earlier than I'm over here, make sure to stop by the house, Sasha. Though if I'm up, I'd love to have breakfast with you."

"You got it, girl. See you in the morning."

Stepping out into the cool night air, I pull Mae close when she shivers slightly.

Minutes later, I unlock the door and relock it after us, putting in the security code that Devil had texted Mae and me earlier.

After slipping off her shoes and hanging up her purse, Sunshine turns on the lights and looks around downstairs. I follow behind her, double checking all the windows are secured. That done, I turn my focus back to the layout. It's a pretty open-concept design. There's a small dining table in the kitchen and if you were cooking, you'd be able to see most of the living room. There's a small laundry room and a half-bath down here as well.

Turning the lights back off, we both head upstairs, where we repeat the process. There are three bedrooms up here, including the master, each with their own bathroom. The only difference is the size of the bedrooms. Sasha had put our stuff in the master bedroom earlier and I hope like fuck Sunshine will want to be in here with me, even if I'm only able to hold her.

Once I check that the other rooms' windows are secure, I head into the master bedroom and can't help but grin as my chest warms.

Sunshine's already set the bags of clothes that she got today on the floor near the dresser and is rummaging through her duffel bag. I'm sure she'll be doing a bunch of laundry tomorrow with the amount of clothes she got. I also notice she's already plugged her phone in and it's resting on the far nightstand. Relief flows through me at the sight.

Walking up to her, I wrap my arms around her just as she pulls out some silky pajamas from her bag. Fuck, tonight's going to be a major test in restraint but I want nothing more than to have her in my arms tonight. Still, I need to hear the words from her.

"You gonna be in here with me, Sunshine?"

Her cheeks turn a little pink and she nibbles her lip. "Is it okay if I am in here? I'm not ready for sex just yet, but I love being in your arms. I feel safe when you hold me."

Groaning, I bend down and kiss her, not being able to resist. After a few moments, I pull back and smirk when she pouts a bit. "I'd love nothing more than to have you in my arms tonight and every night, Sunshine. Why don't you go ahead and change?"

Nodding, she slips out of my arms and heads into the bathroom.

Snagging my bag, I find some gym shorts and start stripping, placing my cut on the dresser. Unholstering my gun, I slip it into the nightstand along with my knives before setting my phone on top of the stand and plugging it in. Normally I sleep in just my boxers or naked, but I know Sunshine isn't ready for that. I've just slipped on a pair of gym shorts when she steps out of the bathroom and I bite back a groan.

Her silk tank top and shorts hug her body like a glove and the tank top shows a fair amount of cleavage. Fuck. I'm going to be having a serious case of blue balls tonight.

"Come on, Sunshine. Let's get to bed. We'll talk more about the club tomorrow and get the last of what you need after Sasha and the guys head out."

Nodding, she walks over to the right side of the bed and slides under the covers. I do the same and shut off the light. Pulling her close to me, I inhale her lavender scent and ignore my raging cock as I drift off to sleep with my Sunshine Goddess finally in my arms.

Chapter 29
Smoke

When Thor and Phoenix dismiss me from Church, I head straight to the bar to grab a couple of beers. I'm going to need them and I feel the need to seclude myself in my room for a bit.

Walking down the hall to my room, I bite back a groan. Axe is leaning against the doorframe.

Just what I fucking need.

He pushes off the wall when I get closer and crosses his arms over his chest.

"Don't get your boxers in a twist. I'm just gonna say my piece and leave." He waits for me to nod and continues. "I get you're fucking mad as hell, Smoke. I would be too if I were in your shoes. What that bitch and asshole did to you was beyond fucked up. All I'm asking is that you calm down and look at everything with a clear, level mind. When you do, you'll see that you're punishing the wrong person. I just hope that she'll forgive you when you pull your head out of your ass."

He turns and takes a few steps before turning back to face me. "And just so you know, Punisher and I both claimed her as our sister. But don't think for a fucking minute that we'll be calling you 'Dad' or anything," he says with a smirk, and I can't help but chuckle at that.

Fuck no, I don't want them doing that shit.

Unlocking my door, I open it and relock it. I don't want anyone barging in here.

Setting my stuff down, I slump down into my computer chair, resting my elbows on my knees and cradling my head in my hands.

I need to calm down, but I'm fucking struggling to. Thor's words keep bouncing around my skull. That I'm acting no better than Preston right now toward Mae.

Fuck.

I never, and I mean *never*, want to be compared to that fat fuck.

Part of the reason why I'm struggling to calm down is that today's letter wasn't the first I'd received. I should have told everyone in Church about it, but for some reason, I couldn't.

Opening a drawer, I pull out the first letter. I don't know who gave it to me, but it was slid under my door during the party yesterday. I checked the cameras, but the guy was wearing a hoodie and didn't show his face. At least it looked like a guy from the build. I have no fucking idea who it was.

Sighing, I take a pull from my beer and open the letter, setting aside the pictures.

> *Her mother taught her well, don't you think? Mae isn't worth protecting. Once a whore and druggie, always a whore and druggie. She has a purpose to fulfill and that purpose is not with you and that pussy-ass club. If she isn't returned by midnight on the 2nd, you and your club will suffer the consequences.*

Anger burns in my veins once again, but I tamp it down. Suddenly, Mae's words pop into my head. That the woman in the picture isn't her. That we both know exactly who is in the pictures.

Spreading out the pictures, I pull out the second set of pictures and compare them. The track marks are still there. Same with the birthmark. Same with how thin she is. Same with her hair.

Fuck.

Mae was right.

Flipping them over, my gaze snaps to the time stamp Mae pointed out to me. Doing the math in my head, in the pictures tied to the first note, Mae would have been either fifteen or sixteen, depending on the picture. There's no way she would have been developed enough to have as big of breasts as the woman in the picture has. Not that they're big, they're just bigger than a sixteen-year-old's would be.

Why the hell didn't I notice the time stamps before?

Scoffing, I shake my head and run my hands through my hair, pulling on it slightly.

I already know the answer.

I allowed my anger and hurt at what Lillian had done to blind me to what was going on with Mae.

Levi and Thor's words come back to me, and I pull up my camera feed, rewinding it to when Mae showed up at the front gate.

Surprisingly, I'm pissed as fuck at the fact that Ethan pulled a gun on her, but thankfully, he never fired at her. But the sheer look of terror on her face when he pulled it on her is like a sucker punch to my gut.

Taking a drink, I settle in to watch the video feed from yesterday, only fast-forwarding when no one's talking to Mae, which is surprisingly very little.

I also see the point in which everyone's drawn to Mae. I know a part of that is because of what I'd done and said yesterday.

However, the more they talk to her, things switch with each person from 'protecting her because she's my daughter' to 'protecting her because of who she is as a person'.

The pit that's been growing in my gut tightens after watching each time that I'd spewed that shit at her yesterday. Seeing her light fading more and more in her eyes with each interaction.

When I reach the end of the feed for the party, I switch and pull up the feed at Timber's house. My chest warms at how my sisters were taking care of her.

It's honestly not surprising that Susie declared Mae her sister around the firepit at Timber's house. Axe must have soon followed suit. I have no idea when Punisher made his claim, but I'm sure I'll find out as I keep watching.

When everyone goes to bed, I lean back in my chair. I could pull up the feed from Timber's house to see more, but with how much of an ass I've already been, I decide not to. Plus, I don't know if I could take it if I saw them getting busy.

I scrub my hands over my face in frustration and look at the clock. Fuck, I've been at this for hours.

My mind replays how Timber treated her all day yesterday. I knew right away, seeing the look on his face when they were at the gate, that he was gone for her. Everything he did since then cemented it, too.

Switching the feed back to the clubhouse, I fast forward until this morning when Drae brought in the letter that had been sent to me.

I had been stewing in anger as I stared into my coffee mug. Instead of watching me, my gaze snaps to my niece and Jordan.

Fuck, the look of fear on their faces fucking guts me. I can't believe I lost my shit so badly in front of them. Thank fuck the Prospects got them out of the room pretty quick. Then it feels like I've been sucker punched again when I watch Mae interact with them before she came into Church.

Needing to finish, I fast-forward to when Timber escorted Mae out of Church. The look on her face is another sucker punch to the gut.

Needing to know more and not caring if Timber gets pissed at me later, I switch the feed back to his house and my heart breaks once again as Sadie and Jordan cuddle up on Mae's lap as soon as she sits down on the couch. How she puts on a brave face for them, but when they fall asleep on her while watching a movie, I don't miss the look of anguish and pain on her face before she closes her eyes.

It's not too long after that that the guys and Levi join them after Church lets out and they head out to go shopping.

Groaning, I lean forward, resting my elbows on the desk and cradling my head in my hands, pulling on my hair. It's something I've always done when I'm frustrated.

The feeling of dread hanging over me grows with each second that passes. *Fuck. Fuck. Fuck.*

What have I done?

A vibrating sound cuts through my thoughts and I look around for my phone, finding it on my nightstand. It's a text from Axe.

> Axe: Preston showed up at the mall. Don't know who the two guys are that are with him. We're going to pack up our stuff and make our way out to the SUV and bikes.

He includes a picture and my blood boils.

I recognize that fat fuck, Preston, right away. What pisses me off even more is that I also know who the other two assholes are as well. Fear snakes down my spine at what this could mean.

Instantly I get to work, pulling information on all three of them as I try to tamp down my anger. I can hit the gym later to work out my anger, but right now, I need to get as much information as I can. If the sick fuck is who I really think it is, then shit's gonna hit the fan.

Even if she never forgives me for what I've done the past two days, I can at least do what I can to give my brothers as much of a heads up to keep Mae safe and out of that sick fuck's hands.

Printing off what I can, I text Thor. We need to have Church.

Now.

Leaving my room, I lock the door and quickly make my way to the main room, grabbing a beer from the Prospect and heading straight into Church. Fuck, this has turned into a major clusterfuck.

My brothers quickly fill the room, but I notice quite a few are missing. Not counting Timber, it's Reaper, Punisher, Doc, Judge and Bear. They must have headed over to Levi's when they heard everyone was coming in hot.

My knee bounces nervously, and I force myself to sit still. That's always been one of my tics and I fucking hate it.

A few minutes later, the rest of the guys come in and I purposefully keep my gaze down. I know it's a chickenshit move, but my mind is still a jumbled mess. I only have enough capacity to focus on these sick fuckers right now, otherwise I'm going to blow and that would most likely get my ass kicked out of the club.

Thor bangs his hammer and everyone quiets down.

"Alright. We all know Preston was spotted at the mall today. Axe snapped a picture of him and two others. Smoke, bring up the picture and tell us what you found out."

I bring them up and then pull out the papers I brought with me.

"The fat fuck in the middle is Preston Cole. To his right is his brother, Phillip Cole. He's had multiple drug charges against him, but somehow, he either gets completely off the hook or just a slap on the wrist. My guess is he's one of the guys supplying Preston with his drugs.

"To his left is Bruce Martin. Now he's a seriously twisted, sick fuck. He's a known womanizer and beater. He also has ties to a gang, the Crimson Adders, who are linked to trafficking women and children. I'm still digging to try and find out more on the Crimson Adders because they have to be working with others to get the women and kids out."

Curses ring out, and I can tell Timber's made the connection first.

"You think they targeted Sunshine."

It was a statement, not a question.

Nodding, but still not looking at him, I sigh. "Yes, but what I don't get is that Bruce offered to pay for Mae instead of just taking her. Maybe he wants her for himself, but something doesn't sit right about this."

I also keep the fact to myself that this isn't the first time Bruce has tried to take a woman for himself. Once I get my hands on that bastard, he'll pay two-fold for what he's done.

"Keep digging and let me know when you have more," Thor says right as there's a quick knock on the door and Drae barges in.

"Sorry for not waiting, Prez, but you and Timber better get out here. Shit's going down with Gigi and Mae."

Everyone files out of the room quickly, and I can't help but grin at seeing Mae beating on Gigi.

"What the fuck is going on?" Thor bellows.

When Mae looks up at him, I advert my gaze. I've still got to get my shit straight in my head, and I can't see the hurt on her face again.

After Mae drags Gigi out of the clubhouse, and Patch attends to her cheek and hands, I grab a beer from the Prospect at the bar. I grit my teeth when Timber takes Mae upstairs.

Fuck.

Needing to escape, I head back to my room.

Right as I'm relocking my door, my computer dings and a I sigh heavily. My chest tightens when I see it's an email from Thor.

Clicking on it, I find attachments for everything Mae brought to Church. Six of the attachments are big and I'm assuming they are Lillian's journals.

God fucking damn. I don't want to read anything of hers, but I know I need to.

After finishing reading all the documents, I push away from my computer. Getting up, I sink down on my bed, holding my head in my hands.

What the fuck have I done?

Bile rises in my throat and my hands start to shake.

Fuck. Fuck. Fuck.

Panic runs through me, making my body shake even more than it was.

My gaze goes to my nightstand, but I don't open it. As tempted as I am to escape the hurt and shame running through me at what I've already done, if I pull out my gun, all that will do is hurt her even more.

Pulling out my phone, I can barely see what I'm doing, but I text the one person I know will be able to bring me back from the ledge.

I hope.

Chapter 30
Levi

SIGHING, I SNUGGLE DEEPER into Thor's side. My head is resting on his chest and Dragon's curled up behind me, holding me. We're watching a movie in our room here at the clubhouse, but I couldn't tell you what it is—I'm not paying attention to it. We got the text about an hour ago that Timber and Mae made it to Junction Creek with Andre and the others. I hope the distance will give Jax the time he needs to come to terms with everything.

My fingers play with the fringe on the edge of the blanket covering me as my mind whirls with everything that's going on with Mae.

Thor kisses my forehead. "Can hear your brain going a mile a minute, Wildcat. Want to talk about it?"

Sighing, I try to put my thoughts in order. "I'm just worried about Jax and how he's taking everything. I'm antsy, like something's going to happen, and I don't know what."

Both Dragon and Thor's arms tighten around me and I don't even have to look to know they're both sharing one of their 'twin' looks.

"Spitfire–"

He's interrupted by my phone dinging, and I sit up, but Dragon beats me to it. He reaches for my phone on the nightstand and passes it to me.

I don't even have to open the text as it's just one word. Frantically, I throw the blanket off me. "I gotta go. I gotta get to him." Quickly, I scoot off the bed, only to have Thor grab my arm.

"What's going on, Wildcat?"

I wretch my arm out of his grasp and I whirl on him, pissed that he's keeping me from going to my brother. "Jax needs me. He texted me our code word."

That gets them both in action. When Jax told me about Mae after claiming me as his sister months ago, we set up a code word for if he ever got back into that dark head space again. While it's only been a few months since setting it up, he's never used it.

Until now.

Not even bothering with shoes, I open our door and race down the hallway as fast as my pregnant body will allow me while dodging around anyone in my path and ignoring their questions about what's going on.

Getting to his door, I curse when I find it's locked.

Fuck! I don't have my keys on me.

"Move, Wildcat."

Hearing keys jingle, I step to the side, but as soon as he has the door unlocked, I throw it open and shut it. My guys will stay close till they know we're both good.

Seeing Jax cradling his head in his hands, his elbows on his knees as he sits on his bed, breaks my heart. From where I'm standing, I can see that his body is shaking.

Quietly crossing the room, I kneel in front of him, resting a hand on his knee.

"Jax, I'm here. You're going to be okay."

He shakes his head and it's only then that I realize he has tears streaking down his cheeks.

"No. I fucked up too much this time. There's no way she'll ever forgive me for what I've done. What I've said. There's no way. No way."

I can't keep my own tears from falling at seeing him beating himself up so much. Yes, he fucked up big time, but he's still my brother.

Pushing him back slightly, I stand and sit on his lap like I had done months ago when he was first telling me about Mae and I rest my head on his shoulder. I wrap my arms around him and he responds immediately, wrapping his own arms around me tight, but not enough to hurt me or the babies.

"All this time, I'd hoped that it was all a lie. That she really didn't die. Then I fuck it all up by not believing her when she shows up here. Instead, I made things so much worse by all the shit I spewed at her. I don't know what to do. She'll never forgive me for what I did to her. Timber either. I should have shown them the first letter, but I don't know why I didn't."

I squeeze him tighter, biting my tongue from agreeing on how much he fucked things up with Mae and instead focus on the new news.

"First things first. You need to tell us what was in this first letter and when you got it. Then, you're going to have to apologize to Mae and not over text. You're going to have to show her that she can rely on you. That you'll be there for her. It'll take time, but I know you'll both get past this."

Neither one of us says anything for a long time as we hold each other. Even though I want to pry about his first letter, I don't.

Not yet, anyway.

Jax's body tenses, and I bite my lip, worried about what he's going to say or do.

"What do you mean 'not over text'? She's still here, isn't she?"

I squeeze him tighter, even more worried about how he's going to take what I say next. "Her and Timber went to Junction Creek with Andre and the rest of his guys for a while. Sasha and a few of our guys went with them as escorts. They'll drive back tomorrow."

He quickly stands and a startled noise escapes me as I stumble off his lap, trying to get my feet under me. Jax paces the room, his hands in his hair.

"I messed up so much I drove her away." His voice is quiet, but I still hear him. The pain and anguish in his voice squeezes my heart like a vice.

Before I can say anything, the door opens and Thor pulls me against him. They must have heard me cry out when I stumbled. Dragon goes over to Jax, resting a hand on his shoulder.

"I fucked up so bad that I hurt her and pushed her away. So much so that she felt she had to leave to get away from me. Fuck, now what am I going to do?" Jax says to no one in particular.

"What you're going to do is get your head on straight. You come down to the gym and spar, workout, whatever. I'll even spar with you if you want. Then once you're calm, you're going to try to call her. She may not take your call, but you gotta at least try. Just not tonight. Both of you have been thrown a major mind clusterfuck. Maybe call her tomorrow or the next day. I know they're coming back for the wedding, Timber said as much.

"If she takes your call, maybe you two could then text a bit the rest of the week. Get to know each other that way before you meet face to face again or even on the phone. You gotta show that you'll be there for her. It'll take time, but you'll get through this. You're not the only one that needs to apologize—I've gotta, too. We'll get through this, together," Dragon tells him.

For a while, they both just stare at each other, and I hold my breath.

Finally, Jax nods and I exhale.

"Spar."

Dragon gives him a chin lift. "Change and I'll go do the same. Meet you down there in ten."

Jax returns the chin lift, and I go over and hug him. "You'll get through this. I know you will." He hugs me back and kisses the top of my head.

"Thanks, Kiddo," he whispers, though I can tell he's still tense as hell. I just hope sparring with Dragon will help him.

I shut the door as we all leave his room and Thor pulls me into his arms while Dragon heads to our room to change.

"They'll get through this, Wildcat. We'll all be there for them, but they're gonna get through this."

Sighing, I nod. I hope they do because if Mae chooses to stay away permanently, even if Timber transfers to Andre's club, it'll kill Jax. And I don't know if anyone will be able to pull him back from the ledge if that happens.

Not even me.

Chapter 31
Mae

THE SUN PEEKS THROUGH the window and I groan. Why didn't I close my curtains last night? Not that they would have helped much since they're so threadbare, but they help mute some of the brightness.

I try to move, but there's a heavy weight over my side and I freeze for a moment before relaxing as everything comes back to me.

I'm not in my dingy trailer bedroom anymore.

I'm with Liam.

Sighing happily, I snuggle back under the blankets, taking comfort in his warmth.

"You okay, Sunshine?"

Oh lordy. Liam's gruff voice when he wakes up shoots straight through me.

Turning, I bite my lip as I nod. "Yeah. It's just for a moment, I forgot where I was. That it was all a dream, and I was back in that trailer."

His hand comes up and cups my cheek before gently rubbing his thumb across it. I find myself leaning into his touch without even realizing it.

"Definitely not a fucking dream," he says quietly as he leans over and kisses me, but this isn't like any of his other kisses. It's sweet and soft yet also passionate. I melt against him and he groans, rolling me over till I'm on my back and he's over me.

My legs open on instinct and a moan escapes me when he grinds himself against my core.

"Fuck, I love waking up with you in my arms, Sunshine." He peppers kisses down my jaw and then down my neck as one of his hands roams down my side, teasing my nipple through the silky material.

My hips roll and I moan again as he grinds himself against me harder before biting down where my neck meets my shoulders, not hard, but enough to ensure the hickey he gave me yesterday will continue to be visible.

"Liam!"

I'm about to combust when he pulls back, scoots off the bed and tugs me to the end of it before scooping me up in his arms.

A shriek escapes me at the quick action, and his chest rumbles with laughter.

"You're not coming without me being able to taste you, Sunshine, but I want to do it a little differently this time."

He walks into the attached bathroom and sets me down on the counter. Seeing my hair tie, I quickly put my hair up into a bun to keep it from getting wet.

He turns on the shower and then his lips are back on mine as his hands roam my body.

"Liam," I plead, even though I'm not sure what I'm pleading for. My heart and body say go for it, but my head is still holding me back by a thread. A thread that's so thin it's about to snap.

"I got you, Sunshine."

He lifts the hem of my shirt, and I raise my hands so he can remove it. His hands go to my waist and I lift myself up a bit to allow him to lower my shorts and panties.

"Fuck, you're so fucking sexy, Sunshine."

His mouth latches onto a nipple and my hands go to his head, holding him there. He chuckles, and I moan when I feel the vibrations against my skin. My core aches, needing more.

Without warning, he lets go of my nipple with a pop and lifts me up off the counter. My legs wrap around his waist and another moan slips past my lips when I feel him hard at my center. I pepper kisses along his neck as I grind myself against him. My body is humming with need.

Liam steps under the spray and he lowers me to the ground. Then he shocks me when he gently guides me under the water before reaching behind me to grab my lavender body wash and luffa. Lathering it up, he washes me, slowly dragging the luffa over my skin. Even though he pays a lot of attention to my breasts, the action is so caring and loving that my knees almost buckle under me.

My heart bursts with love for this man, and I realize there's nothing in the world that can keep me from being with him for the rest of my life. Married or not. Though, I would prefer to marry him. I know he asked me to be his Old Lady, and in the biker world, that's even higher than being married. But I want to tie him to me in every way.

He turns me around and lets the water rinse my front while he washes my back. I bite my lip to bite back another moan when he passes the luffa over my rear. My hips arch back, wanting more contact but he moves out of the way.

When he's done, I rinse the luffa and decide on a little payback of my own. I pull him slightly and reposition him so that his front is in the water. Grabbing his body wash, I squirt some into my hands and start washing his back. As I do, I trace his tattoos with my fingers, wishing I could use my tongue instead. Skipping his delicious bum, I kneel and wash the back of his legs. When I'm done, I run my hands over his rear, and I bite my lip to keep from biting him.

When I'm done, I turn him around and darn near melt into a puddle at his lust-filled gaze. Wanting to continue, I squirt some more body wash into my hands and start washing his chest. My fingers swirl in the dusting of hair there before once again tracing his tattoos with my fingers. When I get to his nipples, I make sure to lightly scratch my fingernails over them. He hisses at the action and I make a mental note of that for the future.

Moving down, I wash his lower stomach but stop when I reach his Adonis belt and move to his arms. He groans and I have to bite my cheek to keep from smirking.

Arms done, I kneel and wash his legs. When I'm done, I trace my hands up his thighs, my fingers brushing his inner thighs. His sharp inhale has my confidence boosting. Meeting his gaze, I move my hands higher and start to clean his length. He hisses and his hips thrust forward.

"You're playing with fire, Sunshine," he rasps, and I can't help but clench my thighs. He groans and I stroke him again, but this time squeezing harder.

"Maybe I want to be burned."

He stares at me for a few moments before hoisting me up and setting me on the bench. He quickly rinses off and kneels in front of me. His lips crash down on mine and I moan when he pulls me flush against him.

The fire spreading through me is building and I rock my hips against him, needing him.

"Liam, please," I plead against his lips.

He rests his forehead against mine. "Sunshine, we either gotta stop or I'll be taking you. Are you ready for that? Is that what you want, beautiful? For me to slide into your tight, sweet pussy, making you mine?"

Moaning, I can't help the shiver that spreads through me. "Yes, Liam. Make me yours."

He stares into my eyes for a few moments and then suddenly he's on his feet, pulling me up with him. He chuckles at my pout and kisses me. "Not gonna have your first time be in a shower, Sunshine."

He rinses off one more time and I do the same. Shutting the water off, Liam passes me a towel and I quickly dry off.

Liam lifts me and I squeal, not having seen him come up behind me. Walking into the bedroom, he lays me down on the bed, pulling me closer to the edge. "Gotta get you ready for me, Sunshine."

A second later, I cry out as he latches onto my clit and thrusts a finger inside me.

Time and time again he brings me to orgasm as he keeps adding fingers, teasing me, or as he said, getting me ready for him.

My chest heaves and a fine layer of sweat already coats my skin. "Liam," I plead, needing him.

Finally, he gets up and motions for me to scoot higher. He follows me and notches himself at my entrance.

"Last chance, Sunshine. Are you sure?" His voice is tight, but I love that he's checking in with me despite him being on the edge.

"Yes, Liam. I'm sure. I want you. Make me yours."

His lips crash to mine and he slowly thrusts into me, allowing me to get used to him. It stings and burns a little, but the feeling quickly gives way to pleasure.

When he's fully seated, he groans and bites down on my neck. "Fuck, Baby, you're so tight."

Slowly, he starts to move and I moan.

Holy goddess of all creation!

I never knew sex could feel like this.

He goes up on his hands and my eyes roll back in my head at the change in angle. "Liam, yes, yes, yes. Right there."

Seconds later, my orgasm rips through me, and Liam curses before he starts thrusting faster and harder. Immediately, another orgasm builds, and when he lifts both of my legs over his shoulder, he goes in even deeper.

"Holy... Oh my god. Liam! Yes."

"God fucking damn, your pussy's tight, Sunshine. It's squeezing me like a vice. Come on, Baby, give me more. Soak my cock."

His words trigger another orgasm and he curses as I clamp down on him. He speeds up and judging by how tense he is, he's close himself.

Grabbing my breasts, I squeeze and play with my nipples. He groans, drops my legs back down, and grabs my hips. He starts thrusting even faster, his gaze glued to my breasts.

"Yes, Baby. Play with those beautiful titties. Pinch those nipples for me." His words have me shivering and I feel another orgasm building quickly as I do as he says.

"Fuck, Baby, that's a beautiful sight. Come on, Baby. Give me one more, soak my cock. Come for me. Now."

My body does as he commands and another orgasm rips through me and, based on his roar, he follows me.

He falls to his elbows and kisses me. Holy mother of all quivering orgasms, this man may just kill me by orgasm.

We're both breathing heavy as we kiss. Pulling back, I stare up at him.

"How do you feel, Sunshine? Was I too rough?"

I shake my head. "No, it was perfect. I honestly thought it would hurt more than that at first, but it only stung a little."

He grins, and I frown, confused.

"I took care of that part while I was eating your fucking perfect pussy. I wanted to take away as much pain as I could, so I broke through it during one of your orgasms."

Surprised, I stare at him and my chest warms that he did that for me. Pulling him down, I kiss him again. At that moment, my traitorous stomach makes itself known and Liam pulls back, chuckling.

"Guess we better get cleaned up again and get you some food, Sunshine."

After another shower, and an introduction into shower sex, which we'll totally be doing more of, I'm finally ready.

Locking our door, we head across the grounds toward the clubhouse. As we get closer, my stomach growls again at the heavenly aroma coming from the open windows.

"Mama Astrid loves to cook, and she's damn good at it," Timber says as he leads me to the porch stairs, his hand on the small of my back.

When we enter, everyone looks up and they all grin. Well, except for the Johnson Chasers. They glare at me and I do my best to ignore them.

Mama Astrid gets up from her chair, heading our way. She loops her arm through mine and I have to laugh at Timber's face when she pulls me from his arms. He follows behind us to the kitchen.

"Whenever we cook, it's always like a buffet. Take whatever you like." She shows me where the silverware and dishes are as well as where the stuff is to make coffee in case I'm ever up early.

"Timber said you usually cook for the club. Is it okay if I help you later? I know we have some errands to do today, but I don't know when we're doing them."

Mama Astrid grins and when she pulls me in for another hug, I have to blink back tears. I don't think I've ever been hugged this much since I was eight.

"I will take all the help that I can get." She pauses as she waves out to the main room in the direction of the Johnson Chasers. "That lot can't cook for shit and if they do, it tastes like it."

A laugh bubbles out of me and I can't help but laugh louder when said Johnson Chasers glare even harder in our direction.

"I love to cook. When I was working in Peggy's diner, I mostly waited tables, but I also worked a lot in their kitchen. She taught me everything she knew."

My chest tightens thinking about Peggy. I hope Preston hasn't tried to hurt her again. Technically, I should have been handed over to Bruce yesterday, so I don't know what's going on now that I left.

"After Sasha and the others leave, we're gonna take you out to get the rest of what you need, Sunshine. That includes hitting the dealership to get you geared up so you can be on the back of my bike."

"Perfect! I'll tag along. Kai told me about a shirt that just came in that he thought I'd like and I want to go check it out," Mama Astrid replies.

I load up my plate with some eggs, bacon, fruit, and one pancake. I don't miss Mama Astrid's look on how little food I grab, but I ignore it for now. Snagging a mug of coffee, I follow her out to the main room and sit down at a seat at their table. Ragnar, Kai, Razor, Sasha, Colt, and Judge are there as well. Timber sits down next to me. Like with Kai, I've started using Odin's real name, Ragnar, since they've taken me in like family.

We all chat as we eat and I feel the same sense of family here as I felt in Forest Creek.

Grabbing my mug, I lean back in my chair, full and slightly upset that I couldn't eat everything. Timber looks at me with a raised eyebrow and I shake my head. I can't eat any more. He snags my plate and finishes what's left of my pancake and bacon.

Mama Astrid looks between us, confused, and I sigh. Might as well tell her. She's going to find out anyway if we are going to be spending time together this week.

"For thirteen years, I was mostly starved. When I was in school, I'd get a free lunch and at home, it'd be the unwanted leftovers from the food bank. I started working at Peggy's diner when I was fifteen and then I was able to get a hot meal whenever I had a shift. There was one time that I tried to eat more shortly before graduation. Unfortunately, Preston took notice and the beating he gave me put me in the hospital. He also went through my bags and my room, taking any money he could find, which was a couple hundred bucks. Ever since then, I've stuck to one meal a day to avoid another beating. Yesterday, I started eating three times a day, but I'm keeping each meal small at first so my body can adjust."

Mama Astrid blinks repeatedly and wipes her eyes. The other guys and Sasha all look like they want to go on a rampage, and my breath hitches at that. No one has ever stood up for me before like these men and ladies have.

Mama Astrid clears her throat. "Well, we'll have you right as rain in no time, Dear. You can count on that. If that asshole stepdad of yours ever shows his face around here, you can bet your booty, these boys of mine and your man's brothers and sisters will make him pay for what he's done to you."

It's my turn, once again, to blink back tears. I'm so thankful that I had the courage to leave the other day to find my dad, even if he doesn't want anything to do with me. By me doing that, I've found the love of my life and a new family I never thought I'd have.

Chapter 32

Mae

AFTER BREAKFAST, MAMA ASTRID tells me that the Johnson Chasers are responsible for clean-up. I giggle at her adopting my nickname for the bunnies and she smiles. She said that since they 'can't cook for shit', her words once again not mine, then they have to take care of all the dishes after each meal. For that, I'm grateful. While I love to cook, I absolutely hate doing dishes.

Dropping off my plate in the kitchen, I walk back out into the main room and Sasha immediately pulls me in for a hug.

"Make sure to text me, girl. Gonna miss your ass and your fucking hilarious ways of cussing."

Throwing my head back, I laugh and once again, thank my lucky stars that I went to Forest Creek after finding out what Preston's plans were.

"I will, and I'll miss you and the others as well."

She squeezes me tighter and I fight back tears when she whispers in my ear. "He'll pull his head out of his ass, trust me."

Not trusting my voice, I nod and blink harder to keep the tears from falling.

Colt, Judge, Tripp, and Ryder also give me a hug before they head out to their bikes.

Arms wrap around my waist, and I lean back into Timber's embrace. "Get your purse, Baby. Nathan's gonna drive you and Mama Astrid in the cage."

Nodding, I give him a kiss and run back to the house to get my purse. If I had known we'd be leaving this soon, I would have just brought it with me earlier.

A few minutes later, I'm back in the main room and I nibble my lip as I look from Timber to Mama Astrid. Pulling her aside, I tell her my idea and she's immediately on board. Guess we'll have one more stop before coming home.

Heading into the kitchen, we take stock of what they already have on hand, and I make up a list of the items I'll need. Just as I put the list into my purse, Timber comes into the kitchen, giving us both a look I can't decipher.

"What you up to, Sunshine?"

I can't help the blush that heats my cheeks and I bite my lip to keep from giggling. "Nothing. We were just doing some meal planning. After we get what I need, can we stop at the grocery store on the way home?"

The grin he gives me has butterflies swirling in my stomach. "Yeah, Sunshine, we can do that. You ladies ready to go?"

Nodding, I follow him out of the clubhouse and get into the SUV along with Mama Astrid and the Prospect who must be Nathan. On bikes, it's Timber, Punisher, Ragnar, Atlas, Cannon, Razor, Loki, and Beast.

We make our way to a large box store and my nerves return, making my hands shake.

"What's wrong, Dear?" Mama Astrid asks, worry written all over her face as she reaches over, clasping my hands in hers.

"After we were done shopping at the mall yesterday, we went to the food court. Preston was there with two men."

I say nothing right now about knowing who the other two men are.

Fiddlesticks...

I should probably tell Timber about that.

Those two men were another reason why I tried to stay away from the trailer so much. They would show up at least twice a month, sometimes more, but their visits were always random. I'd tried to track them in the past but couldn't find a pattern. That is, until these past few weeks.

Both she and Nathan tense at my words, and she pats my arm.

"I doubt they would have followed you here, and I bet my boys will all be on alert. Try to calm down, Sweetie."

It takes me a bit to remember she calls all the guys in the Junction Creek chapter 'her boys'. Heck, she even calls the Forest Creek guys that, too. And all the guys call her Mama Astrid as well from what I've heard. They have a house on club grounds and since she's now retired, she cooks almost all the meals for the Junction Creek guys.

Nodding, I take a few deep breaths and unclench my hands. I hadn't even realized I'd balled them up in my lap. Someone opens my door and I jump.

Jeez, my nerves really are shot. I seriously do hope that Preston didn't follow us here.

Turning, I give a small smile to Timber, who's watching me with concern. "Just worried about a repeat," I whisper.

His face hardens as he gives me a chin lift, but I know he's not mad at me. Taking his hand, I climb out of the SUV.

He keeps his hand on the small of my back as we enter the store, and I immediately grab a cart. I'm surprised when Mama Astrid grabs one herself and gives me a mischievous look.

"Just grabbing one in case we need it."

Even though I don't believe her, I nod. After my experiences yesterday, I have a feeling I'll be coming away from the store with more than I intend to buy.

Shaking off my thoughts, I head to the pharmacy area. I grab the medicines I'm used to getting—ibuprofen, cough drops, allergy medicine, vitamins, eye drops, and such. Hearing items going into a cart behind me, I turn around and frown when I see Mama Astrid grabbing the exact same things that I just did.

She smirks at me. "Trust me, Dear. You're going to want to keep extra of everything you buy like this in Timber's room at the clubhouse. We'll bag it up separate from your other order, so it'll be easier when you all get back to your clubhouse. Make sure you keep extra clothes there too for the times when you don't have a chance to grab a bag and the guys are all out taking care of business."

Pausing, I take in what she's saying. Then I remember the times where Timber had told me not to leave the clubhouse without him. I really need to talk to him at some point to learn more about the club. Taking a deep breath, I nod.

"I hadn't thought of that, but it makes sense. Thank you."

She waves me off and I continue, but this time, I pull two of everything and throw one in each cart.

When we get to the feminine aisle, I blush and keep my head down. It's a necessity, but I still feel weird getting the items with all these men around us. Mama Astrid reaches around me, and I freeze when I see what she's grabbing.

A couple boxes of pregnancy tests.

It's then that I realize Timber didn't use a condom this morning, either time, and I start to panic. I wonder if he realizes he didn't use one. What if I'm already pregnant? Does he even want kids?

"For whenever you're ready or you think you've missed your period. This way, you won't have to wait to go and buy one," she whispers as she squeezes my shoulder.

I bite my lip, mouth 'thank you' to her and tuck them both in the carts, covering them up with some other items. She smiles at me and we continue shopping.

Walking by the clothes, I see a few shirts I like and another hoodie. Since fall's fast approaching, I snag a couple and throw them in the cart.

Turning around, I'm about to head to the checkout when I see Timber grinning at his phone and then he gives me a mischievous look.

"What?"

"Nothing, Sunshine."

I narrow my eyes at him, but he just grins.

"You'll just have to wait until we get back to the clubhouse."

Rolling my eyes at him, I head to the checkout and start piling items onto the belt. The total makes me want to wince, but I hold my card out only to have Timber snagging it back and giving the checkout lady his card instead.

Sighing, I put my card away, then cross my arms as I glare at him.

He steps closer and whispers in my ear. "Can't have you using your card, Sunshine. If they have the means, they'll be able to track where you are."

I freeze, feeling like someone's dumped a bucket of ice water over me. Licking my lips, I nod and wrap my arms around my waist as the reality of the situation I'm in comes crashing back down around me.

Thankfully, we make it out to the car without incident.

"Let's grab a bite to eat," Ragnar suggests, and I nod. I don't miss his frown or Timber's, but I can't help it right now. Not after that reminder.

The car ride to the restaurant is subdued. I want to be excited. To be happy with the new changes in my life, but it's also why I've had to change that's a heavy weight on my shoulders.

When Nathan parks, I force myself to push those thoughts away for right now. Well, as best as I can, anyway.

Timber gets off his motorcycle and after they all look around, he comes around to my door and opens it. I plaster on a smile, but judging by his frown, I'm not fooling him any. He kisses my temple and guides me into the restaurant.

Looking up, it's the same sub chain I ate at yesterday at the mall and I'm glad I'm not trying anything new right now. My nerves, combined with anything new, would probably make me sick.

While we eat, the others keep trying to draw me into the conversation, but I can't really bring myself to answer more than a word or two.

After we eat, we load up and head to the dealership.

My excitement at getting gear to be able to ride on Timber's bike helps push away my gloomy feelings, but they're still there at the back of my mind.

God, I can't wait until the guys catch Preston, Bruce, Michael, Phillip, and X

.

I have no doubt that they'll be dealt with the club way. I've read enough to know that clubs do that as much as they're able to. While I've often doubted a lot of the things I've read about motorcycle clubs, that part is one I always believed. There will be no calling in the cops unless, for some reason, the cops catch their trail. And even then, I don't know if the guys will hand over any of the men to them.

Shaking my head, I take Timber's hand when he opens my door and we walk into the dealership together.

"Ma, Atlas put the shirt for you under the register. Let him know if you need to change the size or color," Punisher, I mean Kai, says before he takes my arm and pulls me away from Timber. His irritated growl has me giving him a smile, a real one, and he calms down before following after us.

"Now, let's start with a jacket, Lil' Bit."

Kai shows me the various styles they have, and I feel out of my element a little. After trying them on, I pick the one that allows me to move the easiest but also has a smidge extra room since I plan to put on weight. I don't want to have to be buying another jacket again come spring if I don't have to.

Next up is gloves. While he says I don't have to wear them all the time, they will help later in the fall before the snow flies. Same for spring when they stop salting the roads.

Once I find a pair I like, they take me over to the boots and I have to tamp down my excitement. I've always loved boots, but other than snow boots, I could never really afford them before. In the end, I get a couple of pairs, both of them have a little bit of a heel but not the two-inch ones.

"Mae," Mama Astrid calls out and I turn, looking for where she is to find her over by the clothing. Kai takes everything I want out of my arms and I hurry over to her, eager to also get a few shirts.

"You've got to try this one on. I think it'll look gorgeous on you."

She holds up a short-sleeve shirt that has a bit of sinching on the sides. Agreeing with her, I look for my size and snag it before looking through the rest of the racks. After a few minutes, I take the few shirts and hoodies I picked out, plus a few others Timber and Mama Astrid picked out, and make my way to the dressing room.

I'm shocked at how well everything looks and that everything fits. The hoodie is, of course, a bit bigger than the other shirts because I love having the extra room with hoodies. Deciding to wear the shirt Mama Astrid picked out for me and a pair of the boots, I put my tennis shoes in the box the boots were in along with the tags from the shirt in the box.

Gathering everything up, I exit the dressing room and come to a halt. Anger rises in my veins at seeing a woman dressed in cutoff shorts and a tank top pressing herself up against Timber. He keeps trying to push her away, but she keeps stepping back into his space.

Chapter 33
Mae

PLACING MY STUFF ON the counter, Kai smirks when he sees me, and I really hope he isn't thinking I'll be taking out the trash again. I don't want to cause a scene in his store.

Stepping up behind Liam, I wrap my arm around his waist and lean on his other side, the one the skank isn't sidled up to. At my touch, his body relaxes a little. Seeing how taut his face is leads me to believe this woman isn't listening to him.

"Baby, who's this?" I ask, trying to keep my voice level, but I can't stop the curl of my lip when I see how much cleavage she's got on display.

"Honestly, Sunshine, I have no idea who she is, and she seems to think I'm lying to her about being with someone."

He wraps an arm around my waist and pushes the woman away again. Her face screws up and my stomach tightens when she sneers at me as she takes me in.

"Are you sure you're even legal, little girl? Run on home to your mama and let the adults here talk."

She turns back toward Timber, batting her fake eyelashes at him as she takes a step toward him, but her smile falters when he sneers at her.

"Bitch, for the last time, I'm not fucking interested. I've got an Old Lady, who is right here, and I have no intention of stepping out on her. Now back. The. Fuck. Off."

She pouts and pushes her arms together slightly as she twirls her fingers, which pushes her boobs out further. At this point, I'm surprised the fabric's even holding them in.

"Oh, you don't mean that, Handsome. We had so much fun together last time. I bet she can't even keep up with a guy of your caliber."

I can't keep from tensing at being reminded of all the women Timber's been with before.

"Well, you better believe it, because I am his Old Lady and I more than keep him satisfied. Now why don't you run along before your nipples pop out of that shirt and you scandalize some of the kids in here."

Timber squeezes my hip and strokes his thumb up and down my side, sliding under my shirt slightly. At the action, I lose some of the tension, but not all. I'm about to say something when Timber squeezes my hip again.

"Like I said before, bitch. I don't know you and I sure as hell have never fucked you before. Now get the fuck out of here before you get yourself banned."

"Stacy, do as he says and get the fuck out of here. My sister is, in fact, Timber's Old Lady, so back the fuck off. Don't want to see your ass around the clubhouse for the next three months, either," Kai growls as he levels her a dark look.

Stacy rolls her eyes and huffs as she walks out of the store, her hips swaying.

I lean more into Timber's side, and he tips my chin up, kissing me.

"Meant what I said, Sunshine. I have no idea who the fuck she was, and I was never with her."

"I believe you, Timber." He kisses me again and steers me over to where Kai is at the counter.

"I put the tag for the shirt in the box for the boots. I wanted to wear both the shirt and boots home—I hope that's okay."

Kai grins at me as he sets down a bag on the counter. Now knowing that I can't use my card while here in Junction Creek, I assume Timber has already paid for the items. Though I have every intention of paying him back.

"That's more than okay, and believe me, you aren't the first to do that. Now, I have a surprise of my own for you," Kai says as he pulls out a large box from under the counter.

I can't help but bounce on my toes in excitement. These last two days have been surreal and add in the fact that I've been almost completely accepted into not one, but two clubs is unbelievable. Everyone keeps saying they're trying to make up for years of birthdays and Christmases since they didn't know about me, which I am still floored by. While yes, it's still awkward as heck, it feels good to be loved and wanted again.

After my tenth birthday party, Preston declared there would be no more presents. That I didn't need material things like that. Not even for Christmas. My grandparents still got me presents, which I had to painstakingly hide, but that ended when they died when I was twelve. It always hurt that all the other kids still got presents from their parents and families for their birthdays, Christmas, and sometimes even on Valentine's Day or Easter. But not me.

Looking back now, I realize it was just another controlling stance Preston made over Mom. It also meant more money for him to do with as he pleases.

Pushing away those thoughts, Kai lifts the lid of the box and my hands fly to my mouth in shock.

There are two motorcycle helmets inside—a full-face one and one that, I believe, the guys call a skull cap. Both of them have Timber's nickname for me, Sunshine, painted on them in beautiful calligraphy. There's even a small sun as the dot for the 'i'. My fingers trace around the scrollwork as I admire the artist's skill.

"When I found out you were going to be getting your riding gear here, I had Atlas work his magic."

My head whips up and my jaw drops in shock. Spinning around, I spot Atlas, knowing he was among the ones that came with us, and he gives me a sheepish grin. I try not to run, but it's hard to. When I get to him, I give him a hug that he hesitantly returns.

"Thank you, Atlas! Your design is gorgeous!"

He pats my back awkwardly, and I pull back, giving him a small smile. I have a feeling that I just overstepped into his personal space too much.

"Sorry if you aren't a hugger or if I overstepped."

He gives me a small, but tight smile, and squeezes my shoulder before heading into what must be a back room or a work area because it's labeled 'employee's only'.

Walking back over to Timber, he wraps an arm around my waist and kisses my temple.

"Did I overstep?" I ask Kai, twisting my hands together in worry.

"Atlas isn't very comfortable about being around women. It's not my story to tell, but I can tell you, that if he didn't want you to touch him, he wouldn't have allowed it."

Nodding, I seriously hope he's right. Stepping forward slightly, I carefully lift the full-face helmet, trying not to touch or smear Atlas' beautiful artwork, and try it on.

Kai smirks at me as he adjusts the straps before buckling them. Then he reaches around to the back and pulls up on the helmet. I look at him, confused as to why he did that.

"Gotta make sure the helmet doesn't come off if something happens, Lil' Bit. It needs to stay snug on your head to properly protect you."

Once he's satisfied it's adjusted correctly and it fits, he unbuckles it. I take it off, running my hand through my hair to make sure it isn't sticking up all over. Next, I try on the skull cap helmet and Kai repeats the process.

"You must have been doing this a long time to be able to pick the right size for me and be confident enough that it'll fit to deck them out in my name." My voice is quiet as my emotions threaten to boil over, but he hears me anyway judging by his smile.

I blink back tears, still not fully believing this is now my life. That I have two brothers, a sister, aunts, uncles, a cousin, and a nephew. Not to mention two more cousins on the way.

Timber's arm wraps around my waist again and he lifts my chin so I'm looking up at him.

"Best believe it, Baby. It's all real. Punisher and Axe. They're real. Mama Astrid and Odin. They're real. Susie and Jordan. They're real. Your aunts, uncles, and cousin. They're real. I'm real, and I'm not going anywhere. None of us are, Sunshine."

My cheeks heat, not realizing I'd said that aloud, but also because of Timber's declaration.

Nodding, I lean forward and rest my head on his chest, breathing deep. His scent of leather and sandalwood that's tinged slightly with smells of motor oil and sawdust surrounds me, calming me. He kisses the top of my head and I look up at him.

"How about you ride with me to the store and then to the clubhouse, Sunshine? A little wind therapy may do you good."

That perks me up and I nod enthusiastically, which has both Timber and Kai chuckling. Being on a bike looks so freeing that I've been looking forward to riding since Timber mentioned it the other day.

Kai rummages through the bag and pulls out my jacket. I take it and remove the tags before sliding it on. Out of the corner of my eye, I see Mama Astrid and Ragnar approach.

"Let me take care of your hair, Dear. With your long, thick hair, you'll be combing out tangles for hours if you don't."

Nodding, I make sure all of my hair is out from under my jacket and pass her a hair tie I always keep on my wrist.

Her fingers make deft work of braiding my hair and she squeezes my shoulder when she's done. Smiling, I hug her in thanks and pick up the skull cap. Timber had said before that they usually only use the full-face helmets on long rides or when they think they'll need to use Bluetooth. Though, he said you can use Bluetooth with a skull cap, it's just a bit harder.

Timber grabs my bags and I turn back to Kai, noting that he's still behind the counter and I can see a door behind him with a 'manager' nameplate on it.

"Kai, do you have to stay and work, or are you coming with us as well?"

He shakes his head. "I need to get some things done in the office for a bit, and then I'll be back at the clubhouse."

"So, if we plan to have supper at 6 pm, is that enough time for you?"

He grins and nods.

Timber snags my hand, tugging me toward the door and a giggle escapes as I follow him. Looking over my shoulder, I wave bye to Kai, which he returns.

Once outside, Timber stows the bags in the SUV and pulls me over to his bike. Another giggle escapes me at his eagerness. He grins at me, and I bite my lip at his heated gaze.

"Been wanting you on the back of my bike since I first saw you the other day." He leans down and gives me a quick kiss.

He flips down two pegs that he tells me is where I will put my feet when riding and to always make sure they are flipped down before I even think of getting on the bike. Putting on his own helmet, he gets on the bike.

"Okay, Sunshine. I'll always let you know when I'm ready for you to get on. Don't just hop on behind me. First, you're gonna put your left foot on the peg, take my hand, put your other hand on my shoulder, and then swing your leg over. Keep your leg and boots away from the exhaust pipes. They get fucking hot, and I don't want you getting burned, Sunshine."

He holds out his hand and I take it. Putting my other hand on his shoulder, I put my foot on the peg, and throw my leg over as I try not to jostle the bike too much. Once seated, I wrap my arms around his waist and he chuckles.

Reaching back, he grabs my hips and scoots me forward even more.

"You're gonna have to hang on tight to me, Sunshine. If you're all the way back there and not hanging on well, you'll go flying off the back, ya hear?"

"Sorry," I squeak out and my cheeks heat when even I hear the hitch in my voice. Feeling him like this between my thighs is turning me on like no other. I want him again.

He chuckles, which makes my cheeks heat even more. He goes over how I should move with him and tells me what to do to communicate with him while riding.

When he starts up his bike, I have to bite back a groan. The vibrations are crazy and they're going straight to my core. Especially with how I'm practically plastered to him. Even though we had sex twice this morning, now I want more.

Chapter 34
Timber

FUCK, I LOVE THE feel of Sunshine being pressed up against me on my bike. I take it easy on the way to the grocery store since it's her first time on a bike. Unfortunately, the ride is over way too soon and I'm backing my bike into a parking space.

When I shut off my bike, I squeeze Sunshine's hands that are still wrapped around my waist and hold out my own to help her off. She stands, flings her leg over, and stumbles a little before she catches herself and hangs onto me to steady herself. But the smile on her face tells me she had a blast.

"Careful there, Sunshine. You'll have jelly legs for a bit, but you'll soon get used to the feeling. How'd you like your first ride?" I ask, even though I know the answer.

Somehow, her smile gets even bigger. "I absolutely loved it! I can't wait to ride again and go for a longer ride!"

After we get what we need here, I might just make that happen.

"We'll stay out here to keep an eye on everything while you guys go in and get what you need," Razor tells me. Giving him a chin lift, I look at Odin and nod. Since it's our ladies that want to get the items, we'll go in together.

Putting down the kickstand, I get off and put my helmet on the handlebars and do the same with Sunshine's while she gets her purse out of the saddlebag. Seeing her decked out in her gear makes me wish I had her cut for her already. Especially when we enter the store. It seems like every fucking guy in here is checking her out.

Odin and I walk behind Mae and Mama Astrid through the store. I make sure I'm not too close to them, but also not too far away in case some asshole tries something. It's obvious they want whatever the fuck they're cooking to be a surprise.

Unfortunately, what I'm worried about happens half-way through the store. Some preppy douchebag walks up to her and slips a number in her pocket.

"Call me," he says with a wink as he blatantly eye-fucks her.

Sunshine's face turns red with anger, and she fishes out the note, handing it back to him.

"You should pick your targets better. Also, you should make sure the woman actually wants you to give her your number before you assume she does. I certainly do not want your number and won't be going out with you. Ever. In case you missed it, my man is right behind me."

I step up to her right as she finishes her speech and place my hand on her hip. Odin does the same to Mama Astrid.

Preppy boy scoffs. "You'd rather be with him than me? Why sink to his level when you could be with someone like me? We'd live the high life where you can have whatever you want. He's a low-life thug, whereas I'm poised to take over my father's office when he retires."

Sunshine raises an eyebrow at him as she crosses her arms under her chest. "And what exactly is it that you do?"

The prick puffs up his chest and gives me a smug look. "I'm a doctor."

I eye him up and down. He's young and doesn't quite look thirty, but I don't think I'd ever keep him as my doctor based on how he's acting. He screams slimy and gives off an air of superiority. I wouldn't be able to trust anything he said or did.

"What's your father's name and which office is his?"

I bite back a smirk because I know exactly what Sunshine is up to, so I keep my mouth shut.

"Dr. Johnson, Andrew Johnson. He has a private office just down the road. I'm Dr. Carter Johnson." Once again, the shit gives me a smug look.

Sunshine turns to me and smirks. "Baby, is that the only doctor's office in this town?"

"No, Sunshine, it's not. And personally, having met the man before, I don't care for Dr. Johnson either." I pause and my gaze goes to the prick. "Neither of them."

Carter's face gets red and Sunshine pats my chest.

"Well, Baby, I never want to go to that doctor's office if I ever need one while we're here. I should probably let Uncle Reaper and my brother, Punisher, know as well to steer clear of the place."

Carter's face pales slightly.

Sunshine turns back to him and smirks. "Oh good! You've heard of them before. Well, you really should have paid attention more because my Old Man is also a Steel Archangel and they are not low-life thugs as you so put it. Now, why don't you scurry along and give your number to some other woman so long as she's single and *wants* your number?" Sunshine shoos Carter away after stuffing his number into the pocket on his polo.

He scoffs. "You'll regret this, bitch."

Sunshine smiles as she leans into me more. "No. No, I won't."

"And you best never hit on or threaten my Old Lady like that again, Junior."

"We'll be relaying our message back to Reaper. You can be damn fucking sure no one in our club or anyone who works for us will be stepping into that fucking office again," Odin sneers at him.

Carter blanches slightly under my hard glare and I'm sure Odin's giving him one as well. Thankfully, the little pussy scurries off.

Before he's even out of sight, Mae laughs and hugs me before kissing me.

"God fuck damn, woman, I love your sassy side."

She hums. "I'm glad you do, Baby. Thank you for letting me deal with the douche-canoe. I know if it had gotten worse that you and even Ragnar would have stepped in, but I appreciate it."

I give her another kiss. "Would have in a heartbeat. Now, let's get the rest of what you need for supper."

"Agreed, Sweetheart. No one messes with my family," Odin growls.

Thankfully, we're able to finish the shopping trip without further incident.

Once everything is loaded up in the SUV, I turn to Odin, talking quietly. "I'm gonna take Sunshine on a ride. We'll be back at the clubhouse before long." He nods.

"I know Astrid will want to put everything away herself," Odin says with a grin that I match.

Yeah, Mama Astrid will definitely want to do that. She has major OCD when it comes to her kitchen. And yes, we all know that's her domain. You fuck with anything in that kitchen, and you'll be getting one very bland and bare-boned meal in return.

"Take Razor and Loki with you. We don't know if that fucker tracked her here. You shouldn't ride alone, but I think a little wind therapy will do her good," he says, and I give him a chin lift.

Walking over to Razor and Loki, I ask if they'll ride with us, which they instantly agree with.

"Can't wait till we get those pricks," Loki growls. "She's too sweet to be having that heavy of a cloud hanging over her."

"Damn fucking agree, brother," Razor sneers.

It's times like these that I love the brotherhood that I have. It's not lost on me how much everyone has taken to Sunshine, and I don't mean it in because she's the club princess. No, she just has something about her that makes everyone feel at ease around her. Even though the others didn't officially claim her, I know they all look at her like a little sister. And if those assholes somehow manage to get their hands on my Sunshine, there's going to be two clubs full of pissed off brothers, aunts, and uncles after them. I know Smoke will go after them, too, but time will tell if he'll accept her as his daughter or n ot.

I give them a chin lift and head over toward Sunshine, who's laughing at something Mama Astrid said.

Stepping up behind her, I wrap my arms around her waist. "How about we go for a ride before heading back to the clubhouse?"

Her eyes light up, and the smile she gives me goes straight to my cock. Fuck, I'd love nothing more than to take her back to my room, but Odin and Loki are right. She needs this.

"I'd love to! But it can't be for too long. I want to get familiar with the kitchen before we start prepping supper. I also need to do laundry at some point."

"Sounds good, Sunshine. Loki and Razor are gonna ride with us. I won't take you out for a really long ride since you're still getting used to the bike. As for your laundry, how about we go back to the house after supper? Get your laundry done then and relax a bit?"

"Sounds like a plan."

She tilts her head and goes up on her toes, giving me a kiss before slipping out of my arms and walking over to my bike. She secures her purse in the saddlebag and slips on her helmet.

I follow suit and soon we're on the road with Loki and Razor riding behind us.

While Loki is technically the Road Captain for Reaper's club, I've been out here so much that I know the roads surrounding the town.

I take Sunshine on the back roads, letting the wind soothe us. The more we ride, the more I feel the tension leaving her body. She relaxes against me more and while I can tell she's paying attention to where we're going, she's also looking around.

An hour later, I pull into the compound and park.

"How was your first long ride, Sunshine?" I ask as I hold out my hand to help her off the bike.

"Even better than earlier! Thank you, Baby, that was just what I needed." She wraps her arms around my neck and kisses me.

Fuck, I think I'm addicted to this woman's kisses. The guys catcall and whistle, causing Sunshine to laugh. Pulling back, she smiles and moves to get her things out of the saddlebag once I get off my bike.

Walking into the clubhouse, Mama Astrid immediately snags Sunshine and the two of them go off into a corner. The grin she gives me over my shoulder twists my insides.

And not for the reasons you might think.

This is how she is when there isn't a heavy cloud weighing down on her shoulders. A weight put there by Preston, Bruce, that X fucker, and unfortunately, Smoke.

Seeing her this happy and carefree makes me even more determined to catch these fuckers.

Chapter 35
Timber

I<small>T'S NEARING SUPPERTIME AND</small> I'm sitting with Reaper, Doc, Loki, Punisher, Odin, and Python while we enjoy a few beers. Though, Python's got his nose in his computer looking for shit on Bruce and Preston when my phone vibrates.

Digging it out of my pocket, I bite back a groan.

It's Smoke.

Taking a deep breath, I answer it.

"You better not be calling me to spew more of that shit."

He clears his throat. *"No, I'm not. I tried calling Mae, but she didn't answer, so I figured I'd try calling you."*

"Sunshine's cooking supper right now with Mama Astrid. They have music on, so I bet she didn't even hear the phone ring."

He sighs and I can almost see him hanging his head. *"Is it... I mean, in the meantime, can we talk? I'd like to apologize."*

Shock fills me, but at the same time, so does relief. *"Just a sec. Let me get somewhere more private."*

He grunts and I mute my phone before leaning in closer to Reaper. It's not that I don't care if the other guys hear me, but just in case he goes off his rocker, I don't want Sunshine to hear it. Not after how happy she's been.

"Hey, Reap. I need to take a phone call but want to stay nearby—can I use your office or Church?"

He looks at me in question and I flip my phone around so he can see that I'm talking to Smoke. He inhales sharply as his features harden.

"Go to Church. That way, you have room to pace if need be. But Timber, try not to put any holes in my walls." The smirk he gives me has me chuckling.

"Well, if I do, it's a good thing I'm in construction."

I slap his shoulder as I get up and make my way into Church, unmuting my phone in the process.

"Okay, shoot."

Smoke sighs. *"I'm sorry. I can't even begin to express how sorry I am at how I treated Mae and you. Especially Mae. I know I'm going to probably be groveling for the rest of my days, but if it means she'll let me into her life, I'll gladly do it."*

Well, fuck. I wasn't expecting that.

"I take it you rewatched all the footage, read through all of Lillian's shit, and took a closer look at those photos."

"Yeah, I did, but that's not what started it all." He pauses, and my gut tightens. *"Someone slipped a different letter under my door during the party the other day. I have no idea who the fucker is. He or she never showed his face to the cameras. I'm pretty sure it's a guy though from the build."*

"What do you mean there's another letter? You should have brought this up during Church the other day." I don't even try to bite back my growl, my anger rising too much and I'm about to put a hole in the wall. *"I can't protect her if I don't know what the fuck is going on, Smoke! What the fuck was in that letter?"*

"I don't know why I didn't bring it up," he growls right back, and I scoff.

I wait a few moments, but when he doesn't say anything else, my anger rises even more. *"What was in the letter, Smoke?"* I grind out.

"It's better if I just show you."

A moment later, my phone vibrates. First, I look at the pictures because I'm sure I'll be fucking pissed if I read the note first. The pictures all look similar to the ones I saw earlier, but I think it's been a few years since the pictures in the other set. Then I flick over to the letter and I see red. It takes every ounce of restraint to keep from doing or saying something I'll regret.

> *Her mother taught her well, don't you think? Mae isn't worth protecting. Once a whore and druggie, always a whore and druggie. She has a purpose to fulfill, and that purpose is not with you and that pussy-ass club. If she isn't returned by midnight on the 2nd, you and your club will suffer the consequences.*

"You do realize that's not Mae, right?" I bite my tongue on the fact that I can guarantee that's not her body strewn about in those pictures since I combed over every inch of Sunshine's body this morning.

He sighs. *"I do now. I checked the timestamps on the backs of these, and Mae would have been fifteen or sixteen. Thor knows about these now."*

He pauses and the feeling of dread running through me grows worse.

"We got something else delivered this morning. Thor and Phoenix know, but it will be brought up to the others in Church later tonight. He was going to ask Python and me to do a video conference, so Reaper's club knows what's going on as well."

After a few seconds, my phone vibrates again and my stomach twists.

The first picture is of a finger on top of bloody rags in a box. Even though I don't want to, I look closer at the finger. There's a tattoo around it.

"Smoke, did you see the tattoo?"

"Yeah, I did," he says quietly, though I can tell it's strained.

There's scrollwork around the name 'Jax' and the edges are hazy, almost like a ring of smoke.

"Was there another letter?"

"No, there wasn't. Ryder dusted the box and papers, but he didn't get any hits on the fingerprints. Other than partials of her bloody ones."

"I know you hate the woman, Smoke, but we got to get her out of there. They'll kill her if we don't."

"I know," he grits out. *"Problem is, they're in the wind. A few of the others drove over to Rixen earlier today, talked to the neighbors and the people at that diner Mae used to work at. No one's seen them since you guys did at the mall. The trailer was completely trashed with blood everywhere. I've got my systems running and if any of our cameras pick them up, I'll get a message. I already asked Python to do the same thing."*

"Fuck, this isn't good." I run my hand through my hair, frustrated that we'd lost them. How the fuck do I tell Mae that her mom is hurt and in danger? And that we don't know where the fuck they are?

"Can you get Thor on the line? I'm gonna get Reap."

"Yeah, give me a few."

I mute my phone and head to the door. Opening it, my gaze locks on Reap's and I nod toward Church. He gets up, but he's not alone. Python, Devil, Punisher and Odin follow him. Devil closes the door after everyone's inside, I unmute my phone and put it on speaker.

"*Timber,*" Thor's voice comes across the line, and I can tell he's pissed as fuck.

"*I've got Reaper, Devil, Python, Punisher, and Odin here.*"

"*Well, fuck. All my guys are here. You just want to do Church now?*"

"*Let me see how much time Lil' Bit and Ma have left preparing super. I'll let the others know we're meeting,*" Punisher says and leaves the room. Python hooks up his laptop and starts tapping away.

"*I've got the club gathered. Timber, go ahead and hang up. Smoke and Python are doing their thing.*"

I do as he says just as the door opens and the guys start filing in. I take a seat, my knee bouncing with anxiety.

"It'll be about forty minutes or so before the ladies are done," Punisher says as he takes a seat. Reaper gives him a chin lift, as do I.

The wall lights up and Smoke's face fills the screen. After a moment, the camera changes to where it's focused on Thor, but I can still see most of my brothers.

Thor fills everyone in on the first note Smoke got the other day and today's package. To say they're pissed he didn't bring it up the other day is an understatement.

"So far, there have been no hits with our cameras here in Junction Creek," Python says.

"Same here," Smoke says. "Last image I have is of three blacked out cars, similar to the ones that tried to run you all over yesterday, heading out of town. The plates all came back stolen. I'm tracking their cards as well as Lillian's accounts, but these guys mostly deal in cash, and I don't know how much they have on hand."

Everyone's silent for a few moments, absorbing what we just learned.

"Smoke, did you happen to find anything out about Mae's dead name?" I ask, remembering one of Lillian's journal entries.

"Yeah, but I'm still chasing down a few things. Preston did, in fact, launder money under Mae's 'dead' name since she was born. He stopped for a while, but about five years ago, he started it up again. I haven't touched anything yet because I didn't want to tip our hand since these fuckers are in the wind.

"However, I do have alerts set for if they do anything with the accounts. There are regular transactions made with five people, but the names are aliases, so I'm still working on that angle. However, whenever we want to pull the trigger, I'll transfer the money to a new account and freeze everything."

The camera changes and Smoke's face fills the screen again. "Timber, I also found something else out. Lillian's parents died when Mae was twelve and left a will. Everything they had was set to go to Mae when she turned twenty-one. There's a sizeable trust fund as well as the house they lived in, their vehicles, and two other cabins that's now in her name. My guess is that Mae doesn't know a damn thing about the will. I've contacted the lawyer and he wants to meet with her when you all are back here. He's based here in town."

"You think Preston was going to marry her off and gain control of her trust fund," I grit out. In my gut I know that's what he's doing. Fuck.

He nods, his face grim. "Yeah, I do. There's been no activity on it, and I've got alerts on it as well for if they try something."

The camera changes again and he pauses as he shuffles some papers. "I looked into Lillian's accounts too. It looks like she gets a couple grand a month from her parents' estate. She gets a disability check every month and up until Mae turned eighteen, she also got a welfare check. There are regular withdrawals each month that barely leave enough in the account to keep it open.

"However, there is a savings account that hasn't been touched in eleven years. And by that, I mean no withdrawals. There have been deposits each month, some from her parents' estate as well. Looks like Lillian also had some of her disability check sent into the account ever since she started getting it."

"If she started creating an 'oh shit' fund, she must have seen the writing on the wall and hoped she'd be able to find a way out. But since there's been no withdrawals, it seems she possibly ended up seeing no way out," Devil says through gritted teeth and the others agree.

We talk through possible scenarios and plans for about another twenty minutes before Thor gets everyone's attention.

"Might as well dismiss for now. Python and Smoke. Let Reaper and me know whenever you find anything out. Timber and Smoke. Let us know the instant you guys or Mae get another letter, package, text or phone call. We've got a hurt woman on our hands and if we can't find anything soon, she may end up dying by their hands. While I get some of you are pissed at what she's done, she doesn't appear to be behind selling her daughter off to Bruce, so we'll help get her free from the assholes and go from there."

Grunting, I get up. I need to set eyes on my woman.

While I'm pissed as fuck at Lillian for putting Mae in this predicament by not leaving Preston, I also get not having the courage or strength or means to leave their abuser.

I know from seeing it firsthand.

Growing up, my dad beat my mother on a regular basis and I often took a lot of his blows to protect my younger siblings. When I got older, I tried to keep him from hitting Mom and sometimes succeeded. However, one time, when I was fifteen, I wasn't so lucky. Neither was my younger brother, Blake. Dad beat us so badly that both Mom, Blake, and I had to be hospitalized. Thankfully, my sister, Olivia, only had a couple of bruises.

That's how my Uncle James and Aunt Sofia ended up with temporary custody of us. Mom was left paralyzed from his beatings, but mine and Blake's injuries healed, thankfully. Dad got forty years in prison for what he did to us. When Mom proved she couldn't take care of us, the temporary custody arrangement turned into permanent custody.

Even with what he did to all of us, Mom still goes to see him every week. He's got his hooks so deep in her that she'll never leave him. I've long since washed my hands of the situation but told her if she ever gets the guts to leave the bastard, then I'll help.

In the main room, my shoulders relax when I see Sunshine through the pass-through pulling something out of the oven.

Then the smell hits me.

Chapter 36

Mae

I BITE MY CHEEK to keep from smiling at Timber's shocked look as he stares at me through the pass-through kitchen window.

I made both my chicken and beef enchiladas tonight.

Mama Astrid's help was greatly appreciated as she helped me with figuring out how many batches I would need to make to feed everyone.

Which was a lot.

I learned a lot from her about planning meals this big and will make use of it whenever I help cook for everyone again.

As I'm setting the last pan of the beef enchiladas on the counter, I feel his arms wrap around my waist and I can't stop my smile this time. I love the feeling of his arms around me.

"You made me enchiladas."

Spinning in his arms, I slide off the oven mitts and wrap my arms around his neck. "Well, I made them for everyone, but yes, I made enchiladas. I remember you saying how much you loved them. I don't know how mine will compare to what you're used to from Susie, but hopefully you'll like them."

"If they taste half as good as they smell, I'm sure I will."

He bends down and the kiss he gives me curls my toes, but I reluctantly pull back and pat his shoulder.

"I gotta help Mama Astrid get the rest of the food out, Baby. Why don't you go out with the others? We'll be ready in a couple of minutes."

The pout he gives me is adorable and something I'm surprised to see on a biker's face. I laugh and swat playfully at his shoulder before reluctantly slipping out of his arms.

I help carry out the rest of the pans of enchiladas to the pass-through along with the Mexican rice, chips, small bowls of salsa for everyone, and a few topping options. Setting out the plates and silverware, I whistle to get the guys' attention.

"Dinner's ready. Come help yourself."

I can't help but giggle as they all rush toward the window, and I have to fight my blush when the guys repeatedly tell me how good it all smells.

Grabbing a flavored water out of the fridge that we picked up when we were in town, I head out to the main room. Surprisingly, the guys don't allow me to wait in line.

"Our rule is those that cook get to grab their food as soon as they step out of the kitchen," Beast says as he gently pushes me in front of him.

"Oh, well, thank you."

Grabbing a chicken enchilada, a little rice, chips, and a bowl of salsa, I make my way over to where Timber's sitting and dig into my meal.

About half-way through dinner, Smithy leans back in his chair and pats his stomach.

"That's it. We're not letting you go back, Lil' Bit. Timber's putting in a transfer and your ass is staying here."

I stare at him in shock and can't help but blush when the others all voice the same thing.

Timber wraps his arm around my shoulders, and I bury my face in his side, overwhelmed by the attention they're giving me. Never have I had so many people praise me for something.

"Okay, ease up, guys. Let's just see how everything plays out," Timber tells them.

Peeking out from Timber's side, the guys all seem a little uneasy about making me uncomfortable. Clearing my throat, I look up at Timber and then at the others sitting with us.

"Well, while I am here, and whenever I visit, I could take requests. We could start with lunch tomorrow and I'll draw a new idea for supper. Though, I'll need to make sure we have everything on hand to make it."

"Send the Prospects out to get whatever you need, Lil' Bit. I'll see if Mama Astrid has a jar that we can use for meal suggestions and put it out on the counter," Devil says as he takes another bite of his food.

Feeling a sense of purpose, and that I won't be sitting around twiddling my thumbs while we're here, I nod. I've always loved when I was able to take a cooking shift at Peggy's diner. Because face it, that was really the only time I was even *able* to cook in a real setting. There was no way I was spending that much time in the kitchen at our trailer with Preston nearby. Not that there would have been enough food in the trailer to cook with, that is.

Pulling out of Timber's arms, I sit up again and continue eating the last few bites as I think about the upcoming meals.

"Let's limit it to one suggestion per person for right now. I want to make sure everyone gets a chance to have their request and when the jar gets low, I'll let the guys know they can put in more ideas."

"What all are you familiar with cooking?" Cannon asks.

Putting down my fork, having just finished, I pause as I think back to everything that I've made over the years.

"A lot, actually. Every now and then, Peggy would switch up the menu to keep things from being the same all the time and she taught me how to make it all. Of course, she had your stereotypical diner food. Burgers. Biscuits and gravy. Eggs. Pancakes and waffles. Sandwiches. Panini. Omelets. Skillet dinners. Salads. Fruit salads. Homemade coleslaw. Steaks on a cast iron skillet. Things like that.

"However, her husband, Glen's family, has some Hispanic roots, so we also had some Mexican food. Quesadillas. Tacos. Burritos. Fajitas. Homemade guacamole. Pico de gallo. And of course, enchiladas. I'm sure there's more, but that's what I can think of off the top of my head for what she would rotate in and out. I also love to bake."

Refocusing on everyone, I see varying levels of shock and that almost everyone had stopped talking to listen to our conversation. And they're all staring at me.

I look around in confusion. "What?"

Timber's the one to break the stare off and squeezes my shoulder. "Sunshine, are you sure you want to run a daycare? Sounds like you could open up your own restaurant. And I can't wait to have more of your food, Baby."

"You learned all that from working at Peggy's diner?" Kai asks in disbelief.

I shrug. "Well, yeah. I started working there when I was fifteen, so it's been six years now. She made sure I knew how to take care of myself, which included how to cook, doing laundry, grocery shopping, handling a checking account. All of that stuff. Her husband, Glen, taught me how to do basic car maintenance and showed me a little self-defense."

"Definitely talk to Levi and see if you can invite them to the wedding, Sunshine. I want to thank them for everything they did for you," Timber whispers into my ear, and I nod, trying to blink away the tears that threaten to fall.

"Well fuck. I'll definitely be thanking them as well. Also, I want to head out to visit them and see this diner," Kai says. "In the meantime, I'm getting seconds."

He gets up from his seat and walks over to the pass-through. As he helps himself, others get up to get seconds as well.

"Hey, you okay, Sunshine?"

Turning toward him, I smile shyly. "Yeah, just a little overwhelmed. While I'm happy that I'll have something to do now so I'm contributing, I've never had anyone respond like this to my cooking. Ever."

Mama Astrid pats my shoulder as she passes us. "I can already tell we'll have lots of fun in the kitchen together while you're here and whenever you visit. This was divine and you can bet your ass I'll be pestering you to write these recipes down for me." She winks at me and goes to get more food. I don't know what parallel universe I've fallen into, but I'm never going back to how things were before.

Pushing back my chair, I go to get up myself when Timber stops me.

"What 'ya need, Sunshine? I'll get it for you since you were on your feet most of the afternoon."

Sitting back down, I hold up my salsa bowl. "I was gonna get more salsa and chips."

Smiling, he takes the bowl from me and a few minutes later; he sets a new one down along with a second bowl of salsa, a heaping bowl of chips, and another water.

I look up at him in surprise, but he just winks at me.

"Wasn't sure how much you wanted, Sunshine, but I can always get more if you want. Or finish off whatever you don't eat."

Squeezing his hand, I dig into my chips. I've always been a sucker for chips and salsa. And personally, I'm just happy I'm eating more in one sitting than I have been before.

A little over an hour later, I get up to use the restroom. After I'm done, I'm surprised to find Timber in the hall, leaning against the wall.

"Is everything okay, Baby?"

His face tightens and my stomach knots. "We should probably head back to the house for the night."

I look at him, confused by his change in mood. Just a moment ago, he was laughing and holding me as I sat on his lap on one of the couches. Plus, it's still fairly early. "Is something wrong?" My shoulders slump as another thought comes to mind. "Ugh, have the Johnson Chasers come out for the night?"

He grins but shakes his head. "Nah. Reaper told them to steer clear of the clubhouse for the night or to stick to their rooms. For those that stayed, Prospects took them some food." He pauses and sighs. "I take it you haven't looked at your phone in a while?"

Confused, I pull out my phone and my body tenses. My dad, er, Smoke called almost two hours ago.

Fiddlesticks.

"You can say that again, Sunshine. Come on, we should call him back."

Crud. I must have said that aloud. Again.

"I didn't even hear it ring or feel it vibrate earlier. It's been in my pocket since we got here."

"No worries, Sunshine. I told him you were cooking and had the radio on, so you probably didn't hear it."

Wait. "Is this tied to whatever you guys talked about in Church earlier?"

He grimaces, and the sinking feeling in my stomach gets worse.

"What happened? Is my mom okay?"

Instead of answering me, he pulls me close and kisses my temple. "Come on, Sunshine. I'll explain more at the house."

Numbly, I let him lead me out of the clubhouse, barely remembering to say goodnight to everyone. Judging by the grim and sympathetic looks on everyone's faces, they know what Timber's about to tell me.

And it's not good.

At the door, Mama Astrid pulls me aside, hugging me tight.

"Trust in your man, Dear. He'll help you through this. Whatever else is going on, know that we're all here for you. You can lean on us in your time of need, and later, you'll be there to help someone through their time of need."

Not trusting myself to talk, I nod and allow Timber to lead me the rest of the way out of the clubhouse.

I barely remember the walk to the townhouse we're staying in.

Unlocking the door, I see the bags we got earlier on the kitchen table, but I ignore them for now. Grabbing a bottle of water from the fridge, I head into the living room and sit on the couch, my back against the armrest. Liam stands in the doorway, looking hesitant and concerned.

"What happened, Liam? Is my mom okay?"

He opens his mouth and closes it a few times before sighing and sitting down on the couch facing me. He takes my hands in his.

"I don't know if I should tell you this, but I'm going to anyway. Smoke got a package delivered today."

I lick my lips nervously. "What was in the package?" Crap, even I can hear the wobble in my voice.

Liam's face falls before it hardens in anger. "A bloody finger."

I stumble to my feet, my body shaking. "It was Mom's, wasn't it?"

"We think so. There was a tattoo on it. Scrollwork, a smoky edge—"

"And inside that scrollwork was the name 'Jax'," I finish for him.

At his reluctant nod, I run my hands through my hair nervously as I pace. I know he probably doesn't need to know this, but I tell him anyway.

"My first memory of that tattoo was when I was around six or so. I asked her who Jax was. She just said it was someone from her past that she had hurt, but he would always have her heart. That was all she would say. Granted, I now know who it was about." I pause, wrapping my arms around my waist.

"When I was eight, I wanted to get Mom something for her birthday. Grandma helped me pick out a ring with a rose birthstone on it since her birthday is in October. She put it on immediately and never took it off. Though, I do remember her changing which finger she wore it on after meeting Preston again. Since he's been back in our lives, she wore my ring over her tattoo and never took it off. I've even seen her wear it in her sleep."

I swallow the lump in my throat as I raise my gaze to meet his. "He's punishing her because I left, isn't he?"

Liam gets up and wraps me in his arms. Laying my head against his chest, I exhale heavily. While I'm here, protected and having a fairly good time, my mom is being hurt because of my actions.

"Both Smoke and Python are trying to track them all down. They have alerts set that will notify them if any of them are spotted."

I swallow thickly, noting that he didn't refute what I said.

"Smoke also found out some other stuff that you should know about."

Lifting my head, I look up at him, confused.

"Let's sit down for this one."

He leads me over to the couch but lifts me onto his lap so I'm straddling him. "Did you know your grandparents, Lillian's parents, had a will?"

I shake my head. Wait. "Well, maybe. I know Mom got a little money each month from their estate. Though, the only reason I found out about that was because shortly after they both died, Preston started yelling at Mom about it. He said they should have got the full amount right away. I think my grandparents set it up that way because they knew Preston would blow through it faster than you could blink."

"You're right that her portion of it is small, but Baby, almost everything went to you. Their house, a couple of cabins, the cars, and a trust fund. I don't know how much is in the trust fund, but Smoke said it was pretty hefty."

Rubbing my temples, I groan as my body slumps. This is so confusing. Why is Preston so insistent on getting his hands on me? Is it just because he promised to sell me to someone? Or did he somehow find out that everything from my grandparents went to me? Is that why he's on such a tear to get to me?

Licking my lips, I sit up again, hoping Liam won't be mad that I didn't say anything at first.

"Um," I pause, nibbling on my lip.

"What is it, Sunshine?"

Taking a deep breath, I decide to just blurt it out. "I know the other two men that were with Preston in the mall."

Surprisingly, Liam just nods. "Smoke also recognized them, so he's tracking them."

Relief sags through me, and I close my eyes as I lean against Liam's shoulder. "Good. Both Phillip and Michael always gave me the creeps whenever they were around." Liam's body tenses underneath me and I sit up, looking at him in confusion. "What?"

Nerves coil inside me when I see him also looking at me in confusion. "Who's Michael, Baby?"

I frown. "He was one of the men at the mall. Phillip was to Preston's right, he's Preston's brother. Michael was to his left. And by that, I mean if you were in the same position Preston is in in that photo, Michael's on your left, Phillip his right."

This time, Liam frowns and he shifts me slightly, keeping one hand on my thigh, before digging his phone out of his pocket. He taps away and when he turns it toward me, it's the three of them at the mall.

I point him out. "That's Michael. Michael Sawyer."

Liam cocks his head and the next thing I know, he's calling someone and Smoke's voice comes through the line. My muscles tense and Liam starts rubbing his thumb across my thigh.

"*Timber.*"

"*Got you on speaker with Mae. Was filling her in on things when she brought something up. Can you look into a Michael Sawyer? The man you know as Bruce was introduced to Mae as Michael.*"

Seconds later, I can hear him clicking on a keyboard.

"Just so we know, what can you tell us about the man you know as Michael? Everything you can remember. I'm guessing Timber told you that the assholes are in the wind. What you know might help us in tracking them down."

I lick my lips nervously. *"Well, uh, are you sure you want to know everything, everything? It's uh,"* I pause as I clear my throat. *"It's not pretty, and it's kind of a long story."*

Liam's body tenses under me and a strangled noise comes over the phone from Smoke. While it seems like he's definitely calmed down, a small ray of hope blooms in my chest that this might be a step towards him accepting that I am his daughter. However, I refuse to call him my dad until he apologizes and starts showing that he really is sorry.

"With those assholes in the wind, we need any advantage we can get. Just, uh, don't freak out if you hear me putting my fist through a wall."

A tremble runs through me, and Liam gives my thigh a squeeze as he keeps rubbing his thumb over my jeans.

"If that happens, I'll patch it up when we're back in town. Go ahead, Sunshine."

Nodding, I take a deep breath, hoping that what I say won't change things.

Chapter 37
Timber

MAE'S BODY IS SO fucking tense that I wish I could hold her in both my arms, but I need to make sure Smoke can hear her. Her voice has barely been above a whisper during the entire phone call.

She opens her mouth to speak, but a knock at the door interrupts us.

"Hang on a minute, Smoke. Someone's at the door."

He grunts, and I pat Sunshine's thigh. She slips off my lap and I get up, walking to the front door. I bite back a groan when I see Odin and Punisher through the window. Then again, if Mae's going to go down memory lane, it would be helpful having them listen in on it so that someone in the Junction Creek club knows what's going on. Not to mention having their support as well.

Opening the door, I step aside so they can come in. My gaze snags on the black backpack Punisher's carrying. Crap, I forgot to grab that from Python earlier.

Both men give Mae a hug, but I don't miss their concerned looks over the top of her head when they realize how tense she is.

"You okay, Lil' Bit?" Punisher asks her.

She shakes her head. "Not really. Timber filled me in on a few things and we were just updating Smoke about some things. Just so you know, he's still on the phone." She pauses as she gestures to my phone in my hand. "You're welcome to stay. Since you're now family, you have a right to know as well."

She fidgets with the hem of her shirt as she shuffles on her feet. It's then that the full reality of how starved she's been for a family sinks in. I mean, I know she's told us before but seeing her so unsure of how Punisher and Odin will accept her strikes me down to my core. And by 'accept her', I mean accepting everything about her, including her past. *Fucking hell.* Smoke's done more damage to her than he realizes.

Odin pulls her in for another hug and kisses the top of her head. She melts in his arms, and I bet that if Smoke were seeing this, he'd really be kicking his own ass even harder than he already is.

"Of course we'll stay, Lil' Bit, but first, we got something for you." Odin pauses and looks at the phone in my hand.

"Smoke, how about we call you back in a minute? Stay by your computer," he says.

"You got it," Smoke replies before hanging up.

Punisher hands me the backpack and I turn to Mae. "Let me set this up and I'll explain your surprise."

She looks between the three of us, puzzled, but eventually she nods.

Walking past her, I unzip the bag and pull out the laptop. Looking over my shoulder, I grin when I notice the guys have her turned as they're talking to her, so she's not looking into the living room. Quickly I set it up, and since I don't know how charged it is or how long we'll talk, I plug it in for good measure. Clicking on the secure program Smoke developed for us, I ring him and make sure everything's good to go.

Miming him to stay quiet, since this is his surprise, I turn toward the others and clear my throat.

Mae turns around and her hands fly up to her face, covering her mouth in shock. Grinning, I walk over to her and hold out the backpack.

"I meant to give you this earlier, but it slipped my mind with everything that was going on. Smoke asked Python to get this laptop for you all set up. There's another surprise in here from Levi," I say as I pass her the backpack.

Hesitantly, she takes the bag and turns toward the laptop as the others sit down. Though I notice they make sure they're in range of the camera. Smoke chuckles at her shocked and confused expression.

"Wanted you to have something better for when you do your certifications or classes for your daycare. Timber told me about your other laptop and how you mentioned it runs slow and is loud."

Her cheeks turn pink, and she licks her lips. "T-thank you, you don't know how much that means to me. I got that one from a friend back in high school and cleared out the viruses she somehow picked up. I cleaned the fan and fixed a few connections, which helped. However, since I was saving my money to get us out of Preston's grasps, I chose not to spend money on replacing the necessary hardware. Instead, I used it only as much as I needed to so that it wouldn't be on for extended periods of time."

Smoke gives her a look I can't quite decipher.

She hesitantly looks in the backpack and pulls out a new kindle and cover. If I hadn't seen Levi, Sasha, and Roxy reading on them so much, I wouldn't know what the fuck it was or what it's for. Though, I bite my lip not to chuckle at her confusion as she looks it over. She looks fucking adorable.

"Um, what's this?"

"It's a kindle, and it's all set up for you with the premium subscription. According to Levi, you can read books for free or buy eBooks as well. Instead of always carrying around a few bulky paperbacks, this will store the eBooks you buy," Smoke tells her.

Her eyes bug out and judging by the way she's clutching the kindle to her chest, I have a feeling she'll be spending *lots* of time reading.

"You guys," she says, sniffling as she wipes her eyes. "You guys and the ladies really are all like fairy and biker godmothers and godfathers with everything you're doing for me and accepting me. Except for my grandparents, Peggy, and Glen, I've never had anyone care this much about me before."

Ignoring the dark look that passes over Smoke's face, I walk over to her and pull her into my arms. "This is the way you should have always been treated, Sunshine. And bet your pretty ass, if Smoke had known about you, you would have had a better life growing up."

"That's for damn fucking sure," Smoke growls.

Stepping back, she puts her kindle back into her backpack and sets it down on the coffee table. Rubbing her arms, she looks around before lowering her gaze to the ground.

"So," she starts and then pauses as she licks her lips before filling Odin and Punisher in on what she'd just told Smoke and me about Michael.

Taking a deep breath, she starts to pace.

"Before I tell you what I know about Michael or Bruce or whatever the donkey butt's name is, you need to know a few other things."

Tension fills the air when she visibly shudders. I want nothing more than to pull her into my arms to give her support, but I have a sneaky suspicion that it'll only make her feel trapped. My gaze goes to Smoke. I fucking hope he doesn't go ballistic because I have a pretty good feeling that whatever she's about to share; it isn't going to be good.

Chapter 38
Mae

"Timber, what I'm about to say will partially explain a question you had the day I came to the club. About why I tried to hide and blend in."

His face softens and then hardens, but I know it's not me he's mad at.

Taking a deep breath as I pace, I lower my gaze to the ground. A part of me still thinks that when they know *everything*, that they'll not want anything to do with me. My chest hurts at the thought, but I try to ignore it.

Here goes nothing.

"You all know Mom and Preston got married again when I was eight. When I was nine, Preston started his tricks and mind games with Mom, trying to break her in every possible way. It got worse in the months leading up to her accident.

"At the time, I didn't think he would turn physical, but I was wrong. It was my tenth birthday. And just so you know, this was about a month before her accident. Anyway, like she had done in years past, she got me a small birthday cake. Then we painted our hands and put our handprints on the side of the trailer. That was the first day Preston hit her. Well, that I was aware of, anyway. Even though she tried to hide what he'd done to her, she couldn't. She walked with a limp and hissed when she had to turn, bend down, or reach up to get something. We never celebrated my birthday since then. Or any other holiday, for that matter."

I force myself to ignore the growing tension in the room and keep my gaze down. If I look up, I'm afraid I'll break down.

"That was also when Preston started bringing sketchy people to the trailer. After the first time it happened, Mom told me to always hide in my room as much as possible when he had guests. Preston rarely went into my room at that point, and if he did, he just told me what he wanted me to do from the doorway. All he could see was my bed on the opposite wall, my nightstand, my desk, and part of my dresser. My closet was along the wall of my door, so he wasn't able to see into it. Though, even if he had seen the closet, he wouldn't have been able to see inside unless he physically opened it. I almost always kept the doors closed.

"One day, while Preston was gone, Mom closed off one corner in my closet with the same paneling as the closet walls. Then she tucked in a small refrigerator and put in some wire shelves above it. When the 'door' was closed, it looked like the jut out in the living room that houses the water heater and furnace. She always kept a few basics stocked in there for me, mostly water, bologna, and string cheese, so I wouldn't have to leave the room whenever Preston had guests over. There was never much in there, but enough to stave off most of my hunger. Especially since I had to ration it out."

Clearing my throat, I risk a glance up at Smoke on the laptop screen. He seems mostly in control, but I can tell by his eyes that he's beyond furious. Swallowing, I decide to add this next part just so he knows exactly how bad it was.

"That was how I mostly survived for the next couple of years. I barely had enough food and was always hungry. Eventually, the mice finally chewed through enough of the wires and I had to unplug it to avoid a fire. If it wasn't for starting to work at Peggy's diner shortly after my fifteenth birthday and the free school lunches, I probably would have starved. Preston made sure to eat almost all the food Mom would bring home. There was no longer a safe way for us to replace the fridge in my room without Preston noticing, so that option was out as well. Later, when it switched to me bringing home the food, he did the same thing and practically devoured everything of worth the same day."

Smoke's gaze turns murderous, but for the first time, I know it's not directed at me. Tearing my gaze from his, I take a deep breath, not wanting to continue, but knowing that I have to. As my thoughts turn to Michael, I can't stop the shudder that runs through me.

"I first met Michael a few months after Mom's accident and she was released from the hospital. I don't exactly remember when, just that it was almost Christmas." My voice hitches, and I push my memories of the edict of no more holiday celebrations out of my head. Shaking my head, I continue.

"Preston made Mom get me from my room so he could introduce his 'daughter' to Michael. The way Michael looked at me freaked me out big time, even back then. Mom quickly excused us and took me to my room. She told me I needed to keep away from him. That he wasn't a good man and that he'd hurt me just like he'd hurt her. It was then that her and Preston's recent fights came back to me. Mom saw who had hit her and caused her accident—Phillip and Michael. I don't know why they did it, but I wasn't going to ask. Unfortunately, Michael's creepiness only got worse with time.

"Since learning about me, Phillip and Michael would come around to our trailer almost every other week. Sometimes every week. Each time, I'd try to hide in my room as much as possible, even though I heard almost everything that happened during their 'visits'. I know Mom lured their attention from me countless times, but I wasn't always able to hide, though. The way Michael looked at me always gave me the creeps. X would sometimes be with them, but never more than once or twice a month. The way X looked at me was even creepier than the way Michael did."

Licking my lips, my mind freezes on X. "I don't remember if I ever described X when we were in Church earlier and I'm sorry." I pause as I bite my lip, trying to find a good comparison. "I'd say he's about a head or so shorter than Timber. Dark tan skin, maybe of Hispanic descent. Lots of tattoos and one of them is of a snake on his neck. Black goatee. Dark brown eyes. Bald. He's not overweight, but he does have a bit of a stomach. Every time I saw him, he was sharply dressed and always made sure you could see his gold Rolex. He liked to throw his weight around, so to speak, and brag about how easily he'd be able to crush Preston, Michael, and Phillip if they crossed him. They always called him 'X' and never by another name.

"The night I lied about my age, all three of them were at the trailer. X and Michael were the most adamant about making me help Mom pay for Preston's debt. Though Phillip said he also wanted a round with me. Michael grabbed me and said that he'd love to take me off Preston's hands. To take me up north to one of his cabins, away from prying eyes and ears to have his 'fun'.

"Then I was pulled from his arms into X's. He said he'd be the one to take me down to his plantation house in Louisiana, where I'd never want for anything. Then told me how his version of 'fun' would be like. When he said that, a bit of his southern accent slipped out. I'd noticed it before. Whenever he got really mad or tried to sweet talk someone, it'd slip out, but he tried to hide it the rest of the time. Fearing they'd steal me away or that they'd act on what they wanted to do to me, I lied about my age."

Another violent shudder runs through me at the memories, and I rub my arms as I pace.

"After that night, X made sure to come around more often. Usually, it was whenever Phillip and Michael came around. To try and avoid them, I hid a step ladder under our trailer so that I could climb into my room through the window whenever they were there.

"On the times I wasn't able to hide, Michael and X would always try to be close to me. Touching me in some way – brushing against my arm, touching my hair, things like that. As I got older, it only got worse. They'd," I pause as I clear my throat, keeping my gaze on the carpet. "They'd try to brush up against me when they walked by me. Not even them believing I was a minor stopped it.

"They usually tried to catch me in the hallway. Sometimes, they'd just push into me more so than they needed to as they passed me, especially if no one was looking. They'd cop a feel as they tried to sweet talk me into doing something intimate with them. Other times..." I pause, swallowing thickly before taking a shaky breath.

"Other times, when they were really wasted and I couldn't always stay hidden, like when I needed to use the bathroom, were the worst. They'd pin me to the hallway wall, face first, before rubbing themselves against me as they groped me. With the way I was pinned, and the fact that I was never strong due to lack of consistent food, I was never able to get them off me, no matter how much I fou ght.

"Mom always stopped it before they could take it too far, but sometimes, especially if the others pinned her down to stop her from getting to me, she wasn't always able to get to me right away. A few times, Michael and X had enough time that they came in their pants as they rubbed themselves against me from behind. They are the reason why I always tried to hide and blend in. I didn't want them to notice me. To touch me." A violent shudder runs through me, and I swear I can feel the ghost of their hands and bodies pressing against me, pushing me into the wall as memories wash over me.

"One night, about a month ago, it was particularly bad. Somehow, Michael was able to sneak into my room even though I kept my chair wedged under the doorknob, since I no longer had a lock. Preston had changed the doorknobs out years ago, with the exception of the bathroom doorknob, that is. That night, I woke up to Michael on top of me, my covers already tossed off me. He... He was trying to pin me down with one hand as the other ripped at my clothes. My elbow connected with his temple as I tried to get free, and it stunned him enough that I got one of my hands free of his. I grabbed the heavy glass lamp on my nightstand and started hitting him on the side of his head repeatedly. Eventually, he collapsed on top of me, knocked out. It was then that I realized he was naked. A second later, he was pulled off me and mom wrapped me up in her arms as I cried.

"Later, she dragged him out of my room and seconds later, I could hear her tearing into Preston to either keep his friends under control or they weren't allowed here anymore. That one of his friends just tried assaulting a minor and she'd call the cops on him if he or any of the others tried to do anything else with me. With the trailer being in her name, not his, that she'd kick him out and get a restraining order against him to protect me.

"She got a beating for talking to him like that in front of his friends, even though she told me they were all passed out drunk. However, her threat worked. No one tried touching me like that or pinning me to the wall since that night. Then again, knowing what I now know, I think they were just biding their time. Nevertheless, I was thankful that they all thought I was still a minor. If they knew I was almost twenty-one, I'm sure my fate would have been different.

"One night, about two or three weeks ago, they didn't know I was home. Mom's car hadn't wanted to start that morning, so I had to walk into town for work. When I got home, I saw all their cars there and could already hear them from outside the trailer. The sight had me grateful that her car hadn't started because otherwise, they would have heard me coming home.

"Instead of going in through the door, I walked around to my small window in my room and used the step ladder to crawl in that way. Though I wish I would have just asked Peggy to crash at her house.

"I could tell by their voices that they were all drunk and judging from Mom's cries, they were taking their payment from her again. X kept calling Mom a 'puta' and that he could do whatever he wanted with her because he owned her. That soon, he'd be taking his payment out on me, too. Him and Michael. They'd take care of Mom once they had me."

Swallowing thickly, I look up at Timber, then Kai, Ragnar, and finally Smoke.

"I think that was what Mom talked about in her journal. That that was the night Preston agreed to sell me."

Licking my lips, I continue. "After that night, they came around daily, but not just to the trailer. Sometimes they'd show up at Peggy's diner or at the grocery store. Thankfully, it was only in the evenings since they thought I was still going to school. I bet if we talk to Peggy, we'd be able to look at her security footage. They put it in three years ago after someone broke the window, trying to rob the place. Then, you'd have a picture to go off of for X rather than just my description."

My body sags when I'm finally done. My mind and my body numb from reliving all those memories. The ghosts of their hands rubbing against me return as the memories refuse to be boxed away in my mind.

Timber, taking that as the cue that it is, snags my hand and pulls me down onto his lap and wraps his arms around me. His touch helps cut through the fog.

After a few moments, someone clears their throat and I look up.

"Thank you, Mae. That gives us more info than we previously had. Can you reach out to Peggy for that picture?" Smoke asks.

"Yeah, but I know she's already in bed since she always opens the diner. Can I ask her in the morning?"

"Of course. Also, Levi wanted me to ask you to invite them this weekend to the wedding. I know I'm not the only one that wants to thank them for what they've done for you."

Tears prick my eyes, so I just nod, not trusting my voice right now.

No one talks for a bit and I just lean against Liam, soaking in his warmth.

I don't know how much time passes when Smoke clears his throat again. My gaze goes back to the laptop, only to find him staring directly at me.

"Can I, can you guys give me a few minutes? I'd like to talk to my daughter."

My breath hitches and I freeze. Did he really just say that? Or am I imagining it?

Timber's arms tighten around me and he kisses my temple before brushing my hair off my shoulder and placing a kiss on the spot where my neck meets my shoulder.

"I'll be in the kitchen if you need me, Sunshine," he whispers into my ear and I nod, refusing to look away from the screen. I'm afraid that if I blink, this will all just be a dream.

He lifts me off his lap and sets me down on the couch. Vaguely, I'm aware of him, Kai, and Ragnar leaving the room, but still I don't look away from Smoke. My dad.

He takes a deep breath and scrubs a hand over his face.

"Mae... I... Fuck. I'm not good at this sort of thing, but I'm fucking sorry about everything I said and did. I can't even begin to say how fucking sorry I am."

Licking my dry lips, I debate not asking my question, but I also need to know. "Why did you say and do those things?"

He hangs his head as he sighs loudly. "I got a letter slipped under my door during Levi's baby shower and I seriously thought it was you at first because of the message."

"What was the message?"

Smoke sighs and before he can even say anything, Liam's at my side, handing me his phone.

My blood boils at the message. Guessing there's more to this than just a picture of the note, I flip to the next picture.

Bile rises in my throat as I flip through all the pictures. Going off memory, I think these were taken a few years after the other set I'd seen in Church. I inhale sharply when I get to the image of Mom's finger. God, I hope she's all right.

"I know now that you aren't the one in the picture, and I'm sorry. I can't even begin to say how sorry I am, Mae, and I'll grovel for as long as I need to. Just... Please don't cut me out of your life. Not when you just came back into mine. I know I royally fucked up, I get that, but even if you can never forgive me, please don't cut me out. I can't lose you again. I wouldn't survive losing you again."

I can hear in his voice how torn up he is about everything and that he truly is sorry. Tears prick my eyes and suddenly, all my emotions come crashing down on me at once.

Burying my head in my hands, fat tears roll down my cheeks, my mind whirling with all the changes over these past few days.

About my anxiety over how my dad has treated me and two days later, is now apologizing. Really apologizing and not placating me.

About finding Liam when I figured no one would ever want me.

About the overwhelming feelings of being accepted by not only one club but two clubs and finding out two men have claimed me as their sister.

However, those things pale in comparison to the two things that are really overwhelming me.

One being my anxiety over what Preston, Phillip, X, and Bruce, or Michael, whatever his name is, have planned for me.

The other is that my mom is hurting somewhere and not knowing what they'll do to her next.

And it's all because of me.

Chapter 39
Timber

AFTER SEEING ODIN AND Punisher out, I stay out of sight, but close enough that I was able to hear what was going on in case Mae needed me. That's how I knew to step in with my phone to let Mae see what Smoke was talking about.

But hearing her gut-wrenching cries strikes me down to my core and I know everything that's happened over the past few days has finally come to a head.

The sound Smoke makes over the laptop at hearing her cry has my chest tightening even further. He knows he's fucked up, but at least he's trying to make amends. Walking over to the laptop, I tilt it away from her so he can only see me.

"How about we talk later? I think everything just came to a head and she needs to process it all."

He clears his throat. "Okay. I'm here if either of you needs me and I'd like to talk to her sometime, whether it's on the phone or text."

"I'll let her know," I reply before disconnecting. Closing the laptop, I pick her up, wrap both arms around Sunshine and hold her as she cries.

After a few minutes, her breathing evens out and I know she's fallen asleep, but I keep holding her for a while longer. One, I love having her in my arms, and two, I don't want to move her right away in case she wakes up again. I have a feeling the last two nights were the only nights since she was eight that she's been able to sleep peacefully from what it sounds like after hearing more details from growing u p.

After twenty minutes, I get up and carry her up to our room. Pulling back the blankets, I lay her down.

Her shirt looks comfortable enough, but I'm not letting her sleep in jeans. Unlacing her boots, I carefully slip them off. Then I slowly slide off her jeans, which takes more work than I realized with them being what I've heard the ladies back at my club call 'skinny jeans'. Even though I jostle her a couple of times, Mae sleeps right through it.

Stripping out of my clothes, I get ready for bed and slip under the covers. Pulling Mae close to me, a little sigh escapes her as she snuggles up next to me. I don't know what I did to get lucky enough to have found Mae, but there's no way in hell I'm gonna question it. Kissing the top of her head, I close my eyes.

The sound of running water wakes me, and I pat around, but find the sheets cold where Mae should be. Looking over at the clock, I groan when the numbers 5 am glare back at me.

Then I hear crying.

Panic runs through me as I throw the blankets off, rush into the bathroom, and rip open the shower door.

There, sitting on the shower floor, is my Sunshine, practically rubbing her skin raw with a luffa.

Not saying a word, I shut the shower door and pick her up, still in my boxers. Sitting down on the bench, I sit her down so she's straddling my legs and take the luffa from her hands.

Her head falls forward on my chest, and she clings to my shoulders as she cries.

When her tears finally stop, she shakes her head, buries her face in her hands, and folds in on herself. "Sorry." Her voice is so soft, I barely hear it above the sound of the shower.

Placing a finger under her chin, I force her to look up at me.

"You have nothing to be sorry about, but I need to know why you were practically scrubbing your skin off."

She pales. Her eyes close and she shakes her head as she tries to get off my lap.

That's not happening.

Releasing her chin, I grip both of her thighs and pull her close to me.

She startles when she feels me hard under her, and her gaze snaps to mine.

"That's not something I can control, Sunshine. I'm trying to ignore the fact that you're naked on my lap, but I am a man. Now, what's going through your head?"

Once again she looks away, shame evident on her face as she wraps her arms around her waist, folding in on herself.

Gently, I grasp her chin and make her look at me. Cocking an eyebrow, her eyes turn misty.

"I could feel their hands on me," she whispers.

Rage flows through me that these fuckers are still hurting her, even when they're not around. Taking a deep breath, I tamp down my anger. It won't do her any good to see that side of me right now.

"Sunshine, if you ever feel like this again, you come to me. I won't have my woman suffering in silence. You give me that weight to bear. You got it?"

Command rings through my voice. Her eyes widen, but I don't miss the way her body responds to my command, either.

A shiver runs through her as her pupils dilate and her nipples pebble. Her skin breaks out in goosebumps despite the warm water. A beautiful, rosy flush rises in her cheeks, going down her slender neck and spreading over her chest.

She licks her lips. "Yes, Liam."

Another time, I'll explore this new aspect, but not right now.

Grabbing hold of her thighs, I stand and lower her feet to the ground.

Turning her so that the water hits her hair, I make sure it's wet before grabbing her shampoo and gently massaging it in. Sunshine's hands come up to my chest as she closes her eyes. While I'd love to have her hands elsewhere, this isn't about me, it's about her.

As I'm washing Sunshine's hair, I'm surprised when I hear her moan. It's then that my sister's words come back to me about how most women love having their hair washed and someone massaging their scalp in the process. When she moans again, I'm guessing Sunshine falls into that category.

I have to bite my lip to keep my mind and hands on task. Her moans and beautiful body have me hard as a rod right now.

Rinsing her hair, I repeat the process with her conditioner and rinse it out as well. I eye her luffa but decide against using it. I bet her skin is probably sensitive after she scrubbed it raw.

Squirting a generous amount of soap into my hands, I start washing her body. Almost immediately, I wish I had grabbed the luffa instead.

Her eyes turn hooded as I run my hands over her body, and her breaths start coming in little pants. Kneeling, I run my hands over one of her legs, raising it slightly to wash her foot. The action puts me right at eye level with her pussy. She's drenched, and I don't mean from the water.

When I put her leg down, a whimper escapes her and I repeat the process with her other leg, purposefully avoiding her pussy.

Standing, my hands run up her torso, only briefly running them over her breasts, which pulls another whimper from her. Turning her, I let the water rinse the soap from her body.

Her head falls back against my chest. A few moments later, she turns, pressing herself against me as she wraps her arms around my neck.

"You have ten seconds to strip, Liam, before I take matters into my own hands. I need you."

Groaning, I lean down, resting my forehead on hers. "Sunshine, are you sure? I wasn't doing all of that to have sex with you. I was trying to chase away the feeling of their hands on you."

She kisses my chest as her eyes soften. "I know, and I love you even more for doing that, but I need you, Liam."

Her hands go to the waistband of my boxers and after hesitating for a few moments to see if I'll stop her, which I don't, she kneels as she pulls them down my legs. Stepping out of them, her hands wrap around my cock.

Moaning, I look down at her and another moan escapes me at seeing her staring up at me as she takes me in her mouth. Fuck, her mouth is hot as she takes me as far as she's able to.

One of her hands snakes down and cups my balls. My hips thrust forward and I feel like shit when I hear her gag. "Sorry, Sunshine. Tap my leg if I do something you don't like."

She shakes her head slightly as she smacks my thigh. I bite back a groan when my dick falls from her mouth. "I liked it, Liam. If you haven't noticed yet, I love putting my mouth on you."

With that, she grips me harder and I moan when she wraps her lips around me again.

Grabbing her hair, so it's out of her face, I thrust slightly. "Is this what you like, Sunshine? What you want? Me fucking your face?"

Her eyes widen with lust and she nods as much as she's able to. She shifts, gripping my thigh with one hand as she opens her legs wider. As I hold her head in place, I thrust into her hot mouth, groaning when she starts teasing her clit with her other hand.

"That's it, Baby. Rub that clit. Make yourself come as I fuck your pretty face."

She moans and, surprisingly, the vibrations damn near push me over the edge. I squeeze the base of my cock, not wanting to come yet.

I thrust a little deeper than I had been going down her throat when she does something I didn't think she'd do.

She swallows.

"Oh fuck," I grunt, as most of my control snaps and I can't help but thrust faster down her throat.

Seconds later, she moans as she writhes. Seeing her come undone, coupled with the vibrations from her moans, has me shooting my cum down her throat.

Even though I just came, I'm still rock hard. With a growl, I pick her up, sit her down on the bench and dive in, running my tongue through her folds, tasting her release.

"Put your legs on my shoulders, Sunshine."

She shakes her head as she tries to push me away. "I'm too sensitive."

"You're going to give me one more before you get my cock, Sunshine." Licking from clit to ass, she's soon grinding herself against my face. After a few passes, I latch onto her clit, sucking, and she cries out again.

Spearing my tongue into her, I press on her star and her eyes fly open as her jaw drops in surprise. She moans and my cock jumps in response. Pumping two fingers into her pussy, I apply more pressure to her ass.

"Not now, but someday I'm going to take you back here, Sunshine. Do you think you'll like that? Me fucking this gorgeous ass?"

She nods, her mouth forming that perfect little 'O' as I apply even more pressure. Pressing the tip of my thumb into her ass, I turn my fingers in her pussy, rubbing over that little bundle of nerves as I latch onto her clit.

"Liam!" Her body bows as she cries out, her hands pulling on my hair as her orgasm rips through her.

I lick up her release, prolonging her orgasm.

Picking her up, I stand and sit on the bench with her straddling me.

"Ride me, gorgeous."

Lowering her onto me, her jaw drops open and her gaze locks on mine. "I love how you feel inside me," she moans.

My chest warms. Gripping the back of her neck, I pull her toward me, crashing my lips down on hers. Her arms wrap around my neck and her fingers run through my hair as she starts riding me. Shifting slightly, I pause when she pulls back from the kiss.

"Oh, fuck. Right there." She rides me faster, chasing her orgasm, her nails digging into my shoulders and arms.

My control snaps at getting her to lose enough control to cuss. Gripping her hips, I thrust up even harder.

"Yes, yes, yes!"

Her hands land on my shoulders again and she meets my thrusts with her own. Her perfect titties are bouncing from our movement and I raise slightly, capturing one of her nipples in my mouth as I continue thrusting in her.

"Yes, Liam. More," she pants, bowing her back and pushing her breast against me. I gently bite down and tease the nipple with my tongue. "More, harder."

Fuck. Watching her closely, I bite down again on the underside of her breast and she cries out, her pussy clamping down on me like a vice. Fuck, this woman is perfect for me.

Pulling out, she whimpers until I lay her down on the bench and bury myself in her pussy in one motion, causing her to cry out again.

I smack her ass and I can feel the walls of her pussy flutter around me. "You like it rough, Sunshine?"

She moans as she nods her head. "Yes, and I love it when you talk dirty."

Smacking her ass again, I grip her hips, raising them slightly as I piston in her, the last of my control snapping. I take her like a madman.

Leaning forward, I capture her other breast in my mouth and give it the same treatment, biting down periodically and then soothing the bites with my tongue.

"Fuck yes, Liam!" she cries out as she comes again, taking me with her.

Panting, I lean forward, kissing her. "You're fucking perfect."

She hums. "And you're perfect for me."

Her breathy voice and 'fuck me' eyes practically have me hard again, but she needs to rest. This was the hardest I've taken her.

"Are you sore? I didn't hurt you?" Fuck, please don't say I took it too far.

She shakes her head. "You didn't hurt me. I loved it. I may be a little sore for a bit, but it was worth it." She pulls me down and kisses me again.

Groaning, I pull back. "Need to get clean before I take you again, Baby."

She gives me a saucy grin as she raises her hips. "I'm up for more."

Groaning, I reluctantly pull out and even though she tries to hide it, I hear her slight hiss.

"And that right there is why I'm not taking you again, Sunshine, even though I want to. Bet your ass I'll be taking you again later. That's a promise, Baby."

She pouts and I can't help but chuckle.

Giving her another quick kiss, I help her to her feet and she lathers up again. The little minx teases me, rubbing her hands all over her body, and I groan.

Swatting her ass, I grab her wrists and hold them above her head against the wall. She moans, and I grit my teeth.

"Sunshine, I'm trying to be a gentleman here. I just took you hard. Harder than I have so far. I don't want to hurt you by taking you before your perfect pussy's had some time to rest."

She squirms and I groan when I see her trying to rub her legs together.

"Does my Sunshine Goddess need to come?"

She whimpers, closing her eyes as she nods. I smack her pussy lightly and her eyes open immediately.

"Eyes on me, Sunshine. Tell me what you need."

Another whimper escapes her as a shudder runs through her.

"I need to come, Liam."

"Good girl." This time, an even more violent shudder runs through her. Seems my woman may have a praise kink as well. Slowly, my finger circles her clit. Trailing kisses up and down her neck, I step into her side, letting her feel my hardness against her as I slowly rub my length against her.

"Later tonight, I'll have to make sure to thoroughly worship this pussy, wringing orgasms out of you until your entire body is limp." I pause, slipping two fingers into her pussy, and I cup it. "Then and only then will I take this pussy again. My pussy."

Her body jerks when I hit that little bundle of nerves again as I swirl my thumb around her clit.

"Tell me whose pussy this is."

She whimpers. "Your pussy, Liam. Only yours."

"Good girl," I whisper in her ear and she moans.

Trailing kisses down her neck, I bite down on her shoulder where I've already marked her with a hickey. I move my fingers and my hips against her faster.

"Your good girl," she replies, her voice heavy with need. "But your good girl also has a dirty side."

A jolt runs through me as my mind wanders to all of the things I want to try with her, and I bite down harder on her shoulder. Those thoughts have me coming, shooting ropes of cum against her side right as she cries out her own orgasm.

Her body sags slightly, her eyes drunk on her post orgasm high.

"Let's get clean and then we can rest for a bit longer. It's still early."

She mumbles an agreement, and both of us are clean and dry minutes later.

Skipping clothes altogether, I pick her up bridal style, carrying her into the bedroom. Her head rests on my shoulder as her fingers trace along the tattoos on my chest.

Chapter 40
Mae

GNAWING ON MY LIP, I try to figure out how exactly I should phrase my question to Liam.

He lays me down in bed before sliding in himself, covering us, and pulling me close to him. Rolling to face him, my fingers continue tracing the tattoos on his chest.

"I can hear your brain going a mile a minute, Sunshine. Talk to me, Babe," he says, his voice huskier than usual. He reaches over and gently releases my lip from between my teeth and I hesitantly look up at him.

"Um... do you..."

He chuckles and my cheeks heat from frustration at my awkwardness.

"Just spit it out, Sunshine."

Taking a deep breath, I decide to do just that. "How do you feel about kids?"

Liam stares at me for so long, a pit starts to form in my stomach.

Then he smiles.

"With you, I'd love to have as many as you want to carry." He rolls us so I'm on my back and he's on his side. Then he leans down and kisses my stomach. "I'm betting you just now realized I haven't used a condom at all while taking you?"

Nodding, I nibble my lip, hardly believing that this is real. His grin widens and he kisses my stomach again.

"That's because, when I saw you at the competition with Jordan and Sadie sitting on your lap, I wanted it to be our children sitting on your lap. Your belly round with my baby as you talked with them, played with them, cooked with them, whatever. You want enough kids to have a football team? I'll add on to the house. I'd definitely prefer to have at least two so that they aren't an only child, but it's ultimately up to you since you have to carry and birth them. How many kids do you want, Sunshine?"

Tears fill my eyes, and I pull him up to me, kissing him.

Pulling back, he cups my cheek as he dries my tears.

"I want as many as I can safely carry with you. I hated being an only child and dreamed of having a large family someday. It's just... I never thought I'd find someone that would want me for me before. Especially with my background and baggage, both emotional and mental."

Fresh tears roll down my cheeks as I lay out my biggest fears to the man I love. His calloused hands dry them before he kisses me softly, yet passionately.

He pulls back, his gaze never breaking from mine. "I don't ever want to go a day without you, Sunshine. You are my heart. My Sunshine Goddess. My Old Lady. I love you and someday, I'm putting a ring on this finger. And hopefully, someday soon, putting a baby in your womb. I want it all with you and no one else."

"I want that too, and only with you. But just so you know, I'm not on anything, so there's a chance I could already be pregnant."

His smile lights up his face and then his lips find mine as he kisses me slowly. Desire curls in my belly, which I'm surprised by since I lost track of how many orgasms Liam's already given me. I can't stop my moan when I feel him hardening against me.

Liam rolls on top of me, and a whimper escapes as I try to wiggle into just the right spot for him to slide into me. I can already feel my thighs slick with my desire.

We both moan when he finally slides into me, taking me slow as he continues to devour my mouth. His strong arms cage me in as his hands slide through my hair.

This is unlike any other time that we've been together. It's slow, it's sensual, and holy mother of all goodness, I swear I can feel how much he loves me with each stroke into me as well as with each kiss.

My orgasm comes out of nowhere and he swallows my cries as my body clamps down around him.

As soon as my orgasm fades, I can feel another one building. He kisses up and down my neck, nibbling, licking, and sucking on my skin. I cry out when his teeth clamp down on my shoulder, my orgasm so close, but it's like he's keeping me right on that edge.

"What does my good girl want?" he whispers into my ear before nibbling on my earlobe.

A shudder runs through me at being called his good girl and I moan when he cants his hips, his pelvic bone rubbing against my clit.

"You, just you."

He hums and kisses my neck right below my ear.

"I wonder how adventurous my good girl is? How dirty you like it? Would you let me tie you up? Put clamps on your pretty tits? Take this ass? Or maybe I'll blindfold you, tie you up, wring orgasms out of you before I fill all three of your holes. Would you like that, Mae? Be my dirty good girl?"

He chuckles slightly and it's only then that I realize I'm nodding my head enthusiastically.

"Say it, Mae."

I whimper as I feel myself reaching even closer to my orgasm as all the images he painted swirl around my mind.

"I'm your dirty good girl, Sir. I want that. Please," I plead as I desperately match his thrusts, needing to come. A shiver runs through him and I wonder if it's because I called him "Sir".

"Does my good girl need to come?"

"Yes, please, Sir. I need to come."

He changes the angle of his hips slightly and my eyes roll back in my head at the pleasure he's bringing me.

"Come for me, my Sunshine Goddess. Now," he commands.

My body obeys him, and I swear I see stars. A scream rips through the room and it takes a bit to realize that it's coming from me. My orgasm triggers Liam's, and he roars as he pumps me full of his cum.

He kisses me as we both just lay there as our orgasms subside, holding each other.

My eyelids droop and I feel sleep creeping in on me. Liam pulls out of me and I whimper at the loss of him inside me. He chuckles and kisses me again.

"Be right back, Sunshine."

Nodding, I close my eyes.

Faintly, I'm aware of him cleaning me up and then crawling back into bed. He pulls me close to him, resting my head on his shoulder.

"Love you, Sunshine."

I hum and snuggle closer to him. "Love you too, Liam."

The faint rustle of blankets is the last thing I remember before sleep claims me.

My pillow moves, and I groan, not wanting to wake up. A chuckle reaches my ear and I feel the vibrations of it on my cheek. It's then that I realize I'm not laying on my pillow at all. I'm still laying on Liam.

"Sorry, Sunshine, but we need to get up. It's already eight o'clock."

I bolt upright. Normally I never sleep in this late, and then it comes back to me why.

My nightmares.

Scrubbing my skin almost raw.

Liam chasing away the ghost of their hands on me.

Multiple rounds of him making love to me.

"I've got to say, I love how disheveled you look when you wake up after being completely sexed up."

Confused, I turn to him to see him staring at me with a goofy smile on his face. He reaches his hand out and runs it through my hair. I do the same and groan when I feel how tangled it is. I never combed it out after our shower, and now it's a rat's nest.

He chuckles again and I playfully smack his chest before gingerly scooting off the bed. I'm deliciously sore, and would love a bath, but I need to get ready.

Hopefully Mama Astrid won't be mad that I wasn't there to help her cook breakfast.

"Laugh all you want, but this is going to be a pain, *literally*, to get untangled. I always have to comb it before bed, even if I don't wash it, to help prevent tangles. Ideally, I would have done a loose braid, but I got kind of distracted by my sexy hunk of an Old Man," I say with a wink as I walk past him to the bathroom, not bothering with clothes since I'm going to shower again.

I shriek as his arm clamps around my waist and he picks me up, throwing me over his shoulder, and smacks my ass. Despite how sore I am, I can feel myself getting wet at the action.

"If my memory serves, you liked my particular brand of distraction," he says as he smacks my ass again.

I'm not sure what comes over me, but I reach down and smack his delicious bubble butt in return. "Darn straight I do, Baby, but you need to stop smacking my tush. My poor honey pot needs a rest, and if you keep doing that, it won't be getting the rest it needs, so we can do some of the stuff you talked about later tonight."

He sets me down on my feet so fast, I get a little dizzy at the change. The next second, he has me pinned against the wall as he devours my mouth in a bruising kiss.

"It's a promise, Sunshine. Though, I'm pretty sure I'll be hard as a rod all day thinking about what I want to do to you," he says before kissing me again.

We're both breathless when he pulls away, and I bite my lip when I see how hard he is. Licking my lips, I wonder if he'd mind if I went down on his love stick.

Laughter rings throughout the room, and I blink, looking at him in confusion.

"Oh, fuck, Sunshine," he wheezes in between bouts of laughter. My cheeks heat and I wonder if I said that out loud without realizing it.

He pulls me close to him again, and the heat in his eyes makes my knees weak.

"I will always accept you, as you phrased it, going down on my love stick."

My cheeks heat even further, but still I tug his arm, making him follow me into the shower.

An hour later, and another mind blowing orgasm as I made myself come as I took Liam in my mouth, I'm finally ready. Looking down at my arms, I bite my lip. Thankfully I didn't scrub my arms bad enough to bleed, but they are raw and still a little red.

For a second, I contemplate changing into a long-sleeve shirt, but shake my head. I can't keep letting them win.

Locking up the house, we walk toward the clubhouse hand in hand when a commotion nearby draws our attention.

Two angry male voices reach my ears and what I hear makes my hands start to shake. A pit forms in my stomach as a feeling of dread washes over me.

"How could you? How could you dishonor her memory by replacing her, you jackass?" a man, who looks a few years older than me says as he gets up into Kai's face. I'm guessing they are related, as their faces look a lot alike, and he also wears his blond hair in the same Viking braids that Kai and his parents do. Only the mystery man's braids go a bit below his shoulders.

"I'm not fucking replacing her! You'd see that if you'd fucking calm down and just talk to her. While yes, she has some personality traits that are similar to Frida's, she's her own person," Kai says in a deadly, calm voice that sends chills down my spine. My brain barely registers that even though Kai says the words, he also signs them.

Neither man backs down, and I seriously think they're going to come to blows.

My gaze bounces around and I notice that the entire club is out here, but thankfully, the Johnson Chasers aren't. Then again, they're probably sleeping everything off after what they do each night for the single guys.

A roar brings my attention back to Kai and the other man as they start fighting. Though I am surprised that Kai doesn't throw a single punch. A couple of punches land, but I have the sneaky suspicion that Kai let them land.

A strong arm bands around my waist, and my throat feels raw. It's then that I realize the other voice that's screaming is mine, as he holds me back from running toward them.

"Stop! Please, stop!"

Both men surprisingly stop, but not before mystery man lands a sucker punch to Kai's jaw. They both turn and stare at me as I wonder what I've torn apart by accepting Kai's declaration of him adopting me as his sister.

Why is it that everything I touch and every relationship I have seems to dissolve before my eyes?

Another pit forms in my stomach as I wonder how long Liam will stick around when my past finally catches up to us. Is our love strong enough to withstand it?

Chapter 41
Punisher

I KNEW WHEN ERIK found out I'd adopted Mae as our sister that he was going to blow a gasket. That's why I didn't tell him on the phone when we talked. I wanted to do it face to face. It's just, I thought I had another week to figure out *how* to tell him that. Instead, he cuts his trip short and the first thing he does when he sees me is sucker punches me. Somehow, he'd found out about me adopting Mae into our family and was fucking pissed.

I let a few of his punches land, but we both know that's all I'll let slide. Even if I don't throw a punch in return.

A gut wrenching scream rips my attention away from my brother and my chest tightens when I see Lil' Bit struggling to get out of Timber's iron grip. Tears streak down her face as she continues to scream for us to stop.

My distraction earns me a punch to my jaw that has black dots swirling around my vision.

"Stop! Please, stop!," she begs.

Seconds later, a familiar voice rings through the air. "Enough!" Pops roars.

He stalks up to us, leveling a dark glare at Erik.

"No one is being replaced, my son. Our family grew when your brother decided to adopt Mae into our family. The woman who is hell bent on getting between you two when you let your emotions cloud your mind and attacked your brother."

Erik looks around before his gaze settles on Lil' Bit, who's still struggling to get out of Timber's grasp, tears still streaking down her face. He's talking quietly in her ear, but I'm not sure if she's actually hearing him.

Surprisingly, a strangled noise escapes Erik and I wonder if he's feeling the same pull to her that I did. While yes, she's fucking gorgeous, I don't look at her that way. From the first moment I saw her, I felt a pull to her.

A pull to be a friend.

A brother.

A protector.

I adopted her because I got the sense that she was alone in the world, aside from Timber, and needed a family. A pull that strengthened when Smoke started pulling all his shit.

I didn't adopt her as my sister to replace Frida, Erik's twin sister who died a few years ago at the hands of her abusive boyfriend.

Despite my rough exterior and the fact that I'm the Enforcer for our club, only a few have seen the real me.

Namely, my family.

The second my gaze locked with Mae's at the competition, and later after talking to her, I knew she'd seen through my walls and saw me. The real me. And the pain and heartbreak I saw in her pulled on my protectiveness. Big time.

Yes, a part of me wants to save Mae from her asshole stepfather and the man, or possibly men, that want to buy her. The part of me that was always protective of my sister, but in the end, couldn't save her. But maybe I can help save Mae.

I know Frida's death is not my fault. She hid her pain well. Too well. None of us realized how bad it was until it was too late. To say that Erik, my dad, and I took out our vengeance on that prick tenfold is an understatement. But at least the asshole won't be hurting any other women anymore.

"Yes, I see you now understand why your brother adopted her. Mae, or Lil' Bit, as we've all affectionately come to call her, is not a replacement for Frida. Once you've sorted through your emotions, talk to her, get to know her, and you'll come to understand that, too," he says, clasping a giant hand on Erik's shoulder and then mine.

"I expect you to make amends," he pauses, his attention turning back to Erik. "If you cannot, then you will be civil when she is around, because whether you like it or not, she is family and she isn't going anywhere."

He clasps both of our cheeks, then turns, and walks toward Mae. Timber finally releases her and she rushes into Pop's arms, fresh tears rolling down her cheeks.

"I didn't want to tear apart your family. I'm sorry, I'm sorry, I'll—" she cries before he cuts her off and I know exactly what she was going to say next. I walk up to them and pull her into my arms, hugging her tight.

"Lil' Bit, look at me," I tell her as I pull back a little and wait for her to do so. She does, and the heartbreak I see in her eyes damn near brings me to my knees. "I knew Erik would struggle with this news and I was waiting to tell him when I saw him face to face. It's just, I thought I had a little more time to figure out how to tell him we have another sister."

"But I don't want to be the reason why your family becomes divided. That seems to be all I'm doing lately. Dividing families and clubs," she says, practically whispering that last part.

A roar sounds behind me and Mae's instantly pulled out of my arms and into Timber's arms. "You aren't the cause of division anywhere, Sunshine. Smoke's the cause of that clusterfuck, and he's trying to make amends. I know where your mind's going, and you need to get that shit out of your head. You hear me, Sunshine?"

She stares up at him, but eventually nods, burying her face in his shirt.

The niggling feeling that I'm missing something intensifies, and I turn back toward Erik. "How did you find out about Mae? I'd already asked the guys not to tell you, so I could tell you face to face."

He scowls at me, but it doesn't have the heat behind it like earlier. "I got a text message with some pictures. I thought it was from one of you guys, since the pictures were of you guys in your dealership and in the clubhouse."

"Let me see your phone," Reaper says as he steps up to us, Python at his side.

Even though Erik isn't officially part of the club, and that he doesn't actually have to listen to Reaper, he does. He's always looked up to Reaper.

Erik even had plans to join the club, but then the accident happened. He can still ride his motorcycle despite what happened, but he's yet to take the chance. I'm not sure what's holding him back, but someday, I'll find out.

Erik clears his throat and it brings me out of my thoughts. He unlocks his phone, brings up the text thread and hands the phone to Reaper.

I look over his shoulder as he reads it, my blood boiling at the message and the pictures.

> *I hate to be the bearer of bad news, but your precious sister's memory has been crushed to ashes and thrown out the window like trash. She's been replaced with a gold-digging, backstabbing whore. Even your parents love her as their own, taking her in and replacing their dead daughter.*

> *If you're not careful, you'll soon be pushed out as well. With your track record for the last year, I'm sure it won't be that difficult. They certainly do love Timber. Soon he'll be accepted into the family and you'll be a distant memory. Forgotten and squashed. Just. Like. Frida.*

> *With their combined poison, it shouldn't take too long for that to happen. Everything she touches burns as relationships get thrown to the curb with her now in the mix. She's better off being discarded into the hands of her true family. If you don't want her toxicity to ruin everything you hold dear, you'll take care of the poisonous rat and push her to the curb.*

Next, Reaper flicks through the pictures. Mae and me in Levi's living room, right after those assholes tried to run over my brothers a few days ago. Mae with me and my parents in the Junction Creek clubhouse. Of Mae and Ma in the kitchen. Mae with Timber and me at the dealership. Mae with my parents at the dealership and the grocery story.

The last one has my blood running cold.

It's of Frida's gravestone.

In pieces.

I know Mae didn't have anything to do with it. In fact, I'm not even sure she knew I had siblings. Even if she had known, I know she'd never do this to anyone.

I need to get there to see if it's truly in pieces.

A hand lands on my shoulder, followed by more, which brings me out of my thoughts. Looking up, my brothers surround me. Small arms encircle my waist as the owner buries her face in my back. I know without looking it's Lil' Bit. She doesn't know what's going on, but she's still comforting me.

"Stay here, we'll go check it out," Reaper says, and I narrow my eyes at him.

"I'm going. I need to see it. I need to—"

"Kai..."

I look over at my brother, surprised. He never calls me Kai anymore, except for moments when he's really hurting.

He swallows thickly, his face grave and my stomach drops.

"It's gone, Kai. I went there before I came here. Frida's tombstone... It's... It's in pieces... just like in the picture... I took a few pictures myself for proof."

A strangled sound reaches my ears, and when Lil' Bits arms tighten around me, I realize it came from me.

She steps around to the front of me, hugging me tighter. Not being able to resist it, my hands land on her waist as I lift her up and bury my head in the crook of her neck, my arms tightening around her waist, her feet dangling in the air. Her small arms encircle my neck.

Then she does something I wasn't expecting.

One of her arms untwines from around me and the next second, my brother's arms wrap around us and I know her other arm is wrapped around him.

Tears burn at the back of my eyes, but I don't let them fall.

Swallowing thickly, I swear I'll find the person or people responsible for this and they will regret defiling my sister's memory.

Chapter 42

Mae

MY HEART BREAKS AS I hold my brothers, their heads resting against mine as we all hold each other tightly. Tears continue to stream down my face, but I don't wipe them away.

I don't know what happened, but I know it's bad when Kai seemed near tears, even though I know he'd never let them fall. Then his face changed and I swear he wanted to go on a warpath. The look on his face combined with how muscular the man is made me think he looks like one of the Viking Gods of old.

It should scare me, but I know Kai would never hurt me.

Tightening my arms around their necks, I turn, kissing their temples. Both of them tighten their arms around me in return, and then they pull back slightly.

Turning toward the man I know now is Erik, I give him a sad smile. "I'm sorry this is how we're meeting for the first time. I truly never meant you any harm." Pausing, I turn toward Kai and giving him the stink eye as I scowl at him. "But you are so in trouble, buster, for never telling me you had siblings!" I say as I flick the tip of his nose.

He scowls at me, but there's no heat behind it. Erik's shoulders shake against me, and I can't keep my scowl in place any longer. A giggle soon escapes me.

"We also have a younger brother, Dominick, but he's spending time with our grandparents, Pops' parents, right now. He'll be at the wedding, though."

Nodding to Kai, I pull them forward until our foreheads are resting against each other's.

"Let's make a promise. When any of us have disagreements, don't let it come to blows. We talk. I can't handle seeing my brothers fighting like that. I don't want either of you hurt," I say quietly, and their arms tighten around me before they pull back and each kiss a temple.

"Promise, Lil' Bit."

"Promise."

Nodding, I hug them each again, and they lower me to the ground. Kai's rough hand drags across the worst section of my left arm, which is also the worst out of both my arms, and I can't contain my hiss of pain.

Worry instantly fills his face as he looks closer at my arms, taking them both in his hands. "Lil' Bit..."

Looking down in embarrassment, I swallow thickly. "After last night... The nightmares came back. I could feel their hands," I whisper. Instantly, I'm pulled back into his arms and I blink back more tears.

"You've relived those memories enough. Is it okay if later I fill Erik in, and then Dom, on what's going on? I don't want to cause you anymore pain, Lil' Bit."

My body sags in relief, and I nod, thankful that I won't have to repeat anything again. He tightens his hug and releases me. Despite the weight on my shoulders, I can't help but giggle when I'm instantly pulled into Timber's arms.

Then, curses ring out behind me, and I turn, only to flinch back slightly at the anger on Python's, Reaper's, and Ragnar's faces.

"Church!" Reaper bellows and I look up at Timber, worried. Is it about whatever caused Erik to attack Kai? About Mom? Preston?

He leans down, kissing me, and rests his forehead against mine. "If it's about Lillian or Preston, I'll give you the cliff note version, but if it's not, don't be surprised if I can't tell you anything about it, Sunshine"

My nerves increase as I remember Levi's talk with me at her house. "Club business?" I ask hesitantly.

He nods grimly. "If it affects you in any way, I'll tell you what I can, but other than that, I most likely won't be able to tell you. Please say you understand, Sunshine."

Nodding, I force a smile onto my face. "I understand, but it doesn't mean I'll always like it." Going up on my tiptoes, I'm thankful that he meets me halfway to kiss me since he's so much taller than I am. Pulling back, I tuck myself under his arm as we follow behind the others into the clubhouse.

Reaper's talking quietly with Ragnar and Erik as they walk, tension radiating off all of them.

Once inside, Timber kisses me once more before giving the Prospect at the bar his phone and goes into Church.

Mama Astrid's face lights up in a smile when she sees me. Then her face turns nervous as she stops what she's doing in the kitchen and comes out to the main room, wringing her hands in worry before she starts to sign as she talks.

"Erik... I... We wanted to tell you, but Kai asked to be the one to tell you since he was the one that brought Mae into our family. I'm—."

Erik cuts her off as he sweeps her up into a hug. Instantly, her body relaxes as she returns the hug. After a few moments, she pulls back, cupping his cheek affectionately.

"It's okay, Ma. It's all sorted out now."

She pats his cheek. "Good. Now how about you sit down with Mae, get to know each other, and I'll bring you out some coffee. Are either of you hungry?"

At that moment, my stomach rumbles and my cheeks heat. I bury my face in my hands, embarrassed, as they both chuckle softly.

"Sit down, and I'll bring you both out something to eat."

We both walk over to a nearby table, and I'm not surprised when he positions himself directly across from me.

Taking a deep breath, I decide to follow their lead and sign as I talk. "So, tell me about yourself."

His jaw drops in surprise and I can't help but giggle. "Someday I want to own and run my own daycare, and figured I should learn sign language in case one of the children attending is hard of hearing or completely deaf. I noticed that you always make sure you can see a person's mouth, or that they'd purposefully turn toward you, even if they were signing. However, if I'm doing something that makes you uncomfortable, please tell me, as that's not what I want."

He stares at me in shock for a few moments before scrubbing his hands over his face. "He was right. If I would have just talked to you, I would have known you weren't capable of doing what the text said." He gives me a sad smile, raising a hand to cut me off before I even say anything.

"When they're done with Church, I'll show you." He looks over his shoulder before leaning closer, and I do the same. "They've got my phone. I think they're trying to track who sent the text, or maybe Python was already able to do it based on their pissed off faces," he whispers. All I can do is nod as I nervously look toward the door leading into Church.

Needing to change the subject, I focus back on Erik.

"So, what do you do?"

I thought it was an innocent question, but at his crestfallen face, I'm not so sure.

"I, uh, I used to be a firefighter. Then, about a year ago, we were out on a call to a house fire around midnight. We knew there were three women living in the old two-story farmhouse. Almost everyone in town knows each other.

"Anyway, my team went in and began searching for them. I was upstairs when I heard over the radio that the mom and grandma were rescued, so it was just the daughter that we needed to find. Then I heard coughing on the far side of the room. The woman was frantically trying to open a window and hadn't seen or heard me yet. Not wasting time, I scooped her up into my arms, and she clung to me as I descended the stairs."

He pauses as he licks his lips, a haunted expression coming over his face. "Halfway down the stairs, they collapsed and we fell through the floor and into the basement below. Debris fell all around us, and I rolled on top of her to stop it from hitting her. Unfortunately, a beam fell and hit me on the head, knocking me out cold. My team reached us in time and got us out, but thanks to me getting knocked out, the woman endured third-degree burns on a portion of her face, neck, chest, and left arm. I have some scarring from burns but my gear protected the vast majority of my body.

"When I woke up in the hospital, I knew immediately something was wrong. I could faintly hear people talking, but most of what I could hear was a whooshing noise. The docs said I lost 90% of my hearing but that they didn't think it'd be permanent. That over time, they were optimistic that I'd regain all of it, or at least a portion of it back. About three months later, I regained about 5-10%, but since then, there hasn't been any improvement. I'm afraid that I'll never be able to do what I love again."

"How's the woman doing now?"

He swallows thickly. "Other than that she lived, I don't really know very much. When I asked about her in the hospital, I was told she was alive but would need multiple surgeries to remove the damaged tissue and, most likely, would need skin grafting. Then, when I asked if I could see her, I was told she didn't want anyone to see her right now. The only ones she let in were her mom, uncle, and grandma, which is understandable as they're the only family she has left from what I'd heard. I know she still lives in town and works at her family's restaurant, but I steer clear of it and her whenever I see her around town. Because of me getting knocked out, she's suffering daily. I don't want to put her in more pain by seeing me."

My heart breaks at the pain he feels for this woman. Without thinking, I get up, walk over to him, and hug him.

"Maybe someday she'll feel brave enough to seek you out. When that time comes, I hope it will help both of you. Who knows, maybe she heard you were injured saving her and she's blaming herself for your injury, just like you're blaming yourself for hers."

Movement catches my eye and I look up to see Mama Astrid staring at us through the pass-through window, wiping her eyes. She mouths 'thank you' to me, and I give her a watery smile back.

When Erik releases me, he turns, wiping his eyes and I pretend not to notice as I retake my seat across from him. A few moments later, Mama Astrid places plates full of eggs, bacon, and pancakes down in front of us. She quickly returns with coffee and hurries back into the kitchen. Thankfully, she didn't load my plate as much as she did Erik's. I'm getting better at eating bigger meals, but it's a slow process.

We sit there talking, our breakfasts long finished. He tells me about his twin sister, Frida, and I wish I could have met her. She seems like someone I'd get along with and could have been friends with.

I quickly find out that Erik has a good sense of humor and it's not surprising when he tells me stories of him and his sister pulling pranks on Kai. Sometimes Dominick, or Dom, as they call him, takes part, but not always.

I'm surprised when he tells me that Dom is slightly on the spectrum, but that he's very high functioning. Apparently, Kai and Ragnar run the Harley Dealership together and have a garage attached to it. While Kai also works in the garage sometimes, he mainly runs the store and showroom. However, it's the garage where Dom shines the most.

"That kid is amazing," Erik gushes, pride evident on his face. "When we were kids, us boys would sit with Pops and Grandpa listening to engine sounds on tape. Then Grandpa would ask us what was wrong with the engine. Dom mastered that game quickly. To this day, he can hear an engine running and he'll be able to pinpoint exactly what's wrong with it. Sometimes he gets excited and could ramble on for hours if we let him about cars.

"I help out at the shop more so than I ever did before, but it's hard when I can't hear the engine very well to help diagnose what's wrong. Usually, Dom and I work together or at least in the bays right next to each other for that reason." He pauses and his face twists into a sneer. "It's also helped for times when we have asshole customers come in and don't want him working on their cars. Since almost everyone in town knows each other, they all know he's on the spectrum. However, those fucking idiots always conveniently 'forget' that he's extremely high functioning," he says using air quotes.

Anger rises in me at the thought of someone doing that to anyone, let alone someone that's now family. "Those hoity-toity jerks better not say any of that if I'm around. I have no problem getting in their faces," I seethe.

His shoulders shake in silent laughter, and I roll my eyes at him. Along with the others, he thinks my version of cursing is also hilarious.

My gaze snags on the clock and I realize the guys have been in Church for almost two hours.

As if they knew I was wondering when they'd be done, the door opens and they all file out. I fight not to shrink back at the looks on all their faces. They're all seething with barely restrained rage.

Timber stalks over to me, picks me up, and sits down with me on his lap. He buries his face in the crook of my neck. I can feel his muscles rippling underneath me with his anger and rage, but for what, I don't know.

Knowing he'll tell me later if he can, I lean into him more as I reach up with one hand, running my fingers through his hair. With the other, I place my hand over his and intertwine our fingers as I try to help him calm down.

Chapter 43
Timber

I STALK TOWARD MAE, needing to feel her to ground myself. I'm fucking pissed at what we've just found out. Now it's just a waiting game until we can get more information. Reaper, Punisher, Odin, and a few others join us at their table.

When Sunshine reaches up and wraps her arm around me, her fingers play in my hair. Her other hand intertwines our fingers together and I place a kiss against the crook of her neck as I take a deep breath of her lavender body wash and perfume.

A shiver runs through her and I can't help my grin and I kiss her skin again. After a few minutes, I finally feel my body relaxing slightly.

Sitting up, I pull her closer to me as I listen to her, Erik, Punisher, and Reaper get to know each other more. She tried to go into the kitchen to help Mama Astrid get ready for lunch, but she shooed Sunshine back out here to get to know her brothers and uncle better. I wish Dom were here, but he goes to a car show each year with Odin's father around this time.

For the next few hours, we all sit around talking. Every now and then Sunshine will slip, referencing what the rest of us know about her background. It's not till Erik's gaze slides to Punisher each time that her body tenses. I wish I could take away her pain, what those assholes have done to her, but I can't. What I can do, is do everything in my power to keep them from harming her further.

As the afternoon wears on, it's all I can do to not jump out of my chair when I hear the unmistakable sound of heels clacking on the wood floor as one of the Johnson Chasers, as Sunshine and the rest of us have started calling them, come out of their rooms.

Candi and Star walk over to the bar to get a drink, swaying their hips. They both look over the room, and surprisingly, when each of their gazes meet mine, they incline their heads slightly, giving me a small smile. I hope like fuck that means they'll leave Sunshine and me alone going forward, but time will tell.

Seconds later, Sunshine stiffens in my lap and when I follow her gaze, I scowl when I see Luscious' hate-filled glare fixated on her when she notices Mae in my lap. Then Luscious' face lights up and I'm guessing it's because Erik's here. He's never done anything with any of the bunnies, that I know of anyway, but it doesn't stop them from trying.

I tense and hope like fuck Punisher talked to him or shot him a text. Movement brings my gaze downward and I see Sunshine signing something. Wait, she knows sign language?

Glancing up at Erik, he gives her a subtle nod. Well shit. Guess that means he told her what happened to him and the accident.

Luscious walks up behind Erik, running her hand down his shoulder and arm. He jerks away from her, ripping her arm off him.

"I thought I told you never to touch me, bitch," he sneers at her.

She bats her fake eyelashes at him as she plays with her hair, an innocent expression on her face as she tries to bring attention to her chest. "Oh, you don't mean that, Handsome. Let me take care of you to relieve some of that stress." She tries reaching for him again, but he swats her hand away.

"Like hell would I ever touch you or your loose as shit holes. Now, if you haven't noticed, you're ruining me and my brother getting to know our sister better. Get the fuck away from us and go bother someone else."

Once again, her hate-filled gaze finds Sunshine as she sneers at her. To her credit, Sunshine doesn't back down. She just smirks at Luscious as she brings my hand to her lips, kissing my knuckles. Placing a kiss on her temple, I level the bitch with a glare of my own.

Luscious huffs and rolls her eyes, thrusting her chest out as she cocks her hip. My guess is she thinks that's sexy, but it just makes her look even more desperate than she already is.

"Keep rolling your eyes there, Luscious. Eventually, you might find your pea sized brain in there somewhere. Then again, you may just be proof that someone can live without having a brain," Sunshine tells her, which has everyone laughing as Luscious' face turns red.

She sneers as she looks over Sunshine's body with disgust before turning her gaze to me and batting her eyelashes. "I don't know why you even bother lowering yourself to slum it with the reject, Timber. She can't be that good in bed or even take all of you. There's no way she can take care of you the way I can. Let's go back to your room and I can remind you how much you're missing out with Miss Skin and Bones here." She runs a hand in between her breasts, and I just want to gag, regretting ever fucking her in the past.

Out of the corner of my eye, Sunshine's smirk deepens as she leans into me further. "Oh, I've definitely taken all of his love stick and have had no problems making sure *all* of his needs are taken care of. Repeatedly."

Grabbing her hips, I pull her closer to me, loving her gasp when she feels exactly how hard I am for her. "Damn fucking right, Baby," I rasp and she moans, grinding her ass against my hard cock through our jeans.

I nibble the skin at the crook of her neck where I left a hickey and grin when her skin breaks out in goosebumps. Fuck what I wouldn't do to throw her over my shoulder and take her upstairs right now, but I can't.

"Get a room, you two," Punisher says as both he and Erik fake gag, but I know they're playing this up to rile up Luscious.

Her face turns redder and she stomps her foot. "You cannot be serious, Timber! What the fuck does she have that I don't have?"

"Kindness," Odin replies.

"A heart," Punisher says.

"Patience," Erik says.

Everyone in the room rattles off traits of Sunshine's that Luscious doesn't have.

I hug Mae tighter when I hear her sniffle. Luscious' face falls a little more each time a person speaks up until I'm the only one that hasn't said anything yet.

When the room turns quiet, I turn Sunshine's face toward mine and kiss her. Turning back to Luscious, I finally tell her my piece.

"Mae has my heart and will always have it. She is my light. She is my Sunshine Goddess. She is my woman. She is my Old Lady. And soon, she'll have my ring on her finger as well as a baby in her womb if it isn't already there. There is no comparison, Luscious. You, and every other woman, will always be lacking to me. Mae is my ride or die and always will be."

Luscious stares at me in shock, and my gut twists when her face turns smug. "We'll see about that," she purrs, as she turns and struts to the bar, making sure to shake her ass.

Sunshine turns toward me and I'm about to say something when the door swings open.

The clack of a metal heel against the wood floor tells me and everyone else *exactly* who's here.

And it's about fucking time.

Chapter 44
Timber

I BREATHE A SIGH of relief when I hear the metal click of heels against the wood floor of the clubhouse as the doors shut behind her.

Turning, I smirk when I see Sasha is dressed to intimidate and while I'd never step out on Sunshine, I can admit that Colt is a damn lucky man.

Sasha's makeup is fierce with dark eyeshadow and blood red lipstick. Her blond hair pulled up into a tight ponytail that's been braided and wrapped into a bun on the top of her head. Her blue eyes are cold as ice, but they also blaze with anger as she glares at Luscious' back. Sasha's dressed in a fitted black club t-shirt with a V-neck and black skinny jeans. However, it's the boots that tell everyone in the club exactly what direction tonight is going to go in.

She's continuing the trend that Levi started.

Red leather knee-high boots with a metal needle heel.

I can't help but smirk when a few guys flinch at hearing her heels.

They're most likely remembering back to a few months ago when we had captured the people that were responsible for kidnapping Levi and Reaper. We handed a few of them over to the FBI but kept the ones that had hurt both of them the most.

Levi had worn boots just like the ones Sasha's now wearing. In the process of getting information out of those fuckers, Levi had driven her metal tipped heel into her uncle's balls as he lay spread eagle on the concrete a few months ago. The fucker was part of a group that was going to kidnap her, rape her, and sell off her babies once she had them.

Now, that's not to say that I don't feel that same ghost of pain Levi inflicted on that asshole, but I'm not letting it deter me. Especially with what this bitch has in motion to do to my Sunshine and what else she's done.

Sunshine moves to get up off my lap, but I tighten my grip on her. "Stay right here, Baby. She's here for a reason. I'll fill you in on what I can later," I whisper into her ear.

She looks up at Sasha, worry evident on her face, but thankfully, she doesn't move off my lap. Though she does tighten her grip on my hand and arm.

Sasha turns her attention to the other two bunnies, who are looking on in confusion and motions for them to leave. Thankfully, they do, but the sound of their quick retreat on their sky-high heels causes Luscious to turn around from the bar to see what's happening.

Her gaze lands on Sasha and she sneers at her. Then her face turns seductive when she sees Colt behind her. She looks around, most likely to see if any other of my brothers from Forest Creek are here and she pouts a little when she sees it's just them.

To their credit, my brothers act like nothing's wrong and Luscious turns back toward the bar, taking the girlie drink from Nathan. Thankfully, the fucker took his time mixing it.

Sasha walks up to the bar. "Can I have a beer please, Nathan?"

Luscious gives her the side eye, most likely wondering why she's ordering a beer since she's a Prospect. She turns and looks down her nose at Sasha.

"Thought you were still in the kiddie pool and couldn't drink yet," she sneers.

Sasha chuckles darkly before taking a long pull of her drink Nathan hands her. "I have a pass to drink tonight."

Luscious huffs. "Of course, you do. Pulling favorites already since your so-called sister is now the Queen B, huh?"

Sasha chuckles again, but this is even darker than before, and it sends a chill down my spine.

She takes another long pull of her drink, swallows, pulls back and then smashes the bottle against Luscious' temple. The remains of her beer spilling down Luscious' face and body as glass shards shatter across the bar and floor.

Luscious sways, giving Sasha enough time to pull back and land a right hook to her jaw. Her body crumples against the bar.

Sasha wrenches her arms behind her, cuffing her wrists. Then she grabs her hair, fisting it as she pulls on it which has Luscious coming out of her daze.

"Someone, help me! Get this bitch off me!"

No one moves as she struggles to get free. A look of disbelief flashes over her face, before it contorts again into one of anger.

"Why aren't any of you helping me? I haven't done anything wrong! After all I've done for you, this is how you repay me?"

I don't have to look around to know that her statement just pissed everyone off even further.

Another click sounds as Sasha cuffs Luscious to the bar. She pulls on her hair again, eliciting another shriek from Luscious, as she steps closer to her, lifting her chin with the hilt of a blade.

"Are you sure about that, Luscious? Are you sure you haven't given information to anyone as of late? Say, I don't know... about a certain someone's whereabouts? Sending false information to rile people up and cause division amongst family? To desecrate memories and reminders of those we have loved and lost? Are you sure you haven't done anything wrong, Luscious?"

Luscious' face pales as her gaze bounces around the room, but I don't have to look at my brothers to know we're all glaring at her. She audibly swallows, knowing she's fucked up big time.

Sunshine's body tenses, and I turn my attention to her. Her face is furious and I know she's now connecting the dots.

She rips my hands from around her and is on her feet, stalking toward Luscious. I warned the guys that Mae would probably want to get in a few punches, so none of us are surprised.

And no one tries to stop her.

Pulling back, she lands a punch straight to Luscious' jaw, but I can tell by the way she's shaking out her hand that she hurt herself in the process.

Fuck!

Sasha tsks at her. "No, no, Sweetie," she says as she takes hold of Mae's fist. "Fold your fingers in like this and your thumb goes here. Now, you need to have a good base as that's where your power is going to come from."

Luscious shrieks in anger. "You can't be fucking serious? Are you seriously giving her lessons right now? Uncuff me! If anyone should be locked up, it's that fucking bitch for coming in and ruining everything!"

Sasha ignores her, and continues to keep her focus on Mae. "Now, keep your wrist locked and in line with your forearm. Good. That will help so that you don't hurt your wrist when you land a punch. Keep your legs spread, but you don't want to be too wide as that will make you unbalanced. Your dominant foot goes behind you. Knees slightly bent.

"Now, picture where you want your punch to land on your opponent. Try to hit something beyond your opponent so that you don't end up pulling your punch. Don't tense as you throw, but make sure to keep your thumb out of the way, otherwise you could break it. In a perfect world, you want your index and middle knuckle to land on your target, not the fingers themselves."

Sasha steps back but stays nearby and nods at Mae. She nods in return, pulls back, and throws punch after punch at various places on Luscious' body.

"How could you? How could you do that to Frida? She was family and you betrayed her, desecrating her memory!"

Luscious grins, her mouth full of blood, but Mae doesn't back down.

"You know nothing of family or how club life works, so save your breath, bitch."

Mae shakes her head, pointing back at my brothers. "You were part of their family, whether you think so or not. Being a bunny meant you were on the fringes, but you were still part of the club family. A family that protected you. Fed you. Put a roof over your head. Paid you—not for the bumping uglies part, but for what you did around the clubhouse. The other part, you signed up for voluntarily. So yeah, I do know what a club family looks like, but it seems you don't." Mae pauses, grasps her chin, and cocks her head as she looks down at her. "Or am I wrong that the club didn't offer all that to you? Tell me I'm wrong, Luscious."

Something flashes in Luscious' eyes, but she doesn't say anything. She knows everything Mae's said is true. Her face hardens.

"You think that just because you're fucking one of them that you are part of their family? Ha! You'll be discarded as soon as Timber tires of you. Once they learn everything about you, they'll dump you like a ton of bricks, tossing you back into the gutter where you belong."

Mae laughs, turning partially as she spreads out her other hand, gesturing to all of us again.

"They all know my background and baggage. Some of them more so than others. If I haven't already been tossed into a gutter to use your words, then I don't think I'm going to be.

"They are all my family now. Not just the Junction Creek chapter, but also the Forest Creek chapter. Timber's my Old Man. Besides finding my blood family, I now have two brothers that are club members, plus two other brothers; a sister; a nephew; three aunts; five uncles; three cousins, two of which are on the way; and another set of parents. Family is not just blood. It can be chosen as well. But when you turn your back on family... hurt them... betray them... you'll quickly find out what it feels like to have their wrath directed at you."

"Ha! You're wrong. Like I said, you're not part of the club family just cause you're fucking one of them. You're nothing. Just like Frida was. She got what she deserved. Just. Like. You. Will," Luscious grits out. Mae smiles darkly and fuck does it go straight to my dick.

"It seems you keep digging your own grave deeper and deeper. I think your purpose in life is about to be fulfilled. The only question is which way? Will you end up being an organ donor or fertilizer?"

My body freezes and Punisher looks at me, a question in his eyes. I shake my head. I never told her we sometimes have to take out the trash. Then again, he did tell me what she said when Levi told her about club business back at Levi's house. Maybe she connected the dots on her own. She's also been reading a lot and is currently reading an MC series. There could be nuggets of truth in those books.

Luscious' face pales before she sneers and strains harder against the handcuffs. She's about to say something when Mae backhands her. Hard. When Luscious turns back toward Mae, her nose is bleeding, but Mae doesn't give her a chance to say anything else. She lands a wicked punch to Luscious' jaw that has her head snapping to the side.

Her body crumples to the floor. Well, as much as her handcuffs will allow, that is.

Seeing that she's not getting back up, I get up, stalking toward Sunshine and pulling her into my arms. After a few moments, I release her, taking her hands in mine, and looking them over.

Her knuckles are a little raw, and her thumb looks a little swollen. I wonder if it was injured during the first punch. Someone steps up next to me and sets something down on a table nearby.

"Let me see those hands, Lil' Bit. I'm gonna clean the blood off before I take a closer look at them," Doc says.

After a few moments, he examines both hands, and she hisses slightly when he bends her right wrist backward and moves her thumb. "Nothing's broken, but you have slight strains, most likely from your first punch. Ice them and take some ibuprofen to help with the pain and swelling. You did good, Lil' Bit."

Doc places the ice pack on her hand and my chest tightens when I hear the hiss she tries to suppress. He hands me some packets of ibuprofen that I put in my pocket. I'll give them to her later when I get her a drink.

Pulling my Sunshine back into my arms, I worry how she's going to process everything after this. I don't want her to have any regrets. Another worry is that if she learns what we're going to have to do, will she look at me differently afterward? Fuck, I hope not. I can't lose my Sunshine Goddess.

Chapter 45

Timber

SUNSHINE'S BODY TREMBLES IN my arms slightly, but I'm not sure if it's from anger, worry, or fear. Tilting up her chin so that she looks at me, her eyes swirl with emotions.

"Are you okay, Sunshine?"

Her face hardens, and she gives me a curt nod.

She turns, slipping out of my arms, and wraps Sasha in a hug. The two of them whisper for a few moments. A dark grin forms on Sasha's face as she nods and hugs Sunshine tighter.

Sunshine steps back into my arms and Sasha uncuffs Luscious from the bar, but she keeps the cuffs around her wrists in place. Gripping her hair, Sasha drags Luscious' body behind her as she heads down to the cellar. Her metal heels echoing down the hallway send a foreboding chill through the air.

I know when they get to the stairs because Luscious' screams start back up again. I smirk, knowing Sasha let her ass hit every single stair on the way down.

The guys all get up, following after Sasha.

Picking up Mae, I walk over to the couches, thankful that Mama Astrid and Erik have also moved to sit on the couch. Setting her down, I put the ice pack back on her hand.

"I'm gonna go get you something to drink so you can take these pills," I say, fishing the packets out of my pocket and giving them to her.

Quickly, I cross the room, grabbing one of her flavored waters from the mini-fridge behind the bar, and walk back over to her.

Kissing her forehead, I kneel down in front of her. "Stay in the clubhouse, Sunshine. We'll be back up after... After we talk to her."

Sunshine huffs, a smile tugging on her lips. "Baby, I know what's gonna happen and I'm okay with it. However, I want you to promise me a few things."

Hesitantly, I stare into her eyes. "I'll do what I can, but it depends on what you want, Sunshine."

She gives me a sad, small smile. "Find out why she smashed Frida's gravestone. Why she said 'she got what she deserved'. Who did she tell where I was and why? I know she's furious that she lost her chance at you, but find out if there's something else behind her anger and hate toward me. I have a feeling that it's more than just you and me being together."

Relief courses through me. Those things I should be able to find out. In fact, they were among the questions we already wanted to ask her about.

Nodding, I lean forward, giving her a chaste kiss. "Hopefully we'll get those answers from her as we want to know them, too. Again, stay inside. If you get tired, I bet Mama Astrid would be able to find a spare room for you to crash in."

"She can crash in our room here, and I'll stay with her, son," Mama Astrid replies and I give her a chin lift.

"Be back when we're done." I kiss Sunshine one more time before standing and walking down the hallway to the cellar.

As I pass the bar, I notice that the Prospects are already wiping it down and the floor, making sure they get any blood splatters. Next, I'm sure they'll scour the shelves behind the bar to make sure they don't miss anything.

My boots echo off the floor as I hurry down the stairs. I know they won't start without me, but I also don't want to miss anything that Sasha puts that bitch through.

Punching in the code, I enter, making sure the door shuts securely behind me.

In the center of the room, on a metal chair, sits Luscious. There are ropes tying her torso to the back of the chair. Her arms are bound to the arms of the chair and her legs have been bound as well. Her heels are missing, but I know that's because if she got her legs free, they could be used as a weapon. There's a plastic tarp underneath the chair she's sitting on. Not to mention there are tarps hanging from the back wall, side walls, and ceiling near where she's sitting.

The guys are spread out on the side closest to the door and I turn to my right when I hear rummaging noises. Sasha's looking through Punisher's toy closet as he calls it. The bag Colt had been carrying previously sits on a table nearby. He stayed upstairs with the others since he's not patched in yet. Actually, I'll have to ask the guys about that. His year is coming up in a few months.

I'm brought out of my thoughts as Sasha walks toward Luscious, a serrated blade in her hand. She circles her, gently dragging the blade across her skin. Not deep enough to cut, but enough for her to feel the edge of the blade.

"Why did you send that text message to Erik?"

Luscious glares at Sasha, and somehow manages to sit up taller. "You can't hurt me. The club doesn't hurt women or children. Release me."

Sasha chuckles darkly. "To quote our Queen, I don't have a dick and I wear my balls on my chest, so there's nothing in the bylaws that prevents me from handling women issues when the need arises." She pulls hard on Luscious' hair, making her look up at her. The cold, hard smile Sasha gives her sends a chill down my spine. "That means we're going to be spending a lot of time together until I get the information I need."

She pauses, pushing the knife a little harder against her throat. A small trickle of blood runs down Luscious' throat. "Why did you send that text message to Erik?"

Luscious' face twists into a sneer. "Because it's true. Frida's being replaced by that fucking bitch. Even her parents seem to have fallen under that bitch's spell. It's sickening to see everyone falling at her feet and eating up the lies she spews. If she would never have come around, things wouldn't have changed and I would have had what should have been mine to begin with."

"And what should have been yours?"

"Timber. All I needed was to show him how much I could do for him and then I would have been his Old Lady. Not that worthless trailer park piece of whoring, druggie trash," she seethes.

I narrow my eyes at her and look at my brothers. Judging by the looks on our faces, I know we're all thinking the same thing.

"What makes you think Mae's trailer park trash? That she whores herself out or is a druggie?" I ask her.

Luscious huffs as she rolls her eyes. "It's not hard to find out. You guys don't exactly whisper, you know."

Stalking toward her, I yank her head back by her hair, hard enough for her to know I mean business, but not enough to hurt her too much.

"That's the thing. We've never talked about where she lived or about certain things related to her background outside of Church. So, I'll ask again. Where did you hear those things about her?"

She smiles, and I seriously think she's trying to be seductive as she bats her eyes at me, but it just sickens me. "It's the talk all around town. You can't really blame that on me, now can you, Handsome?"

My lip curls in disgust as I look down at her. "Who did you hear it from?"

"I overheard it at my doctor's appointment."

"Who did you go to?" Odin asks and I'm sure he's remembering the clubs' edict after that run-in with that asshat Dr. Carter Johnson.

She rolls her eyes at him. The disrespect is starting to really get on my nerves. Judging by the others' faces, they're feeling the same.

Sasha backhands her. "Show some respect for the club, you bitch. These are the men that took you in off the street to protect you from your father and brother. Or have you forgotten that?"

Luscious' face pales at the reminder, and she lowers her gaze before clearing her throat. "Dr. Johnson. I know you guys said we aren't supposed to go there anymore, but he's been my doctor since I was a baby and has never done anything wrong or inappropriate. Why should I have to change doctors just because his son hit on that bitch?"

"He disrespected the club. Everyone in town knows not to mess with our brothers and their women or there will be hell to pay. Timber was with Mae when Junior decided to step out of line, and he's going to have to deal with the fallout. Especially since he threatened an Old Lady," Reaper says as he steps forward. Luscious shrinks back at his cold stare. "And you disrespected the club by going against our rules. Not only the one about the doctor, but other ones as well." He pauses as he glances at Sasha. "Continue."

I step back in line with the others.

"Who did you tell that Mae was here in Junction Creek?"

When she doesn't answer, Sasha drags the blade across her cheek, drawing blood. Luscious screams, but Sasha ignores her, doing the same on the other cheek before moving to her arms.

"Anytime you want to speak up, the pain will stop. Well, until you lie to me again, that is."

After a few more cuts, which look pretty deep, Luscious finally caves.

"I don't know who he is, but he's been asking around town, flashing that bitch's picture around. Said he was trying to find his daughter and that she ran away from home."

I grit my teeth, knowing it's one of four possible men. "Describe him."

"He's older. Has black, slicked back hair. Dark brown eyes. Tan skin. Sharply dressed. Drove a fancy car and had a Rolex."

X.

Mother fucker. The last thing we need is for him to get his slimy hands on Sunshine.

"What'd you tell him?" Python asks.

She shrugs. Well, as much as she can while restrained. "That she was here at the compound."

I narrow my eyes at her when her gaze once again shifts down to the left. It's always been a tell of hers.

Sasha notices and starts cutting again. "Try again."

After a few more minutes of cutting, Sasha puts down her blades and grabs the pliers off the bench.

In the aftermath of her and Levi handling our previous female guests, we made sure that the women's hands would be able to be secured to their chairs in case of scenarios like this, where we only have one of them that's doling out the punishment. In all honesty, it'll help with men too, depending on how many we are entertaining.

For the women's chairs, Smithy measured both Levi and Sasha's arms. Then he went back to his shop and welded us chairs that we could use at both of our compounds. Drawings were sent to the other chapters for them to make their own since they are further away. There is a plate where their hands are positioned palm down and holes in the plates for the rope or zip ties to be threaded through. He even took care of making sure that the edges of the holes were soft and rounded enough that our guests couldn't try to use them to 'cut' through the ropes. Same for the other surfaces of the chair as well. There're also eyebolts welded in on various spots where we can further secure them to make sure they can't slip the ropes off.

Luscious eyes the pliers warily, but when Sasha bends back the first nail and then rips it out, her screams bounce off the walls.

"Care to tell us the truth this time?"

She glares at Sasha, who just smirks at her before lining up to rip another nail off.

"That she's staying here and stole my boyfriend from me."

I say nothing about the boyfriend comment even though it kills me not to. I've never been hers and never will be.

"Then what?" Sasha asks as she tugs on the next nail.

"He promised that Timber would be mine again if I helped him get his daughter back," she says with a smug smirk.

That has all of us laughing.

"I knew you were stupid, but I didn't think you were stupid enough to believe something like that," Razor says when he catches his breath.

"I'm not stupid!"

"Yes, you are. Even if you had succeeded, there's no way I'd take you for an Old Lady. Or ever tapped your ass again." Bending down, I stare straight into her eyes. "You were always just a fucking release. You are nothing to me. Same for all the other bunnies. None of you are Old Lady material to me. I have never wanted an Old Lady that's taken all my brothers in all her holes. You had to have realized that the asshat, who by the way is *not* Mae's father, was playing you. He got what he needed out of you and left you to the wolves. Smoke's her father, not the man you talked to. That makes Mae legacy."

Stepping back in line, she stares at me in disbelief. Her eyes are glassy with tears, but I don't know if it's from the pain or what I just said. Either way, I'm not losing sleep over it.

"Why did you destroy Frida's tombstone?" Sasha asks her which has Luscious narrowing her eyes at her.

Next to me, Punisher's body tenses. This has got to be dredging up painful memories for him and I can't wait until Sasha makes her pay for bringing this pain back up to the surface.

"I don't know what you're talking about." Her gaze lowers to the left.

I grit my teeth. She's lying.

Again.

Sasha rips the rest of her fingernails out, one by one, not pausing in between each one. Tossing the last nail into the trophy box, as Levi's taken to calling them, she puts the pliers down and grabs a sledgehammer out of the closet.

Luscious' eyes roll into the back of her head at the sight, her body slumping as she faints.

Sasha sighs, sounding bored. "Can one of you wake her up, please?"

"Gotcha covered, Chica," Loki replies.

He turns around, lifts the bag of ice out of a bucket filled with water and puts the bag in the utility sink. Picking up the bucket, he walks around in front of Luscious and dumps the ice water on her. She wakes up, sputtering, and instantly starts shivering from the cold.

She looks around confused for a moment. When she notices Sasha with the sledgehammer resting on her shoulder, a bored expression on her face, her face pales even further.

"I'll ask again. Why did you destroy Frida's tombstone?"

"I-I didn't. I didn't, but someone else did. It was a message."

"Who?" Punisher grits out. His hands are fisted at his sides, and I know it's taking everything in him not to step forward.

"Her boyfriend."

That has us all frozen in place. I know for a fact that Punisher, Odin, and Erik killed the fucker.

"Her boyfriend's dead. He died years ago."

Luscious huffs as she straightens herself in the chair, despite shivering like crazy. Something has given her a boost of courage, and I want to find out what it is.

"That sick fuck wasn't her boyfriend. He was the front. Sure, they fucked and he doled out punishments to her, but that wasn't her boyfriend."

Fuck......

"What do you mean, he wasn't her boyfriend? Then who was?" Reaper asks as he steps forward.

Luscious grins darkly at him and then her gaze goes to Punisher. "He asked Frida out multiple times, but she denied him each time. Finally, he took matters into his own hands. He knew she liked someone else, but he wasn't going to lose her to anyone else. Especially when he saw how doting and protective you all were of her.

"He kidnapped her after work one day and held her all weekend. Used her phone to send texts to her parents and brothers that she was going out of town for work unexpectedly. By the time the weekend was over, he had her hooked on his drugs. She voluntarily came back after that just so she could get her next hit."

I swear you could have heard a pin drop in the room.

"What the fuck?" someone whispers.

Punisher stomps up to her. "Who. Is. He?"

She smirks at him. "You'll have to figure that out. Use that brain you're so proud of." Punisher's arm pulls back, but Sasha beats him to it, backhanding her so hard a couple of teeth fall out. It takes me a bit to realize she'd put on brass knuckles before hitting her.

"So your conscience is clear, brother."

He gives her a curt nod and turns his deadly gaze back to Luscious. "I repeat. Who. Is. He?"

Instead of answering him, she turns her attention to me, and her smirk deepens. "Your worthless whore will be experiencing the same treatment soon, if she hasn't already."

Suddenly, the door is thrown open. We all turn and see Mama Astrid standing there with Erik supporting her, blood dripping down her face from a nasty cut on her forehead. Her frantic gaze lands on me and I know.

"Mae's gone. Bastards snuck in and took her when she went to the restroom. Colt and Drake took off after them. Nathan went to watch the gate. They took that bitch's car, so the gate let them out right away." She pauses, her gaze returning to me and her face crumples. "I'm so sorry, Timber. I tried to stop them."

"Who? Who did this to you and took my Sunshine Goddess?" I grit out, barely able to restrain myself from going after them this instant.

"Carter Johnson. I didn't get a good look at the other one."

Chapter 46
Mae

MY HEAD FEELS LIKE there are tiny little jackhammers trying to split my brain apart. Groaning, I crack open my eyes and immediately shut them against the harsh light.

What happened?

Racking my brain, I try to remember, even though it makes the pounding worse. Another groan escapes me as little bits and pieces start to come back to me. Then it's like a tidal wave of memories wash over me.

Luscious trying, and failing, to stake her claim on Timber. *Again.*

The club saying all those kind things about me.

Timber's declaration that I'm his in every way.

Sasha coming and dealing with Luscious.

Me getting in a few swings at Luscious and Sasha showing me how to throw a punch correctly.

Sitting down and watching a movie with Erik and Mama Astrid.

Then I frown. I remember getting up to go to the restroom, but then... nothing.

An unfamiliar muffled voice from the next room has my eyes flying open, despite the harsh light. Panic starts to set in when I realize I'm tied down to a bed spread eagle. I still have my clothes on, but since I'm spread out, there's no way for me to stop them from removing them.

Wiggling, I can feel the bracelets Levi gave me shifting against the rope and my skin, but with how I'm tied up, I'm not able to make use of them.

The voice comes closer and ice runs down my spine.

It's the douche canoe from the grocery store.

Carter.

It's then that I remember him and another guy grabbing me after I walked out of the bathroom. I had planned to head back to the main room and I kick myself for not being more aware of my surroundings, but I thought I was safe in the clubhouse. I never thought someone would be able to sneak in.

I close my eyes as I remember what happened next.

Something pricked my skin on the back of my neck right as Mama Astrid rounded the corner. The other guy hit her across the head with the butt of his gun. I tried to yell out and get to her, but then everything went black.

Panic seizes me again. Please let Mama Astrid be okay!

"Yeah, we got her," Carter says and then pauses. I can hear him getting mad at whoever is on the phone as he huffs and paces, his steps getting louder and louder. *"Don't forget our deal,"* he seethes. *"I will get my revenge and then you can have her."*

He growls and I jump, well as much as I can, when I hear something fall to the ground, breaking. He stomps over to the door to the room I'm in and I'm surprised that I can hear him breathing heavily through the door. If he comes in here already spitting nails, then it's not going to end well for me.

Fear seeps in even more at what he must have planned for me if my position and restraints are anything to go by.

I release a breath I hadn't realized I was holding when it sounds like he's heading into another part of the house.

A few minutes later, the sound of something else heavy hitting the wall and breaking reverberates through the house.

"Where the fuck is she? She was supposed to be here by now," Carter says, his tone cold and hard.

"Maybe those assholes caught onto her. I knew we should have never used her to do this," another man says. Just going off of his voice, he sounds older than Carter... and almost hesitant? Maybe if I got him alone, I could convince him to let me go?

"She got us in since that bitch hasn't stepped foot outside after I saw her yesterday. She'll pay for publicly embarrassing me and threatening my business."

"Just remember, it's not your business yet, and I won't tolerate *anyone* disrupting my business," the other guy replies harshly.

I swallow thickly. Ooookay, maybe that wasn't hesitancy in his voice earlier. And did they really kidnap me just because I turned down Carter and said I was going to tell Kai and Reaper not to use him or his dad as their doctor?

A chill runs down my spine. If they're that put off by that, then I wonder exactly how dangerous these men really are.

Futtenfarter...

What if they've done this to someone else before?

Trying to tamp down my panic, I look around the room I'm in. There's a small closet, but it looks completely empty from what I can see. Other than the bed and a chair that's in the corner, there's no other furniture.

My gaze snags on a small window, the only window in the room, which is a few inches above ground level near the ceiling of the room. That must mean I'm in the basement. But if I can manage to get free, maybe I can crawl through it and escape. Since I'm so skinny, I shouldn't have any problems fitting through it. Yeah, I'm sure I'll have some scratches, especially around my chest and butt since my starvation seems to have not affected those areas much, but the scratches will be worth it if I can escape. It looks near sunset, but there's no way to tell if it's still the same day or not.

Tilting my head up, I start wiggling my right arm, trying to loosen the ropes. If I can get one of my hands free, I can get to the hidden blade in my bracelet.

Biting my lip, I push the pain of the ropes biting into my skin and rubbing it raw out of my mind. Thankfully, I didn't scrub my wrists as rough as I did my arms this morning. If I had, I'd probably already be in a lot more pain as I tried to get free.

Feeling the ropes loosen a little more gives me hope and start trying to free my left hand as well.

After a few minutes, the ropes loosen a fraction more, but the sound of stomping boots approaching has me freezing and closing my eyes. Maybe I can convince them that I'm still passed out from the drug?

Taking a few deep breaths, I try to calm my racing heart.

The door flies open and I force myself not to flinch as it bounces off the wall. Keeping my breath low and steady, I will my limbs to remain lax as whoever it is approaches the bed.

A smack rings through the air as my head whips to the side and a cry escapes me despite my best efforts to keep silent. I feel a trickle down my face and know he cut me somehow. My gaze goes to his hand to find a ring with some stones inlaid on it.

Wait.

He's married and he's doing this to me?

A shiver runs through me at how he must treat his wife.

The stinging feeling around my eye worsens, but I blink to keep the tears at bay. How is it that men know just the right spot to hit a woman's face?

Turning, I fight not to flinch at the angry look on Carter's face. The man standing behind him is also angry, but he's also looking at me in a calculating way. It's similar to how X first looked at me as his eyes raked over my body.

Movement has my attention turning back to Carter. Gone is his anger, and in its place, concern. I'm not buying it for a minute. I've seen Preston pulling this same trick with Mom before.

"Now, see what you made me do, Love? If you would have just accepted my invitation, none of this would have had to have happened."

He cannot be for real right now.

"Yeah, about that. You gave your number to a woman in a committed relationship. Why would I step out on the man that I love? Not to mention, you're married yourself."

That response earns me another, and somehow harder, backhand to the face.

Crickey, that hurt! You can do this, Mae. You can do this. Stall. Somehow, Liam will find me and rescue me. I just need to stall.

"Why do you keep making me hit you? Does that lowlife thug not know anything about keeping a woman in line? Regardless, I'll teach you the right way to behave. And as for my wife, she knows how to behave properly. She's just one of many."

He reaches for his belt and I panic, trying to scoot as far away from him as I can. The other man walks over and flips open a switchblade. I freeze, my eyes tracking every movement of the blade.

Oh, sugar honey ice tea.

This is it. They're going to rape me at knifepoint.

The man grabs my shirt and I try to wiggle away from him despite the knife. Fabric tears as he cuts up my shirt and opens it. He backs away but doesn't put away the knife.

Relief flows through me that he isn't cutting off any more of my clothes, but that relief is short lived.

He sets down the knife and yanks my pants down before cutting them off. Surprisingly, he keeps my panties in place. I bite back a sob as the man picks his knife up again with one hand and rubs himself through his jeans with his other hand.

Seconds later, I scream as the metal part of Carter's belt lands on my stomach. The sting from the metal and leather lingers and I don't need to look to know that he's drawn blood. I can feel it trickling down my side.

Futtenfarter... I was so distracted by watching the knife that I stupidly didn't pay attention to Carter.

Closing my eyes, I try to block out the pain, but the next hit is even harder than the first before he backhands me again and twists my nipples painfully through my bra. If he keeps this up, my eye will be completely swollen shut.

"Look at me when I'm punishing you, bitch! Remember, you made me do this. You will learn your place. Women are nothing but birthers, there to please their owners in the bedroom and obey their master's commands. Nothing more. Now, shut up and take your punishment."

Lash after lash of his belt lands on my stomach, hips, and periodically across my chest. So much so that I lose count of how many times he's hit me. On top of using the belt, he periodically hits my breasts with his hands and twists my nipples painfully. My screams bounce off the walls. There's no way to keep them in with the amount of pain he's inflicting on me.

Finally, he lowers his arms, and I pant as I try and not pass out from the amount of pain coursing through my body.

I don't even want to look at my stomach, chest, or hips. I know the skin is shredded. Why he spared my legs, I have no idea.

"You bleed and bruise so beautifully for me. Rest up, Love, you'll need your strength for what's next," Carter says as he smiles wickedly, an evil glint in his eyes.

Carter smacks my va-jay-jay hard a couple of times. Ignoring the shooting pain, I wiggle as best as I can to keep away from his fingers. He takes the knife from the other man and slices through my panties, ripping them off. He cups me again and I cry out when he forcefully shoves his fingers into me. Roughly, he pumps his fingers a few times into me as I keep trying to get away from him. Each time earns me a smack to the side of my breasts, but I don't care. I want his fingers out of me!

Finally, he pulls his fingers out of me and I almost puke when he brings them to his face, sniffing his fingers before licking them clean.

Both men have small bulges in their pants, and my stomach sinks even further at the wicked and lustful looks on both of their faces.

"Can't wait to have more of you, but that will happen soon enough when our friend arrives. Sweet dreams, my Love," Carter says before he slaps my face again. My eye stings even more from all the hits he landed to the same place on my face.

Both men leave, locking the door behind them.

A sob escapes as tears stream down my cheeks.

God, what did I do to deserve this?

Just as my life was finally turning around. Why did this have to happen?

Black dots swirl around my vision from all the pain as my tears come harder.

Liam, please hurry. I'm not sure how much more I can take.

Chapter 47
Timber

I stare at Mama Astrid, frozen in place as her words bounce around my mind.

Mae's gone.

Luscious' maniacal laughter from behind me has me snapping out of my thoughts. Turning, she doesn't even flinch from my glare. She just laughs harder until Sasha nails her with a punch to her jaw. She spits out some blood and a tooth as she grins darkly at me.

"Your whore is getting what she deserves for taking you away from me. For denying Carter. For running from her owner and master. Soon, there won't be anything left for you to save. Just like Frida," she seethes.

This bitch really is crazy. Stalking toward her, I get right in her face and let her see the monster in me she's released. One that only a few people have ever seen. Her face blanches as her mask cracks.

"Looks like you just earned an extended stay in our lovely accommodations. Now, I'd tell you to stay put, but there's really no place for you to go and you won't be released for anything. Not even if you have to piss. You'll be pissing and shitting in your own pants as you sit in your filth. We'll be back and we *will* be continuing this conversation."

Turning, my brothers and I file out of their interrogation room. Odin carries Mama Astrid upstairs with Doc hot on their heels.

In the main room, I notice Python, Reaper, Devil, and Punisher are all talking in hushed tones and I head their way.

Reaper sees me approach and gives me a chin lift.

"FYI, I called Smoke, and he's on his way. However, these fuckers are dumb-asses. Python said they kept her phone, and it's pinging from the same location as the trackers in her bracelets. They're at a cabin about ten miles north of here.

There's a nearby old service trail we can use. Like usual, we'll walk the last bit to the cabin so they don't hear us." He pauses, his face hardening as his gaze cuts to Mama Astrid and then to Odin as he comes up to us.

A low growl comes from Python as he watches Doc fix up Mama Astrid. "Fuckers knocked out three of my cameras. My guess is Luscious told them about them, but I don't know how she knows where they are. I never watch camera feeds in the main room and I sure as fuck haven't had her in my room before. Later, after we get your woman back, I'll look further back in history to see if I can find anything."

"Did you get anything off of the cameras at the gates?" I ask him, itching to know who else put their hands on my Sunshine.

He gives me a chin lift. "The two fuckhead Johnson doctors. Though senior had enough sense to wear a hooded sweatshirt and baseball cap while sneaking in here. He took them off right before they got to the gates."

"Alright. Python, send coordinates of the cabin to everyone's phone. We'll split up and take the trucks so they won't be able to hear us. It's pitch black out, so that will help us with cover. Get your gear and meet out front in five. Timber, follow me," Reaper says as he turns and heads to his office.

He signals for me to shut the door and he turns, opening his gun safe. He passes me an extra magazine that I tuck into my cut. All of the club members have at least one gun that is the same as everyone else's, and if they are traveling, they have to take it with them for this reason. The ability to share ammo when in a pinch. I have more ammo at the house that I brought, but I don't want to waste time going and getting it.

"When we get back, you'll lead the interrogation since she's your Old Lady. Though, I've seen the same cut of cloth in Mae as I see in Half-pint and Sasha. She'll probably want to get a few hits in herself, talk to them, or at least state what she wants to happen. Just know, I'll support whatever she chooses. Those fuckers messed up by going after my niece and stepping foot in my home."

It's moments like these that remind me exactly how terrifying Reaper can be. He can be a scary dude on a normal day, but if you mess with his family, the fucker looks like someone from your worst nightmare. On top of his tattoos and with how massive he is, both in size and how muscular the fucker is, the scars from

what he endured a few months ago add an even more deadly air than he already h
ad.

Giving him a chin lift, we head outside toward the trucks. Reaper splits everyone up, leaving a few brothers here to protect the clubhouse in case X or anyone
else tries to come back.

I get into the truck that Punisher and Python are already in and Reaper slides
in next to me in the back seat. Normally, Reaper would be up front, but at times
like this, the navigator is always up front so they can clearly see where we're going.

As soon as we leave the compound, Reaper's phone beeps with a message. He
grunts as he reads it and tucks it away after silencing it.

"Colt and Drake tracked them to the same cabin. It's only Carter and Andrew
inside, though the idiots have a window cracked. It sounds like they are waiting
for Luscious. Colt said that Carter got off the phone with someone who doesn't
seem to want to hold up the deal that Carter gets his revenge before the person
on the phone gets Mae."

I grit my teeth and clench my fists. Those fuckers better not touch my Sunshine
Goddess. I'll make them pay tenfold whatever they do to her.

Pulling out my own phone, I text Doc.

> Timber: Doc, in case those assholes hurt my Sunshine,
> there's a chance she could be pregnant.

> Doc: No problem, Timber. I'll make sure she's taken care
> of. Is your preference to bring her back to the clubhouse?

> Timber: Yes. Don't want to go to the hospital unless we
> have to with those other psychos possibly circling.

> Doc: Got it. I'll let you know once I see her.

Just as we're pulling up to where we'll leave the trucks, Reaper digs his phone out of his pocket. His face darkens as he reads the text and he clutches his phone, his fingers turning white. With how tight he's holding it; I'm surprised it hasn't broken yet.

His gaze locks on mine, and I know.

Someone is going to die for hurting my Sunshine.

Also, thank fuck I already had that conversation with Doc.

Punisher parks the truck and we all get out. He immediately places a hand on my shoulder, but even though I know I need to get to Mae, we need a plan so no one else gets hurt or killed. Still, it kills me to wait. Especially since he could be hurting her still.

"Timber, Punisher, Devil, Smithy, Doc, and I will be the first wave. Mae's being held in a room in the basement. There's a small window, but that's it. Punisher, Devil, and Smithy will neutralize anyone in the house while Timber, Doc, and I head to the basement. The rest of you, secure the area and be ready to move in if you get the signal." He pauses as he looks at each of my brothers and my gut twists. "Mae's hurt and Colt advises we carry her out on the stretcher. Once Doc says she's good to move, I'll send for the stretcher, but I need someone on the perimeter team to carry it with them."

Odin slaps my shoulder and moves out with the others that will secure the perimeter. I'm honestly surprised he didn't stay with Mama Astrid; however, I also know how important Mae's become to both of them. He'll no doubt be wanting a piece of these bastards when we get them to the cellar.

My heart clenches at what they could have done to Mae for Colt to suggest taking her out on the stretcher.

I know both Doc and Patch keep two types of stretchers in their trucks. The normal hard backed one, but also another one with a sturdy cloth stretched across two long poles. Right now, Razor's carrying the hardback stretcher as he follows after Odin, the guys spreading out to the left and right of the trail.

I follow my brothers up the trail and when we get close enough; I hear a bird call off to my right. Turning, I spot Colt and quietly but quickly make my way to him with Reaper at my heels.

"There are two entrances, this one," Colt whispers as he points to the door nearby, "and one on the backside of the house. Drake's watching that one. Still just the two assholes inside and neither of us have seen anyone else trying to approach. No idea who Carter was talking to on the phone."

Drake must have told him who the two men were.

Reaper gives the signal, and our group heads toward the cabin.

Hang on, Sunshine, I'm coming.

Chapter 48
Timber

WITH THERE BEING TWO doors, Reaper changes the plan and our groups split up when we get closer.

Via text, we coordinate the countdown, and Reaper kicks in the front door right as Devil kicks in the back door. A couple of shots ring out and I'm hoping it's just to neutralize the assholes and they don't hit anything vital. I want these bastards alive.

Hot on Reaper's heels, Doc and I enter the living room and I would have laughed if it were any other type of situation.

A porno is on the TV and both men have their pathetic cocks hanging out, most likely from jerking off. Andrew is on the ground by the couch and Carter is by a chair. Behind Carter, there's a railing and some stairs that lead down to the basement.

My brothers secure both of the assholes easily, using zip ties to tie their hands behind their backs and secure their ankles together. Both men have gunshot wounds in their legs.

I stalk to the stairs and Carter yells at me.

"Stay away from her! She's mine, you lowlife thug!"

Not even bothering to reply, I continue downstairs and Doc, Reaper and I make our way, room by room, making sure each one is secure.

We get to the last room and I scowl when I see there's a heavy-duty padlock on the door. I'm about to try and kick it down when footsteps on the stairs draw my attention.

"Here, found this on the table," Punisher says as he hands me a key.

Quickly, I unlock the door, open it, and freeze for a moment when I see Mae.

Spinning on my heel, I turn toward the guys, who thankfully, have their eyes adverted. "Give me a sec to get her free and covered."

Shutting the door, my legs eat up the distance to her and I gently cup her face in my hands, kissing her.

"Liam, oh my God, Liam. You're really here," she cries, and it takes everything in me not to comfort her further right now.

"I'm gonna get you free, Baby."

She nods and I grab my knife out of my boot, getting to work, cutting her feet free before moving to her hands.

Her stomach is shredded with areas of raised welts. There are a few on her chest and hips as well, but the assholes at least left her bra on. It doesn't escape my notice that her panties are gone and I hope like fuck those assholes haven't raped her. If they did, their punishments will be severe.

As soon as her second hand is free, I scoot closer and she wraps her arms around my neck as I rest my forehead against hers, holding onto her arms. I'm scared to touch her anywhere else on her torso with how much damage those fuckers have done.

Pulling back, I slip off my cut, pull my shirt off, and drape it over her chest. Putting my cut back on, I lean in, kissing her hard.

"I'm sorry we didn't get here sooner, Sunshine." Tears prick my eyes as I cup her cheeks.

"I knew you'd come. I'm sorry I didn't pay closer attention in the hallway. I'm sorry, so sorry," she sobs, and I kiss her again.

"Shh, you have nothing to be sorry for, Mae. Those two assholes will get what's coming to them, I promise."

She nods, but I'm not sure if she believes me.

"Doc, you can come in now," I shout and seconds later, he's at my side.

"I'm sorry, Lil' Bit, but I need to take a peek at the damage before we get you on the stretcher."

Swallowing thickly, she nods. "The worst is my stomach. There are some marks on my upper chest and hips, but they aren't as bad as my stomach. And of course, my face."

Since she still has her bra on, I pull down her shirt, but keep her pussy covered.

His face hardens, and when he looks at me, he nods. Thank fuck that he'll be able to do this at the clubhouse. I cover her back up with my shirt.

Standing, he lets the others in.

"I'm sorry, but this is probably gonna hurt as we transfer you," Doc says as he lays it out on the floor.

Mae's face hardens. "I don't care. I just want out of this place. Carter was talking on the phone to someone about getting his revenge before the other person could have me. They were also waiting for someone. I have no idea when the handover was supposed to take place or where, but I don't want to stay in this bed or this house another second."

I carefully get my hands under Mae's hips while Doc slides his hands under her shoulders. Reaper takes her feet. Together, we lift her off the bed and onto the stretcher.

I pick up the poles by her head, and she reaches up, wrapping her hand tightly around my wrist while the other grabs onto the stretcher. Doc picks up the other end. She gnaws on her lips but doesn't make a peep as we make the trek upstairs and outside. Thankfully, someone pulled up a truck closer, so we don't have to carry her down the trail.

Reaper comes up and takes the poles from me, and both Punisher and I hop in the backseat almost in unison. It takes a bit of effort and maneuvering, but as careful as we are, we still jostle Mae a few times as we get her positioned so that she's laying across Punisher's and my lap. Through it all, she doesn't make a sound, but I notice her tears haven't stopped and her face is tight with pain.

Her sapphire eyes stay locked with mine as I dry her cheeks. She still has a tight grasp on my wrist, as if she's afraid I'll disappear. I won't, but I worry she's going to have nightmares about this for a while.

Her eyes start to droop as we get closer to the clubhouse.

"Sleep, Sunshine. You're safe now."

She slightly shakes her head. "I don't want to sleep. Not yet. They injected me with something at the clubhouse, but I don't know what. I was out pretty quickly."

"I'll draw blood to get it tested, but I'm going to bet it was a sedative," Doc says from the front seat. Reaper's knuckles tighten around the steering wheel.

Once Mae's taken care of, I want to find out how the fuck those assholes got onto the property in the first place. My bet is they were in Luscious' car, but I need to know.

The gate opens as soon as we approach, and Reaper parks right in front of the clubhouse doors.

Before I can do it myself, my door is opened and a sob escapes Mama Astrid when she sees Mae laying on our laps. Glancing at her forehead, I'm relieved to see that she's already been bandaged up.

She steps back and we carefully slide out of the truck. One of my brothers helps hold the stretcher poles up high until Punisher is out of the truck, and then we lower her before carrying her up the steps.

Sasha and Mama Astrid open the front doors and once we're inside, I'm directed to a room next to Doc's. Judging by the supplies, this must be where he patches up my brothers when needed. Fuck, I wish we had a room like this.

"Lay her on the bed. We'll slide the stretcher out from under her," Doc says and Punisher and I comply.

Once she's on the bed, he expertly pulls the stretcher from underneath her and turns around. It's then that I notice as many people cramming into the room or looking over shoulders as possible.

"Okay. Mama Astrid, Sasha, and Timber can stay. The rest of you need to scram. You'll all be able to see her once I get her patched up and she's rested."

Despite the grumbles, everyone comes in and says something to Mae before leaving. More than one cause tears to spring to Mae's eyes and almost everyone places a kiss on her forehead before stepping aside for the next person.

When the door finally shuts, Doc gets to work and covers her legs with a sheet, sliding it under my shirt to cover her.

"Mae, I'm gonna hook you up to an IV first."

She nods in response as Doc gathers everything he'll need.

After hanging up the fluid bag, he turns his attention to my shirt.

Stepping forward, I give her a quick kiss before I slowly take my shirt off her in case any blood dried to it.

Seeing her shredded stomach, chest, and hips again has rage boiling in me. Blinking, I force my tears not to fall. Those fuckers will pay for putting her through this.

"Oh my," Sasha says as her hands fly to her mouth. Both her and Mama Astrid look near tears.

"What was used to cause this?" Doc asks and I notice even his eyes are glassy with unshed tears.

Mae swallows thickly. "His belt. The buckle end."

My gaze goes to her legs. "Did he…" I swallow, not able to finish the sentence.

She sees where I'm looking and shakes her head. "He touched me, but he didn't rape me. He said he was waiting on someone before he was going to take it further."

Taking a few deep breaths, I tamp down my rage. That's not what Mae needs right now.

Spotting a chair, I move it to be right by the head of the bed and sit down. Immediately, she reaches out to me and I intertwine our fingers, kissing the back of her hand.

Doc washes his hands and then wheels over two trays, one on each side of the bed. He stands next to me and Sasha and Mama Astrid stand on the other side of the bed, already with gloves on.

"Mae, we're going to start by cleaning you up first, and then we'll see what needs stitches and what doesn't. But I will say, there are already three areas where I know for sure that you'll need stitches. Now, do you want to stay awake or do you want me to put you under?"

"Awake," she says before he's even finished his sentence. She swallows thickly. "Please don't put me under. I'm not ready for that yet."

Fresh tears pool in her eyes, and Doc nods, blinking rapidly. Both women dab their eyes before helping Doc get to work.

Chapter 49
Timber

THROUGHOUT THE WHOLE PROCESS, Mae hardly made a peep, though her tears were almost constantly running down the side of her face. I knew when Doc was working on the worst of the wounds because she would occasionally whimper and her face would scrunch up in pain as she squeezed my hand hard.

In the end, there were eight wounds that needed stitches, ten that he applied some skin glue stuff to, and the rest he said should heal naturally on their own. She got lucky with the cut by her eye and that her eye wasn't damaged. While the cut was a little jagged, Doc wanted to try skin glue first rather than stitches.

"Okay, I think we're good to go. I gave you some pain meds and antibiotics in your IV, so that should help keep your pain at bay for right now. Timber mentioned there's a possibility you could be pregnant, so I made sure everything would be safe in case you are."

Sunshine looks up at me, her cheeks flushed, and I can't resist leaning down and giving her a quick kiss.

"All the skin glue seems to have set. Until everything heals up, no baths and keep your showers quick. You don't want the wounds getting soaked. Let them air dry and keep your clothes loose until the wounds heal. For tonight, don't wear a bra. Tomorrow you should be able to wear one as long as it isn't too tight and doesn't rub on your wounds.

"If anything starts to look infected or red and irritated, let me know right away. I'll be checking in on you every now and then to see how you're doing and how you're feeling." He pauses, pulls out an icepack out of his mini-fridge and wraps it in a towel.

"Now, I'd prefer you don't put this directly over that wound by your eye for right now to ensure the glue is fully set, but you can position this around your eye in the meantime. Tomorrow, you should be good to place it directly over the wound, but no more than ten minutes at a time."

"I grabbed a club tank top that should be pretty loose for you. As a bonus, it's black in case it gets any blood on it. Sasha also got you some underwear and sweats, so you'll be a bit more comfortable," Mama Astrid says.

Mae tries to sit up but winces. Stepping closer, I carefully slip my hands under her back, and slowly raise her up, making her bend at the hips rather than her waist. She still winces slightly because of the couple of wounds on her hips, but not as badly as before.

They both help her slip the tank on and then I gently lower her back down to the bed. She exhales deep and slow, closing her eyes for a moment once she's fully horizontal again. Sasha wiggles the cloth of the tank top down until it's flat and not bunched up underneath her back. Then, they help get her into clean panties and sweats. When they're done, they both squeeze her hands.

"Get some rest, Dear. I'll make you some soup that you'll be able to drink through a straw, so you don't have to sit up or move for a while." Mama Astrid squeezes her hand and kisses her forehead. She steps out and Doc follows her.

"I'll come find you tomorrow. Colt and I are staying here, and we'll all drive back with you for the wedding," Sasha pauses and swallows thickly. "I know it's hard right now, but it will get better. Remember, we're here for you when you need it." She bends down, resting her forehead on Mae's like I've seen her do with Levi and her brother before.

After a few moments, she straightens and steps out of the room.

Mae shivers, and I pull up the light blanket over her. I'm about to ask how she's doing when there's a knock on the door.

Getting up, I'm surprised to see Smoke standing there. Then I remember Reaper saying he called him. He must have booked it to get here in three hours.

"Come on in." I step aside and go to the opposite side of the bed, taking the chair there and letting Smoke sit where I had been.

"Dad," Mae whispers and Smoke leans closer, torment and anguish written all over his face. His hands hover over her like he wants to hug her, but he's not sure of where it's safe to touch her.

She reaches out to him, and he takes her hand before resting his forehead against hers.

I'm about to step out to let them have a moment together, but Sunshine stops me, squeezing my hand.

"What happened? Reaper just said you'd been kidnapped, and they were on the way to rescue you," he asks as he sits down but doesn't release her hand.

Mae swallows thickly. "Carter, one of the doctors here in town, somehow got into the clubhouse. I went to use the bathroom, and he grabbed me right as I stepped out. He injected me with something and kidnapped me. The other man—"

"Andrew, Carter's father, who is also a doctor here in town," I interrupt and she scrunches up her face in disgust. Smoke's scowl deepens. He's been here to Junction Creek enough to know who we're talking about.

"Ew, that just makes that worse," she says before shuddering.

She continues, filling him in on what happened as well as what happened at the grocery store yesterday.

When she's finished, his gaze goes to her stomach, and she nods, even though he doesn't ask. She takes a deep breath and I gently squeeze her hand before letting go. Standing, I pull back the blanket and she rolls up her shirt to her breasts.

"There's a few more on my upper chest and hips, too," she says quietly.

Smoke's face morphs into one of rage when he sees the crisscross of wounds from the belt over her stomach and her swollen face. His gaze goes to mine and I nod, knowing what he's silently asking.

The fuckers are in the cellar.

I pull down Sunshine's shirt and cover her again with the blanket. A knock on the door breaks the tension and Mama Astrid walks in.

"I just stuck with a gentle tomato soup for right now, Dear. Tomorrow we'll see how you're feeling and go from there. If you want more later, I made extra and there's some in the fridge. Just warm it up in the microwave." She hands me a couple of large, insulated thermos with straws. Looking back at Sunshine, I wince when I realize this is going to hurt her.

"Sorry, Sunshine, but we're gonna have to move you to do this. Doc doesn't have a raising bed like they do in a hospital."

She gives me a small smile. "I kind of figured. And thank you for bringing me here rather than the hospital. With Preston, Phillip, Bruce, X and who knows else running around, I'd rather be here so long as Doc had everything he needed to patch me up."

Smoke and I share another look. Yeah, we're happier with her being here as well.

Setting down the thermoses, I walk around by Smoke and between the two of us, we get her situated closer to the edge.

I hand Smoke one of the thermoses, to which he gives me a surprised look, but I know they need to bond and he needs to work to repair the rift he caused. Not being ready to leave her side, I take her hand in mine and lazily rub circles on the back of her palm with my thumb.

Neither one of us says anything while Sunshine slowly sips her soup.

About twenty minutes later, she can barely keep her eyes open.

Letting go of her hand, I slip off my cut, set my phone down on the counter along with my gun and kick off my boots. Looking through some cabinets, I thankfully find some pillows and grab two out before handing one to Smoke.

Seeing that Doc had ordered a larger than normal sized bed, most likely because so many of my brothers are huge, I lay down on my side next to Sunshine on the bed. Even laying this way, there's plenty of room for both of us. Plus, there's no way that I'll be able to take my eyes off her tonight. Hell, most likely for a lot longer than that. Hopefully she won't be pissed off about it, but with this incident, she's going to have to go on lockdown.

"Sleep, Baby Girl. We'll be here if you need us," Smoke tells her.

With a yawn, she nods and slips her hands out from under ours and places them on top of ours. "Please don't hold down my hands. I have a feeling that could be a trigger if I can't free them while sleeping," she says as she yawns again.

Leaning down, I kiss her. "Night, Sunshine. Love you."

She looks up at me with a sleepy smile. "Love you, too, Liam." She pauses and turns toward Smoke.

"Thank you for coming to see me, and even though we're still on the outs, I still love you, Dad."

He swallows audibly and blinks repeatedly. "They wouldn't have been able to keep me away with you hurt like this. Love you, too, Baby Girl."

She gives him a small smile. "We still need to talk, though. You hurt me with everything you said and did."

He gives her a curt nod. "When you're ready, we will. Right now, you focus on getting better."

Once her eyes close, Smoke repositions his chair slightly and puts his pillow behind his head as he leans against the wall. He's going to be stiffer than fuck in the morning, but I already know without asking that he's not going to leave. Unfortunately, Doc only has the one bed in here.

A few minutes later, her breathing evens out and he clears his throat.

"Thank you for getting to her so quickly," he says quietly.

"Of course. She's my everything." I pause as my thoughts go back to those assholes. "They're both downstairs and I'm sure our brothers will keep them entertained until we get down there."

He gives me a chin lift, his face hardening. "On my way in, Reaper told me the phone call to Carter was made from a burner phone, so we're up against the wall on that one."

"Maybe and maybe not."

I then go on to fill him in on the interrogation with Luscious.

To say he's fucking livid is an understatement. He was pulled in to help on some of the work when stuff was going down with Frida, and not even he knew about Carter being involved.

"She's still down there as well, so we'll get more answers later. Tonight, let's try to sleep. I have a feeling it's going to be a rough night." My gaze goes to Mae, and I softly caress her cheek when I see her brow furrow in her sleep.

Smoke grunts and closes his eyes, his giant hand still resting underneath Mae's.

I wish we could take her back to our house so we could all rest easier, but Doc wanted her close by for tonight, so this will have to do for now.

Chapter 50
Mae

IT'S BEEN A COUPLE of days since the club rescued me and I'm finally able to move around easier. So far, everything looks like it's healing properly, which is a relief in and of itself.

After breakfast that next day, Doc gave the okay for me to sleep back at the townhouse, and a part of me wonders if it's because he could hear me screaming at night or not. I'd woken up three times that night from my nightmares. All three times, Liam and, surprisingly Dad, helped calm me down and coaxed me back to sleep.

However, as soon as I got back to the townhouse, I've pretty much been stuck here. Whenever Liam wasn't here, someone else came to keep me company, which was usually Sasha or Mama Astrid. Sometimes both of them.

Dad opted to stay in the town house next to us, and he's been over here multiple times. Unfortunately, I'm never alone with him so we haven't been able to really talk much.

He's told me more about his life. Growing up. His parents, who I wish I could have met, and about Nikki and Sadie. When I asked about Sadie's dad, for some reason he shut down and just said he's not in the picture. I wanted to pry more, but again, we weren't alone.

Shaking my head, I set my coffee down on the table. My hands graze over the blue and black journals Sasha gave me yesterday, as well as a pack of colored pens. We ended up having a video call with Levi, who apologized profusely for not being able to come to see me, but I totally understood and told her that. Her wedding is in a couple of days, and she needs to finish getting things ready.

During the video call, Levi told me her story. About being kidnapped a bit before her sixteenth birthday. About Scott and then about Black Plague when they kidnapped her again earlier this year.

She showed me her scars, and I burst into tears at seeing what they'd done to her. She said Reaper's scars are far worse than hers, and I'd bet anything it was because he tried to draw their attention away from her. On top of the normal protectiveness I've seen toward Old Ladies, they'd just found out that she was pregnant with twins the day before she was kidnapped.

I showed her what Carter had done to me, which had both of them in tears as well, even though Sasha had already seen them. Knowing what Levi had been through, and that it was sorta similar to my situation, helped me open up about it more to them.

Then they told me about the journals.

When she held up her own journals for the first time, it finally clicked. I'd seen Reaper writing in some notebooks like hers after breakfast each day. Sometimes multiple times throughout the day. When I said that, she gave me a small smile and said in the hospital after they were rescued; she told him about the journals. Her family uses them as well.

My mind wanders back to our conversation.

"Besides talking to family and friends about things, or sparring, or throwing knives, I also keep two journals. I always have a stack of each color for when I fill one up and I never let the stacks run out. You never know when something will trigger a memory, or your emotions, and you'll have the urge to use the journals.

"The blue one is my everyday journal to chart how I'm feeling. I use whichever color pen strikes my fancy but never black or red for the lengthy daily journal entries.

"On days that are exceptionally hard, I make a note, like this one," she says as she points to an entry in her own blue journal. It had the date and just a simple note of 'used the black journal'.

"If I feel like I'm in a really dark place, I'll make a note like that in either black or red ink. That's how I track how frequently I use it. I only use black or red pens when I'm writing in the black journal, no other colors.

"In the black journal, I'll jot down everything that I'm feeling. Times where it seems like I'm caught in the clutches of darkness and trying to claw my way out. I would write out every dark, and often torturous, action I'd do to my captors.

"When I found myself crawling out of that dark hole, I'd go out back to our firepit and light a fire. Then I'd rip out those pages and tear them up before rolling them into little balls and throwing them into the fire, letting the fire burn away my hateful and gruesome thoughts.

"After each... incident I'll just call them, the time periods between needing to write in the black journal were usually pretty frequent. Dad had heard of a saying that some therapists use with their patients to gauge how they're doing. He'd ask me 'how long?'. Meaning how long has it been since I felt the urge to write in the black journal and I'd always answer truthfully.

"Over time, the time periods between using the black journal and burning the pages lengthened. I found myself being able to process my emotions better and not needing to use the journals. Once I feel like I'm in a good place to put it all behind me, then I burn the blue ones as well."

Blinking, I pick up the notebooks and pens and put them in my backpack along with my Kindle. Reading has helped me pass the time since I've been stuck here for two days.

But that ends today.

Yesterday, Mama Astrid brought over the little golf cart she sometimes uses when carrying things back and forth between the clubhouse and their house. Since Doc doesn't want me exerting myself too much yet, she said I could use it to get around.

Putting my phone in my pocket, I slip on my flats and head out, locking the door behind me.

"And where do you think you're going?"

I jump, startled, and twirl toward the voice. Scowling, I curse myself for forgetting Timber has a Prospect watching our house since Carter and Andrew were able to sneak onto club grounds.

Colt stands a few feet away, his arms crossed with a stern look on his face, but his eyes dance with amusement. Like he knew I'd crack soon.

Squaring my shoulders, I lift my chin, not breaking his gaze. "I'm going to the clubhouse. I have to get out of this house. Plus, a few minutes of fresh air would be nice."

He frowns. "My orders are to keep you here and keep anyone not related to the club out."

"I need to see something other than these four walls. Besides, Doc cleared me to be more active, so there's nothing wrong with me going to the clubhouse."

His gaze narrows on mine and I cross my arms. The skin around my stitches pulls a bit at the action, but I refuse to show it. "You said you're supposed to protect me, right?"

"Yeah," he says, his gaze narrowing even more.

"What better place to protect me than where all the club members are all at?"

His face softens as he frowns again. "That's also where you were taken from."

My stomach rolls at the reminder, but I have to do this. "I know, and I also know that Python figured out what happened to his cameras and has fixed them. I'm guessing you also know about what else he did."

He'd placed even more cameras and changed up some of their locations, but there was no way I was saying that out loud.

"Please, Colt. I'm going to go crazy if I have to stay in the house another day," I darn near beg.

Finally, he sighs, his shoulders falling a little. "Fuck, I better not get in trouble because of this," he groans.

"If you do, you can blame it on me."

I spin around, not having heard anyone approach us.

Leaning against his door, my dad grins at us.

"Us Witlocks tend to go stir crazy faster than most, and it seems you've inherited that trait." He pushes off the door and walks toward us before gesturing toward the golf cart. "However, the only way I'll allow it is if you ride in the cart and we go in through the back door. Don't want you overexerting yourself. Or letting someone get a good look at you if they're watching the front gate."

I can't hold back my smile, which has Dad grinning even wider. "That was my plan."

Dad slides in behind the wheel and I sit beside him. The golf cart shifts as Colt sits on the back, um bench, for lack of a better word. There's no seat back there, but the bench is about three feet deep and as wide as the cart. Mama Astrid said that's where she usually puts her dishes when she brings them to the clubhouse.

I bite my lip, not sure if I should state my worry or not.

Dad laughs. "Odin and Dom beefed this golf cart up big time and it can easily carry four of us fuckers without breaking anything."

My shoulders relax and I can't help the giggle that escapes. "Sorry. I don't know too much about cars or other vehicles, so I wasn't sure if these things had a weight limit."

"You saying we're fat, Lil' Bit?" Colt asks and I turn, trying not to move too fast or pull my stitches and glue too much.

"No! It's just that you're all so," I pause, gesturing up and down both of their bodies, "so muscular. Mama Astrid lent me this, and I want to make sure nothing would happen to it. It's poor etiquette."

Both of them laugh and I turn around, facing the front again with a huff.

Men.

Dad pats my knee. "Don't worry, Baby Girl. We'd never intentionally break it."

I don't reply, because my gaze locks on the back door of the clubhouse as we get closer.

I try to control my breathing as we get closer but judging by how both of them are watching me, they know I'm nervous.

Dad parks off to the side of the door, so that he's between me and the door.

"Take all the time you need, Baby Girl. It's going to be hard, but it will get better. I promise."

Taking a few deep breaths, I nod and slide off the seat before slipping my bag strap over my shoulder. Slowly, I walk to the door, my hand hovering over the doorknob.

I swallow thickly, pulling back my hand and rubbing my hands against my jeans, wiping off the sweat.

Squaring my shoulders, I reach forward and open the door, only to freeze right inside the door. My gaze locks on the scuff mark on the wall.

"What is it, Mae?" Dad asks.

I open my mouth, only for nothing to come out as I point toward it. It takes a few times before I can actually say what I need to.

"That scuff is from when Andrew hit Mama Astrid in the head. As he brought the gun back, the handle made that mark," I whisper, and both of them curse behind me.

Dad wraps his arms carefully around me, forcing me to look away from the wall. "We'll get that taken care of, Baby Girl. I'm sorry. I'm not sure how we missed that."

Nodding, I take another deep breath and allow him to guide me down the hallway. My feet try to stop when we reach the bathroom, the spot where Carter first grabbed me, but Dad urges me to keep walking rather than dwelling on it.

Once we're in the main room, I'm able to breathe easier.

That is until I look around.

The Johnson Chasers are out and Timber's talking to both Candi and Star.

My heart squeezes when Candi places a hand on Timber's arm as she smiles up at him sweetly and he doesn't shove it away.

Is this what he's been doing when he hasn't been home? Spending time with them doing God knows what?

Turning away from him, I force myself not to cry. Why am I always the one that has to fight to keep Timber with me? He should be making sure they don't cross any lines as well.

Instead of going to Timber, I make a beeline for a spot I know will keep me somewhat hidden, but my feet pull up short when I get there.

Reaper is sitting on the couch in the middle and it looks like he had the same plan I had. He's writing in his journals.

Looking over my shoulder, Candi's hand is still on Timber's arm and he laughs at something she said. My heart breaks a little more and I quickly wipe a away as I turn back toward Reaper.

Clearing my throat, I clutch my bag closer to me. "I-Is it okay if I sit by you, Uncle Reaper?" I ask, my voice probably no louder than a whisper, but he still hears me.

He looks up at me, his face quickly turning to one of worry before his gaze bounces across the room and when it narrows, I know what he's finally seen. I'm surprised he doesn't say anything about my 'uncle' slip since I know they like to go by just their road names, but he doesn't say anything about it.

He pats the spot to his left, and I carefully sit down. I learned the hard way that moving too fast while sitting down or getting up pulls a lot on my wounds. Slipping off my flats, I cross my legs and set my backpack on my lap, using it as a bit of leverage before pulling out my journals.

Reaper looks at me, his eyebrow raised, and I give him a soft smile.

"How long?" he asks me and my smile falls.

"An hour," I whisper and he grunts, patting my knee before going back to writing in his own journal.

Settling in, I get to writing, though every now and then, my gaze always finds Timber. Each time, my chest tightens further. He's still talking to the Johnson Chasers with his back toward me.

And when one of them notices me looking, they touch him.

Every time, I hope that Timber will push them away or turn and notice me, but he doesn't.

This time though, it's a scuffle that has me looking up from my journal and pulling my attention across the room.

Dad has Timber pinned against the wall, their voices hushed. Timber's gaze looks around the room and the surprise on his face when his gaze finally lands on me has my chest tightening even more.

Out of the corner of my eye, I notice the clock above the bar reads 11 am. I've been writing for two hours. Two hours and Timber hadn't even noticed I was in the room the entire time.

Turning and shifting, I lean my back against Reaper's shoulder, effectively giving Timber my back, and go back to my writing.

Well, at least I try to.

I bite back a sob as tears threaten to fall. Pain courses through me once again, but it isn't from my wounds.

It's from Timber.

The man who swore he'd always love me and protect me.

Doubts swirl around my mind once again. Wondering if he doesn't believe me about not being raped. Does he think that I'm damaged now that I'm all scarred up and someone else put their hands on me? Not to mention him flirting with two whores for at least the past two hours. Who knows how long it was going on before I came in here? I'm not the only one in the room that notices his actions either. Has he been doing this for the past two days as well?

Hastily, I wipe my face, angry at everything that's happened and from the pain of being ignored by the love of my life.

Taking a deep breath, I force myself to focus on the words when a shadow falls over me.

I don't look up. I know who it is.

My body always prickles with awareness whenever we're in the same room. Too bad it's never worked in reverse.

"Sunshine," he whispers as he shifts on his feet.

I shake my head, not wanting to talk to him right now.

He sits down on the coffee table and reaches out for me, but I don't move a muscle. I can feel Reaper's body tensing against my back.

"You're supposed to be at the house."

Anger rises in me and I finally look up at him, letting him see the hurt, the pain, the anger I'm feeling. His face blanches as he flinches back.

"Why? So you can continue to flirt with your whores? Have they been keeping you company all this time when you made me stay at the house? Have you been with them since we got here?"

"No," he replies angrily. "How can you even ask me that?"

I huff. "How? Let's see. I've been here for two hours. Two hours and you only just noticed me, and that's only because Dad made you. Instead, you've been flirting with those two whores since before I came here. When they touched you, you never brushed them off. Instead, you laughed and flirted back with them. They both knew I was in here and whenever they saw me watching, they'd touch you. Give you soft smiles while rubbing it in my face that you weren't paying attention to me. Your Old Lady. Am I even that anymore?"

His face darkens and his hands clench.

"Do you know how much it hurts when the person you love the most doesn't even want to touch you anymore? When you kiss me, it's barely even a peck on the lips. You never hold me anymore. If I sit next to you and lean against you, you move away or get up. In bed, you lay as far away from me as possible and turn your back toward me.

"Before I was kidnapped and we were in the same room, you always found a way to touch me. Every kiss, even the chaste ones, held more love than what you've given to me the last few days. Instead of being by my side, I felt like I was locked away again since I wasn't allowed to leave the house.

"Or is it that you don't believe me about not being raped? Or do you not want me anymore because you see me as damaged? Scarred for life because of what that asshole did to me? If that's the case, if you don't want me as yours anymore, tell me now and I'll leave you to your whores."

He doesn't answer me. He just stares at me, shock written all over his face.

My heart cracks further and I hastily grab my things, ignoring the pain of getting up too quickly and stalk toward the back door. Tears streak down my face, but I make no move to wipe them away.

Getting in the golf cart, I floor it toward the townhouse. I'll pack the necessities, grab my stuff out of the safe, and leave.

Dad gave me a fake ID the other day in case I ever needed it, along with a credit card, so that I'd always have an escape route if need be since we don't know the lengths Bruce, X, Preston and Phillip will go to get me.

I think it's finally time for me to see the ocean and get as far away from Timber as I can. I'll pay Dad back later—I'm sure he'll understand. There's no way I can stay here and continue to see Timber flirting or screwing those women. It would shred what little's left of my heart.

Chapter 51
Timber

WHAT THE FUCK JUST happened?

Candi and Star had come up to me earlier and apologized about hitting on me before. Then I found out they were both taking online college courses and we got to talking about that which spiraled into other things. I'd never really just *talked* to them before, but they're pretty cool. I had no idea that we'd been talking for over two hours, or that Sunshine had come to the clubhouse.

Shame rolls through me at not even noticing her come in. Normally, I'm aware of wherever she is and always gravitate toward her.

A punch to my jaw pulls me out of my thoughts and I barely catch myself before falling off the coffee table and onto the floor.

"You fucking bastard," Punisher seethes as he towers over me.

Instantly, I'm on my feet, but Reaper pushes us apart.

"Enough. There's been enough damage done today." He turns to me, and I force myself not to flinch back from the dark look on his face. "Go to your woman and fix this before you lose her forever. I've known you for years and know you'd never cheat on a woman, especially someone you'd make your Old Lady. I'll deal with the bunnies. They knew what they were doing and did it anyway."

Not wasting another minute, I stalk toward the backdoor, ignoring everyone else, though I do notice enough to know that they're all pissed at me. In the hallway, I pull up short, pissed as fuck that he's blocking me.

At the end of the hallway, Smoke's standing in front of the door, arms crossed.

"You don't fix this; you will never see her again. Got me?"

"I get you, but I will fix this. I'm not losing my woman," I grit out as I push past him and out the door.

Turning, I run toward the house, hoping she hasn't found a way to leave yet. I can't lose my Sunshine Goddess.

Once inside, I flip the lock and instantly know she's up in our room. I can hear her hastily going through drawers. That hits me like a punch to the gut.

She's going to leave if I don't set things straight.

For once, I'm thankful the house has carpet everywhere but the kitchens and bathrooms so that it can help muffle my steps.

Before I even reach the stairs, I can hear her sobs and my gut twists. I fucking hate hearing Sunshine crying on a normal day, but the fact that she's crying because of me makes it ten times worse.

Only the fact that I can see the bedroom door is open is what keeps my footsteps steady as I climb the stairs. I don't want her shutting the door and putting up another barrier between us.

When I reach our room, I shut the door behind me. She's standing at the edge of the bed with her back to the door as she shoves clothes into a bag.

It's then that she notices she's not alone.

She spins on her heel and levels me with a hateful glare. It pisses me off even more that that look is on her face because of me.

"Leave, Timber. I'll be out of your life shortly and you can go back to your fun," she spits.

Quickly, I cross the room toward her, but she backs away toward her side of the bed, trying to keep distance between us.

That's not happening.

I follow her and gently grab hold of her shoulders, careful not to touch any of her wounds.

Before she can say anything else, I slam my lips down onto hers. She refuses to open, but after a few moments, she melts against me.

I should have known it was too easy, because the second she lets me in, she bites down on my tongue as she pounds her tiny fists against my chest.

"What the fuck?"

"What the fuck? What do you mean, what the fuck? How dare you kiss me with the mouth you had on *them*, Timber!" she screams as she continues to beat on my chest.

"I've never kissed or been with anyone else since we've been together, Sunshine. And I'm not Timber to you when we're alone. I'm Liam."

"Liar! And I'm not your Sunshine. Not anymore. You didn't deny anything just moments ago. You just sat there and stared at me. Ripped my heart out and stomped on the shredded pieces."

The knot in my gut twists even harder at that. "I swear, I never touched them or anyone like that. How can I prove it to you? You're my everything, Sunshine. My Old Lady.

"You want to know why I wasn't here? Aside from when I had to be in Church, it's because every second I saw you, I had to remind myself that I couldn't touch you like I wanted. It was so fucking hard to step away because I still felt the urge to have eyes on you all the time. But I had to take things slow. It would kill me to know that I caused you pain because of my selfish needs. I was waiting for you to let me know you were ready for more. I never meant for you to take that as rejection. It's been killing me that I couldn't touch you or sink into you like I wanted to."

Her bright blue eyes search my face, but she won't find any lie in what I'd said. It's all true.

Then her jaw clenches. "Then why did you not brush off those two whores touches earlier? Was this the first time you talked to them like that? That they touched you like that?"

Groaning, I shake my head. "Honestly, I don't know why. I thought they were just being friendly, and I didn't know they were stalling me or rubbing it in your face. I swear."

"What did you talk about?" she practically whispers as another tear rolls down her cheek. Surprisingly, she doesn't pull away from my touch when I wipe it away. Hope flares in my chest that I haven't fully lost her.

"They apologized for hitting on me before and causing problems. I found out they were taking online classes while being here, and it kind of just spiraled from there. I had no idea they were creating another problem." Pausing, I lift her chin and make her look at me again. "I mean it, Sunshine. There's no one else for me. I can't live without you by my side. I need you. Please believe me, Baby."

More tears escape down her cheeks, and I wipe them away. "This can't happen again, Liam. I don't care who the fuck they are. They touch you; you step away. I'm tired of always being the one that has to fight to keep you. I need you to fight to keep me, too."

"Always," I say right before I slam my lips down on hers.

She moans as she melts against me. This time, she opens right away, her tongue dueling with my own.

A moment later, she pulls back, tugging on my shirt. "I need you. Please, Liam. I need your touch. To prove I'm not damaged. To prove you still love me."

Stepping back, I take off my cut and lay it on the dresser, all the while, my gaze staying locked on hers.

Slowly, I strip for her, loving how her eyes eat me up and she licks her lips as she stares at my cock.

Waiting, I watch her gaze rise and her hands fly to her mouth in shock, her eyes wide.

Walking toward the bed, I pull back the blankets, throwing them on the floor. Crooking my finger at her, she lowers her hands and smirks but walks toward me.

When she's close enough, her hands go to my chest, but thankfully, she doesn't touch the tattoo. It's still pretty sensitive.

"Told you you're my everything, Sunshine. I wouldn't have gotten your name tattooed on me if you didn't own my heart."

I'd gotten the same 'Sunshine' design that Atlas had put on her helmets tattooed above my heart. I also had them add similar scrollwork underneath it with Mae's name included in it.

She leans up on her tippy toes and pulls me down, kissing me.

After a few moments, I pull back. Without a word, I lift her t-shirt and she raises her arms for me to take it off. Leaning down, I kiss her as I reach behind her, unclasping her bra. She pulls the straps down her arms and flings it somewhere in the room.

Running my hands down her back, I grip her ass as I kiss along her jaw, making sure to pay special attention to the two very sensitive spots on her neck. Right below her ear and at the crook of her neck. As soon as I lick the first spot, she's panting and rolling her hips against me.

A whimper escapes her when my teeth scrape the crook of her neck, and not being able to resist it, I bite down. Hard. I'm sure it'll leave a mark later, but I don't care.

"Liam!" she cries out, her hands tangled in my hair, tugging on it as she rubs herself against me.

Kneeling, I make sure to look her straight in the eye as I start to kiss down her chest, kissing every mark that fucker gave her.

"That fucker may have marked you up as a punishment for denying him, but I see you as a survivor, Baby. You didn't cave into him. You fought and will go on to be stronger because of it."

Something shifts in her eyes as they turn misty. She tries to pull me up, but I smirk. "You are wearing entirely too much clothing, Sunshine. Need to take care of that first."

Instantly, her eyes darken with lust as she bites her lip.

Undoing her jeans, I lower them, along with her socks, and toss them to the side after she steps out of them.

My gaze locks on her little black thong, which already has a dark stain on it, and my cock twitches. I'm surprised she's wearing it since she was pretty adamant about not wanting, in her words, 'a piece of floss between her ass cheeks' not that long ago, but fuck does she look sexy in it.

Leaning forward, I run my tongue over her slit through the thong, the silky material getting wetter with each pass, both from me and her. I groan as her juices soak through, and I almost break my resolve, but this is about her right now.

With my teeth, I tug on the material, nipping her skin on purpose before lowering it. Her skin breaks out into goosebumps. She shivers and quickly steps out of the thong.

Watching her the entire time, I lift one of her legs, kissing from her ankle to her knee and up her thigh. I stop right before I get to her pussy, which is already dripping juices down her other thigh. She whimpers when I set her foot down.

Lifting her other leg, I repeat the process, and when I get to that little trail, her breath hitches when I lick it all the way up to her pussy.

"Oh, God, Liam!" she cries out when I run my tongue through her folds.

Propping her leg on my shoulder, I grab her hips and damn near devour her.

Her hands fly to my head, her fingers grabbing onto my hair.

I bring her to orgasm two times like this before pulling back slightly and biting her inner thigh.

"Does my good girl want to be a little adventurous?"

A shudder runs through her and I move down a little further, biting her thigh again.

She whimpers. "Yes, please."

"Sit on the edge of the bed and close your eyes."

Her eyes widen a little at the command in my voice, but then she scrambles to do as I asked, though thankfully, she remembers not to sit down too quickly in the process.

She may not have thought I caught her wince when she sat up earlier at the clubhouse, but I did.

When she's in place, I go to the closet and get down the box I'd set up there late last night. One of the things I'd done yesterday, besides getting this tattoo, when I had put some distance between us, was to go to the adult store on the edge of town.

I'd gotten a variety of things, both for now and for when she's fully healed. Once they were charged and washed, I stowed them out of sight. I had hoped that with time, I could erase the memories for how she'd been restrained.

Sitting the box on her lap, I kneel in front of her, so that my face is level with hers.

"Open your eyes, Sunshine."

She blinks and smiles before turning her attention to the box. "What's this?"

Clearing my throat, I feel my cheeks heat a bit. "I know now that staying away hurt you rather than helped, but one of the things I did yesterday was to go and get these items."

Her face lights up in excitement, but I stop her from opening it just yet. She looks back up at me in confusion.

"There is something in here that I got that ties into something we talked about before..." I pause, and clear my throat, not wanting to say that asshole's name in our bedroom. "Anyway, you may not want to try it now, but know that when you do, it will be done with trust and you'll have a safe word. I thought about just keeping them hidden in the closet, but I didn't want you to freak out if you found them. Just remember, this will always be on your terms."

She swallows nervously, and I think she knows what I'm talking about, but neither of us says it out loud. This time when she goes to open the box, I let her.

She pulls out each item and lays them on the bed—a couple of vibrators, including a double penetration one, butt plugs of various sizes, a couple of clit stimulators, nipple clamps, a flogger, a blindfold, some soft rope, and a restraint system with cuffs. There are also a couple of different types of lubes.

Her breathing starts to quicken, and I cup her cheeks, making her face me instead of the toys.

Fuck.

Her eyes are clouded and I know where her mind's at. "Look at me, Sunshine. You're here with me. You are in my arms. We're in our bedroom. You aren't there or with him anymore. You're with me, Liam."

Finally, she blinks and her eyes start to clear. She tries to look away, but I don't let her.

"There's nothing to be ashamed of, Baby. We're going to take things slow. You pick out what you want to try and we'll go from there. Am I expecting to use all these today? No. In fact, we don't even have to use any of the items. It'll always be on your terms.

"And if there's something you want to try that isn't in this box, then we can either order it online or go to a store together to get it." I pause, leaning forward and kissing her gently before resting my forehead against hers. "It's all up to you, Baby."

Taking a deep breath, she pulls back, and although I notice she's a little shaken still, she turns back to the array of toys.

Chapter 52

Mae

I CAN'T BELIEVE I'M even considering this, but I want to try.

I'd prefer the way Liam described after our shower the other day, but I know that's not an option, since my wounds are still healing. Not to mention the apprehension of being tied up again, but as they say, taking baby steps is still progress in overcoming your fears.

Knowing that part of the time Liam was gone the last couple of days was to get that beautiful tattoo and these toys blows me away. Those actions also help lessen some of the sting of what he's done. He's not off scott-free by any means, but I'm giving him another chance. I just hope he doesn't let me down again.

Grabbing the box, I put away the nipple clamps, silk rope, flogger, blindfold, and as for the rest of the stuff, I leave them out.

Looking back up at Liam, I can tell he's apprehensive, but excitement also shines through his eyes.

"These are things that I'm willing to try right now. I'm not saying no to this other stuff, just not yet. Also... don't make me close my eyes. I need to be able to see you. And no hitting my breasts or down there. As for teasing my nipples, I'll probably be okay since it's you, just don't twist them, please."

His face darkens with anger, but I know it's directed at those two twattwaffles they have hidden somewhere on the property. I'm not dumb. I know the club will deal with them and that the cops won't be called in for this. Just like I know they're dealing with Luscious.

"Understood, Sunshine," he replies right before his lips slam down on mine. I moan as his giant hands slide up my back, holding me gently against him.

After a few moments, he pulls back, both of us breathing heavily.

"Do you want a singular safe word, or do you want to use the color system? Green for good, yellow for caution, and red for stop."

Nibbling my lip, I nod. "Color system. That should be easier to remember."

He kisses me again and gently guides me until I'm on my back. "Scoot up until your feet are hanging off the bed and put a pillow under your head."

I do as he asks, and lay with my elbows bent, my hands laying on the mattress on either side of my pillow. He picks up two of the cuffs along with some straps, and instantly, my body tenses, but I force myself to relax.

This is Liam.

He won't hurt me.

"Still green?" he asks, and I notice he's now standing up by the head of the bed to my right.

Nodding, I make sure not to look away from him. "Still green."

He hooks the strap to something on the bed and attaches the cuff to my wrist. "I'm not going to fully restrain you in case you panic. If you're okay with it this time, maybe next time we tighten it more."

I test how much range I have and, if I wanted to, I could raise my forearms straight up. Relief fills me, and he leans down, cupping my cheek.

"I want you comfortable, not panicking. Remember, if at any time it becomes too much, say the word and I can pull on these Velcro straps on your wrists to free you." To emphasize his point, he undoes the Velcro strap and proves just how quick it'll be to free me.

My body relaxes further at that. Guess I must have been showing more of my emotions than I thought.

Walking around the other side of the bed, he secures my other wrist the same way before moving to stand at the edge of the bed and puts the other two back in the box.

He catches me watching him and gives me a small smile. "I'm not gonna do your ankles. We'll ease into that when you feel more comfortable with the restraints."

These little things are adding up so much that it's about to make me cry with how much he's helping me walk through my insecurities.

He repositions the rest of the toys so they'll be in easier reach for him and then crawls in between my legs, kissing my thighs.

"I think I want another snack before we get to the main event," he growls before diving in and practically devouring me.

My thighs clamp around his head and my back bows off the bed when he licks from my star to clit and then circles around my clit before doing it all again.

He brings me twice like that, and when he pulls back, I'm panting like crazy and my body is covered in a light sheen of sweat.

The snick of a bottle has me curious for what he's planning next, and when I see the smallest butt plug, I bite my lip. While it's small, I've also never done anything anal before other than when he put the tip of his thumb in me. I'm nervous, but I'm also excited to try it out. Surprisingly, Liam also grabs one of the vibrators with some sort of additional protrusion with little bumps all over it. He grabs another pillow and lightly slaps my thigh.

"Raise your hips, Sunshine."

I do as he asks and then he places the pillow under my hips before slipping the vibrator inside me. Not surprisingly, it goes in without any resistance since I'm so wet. It's then that I realize that protrusion is the clit stimulator. He turns the vibrator on, and my eyes roll back in my head as another orgasm starts to slowly build.

Liam starts thrusting the vibrator in and out, making sure to rub the small tip against my clit each time.

After a few thrusts, I feel something cold press against my star.

"Relax your body, Sunshine. I know it sounds a little weird, but push out while I push in. I'll go slow. If it gets to be too much, let me know."

Nodding, I keep my gaze locked on Liam's as I try to force my body to relax, focusing on the vibrations and thrusts from the dildo in his other hand. The pressure increases, and my body clenches without me even realizing it.

He increases the vibrations, and I cry out in surprise, my orgasm cresting immediately. Liam takes that moment to push the plug in further until it's fully seated.

My thighs shaking, I moan at how full I feel.

"Does my Sunshine like having herself stuffed full like this?"

"Yes." My voice sounds foreign to me, huskier and lower.

"Do you want more?"

He slows the thrusts of the vibrator and plug, and a whimper escapes me. I'm already so close again. "Yes, please give me more."

Liam grabs a piece of silky fabric and loops it around the end of the vibrator before snaking it around my hips and tying it off, effectively making sure it won't slip out of me. He adjusts the setting again, and I cry out from the intensity.

He kisses up my stomach until he devours my mouth. Knipping my lip, he pulls back and crawls forward more and my mouth waters as his cock stops right in front of my lips. A bead of precum oozes out of the tip and I stick my tongue out, licking it up.

He moans and I open my mouth, slightly tilting my head back so he can slide further down my throat. That's all it takes to snap his control because the next thing I know, he's fucking my mouth like he did in the shower the other day.

"Fuck, you look so good with all your holes stuffed. My dirty good girl."

I moan, rubbing my thighs together, wanting more friction. I'm so close again. His words are turning me on even more, but they also have me wanting to be even dirtier for him.

As if he's reading my mind, he moans deeply.

"Fuck, your mouth is perfect, Sunshine. Next time, I'm going to stuff you even fuller. Maybe use the dual vibrator until you're begging for me to fuck you into oblivion. Or maybe I'll tie you up in a sex swing, taking my pleasure from each of your holes before fucking you so hard you see stars and pass out."

The mental images he's painting tip me over the edge, and I cry out as much as I can with his cock in my mouth.

Suddenly, he pulls back, takes out the vibrator and slams into me in one stroke.

"Yes! Liam, oh my God, yes!"

He pistons into me harder and I love the way he feels at this angle.

"Harder, Liam. Fuck me harder."

I don't know what's come over me to be cursing so much, but it seems to snap something in Liam every time that I do it.

He leans forward, his hands on either side of my face and my eyes roll back as his cock hits me deeper. I moan when his lips slam down on mine. His pelvic bone hits my clit just right with each thrust, the tingling in my belly increasing with each touch.

"I want you to come with me, Sunshine. Milk my cock with your sweet pussy."

My legs tighten around his waist.

"I'm so close," I whimper.

"Come, now," he commands right as he bites down on the crook of my neck. My orgasm rips through me as little black dots swirl around my vision. Liam roars seconds later and I feel him filling me full of his cum.

I know I'll probably have a huge hickey later, *again*, but I don't care.

His lips find mine. We lay there for a little while holding each other and kissing as he slowly keeps pumping into me.

Pulling back, he brushes some hair off my face. "Love you, Mae. Always," he whispers before leaning down and kissing me again.

"Love you, too, Liam. I'm giving you another chance. Don't make me regret it."

His eyes soften and he kisses me again. "I won't, Sunshine."

Chapter 53

Timber

I CAN'T HELP BUT smirk when Mae whimpers as I pull out of her. "Need to get you cleaned up, Sunshine, and get some food in you. You'll need it for later tonight."

Her eyes light up and I grin. I'm still thanking my lucky stars that she didn't leave me. I was a fucking idiot for thinking the way I did. If only I would have paid more attention to her subtle cues when we were together the last few days, this could have been avoided.

Looking back, I see them now, but at the time, I was stupidly only thinking about my needs. Not what she needed.

Leaning forward, I undo her wrist restraints, pull the plug slowly out of her and pick up the dildo I'd used on her. "Be right back."

Walking to the bathroom, I quickly clean both toys and then wet a washcloth. Back in the bedroom, my chest warms at the blissed-out look on Sunshine's face. The way she bites her lip as I clean her up and then myself has me already half hard for her again.

Putting the toys back in the box, I unhook the restraints from the bed slats and help her up.

"Let's get cleaned up and then get some grub."

She nods, but then her face pales. "Fiddlesticks... With everything going on, I haven't been able to cook for the guys like I said I would!"

Grabbing her arms before she can dart off in a panic, I can't help but chuckle. "Baby, the guys all understand. Trust me when I say they'd rather you take care of yourself and get back on your feet. It's not like we're never gonna come back here. We'll make sure that when we do, it's for at least a few days so that we can spend time with everyone and you can cook more then. Okay?"

She relaxes in my arms, leaning her head against my chest and sighs. "Okay, but I still want to help with supper and at least breakfast. I'm not sure when we're heading out tomorrow."

Her fingers trace around the edges of my new tattoo, and I hold her in my arms for a few moments, before kissing the top of her head.

"Let's hop in the shower, Sunshine."

She smiles before sashaying her cute little ass toward the bathroom. However, it's the mischievous glint in her eyes that has me pausing. Unease twirls in my gut and I wonder exactly how much Levi and Sasha have shared with her about living on club grounds for the past few months.

And if they told her about their versions of punishments.

Swallowing thickly, I follow her into the bathroom.

Walking up to the backdoor of the clubhouse, Mae pauses a few feet from the door. I squeeze her hand, but don't nudge her to keep moving.

My chest tightens that I wasn't here to help her through this earlier this morning. I hate that Smoke was the one that pointed out I was being an idiot and fucking everything up, but at least she had him there for her when she needed him. Colt, too.

She takes a deep breath, opens the door and hurries down the hallway, not stopping. The smell of fresh paint lingers in the air and it takes me a bit to realize they'd painted over the scuff mark that was on the wall. Another thing I should have picked up on if I had been paying attention.

It's only once she's past the bathrooms that she slows, exhaling heavily.

I pull her into me, kissing her temple. "You did good, Baby. Let's get you fed."

With a hand at her back, I guide her into the kitchen and wince at the look on Mama Astrid's face. She studies Mae for a bit before her harsh glare cuts my way again.

Shit.

Here I'd been worried about what Mae might make me do to grovel when I should have been worried about facing Mama Astrid. For the first punishment, I mean.

Walking up to me, she lands several whaps with her wooden spoon on my arms and the back of my head. Fuck that hurt, but there's no fucking way I'd ever verbalize that.

"You best treat her right or the next time, it'll hurt much worse than that," she hisses as she shoves a bowl of oatmeal into my hands. Sunshine giggles and smirks at me when I glare at her, but it has no heat behind it. I know I fucked up.

You know when Mama Astrid is pissed at you because you don't get to eat what everyone else is. Oatmeal is her go to, but if you really pissed her off, you'll be eating bare bone meals for a few days. From what I'd heard, it's a few hard-boiled eggs, a sandwich that usually had just cheese on it and possibly bone broth.

"Serves them right," Sunshine says softly.

Looking over at her, she's smirking at something. Following her line of sight, I can't help but smirk as well.

Looks like Candi and Star are getting Mama Astrid's bare bones menu. And it seems that Sunshine already knew about Mama Astrid's punishment system.

Pushing that thought out of my mind, my gaze narrows on the bitches. They'll be getting a piece of my mind later. Focusing back on Mae, I realize she hasn't grabbed a drink yet. "Baby, which flavored water do you want?"

She looks over the buffet of fruit salad, cold cut sandwich and sub fixings, apple crisp, cinnamon rolls and corn on the cob. My stomach rumbles, but I don't act on it. If I did, I'd be in even bigger trouble with Mama Astrid.

"Um, lemon please."

Nodding, I walk over to the fridge and grab her one before waiting while she fills her plate.

My chest warms at seeing her plate nearly full. She's been able to eat more and more each day, which is good. When we get our hands on that fat fuck of a stepfather, he'll regret everything that he's done to my Sunshine.

"Hey, you okay?"

Sunshine's voice brings me out of my thoughts and I smile. "Yeah. I'm happy at seeing how full your plate is."

The blush that spreads across her cheeks is cute as fuck. I don't think I'll ever get tired of seeing it.

"Then what was that angry look at the end?"

Sighing, I lean down, kissing her temple as I pull her into my side, careful not to make her drop her plate.

"Just hating what that fuckwad put you through and that I can't wait to get my hands on him."

Her eyes turn a little misty as she turns, hugging me as much as she can. "Thank you," she whispers.

Tilting her chin up, I make sure she can't look away. "Always, Sunshine. And that's a promise." Leaning forward, I give her a quick kiss and squeeze her waist gently. "Now, where do you want to sit?"

She looks out over the main room and smiles. Reaper and Smoke are waving us over and while Punisher's still glaring at me, at least he doesn't look like he's gonna punch me again.

"Good to see you've pulled your head out of your ass, brother," Punisher says with a grunt as we sit down. Sunshine playfully swats his arm, and he winks at her. "Just looking out for you, Sis."

Reaper clears his throat. "Star and Candi each earned their first strike with their display earlier. Since you were impacted, I wanted to discuss with you, Lil' Bit, about their punishment."

Mae looks up at him, wide-eyed with her fork frozen halfway to her mouth. "Is that allowed?" she whispers, which has all of us laughing.

"Sunshine, he wouldn't have brought it up if he wasn't okay with it."

"Oh," she says as a blush stains her cheeks. She sits her fork down and her gaze narrows on Candi and Star. "Two months of them being fully clothed at all times since their display went on for two hours. They'll probably hate that, seeing that the clothing they always wear barely covers the important bits.

"I get that the single guys want easy access, but I wish there was a minimum dress code. I'd hate for one of them to be walking out like that or how Gigi was dressed when Jordan and Sadie were there. The kids shouldn't have to see that." She pauses, and her gaze narrows even more. "I'd love to pull a card out of Levi's book and make it so they can't have sex during that time, but they are also your only two bunnies right now. How about I leave that decision up to you, Reaper?"

From the glances my brothers and I are all sharing, we're all feeling a little ashamed right now as her words sink in. I'll be bringing it up at our club, too.

Reaper clears his throat. "I'm ashamed to admit that I never thought about that, but you're right. If Sadie, Jordan, or Half-pints twins were here, I wouldn't want them around that either. I'll be fixing that. Now, as for their punishments, I'm all for the clothing one. As for the sex, since they are our only two and Luscious quit, we'll have them trade off. Only one of them will be available to the guys at a time. I'll work out a schedule and post it so everyone knows."

I bite my tongue at the Luscious comment, but I can't help my smirk when I see the mischievous glint in Sunshine's eyes. She damn well knows Luscious didn't quit, and I'm beyond relieved that she doesn't think differently of us for what we're doing.

Taking another bite of oatmeal, I wish I had a little cinnamon to sprinkle on top, but I'm not about to ask for it.

"Can I try a bite?" Sunshine asks me as she nudges my shoulder.

I turn toward her and frown at her excited look. "You've never had oatmeal before?"

She shakes her head to my relief. "Oh, no, it's not that. I've always considered it a treat when I was able to have it. It was only when I was working at the grocery store that I got to have it because they had a little kitchenette. I even broke down and splurged, buying a little container of cinnamon that I always carried around in my purse so I could sprinkle it on top. Granted, that was once, maybe twice a week that I got a shift at the store, but yeah, I loved being able to use their microwave to cook up my little treat. I could have had it while working at the diner, but I chose to take the more filling meals that I got there over the oatmeal."

I stare at her in shock for a few moments before the anger starts boiling up inside me.

"Did I say something wrong?" she whispers, her eyes wide as her gaze bounces between my brothers, her dad, and me at the table.

Pushing down my anger for now, I scoop up a big spoonful and hold it out for her. Her eyes light up and she eagerly eats the oatmeal, practically bouncing in her seat with happiness.

A chair scrapes as I give her another spoonful, and it's like a sucker punch at the sheer joy she has from eating a bowl of hot, plain oatmeal. Something she considered a treat. That she couldn't have it at home because of fear of being around that asshole for too long while it cooked.

That fucker is so dead.

I'm brought out of my thoughts when someone plops down a jar of cinnamon on the table. Looking up, I realize it was Smoke that had gotten up.

"Mama Astrid says she'll make you up a bowl if you want, but she said to first eat some of your other food first so you have a bit more balanced food groups."

Sunshine pouts, but nods. I reach over, squeezing her knee.

"I'll make sure to have the Prospect add some oatmeal and cinnamon to the list when he goes out today to stock up for me, since we've been gone for a week."

The smile she gives me simultaneously warms my chest and squeezes it.

The little things that we all take for granted are the things that bring her the greatest joy and happiness.

As we finish lunch, we talk about random things. Mae polishes off three-quarters of her plate and asks if she can have a small bowl of oatmeal which Mama Astrid happily makes for her.

Glancing at Mama Astrid in question, she nods and I finish off what was left on Mae's plate. One, I know she's still pissed at me but I wasn't going to eat it without asking since I'm still being punished by her, but on the other hand, neither of us like wasting food either.

That said though, none of us have the heart to deny Mae her treat.

Chapter 54

Timber

SUNSHINE INSISTS ON HELPING Mama Astrid clean up from lunch and takes our empty dishes into the kitchen.

"I'm going to love beating her stepfather when we get our hands on him," Devil seethes as he clenches and unclenches his fists.

"Agreed, but you're going to have to get in line," I reply, my voice hard and cold.

The others give me a chin lift. Smoke and I share a look. That fucker's going to regret ever laying hands on Mae.

About twenty minutes later, Reaper stands up, his chair sliding on the tile. "Time to go talk to our guests."

Standing, I tilt my head toward the kitchen. "I'll talk to Mae," I tell them and follow after her.

Once in the kitchen, I step up behind Sunshine and gently wrap my arms around her waist.

"Need to talk to you about something, Mae. Are you almost finished in here?"

She turns in my arms, wrapping her arms around my waist. Mama Astrid slips out of the kitchen, giving us privacy.

"We just finished."

Leaning down, I give her a chaste kiss before pulling back.

"We're going downstairs to have a talk and we wanted to ask you if you wanted to be there? You can say no, obviously, but if you wanted to ask them something or join in, you can."

She stares up at me in shock before her face hardens and she nods. "I want to be down there. To find out the real reasons why they took me and did this to me. I also want to join in." She pauses, looking away before her gaze returns to mine hesitantly. "I hope you won't be mad, but I also talked to Sasha and Levi. Sasha got me something that I want to give them. If that's okay, that is."

I can't help my grin. Seems like my little ray of sunshine also has some darkness in her. "More than okay, Baby. However, if it ever gets too much, say the word and I'll get you out of there. Okay?"

"I understand."

Taking her hand, I lead her out into the main room and down to the cellar.

At the door, I pause, looking back at her. "Ready?"

She takes a deep breath, squares her shoulders and raises her chin. It's like a switch has been flipped in her. Fuck, seeing her like this has me ready to take her again, but we need to get more information from these fuckers.

"Ready."

Damn, am I proud of her for this. Punching in my code, I open the door.

Carter, Andrew, and also Luscious are now hanging from their wrists from the ceiling with their toes just barely touching the ground and their ankles are chained to the ground. The gunshot wounds Carter and Andrew received are patched up just enough so that they won't bleed to death, but I know from past experience that the bullets are still imbedded inside. All three still have their clothes on.

My brothers step aside to let us through.

As soon as Carter sees Mae at my side, my arm around her waist, he starts thrashing against his restraints. "Get your hands off her! She's mine!"

Ignoring him, Sasha grins darkly when she sees Mae, and I'm surprised to see the same expression mirrored on Mae's face.

"So, per the plan?" Sasha asks her.

Wait. Plan?

"Yes."

"Perfect!" Sasha says as she clasps her hands, her dark grin widening.

She goes over to the cabinet and comes back with a box wrapped like a birthday present that she hands to Mae. It even has a bow and everything.

"So, we have a little surprise for you. The other day when Levi and I asked you if you were given the option, what you would do or want to ask, I kinda went behind your back and talked to Smithy, Dragon, Reaper and Punisher afterward.

Between the five of us, we think you'll enjoy using this better than what you had originally planned on."

The glint in Sasha's eyes as she hands Mae the present has me on edge slightly, but I'm also not surprised she talked to Mae about this. Even if Mae hadn't wanted to come down here, Sasha would have ensured that Mae's desires were carried out. Fuck, I wish I had been the one to talk to her about this, but again, I was a stupid motherfucker.

With a dark chuckle, Mae unwraps the present and pulls out a card that she quickly reads. A grin spreads across her face before she tucks it back into the box and pulls out a small whip. I know for a fact the size of it was on purpose so that she wouldn't overexert herself. However, instead of normal whip ends, they are all metal buckles.

Mae holds up the ends, inspecting them, and it's then that I see they aren't normal buckles.

Smithy's been busy working his magic.

The buckles have metal tips and barbs on them, much like Dragon's cat o' nine whip tail ends, going in various directions. Just looking at them, I know they'll hurt like a son of a bitch and will shred their skin. The rest of the whip has some sort of intricate weaving pattern of black and red leather. Honestly, it looks like the pattern that's similar to Dragon's whip that he made himself years ago.

Mae turns and smiles. "Thank you, Sasha and gents, this is perfect. I'll have to remember to thank Dragon later as well."

They all grin darkly at her, dipping their heads.

Turning her attention back toward our guests, her face hardens before her gaze focuses on Reaper, an eyebrow cocked in question.

"The floor is yours, Lil' Bit. If you want something done that you aren't comfortable with doing yourself, I know a room full of people that would be happy to step in," he says with a wink and the laugh that bubbles out of Mae warms my chest.

Punisher, who's standing next to me, leans down and whispers in her ear. "Or if you want them to hurt even more than what you're able to inflict. We're here for you, Sis."

She looks up at him and smirks as she dips her head in acknowledgement before turning and walking up to Carter, stopping six feet in front of him.

Sasha walks over to the levers controlling the chains as Punisher and Smithy walk over and behind Carter, each with chain restraints in their hands. She lowers the chains, and Punisher and Smithy quickly secure Carter's legs, making him kneel before chaining him to the floor so he can't stand up. I guess Sasha must have filled them in on Mae's ideas.

Mae pulls something out of her pocket, fiddles with whatever it is, pulls back, and lands a punch, right to the side of Carter's left eye. When she lowers her hand, I chuckle at seeing her wear brass knuckles.

Fuck, I love my girl.

Carter cries out and Mae's grin darkens at the sound.

"Why did you kidnap me? The real reason. Not some bullshit answer about me turning you down publicly. Not about us saying that none of the Steel Archangel's or their employees will be using your office again."

Carter glares at her. "You'll pay for this. You need to be taught your place and it isn't with those thugs. Your behavior is unacceptable and you will be punished."

Her gaze narrows on him. "Yeah, wrong answer. I know my place in life and it's right over there with my Old Man."

That has Carter struggling against his restraints harder. Mae walks around him, and he twists, trying to keep her in his line of sight. Both Andrew and Luscious eye her warily. No doubt wondering if they'll be hit by her whip as well.

Mae uncoils the whip and lands a brutal hit across his back that has Carter crying out in pain. Lash after lash she lands as Carter's cries of pain fill the room. Though I do notice that her arms don't arc out as much as Dragon's does when he's whipping our guests.

My gaze goes to Sasha in question. When she feels me looking at her, she turns and winks at me, smirking, but she also has a look of pride on her face.

Son of a bitch.

While I was being an asshole, seems Sasha was teaching Mae how to properly wield a whip because not once does Mae hurt herself while doling out her revenge. I don't even see her wincing, so her movements must not be pulling too much at her stitches.

Either that, or the adrenaline is masking part of her pain.

I make a mental note to watch her closely later to make sure she's okay. While I don't want her to overexert herself, I also know she needs this.

When Carter sags against his restraints, she pauses, then walks around and stands in front of him. With the handle of the whip, she places it under his chin and makes him look at her.

"Ready to tell me the truth? If not, I'll gladly see what's in my brother's goodie closet and pick a different toy to use on you."

Carter hesitates before his face contorts in anger and he presses his lips together tightly.

"Kai?"

Punisher walks over to his tool cabinet and opens it for her. She walks over to him and looks through everything. I'm shocked when she pulls out an acetylene torch and hands it to him.

He reaches into the cabinet and hands her a bandana, to which I'm glad he gave her one in case the smell gets to be too much for her. Then he leans in close, both of them talking in hushed whispers.

Nodding, he walks in front of Carter, making sure the torch is in front of him.

"You laid your hands on my sister and my brother's Old Lady. That was a pretty stupid thing for you to do, Carter." He pauses and lights the torch, adjusting the flame a few times. Carter visibly swallows hard, his gaze locked on the torch.

My gaze cuts over to Andrew, who's sweating like a pig as his worried gaze bounces between Carter and the torch. Luscious, on the other hand, looks smug as she watches them.

Why?

"Now, you're going to answer her questions or you're going to be in for a real... treat," he says with a wicked grin.

"Wait," I call out, walking toward Luscious.

She looks up at me, batting her eyes, but her mask cracks at the dark look on my face.

"You looked like you wanted to say something. Care to share with the class, Luscious?"

She tilts her chin up, trying to look defiant. "Just waiting for you to realize that you deserve better than that damaged and scarred whore who spreads her legs for anyone. That you'll come back to me, just like you always should have. You were meant to be mine, Timber. Not shacking up with that trashy bitch," she says, curling her lip as she looks down her nose at Mae.

What the fuck will it take to make her realize that I want nothing to do with her?

Mae saunters up to my side, swaying her hips as she places an arm around my waist. Her other hand still holds the whip at her side.

"You're delusional, Luscious. Why would Timber want you? You take a man, any man, in all of your holes. Sometimes all at once. I've even seen you take two in your va-jay-jay at once. Who would want to fuck your worn out, loose as shit holes? I mean, can you even feel their dicks when they fuck you? I bet you can't even orgasm anymore."

Luscious thrashes against her chains as she spews obscenities at Mae whereas my brothers all bust out laughing at Mae's words.

"What did they promise you for helping them?" I ask.

Sasha takes the acetylene torch from Punisher and walks to my other side. Luscious pales when Sasha holds it close to her face. Her eyes stay fixed on the flame, but she doesn't answer me.

Mae steps forward and grips Luscious' chin hard, preventing her from moving. Sasha brings the flame closer, burning her cheek, but making sure not to burn Mae in the process, either. Luscious' screams fill the air. Sasha hovers the flame up and down her cheek. The scent of burned flesh and hair soon fills the air.

A few moments later, she finally cracks.

"Stop! I'll talk! I'll talk!"

Sasha pulls the flame away and shuts it off. Mae releases her chin, steps back, and wraps her arm around my waist as she leans into me. I do the same and squeeze her hip slightly before repeating my question, along with a few others that have been bugging me.

"What did they promise you for helping them? How did those two assholes get on the property? What was your role in all of this?"

"Don't tell him anything, you cunt!" Carter shouts.

Andrew frowns before a resigned look comes over his face. I wonder what his act was in all of this.

"I'm not going to be tortured just to keep your secrets, you asshole! You were the one that couldn't follow his instructions in the first place!" Luscious shouts at him before turning her attention to Mae, glaring at her.

"Those two were supposed to text me when they snuck out of my trunk, but they never did. If they had, I would have slipped out for a smoke while waiting for their next text. I was supposed to be their getaway driver. They were in the trunk when I came in tonight.

"After getting that bitch to the cabin, Carter was going to make her pay for embarrassing him publicly. Not to mention, their whole conversation in the store was overheard by Betty Lou, who is the town's gossip queen. Before you guys had even left the store, the whole town had heard about it. It didn't help that Carter is married to the daughter of a bigwig in town and he was pissed that Carter was stepping out on his daughter. He threatened to pull his funding for expanding the Johnson's office building because of it.

"On top of threatening you, he was supposed to warm you up and start breaking you down for your new owner. Your dad was in on it."

Mae snorts. "Uh, yeah. My dad was most definitely *not* in on it as my dad is Smoke, who is right over there. Describe the man who you thought was my dad."

Luscious stares at her in shock, her gaze bouncing between Smoke and Mae. I'm not sure why she's shocked because we told her Smoke was her dad before leaving to rescue Mae. Unless she didn't believe us earlier.

I turn toward Mae, frowning. "She described him earlier, Baby. It's X."

Mae scowls. "Figures," she huffs, shaking her head before refocusing on Luscious. "Then what was supposed to happen?"

"Your dad, or X or whatever his name was, was supposed to arrive at the cabin at midnight. That's when the handoff would have happened. Until then, Carter could have his way with her."

Fuck, we came so close to having our hands on that asshole but didn't know it. Also, so close to losing Mae.

"What were you getting out of this besides the delusion that I'd suddenly be interested in you?" I ask her.

"X knew a plastic surgeon that would make me look like your bitch. Then I'd dye my hair and get a wig."

A humorless laugh escapes me. Plus, I wonder if her hair would have turned out green since it's currently bright blue and Mae's hair is blond.

"Well, to once again quote our Queen, you can change the package, but I would have known you weren't my Sunshine."

Luscious scowls at us and I can't help my smirk or pulling Mae closer to me.

Mae squeezes me and then pulls away before walking over to Andrew. With the handle of her whip, she raises his chin, making him look at her. "What was your role in all this?"

He sneers at her. "You mean besides trying to save my business? Easy. I've known X for a while and our tastes are similar," he says as his gaze blatantly rakes over her body.

Before I can get to him, Smoke punches him and yanks his head back by his hair.

"That's my daughter you're leering at, asshole. Now, how *exactly* do you know X?"

Andrew huffs. "And why should I tell you? You're going to kill us anyway."

Smoke chuckles darkly. "Because if you don't, we'll stretch out your fun for days. Weeks. Months. Fuck, I'll keep you alive for years until you tell me what I want to know. However, if you're a good boy and answer all of our questions truthfully, your death will be less painful. It will still hurt because of what you've done to my daughter, but it won't hurt nearly as much as the other option would."

They stare at each other for a few moments, and then Andrew's lips press in a fine line.

"Have it your way." Smoke turns around, walks to Punisher's cabinet, and pulls out a wicked knife with a partially serrated blade before walking back over to Andrew.

Smoke cuts off his shirt and I grin when a few of the cuts sink into Andrew's chest along the way. Next, he cuts off his jeans which are quickly followed by his boxers.

"Someone hand me some gloves," Smoke asks. Loki gets some out of the cabinet he was leaning on, hands them to him and Smoke puts them on.

Mae's lip curls when she looks down at his dick. "No wonder you're acquainted with X. You're suffering from small dick syndrome. You have to pay or kidnap women so you can rape them, since I doubt anyone would want to fuck you willingly with a dick that small and tiny."

The guys all chuckle darkly, but it's true. I wonder how a woman can even feel his dick since it's only a few inches long and really thin.

Andrew's face reddens, but before he can say anything to Mae, he screams as Smoke grabs his pathetically small dick, slicing it clean off.

Punisher steps forward and takes the torch from Sasha. He walks over to Andrew and cauterizes the area so he won't bleed to death.

Andrew passes out and like Sasha had done before, Punisher looks at Andrew with a bored expression.

"Loki?"

"Coming up," he replies right before he dumps a bucket of ice water on Andrew. He sputters as he tries to catch his breath.

"Want to try again?" Smoke asks as he holds up Andrew's dick for a second and then tosses it into a biohazard bag that will be burned later on.

Andrew's chest heaves as tears streak down his face and he nods.

"How do you know X?"

"H-he's who I b-bought my first w-wife from."

Curses ring out and Mae steps forward, but I grab her by the hips. Her whole body is trembling with anger.

"What do you mean 'first'?" I ask.

Mae freezes. "Wait. Are you like Carter? He told me his wife is one of many. How many wives do you both have? Are all of them unwilling?"

Andrew grins wickedly even though the fucker has to be in a shit ton of pain and is shivering like crazy. "I-I have eight wives and he has s-six. They all know their p-places, unlike you two b-b-bitches who think they can b-b-belong in a man's world. The only t-things a woman is good for are sex, obeying our o-orders, having k-kids, and k-keeping the house in order. T-that's it. T-they know to obey our every c-command, otherwise they'll be s-severely p-punished."

What the fuck...

Chapter 55
Mae

My stomach churns at Andrew's words and his words bounce around my mind. I have a nagging feeling like I'm forgetting something.

Then it hits me like a ton of bricks.

Michael said the same words to me when he tried to rape me.

Futtenfarter...

Are they part of a cult or something? Michael had mentioned 'the Oasis' a few times over the years and the things he and X would say always sounded like they belonged in the history books. Of course, they didn't know I'd heard all that, but when they were drunk, they were loud. I could hear every word of theirs through the paper-thin walls.

To them, women are there to serve their every need and obey their every word. Apparently, the women also had to dress a certain way, and they weren't allowed to leave without their husband. As soon as a woman could no longer bear children, they were demoted from their status, moved into a rickety hut and given even more chores. Usually, they were despicable ones at that. That was their lives until they died and even then, they were buried in unmarked graves.

Crap...

How am I going to go about getting the information out of them and find out where Oasis is located without me outright asking them? Right now, I really wish I knew how to speak Russian so I could at least ask Sasha for advice.

Feeling eyes on me, I look around to see Loki looking at me oddly. I raise an eyebrow in question, but don't look away. He continues to stare at me for a bit before ever so slightly dipping his chin.

Pushing off the cabinet, he stalks toward Andrew, yanking his head back and baring his neck to Dad.

"So, you're that pathetic that you have to kidnap or buy your women? How are you even able to hide that you have so many wives?" Loki asks Andrew.

Holy crap... Is the man psychic?

Andrew doesn't answer right away and Dad starts cutting him in various places, making him cry out, but Loki never lets go of his grip.

"O-only my f-first wife and I-I live in town. The others l-live somewhere else. Same with Carter."

"Did you get all your wives from X?"

When he hesitates, Dad cuts him again, deeper than before.

"Y-yes! Yes, I b-bought them all from him. He k-knows the type of women I l-like and w-when he has one that fits my r-requests, he lets me k-know about them.

"Where? Where are they?" I ask, trying to keep my voice as level as possible.

"I c-can't tell you that."

Dad huffs. "Yes, you can. You're going to die anyway, so you don't have to worry about someone else killing you for telling us."

Andrew presses his lips together tightly, refusing to answer.

Anger rises in me, and this time when I step forward, Timber lets me go.

Walking around behind Andrew, I give a flick of my whip, making it crack in the air. "Answer me."

Dad looks up at me in question and I realize I let more of my anger out than I had intended, however, he doesn't say anything.

Yet anyway.

I know I'll have to fill them all in on what I remembered, but not right now. Not unless they give me the information I need.

"F-fuck you, b-bitch," Andrew seethes.

Dad steps back and I let my whip sail through the air, landing a hard hit on his back.

Andrew's cries ring through the air until his back is as shredded as Carter's.

When he sags in his chains, I stop. Waiting.

Walking around to the front of him, I notice he's passed out again. Before I can even ask, Dad pulls me back slightly and Loki tosses another bucket of water on Andrew. Once again he sputters while gasping and turning a tired glare my way.

"Well?" I ask after a few moments of silence.

"Dad, no!" Carter yells as he thrashes in his chains.

"T-there's n-no point, C-carter. They're r-right. We aren't g-getting out of here." Sighing, he nods. "It's almost f-fifty miles n-north of F-Forest Creek on p-private land. T-thirty acres. The f-forest h-hides it from o-outsiders."

"How many men live there permanently?"

"T-ten."

"How many men have the same living arrangements besides you and douche canoe here?"

"F-five. Only the M-masters can l-live like we d-do."

"How many women? Children?"

He doesn't answer me, and I walk behind him, whipping him again.

"F-forty women of b-bearing age. T-twenty-three kids."

Rage fills my veins. "And how many women that can no longer have kids?"

He hesitates again, but right as I raise my hand, he whispers his answer. "T-thirty-six."

Coming back around in front of them, I let them see how angry I am. "How does Frida fit into all of this?"

Carter smirks at me. "She was one of my wives. I knew I had to have her and did what I had to do to ensure it. After a couple of days, she was hooked and I got what I wanted. She committed to me in a ceremony. I almost had her to the point where I could indoctrinate her when she decided to grow a conscience. She started defying me more, so her punishments increased."

"What did you do or say that made her change her mind?" I asked.

He sneers at Timber, and I look between them, confused. "I had asked her to move in with me. She didn't know about my wife because I keep her under lock and key most of the time. I never wear my ring out in public, only when I'm around my wife.

"It was when I said she'd have to cut contact with her family that she started rebelling. She'd refuse to answer my calls, texts, or summons. Ignoring those goes against our rules. Slaves do not disobey their Masters. I knew she had feelings for you, Timber, but I thought I had snuffed those out when she committed to being mine. Turns out I was wrong."

Shock goes through me at that, and judging by Timber's equally shocked face, he had no idea Frida felt that way toward him.

"She refused me for a week when I'd had enough. I told one of my fuck boys to bring her to me, and he did. In public, per my orders, he acted like her boyfriend to keep suspicion off of me." He pauses, his bloody grin widening as he turned his hateful gaze to Kai. "She bruised and bled so sweetly for me. She begged me to let her go, but she was mine. The only escape was death, which was her punishment for her disobedience and disloyalty to our cause."

Kai's in front of him faster than I can blink as he rains down punch after punch to Carter's body.

It isn't until Carter's body sags as he passes out that Reaper steps forward, putting a hand on Kai's shoulder. He turns and looks at everyone before his gaze lands on me, and I nod, already knowing he wants me to tell him what I remembered.

"Church."

Sasha holds her hand out for the whip and I give it to her before following Reaper out of the room. He stops in the large room just outside of the cellar and turns to me.

"I know Sasha must have given you pointers on your clothes. You can freshen up in the shower and then meet us upstairs." He pauses, his gaze looking me over from head to toe. "It looks like you'll be able to salvage your clothes, but your shoes will need to be burned."

"I'll go get you fresh clothes and shoes, Sunshine." Timber steps forward, gives me a chaste kiss and heads upstairs.

Kai steps forward and holds his hand out. I slip off my flats and hand them to him before turning and going into the bathroom Reaper gestured toward.

Once inside, I look around. It's like a locker room with individual stalls. Walking to the first one, I turn on the water and strip on autopilot. There's a bag of bags on a hook nearby and I grab one to stuff my clothes in.

When the water's warm, I step in and close the curtain. I'm surprised when I see women's shower gel, shampoo, and conditioner in the stall along with men's stuff. A soft chuckle escapes me as I shake my head. I'm going to bet they have this for when Sasha and Levi have to handle stuff for the club.

As I quickly wash my hair and body, my mind reels from everything Andrew, Carter, and Luscious told us.

I know you always hear about bad people on the news or radio, but to actually have almost been thrown into that life when they kidnapped me, has me about ready to break down, but I can't. Not yet anyway.

Shutting the water off, I dry off right as there's a knock on the door.

"It's me," Liam says before opening the door, stepping inside and closing it behind.

He drops the bag on a nearby bench, quickly crosses the room and engulfs me in a hug.

After a few moments, he lets go and lifts my chin.

"How are you holding up, Sunshine? Where's your head at?"

I can't stop my sniffle. "That I was hours away from being thrust into that life and I can't even begin to thank you and the guys enough for finding me so fast."

Tears stream down my face and his calloused hands attempt to dry my cheeks, but I can't stop my tears.

"Come here, Baby."

He pulls me tighter to him and I clutch his cut as I sob.

I don't know how long we stand like that, but when I pull back and wipe my face, my cheeks heat at seeing how drenched his shirt is from my tears and wet hair.

"Oh, my gosh, I'm so sorry, Liam!"

He chuckles softly. "It's nothing, Sunshine. Now, you need to get dressed before I sink into you."

I roll my eyes at him. "There's no way you could want me after what happened in there."

He grabs my hips, pulling me tight against him, and I gasp when I feel how hard he is.

"On the contrary, Sunshine. You were fucking amazing in there and hot as fuck as you doled out your revenge." He leans down, giving me a searing kiss. "Later, I'll show you exactly how much I wanted to fuck you in there, but we need to get to Church."

Just like that, it feels like a bucket of ice was thrown on me.

"Right," I almost whisper as I step back from him and over to the clothes he brought for me. Lowering my towel, I get dressed before drying my hair a little and loosely braiding it to keep it semi-contained.

Sensing my change of mood, Liam reaches out and grasps my hand in his, threading his fingers through mine and squeezes my hand. Picking up my bag of soiled clothes, we leave the locker room and find Mama Astrid waiting for us. She hands me a water and takes the bag from me.

"I'll get these started and when they are finished, I'll bring them over to the house," she says before disappearing.

Seeing my confusion, Liam chuckles. "Someone probably asked her to come down. Though some of us swear she has a bit of witch blood in her. She sometimes just knows stuff without anyone saying anything." He pauses, shaking his head. "Come on, Sunshine. Everyone's waiting."

Nodding, I numbly follow him up the stairs. He puts our phones in the basket and grabs a beer from Colt before leading me into Church.

He takes a seat next to Dad, pulling me down onto his lap.

Reaper bangs his hammer on the table. "Alright, shut the fuck up, assholes. We need to talk about what just happened." He pauses as his gaze lands on mine. "Fill us in, Lil' Bit."

I clench my hands under the table, hoping to keep them from shaking too much as I tell them what I remember about what Michael and X said about the Oasis over the years.

When I'm done, curses ring out through the room.

The weight of Reaper's gaze on me, along with several others in the club, has me wilting under it.

"I'm sorry. I'm not sure how I repressed those memories. I would have told you sooner if I had remembered it."

Timber's arms tighten around me. "It's not your fault. Honestly, with everything you've been through, I'm not surprised that you repressed memories to protect yourself. None of the blame is on you, Sunshine," he says, his voice full of anger.

Risking a look up at him, I'm surprised to find him directing his anger at Reaper. After a few seconds, Reaper sighs, his face and eyes losing some of his anger.

"I'm not angry at you, Lil' Bit. It's actually the opposite. I'm pissed that we came so close to you being sold off into that sort of life. Also, I wish we had known about the exchange at midnight. We might have been able to nab X and whoever was with him." He pauses and looks at Python and then Dad. "I'll fill Thor in on this, but Python and Smoke, start looking into Oasis and see if you can find anything else out about it. We're not going in blind on this. We also need to figure out who's at the top of this. Is it X? Or does he report to someone else?"

"You got it, Pres," Python replies.

"Got it," Dad says.

"Now, let's discuss what all we've learned so far."

After a couple of hours, Reaper dismisses us. I'd been able to contribute more information as they talked. More and more memories started to surface and I hated that I'd suppressed them unintentionally. If only I had remembered them all in the beginning, maybe we could have already had a head start on this cult.

Dad had found some information about the Oasis Masters, as Andrew called them, and it wasn't pretty. Those men's tastes run dark.

Really dark.

He'd even found the listings for a few members about what type of women they wanted and what they wanted to do to them.

There were a few times where it felt like I shouldn't be there, but no one said anything about it. I know I'll never repeat anything they said outside of Church, and I think they know that I won't either.

Shaking my head, I can't help but smile when I see Mama Astrid and Sasha in the kitchen through the pass through.

Turning, I'm about to tell Timber I'm going to go help them with supper when I feel him tense against me.

Looking up at him, he's glaring at someone behind me. I turn around and can't help my scowl when I see Candi and Star strutting into the room with an air of superiority. They both smirk when they see me, and I wish I could wipe that look off their faces. However, a thrill goes through me at seeing both of them fully clothed, though they still have on their stripper heels.

They wander off to the side of the room and I sigh, trying to let go of my anger. "Timber, I'm gonna go help with supper." Leaning up on my toes, I intend to give him a quick kiss, but he deepens it as he pulls me tight against him.

I whimper as a current of need runs through me at the feeling and I ignore the tinge of pain I feel at him pressed up hard against a few of my deepest wounds.

When he pulls back, both of us are breathing heavily and I'm sure my cheeks are bright red. He lightly smacks my ass and his arms loosen around me.

"Behave," I whisper as I playfully swat at his chest.

That earns me a growl as he pulls me closer to him again. Leaning down, he nips my ear and then the crook of my neck where he'd left a hickey earlier. "Never," he growls again and I shiver as his voice rolls over me and feeling the vibrations in his chest.

He kisses me again before letting me go, and I walk, almost in a daze, into the kitchen.

The look Sasha gives me has me turning beat red as she fans herself. "Girl, you are getting it tonight," she sasses as she does the little licking her finger and sizzle thing which has all of us laughing.

Nibbling my lip, I roll my eyes at her, waving her off. I'm still uncomfortable talking to them about sex, but I have a feeling I'll get used to it before long.

"Alright, ladies, let's get to cooking," Mama Astrid says with a wink.

Tonight, we're cooking Devil's request for chicken fried steak with biscuits and gravy and a side of green beans. It's one of my favorites, so I'm definitely looking forward to it. We're not leaving till after breakfast tomorrow, so I'll be able to cook one more meal for everyone. I hate that I forgot about it while I was healing, but like Timber had said, more than one of the guys had mentioned that it wasn't a big deal and they'd save their requests for when I visit again. I had surprised them when I countered that I'd cook for them while they were in Forest Creek as well whenever they were there in the future and that I'd work something out with Mama Astrid so that we both could keep track of the requests.

Shaking off my thoughts, I go over to the pantry and start pulling out the ingredients.

Chapter 56

Mae

WE'RE LOUNGING IN THE main room on the sofas with Dad, Devil, Loki, Kai, Ragnar, and Razor talking about random things after supper. Timber has me on his lap and I'm soaking in his warmth, having missed it the last few days.

A throat clearing has me looking behind me. Reaper has me pinned with a look that I can't quite decipher, and it makes me nervous.

"Lil' Bit, is it okay if we talk for a bit?"

Timber must sense my nervousness because he squeezes me and kisses my temple. "It's okay, Sunshine. He probably just wants to make sure you're okay after everything," he whispers to me, and I nod.

My body slightly relaxes at that and I carefully slide off his lap so that I don't pull at my stitches. I hadn't felt any pain when we were downstairs, but I'm guessing my anger was masking it. It wasn't until we were sitting in Church that I felt the soreness and tenderness setting in.

I follow him into his office and he shuts the door behind me.

"Have a seat, Lil' Bit," he says, gesturing to the sofa in front of his desk.

I sit down and he sits on his desk, facing me.

"Timber was right, I just wanted to check in to see how you are handling everything that happened downstairs."

Exhaling, I nod. "I did have a little breakdown after I'd freshened up. That I had come so close to being forced into that lifestyle." I pause, my body tensing as my anger grows at what they'd done and were involved in. "As for the other stuff that I'd done and said, I don't regret any of it. Honestly, I wanted to hurt them even more for what they'd done to me. What they'd done to Frida. What they've done and are doing to all those women and children. I want them to pay for all of that and I want to free those women and children."

He stares at me for a bit before he smirks. "I knew you were cut from the same cloth as Levi." He shakes his head, and the look on his face softens. "Everything okay between you and Timber?"

Swallowing hard, I nod. "I think so. I told him I can't be the one to always fight for him. He has to fight for me, too. Which means not letting other women touch him like Candi and Star were and not flirting with them. He told me he thought they were just talking. He didn't know they were rubbing it in my face. Honestly, I'd love to bitch slap them both, but it wouldn't do any good."

A booming laugh comes out of him and I jump slightly at how loud it is as I'd never heard him laugh like this before.

"Fuck, I love when you get so riled up that you actually curse instead of your usual way of cursing." He shakes his head, still smiling. In all honesty, I hadn't even realized I had cursed.

A moment later, he sobers and opens his mouth to say something, but then closes it. After a few moments, he turns, facing a shelf as he gnaws on his lip.

"I'm not sure how to ask this, so I'm just going to say it. I was wondering if we could talk some as we burned our black journal pages? I'm a little ashamed that I haven't gotten to know you much this past week."

Grinning, I get up, ignoring the twinge of pain as I wrap him in a hug. His body tenses at first and then his arms wrap around me, too.

Pulling back, I can't help my giggle at his surprised face. "I'll go get my journal and meet you out by the firepit. Okay?"

Still slightly stunned, he nods, and then he masks his emotions again.

"Sounds good, Lil' Bit."

Feeling brave, I lean up and kiss his cheek, right over his worst scar on his face. I don't react when I feel him tense even further under my touch, and I smile at him when I lean back. "I want to get to know you better, too, Uncle Reaper. See you in a few!" I say with another smile before spinning on my heel and heading out into the main room.

I make a beeline for Timber and tell him where I'm going to be at. I know I don't have to, but I don't want him to worry. Likewise, I'd want him to tell me if he was going off to do something as well.

He grins and lightly smacks my hip, telling me he'll find me out there later.

With a skip in my step, I hurry toward the backdoor and force myself not to slow down by the bathrooms, even though memories bombard me. Hopping into the golf cart, I drive the short distance back to the house. Once inside, I grab my backpack with my journals and pens in it, and after hesitating a few moments, I slip on my hoodie. The wind has had a bit of a chill to it the last couple of days, but the fire should chase most of it away. Still, I'd rather be prepared than freezing later.

In no time, I'm pulling up next to the firepit that Reaper's at. He's already got it lit and is adding a few more logs to it. Then he sits down on a bench.

Not sure if he wants me that close, I grab my bag off the seat of the golf cart and sit in one of the chairs next to him criss-cross style. Nibbling on my lip, I pull out my red pen and black journal and jot down a few of my emotions from earlier. I know I'll need to write more later and process things better, but still, I want to watch those pieces of paper burn.

Reaper tears out his pages from the journal and I follow suit.

We don't say anything as we tear the first few pages up into little balls and toss them into the fire.

He clears his throat, a pained look coming over his face. "If you know about the journals, I'm going to guess that Half-pint told you her story?"

It takes me a bit before I remember that's his nickname for Levi and I nod. "On Tuesday, she told me, and that's when Sasha gave me the journals and pens." I pause, swallowing thickly as my emotions tighten my throat. "I'm sorry that you both went through that. For what they did to both of you. They didn't tell me everything that was done to you. Just that your scars are worse than Levi's."

A tear slips down my cheek and I quickly wipe it away, but he sees it anyway. He scoots over and pats the bench next to him. I get up and sit by him. Taking a risk, I rest my head against his shoulder.

As expected, his body tenses at the contact, but I don't react, waiting to see if this is okay.

After a few moments, his muscles relax a little.

"For the record, Reaper, I don't see you any differently because of your scars. In fact, they make me feel safer with you."

That remark earns me a scoff and he angrily throws a ball of paper into the fire. "Safer? How? People have always given me a wide berth before, but now it's even worse. I mean, they take one look at me and run the other way."

Holy snickerdoodles...

The pain radiating off him is intense. How people have been treating him makes my anger rise. I jump off the bench, ignoring the pain, and stand in front of him with my fists on my hips.

"Then fuck them all! You don't need people like that in your life. To me, I know I'm safe with you and not just because you're a badass biker who's a mountain of a man with arms that look like if you squeezed someone's neck, you could pop their head off."

He huffs but I also see him trying not to smile, too.

"Your scars tell me you're the toughest and most dangerous person in the room. You know why?"

Apprehension and nervousness fill his eyes as he looks at me. "Why?"

"Because they tell people that you will go to any length to protect those you care about. Even if that means you are hurt in the process." I step forward and cup his cheeks in my hands. "If those people don't take the time to look past your skin, then they aren't worth knowing. They're judging a book by its cover when, in fact, there's an amazing story hidden in those pages. You are Reaper, the President of the Junction Creek Steel Archangel's MC. You are Tony Leyton. An amazing man who deserves to be loved, just like he is."

He stares at me in shock and I give him a small smile before kissing his cheek again and retaking my spot next to him. I rest my head on his shoulder as I tear another section off, wad it up, and throw it into the fire. I honestly think he's going to ask how I know his real name, but he never does. Levi had told me it the other day during our video call.

For a few minutes, Reaper doesn't say anything as I continue throwing my little balls of paper into the fire. His giant hands grip his sheets of paper tightly as he stares at the fire.

I start to worry that maybe I overstepped when suddenly, he rips all the pages, multiple pages at once, into small little pieces of paper that he deposits on his lap. Then he surprises me by lifting his arm, pulling me closer into his side and draping his arm over me.

Smiling, I throw another piece of paper into the fire.

We stay like that for a few hours as we get to know each other more. I find out that he has a sister, Julia, but that they don't speak anymore.

"My nephew, Chris, was visiting me two years ago. He was fifteen at the time and looking forward to getting a car. I had a bike all lined up for him, too."

My stomach twists and I know this isn't going to be good.

"He loves cars and bikes and wanted to go to the garage to work with the guys. I got him all suited up, and he rode behind me on my bike. We've ridden together hundreds of times before. He knew he always had to wear his gear, and he knew what not to do and what to do. Julia's ridden with us a lot, too.

"On our way there, someone clipped me and we went down. Hard. As soon as I looked up from where I landed, I knew it wasn't good." He pauses, taking a few deep breaths.

"Chris ended up being paralyzed from the waist down. Julia blames me for hurting him and won't let me see him anymore. We text, but we can't do any more than that. I see him around town every now and then, but that's it.

"After the first few times that Chris and I talked in public and her reaming me out afterward, I stopped talking to him publicly. I know he doesn't blame me, but it kills me that she's cut my nephew out of my life because of someone else's actions. Especially with him being right under my nose and not being able to spend time with him. She takes my money since I've been helping them for years even before the accident, but yeah. Can't see him anymore."

My heart breaks at the pain he's been carrying.

I loop my arm around his waist, squeezing him, but have no idea what I could possibly even say to him. I could never imagine cutting my child off from a relative like she did. Especially when it wasn't even his fault. If I ever meet her, I'm giving her a piece of my mind.

We sit there for a while after that when I hear the back door open and close. After a few minutes, Timber hands Reaper a beer and me a water before sitting down where I was previously.

Not too long after that, others wander out and before long, all the fire pits are lit and everyone's relaxing together.

Reaper squeezes me tight. "Thanks, Lil' Bit."

I look up at him, confused. "For what?"

He grins. "For kicking me in the ass earlier, for getting to know you better, and for listening to me."

I return his grin. "Anytime, big guy. But if your sister ever reams you out in front of me, I'm warning you ahead of time that I'll be throwing down. What she's doing is wrong. She probably knows it too, but needs someone to blame. I'm sorry that you're the one she's blaming."

He leans down, kisses my forehead, and releases me. Almost instantly, I'm picked up and Timber sits me down on his lap. I giggle, but I don't say anything.

Two hours later, I'm beat. I yawn and I feel Timber's chest shaking against me. Playfully, I swat his chest. "Oh, shush you. You know I'm still taking those pills Doc gave me and they make me sleepy."

"Well then, how about we head out? We still need to pack for tomorrow, too."

Nodding, I stand and start saying good night to everyone. Devil snags me when we get to the outskirts of the group and gives me a hug.

"Thank you, Mae. I didn't mean to overhear, but I did. I think what you told him will help. For both topics."

Tears prick my eyes and I nod. "I hope so, too. And I hope things improve with Julia and Chris, too."

He nods. "Same. He turns eighteen early next year, so hopefully that will help things."

"Fingers crossed," I reply with a smile, and he lets me go. I slide onto my seat of the golf cart while Timber gets behind the wheel.

As we drive back to the house, I really do hope things improve between Reaper and Julia. It's not fair to Chris or Reaper what she's doing.

"You okay, Sunshine?" Liam asks as he locks the door and resets the code. I shrug as I slip off my shoes.

"Aside from getting to know each other, Reaper also told me about his sister and Chris. I hate what she's putting him through. It wasn't Reaper's fault. He did everything he could to protect Chris."

Liam scowls. "I hope that when Chris turns eighteen early next year, he's able to get a place of his own. I know Reaper has a place he can move into that's wheelchair accessible if he wants it. I helped him remodel it. He hasn't put it on the market yet in case Chris wants it."

My chest warms at them making sure Chris has what he needs, and I'm also happy that Liam helped him with the remodeling.

I walk over to him, wrapping my arms around him and kiss his chest.

Once again, I thank my lucky stars that I made the decision to seek out my dad. Even though I had to go through all that crap with him and with Carter kidnapping and attacking me, I still would have done it again. Because in the end, it brought me Liam.

Chapter 57

Mae

THE NEXT DAY, WE pull into the gates at the Forest Creek clubhouse around early-afternoon and Sasha parks the SUV by all the bikes. I tried to ride with Timber, but just after sitting behind him for a few moments, I knew I wouldn't be able to hold that position for the entire trip. Sasha was already driving back the SUV, so I hopped in with her. Thankfully, Timber promised to take me out for a ride soon.

Levi, Sadie, Nikki, Jordan, and Susie all barrel out the clubhouse doors at our arrival and I smile. Man, I missed them.

Unbuckling, I don't even have a chance to open my door. It's pulled open for me and my smile widens even more.

"Welcome back, girl! We missed you," Levi tells me as I gently ease out of my seat.

As soon as both my feet are on the ground, I'm swarmed in a massive hug pile.

"Can you please let my Sunshine breathe, ladies and gent," Timber teases from behind them.

We all chuckle at that and as soon as they all step back some, Timber steps forward. However, before he can get to me, Axe wraps me in a hug as he dances back a few feet outside of Timber's reach. His antics have several of us laughing and my chest warms at seeing the smile on my dad's face as he watches all of us.

After a few moments, Timber growls and Axe's chest shakes with laughter, but he finally lets me go. Instantly, I'm swept up into his arms and he leans down, kissing me.

"Hey, I can walk, Timber!"

He winks at me. That combined with his sexy grin has my lady bits tingling. Even though he kept me up for a few hours last night, I already want him again.

"I know you can, Sunshine, but I miss having you in my arms."

And there's the cue that has my stomach filling with butterflies. My man is frickin' sex on a stick, and I wouldn't change a thing about him.

He carries me into the clubhouse and stops inside the door. My hands fly to my mouth in shock and I feel him gently lowering me down to the ground.

There's a banner hanging over the bar that says 'Welcome Home Mae & Timber'. Streamers decorate the main room, but my attention is glued to the two people under that banner.

Peggy and Glen.

Peggy opens her arms, and I don't even hesitate. I run to her and she wraps me in a hug. Seconds later, I feel Glen's arms wrap around us.

Tears prick at my eyes, but I make no move to wipe them away. I just hope my waterproof mascara does its job and doesn't run or turn into raccoon eyes.

They pull back after a few moments, and I finally wipe my eyes.

"I didn't think I'd see you two until tomorrow."

They both chuckle.

"Well, your aunts, sister, uncles, brother, nephew and cousin were very convincing," Peggy says with a wink that has me laughing.

Oh, yes. They definitely can be.

I've talked with all of them multiple times this past week, as well as texting. We even have a group chat with all of us women in it. There is also a more secret thread that's just Levi, Sasha, and me in it. Same as one for just Levi and I since we're the only two Old Lady's right now. Those two are for if we need to discuss something club related that's also text safe. Or at least vague as heck.

It's how I knew that even though Levi's wedding is tomorrow, we're still on lockdown. Thankfully, the guys haven't limited the guest list, but since everyone outside the club are either friends or coworkers, they know a little about club life. That's also why it didn't take much to get pictures of the few people that the club members didn't know, including the caterers, and every club member was ordered to memorize faces and names. Even the Prospects, me, Nikki, and Susie. That way, if someone sneaks in, it'll be easier to spot them.

That's the hope anyway.

Turning, I spot Timber talking to Dad, and I wave them both over.

"Peggy, Glen, I'd like you to meet my dad, Smoke, and my Old Man, Timber."

Like I suspected, Peggy rushes forward, hugging both of them. I giggle at the looks on their faces when she pulls them both down and kisses their cheeks, leaving a pink lipstick stain both times.

"Thank you, Timber, for protecting our girl," Glen says and they both do that shoulder clap and handshake thing men do.

He turns to Dad and cocks an eyebrow at him. "I don't know all the details except that you were lied to, but I hope that you'll be the dad she needs going forward."

Dad's gaze flicks to me and he smiles as he pulls me into his side, wrapping an arm around my shoulder. "I plan to," he says as he kisses my forehead.

Glen steps closer and motions for Timber to do the same. "The others already know, but on our way here, I swore I saw Preston and Bruce driving a black SUV around town. Thor said I could tell you guys and he, Dragon, and Phoenix were going to tell the rest of the people that drove over with you."

I freeze and can't help the shiver that runs through me.

Dad leans in close to my ear and whispers to me. "You need to relax and act like you don't know about them. They're most likely watching us, which is why Thor is having everyone being informed like this. It's how we do things. It also means that Glen and Peggy have proven to Thor that he can trust them as well."

Nodding, I force my body to relax and smile as I watch him and Timber chatting with Peggy and Glen as they all get to know each other.

We're relaxing in the main room when Sasha gestures for me to join the others in the kitchen.

Turning to Timber, I give him a quick kiss. "I'm going to go help the ladies with supper."

He squeezes my hip and gives me another toe-curling kiss that has me wanting more, but I know we can't right now. He releases me and I head toward the kitchen.

I force myself not to scowl when I see two people I really didn't want to see. I know that even though Thor deemed this a family night; the bunnies are still out, just dressed in normal clothes. Something that I can instantly tell that Gigi and Crystal absolutely hate.

As soon as Gigi sees me, she glares at me and I can't help but crack my knuckles in response. If she tries anything with me or Timber, she'll be paying for it. One way or another.

Rounding the corner to the kitchen, I grin when I see Mama Astrid, Sasha, Nikki, Susie, and Levi all in here. Though Levi's sitting on a stool at the large island with a cutting board in front of her.

She must feel my eyes on her because she turns, grins, and rolls her eyes. "The guys said I needed to rest more, but I still wanted to help, so we compromised. As long as I stay off my feet, I can continue to do stuff."

Nikki tsks at her. "You know it's for the best, Levi. You were running yourself ragged and your ankles were swelling. I had to pull the guys in on it so you'd be okay for tomorrow. Besides, you can still tell us what you want us to do while sitting your ass down. We need you looking sexy for your men tomorrow," she says with a wink, which has all of us grinning, and a few trying to hide their laughter.

"I hear you, I hear you," Levi mumbles as she tries to hide the fact that she's smiling.

"So, ladies, what are we cooking tonight?" I ask, and Mama Astrid winks at me.

"I told them about your idea and they all loved it. Your guys have already filled up their jar for all of you to start with on Monday. So, since we're in town, we're going to continue with the Junction Creek suggestions. Tonight is pan-seared steaks, mashed potatoes and gravy, asparagus, and corn. It was Beast's idea."

My chest warms and when I look over at Levi, she winks at me, pointing over to the open shelves above a counter. My grin widens when I see a large glass jar, and true to Mama Astrid's words, it's already stuffed full of suggestions.

Shaking my head, I get to work prepping the potatoes and asparagus alongside Levi and Susie.

We're almost done when I hear a commotion from the main room. I place the lid on top of the potatoes to help keep them warm and then look through the pass-through window. What I see has my blood boiling.

"I said fucking no, bitch. Now get the fuck off me," Timber yells as he grips Gigi by the shoulders and literally throws her off him. She trips in her heels and falls on her ass.

He stands and zips himself back up and that's all it takes.

Timber sees me making a beeline for Gigi, and the look in his eyes is begging me to believe that he didn't do anything with her. I believe him, but she's going to pay.

I pull my brass knuckles out of my pocket that Sasha gave me this morning in case I ever needed them, and slip them on. Stepping up behind Gigi as she tries to get to her feet, I kick her feet out from under her and she falls forward onto her hands and knees. Gripping her hair, I yank her back and land a punch to her face. Then, I pull on her hair harder so that her neck is barred and she's looking up at me. Her hands fly up, scratching at my hand and arms with her fake nails. Grabbing the leather band out of my pocket that Sasha also gave me this morning, I quickly wind it around her wrists and then twist the band.

Hard.

She screeches as she tries to get out of my hold, but with how I have her, it's like I have a leash tied around her wrists.

From the kitchen, I can hear Sasha cackling followed by what I think is the sound of a high-five. When Sasha gave me the items before we left this morning, I never thought I'd need to use it this soon. Thankfully, I kept them in my pocket rather than putting them into my purse or backpack.

"What have I told you about touching my Old Man, Gigi?" My voice is low, cold, and surprisingly, dark.

Then again, maybe I shouldn't be surprised after yesterday.

I'm still processing everything I learned and did. Maybe it is like Timber said. That I have a little darkness in me. That I'm not all sunshine and roses. I mean, I knew I wasn't all sunshine and roses, but I never knew I was capable of the things I've done recently. That said, I don't regret a single second of i t.

Gigi snarls at me. "He shouldn't have to lower himself to being with trailer park trash. Especially one that's all scarred and damaged. He deserves someone beautiful at his side who knows how to properly take care of a man."

Her words have me narrowing my eyes at her. As far as I knew, she shouldn't have known about me being injured or what happened to me. Levi told me that what happened has been kept hush hush here.

Same as for at Junction Creek.

Star and Candi just think I have some bruised ribs which covered up how slow I sometimes moved. Only club members, Sasha, and Mama Astrid know what happened. Well, Sasha may have told Colt, but I don't think she did.

"What makes you think that I'm scarred? Damaged?" I ask and seconds later, growls ring out throughout the room.

The room goes silent and Gigi pales as she visibly swallows hard.

"I—I..." she stutters but doesn't continue.

Shuffling sounds reach my ears, but I don't take my focus off Gigi. However, I can hear people walking down the hallways and a few doors closing. I know the guys have circled around us, but until someone tells me otherwise, I'm not letting her go.

Someone steps up in front of Gigi.

"Answer her," Thor says and somehow, Gigi pales even further as she flinches. I break my gaze with Gigi and look up at Thor.

His face is thunderous and I swear I can see storms brewing in his dark blue eyes that almost look like they have flecks of smokey grey in them right now.

Gigi pulls, trying to break her arms free, and I tighten my grip on the band as I look back down at her.

"What does it matter where I heard it? It's still true. Timber shouldn't be with someone who spreads her legs for anything with a dick."

I can't hold back my laughter with that one. "Wow, and you think you qualify for that since you spread your legs for all his brothers? You really don't know anything about him." I shake my head and she scoffs.

"Like you do, bitch."

Grinning, I yank back harder on her hair. She cries out as she squirms in my grasp, trying to break free.

"Actually, I do. And I know for a fact he wouldn't take a club bunny for an Old Lady. Now, answer my question for real this time."

She purses her lips as her gaze bounces from person to person, but no one steps forward to help her. Uncertainty fills her eyes, and I wonder if she'll actually answer me or not.

"I got a text message a few days ago saying that you were going to get what was coming to you. That you'd pay for taking a club brother off the market. A few hours later, I got a picture of a torso that was practically shredded."

Dad steps forward and pulls her phone out of her back pocket. He scowls when he finds it locked and takes her right index finger to press her fingerprint to it. She struggles in our hands, but he manages to unlock her phone.

He fiddles with her phone and then lets out a long whistle before handing the phone to Thor. Thor pulls out his own phone, his fingers instantly flying over the screen. Drae and Sasha head down the hallway that leads to where the bunnies' rooms are. Seconds later, I hear boots heading toward the door and see Colt, Ethan, and Alexei rushing out of here. Their bikes fire up outside before fading as they drive off.

I thought his face was thunderous before, but the look on his face now is darker and deadlier.

Thor steps forward and grips her chin harshly. Gigi cries out but then falls silent at the look on his face.

"You're done here, Gigi. We're keeping your phone too, since it's a club one. You seriously thought you could pull this shit over on us? Well, guess what? You're not only done here, but you're also now homeless.

"You are never to step foot in a Steel Archangel's establishment again or else you won't like what happens to you. Now you're going to wait here while we strip your car of its remote and make sure you don't have any spare keys you've copied to the apartment or your room here. Then you're going to walk your ass out of here and never look back. Do you understand me?"

Anger flashes in her eyes as her cheeks redden. "Yes," she grits out.

"Good. And if you ever lay a hand on any Steel Archangel member, which includes Old Ladies and family members of the club, we will rain fire and brimstone down on you. Do you understand?"

The muscle in her jaw ticks as she spits out another 'yes'.

The malice in her voice sends a shiver down my spine and I know my lockdown timeframe just got longer.

Whatever Dad and Thor saw on her phone was damaging enough to kick her out but not enough to question her further. Which means she might just have a warning on her phone or somehow got information she wasn't supposed to have.

Regardless, I'm going to have to keep my head on a swivel going forward.

Chapter 58
Timber

IT'S BEEN TEN MINUTES, but Thor doesn't budge from in front of Gigi, his arms crossed against his chest as he stares down at her. Gigi is still kneeling on the floor and Mae still has ahold of her hair and hands. I hope like fuck that position isn't hurting her, but I have to trust that she'll let us know if she is.

I want to know what the fuck he and Smoke saw on her phone, but thank fuck Mae knew her injuries were kept hush hush. I don't think anyone else put the pieces together faster than she did.

A phone dings and Thor grunts before putting his phone back in his pocket. Sasha and Drae come down the hallway and toss two trash bags stuffed full down on the ground by Gigi.

"Take your shit and get the fuck out of here, Gigi. The others have cleaned out your apartment and changed the locks. Your stuff is out by the dumpster. If you don't pick it up, then it'll be considered trash." He levels her a hard look that has her flinching back.

"Remember, you aren't to set foot in any of our establishments. If you see one of us, our Old Ladies, or one of our family members, you are going to go the other way. Cross the street. Leave the store. But if you ever approach one of us again, we'll bring the Steel Archangel's wrath down on you and ruin you. Do you understand?"

"Yes," she spits out.

Thor gives Mae a chin lift, and she undoes the leather band that was twisted around Gigi's wrists and let's go of her hair before stepping back by Thor.

"Now get the fuck out of here," Thor growls and Gigi scrambles to her feet, grabs the bags, and struts out of here like she hasn't just been banished.

She sneers at Mae as she walks past her and my stomach knots. Her gaze promises retribution. Dragon and Ryder follow her out, most likely to make sure she actually leaves and doesn't do anything funny on the way out.

Once the door closes after them, Thor leans in close to Mae and whispers something to her. I walk toward her, but my worry evaporates when I see the wide smile that spreads across her gorgeous face.

"Thank you, Thor," Mae says quietly.

I wrap an arm around her waist and she leans into me. Thor looks over at me and gives me a chin lift. "Church," he bellows and then walks over to Levi. They talk quietly and then Levi heads back into the kitchen, only to reappear a few minutes later and heads into Church.

Grasping Mae's chin, I give her a quick kiss. "Not sure how long we'll take. And I swear, Sunshine, I moved as fast as I could to get her off me."

She nods and gives me another quick kiss. "I believe you. Now, you guys do what you gotta do. We've got the food on the warmers, so it still should be good by the time you're all done. Unless you guys want to take food into Church?"

"It should only take a few minutes, Mae. I just need to fill the guys in on what was on Gigi's phone," Thor says as he walks back up to us.

Mae smiles. "Alright. We'll get everything set up for you when you're done. Tonight, we're having Beast's meal suggestion of pan-seared steaks, mashed potatoes and gravy, asparagus, and corn."

"Yes!" Beast yells as he hurries over to Mae, picks her up, and twirls her around. Her laughter rings out, but I scowl.

"Easy, Beast." Fuck, I hope he hasn't hurt her by pulling that stunt.

Beast blanches and quickly sets Sunshine down.

"Fuck, I'm sorry, Mae. I didn't think. I just got so excited about your cooking. Did I hurt you?"

Mae shakes her head and hugs him again, which he returns. "You didn't hurt my ribs, you're good. And I'm glad you're happy to eat our food. Now scoot on into Church. We'll have everything done by the time you guys are finished," she says with a shooing motion which has all of us laughing.

We may all be badass bikers, but these women have us wrapped around their fingers like you wouldn't believe.

Shaking my head, I follow the others into Church.

Once everyone has taken a seat, Thor bangs his hammer on the table.

"All right. Smoke's already tracking Gigi's phone to see who sent the messages, but somehow, someone did get a picture of Mae in the cabin while she was tied up. And yes, it was after Carter whipped her. The cabin is ashes now, so I have no idea if there were cameras in there or not. Smoke, put the messages up on the screen."

Smoke nods and after a few clicks on his keyboard, the wall lights up with a message.

"This is the first message. There are two," he says.

> That bitch pain in the ass will be taken care of tonight. You won't have to worry about her ever finding her way back from where she's going.

"And the last one."

> She bleeds so pretty for me and will be doing so much more for me soon. In a few hours, he'll be on the market again, but you've got competition. Best strike while you can.

Attached to that message is a picture of Mae tied down on that filthy bed, only wearing her bra. It must have been not too long after Carter whipped her, because I can see fresh tears on her face. Her eyes are closed but I don't know if she passed out or not afterward.

"According to Gigi's phone, the messages came from Carter's phone, but I've already been through his phone and they aren't there, so he must have deleted and cleared out the thread. Also on her phone are other conversations with Luscious and Carter, where the three of them planned what they wanted done to Mae. Gigi just wanted her gone. Luscious wanted her to be raped, to be hurt and to bleed before being sent off to her owner."

I clench my fists, wishing I had beaten Carter and Andrew worse before we left. I would have loved to get in some licks on Luscious, too, but I can't. Fuck, if Sasha gets wind of this, she'll probably drive back to Junction Creek to dole out more punishments for her.

"Lockdown will be continuing with the exception of the wedding, but we know who all is supposed to be here. Make sure you memorize their names and pictures. They could try and slip in thinking we're distracted with the wedding." Thor pauses and turns to me. "Have you thought about tying Mae to you in every way in case those fuckers get their hands on her?"

I clear my throat and scratch the back of my neck. "Thanks for ruining it, asshole."

"Wait, seriously?" Smoke asks, looking up at me from his laptop.

"Yeah, I had planned to ask her after the wedding so that we didn't draw attention away from your big day. Tripp texted me this morning that he has her cut and I was going to give it to her tonight after supper. As for tying her to me completely, she's not on anything and we aren't trying to prevent a pregnancy, so who knows? She could be pregnant already, but it's too soon to tell."

It's only been a week, which still boggles my mind, since Sunshine came into my life. Already I can't imagine being without her in my life.

The guys and Levi all hoot and holler as they congratulate me and tease me all in one.

"You know, I could marry you on paper and you guys have your ceremony later?" Smoke suggests when everyone settles down some.

Frowning, I shake my head. "I'm not going to decide on that until I ask her. She told me she never thought she'd find someone who wanted her for her and part of that is because of her fucked up stepdad filling her head with a bunch of fucking lies and starving her. If she wants a full-on wedding, I'll give it to her. I'm not taking her choice away from her."

Smoke grins at me and dips his head. "Good man. Let me know if she decides the paper route and I'll get it done."

The guys razz me some more when I feel eyes on me. Looking up, Levi, Thor, and Dragon are talking quietly together. Levi winks at me and gestures for me to join them. What are they plotting? And if it's what I think it is, is it something Sunshine will want?

Everyone's finishing supper when Tripp walks up and puts a box on the bar, tipping his head at me.

Grinning, I stand up from my seat. Sunshine looks up at me, confused, but I wink at her. "You'll understand in a second."

She frowns, but nods. I feel her gaze on me as I walk over to the bar. Turning to face everyone, I whistle to get their attention.

"Quiet down, assholes and ladies."

Chuckles ring out but I wait a few moments for everyone's full attention. My gaze passes over the room and I fight to curl my lip at the seductive look Crystal's giving me. Fucking hell. Even though I know my single brothers like them, I wish we didn't have bunnies. It would save a lot of fucking headaches.

"Sunshine, can you come up here, please?"

Worry flashes across her face, but Smoke nudges her, most likely reassuring her it's nothing bad without giving it away.

Hesitantly, she gets up and weaves through the tables until she's at my side.

"A week ago, you came into my life, and with one look, I knew you were the woman for me. In fact, that same day, I told you I wanted you to be my Old Lady. You accepted the next day and now," I pause as I hand her the box. "Now, everyone will know you're my Old Lady."

She looks up at me in shock before grinning and opening it. She pulls out her cut and chuckles at her road name.

Sunshine Goddess.

She slips it on and I pull her to me, slamming my lips down on hers.

Catcalls erupt from everyone, and she laughs at their antics when she pulls away. I raise my hand, quieting everyone down again.

"There's something else." Turning toward her, I take her left hand in mine, kissing it. "You are my world, Sunshine. There's not a day that goes by that I thank the stars that you're my woman. And I hope, you'll be my side forever."

She gasps, her other hand coming up to her mouth in shock as I kneel in front of her and pull out the ring I had picked out for her. It's a princess cut with diamonds surrounding it and along part of her band. On the inside, I had them engrave 'My Sunshine Goddess'. I had overheard her and the ladies talking about rings once and Sunshine had said her favorite cut was the princess cut. There was no way I was going to get her anything but that style.

"Will you marry me, Mae Rose Witlock, and be my Sunshine Goddess forever?

"Yes!" she cries as she throws her arms around my neck and kisses me.

Relief flows through me even though I was certain she would say yes. Everyone stands up, congratulating us, as they clap and cheer. Well, I notice Crystal scowling at us as she claps slowly so as not to draw too much attention to herself.

Wrapping my arms around her, I stand, carefully twirling us before setting her back down on her feet.

"As for our wedding, we'll do whatever you want, whenever you want. You hear me?" I whisper to her and she nods as her eyes turn misty again.

The ladies rush forward, and I grin as they surround my woman. They hug her, all of them wanting to see her ring. They start to pull her over to a table at the back when she looks over her shoulder, a question in her eyes.

Smiling, I nod and the blinding smile she gives me washes away any doubts I might have had about asking her tonight. I hadn't wanted to encroach on the eve of Levi's wedding, but she did raise some valid points and concerns to marrying Mae as soon as possible.

Now, it's up to what Mae wants, as I would never deny her the wedding of her dreams.

Chapter 59

Mae

HOLY CANNOLI...

I can't believe I'm engaged!

I stare down at my beautiful ring and tears prick my eyes. The ladies are gushing, but something someone says pulls me out of my thoughts with a jerk. "Wait. What did you say?"

Sasha laughs and wiggles her eyebrows. "What if you two had a double wedding? That would be so cool!"

Instantly, I shake my head. "No, no, no. I couldn't do that! There's no way I'm taking Levi's day away from her."

Levi stands and holds out a hand for me. "Hear me out?"

I gnaw my lip as my gaze goes from woman to woman. Friend to friend. Family member to family member. They're all nodding and giving me encouraging smiles. Do they know something I don't? My gaze returns to Levi's and I hesitantly put my hand in hers as I stand.

She pulls me into Thor's office, shuts the door, and sits on the couch, patting the spot beside her. I sit down, facing her and my worries and nerves come back full force. Did they find something out when they were in Church?

"Mae, I want you to know that I am in no way pressuring you into this, but I ask that you hear me out, okay?"

Hesitantly, I nod again and she smiles.

"Personally, I think it would be a good idea to marry Timber sooner rather than later. For one, if those assholes manage to get their hands on you, you'd have even more backing in the club because not only are you his Old Lady, you're also his wife. Being his wife also brings in support from outside the club as well. They don't understand that in the biker world, the guys see Old Ladies as even higher than a wife. Though these guys seem pretty intent on tying us to them in every way," she says with a giggle as she caresses her stomach.

I giggle in return when I remember how adamant Liam was about getting me pregnant.

"You love Timber, right?"

"With all my heart," I whisper as I fight not to cry.

"And you're going to get married eventually, so why not consider marrying him tomorrow?"

I hesitate as my head spins. This is all happening so fast.

"There's also another way you could go about this. Smoke could legally marry you on paper, and you could have your ceremony at a later date."

My jaw drops in surprise. "He can do that?"

She laughs at my shocked expression. "That man can hack into anything. Even the government comes to him for jobs sometimes."

I'm not sure it's possible, but it feels like my jaw drops even more at that. I had no idea Dad was that skilled with what he does. Then again, I'm not sure of everything that they do with their security company, though, that's probably for the best.

Shaking off those thoughts, my mind whirls as I contemplate what Levi's saying.

"The question of the hour is, what is it that you want? Not Timber. Not your dad. Not your mom. Not anyone else. You. What do *you* want?"

Closing my eyes, I swallow hard as I think about Mom. Wondering where she is and if she's been hurt again. God, I wish we could just find her so that I know she's safe. Taking a deep breath, I will myself not to cry and refocus back on Levi's question.

Gnawing at my lip, I fight back tears as the memories wash over me. "In all honesty, I never thought I'd even be at this stage of my life. I had it drilled into me that no one would want me for me. That I was worthless. That I was lower than the gum on someone's shoe.

"When I was a little girl, Mom would read me a bunch of books and I would dream about my white knight. But then Preston came into our lives and not only did those stories stop, but he also shattered any dream I ever had at that point. As

I got older, the only ones he wasn't able to take from me were getting Mom out and owning and running my own daycare."

Taking another deep breath, I close my eyes and dare to let myself dream. About my life with Liam.

Opening them, I see Levi smiling at me, and I return her smile. "I want a white dress. Nothing too fancy, as that isn't my style, but I want it to hug my torso and hips before becoming a little looser so that it's easier to walk. Timber doesn't need to wear a tux. That's never mattered to me, but I definitely want a nice dress. For Dad to walk me down the aisle." My breath hitches as my chest tightens. "I'd love for Mom to be there, but I have no idea where she even is right now or if she's even alive."

A tear escapes and I hastily wipe it away. I'm so mad at Preston, Phillip, Bruce, and X for what they've done to us over the years and what they're doing to Mom right now.

Surprisingly, dark thoughts start to creep in at what I'd do to them as punishment, however, I push those thoughts aside for right now.

Levi gives me a sad, small smile. "I completely understand wanting your mom there. I just ask that you at least think about my suggestions. I know your mom would understand that what we're proposing is to add another layer of protection around you, but only you can make the decision about what you want. No matter what you decide, you'll have the club's backing."

I think over her words when my brain skitters. "What do you mean, 'what we're proposing'? Who's we?"

She grins. "My men and I would love to share our day with you, so if that's one of your worries, you can put it to bed right now. We wouldn't have offered if we weren't okay with it. It would be an honor to share my day and future anniversaries with my niece."

"But... Don't you have to have a marriage license like three or four days in advance?"

Levi laughs again. "Four days, but did you already forget about the part where your dad is an insanely talented hacker?" she asks as she wiggles her eyebrows at me, which has me laughing nervously along with her.

I look down, my fingers running along the seam in the leather cushion of the couch and my gaze catches on my engagement ring as I contemplate her suggestion.

Would it be so bad to marry Liam tomorrow? I want to, but there's still a tightness in my chest at the thought that Mom won't be there. Then again, what I said before is true. I don't know if she's alive still. And I know Levi's right. Mom would want me to protect myself, she said so herself multiple times in her journals. The club has already shown that they're willing to protect me, too.

Plus, Levi's right. Being legally tied to Liam would give me more protections outside of the club. More resources to call on should we need them. Should I go ahead with the ceremony or just have Dad marry us on paper?

Shaking myself internally as Levi's words come back to me about what I want, no one else, I will myself not to cry.

"Even if I wanted to, there's no way I'd be able to find a dress. Your wedding is tomorrow."

She grins at me. "Is that your only concern left?"

Nibbling on my lip, I nod.

"If I could find you a dress, do you want to get married tomorrow?"

"Yes," I whisper.

The smile that lights up her face pushes away my doubts, but my nerves remain. "Well, then. I have a call to make."

Chapter 60
Timber

A HALF HOUR AGO, Levi and Sunshine came out of Thor's office, grabbed the other ladies, and made a beeline for the door. All I got in passing was a kiss on the cheek and Sunshine telling me that she'll be at Levi's house.

I did catch a few little slips about wedding dresses and I wonder if Mae will take up Levi's suggestion of marrying me tomorrow.

Someone's hand lands on my shoulder, squeezing it.

Turning, I grin, seeing Dragon standing behind me before he comes around and sits next to me. I'm still pissed at him, but he's also one of my best friends.

"Sounds like we might be both getting hitched tomorrow."

Shaking my head, my grin widens. "I definitely wouldn't be against it. I wanted to marry her the day I met her, but I knew she wasn't ready."

He laughs but also nods before his face turns grim. "I'm sorry for all the shit I said about her. I didn't realize how drunk Smoke was when he said that stuff about Mae, but still, I shouldn't have just taken his word about who she is."

My jaw clenches as I remember all the shit he spewed last week. "Please say you've pulled your head out of your ass and won't say any of that shit to another brother when they bring someone around."

His face hardens. "I won't, and I've been kicking myself for it ever since. I've known you for years and should never have said that shit."

Giving him a chin lift, we clink beers. Having known him for so long, I know he's not good at this sort of thing, but at least he said he won't pull that bullshit with anyone else.

All of us have been shooting the shit for the past couple of hours. Most of us have been giving shit to Thor and Dragon about this being their last night before being fully shackled.

They both share one of their twin looks and I grin, shaking my head.

I still don't know if Mae wants to get married tomorrow, and it's taking everything in me not to storm over to their house and ask her.

"Never know, could be another one fully off the market tomorrow and shackled just the same," Reaper says as he laughs.

"Just you wait till you find the one that knocks you off your feet, Reaper. You'll do anything for her once you find her," I growl at him in response, but there's no heat behind it.

A look crosses his face and I clamp my mouth shut. Fuck, I shouldn't have said that after everything that's happened.

Then, surprisingly, he gives a small smile and shrugs his shoulders.

Well, fuck.

Sunshine told me a little about their talk and that she gave him a piece of her mind when he said no one would want him because of his scars. Maybe he's taking her words to heart. If anyone deserves to be happy, it's him after all the shit he's been through.

A whoop sounds and I look over to see Thor and Dragon looking at something on Thor's phone. They look up at me and grin.

My phone vibrates and I pull it out.

> *Mae: Will you marry me tomorrow?*

> *Timber: Fuck yes, Sunshine. I'd marry you tonight if I could. Fuck, I would have married you the day I first saw you.*

She sends me a bunch of heart emojis and I chuckle.

> *Mae: Love you.*

> *Timber: Love you, too, Sunshine.*

More whoops and hollers go up, but there's nothing that's going to shake the smile off my face.

All of a sudden, music starts up and Loki and Punisher both start singing *'Another One Bites the Dust'* by Queen, which has everyone in an uproar.

Well, fuck. I watch them in shock as they both sing the entire song. Loki even busts out some moves. I had no idea the fuckers could sing, let alone that they were that good. Based off a few other looks, I know I'm not the only one shocked at this revelation.

"Get your asses up here for some shots," Phoenix yells after the song ends.

Once everyone has their drink, Phoenix whistles to quiet everyone down again.

"Not only is our fearless leader and our Enforcers tying the knot tomorrow, but Timber and Lil' Bit will be as well. You fuckers know I'm not good at making speeches and all that shit, but here goes nothing." He pauses as a few of us chuckle in agreement. The man hardly says anything, and he definitely hates having attention on him like this.

"All three of you have found women that have made you all better men. Though why they want to be chained to your ugly mugs for life, I'll never know." Laughter rings out at his statement, but after a few moments, it dies down again. "I'm happy for all three of you and I can only hope that the rest of us fuckers will be as lucky as all of you when the time comes for us. Let's hear it for Thor, Dragon, and Timber!"

Cheers ring out again before everyone drinks their shot. The alcohol burns down my throat, but I barely feel it.

I'm getting married tomorrow.

It's nearly midnight when I leave the clubhouse and head toward Levi's house. I've got a good buzz going, but I'm not as drunk as some of my brothers who will definitely be feeling it tomorrow.

I paced myself because I wanted to remember everything tomorrow and not be wincing at every bright light or loud sound.

As I climb the steps up to Levi's house, I can hear laughter from inside.

I knock and then enter. Instantly their laughter dies down and I hear some ruffling of pages or something.

"Is it okay to come in?"

After a few moments, Mae comes out of the living room into the hallway, sliding the last foot or so in her socks on the hardwood floors before coming to a stop right in front of me. Briefly, I worry the action pulled at her stitches, but I don't see her wincing or her eyes tightening with pain. Instead, they are bright and a huge smile lights up her face.

"Hey!" she says before pulling me down and kissing me like her life depends on it.

I'd been sporting a semi all night thinking about marrying her tomorrow and this kiss has me hard as steel for her.

"Bow-chicka-wow-wow," Sasha sings sassily, which has the ladies laughing again.

Pulling back, I set her back down on the ground. "Do you need to still figure some things out, or can I take you home?" My voice comes out huskier than normal and her pupils dilate instantly. Fuck, I need to get her home.

"Let me just grab my things. I'll need to come over tomorrow after breakfast."

"Not a problem, Sunshine," I tell her before leaning in closer. "But get your ass moving before I throw you over my shoulder and haul you home with my hand on your ass."

A shiver works through her before she rushes back into the living room and a few moments later, reappears with her backpack.

I take it from her and without warning, lean down and scoop her over my shoulder, mindful to put more pressure on her hips since those wounds have mostly healed.

"Timber! I thought you said if I hurried you wouldn't do this," she says as her little fists pound on my back.

"I changed my mind." Turning to the ladies, I wave goodnight and head back out into the night as their laughter rings out.

"Timber, put me down! I am perfectly able to walk on my own."

Bringing a hand up, I spank her ass and keep walking. "I've been thinking of you all night, Sunshine. I need my fiancée home, in my bed, and buried in her sweet pussy."

A shudder runs through her, and I grin as I smack her ass again. She moans and fuck, does that make me even harder than I already was.

I pick up the pace and as soon as I'm in my house; I lock it back up and take the stairs two at a time.

In our bedroom, I lower her onto the bed. She bounces a little and fuck do I love how her perfect tits bounce. I crawl over her, letting her feel me against her as I take her mouth. She melts against me and a few beats later; I feel her grinding herself against my length.

"Fuck, Sunshine. I need to worship my fiancée."

She moans as I kiss down her neck, scraping my teeth over her collarbone. "Yes, please, Liam. I need you."

Her hands push at my cut and I pull back, slipping it off and setting it on the dresser along with my gun.

"Strip."

Her eyes dilate further at the command in my voice and I can see her skin break out into goosebumps from here.

I take my time slipping off my boots and clothes. Her eyes drink in my body and tattoos and fuck do I love when she licks her lips as she stares at me.

I want to explore things with her, but right now, I just want my fiancée. "On your hands and knees toward the head of the bed. I want that ass in the air. Later we'll play more, Baby. I need you too much right now," I tell her as I stalk toward her.

She quickly does as I ask, her pretty pink pussy peeking out at me as she gets into position. Not being able to resist, I crawl under her so I'm on my back, grab her hips, and lower her onto my face as I devour her.

"Liam!" she screams. She tries to pull her hips up and I smack her ass. This is the first time I've eaten her pussy like this, and she looks down at me hesitantly.

"Ride my face, Baby."

She moans when I flatten my tongue and lick her, flicking her clit. It takes her a bit to get into a rhythm, but when she does, fuck do I think this is my favorite position to eat her sweet pussy and see her tits bounce and sway as she moves.

Running a finger through her juices, I tease her ass. She tenses at first, but soon relaxes enough that I'm able to push my finger inside.

"Oh, that feels so good, Liam!"

Her pace picks up as I continue to devour her pussy and finger fuck her ass.

After a few moments, her thighs start to tremble and I know she's close. Biting down gently on her clit, she cries out as she comes and I lap up her juices, but unlike I usually do, I don't keep licking her as the tremors subside.

Instead, I slide out from underneath her and get on my knees. Grabbing her hips, I slam into her in a single thrust, burying myself to the hilt.

"Liam!" she cries out as another orgasm suddenly rips through her.

I start thrusting, fucking her through her orgasm. The need to keep her screaming and on edge consuming me.

"Oh my god, oh my god, oh my god."

"That's it, Baby, scream. I want to hear you as I fuck you. My fiancée."

She does just that as I bring her three more back-to-back orgasms before her last one has me coming hard inside her.

Her upper body slumps down on the bed. Wrapping an arm around her waist, I pull out, gently lowering her to the bed as I lay down next to her.

Pulling her close, she goes up on her elbow, kissing me as I cup her cheek.

"If I lose my voice for tomorrow, I am going to kick your hiney, Mister."

I chuckle, pulling her in close and kissing her again.

She moans as she grinds against me.

"Does my fiancée want more?" I reach down, rubbing circles on her clit.

Her voice turns sultry as she moans deeply, rubbing against me even harder. "Yes, Liam. I need my fiancé's cock in me. Filling me up and making a baby."

This time, it's me that moans. Grabbing her hips, I pick her up and roll onto my back.

Her little fingers grab the base of my cock and we both moan as she lowers herself onto me.

Her hips start moving and fuck, do I love the way her body moves when she's on top of me. With one hand on my chest, the other pulls her hair off to the side. The sultry look she gives me while doing that simple action has me almost rolling her onto her back and fucking her harder than I ever have before.

"That's it, Sunshine. Ride my cock like a good girl."

My words seem to flip a switch in her because she picks up the pace. Keeping one hand on her hip, my other lowers until I'm able to rub her clit with my thumb.

"Oh, fuck. Right there. Don't stop."

I bite my lip to keep from doing anything different, but the fact that she's cussing has my control barely holding on.

She cries out as she clamps down on me like a vice.

Not being able to take it anymore, I roll us and kiss her, swallowing her cries as her body shudders from her orgasm.

She kisses me back passionately, and I feel the change in both of us. Yes, I still want to fuck her hard, but instead of that, I do slow, deep thrusts as I make sure to rub her clit on each thrust with my pelvis.

"Fuck," she hisses, her nails raking down my back as I kiss down her neck, making sure to lick and nibble her most sensitive parts.

Her moans fill the air, and soon, I can feel her body tensing and trembling against me.

"I'm so close," she whispers.

Nipping at her skin, I growl. "Not yet. You'll come when I say you can come."

She whimpers and I can feel my own orgasm getting closer as I continue my same pace.

"Liam," she gasps and claws at my back harder. Fuck, I think she might have even drawn blood. That image brings me closer to my own orgasm.

"Now. Come for me, Sunshine. Milk my cock."

She cries out and her pussy clamps down on me, triggering my own release. I continue thrusting as I fill her up with my cum.

A tear slides down her cheek and I wipe it away with my thumb. "You okay, Sunshine?"

She nods and smiles. I wipe another tear that escapes.

"Happy tears. Everything just felt so intense. I love you, Liam, and I can't wait to marry you tomorrow."

Grinning, I kiss her again.

"Love you, too, Mae. Can't wait for you to be my wife."

We stay like that for a few moments before I pull out. My cum leaks out of her, and I can't help it. I run my finger through it and push it back inside her.

"Liam!" she gasps, but then giggles.

I cock an eyebrow at her. "Well, you did say you wanted me to put a baby in you. Gotta make sure it all stays where it's supposed to be."

Her eyes darken, but I need to let her sleep. It's already past one and we have a big day tomorrow.

"Be right back, Sunshine."

Walking into the bathroom, I wet a washcloth, and head back into the bedroom to clean her up. Turning off the light, I throw the washcloth toward the hamper, lay down, and pull her close to me as I cover us with the blankets.

She sighs as she nestles up close to me, and soon, her breathing evens out. I kiss her shoulder, smiling against her skin when she breaks out in goosebumps. Kissing her shoulder again, I close my eyes, letting sleep take me.

Chapter 61
Timber

I PULL AT MY collar, hating it, but at the same time loving it. After Sunshine had gone off with the ladies this morning to get ready, I quickly ran into town to get a quick trim and pick up a nicer white long-sleeve button-up shirt. I already had one that I had planned to wear, but since I'll also be getting married today, I felt that I should get a new shirt.

Thor and Dragon had told me the place they went to get theirs, and I took their recommendation. The guy that runs the place hooked us up, and in less than two hours, we were all back at the compound. Smoke, Axe, Punisher, Erik, Dominick, and Gunner had gone with me. With the exception of Smoke, they'll be my groomsmen, along with Thor and Dragon. Though Dragon will be my best man. Since Smoke already had a white shirt for Levi's wedding, he got a royal blue shirt for when he walks Mae down the aisle.

Dragon being my best man had made Mae a little hesitant because of their history, but she also knows he's one of my closest friends. I hope like fuck he apologizes to her and they're able to get to know each other better.

Shaking off those thoughts, I look around the main room again. Ashley, Ginger, Amy, Sarah, Mama Astrid, and Peggy are all putting the final touches on the decorations. The place is buzzing with excitement as guests start trickling in.

Frowning, I notice Patch sitting at the bar with a beer as he stares at his phone. Even from across the room, I can tell he's anxious as fuck. Sliding onto the barstool next to him, I motion for Lex to bring me a beer.

Turning toward Patch, my frown deepens. "What's going on, man?"

He sighs. "Remember that woman I told you about that's been in and out of the ER multiple times the past six months?"

"Yeah. Her name's Mary, right?"

He nods glumly. "Yeah, well, back in the day, she was my best friend. She, Allison, Brady, and I were close as could be. We were always together, though it helped we all lived next to each other, and our parents were all friends.

"In high school, Mary and I started dating. We were each other's firsts. Then about a few of months later, she disappeared with no warning and her house was put on the market."

He pauses and I get the feeling he isn't telling me something, but I don't push him on it.

"I never heard from her in the past nine years until I saw her that first time in the ER six months ago. Every time she's in there, her injuries are worse than the last time," he says, his lip curling.

"I know you can't tell me specifics, but I hope like fuck you aren't suggesting her husband is beating her."

He turns toward me and fuck, do I know that look.

"Fuck. Who's the dead man walking?"

His face turns thunderous and his hands tighten on his phone so much that his fingertips turn white. "Fucking Deputy Chief Stephen Haynes."

"You've got to be fucking shitting me," I snarl. "I always knew I hated that fucker. I don't know how he weaseled his way into our town, but I knew he was crooked from the first time I saw the slimy bastard."

Patch's sneer darkens. "He always plays the doting husband in public, but at home, it's a fucking shitshow. I know because one of her kids told me when the fucker stepped out of the room. I gave her my number and the club's number. Told her oldest to memorize it as well. That if they're in danger, they can call us and we'd get them all out of there."

I narrow my eyes at him. "What aren't you telling me?"

He looks over at me nervously before looking around, but no one's paying us much attention. His Adam's apple bobs as he swallows thickly. "I think her eldest, Asher, is my son. She's been away for nine years and he's nine. I had suspicions that she was pregnant before she disappeared, but that's all they were, unless you count a home pregnancy test that was found in her trash. However, we all know they can give false positives. She has two other kids that are younger, Isaiah and Cassie, with Cassie being the youngest. Asher, or Ash as she calls him, looks just like I did when I was that age if you change the hair out. While all three kids have Mary in them, all of them but Ash have bits of Stephen in their looks," he w hispers.

Fuck.

Large hands land on both of our shoulders, and we both jump as Thor chuckles at our surprise. "We've got your back, Patch, on whatever needs to be done to get her and her kids away from that fucker. Later, come find me and fill me in on what's all happened so far. Keep me posted."

And with that, he walks off and heads upstairs.

"Fuck, I didn't even hear him walk up to us," Patch says with a sad laugh as he shakes his head.

"I swear he's been taking stealth lessons from Lex and the others," I reply, laughing.

Lex grins from behind the bar, which has us both laughing harder.

"Timber," Kristy yells from upstairs. I finish my beer and clasp Patch's shoulder.

"Like Thor said, I've got your back on this. Let me know if you need me for anything."

He gives me a chin lift and I head upstairs to see what Kristy wants.

I grin as I think back to when Kristy first came here this morning. She's got to be no more than five feet tall, with long wavy brown hair, and her body is curvy as fuck. I saw more than one brother looking at her appreciatively and I know more than one loves the fact that her waist is not small. I wouldn't call her overweight, but from past conversations, I know a few of my brothers love their women to be heavier and curvier.

Regardless, the woman is a hurricane—a force to be reckoned with. She didn't even bat an eye at being surrounded by a bunch of muscular, tattooed men that tower over her. The second she was inside, she started barking orders. It was almost comical to see my brothers jump to do whatever she needed.

Shaking off those thoughts, I enter the room that us guys in the wedding party are using. I guess I should say wedding parties. With so many of us now, it's a tight fit in here. There are fifteen of us in this little room, but only Jordan, Smoke, Thor, Dragon, and I are in both weddings.

Kristy nods as she looks me over in my black jeans, boots, cut, and new shirt. Mama Astrid had taken our shirts as soon as we got back to wash and press them, which I was grateful for. The material had scratched my skin like crazy when I was trying it on in the shop.

"Good, you all are looking handsome. Now just don't fuck it up or get into any fights in the meantime. For now, Axe, Punisher, Erik, Dom, and Gunner, you all can take a seat in the audience when you are ready. Before we begin Levi, Thor, and Dragon's wedding, I will make an announcement that instead of just one wedding, there will now be two, one right after the other." She pauses right as I open my mouth to ask her something and she waves me off.

"Don't get your boxers in a twist, Timber. We'll make sure to give Levi and Mae enough time to change dresses and freshen up in between, and then we'll get to your wedding. After Levi, Thor, and Dragon's wedding, that is when Axe, Punisher, Erik, Dom, and Gunner need to make their way back and stand in the hallway near the room the ladies are using.

"Don't forget, we're going to get a few photos of the wedding party before we start getting ready for Timber and Mae's wedding. Once we're done with pictures, it shouldn't take too long for the ladies to get ready, and then we'll get you all paired up again. Now, do you all understand? Any questions?"

When all of us tell her we're ready, she nods. Grinning, I can only shake my head. Kristy is really a force to be reckoned with.

"Okay, those of you in the first wedding, wait in here while I go and check on the ladies. I'll text Phoenix when you can all come over to their room to get paired up."

The room the ladies are in is off down a hallway on the first floor. To help with keeping us separate and so that neither Thor, Dragon, or I could see our fiancées before the wedding, we're in a spare room up on the third floor.

Once the others step out, I'm able to breathe a little easier, but I'm nervous for some reason.

"Take a deep breath. You're going to do just fine," Roy says as he clasps my shoulder.

"I don't know why I'm nervous," I whisper, and he smiles.

"It's normal. Honestly, I think everyone gets the pre-wedding nerves, even if they won't admit it. You'll be able to see your lovely bride in just a few minutes. Levi told me this morning that she rearranged the lineup so that you two could be together."

I look at him in shock and he smirks at me. I was supposed to walk Erin down the aisle. But that was also before Levi asked if Mae could also be her bridesmaid right before we left for Junction Creek. Mama Astrid had taken her into town when we were there for her to pick out her dress and shoes. I never thought she'd change the lineup, but fuck, am I grateful she did.

"Who's walking Erin down the aisle now?"

"Well, since she was already changing it up, she changed up a couple of people as well. Susie and Tripp will be together and then Erin and Ethan will walk together."

I glance over at Tripp and smirk. I know he's got it bad for Susie, but I didn't think he'd actually act on it. He's been wanting her for a few years now but has always been worried about how Axe would take it. Not that I blame him. Axe is very protective of Susie and Jordan. Though, I think it would be a plus in Tripp's favor since he and Jordan get along so well.

Actually, now that I'm watching him, he seems more nervous than usual.

Shaking my head, I take a sip of my water and wait for Kristy to tell us we can head downstairs. Fuck, I can't wait to see Sunshine.

Chapter 62

Mae

SLIPPING INTO MY DRESS, I try to calm my nerves.

For my bridesmaid's dress, I'd chosen a dark blue dress with spaghetti straps that goes down to the floor. There's a fair amount of cleavage, and the slit on the side goes up to mid-thigh. At first, I thought it was too much skin, but when Mama Astrid had me text Levi and Sasha pictures of me wearing it, both of them insisted I buy it. Eventually, I caved and got it. To go with it, I got silver strappy heels.

After my attack, I was worried that I should get a different dress since this one will show so many of the scars on my chest. It wasn't until after a long tear-filled call with all the ladies that I finally decided to keep it. Remembering Levi's words has me tearing up and I blink rapidly to keep them at bay.

"Our scars do not define us," Levi told me. "They are a sign that you have been through the unthinkable and have come out on the other side stronger than before. A survivor. Those scars are your badges of bravery. Even if you didn't feel very brave at the time. They didn't break you and nothing will. You are a Steel Archangel's Old Lady, Mae. Like our men, we are as strong as steel. Our club does not bend to the enemy. Our club does not break—our bonds with our brothers and sisters make sure of that. Your scars do not own you. You own them. Wear those scars with pride, Babe."

Earlier, Kristy had done my hair so that it was half-up and half down and kept my makeup semi-light. She said she'll pin the rest of my hair up and tweak my makeup when we're done with pictures for Levi's wedding.

My gaze goes to my wedding dress hanging up in the corner and I can't help but smile as I remember last night.

"Okay, all you fabulous and gorgeous ladies! Everyone's hair and makeup is done! Let's get Levi in her dress and then you all can slip into your dresses or finish getting ready," Kristy calls out as she claps her hands, pulling me out of my thoughts.

She goes over to Levi's dress in the corner and unzips the bag. Even though I saw it last night, I still love it.

Levi had chosen a sexy spaghetti strap dress with a deep V-neck. It's sort of a mermaid style floor-length dress that has straps crisscrossing on her back a few times. It also has a slit that's about mid-thigh on her. Eh, maybe a bit higher but not high enough that you'd see her panties. There's a small train, for which I'm sure she's happy for as I can imagine it would be cumbersome for her if it were longer. It wraps snuggly around her baby bump and she looks absolutely gorgeous in it.

The shoes she paired with it are strappy silver stiletto heels that have little rhinestones on them and the straps wrap around her calves a few times.

While Sasha, Allison, and Kristy get Levi into her dress, I get her shoes ready.

After that, Sasha helps her slide on her garter belt and a little surprise that I know her men will like. Especially Dragon. I've heard more than once that he loves seeing her armed.

I was surprised when Sasha told me that Levi is the club's unofficial second Enforcer. Though, that does make sense with her knife obsession and how well she handles blades. My cheeks heat as I remember some of our conversations where she's told us *exactly* how much Dragon loves to see her armed.

A few minutes later, she's ready, but I notice she's staring at the picture of her mom. Her eyes turn glassy and Sasha rushes back to her side, fanning her face. I step away, giving them some privacy when a knock comes at the door.

"Everyone decent?" Phoenix calls out and a few seconds later, Levi responds. "Yes."

Phoenix and the rest of the guys enter, but I only have eyes for one man. *My fiancé and soon to be husband.*

He stares at me, mouth agape, but his eyes burn with desire as his gaze slowly slides over my body.

"Fuck, Sunshine. It's gonna be damn near fucking impossible not to be hard out there. Fuck, Baby." He whispers the last part as he kisses down my neck.

"You? I'm going to be drooling onto my dress."

A whack sounds and I look around startled as to what happened.

"Ouch! What the fuck?" Timber suddenly calls out as he flinches back from me.

I giggle as I try to hide my smile with my hands and he glares at me over Kristy's head, who had stepped between us.

"Back off, you horny animal! I had to use so much concealer on her neck that you better not even think of putting another mark on her until after the ceremonies and pictures are complete. Do you understand?" Kristy says as she continues to stab her finger into his chest.

I try to stifle another giggle as he stares down at her in surprise, but when he glances up at me when my giggle escapes, his eyes hold a promise.

Oh, sugar honey ice tea.

I may have bitten off more than I can chew with this outfit.

And he hasn't even seen my wedding dress yet, which is even more bold and sexier than this one is. At least in my opinion, anyway.

"Baby Girl, you look beautiful," Dad says as he comes up and hugs me.

"Thanks, Dad. You look quite handsome yourself."

"Places!" Kristy calls out as she ushers us all into line and I loop my arm through Timber's. She bends down to talk to Jordan and Sadie and then slips out of the room. Kristy left the door open and I can hear her getting everyone's attention out in the main room.

"Ladies, gentlemen, and bikers," she starts, which has several people chuckling. "We have a surprise for you. You are all here to witness the marriage between Levi Wallace, Ryan Gilbert or Thor to the club, and Nick Gilbert or Dragon to the club, but there will be another wedding after this." She pauses again, and I shift on my feet nervously as I hear the excited chatter.

"Last night, there was another proposal in the club and the newly engaged couple are very close to the three you are here to see get married today. Close as in best friends and family, close." She pauses yet again, and the 'awws' damn near have me crying. I fan my face to keep the tears from falling, and Timber places his hand on my arm, squeezing slightly.

Sasha turns around and gives me a thumbs up before blowing me an air kiss that I return. I had no idea Kristy was going to say all of this.

"Another person very close to the two couples suggested they both get married on the same day. The two brides-to-be couldn't turn down their sister and aunt's request as they both equally loved the idea as much as the woman who suggested it. Long story short, you will also be witnessing Liam Caldwell, or Timber to the club, and Mae Witlock exchanging vows after Levi, Thor, and Dragon's wedding. There will be a brief interlude in between both weddings. Now, without further ado, let's welcome the wedding party for Levi, Thor, and Dragon!"

Seconds later, the music starts up and then Jordan revs his mini-motorcycle.

"Not too long now and it'll be our turn," Timber whispers in my ear and my breath catches when I feel his hot breath against my skin.

Turning to look up at him, I smile. I wish I could kiss him, but that would smear my lip gloss. "I can't wait."

The guests cheer as Jordan rides out on his mini-motorcycle with Sadie sitting behind him. I really hope they're getting a video of them. I saw them practicing last week when Susie and I had talked and then again yesterday afternoon, but it won't be as special as right now.

We're all walking out to *Born to be Wild* by Steppenwolf, and for half of it, we're going to be dancing until we get to the chairs and when the aisle narrows.

Cheers and whoops ring out as Susie and Tripp make their entrance. Then it's Erin and Ethan, Allison and Ryder.

When they step out, I take a deep breath, nerves fluttering in my belly.

We had all been practicing what we were going to do, and I'm nervous since I've never really danced before. And then adding heels on was another layer of complexity on top of that.

When it's our turn, we step out and for the first few steps it's normal so that Kristy's photographer can get a few pictures and then Timber takes my hand, spinning me before we start dancing.

Surprisingly, I nail each move and am smiling widely when I retake his arm to walk the rest of the way down the aisle. Liam leans in and gives me a chaste kiss before parting and I feel my cheeks heat as I hear a few 'awws'.

Then it's Nikki and Dad followed by Roxy and Alexei; and finally Sasha and Phoenix.

When it's Levi's turn, I blink away tears at how beautiful and happy she looks as she walks down the aisle on Roy's arm. He passes her off to Thor and Levi turns, giving Sasha her flowers.

Reaper starts the ceremony, but almost immediately, my attention and focus shifts to Timber, who not surprisingly, is staring at me heatedly.

I cheer and clap when Levi and Thor kiss and then he switches places with Dragon.

Even though I try to stay focused on their vows, I can't. My gaze once again goes to Timber who is looking especially drool-worthy in his crisp white button-down long-sleeved shirt with his cut on over top. He's wearing black jeans and his best black boots that he cleaned up so that there wasn't any oil on them.

Cheering has my gaze snapping back to see Dragon and Levi passionately kissing.

"I didn't say you could kiss her yet, asshole," Reaper grumbles as he tosses his hands in the air, which has more laughter ringing out.

"Since when do I need your permission to kiss my woman?" Dragon retorts which has more laughter filling the air.

Reaper glares at Dragon, but I see the corners of his lips twitching.

"Every fucking time," he mumbles and then looks out at the crowd. "Well, since this asshole jumped the gun, let me officially introduce Mr., Mr. and Mrs. Ryan and Nick Gilbert!"

Once again cheers erupt, louder this time, as Thor comes to stand at Levi's other side and the three of them walk down.

We all file out through the back of the clubhouse where we'll take some pictures—of all of us as a group, of us partnered up, and of course, a lot of Levi and her men.

About twenty minutes later, we head inside and Kristy turns to me, wiggling her eyebrows.

"Now it's your turn, Mae. Let's get you sex-ified for that husband-to-be of yours," she says and I can't help but laugh along with her.

She's fast become a friend of mine and I can't wait to hang out with her more.

Chapter 63

Mae

KRISTY'S ALREADY PULLED THE rest of my hair up so that it's off my shoulders and is in some sort of a fancy, braided bun at the base of my head. For my makeup, she went a little smokier with the eyeshadow and I wiped off my light pink lip gloss, switching it out for a bright red lipstick that Kristy swore was smear proof.

When she's done, I slip out of my bridesmaid's dress and take off my silver strappy heels. I'm standing in my white thong and nothing else when Kristy unzips the bag holding my wedding dress.

Kristy's sister, Emily, owns a wedding dress store. Levi, the ladies, and I all had a video chat with Emily last night as we talked about what I was looking for. An hour later, she showed up at the clubhouse with a van full of dresses for me to choose from.

I ended up choosing a dress that I had never imagined myself in.

It's a white mermaid dress with black lace on the torso and on the bottom of the dress. On the top, there is a nude material on my arms and chest with the black lace overlaying parts of it. The nude material follows the lace, which I'm thankful for, otherwise if it were straight across my chest, it would have rubbed on some of my stitches that haven't fully dissolved yet.

The nude material and lace go up my shoulders into a narrow strap and then on the back, it changes. There's a small section that buttons up at the base of my neck, but the nude material and lace follow along my sides, leaving my back open until it meets the white material near the small of my back. There's absolutely no way to wear a bra with it, so Kristy used something she called pasties to cover my nipples. Then she used some sort of similar tape to support my ample chest and prevent a wardrobe malfunction.

The white part of the dress starts at my chest and goes down to the bottom hem of the dress. The black lace dips down into a deep V at my chest, revealing more cleavage than I ever have before. There's a slit in the gown that is darn near as revealing as Levi's was. For shoes, I chose black strappy stilettos with rhinestones and the straps go up to almost my knees.

Wearing this dress brings Timber's words back to me. That I'm his Sunshine Goddess with a bit of darkness in me.

Kristy and Sasha bring over my dress. Carefully, I step into it, not wanting to tear the delicate nude material. They button me up right as there's a knock on the door.

"It's Smoke."

I quickly glance at Levi and see that she's changed into her bridesmaid's dress, which Emily brought over for her last night as well.

"Come in," I call out.

He quickly enters and shuts the door behind him. When he looks up, he stops in his tracks as his gaze sweeps over me.

"Fuck, Baby Girl. You look fucking gorgeous."

Tears prick my eyes and I fan myself to keep them from falling. "Thank you, but don't you dare make me cry, Dad! I almost did multiple times during Levi's wedding, so I'm really on edge right now."

He shakes his head and steps forward with a box in his hands.

"Levi and Sasha helped me pick these out earlier. I wanted to give you something to go with your dress but wouldn't be too much since they said there's a lot of detail to your dress, and fuck, they weren't kidding around about that."

Instantly, my nerves go into overdrive. "Too much?"

He shakes his head. "No, Baby Girl. This dress is fucking gorgeous on you and fits your personality perfectly. Until that one meeting, I didn't understand Timber's comment about you being his Sunshine Goddess with a bit of darkness in you. After that meeting, I totally understood his comment and this dress almost personifies that. It was made for you, Baby Girl."

"Thank you," I whisper as I blink back more tears.

He hands me the box and I open it, revealing drop diamond earrings, a diamond necklace and a diamond bracelet. There are also black rhinestones mixed in on all the pieces. My hand shakes as I stare down at them. "Dad..." I whisper, barely able to even get that out.

He clears his throat. "My Baby Girl only gets married once, and I wanted you to have something fitting for the occasion, so don't you fucking dare tell me it's too much."

His words have all of us laughing and I pass him the box to hold while I put on my new jewelry.

As I'm clasping my bracelet, he clears his throat. "I have one more thing for you," he says as he pulls another box out of his cut.

His fingers rub the edges of it as he stares at it, and I get the feeling that whatever is in this box is really important to him. When he looks up at me, my feeling is confirmed when I see his eyes are glassy.

"This..." He pauses as he clears his throat and Nikki comes up next to him, wrapping her arm around him. "This was our mom's. Both of us would be honored if you wore it."

Oh, fiddlesticks.

If they keep this up, I'm going to be a blubbering mess before I even get out there.

Nikki places her hand on Dad's and together, they both hold out the box to me.

Hesitantly, I take the box and when I open it, my other hand flies to my mouth in shock.

Nestled inside the box is a beautiful antique comb with diamond and black alternating stones across the top.

"As soon as Nikki showed me a picture of the black lace on your gown, we both knew that this was meant to be yours. Like you, Mom had a bit of darkness in her as well. Despite the fact that her dress was looked down upon at the time, Mom also had some black on her dress, though not as much as yours. With her being an Old Lady, Dad thought it was fitting. It seems like you're carrying on the tradition without even knowing it, Baby Girl."

Looking up at Nikki in shock, I remember what she had said last night, only to find her grinning at me.

"I told you that dress was perfect for you and that you'd be doing the family proud by choosing it."

I hug both of them before handing Kristy the box. "Kristy, could you?"

"Of course, Mae. Nikki told me about it this morning and sent me a picture, so I made sure the wedding hairdo I did for you would suit it."

Smiling, I shake my head.

When she's done, I look up and give a bit of a twirl. "How do I look?"

Dad's eyes turn a little glassy again, but they're also filled with pride. I'm also shocked to see Nikki, Levi, Sasha, and Susie all blinking away their tears as well. The others are grinning as they watch.

"Fucking beautiful, Baby Girl."

"Beautiful? She's fucking hot and as soon as Timber lays eyes on Miss Sexy here, he's going to be stealing her away the first chance he can get," Allison says which has everyone laughing but Dad.

"Please, for the love of God, I do not need the image of my daughter having sex in my head, Alli," Dad growls at her, but there's no heat behind it and she knows i t.

Allison's grin widens as she wiggles her eyebrows and Dad groans again.

"Alright, are we ready?" Kristy asks.

Looking around, everyone gives me a nod, and I nod to Kristy, not trusting my voice right now.

She grins at me. "I'll get the guys then and, in a few minutes, I'll make the announcements for everyone to retake their seats."

Kristy disappears down the hallway and minutes later, the door opens up. My brothers lead the charge with Punisher in the front, Erik, Dom, and Axe behind him with Dragon, Thor, and Gunner not too far behind them.

However, Punisher stops a few feet in, which has the others running into his back.

"What the fuck is your..." Dom says before he follows Punisher's line of sight and they all stare at me, stunned. "Fuck, Sis. I mean, I knew you were gorgeous before, but fuck..."

His statement has my cheeks flaming and I turn, embarrassed, as I stare at the ground. "Is it too much? My scars?"

Axe is instantly in front of me, kneeling so I can look straight into his eyes. "Lil' Sis, this dress fits you perfectly and you shouldn't give a flying fuck if anyone says anything about your scars."

Cheers of 'hear hear' ring out and I blink, struggling to believe this is real.

"It's real, Lil' Sis. Now, shake off those nerves, dab at your eyes, because I know someone is dying to lay his eyes on you already. Fuck, I can't wait to see his reaction when you step out on Smoke's arm. I have $20 that he's going to be sporting wood the second you walk out."

I stare at him in shock. "You had better not be betting on my man's love stick, brother dear!"

This causes laughter all around.

"Hun, we all placed bets, but it wasn't just on Timber. It was also on Thor and Dragon."

I sputter. "How did I not know about this?"

Susie grinned. "Because we also knew it would almost instantly wipe away any tears you might have. Though I'm surprised it didn't leak out while we were getting ready for Levi's wedding. She had no idea as well."

Levi nodded as she laughed. "I had no idea until afterward, but fuck is that funny. I would have put money on Dragon first."

"Oh, he won for your men," Sasha tells her with a wink, and I narrow my eyes at her.

"So, who exactly is staring at our men's love sticks and judging these bets?"

"My sister, Lizzy," Erin speaks up. "She's a lesbian and offered to judge so there'd be no hard feelings."

Even though it didn't seem intentional, her words cause a whole 'nother round of laughter.

A knock on the door has all of us settling down and Kristy pops her head in. "I didn't want to interrupt since I wanted to give you all a few minutes," she says and then winks at me. "And I knew about the bets, as well. My money's on 'at first sight' for Timber. And with that, I'm going to go make my announcement."

I shake my head as she walks down the hallway, leaving the door open like she had before.

Taking a deep breath, I try to settle my nerves.

I'm getting married to the love of my life and I can't wait to start our lives together.

Chapter 64
Timber

KRISTY GIVES REAPER AND me the signal and I follow him up to the arch. Taking a deep breath, I try to calm my nerves.

"Don't worry, brother. Everything's going to be just fine and in a bit, you'll be married and your balls will be firmly secured in her purse."

I laugh quietly as I shake my head at him. "Just you wait till you find the one, man. Without her, I was a shell of myself. She's my breath. Her and our future kids, they are my reason."

I know without even looking at him that he knows what I mean. Even though I'm part of the club, she's my everything. Without her, I'd crumble. And if something ever happens that endangers her or our kids, then the fucker had better have his shit in order because he'll suffer at my hands before meeting a very painful death.

Kristy steps out of the hallway, and I straighten, knowing it's almost time. She comes to stand in front of us and quiets everyone down.

"Thank you for your patience. Without further ado, let's welcome the wedding party for Timber and Mae!"

Cheers erupt as *Ride the Wind* by Poison comes on.

This time, Jordan and Sadie come out of the hallway dancing and they go all the way up until they are near us. They part with a fist bump and I give Jordan one of my own as he comes up to stand by me.

"Nice moves, J-man."

His face lights up and then he turns, watching Roxy and Gunner dance in.

After them, it's Allison and Erik, Nikki and Dom, Erin and Punisher, Susie and Axe, Levi and Thor, and finally, Sasha and Dragon dance in.

At first Mae was worried about having Sasha be the maid of honor for both weddings, but I knew they bonded hard and fast with all the bullshit with Luscious, Carter, and Andrew.

The music fades and *The Keeper Of The Stars* by Tracy Bird starts up.

I blink back the emotion at this song and I find my Aunt Sofia's eyes in the crowd. This was hers and Uncle James' wedding song. Her hands fly to her mouth in surprise and I dip my head, smiling at her. I had sent the link to the song last night as Mae and I were texting. She fell in love with it immediately.

Fuck am I glad they were able to make it today along with my sister, Olivia, and brother, Blake. Both of them are grinning at me even though Olivia's wiping her eyes repeatedly. They were all ecstatic when I told them last night that I was getting married, though they were all hesitant to hear that it was happening today. I swore that once they met her, they'd understand that she's the one for me, and I can't wait to introduce her to them later. Not to mention, introducing them to Peggy and Glen, too.

Mae steps out on Smoke's arm, and the breath leaves my body. She's always been gorgeous to me, but fuck... She's absolutely fucking stunning.

My gaze roams over her black and white dress, and fuck does it fit her perfectly. My Sunshine Goddess with a bit of darkness in her. Then I see the flash of leg and strappy heels. That coupled with the neckline of her dress, which is drool worthy, makes me want to cover her up but also show her the fuck off because she's mine.

And soon, she'll be mine permanently.

Smoke places her hand in mine and she turns, passing her flowers off to Sasha before turning to face me fully.

Her eyes are shiny with unshed tears and I squeeze her hands as she smiles up at me.

'I love you,' she mouths to me, which I return.

Reaper clears his throat. "We are here to celebrate the union of Liam Caldwell with my gorgeous niece, Mae Rose Witlock."

I tune him out as I drink in the sight of Mae. Her dress enhances her natural beauty and I thank God that she didn't get anything that hid her scars. I think they are sexy as fuck, plus they show that she's survived the unthinkable.

I'm brought out of my thoughts when I hear Reaper say, "Do you have the rings?"

Turning to Jordan, who reaches into his pocket and hands me both of our rings, I pass them to Reaper.

However, the second I retake Mae's hand, I get lost in her sapphire eyes again. It's not until I somehow register Reaper asking me a question that I manage to reply on time.

"I do."

A few moments later, she repeats the words. Mae's blinding smile has me smiling like a loon.

"Finally, bikers who actually listen," Reaper says under his breath with a side eye toward Dragon. Though it's loud enough for most of our guests to hear, judging by their quiet laughter.

"I present Mr. and Mrs. Liam Caldwell. You may kiss your bride."

Pulling Mae toward me, I don't keep the kiss short and sweet. My need for her has me dipping her and kissing her deeply.

"Alright, that's enough biker boy, there are children present," Reaper chides.

"Eh, he's fine," Jordan quips, which has us all laughing and when I look over at him, he's smirking. Man, that kid is going to grow up to be a handful.

Mae slips her arm through mine and like earlier, we head out to the back to take some pictures.

It's nearing ten o'clock as I look around at everyone celebrating and having a good time. I had been relieved when Mae got along so well with my aunt, uncle, brother, and sister. She introduced them to her dad and then to Peggy and Glen, although I know I'll owe them some information later on. None of them said anything about her scars, but when her back was turned, they looked at me in question and worry. I wasn't going to fill them in now about it, though. Today is our day, and I'm not going to taint it by bringing that up.

"Good boy," Mae coos and I turn, smiling when I see her bent over and petting Bastion, Levi's dog.

Last week, she wasn't able to really see him because he was recovering from getting stitches, so they kept him indoors while he healed. She said he had cuddled up to her a lot last night while the ladies were planning things and she absolutely loved it. Mae had told me before that she always wanted a dog and a cat but was never able to have one. I have a sneaky feeling we'll be making a trip to the animal shelter at some point in the near future.

We still don't fully know what happened and how Bastion got hurt last week before Mae came. However, when Lex was walking the fence perimeter, he saw a small section that had been cut and a wire was left pointing in toward our property. It had blood on it.

Smoke couldn't find anything on the cameras, but we had made sure to fix that section. After that, we looked closer at the rest of the fencing, but didn't find anything wrong.

Growling has me returning my focus back toward Mae, who is still crouched down next to Bastion, but he's turned, facing the gate.

"Thor," I say, nudging him, who just so happened to be nearby. He turns toward me, but then stops when he hears Bastion's low growl, too.

"Fuck," he hisses under his breath and then digs his phone out of his pocket. Drae's name lights up his screen.

Since he's right next to me, I can hear every word.

"There's a package that's been dropped off. I was scanning the monitors when I saw his back as he walked away from the gate. I called out to him, but he just kept walking. After he left, I rewound the tape, but whoever it is kept their face covered. I'm sorry, but I have no idea who it was. What do you want me to do? I haven't opened the gate to get it."

"Stay put. I'll get some men around and we'll be up there in a few."

"Yes, Sir."

Thor ends the call.

Fuck, I hope this has nothing to do with Mae.

Thor steps closer to me. "I'm going to send out a text to alert everyone. I need you to go to Mae. Make sure she stays here and with the club. I'll send Levi over to her in a moment."

"You got it, Pres."

I stalk toward Mae when I feel my phone vibrate with his text and she looks up at me, worried.

"What is it? Why is Bastion growling?" she asks anxiously and I pull her into my arms, laying her head against my chest.

"We aren't sure yet, but something was left at the gate," I whisper to her and close my eyes in frustration when I feel her entire body stiffen against me. "Stay with Levi. She'll be over here in a moment. Listen to whoever Thor leaves back here to guard everyone. Try not to give away that something is up in case they are watching us."

She pulls back slightly and reaches up, her hands cupping my face. She pulls me down and I kiss her.

"Be safe. Come back to me," she whispers, and I kiss her again.

"Always, Sunshine."

With one more kiss, I head toward the gate. Smoke gives me a chin lift as he walks toward Mae. Looking over my shoulder, he wraps and arm around her and guides her over toward the drink table. Levi joins them and my shoulders relax at his move. The drink table is right by the back door of the clubhouse, so if anything happens, he'll get them inside quickly. A moment later, Jordan and Sadie are at their sides and something pulls at my chest at seeing Mae crouched down and talking to them. Fuck, I can't wait until she's doing that with our kids.

Someone claps my shoulder and I turn, seeing Reaper there. Bastion steps forward to follow us, but Levi calls him back to her.

"Come on. Let's go see what the fuckers left for us."

Chapter 65

Timber

WE APPROACH THE GATE and Drae comes out of the gatehouse.

"Sorry that I couldn't see his face, Pres. I didn't go after him because I didn't want to leave the gate unmanned."

"It's not your fault, Drae, and that was the right call not leaving your post." He pauses and looks down at his phone. "Lex said he pulled up the road cameras and there hasn't been any motion since the last guest arrived until this mystery person showed up. He couldn't see his face either, but from the build, he's guessing it was a guy."

Thor looks around at everyone that's gathered, though his gaze lingers on Dragon's and mine for a moment.

"Guns out, be prepared." He turns back to Drae. "Open the gate."

Drae walks back toward the gate and I draw my gun.

Thor steps forward, but Phoenix puts a hand on his shoulder. "I've got it, Pres."

He gives Phoenix a hesitant look but eventually gives him a chin lift.

Ryder, Devil and Razor all step up behind Phoenix as they approach the package.

Suddenly, Phoenix holds up a hand and the others stop. Everyone goes quiet when he gives the sign to be quiet.

Then he turns on his heel toward the gatehouse. "Run!" he shouts and grabs Drae by his cut, dragging him out and back toward the clubhouse.

We all back away quickly, and I duck behind the side of the clubhouse when the package explodes.

When the dust and debris settle, I peek around the corner, my gun still drawn but I don't see anyone that shouldn't be here.

Turning toward the men at my side, my gaze rakes over them all, but other than being dusty, no one is injured.

Thor gives the signal and we all approach slowly. Quickly, I glance inside the clubhouse through the windows and see the guests starting to file into the main room. I release a breath I hadn't realized I'd been holding when I see Mae inside. Refocusing, I cautiously approach the gate.

There's a charred hole in the pavement where the box was, but nothing remains of the box. Which doesn't surprise me. I turn my focus back to the gate I'd helped install and frown when I see the damage to it and both gatehouses.

We're going to need a better gate and gatehouses. This can't happen again.

"Four men guard the gate until we're able to get it replaced. Four-hour shift rotations. Timber, we'll discuss a plan later."

"You got it, Pres."

I already know what I want to do and if another bomb goes off in the future, there will be no damage to the gate or gatehouse. There will also be no serious injuries to whoever is guarding the gate.

"First round is Prospects while we meet. Party's over. Everyone, help the guests get out, then we'll have Church."

Tucking my gun away, I make a beeline for the clubhouse. Thor and Dragon join me at the front while the rest of our brothers fan out.

Pushing open the door, Thor clears his throat and whistles to get everyone's attention. "Our apologies, but the evening will have to be cut short. As I'm sure you all just heard, there was an explosion at the gate. Thankfully, no one was injured. We don't know any other details at this time, but for your safety, you will all need to leave."

Murmurs spread throughout the crowd, but I ignore them as I make my way toward Mae and sweep her up into my arms. "Don't say anything about it till everyone's gone," I whisper in her ear and feel her nod against me.

It takes about twenty minutes for everyone to leave except family members who had already planned on staying at the compound. Those that are staying have already gone to whoever's house they are crashing in.

When it's just club members, the Prospects, and Mae, Thor's about to say something when a phone rings.

It's Drae's, who Patch was looking over since he and Phoenix were the closest ones to the bomb when it went off. Thankfully, either were hurt seriously, just a few scratches.

Drae looks hesitantly over at Thor and Smoke sits down at the same table as Drae, opening his laptop that he'd already grabbed. Thor gives him a chin lift and Drae answers it, putting it on speaker.

"Hello?"

"Did you like my little display? You didn't listen to us before, and now you're going to pay," a voice seethes through the line and Drae pales.

"What the fuck do you want, Ghost? I told you I was never going to be coming back. You all are dead to me."

Oh, fuck... His dad.

I shoot a nervous look at Thor, who's beyond pissed. I thought the feds cleaned them out.

A dark chuckle comes through the line. *"Yeah, that's not how it works, son. You thought you were all so clever joining with the Feds to wipe us out, but they didn't get all of us. Now tell me, have you heard from your lovely Jane lately?"*

Drae pales further, his Adam's apple bobbing as he swallows. *"She texted this morning and sent a picture of them at the zoo."*

"Hmmm. You might want to take a closer look. I mean, they've been at her parents for two weeks now. I'm surprised she hasn't contacted you more."

"How did you know they were at her parents?"

More laughter comes through the line. *"We've been following you three around for a while now. Time is ticking, son. Will you find them before time runs out? They aren't the only ones in danger, either. A certain woman who is very close to someone in your club has been here for about a week and she's very lovely. Would be a shame if they all met an untimely demise."*

The call is cut and I feel Mae's body stiffen against me right as her phone vibrates in my cut. Earlier she had gotten it from the room they were getting ready in and asked me to hold onto it.

Pulling it out, there's a text notification from an unknown number.

"Do you want me to see what it is first?" I ask her.

She bites her lip and nods as she steps back a bit, wringing her fingers together. Punisher steps forward, pulling her into his arms as they watch me.

Opening up the text, I feel like I want to puke.

There are numerous pictures of Lillian being taken by different guys. Her body is all black and blue, and I'm pretty sure her leg is broken. The last is of her chained up in a cell as multiple men piss on her. There's also a video attached but I'm not playing it. Not right now, at least.

It also doesn't escape my notice that whoever took the pictures made sure that Preston, Phillip, Bruce, and X were involved in everything.

I forward everything to Thor, Smoke, and me before tucking her phone back into my cut.

A strangled noise has me looking up and I'm betting that fucker sent Drae pictures of Jane and Lindsey as well.

"The text was about Mom... wasn't it?" Mae asks me and I pull her back into my arms.

"I'm sorry, Sunshine," I whisper to her and feel her body shake as a sob escapes her.

"Alright. Ladies and whoever was in the weddings, how about we all change? We'll all meet back here and have Church. You too, Drae and Mae. Sasha, Lex, Colt, and Ethan will guard the gate first."

I guide Mae back toward the room where her stuff is and help her gather everything up before heading up to my room here at the clubhouse. Once inside, I lock the door and lay everything on the bed.

Mae sinks down on the bed, her face streaked from her mascara that's running. "They were in the pictures, weren't they?" she asks me.

I kneel in front of her, taking her hands in mine. "I'm sorry, Sunshine, but yeah, they were. All four of them."

She takes a deep breath and squares her shoulders. "I want to see pictures."

I hesitate and her face hardens. "Please, Liam. I don't want to see them for the first time in front of everyone."

Sighing, I pull out her phone and hand it to her. She takes it, her hands shaking slightly, and a sob escapes her as she goes through the pictures. When she gets to the video, she hesitates again, but hits play.

The fuckers recorded beating Lillian until she passed out and then raping her while she was unconscious.

Finally, the camera turns and Bruce's face fills the frame.

"You know what I want, Mae. You were mine and you gave what was mine to another man. You had the audacity to marry someone when you were bought by me. Like that will protect you. Those men and your dear husband will all die by our hands. If you don't turn yourself over, more people will pay. What we do to them—their injuries, their blood, their torture, and possibly even their deaths—they will all be on your hands. Time is ticking, Precious."

His evil laugh comes through and is joined by others laughing as the video cuts out.

Looking up at Mae, her face is paler than before and I take her phone, slipping it back into my cut. "I'm not giving you up, Sunshine. And don't believe a word he said. What they do is *not* on your hands. It's on them. They are responsible for their own actions. Not you."

Numbly, she nods. "I just hate that they always find a way to taint something that makes me happy. Why can't they just let me be happy?" she says as another sob escapes her and she buries her face in her hands.

Standing, I scoop her up and sit with her on my lap as I hold her.

My anger has me tightening my arms around her as I listen to her sobs. I will make those fuckers pay for what they've been putting Mae through. Drae too, for that matter, if they really do have his girlfriend and daughter.

Suddenly, Mae sits upright in my lap. "How did I miss that before?"

"What?" I ask her, confused.

Instead of answering, she slides off my lap. "Help me out of this. We need to change and get down there, quickly."

My fingers make quick work of her buttons while she takes off her jewelry. When she slips out of the dress, I groan internally. Seeing my Sunshine in just a thong, garter, and heels has me as hard as steel.

"Later," she purrs as she starts to take the tape off her breasts. She winces slightly as the tape pulls at her skin. Once it's removed, she bends over to unlace her heels.

"Fuck, Baby," I groan as I stare at her gorgeous ass in that thong.

She giggles.

Fucking giggles, and I swear she puts extra sway in her hips as she goes to the closet to grab clothes.

"You're gonna pay for this later, Sunshine," I growl and she winks at me from over her shoulder before sliding on a bra, followed by her clothes.

Slipping off my cut, I take off my button-down shirt, pull a t-shirt out of my dresser and put it on. Mae slips into the bathroom as I put my cut back on and I lean against the bathroom door frame as I watch her.

She wipes off her makeup and then starts taking out the comb and bobby pins from her hair. Stepping forward, I help her and soon she's got it brushed out and pulling it up into a messy bun on top of her head.

Mae walks over to the door and grabs her cut off the hook, slipping it on.

"Fuck, Baby. You are downright sexy in my property cut." Fuck, I wish I could rip off her pants and bury myself in her from behind.

"Later, Sexy. We need to get to Church, and I need to talk to Drae. He showed me some pictures of his little girl yesterday and something was bugging me about them, but I couldn't put my finger on it at the time. Now I know what it was. They were doctored."

I stare at her for a moment, and curse before we both rush out of the room, locking it on our way out.

Moments later, I take my usual seat, pulling Mae down on my lap and internally grimace when I realize we're the last ones in there.

"I'm sorry for making us late. I had a bit of a breakdown when I saw the pictures," Mae says quietly as she shifts on my lap.

"I'm sorry, too," Thor says softly to her and she dips her head in acknowledgement. "Drae has shared the pictures he received the past few weeks with Smoke, along with the text messages, and we were about to put them up on the screen," he says.

Smoke hits some buttons on the computer and multiple pictures appear on the screen.

"That one," Mae says as she gets up, walks up to the projector screen and points to the middle one in the top row. "I was just telling Timber this when I was changing that something felt off about the pictures Drae showed me the other day, but I couldn't put my finger on it at the time."

"What did you notice? I'm not following you," Thor says as he steps closer to the screen.

The picture is of Lindsey sitting on a chair reading a book in what looks like a living room.

"The light and shadows in it are all wrong. This picture was pieced together. It's not real."

Curses ring out throughout the room.

"Are the others fake, too?" Devil asks.

Drae gets up and steps closer. "Show me," he asks her and she nods.

"Dad, I need your laptop. Do you have a stylus?" she asks as she walks over to him. He gets up, hands her a stylus, and she sits in his seat.

The picture she pointed out enlarges on the screen and she starts drawing on it.

As she dissects the picture, I can practically feel Drae's fury rising.

He points to the lower portion of the picture. "This is part of a chair from Jane's parents' basement. I don't recognize the curtains, pillows, lamp, nothing else from the picture. I tried calling Jane's parents and her cell, but no one picked up. Her parents live about four hours south of us, near the Illinois border."

She goes to the next picture, studying it for a little bit before doing the same thing.

To every single picture.

When she's done, she puts them all together on the screen like Smoke had at the beginning, so we can see them all at once.

Mae fidgets in her seat as we all look at the pictures, and I wish she were back in my arms.

Smoke pats her shoulder. "You did good, Baby Girl."

"Maybe, but it leaves us with more questions than answers. It doesn't show us where Jane and Lindsey are being held, my mom, or anyone else they could have taken."

"That may be, but now we know that Drae has been being manipulated for the past two weeks."

"Were there any hints in the text messages?" Levi asks.

Drae shakes his head. "No. And we've talked since she's left too, but I didn't notice that there was anything wrong. She sounded like her normal self. Though only once was Lindsey awake when I called. The other times, she was either napping or already down for the night. At least, that's what Jane told me."

"My money is on someone threatening her to not give anything away. Probably used Lindsey as leverage," Phoenix growls.

"Okay. Judge, I want you in on this and I'll need four other volunteers. You five will ride with Drae down to check out Jane's parents' place. We're the closest ones to them, so I'm not calling in any other chapters on this one yet. Leave first thing in the morning and keep me posted. Now, let's switch gears. Only Smoke, Timber, Mae, and I have seen what she was texted when Ghost was talking to Drae. It's up to you, Mae, if you want everyone else to see the pictures and video."

Mae visibly pales, and Smoke rests a hand on her shoulder as she takes a deep breath.

"You can show them. Someone might see something that could be a hint or something about where they are. I'm not going to lie, I didn't look that long at the pictures the first time, so I could have missed something, too."

"Come here, Sunshine," I say and she gets up, walking around and sits back down on my lap. When I feel her body trembling slightly, I tighten my arms around her.

After a few clicks, six images appear on the screen. "There's more and a video, but I thought I'd split them out, otherwise they'd be too tiny to notice anything," Smoke says.

Levi, who is sitting next to me on my left, reaches out and takes Mae's hand, squeezing it.

"The snake tattoo on the man's wrist in the third picture is just like the one Michael has on his wrist. I mean, Bruce. It's the same color, orientation, everything. And the left arm with the voodoo doll image is just like the one X has. Since they were in the other photos and the video, I'm assuming that it's also them in these pictures. I bet that the heavy guy is Preston because of the scar on his stomach. During the summer he loved walking around without a shirt on, so

I've unfortunately seen it a lot over the years," Mae says as a shiver works through her.

"Here are the last five images," Smoke says as he clicks to the next group.

Levi leans forward. "Is that... Yeah, that looks like a part of a little teddy bear in the bottom corner of the last picture."

Drae curses as he runs his hands through his hair. "It's Lindsey's." His voice is thick with anguish. Then again, I'd be feeling the same if someone had kidnapped Mae and our child.

Smoke looks over at Mae, regret in his eyes. "You don't have to listen to the video again if you don't want to, Baby Girl."

Mae's body tenses, but after a few moments, she shakes her head. "Play it."

Smoke hits play, and even though I don't want to watch it again, I do.

About halfway in, Drae raises his hand. "Pause it. Okay, back it up just a little."

Smoke does as he asks and Drae's head drops. "The woman with her back to the camera with the shamrock tattoo on her right hip is Jane. They're both being held in the same place as Lillian."

My chest hurts as I see the condition Jane is in. Her body is almost as black and blue as Lillian's and she's lost weight since the last time I'd seen them, which was about a month ago.

Smoke restarts the video and after Bruce's threats at the end, curses fill the room.

For a few moments, no one says anything. Then I notice Mae gnawing on her lip as she stares at the screen.

"What is it, Sunshine?"

"Dad, can you go back to the pictures that I was sent?" she asks instead of answering me.

She stares at the pictures for a bit and signals for him to go to the next set. After a few more minutes, she asks to see Drae's pictures again.

"What are you thinkin', Lil' Bit? Talk it out, it might help," Reaper says.

Mae furrows her brows more. "It's just that for some reason, the background of some of those pictures seems familiar to me, but I can't place where I've seen it. And some of the background sections in Drae's pictures also seem to match the background of the pictures I received."

"If you think of anything else that can help narrow this down at all, let me know immediately," Thor says and Mae nods.

"At first, I thought it was the cabins my grandparent's own, but they never had wallpaper in them. However, the last time I was there, I was eleven. Things could have changed since then."

"Well, that ties into something I wanted to remind you both about. Your grandparents' lawyer wants to meet us Monday morning at ten to discuss their will. Maybe he has keys to the cabins. We could always ride out there and scope it out afterward to make sure there haven't been changes since the last time you were there. And if there have been changes, we can see if they fit these pictures."

"I'm up for that. The sooner we can find out the better."

I give Smoke a chin lift. "I'm good to meet them. Blake told me he'd take the reins right now in the office until things settle down. We weren't going to go on our honeymoon till after everything's said and done with these assholes."

Thor sighs and looks around. "Is there anything else we need to discuss right now?"

Everyone shakes their heads no.

"Alright. You three check in with me after you get back from the lawyer's office. Keep me posted if any of you get anything new in the meantime. For now, let's call it a night. Unless it's an emergency, don't bother us newlyweds until tomorrow," he says as he bangs his hammer. Laughter and jokes ring out through the room.

Mae turns toward me, and I smirk as I see her cheeks pinken and she squirms on my lap a little.

Time to take care of my wife.

Chapter 66

Mae

IT'S MONDAY MORNING, AND with everything going on, Timber, Dad, and I are in Timber's truck as we head into town to see my grandparents' lawyer, Mr. Worthe.

Neither Dad nor Timber wanted me on the back of Timber's bike today. Even though I missed riding, I didn't want to risk it either. Ethan and Colt are in a truck behind us, since we don't know how long we'll be. Mr. Worthe had told Dad that he cleared the day for us just in case things took a while. Ethan and Colt will keep an eye out while we're inside at the appointment.

I fidget as I remember yesterday's conversation. We had heard back from the group that went with Drae yesterday that no one was home at Jane's parent's house and that nothing looked suspicious. Though, both of their cars were gone. The team is going to stay a few days and watch the house to see if anything changes or anyone shows up. Timber squeezes my hand, and I blink a few times before looking around only to realize we're already at the lawyer's office.

"Stay inside until Smoke opens your door, Sunshine."

I nod as I stare at the door of Mr. Worthe's practice. My nerves are shot and in the back of my mind, I worry that my grandparents' cabins are the place where my mom, Jane, and Lindsey are being held.

Dad opens my door and I jump a little. He gives me a small smile and holds his hand out so that I can get down easier. I don't know what it is about men and wanting their trucks so high up off the ground, but I almost have to jump to get in and out of it.

"Definitely need to get those steps for you, Sunshine," Timber had muttered to himself when he had to help me get into the truck earlier.

Standing in front of Dad, I wait for Timber to join us and step up behind him. They had previously told me that they wanted to walk in this way to better protect my front and back.

A little bell rings over the door as we come in and a nice-looking older lady smiles at us when she looks up. Dad steps around me and I step off to the side so I'm out of the way of the door.

"Hello, Jaxon. Good to see you again."

"Good to see you again, Alicia. How are things with you and Tom?"

She rolls her eyes, but there's a smile on her face. "He was off fishing like usual this weekend. Trying to fill the freezer before winter. You know how it is with fishermen and hunters." She pauses and her eyes widen when she sees me. "You must be Mae." Alicia clicks her tongue and points at Dad. "She looks just like you when you were younger."

Dad chuckles at my confused look. "Alicia and Tom live next door to the house where my parents used to live."

Alicia waves him off. "His mom, Sarah, and I were best friends. Heck, I even changed some of your dad's diapers," she says with a mischievous grin.

A giggle escapes me, and Alicia winks at me while Dad scowls at her.

"Is Al ready for us?"

"Let me check," she says as she gets up and walks down the hallway.

"So, I guess if I want any embarrassing stories about you, I just need to ask Alicia?"

Dad glares at me, and I giggle again.

"Baby Girl," he growls.

"He's ready for you, Jaxon," Alicia says as she walks back toward us.

He sighs. "I'm never going to get you to call me Smoke, am I?"

"Nope. Like I said, I helped change your diapers. I've earned the right to use the name your mother gave you," she tuts and Dad sighs again. Then she leans in closer to me. "And yes, I have tons of stories I can tell you," she says as she winks at me.

I laugh even harder when Dad glares at me.

"I'll tan your hide, Baby Girl, if you do any such thing."

"Sorry, Dad. Timber's the only one that'll be spanking me going forward."

My statement has Alicia howling with laughter as Dad's face blanches.

"Timber, reign in your wife," Dad says with a sigh.

"Sorry, Smoke, but no can do. I like my wife feisty," he says as he winks at me and I fight my blush. This banter is making me want him again, even though we spent most of the day yesterday in bed.

Dad grumbles and turns on his heel, walking down the hallway. What we're here to go over hits me full force again and I slip my hand into Timber's as I try to calm my nerves. The banter with Alicia helped get my mind off it, but I'm going to have to deal with my grandparent's will at some point anyway. May as well be now. Timber squeezes my hand and we follow Dad down the hallway.

We enter an office with windows overlooking the park across the street. A dark desk separates the room and behind it are bookcases with the same dark finish and multiple filing cabinets. An older gentleman looks up from his computer and fixes his wire glasses before breaking out into a grin.

"Smoke, it's good to see you again," he says as he rises and shakes Dad's hand. "And this must be your lovely daughter, Mae, that you've told me about. I'm Allen Worthe, but you can call me Al."

I nod and step forward, shaking his outstretched hand. "Yes, and it's nice to meet you," I say as I step back gesture to Timber. "This is my husband, Timber."

"Ah yes, I heard about your nuptials this weekend. Congratulations to the both of you," he says as he shakes Timber's hand and then gestures to the seats in front of his desk. "Please, have a seat."

He walks around us and shuts the door before going back to sit behind his desk. Taking some keys out of his pocket, he unlocks and opens a drawer, ruffling around a bit and then pulls out a large accordion folder. He empties out the contents and then grabs a fresh legal pad.

"Smoke told me you had no idea your grandparents left you an inheritance. Is that correct?"

"Yes, that's correct. I know that my mom gets some money from their estate each month, but other than that, I don't really know anything else about the will."

He frowns and nods. "I'll do a reading of their will first, then. Are you okay with your dad and husband hearing what is in it? I can read it to you in private if you would prefer."

Immediately, I shake my head. "They can both hear it."

For the next half hour, I stare at Al, half in shock and half in disbelief. I never knew Mom's parents came from old money.

They left me almost everything.

Their house that is worth a half a million dollars.

Grandpa's old sportster and BMW as well as Grandma's Lexus.

Their two cabins that they rent out year-round which are situated on sixty acres of land north of here.

Shares in two companies that Grandpa was on the board for.

A trust fund worth the rest of their fortune. *Ten million dollars.*

"The shares and voting rights for both companies have been managed by Gene's long-time friend, Alfred Rossen, since his passing. He said that he is willing to continue to vote in your name if you so choose. He has also offered to buy them if you choose that you don't want them."

I turn to Dad, lost for what I should do. I don't know this Alfred guy. Is he even trustworthy?

"I've looked into the companies and they are both sound ones. Alfred's a good guy, too. Good head on his shoulders. Doesn't take shit from anyone."

Turning toward Timber, I cock an eyebrow.

"It's up to you, Mae. If Smoke's vouching for him, I'd trust him."

Nodding, I turn back toward Al. "If Alfred could continue to vote in my stead, I would appreciate it. As for the shares, I'd like to keep them, but if I ever decide to sell, I'll get a hold of him."

"Wonderful. I'll let Alfred know your decision. In this folder is his contact information should you have questions for him or if you someday decide to sell your shares," he says as he tucks that paperwork back into the folder.

"These are the keys to their house, along with sealed envelopes with further information for you, Mae. The keys for the vehicles are in here, too. Shortly after they died, they were serviced and a trusted friend of theirs makes sure they are well maintained. They also have a handyman that keeps the house in good repair. Both men have keys for those purposes, and when you meet them, they will hand them over. Their contact information is in here as well.

"The two cabins are about fifty miles north of here on sixty acres of mostly wooded land. I've contacted the woman, Martha, who has been taking care of the cabins along with her husband. She handles the bookings.

"When Smoke confirmed you would be able to meet today, I reached out to her to see if anyone was staying there currently in case you wanted to go up and see them yourself. She said there are currently tenants in both cabins with one of their stays ending this Wednesday and the other this Friday. She doesn't have any other tenants scheduled at this time, and I have asked her to keep it that way. Her contact information is in here as well."

"Mae?" Timber asks and it's only then that I realize I'm squeezing his hand tightly.

Clearing my throat, I will my voice to stay level. "Where did you say the cabins were located?"

Al looks back down at the paperwork. "About fifty miles north of here, outside of a small town called Ravenwood."

"Do they rent out any of the land? Or is it more for like hunting and things like that?"

"They do rent out some land to a group of homesteaders. Martha is also the one that handles depositing those checks for now. She can continue to be the middle person unless you would rather take on that right away?"

"Um, let's let Martha do it for right now. We can talk to her more when we go up to check on the cabins."

I turn, looking at Dad, wondering if he's putting the pieces together. His eyes widen slightly, but then he schools his features, giving me a small nod.

"Thank you for asking to keep them vacant after these tenants leave. We'll go up there this weekend to check them out. Timber actually works in construction and owns his own business. With winter coming up soon, it might not be a bad idea to take a look at the cabins for ourselves to make sure nothing needs to be repaired or brought up to code. Like Mae said, we'll talk to Martha about everything at that time."

"Perfect. Martha said that she could continue to run your bookings for you if you so choose. Both her and her husband, George, tend to the cabins after each visit and restock things as necessary. The software she uses for the bookings is the one Gene requested because it allowed him and Laura to log in and check it themselves. I have set you up with a log-in and temporary password. Once you are in, you can change the password. Now all that is left, is to discuss the transfer of your trust and the properties."

It takes another hour to discuss all the finances, sign papers to transfer everything into my name, and to put Timber on the accounts.

Finally, we're able to step outside, the file folder safely tucked into my backpack. I take a deep breath of fresh air before remembering someone could be watching me and I hurry to the truck.

When Timber backs out and puts the truck in drive, he reaches over and takes my hand.

"What was that about in there? With the cabins?"

I sigh. "It could be nothing, but that's the general vicinity of where Andrew said the Oasis is located. Granted, my grandparents' land size is larger. Andrew could have just been talking about how much land the Oasis was renting. However, what if it's my own grandparent's that have been providing those jerkwads a place to live while they're treating those women and children so badly?"

"I guess that could be an angle if Preston, Phillip, Bruce, and possibly X are involved with that. Maybe Preston somehow found out. You've said before that you wondered why Preston seems to have it out for your family. Maybe this is a small part of it. Find a secure place for them to do what they want right under someone's nose, and if things go sideways, the blame could be put on your grandparents since they own the land," he says and it feels like I've been sucker punched.

Oh, sugar honey ice tea.

I groan. "That would make sense. I mean, I know Preston had a hand in my grandparents' deaths and I suspect he also had a hand in Mom's accident."

Both of them curse. "When we get back, let's talk with Thor. That way, you don't have to repeat anything. That and we should tell him what we found out about the cabins as well as our suspicions."

"I didn't mention it before because I didn't think they were related to what's going on now. I'm sorry."

"It'll be okay, Baby Girl."

I nod glumly as I stare out the window. This is such a dumpster fire.

Twenty minutes later, we pull up to the clubhouse and when we walk in, the ladies have just finished spreading out food for lunch.

"Let's grab some lunch and then sit with Thor. I'll ask that he calls Church after lunch for those that can make it," Dad says before kissing my temple and walking off toward Thor.

Sighing, I head to the kitchen. I try to put on a positive face, but judging by Levi's surprised look, I've failed.

"Did things not go well at Al's?"

Sighing again, I start filling a plate. "Yes, but it also raised some suspicions. Dad's talking to Thor and asking if we can call Church afterward for those that can make it."

Her phone on the counter buzzes and she nods. "He just texted everyone to meet in a half hour. Eat up, girlie. It'll be okay."

I eat my sandwich and fruit, but don't taste any of it. It sits in my stomach like cardboard. My memories from my past bombard me. How could I not see it before?

"Hey, Sunshine. Time to go," Timber says as he stands, squeezing my shoulder, before taking my empty dishes to the kitchen.

Chapter 67
Mae

STANDING, I WALK UP to put my phone in the basket, but Lex waves me off. "Thor said you could have your phone in there in case you get any more calls or messages."

Timber's hand lands on the small of my back, and I nod, slipping my phone back in my pocket. Heading into Church, I walk to Timber's chair, and when he sits down, I sit on his lap. I'm thankful he loves to hold me while in Church, because I think I'll definitely need his strength right now.

Thor bangs his hammer and calls the meeting to order.

"Smoke, Mae, and Timber. How about one of you fill us in on what happened this morning at the lawyer's office?"

Dad starts filling them in on everything and my shoulders relax that he's taking the brunt of this off my shoulders.

"I'd like to propose that we ride out and see if we can get eyes on who the tenants are. If our suspicions are correct, then the Oasis group is renting land from Mae's grandparents' without them realizing who they are. It would make sense that members also rent the nearby cabins, too," Timber says and I can't keep my body from tensing.

"Recon only. Any volunteers to go with Timber?"

Dragon, Bear, Reaper, Punisher, and Dad all volunteer to go with him.

"Okay, now on to the other part. Mae, you said you suspected Preston had a hand in your grandparent's deaths and your mom's accident. You told us about your mom's accident before. Fill us in about your grandparents."

Taking a calming breath, I nod. "They never approved of Preston and never gave Mom their blessing when she married him again. Because of that, I didn't see them as much as I did before they were married, but whenever I did, Preston tried to weasel in and attempt to smooth talk them as Grandma would say. After Preston did that a couple of times, they demanded he never be present or come to visit them.

"Shortly after my grandparents forbade Preston from coming when we would visit, they started getting sick frequently. Six months later, Grandpa died and two months after that, Grandma died. I know Preston's behind their deaths because he went on a rant afterward about what he'd done and how they should have gotten everything from their estate all at once rather than a few thousand dollars a month.

"After learning everything that they left me today, I wonder if Preston had hoped that they'd leave everything to Mom and then he'd have the money, the land, the cabins. Everything. Then that Oasis group, if they really are living on my grandparents' land, could do whatever the hell they wanted and stay out of society's eye since they would then own the land rather than renting it.

"I didn't mention my grandparents' deaths before because, at the time, I didn't think it was related to Oasis. It wasn't until we heard about the cabins and land this morning that I started to connect the dots with what we learned from our guests still at Junction Creek. I didn't realize the cabins were that far north of here. I thought they were closer to Forest Creek, but the last time I was there was when I was eleven."

Timber squeezes my hip and I bite my inner cheek, hoping they won't be mad. But then Thor pins me with a look and I think he's getting frustrated with me. I try not to squirm on Timber's lap. I wasn't kidding when I thought it was irrelevant. Stupid me for not realizing I should have said it before, even if I didn't think it mattered or was relevant.

"Is there anything else you can think of?" he asks.

I hesitate as I try to think back. "I don't think so, but if I remember anything else or if something we learn triggers a memory, I'll let you know right away." Nibbling my lip, I look over at Dad. "Do you have cameras that work well out in the elements?"

"Yeah, I've got some and can make more if need be. Why?"

"I was curious about when we go to meet Martha and see the cabins this weekend if it's possible to put cameras around them to monitor who goes in and out? One that can maybe even keep a date and possibly time stamp on the feed? Once I get logged into the system that Martha uses, I wonder if we'll be able to tie future renters to whatever name or alias they are using and get more information.

"Al mentioned that there is a history log tied in with the program, but didn't mention how far back the log goes. If they're related to the Oasis, the men could be using an alias. Unless they live close enough or are well known enough that they have to use their own names. If X, Bruce, Phillip, or Preston show up there in the future, we can possibly find out any more aliases they have."

He nods. "I'll bring some and we can put them around once we have eyes on the cabins. Let me know if you need any help with that program."

After a few minutes of talking about when Timber and the guys will head out, we all file out into the main room.

Turning to Timber, I lean up and kiss his cheek. "I'm going to try logging into that program to see if I can find any information out."

"Stay out here in the main room or up in our room. Let me know if you want to go to the house."

Nodding, I grab a water and find a table back in the corner where I should be out of the way. It bugs me a little that I have to tell Timber or Dad wherever I go, but I also know it isn't forever. They're still on edge from me being kidnapped last week.

"That's interesting," I mutter to myself as I scroll back through the bookings.

"What's interesting?" Kai asks as he plops down in the chair next to me. He and the other Junction Creek guys are heading back at the end of the week. I'm going to miss seeing all of them, but they all have jobs they need to get back to.

"Huh? Oh. Well, the guests that are supposed to be there through this Wednesday are Krista and Grant Williams. The one staying through Friday is John Creighton. They frequently book the cabins together. Frequent as in almost every month, and it's usually for a week at a time. They aren't the only ones that have this same pattern either.

"If these people keep up this pattern, the next ones that would check in would be Elisa and Joseph Dean and Warren Crowley. Probably in the next two weeks if the cabins remain un-booked by anyone else. They tend to drop in their reservations one or two days in advance. Though Al did say he had asked Martha to make sure no one books the cabins after these guests leave so that we could come up and look at them."

"Do you think this Martha person might know about them and tries to keep it open for them?"

I chew on my lip. "I don't know. I need to call her to set up a time to meet her. Time will tell, I guess."

"How about you call her now?"

I look around the room. There aren't too many in here and those that are are either chilling at the bar or playing pool. Most people went back to work.

Nodding, I fish out my phone and I'm about to dial when Kai stops me.

"Wait a minute," he says before he whistles. "Hey, Smoke, Timber, come here. The rest of you assholes quiet down. Mae's gonna make a call and I want her to put it on speakerphone."

I shake my head but smile.

Dad, Timber, Thor, and Levi all come over and sit down with me. I fill them all in on what I found out.

"When you talk to her, see if you can fish out any details for if someone has called but is now on the waiting list to book? Or if she has any guesses for when the next one might be per history?" Levi asks and I nod.

"Those were going to be my questions, too, along with setting up a time to come and see the cabins this weekend."

Holding my phone, I dial the number Al gave me and put it on speaker. After a few rings, she picks up.

"Hello?"

"Hello. Is this Martha Wells? This is Mae Caldwell. My lawyer, Allen Worthe, gave me your number about my grandparents' cabins."

"Oh yes, hello Dear. However, I was told your last name was Cole?"

"It was. I got married this past weekend."

"Well, congratulations, Dear! What can I do for you?"

"I was wondering when would be a good time to come up to meet with you this Friday or possibly this weekend? I'd like to also see the cabins and see if we need to schedule any upcoming repairs or updates."

"That won't be a problem. Allen had asked that I keep the books open for a bit. Originally, one couple was supposed to check out this Wednesday and another gentleman this Friday, but they had to cut their visits short. They'll both be checking out tomorrow instead."

My eyebrows rise in surprise and I glance at the others. *"Oh. Well, I hope everything is okay with their families and that no one is injured or sick or anything."*

"Oh, no, nothing of the sort. John and Grant work together at the same company and they have an emergency with one of their accounts, which is why they need to leave early."

"Well, that's a relief then. I guess if they are checking out early, would it be possible to come up and meet with you earlier then?"

"That won't be a problem. We live on a farm that neighbors your grandparents' land, well I guess now it's your land. The close proximity is why your grandparents asked if we would be willing to do this for them. Will you still want us to continue handling things for you?"

"Well, I would first like to meet you and your husband, but as of right now, I am leaning toward having you both continue to handle things. My husband and I live in Forest Creek so we aren't too far away if you would need us for anything. Going forward, I'd like to pop in regularly to check in with you both and check on the cabins."

"That won't be a problem at all. Just give me a jingle when you want to come and we'll be here. As for this week, how about Wednesday around 1 pm? Grant had mentioned that one of the toilets was running a lot, so after they check out, George was going to take a closer look at it and run into town for any parts he might need to fix it."

Ice runs down my spine, but I force the feeling away for now. Looking up at Timber, he nods.

"*That sounds perfect! Oh, I was going to ask. Just in case we do need or want to do any repairs or updates, was there anyone on the waiting list to check-in? My husband works in construction, so he would like to make sure everything is good, especially since it won't be long until it's winter.*"

"*Well, let's see. Usually the Deans and Crowley gentleman like to reserve the cabins sometime in October. They like to hunt out here and they usually have good luck, too. Besides them, the weekends will start to book up as well for other hunters. During the week would be the best time for repairs unless you want me to blackout certain dates?*"

"*How about we decide on if we need blackout dates once my husband has a chance to look everything over?*"

"*Sounds like a plan, Dear.*"

"*Alright, so we'll see you at 1 pm on Wednesday. Please keep us posted on the toilet repair, especially if it turns out to be bigger than expected.*"

"*Will do, Dear. See you on Wednesday. Goodbye.*"

"*Goodbye.*"

As soon as she hangs up, I drop my phone, grab my cable out of my bag and plug in my phone to my computer.

"Mae?" Thor asks.

Hesitantly, I look up at him. "I... I think they're in on it. The renters. I'm pulling up my pictures so I can see them better. Wasn't one of the women handcuffed around a toilet?"

"Fuck, I think you're right," he says, and they all come around to stand behind me.

Clicking on the folder, I find the picture I want and enlarge it.

"*Fiddlesticks...*"

Unfortunately, by enlarging the picture, I realize who it is from her tattoo.

"Jane..."

They all curse.

"This changes things. Timber, you and the guys need to head up today. Stay hidden and try to get pictures of these assholes. We need recon."

"We'll gather our gear and head out. We planned to take the black SUV. Should we still do cameras or wait to do that on Wednesday?"

"Let's wait for now, but we need pictures and or footage of them when you see them. If possible, try to put trackers on their vehicles."

"And if we see the women?" Kai asks, his hands clenching into fists.

"Only if you are sure you can out-gun them. Do *not* do anything stupid. If you're able to put trackers on them, we can regroup and go after them then when we have more manpower."

"Wait. What if they have their cars in the garage and you aren't able to get in through a door? I mean, they have a side door from the pictures I pulled up, but what if they are blocked?" I point out.

"You best not be volunteering, Sunshine. I don't want you near any of those fuckers," Timber darn near growls.

I shake my head. "No, and I know neither you nor Dad would allow it. Not with everything that's going on. But Dad, Dragon, Bear, Reaper, and Kai all volunteered to go with you. If your only access point is that window," I pause and point out said window in one of the pictures. "Then none of you will be able to fit through it. Plus, you'll probably need to split up because the cabins are about a half-mile apart, it looks like."

Thor nods. "Take Lex and Colt, too. They aren't small by any means, but they're smaller than you guys. Plus, Lex is stealthy as shit and Colt's been improving in that area as well." He squeezes my shoulder. "Good thinking, Mae."

Pride runs through me, and when Levi winks at me, I can't help my smile.

Chapter 68

Timber

IT'S MID-AFTERNOON BY THE time my group finally sneaks up to the first cabin. Smoke had found us an old, overgrown farm road on the maps to park the SUV. Since it was about a half mile trek to either cabin from there, we had thought about using hunting as a cover, but we didn't want to draw attention to us by wearing bright orange. At least we all have camo gear to help us blend in.

Voices from inside the house bring my attention back to the cabin. It's a two-story cabin and looks like it has two, maybe three bedrooms depending on the sizes. Luck seems to be on our side because this cabin's garage door is open and the forest is close to the house on the backside by the garage. There are two cars in the garage and a third in the driveway.

"L, go around the back and when the coast is clear, sneak into the garage and put the trackers on the cars," I whisper through our coms. I still have no idea how Levi got a hold of these communications devices, but I'm thankful as fuck right now.

"Got it."

Out of the corner of my eye, I see Lex stand slightly so that's in more of a standing-crouched position, and then he's gone. The fucker really is like a shadow.

The voices get louder and my frown deepens when it sounds like they are arguing over something. I hope like fuck that Lex can get the tracker on before whoever is inside decides to leave.

Pulling out my phone, I ready my camera and take a few pictures when the front door opens. Cursing, I quickly switch to video. A man comes into view that I don't recognize carrying a large black duffel bag. He pops the trunk of the car in the driveway and puts the bag inside, leaving the trunk door open before heading back inside.

Movement off to the side has me holding my breath as Lex shimmies slightly under said car to place a tracker, and then places two others before slipping into the dark garage.

A few moments later, I see him retreat back into the forest and his voice comes over the coms.

"Three vehicles marked, three on each at location A. Verify they are live."

I look down at the handheld device Smoke gave me and nod. *"They are all live."*

"The bag had a person in it, T. I heard her whimpering when I was by the trunk."

Fuck... *"We need a headcount. We only have four men at this location."*

"There are a few large, bushy trees that will block me if I climb the one behind me. Want me to see if I can check the windows of the upstairs rooms?" Lex asks.

I hate to expose him, but we need to know who we're dealing with and how many there are. *"Do it, but don't be seen."*

"I have one male in the kitchen. From here, it looks like Bruce. Pictures taken," Bear says.

"I can see two males in the upper south bedroom. Don't recognize any of them. Pictures taken. Descending," Lex says, mimicking Bear's response.

"There's a woman in the upper north bedroom. She's packing and not looking frazzled. Pictures taken. Descending," Punisher adds.

"I got pictures of the man who put the duffle bag in the trunk. Stay put and capture anything else that may happen."

"Roger," they all reply.

Over the next half-hour, nine more large duffle bags are brought out of the house, and I can barely contain my rage. I've also seen the men are packing serious heat.

The men and woman load up into the cars and I watch the monitor as they all start moving.

"Team B, our three are on the move. What's your status?"

"We have two on the move now. All live. They loaded up eight duffle bags. Colt said he heard whimpering out of some of the bags," Smoke replies.

"Meet back at the car," I tell them all.

I try to keep my steps light as we backtrack, but it's hard with how pissed off I am.

Eighteen women.

And that's only if there was only one woman per bag. There could be more if some of them held children, but aside from Lindsey, we didn't see any other children in the pictures.

There must be a basement or something where they're holding the women, since neither Lex nor Punisher mentioned them in the upstairs rooms.

Fuck, I can't wait to find out where these fuckers are taking the women.

Back in town, we're finishing up a quick lunch that we grabbed from a fast-food place when Smoke grunts from next to me.

"Trackers stopped and they aren't too far away. If the maps are accurate, they're still on Mae's land. They're near a clearing," he says.

"Do you think that could be where those Oasis fuckers are hiding?" Reaper asks.

"Possibly. If we can get close enough, I can fly a drone out and take some pictures."

"Won't they be able to hear it?" Dragon asks and Smoke shakes his head.

"No, this new prototype I made barely makes a sound. The only way they'd be able to hear it was if they were in the tree next to it."

He reaches under his seat and pulls out a silver briefcase. Unlocking it, he pulls out the drone that's no bigger than Mae's palm and a remote. He turns it on and has it hover over the console.

"Fuck, that's some good shit, man," Bear grunts and I have to admit he's right. You can only hear a slight whisper from it.

"Let's check in with Thor, but my vote is we launch it," Reaper says as he digs his phone out to call Thor and update him. Minutes later, we're on the road following Smoke's directions.

About ten minutes later, Smoke has us stop on the side of the road. He rolls down his window, and the drone flies out. I look over his shoulder, watching the laptop screen as the drone flies closer.

"Fuck," I grind out when the homestead comes into view, along with the three cars we saw earlier.

"No shit. And these two that just pulled up are the ones we tracked."

The woman stays in the car, but Bruce leads the men toward the back of the property and Smoke carefully follows behind them with the drone. They stop at a worn-down shed.

"This here will be the perfect spot to secure those two bitches and that brat. Especially since those two imbeciles must have been captured seeing as we haven't been able to get in touch with either of them. As a result, we're running low on our special sedative," Bruce spits as he enters and the door closes after the last one goes in.

"Fuck, I can't follow them. It's too close and they'll see it or hear it. Though I can switch it to night mode and the color of the drone will fade to black," Smoke hisses in frustration.

"Hover there for now, unless you can have it land somewhere safe."

Smoke nods in response to Reaper and lands the drone on a large branch hanging over the shed. He maneuvers it around in a circle to get a better idea of the layout.

There's nothing on three sides other than bramble and thick trees.

A few minutes later, the men reemerge, chuckling darkly to themselves.

"Yes, this will be perfect, my friend. We will watch them for you while you deal with those pests and the bitch," one of the male homesteaders says as he chuckles.

Bruce suddenly whirls on him, grabbing him by the throat and pinning him against a nearby tree. "That bitch is to be my wife when I get rid of that biker trash. Do not speak about her that way," he snarls.

The man visibly pales and nods. "Yes, Sir. Sorry, Sir. My mistake. It won't happen again, Sir."

"See that it doesn't," Bruce says before releasing him and turning toward the clearing. "Unload the cargo. We leave immediately."

Smoke videotapes them unloading the bags. Three are taken to the shed, but the others are dispersed to the surrounding houses.

When Bruce and the others leave, Smoke starts guiding the drone back to us when a gunshot rings out.

All of us duck and Smoke pushes on a bunch of buttons on his remote as Reaper starts to drive. "Fuckers are trying to take out the drone. Somehow they spotted it."

Looking behind us, I spot a black car tailing us. Just before we're about to turn onto another road, the drone flies in the window and Reaper floors it, going even faster than before.

More gunshots ring out as another black car emerges from behind some trees, making it two cars that are tailing us while the others break off into a different direction.

"Fuck, they must have put in some roads or something through the trees that wasn't showing on the maps."

Reaper's knuckles turn white as he races through town and onto the busy interstate. The bullets stopped when we got into town, thankfully, but we still need to lose them.

We manage to stay ahead of them thanks to the busy roads. Reaper exits two exits before we normally would and takes the winding back roads.

"I don't think they followed us. Or if they are, they're far enough back that I can't see them," Punisher says from the backseat.

"We'll be at the compound in ten minutes, so long as those fuckers don't suddenly show up again," Reaper grits out.

Thankfully, we don't encounter any problems the rest of the way, but still... I can't shake the feeling that we're being watched.

Reaper parks, and as soon as Thor sees us, he frowns. "Church," he bellows.

Sunshine whirls in her seat, smiling when she sees me, but then it falls at our expressions.

Stalking over to her, I lean down, kissing her quickly. "Stay inside. Don't go outside, even to go to our house."

She presses her lips together and nods. "Ragnar forwarded me a message, which Thor now has. Didn't want to send it to you guys in case it distracted you or something. I asked Ragnar if someone in Junction Creek could get the names of the other Masters out of Andrew or Carter, and he had Cannon and Atlas go down to talk to our friends."

"Good job, Sunshine." Stealing one more kiss, I head into Church.

Thor bangs his hammer on the table. "Fill me in."

Thirty minutes later, everyone's been filled in and we looked at the pictures and videos.

"Where are those five cars now?" Thor asks.

Smoke clicks away on his computer and the screen switches to a large map of the surrounding area. "They're all within an hour radius of the homestead, and no two are in the same town. Seems Andrew and Carter were the only exceptions to that rule. That and they lived further away from the homestead than the others."

"Maybe it has something to do with that sedative Bruce mentioned. They must have needed a doctor to get it, or the ingredients, and they were the only doctors in the group per the list that Cannon and Atlas sent us," Phoenix says.

"We need to stake out these houses and see if they have any other women captured there or if they are all at the homestead. Let's make a plan," Thor says.

Scrubbing a hand over my face, a foreboding feeling settles over me. Something's going to happen and soon.

But what?

And when?

Chapter 69

Mae

I DON'T KNOW WHAT'S going on, but all the guys and Levi have been on edge for the past almost six weeks. It's making me nervous. Drae, too. We haven't gotten any more messages, at least that I'm aware of, anyway. It's like everyone's just waiting for the other shoe to drop.

Our trip up to see the cabins was uneventful but informative. They're in great shape, but unfortunately, wallpaper was installed and it matches the background of the pictures we were sent. However, Timber and Dad didn't seem surprised for some reason. Unless they saw it when they did their recon mission. We also decided to keep Martha and George running things and I'll have regular check-ups with them.

Shortly after we got back from checking on the cabins, Timber helped install the new gate and fill the hole that the bomb had left in the concrete. The gatehouses took longer, but now they should all be blast-proof. Not to mention being reinforced so that a car can't crash through them.

Shaking my head, I refocus on finishing seasoning the meat. This weekend is forecasted to be the last good one in October, and everyone voted to have a barbeque. We're having steaks, potatoes, green bean casserole, corn, and biscuits.

Walking over to the sink, I wash my hands and put the seasonings away before heading outside. Gunner and Judge are manning the grills tonight.

"Hey, guys. The meat is all ready. Are the grills ready?"

"Yup. Go ahead and bring them on out."

Spinning on my heel, I head back inside to the kitchen. "They're ready for the meat," I say as I pick up one of the trays.

"I'll get the other one. The rest of the food just got done, so they're on the warmers," Sasha says and we both head outside.

Setting down the tray on the tables near the grills, I squeal when a large arm bands around my waist, pulling me back. "Timber!"

He leans down, nipping my shoulder. "You've been teasing me all day in this sexy as fuck sweater that shows off your delicious skin, skintight jeans, and sexy knee-high boots. And to top it off, my property cut."

I groan when I feel him hard against my rear. I've been insatiable lately, wanting him all the time, and it seems he's more than happy to keep up with me. We've already snuck off once today, but I want to enjoy the barbeque.

"Tonight, Baby," I hiss at him as I turn in his arms. "I want to hang out first. The next time we have a barbeque, I'll probably have to be bundled up like an Eskimo if we sit outside."

He pouts but leans down and gives me a kiss. "I'm gonna go grab another beer. Need anything?"

"Can you grab me a raspberry-lemonade?"

"You bet, Sunshine." He kisses me again and lets go of me before heading inside.

Dad waves at me and I smile as I head over to him.

A week after Timber and I got married, Dad and I were finally able to sit down and talk about everything that happened when I first arrived. While what he did and said still hurts, he's been trying really hard to make up for it.

When I reach him, he pulls me into his side, and I wrap my arms around his waist, hugging him. He kisses my temple and goes back to talking about our upcoming Halloween drive.

With colder weather coming soon, we're asking for donations of old coats, gloves, hats, snowpants and boots, the whole works. Then we're going to do a Halloween drive for those that can't afford new ones. This will be the first event I'm a part of and I'm excited to help.

However, a few minutes later, the hairs on the back of my neck stand on end, and I look around cautiously.

"Hey, what's wrong, Baby Girl?"

It's only then that I realize my entire body has tensed up.

"It's probably nothing, but I feel like I'm being watched," I whisper.

Out of the corner of my eye, I notice them all tense but then relax.

"Let's get you," he starts to say, but then a commotion off to the side of the property draws our attention.

My eyes widen when I see a guy peering over the top of the cinderblock wall with a gun.

Pointed straight at me.

I start to run and a couple of shots ring out. The next thing I know is I'm being tackled and we're rolling on the ground as I hear shouts all around us and a few motorcycles starting up.

When we stop rolling, I stare at Dad in shock, but then notice his face is taut with pain.

"No, no, no, no," I cry out as I push him off me, only to see a bullet wound on his side. "Dad!"

"Mae, here! Press this on his wound," Patch says as he kneels beside me.

I take the towel, push back his cut, and press it onto Dad's side. He winces, but I know I shouldn't back off on my pressure. I don't know much about bullet wounds, but I do know that.

"Sorry," I say quietly, wincing as tears start to fall.

"It's okay, Baby Girl. I'm just glad I got to you in time," he says as he lets out a long breath, his face paler than before.

Patch gets Dad's cut off somehow and calls out for more towels. "It's not a through and through and there's a graze as well, which isn't good. You're losing too much blood. We gotta take you in." He pauses as he looks me over. "Is that all his blood or are you hurt, too?"

I look down at my torso and more tears fall. Shrugging off my cut, I don't see any bullet holes. There is a graze, but it didn't go all the way through the leather. To be sure, I pull up my sweater to check. Relief flows through me, but then it's instantly replaced with worry and nerves as I shake my head, staring down at Dad, whose shirt is darkening with blood.

"No, it's all Dad's blood. The leather stopped the bullet from grazing me," I say, biting back a sob. I see Dad's cut on the ground next to me and wipe some of the blood off my hands onto my jeans before carefully picking it up, trying not to get blood on his patches. I pick up my cut and clutch the both of them like a lifeline as I watch Patch work.

A sound of an engine has me looking up to see Thor pulling up in the club SUV and he hops out.

"I have your kit, Patch. We'll get him there faster if we take him ourselves. Mae, you should get cleaned up and meet us there."

Strong hands pull me back out of the way, and Timber scoops me up into his arms.

"Come on Sunshine. They'll take care of him. This isn't our first rodeo. Let's get cleaned up and throw a bag together, then we'll head to the hospital."

I can only nod numbly as I look over his shoulder, watching the guys load Dad up into the SUV. He sees me and lifts his hand in a weak wave. Swallowing a sob, I wave back and then the doors close. Thor carefully loops around the clubhouse and then he's gone.

When the SUV disappears from view, my tears come harder as the reality of what just happened sinks in.

My dad just took a bullet for me. Two if you count the graze.

Up in our bedroom, I don't pay attention as Liam strips me out of my clothes, tossing them on the floor. He picks me up again after shedding his clothes and carries me into the bathroom. After starting the shower, he grabs a hairband off the counter and starts to put my hair up, but then stops.

"Sorry, Baby, but you have blood in your hair," he whispers.

I nod and turn, walking into the shower on autopilot and start washing myself.

I scrub at my hands, arms, and stomach where Dad's blood seeped through my shirt.

Liam's large hands stop my scrubbing, and I look up at him, his face blurry through my tears.

"Let me, Baby. You're rubbing yourself raw."

I can only nod again in response, not trusting myself to talk right now.

Liam takes the luffa from me and starts washing the rest of my body before tilting my head back and rinsing my hair. He squirts some shampoo in his hand, and I close my eyes as his hands work through my hair.

Even though the sight of my dad laying bloody on the ground instantly bombards me, I can't look at the pink water as it circles the drain.

Liam shuts off the water and grabs a towel off the rack, wraps it around me and starts drying me off.

"Let's get dressed, Baby."

That has me slightly snapping out of it and I loosely braid my hair after combing it quickly. Once that's done, I hurry to the dresser and pull on clean clothes. Grabbing a bag from the closet, I pack a few more clothes and then grab my backpack and purse. Seeing my cut and Dad's on the dresser, I take them into the bathroom and wipe off the blood before putting it on. Then, I wipe the blood off Dad's cut as best as I can before tucking it safely into my backpack.

Liam's waiting at the door with his own backpack, looking down at his phone.

"Levi texted that she called Nikki. Her and Sadie are on their way to the hospital. They were just about to leave their house to head here when Levi called. Levi said she grabbed a bag of Smoke's clothes and his laptop. Dragon's driving her in."

"Okay. Let's go," I whisper and then hurry out of the house getting into Timber's truck. We've been looking for a car for me but haven't bought one yet. I want to wait until this mess is done with and we can find Mom.

I still worry that we haven't heard anything the past few weeks, but it's nothing compared to what Drae's going through since there has also been no word on Jane or Lindsey. At least, not that we've heard anyway. I realize the guys may know more, but if they do, there must be some reason why they haven't said anything to us.

Liam speeds through town, for which I'm grateful. Instead of the usual twenty minutes, it only takes fifteen.

As soon as he has the truck parked, I fling open my door and race inside, ignoring his growl of annoyance. I know it's only been about a half hour, but I need an update on my dad.

Chapter 70
Timber

CURSING, I HURRY AFTER Sunshine. I get she's freaked the fuck out, but I wish she would have let me make sure the area was clear first. Especially since she doesn't know about all the threats that we've kept from her and Drae.

I couldn't bring myself to tell her that for every week that's passed, we've gotten more demands and pictures. Fuck, just last Friday they sent us a severed hand that we think is Lillian's. Only thing is, there were three dismembered fingers and a thumb in the box too. We have no idea who the fingers and thumb belong to. The pads of the fingers were all burnt off, so there's no way to run fingerprints on them.

Mae's probably going to ream us to high heaven over this, but we all thought we were protecting her. Smoke included. Drae doesn't know about everything either, but we haven't gotten as much about Jane or Lindsey as we have about Lillian.

Not too long after we saw Bruce dropping off the bags we suspect were full of women at the homestead, he came back and went back into the shed. Later, he and his men came out carrying three heavy duffel bags which we pegged as possibly holding Lillian, Jane, and Lindsey. Smoke had another thinner drone that was just as silent as the first one that he flew to the shed and inside it. There were heat signatures, but they were already fading fast, so those areas must have been where the three women had been held. There was no one else in the shed.

Smoke also used his drone to check the other houses, but no one resembling Lillian, Jane, or Lindsey were there. However, while we suspect they were the ones in the bags, we have no proof if it really was them. Or where they are now being held. There were just as many people there at the homestead as last the time Smoke had done recon before they started shooting at us, so we don't know where the other eighteen women we suspected were in the bags went.

Since then, no one has been back to the cabins this entire time and we haven't seen anyone new at the homestead either. We're grasping at straws, but the fuckers are back in the wind. We staked out the houses that vehicles we tracked went to, but those were a bust too as they are now abandoned with no trace of anyone being there before. I know I'm not the only one going out of their mind wondering where in the fuck they are—I've seen more than one of my brothers and sisters offering to help Smoke track these assholes down.

Mae speed walks right up to the check-in station, startling the woman there.

"I'm sorry. I didn't mean to startle you. My dad, Jaxon Witlock, was brought in here a little bit ago. Is there any update?"

"What's your name?"

"Mae Caldwell."

Despite what's going on, I fucking love hearing her say my last name.

"He's still in surgery. When there's another update, the nurse or doctor will come out to get you."

A second later, I hear someone running toward us as they call Mae's name, and I turn, seeing Sadie barreling toward us with tears streaming down her face, Nikki not too far behind her. Bending down, I scoop Sadie up and she buries her face in my neck.

Mae looks behind her and then back to the nurse. "Can you make sure Nikki Witlock is on the list too? She's Dad's sister," she says right as Nikki walks up to us.

"Of course."

"Thank you," Mae replies and when she turns, Nikki wraps her into a hug. After a few moments, they pull apart and I guide them over to my brothers.

Levi wraps Mae in a hug and then suddenly, Mae jerks back. "Crap! I need to add you, Sasha, Lex, and Ethan to the list!"

Levi puts a hand on her arm and shakes her head, stopping her from walking back to the check-in station. "No, you two need to see him first. We can wait until afterward."

Mae hesitates. "Are you sure you want to wait? You're just as much his family as we are."

She sniffles but nods. "Thank you, but you're his blood and you two should see him first."

Mae hugs her again, and this time when she pulls back, both of them are chuckling softly. Mae touches Levi's stomach before smiling widely and bending down, kissing where her hand had been.

"Hey, Princesses. Be good in there and don't beat up your mama's insides too much."

Levi groans and then looks down at her stomach as she caresses it. "And stop laying on my bladder. It isn't a pillow."

The ladies all sit together and Sadie wiggles slightly in my arms. I set her down and she crawls up and into Nikki's lap.

Walking over to the others, I step up to Thor. "Any news?" I ask, pitching my voice low.

"They lost them. Jackasses were on bikes and were gone pretty quick. Dragon took Bastion out there but, the trail was localized to the area around where the shooter was."

Swearing, I scrub my hand over my face and settle in to wait for an update.

It's been five long fucking hours and Mae is getting antsier by the minute.

"I shouldn't have had that soda. I need to pee but I don't want to leave in case they come out," she moans as she wiggles slightly on my lap again.

"Tell you what. I need to pee again too, so we'll go together," Levi says as she gets up and I pat Mae's hip.

"I'll come knock on the door if they come out. Take Lex with you," I say since he's the only Prospect here right now. Ethan went to get some drinks from the cafeteria a few minutes ago and Colt, Sasha, and Drae are back at the clubhouse.

They all wanted to be here, but we can't leave the compound unattended either. They're there with Bear, Phoenix, Bones, and Axe, as well.

Mae grumbles but gets up. She doesn't like having a shadow, but she understands, too.

Lex follows behind them as they walk down the hall and around the corner to the restroom since the one just outside the waiting area is occupied.

Ten minutes later, they still aren't back, and I exchange worried glances with Dragon and Thor. All three of us stand and head down the hall.

"Where the fuck is Lex?" Thor asks when we round the corner and a feeling of dread washes over me when no one is standing outside the women's restroom.

I hurry down the rest of the hallway and knock on the door. "Mae? Levi?"

No one answers and I share another worried glance with the others.

I try knocking louder, but still no response.

Turning the handle, it opens and my stomach bottoms out.

It's empty but there's blood smeared around on the stall doors, the sink, and the floor.

"Fuck," I growl and pivot on my heel, but then stop.

Thor and Dragon push past me, but I stop them and signal them to be quiet.

A banging noise is coming from further down the hallway. As I get closer, I can hear grunting as I see the door rattling like someone's trying to break it down from the inside.

Hurrying the rest of the way down the hall, I bang on the door. "Lex?"

"Timber! Fucking assholes got the drop on us and locked us in here."

"Please say my Sunshine's in there with you and Levi?" I ask as Dragon starts picking the lock.

Seconds later, the door swings open and anger flows through me at seeing a deep gash on Lex's head as well as a few others on his arm and one on his neck. Behind him, Levi slouches against the wall, blood running down the side of her face as she holds her shoulder with one arm, the other cradling her stomach.

The defeat in her eyes tells me all I need to know.

"I'm sorry, Timber. We tried, but Bruce got her."

Nausea swirls in my stomach as a white-hot rage fills my veins.

"How many were there?"

"Three other men beside Bruce and a female nurse. They were all in scrubs," Lex replies to Thor and then he turns toward me. "Do you have Mae's or Smoke's laptop?"

I immediately nod.

"Good. I can route into the program and track her. Last I saw, she still had on her cut and bracelets," he says as he takes off down the hall.

Thor scoops up Levi in his arms and we all follow them, only to get stopped by a wide-eyed nurse.

"What's going on? Oh my gosh, we need to get you both back in the ER right away."

"First you're going to page Mr. Thatcher and have him get his ass down here. Then page Luke or Allison to come look at these two," I bark at her.

She presses her lips together in a thin line. "Sir, I don't know who you are, but I will not tolerate you ordering me around like this."

"Stop right there, lady," I hiss. "My wife was just kidnapped from your hospital and my friends are injured from said attack. As you can see, she's pregnant," I say, gesturing to Levi. "We will be requesting guards on their rooms as well as our brother's room, Jaxon Witlock, who is in surgery. Now get me Mr. Thatcher so we can talk about the guards before I go above your head to get it done."

I don't know if the nurse finally comes to her senses and realizes that she's not going to get me to back down, but she turns on her heel and we follow her.

My brothers all practically stampede toward us when they see Levi and Lex.

"Mae?" Tripp asks, but then his face hardens as he sees the answer written all over my face.

"Get Bones here. At least until Smoke or Lex is good again. Warn the others. Call Reaper."

He gives me a curt nod and he and Ryder both pull out their phones.

Grabbing Mae's backpack and the one Levi had packed for Smoke, I follow the others back into the ER. As soon as they get Lex on a bed, he gestures toward the bag and I hand him the laptop.

"Sir, you really need to lean back and rest," the same nurse tells him, and the glare he gives her has her shrinking back.

"My niece was just kidnapped from your hospital. Get Luke or Allison in here. I don't want you fixing me up. If they aren't available, I'll wait till they are," he says as he continues to glare at her.

Finally, she nods and scurries out of the room.

"I also don't know if she's in on this and in no way do I want her to see anything I do," he mumbles under his breath as he starts clicking away.

Walking over to the counter, I grab some gloves, gauze, tape, scissors, and wet down some paper towels.

"I'm no Patch or Alli, but I can at least clean you up and put pressure on your wounds," I say as I get to work.

To his credit, he doesn't flinch at anything I do and I finish up just as Mr. Thatcher comes in.

"Thor and Levi told me what happened. She's getting checked out. In fact, they were just wheeling in the ultrasound machine as I left. All three of you will have the guards you need when you are here and later if it's deemed you and Levi need to stay for observation. Now, with that said, what can I do to help in tracking down the assholes who kidnapped your wife, Timber?"

"We need to see your security footage and we'll need a copy of it," Lex says before I can say anything.

"Done and done. I'm going to assume that I need to keep the cops out of this?" he asks as his gaze cuts to mine, his eyebrows cocked in question.

Fuck, I knew I liked this guy.

"If at all possible, yes. And just so you know, when Smoke comes around after surgery, any monitors he's hooked up to are going to freak the fuck out when he finds out Mae's gone."

Mr. Thatcher frowns. "They're close?"

His face falls slightly at the look on my face and his worry increases.

"Mae's his daughter and he took two bullets to save her."

"Fuck," he hisses as he scrubs his face, but then nods. "Anything you need, you'll have it. If anyone gives you trouble, call me. In fact," he says as he digs in his pocket and hands me a card. "My numbers, so any of you can call me anytime—day or night."

"Here, Timber," Lex says as he turns the laptop slightly so I can see what he just brought up.

I clench my fists when I realize where her locators are pinging from. They're on the move, but I have a pretty good idea where they're taking her.

Fucking asshole.

"Thanks, Lex." I pause as I tuck the laptop under my arm, noting that it's already after midnight, and turn to Mr. Thatcher. "Let's go see security."

Chapter 71

Mae

I GROAN AS I blink my eyes open, but then close them against the harsh light.

Another groan slips past my lips when I remember that mother trucker Bruce frickin' drugged me.

Taking a deep breath, I slowly open my eyes, ignoring the jackhammers in my head. I feel just like I did last time when Carter drugged me, so they must have used the same sedative or something that's close enough.

Once I've adjusted to the light, I look around and grimace. I'm in a room that has cinderblock walls and a cracked concrete floor. There's a bed in the corner that looks newish, but I hope like heck they don't put me on it. A shudder runs through me as I remember the pictures and videos Bruce and his minions sent me.

I know without looking down that I'm no longer wearing the clothes that I had on earlier. I can feel the cold concrete under my feet and the cool air on my bare legs and arms. Taking a deep breath, I suppress my groan when I realize I've been put into one of those white, almost sheer dresses that the other women wore in some of the pictures.

Forcing my attention away from my clothes and the bed, I take in the rest of the room. The walls are kind of mossy and it smells like mold in here. The ceiling looks similar to the floor—cracked concrete that's been pitted in places. Also, there are areas in the ceiling where water drips down into the room. Thankfully, the water isn't dripping on me and I'm not chained against the disgusting walls. Unfortunately, that means I'm secured in the middle of the room.

Looking up, I groan when I see they've secured metal shackles around my wrists and the chain that connects them is wrapped a few times around a pipe that goes from wall to wall. Glancing down, I realize my ankles are shackled as well. Each one is connected through a metal loop that's been secured to the floor which has my feet spread about shoulder width apart.

Then I notice the rust on the loops.

When I test them, the bases of the metal loop in the floor jiggle. Looking up, I'm about to test the pole when a nearby whimpering sound has me straining and looking around again.

I'd somehow missed that there was an opening in the wall with metal bars looking into the next room. Looking at the other wall, there's one there, too.

Or I should say cell, not room.

"H-hello?" I asked hesitantly.

Instantly, the whimpering stops.

Nibbling on my lip, I try again. "Hello? My name is Mae. What's yours?"

"I'm not falling for that again. Last time that happened, they beat me and hurt Mama."

Oh dear lord... She sounds like a little girl. Could it be?

"Lindsey?"

She doesn't answer me right away. "How do you know my name? You're one of them. That proves it," she whispers.

"No, I swear to you I'm not. I know your daddy, Drae. I'm Smoke's daughter. A little over a month ago, Timber and I got married. I'm also trying to find my mom. My stepdad, Preston, took her away and has been hurting her."

Silence meets my words before I hear the chains moving and then her little face appears through the window as she leans against the back wall.

"Oh, Pumpkin," I whisper when I see how thin she's gotten compared to pictures I've seen of her before she was taken.

"What's your mama look like?"

Frowning, I decide to answer her question to keep her talking.

"The last time I saw her, she had long blond hair, but it was dyed and she had about a half an inch of brown roots at the top. The brown sections are probably longer now. Do you know what I mean by that?" I ask and she nods her head.

"Mama was the opposite. Her hair was blond and she dyed it brown."

I nodded, relieved when I noticed the little girl is relaxing further the more I talk to her. "Other than that, she has blue eyes like mine, she's really really skinny, and…" I pause and swallow thickly "And she's missing a finger on her right hand."

Lindsey frowns, her eyes darting over to her right before quickly looking back at me.

"What was your mom's name?"

"Lillian Cole."

"So you're telling me the truth, then? You aren't with them."

I nod. "That's right, Pumpkin. I'm not with them. I really am friends with your daddy and we've been looking for you and your mom for a long time."

She sniffles and hugs her legs. "I miss Daddy. He calls me Pumpkin, too."

My heart breaks even more at seeing her tears streak down her dirty face.

After a few minutes, she dries her eyes.

"Mae, your mama… She's in here with my mama."

Hope springs into my chest, but it dies immediately when I see her crestfallen face.

"Are… are they sleeping?"

More tears well in her eyes as she shakes her head.

"Your mama stopped moving the day after they cut off her hand. Mama stopped moving three days ago. The mean men hurt her really bad after cutting off some of her fingers, too."

"Futtenfarter," I mutter under my breath. Drae's going to be so devastated.

The sound of a grate above us scraping over the floor has her eyes widening in fear before she scoots out of my view.

Footsteps echo down the stairs and from the sound, it almost sounds like dress shoes.

A face appears on the other side of my door through the barred window and I scowl.

"Bruce," I spit.

If he's surprised that I know his real name, he doesn't show it.

"Now, now, Precious, that's no way to meet your future husband," he purrs, and my scowl deepens.

"You aren't my husband and will *never* be my husband."

"Not yet, and with that biker scum now out of the way, you're free to be where you belong. With me. Your marriage has been dissolved and soon, you'll be my wife."

"You're nuts if you think I'll marry you. I'm never divorcing Timber."

He chuckles. "Well, see now, Precious, that's where you're wrong. He's already submitted his paperwork and is having fun with his new fiancée now that you're out of the picture."

Bruce fiddles with his phone before turning it around for me to see and my stomach roils at seeing Liam fucking another woman. But then the woman's voice comes over the video.

Gigi.

Liam has never been with Gigi, though. My gaze cuts to his chest and I smirk.

"Seems you got played, Bruce. Either that or you didn't count on two things. One, I know Timber hasn't been with Gigi in any sense—sexually or orally. And two, that is a video that's been pieced together and hodge-podged. Not to mention, it's an older video of Timber. See, he's had some new artwork done which isn't in that video. The fact that my name is now inked on his skin, tells me he's not going to be giving me up without a fight," I tell him with a smirk.

His face turns red, and he backhands me, hard, before grasping my jaw to the point where I know I'll have bruises.

"I'll teach you some respect, girl, if it's the last thing I do. It's bad enough you ran away, but then you let that biker scum in between your legs, taking what was my right to take. I paid for you outright you fucking bitch, and you will be mine," he hisses and steps out into the hallway, only to come back with a flogger. This one, though, has pronged tips that I know are going to hurt like hell.

Futtenfarter.

He steps behind me, and immediately a cry escapes me when it lands, even though I try not to let it out.

I'm not sure how much time passes when Bruce finally stops.

He comes around in front of me and grips my chin again, hard, and I glare at him.

He grins. "So defiant. I look forward to breaking your spirit."

I spit and grin when it lands on his face. "Fuck you. You will never break me."

His hand grasps my throat and squeezes. I pull on my restraints, trying to get away from him, but stop when I hear the metal groan above me right as the door opens up on top.

Bruce releases me, and I start coughing when I inhale sharply.

"Boss, they're here," a man says as he stops just outside my door.

Even though black dots are dancing across my vision, I try to catalogue him, burning his image into my memory.

Bruce scowls and pulls out a handkerchief, wiping my spit off his face.

"Fuck, they weren't supposed to be here until later tonight." He pauses and then turns back to me. "Rest up, Precious. I'll be back to play later, and I know it'll be one that I'll greatly enjoy," he says as he leers at me and his eyes roam over my body. He adjusts himself as he licks his lips.

Ice rolls down my spine, but I don't let it show.

Bruce leaves, and the new guy locks the door behind him before leering at me as well. That look tells me all I need to know.

He's also been hurting women along with the others.

And if I don't get out of here, they're going to rape me like they have all those other women.

I wait for a little bit after they leave and glance up at the pole above me. Summoning all the courage I have, I try and force my voice to be as level as possible, so I don't scare Lindsey more than she already is.

"Lindsey, are you still awake?"

A shuffling sound reaches my ears and then she re-appears in the window. "He hurt you. He used that on them a lot, too," she whispers.

"Yes, he did hurt me, but when your daddy and my Old Man get here, they are going to make them pay for what they've done to all of us." I pause, letting her see the confidence in me.

Because what she doesn't know is that when I pulled on my arm restraints, I felt my bracelets.

They can track me.

Unless Bruce has jammers...

Crap, I didn't think about that, but I'm going to hope like heck that they don't.

"Now, Lindsey, can you see the bar above my head?"

She comes forward before her chains stop her, but then she nods her head.

"Does it go into your room, too?"

"No, it doesn't. I'm only chained by my ankle, which is chained to the wall. Mama and Lillian were chained to the wall along with their beds."

I try not to shudder at that thought and pray that the beds are there for them to only sleep in and nothing else in front of Lindsey.

"Can you do me a favor? Take a look at the bolts connected to the wall for your shackle. Are they brown with rust? If you tug on the chain, does it wobble?"

She disappears from sight and then I hear her rattle the chain. I grin when I hear her little shriek of joy that she quickly cuts short.

"Yes, they are rusty and it wiggles a lot."

"Okay, I want you to pull on it with all your might. Tell me if you get it to come loose. I'm going to work on mine, okay?"

"Okay."

Chapter 72

Timber

It's after 1 am before I'm able to get the security tape from that freaking guard. Even with Mr. Thatcher with me, he still bitched and moaned. I made sure to memorize what he looked like just in case he shows up on the footage—both here and at the clubhouse.

Sighing, I head back down to the ER since Thor said that's where he still is with the others. Mr. Thatcher is following me on my heels, making sure no one continues to mess with us anymore.

The nurse at the desk tries to stop me from entering the room Levi's in, but Mr. Thatcher waves her off.

Fear snakes down my veins when I see all three of them crying as Thor and Dragon are on either side of Levi's bed.

"Oh fuck. Please say both jellybeans are doing good?"

Levi nods. "These are happy tears of relief. Other than getting a few stitches and them popping my shoulder back into place, I'm doing good. Now, tell us what you found out in the security room."

Before I answer her, I turn on my hotspot and refresh the page Lex brought up. Then, I turn on the jammer Lex had on him before turning back to Levi, Thor, and Dragon.

"We already knew Bruce was in on it, but I don't recognize the three thugs that were with him or the getaway driver. The nurse, however, is someone we all know quite well."

"My money's on Gigi," Levi mutters under her breath and at my nod, all three of them curse.

"She had on a wig and face mask, but she took them off before hopping in the car. I texted the plate number to Bones and Lex but I'm gonna bet the plates are stolen." Pausing, I turn around Mae's laptop. "Fuckers must not think we're very smart because they didn't ditch her phone, her cut, or her bracelets. All of them are pinging at the same location."

I hand Levi the laptop and they study it. Thor lifts his gaze to me in disbelief. "The asshole took her to her grandparents' house?"

"Yes. Bones was also able to hack into their security system and judging by the map he sent me; Mae's being held in an old rundown garrison-like building that is on the corner of the property. Preston and X are there, however, there's no sign of Phillip. There's also another woman there, but I think she's there by force because of how they're treating her. Luckily, there's no video surveillance noted where Mae's being held, but it borders along a small thicket of woods."

"That could be our way in, then."

I nod. "That's what our thoughts were, too." I pause when someone knocks on the door. Quickly I disconnect the hotspot, close the laptop and stow away the jammer before opening the door.

Thankfully, it's just Patch. "Lex is all stitched and bandaged up. He also filled me in. Smoke is awake and asking for Mae. Nikki is in there now with Sadie. I think he knows something's up and is about to lose it. Also, I have Levi's discharge paperwork along with Lex's. I worked my magic and got you both out of here sooner than they wanted, but they let it go since I'll be able to keep an eye on you at the compound."

Sighing, I nod. "I'll go tell him, but then I need to get back to the compound to plan. Bones and the others are working on a plan as we speak." I pause and turn to Patch. "I know as soon as he hears about Mae that he'll want to be discharged too. What are the odds they'll let him?"

Patch groans. "That is going to be a harder sell. I can try, but he might not get released until after twenty-four hours at a minimum. The risk of infection is high. Thankfully, they didn't have to give him any blood, but it was a close call. They almost pulled the trigger on that, and if they had, it would have been a minimum of twenty-four-hour watch with no way of me being able to get him out of it."

"Can you look into it so that way we can at least know?"

Groaning again, he nods and slips out after giving Levi her paperwork.

Thor's phone dings, and he digs it out before nodding and putting it away. "Reaper and a few others just rolled in at the clubhouse, so they'll be able to help. They left as soon as they heard Smoke was shot."

Taking a deep breath, I grab my stuff. "I'll go talk to Smoke. Wish me luck."

The fuckers chuckle in response, and ignoring them, I head out into the pod. Mr. Thatcher points to another room and I guess that means it's Smoke's room.

Knocking, I enter and Nikki gives me a relieved look before standing. "Timber may have some answers for you, but as I've told you, I don't know. You know how they are about club business." She bends down, picking up Sadie who had fallen asleep cuddled up to Smoke's good side. "I'll let you two talk."

I wait until she slips out and sigh as I sink into the chair Nikki just vacated and rub my tired eyes.

"They got her, didn't they?"

Nodding, I dig the jammer out and fill him in. The more I say, the darker his face gets.

"Get me out of here. I want to help plan this. I need to be there for her."

"Patch is already trying to see what they say, but you and I both know they might not let you. You almost needed a blood transfusion, man."

"Did we get the assholes?"

"Not yet, but maybe the guys on our security pictures match the guys on the hospital security cameras or at her grandparents' house."

Smoke huffs. "It's not a house. It's a fucking mansion with a lot of secret tunnels."

That has me sitting up straighter. "Wait, what now?"

He nods grimly. "Yeah, fuckers messed up by taking her there. It's in the countryside outside of Rixen on ten acres. Been forever since I'd been there, though, so they could have changed things over the years."

A knock has me pocketing the jammer and Patch comes in scowling. "Had to pick up some extra shifts, you asshole, but I got you cleared by promising you'll be an obedient little patient. However, your ass does *not* leave the clubhouse. Bones or someone else can be your eyes and can wear a fucking camera or something."

I try to bite back a laugh at the obedient part, but I must not be successful because Smoke turns his glare on me.

"Hey, it's either obedient patient or your ass is stuck in the hospital," I tell him.

"Fine," Smoke grumbles. "Help me get into my clothes."

I grab his jeans out from the cupboard and then plop them on the bed before grabbing a backpack that Nikki must have left in here. I had left it with Lex, but he must have somehow got it to Nikki.

"Levi grabbed you some clean clothes, which is good cause those jeans are going to need to be burned."

Patch starts unhooking Smoke from the monitors and takes out his IV. "Just know the IV is going back in when we get back to the clubhouse."

Smoke snorts and then groans. "So that's why you had to pick up extra shifts."

"Yeah, cause I sure as fuck am not going out with that bitch. I wish we had a setup like Doc's."

That has me pausing. "I'll talk to Mae, Thor, and Phoenix. Maybe we can set something up that's similar."

"How the fuck is she going to... oh... never mind," Patch says as he nods his head.

This time it's me that snorts. As soon as there was a bit of downtime, Mae sat down with Thor and Phoenix and asked if they needed anything for the club. They hadn't wanted to take her offer for money at the time, but they may change their minds after this.

It takes some maneuvering, but we get Smoke dressed and I pull his cut out of Mae's backpack.

"She wasn't able to give it a good cleaning since we rushed straight here, but she did get most of the blood off. Wasn't sure if you wanted me to put in an order for another one or not. Mae's cut just has a graze mark on hers. Though who knows what these fuckers have done to it now."

He takes his cut from me and rubs his thumb over the leather, his eyes turning glassy a little before he clears his throat. "Order new ones for both of us. I'll pay for them. I don't want her seeing the marks on a daily basis and being reminded."

I start to argue about him paying for them when he cuts me off.

"You just got married, Timber, and even though I don't want to think about it, you two fuck like rabbits. Since I know neither of you are trying to prevent it, she very well could be pregnant right now. I know our cuts aren't that expensive, but babies sure as hell are."

That pulls me up short and I damn near drop Mae's backpack.

Shit...

"Oh fuck," Smoke mutters and then Patch swears as they both stare at me.

"Has she had her period at all while she was here?" Patch asks and I shake my head.

"No, and now that I think about it, after we talked about kids, she said we'd probably know in a few weeks, since that was when her period was due. That talk happened when we were at Junction Creek. Then she was attacked a couple of days later. I guess with all that was going on around that time, we both forgot."

"What time is it? We need to get a plan finalized and fast. I don't know what those fuckers will do if they find out she's pregnant," Smoke grits out, his face paling slightly as he tries to put on his shirt.

"Fuck, it's almost 2 am," I grunt and then step forward when I see the shirt getting caught on the tape.

Patch leaves and comes back in a minute later with a wheelchair.

"I don't care how much you complain. Your ass is going in this chair and you are being wheeled out of here. I already texted Levi and they are near the exit with her SUV since that would be the easiest vehicle for you to get in and out of."

He grumbles, but carefully maneuvers into the chair. I know he'd never say it, but I think he's grateful to have it right now. Especially if he wants to have the energy to plan things with us.

"Alright," I say as I pick everything up. "Let's bust you out of this joint."

Twenty minutes later, we pull up in front of the clubhouse and quite a few eyebrows raise in shock at seeing Smoke stroll through the door into Church.

"Well, fuck," Devil starts and Smoke cuts him off.

"Don't even start with me Devil, but this is my daughter and grandbaby we're talking about. I'm going to be a part of this and will be on cameras on this side of things."

"Grandbaby?" Devil asks as his gaze shoots to me along with everyone else's.

"Possibly. Though I would like to say, to my knowledge, she hasn't taken a pregnancy test. Smoke was pulling my leg about babies when I realized Mae should have had her period two weeks ago."

"Fuck," Levi, Reaper, Punisher, Axe and Odin all say at the same time.

"Patch and Doc, you definitely need to go with them as a just in case," Levi tells them. "I can watch over this stubborn ass to make sure he doesn't overdo anything."

Smoke narrows his eyes at her, taking in her fresh bandages. "And who will be making sure *you* don't overdo things?"

"Oh, shut up. Let's get back to planning so we can bring our girl back home," Levi sasses him back.

It's a little after 6 am when we pull up into the driveway of an abandoned, run down field that's on the backside of the Cooke estate.

We've split up into two teams. The larger group is heading toward the house because as of our check-in a few minutes ago, Preston, X, Gigi, four thugs and an unknown woman are at the main house. We didn't see Bruce on the cameras and I worry that means he's with Mae or on his way to where she's being held.

We've all got cameras clipped onto us just in case we come up to an obstacle that Smoke might need to walk us through. Though that will most likely be the house crew more so than us since they're planning on entering via an old servant's entrance.

Punisher, Judge, Tripp, Axe, Drae, and I sneak our way through the thick grouping of trees when the sounds of struggling and the sound of metal on metal reach our ears.

Drae and I damn near launch forward, but Punisher holds us both back, pointing to the house without uttering a word. A guard is pacing by the window, holding a gun in his hand.

When he turns his back, we dart to the far side of the garrison-like building and find that the door's been left slightly ajar. Double-checking the window, I nudge the door open a little wider, relieved when it doesn't squeak.

The shuffling sound increases, but I force myself to stay calm.

Hang on, Sunshine.

Just as I'm about to step inside, I hear something I wasn't expecting.

Chapter 73

Mae

My ankles and wrists are a bloody mess, but I don't care.

I'm free.

And so is Lindsey.

Well, free as in our shackles are no longer secured to the wall, floor, or pipe. They're still attached to our bodies, unfortunately. Once she had gotten her chains free, I had her brush any cinder block dust off her little mat and carefully slide the bolts back in place.

The look she gave me when I told her to do that damn near broke me, but it needed to be done. Especially after her telling me what she'd seen and who had hurt our mothers. I hope she hadn't left anything out but the fact that she said there was nothing sexual going on in front of her gives me hope. Unless she just isn't telling me about it. God, I pray that isn't the case.

"If they come in and check on you when you're asleep, everything needs to look like you're still their captive. Only you and I will know the truth."

"But can't I cover up Mama and your mama?"

My throat burns as do my eyes with unshed tears at her words. "When I give you the signal, you can cover them, okay?"

"Okay," she grumbles, but does as I ask.

"Can you sing me a song, Mae?"

"Of course, Pumpkin, so long as I know it."

"Do you know 'We Don't Talk About Bruno' from the movie "Encanto"?"

I definitely know that one. One of the other ladies at the diner would sometimes have to bring in her daughter if she didn't have a babysitter. Her daughter loved "Disney" movies and would regularly watch "Encanto".

Grinning, I start singing as I get to work on my own chains.

I had been able to break the pipe free from the walls that the chains for my hands had been wrapped around. Unfortunately, I wasn't able to loosen any of the links with the edges of the pipe, but at least my feet are free for if I have to run. Prying the bar down had been nasty since it had some putrid water in it, but at least I got it free before Lindsey fell asleep because it was kind of loud.

Now I just have to wait for a guard to come down to try and get their keys from them. Lindsey said they tossed stale bread into our cells each morning, but the time would vary based on their whims.

Feeling a trickle on my arm, I look down at the pile of strips of cloth that I'd torn from the sheet that was on my bed and try to clean up the blood from my hands and arms. I need to keep them as dry as possible in case the guard comes soon.

Light catches my eye and I shift slightly. From Lindsey's window, I can see the sky starting to lighten with the sunrise.

Somewhere nearby, a rooster crows and I jump, startled before chastising myself. Though, at least that tells me we're in the country somewhere.

However, minutes later, the door scrapes open and I quickly get into position, lifting the metal bar above my head, even though the action makes the wounds on my neck, shoulders, and back burn. I hear Lindsey's chains rattling, and I wonder if it's to help hide the noise my chains just made. I pray she stays quiet like we talked about. She doesn't need to be hurt any more than she already has been.

The sound of dress shoes on the steps reaches my ears, and I wonder if it'll be Bruce or someone else.

The footsteps go to Lindsey's cell first and I hear a soft thump against the floor, so it's most likely her piece of bread.

Then I hear the curse when the person gets to my door and right before the door opens, I hear the click of a gun's safety going off.

Fear runs down my spine at the fact that he has a gun, but I force it down. The door opens and as soon as his arm is inside the cell; I bring the pipe down hard on his arm. He cries out and, thankfully, drops the gun from the pain. The gun skitters across the cement into the corner of the room.

I get another good hit on him and he staggers enough for me to pull back even more and thwank him up alongside his head. He goes down to his knees. Another whack to the head has him going down hard.

I grab his gun and then his radio that's clipped to his belt before grabbing the keys out of the door, and I lock him inside. I stash the radio and gun on my pile of things just outside the door, surprised that everything's actually there, and rush to Lindsey's door.

When I get there, I see she's already covered both our moms up like she had wanted to.

She rushes into my arms as soon as the door opens and sobs into my neck. Her arms tighten around me but I swallow my pain when her arms lands on multiple wounds.

"We did it, Pumpkin. We're free of our shackles. Now we just gotta get out of here."

"Before we do that, can I hit him for what he did to Mama? For hurting her?"

I freeze, but then go and look at Bruce through my door's window. He's still knocked out and blood is dribbling out of his ear. I must be insane because I'm actually considering it, but then I look back down at her.

"Pumpkin, we need to get out of here. I don't know if he's faking it, and I don't want to risk your safety. However, I know your daddy and my Old Man are on their way here. Do you know how?"

She shakes her head.

I shift the shackle on one of my wrists and wiggle down my bracelet that is coated in fresh and dried blood. "There's a tracker in here, Pumpkin. So long as we stay together, they'll be able to find us. Once we're back home, I'll talk to your daddy about letting you get in two hits on him, since I have to say no right now. Okay?"

"I think that can be arranged, Pumpkin," Drae's voice comes from behind me, and I spin on my heel, covering my mouth with my free hand as a sob escapes me at seeing Liam right behind Drae.

Tears roll down Lindsey's cheeks as Drae carefully takes her out of my arms and it's then that I see my wrist wounds under the chains are bleeding even more than before.

Liam scoops me up in a hug but immediately releases me when a hiss escapes.

"Fuck," he hisses when he turns me around but then I immediately scramble out of his arms to get in front of Drae, who is moving toward Lindsey's cell. Standing in front of her door, I spread my arms and legs wide, blocking him from entering.

"Please believe me, Drae, you are going to want to wait to see her until I, or someone else, cleans her up. Please," I whisper. I know I have no right to ask this of him, but I also think Lindsey needs him to be strong right now for her.

"The bad men hurt Mama and Mae's mama, Daddy. I saw most of it. Mae's mama stopped moving the day after they cut off her hand and Mama stopped moving three sunrises ago after the mean men hurt her really bad. Worse than they had before. They even cut off some of her fingers."

Tears cascade down my cheeks at rehearing Lindsey say what our moms went through, and they fall harder at seeing the anguish on Drae's face.

He nods, turning away, and I push through the other men to the corner and grab my things, stuffing them into a bag that Liam holds out.

"I don't know what you want to do with his radio or gun, but just so you know, I touched both. Same with these keys," I say as I hold them up.

Liam touches his ear and it's then that I see he's wearing some sort of communications device. Kai gives me his and I put it my ear.

"Front team, status check?" Liam asks.

"Just got the bitch and assholes all trussed up. The unknown woman is actually Jane's mother, Elvira. Bastards ran their car off the road. That's how they got their hands on them. Jane's dad, Douglas, died in the car accident," Bones replies.

"What about 'you know who'?" Drae asks Liam and I'm sure whoever Liam's talking to.

Since Lindsey's still in Drae's arms, I reach up and cover her ears so Liam can say it. Drae nods at me in thanks.

"Is Ghost among them? Also, we have Bruce locked in a cell out here. He's breathing, but he's in rough shape. Sunshine got in quite a few good hits."

Bones chuckles softly. *"Kuddos to Mae. Ghost's body was found in the basement, gunshot wound to the head. We already called for a cleanup crew, so you guys are good to head back with the ladies."*

Drae's body relaxes and I let go of Lindsey's ears. She shifts in his arm and wraps her arms around my neck.

I lean up kissing her temple, and she rests her forehead on mine since she's higher up than me.

"You were so brave, Pumpkin. I'm proud of you," I tell her.

"I couldn't have done it without you, though, Mae. I was so scared after both our moms stopped moving. I didn't know what they were going to do with me."

Tears prick my eyes again, and I pull back before leaning my side into Liam's chest.

"How about we get you ladies out of here and back to the clubhouse for some medical attention. Doc came down and brought a whole bunch of stuff that I think will help both of you," Liam says as he carefully wraps an arm around my waist.

Mention of medical stuff has me remembering where Bruce and his minions grabbed me. "Wait! How's Dad?"

Liam chuckles and then taps his shirt button and points to the earpiece. "Wave and say hello."

Frowning, I look down at his button. *"Dad?"*

"Fuck, Baby Girl, it's good to hear your voice again."

I narrow my eyes at the button and then at Liam. "He wouldn't do this from the hospital. You all busted him out, didn't you?"

At his sheepish nod, I turn my scowl back at the camera and stab at it without really hitting it.

"You pop one stitch and I will have your rear carted back in there. You understand me?"

His laughter is music to my ears, but it still sounds strained.

"Dad, get someone to help you to your room and take a pain pill. We'll be back soon. Hopefully anyway, since I don't know where we are."

He groans through the earpiece. *"I'm gonna be bossed around forever by you, aren't I?"*

"You bet your booty and I will tan your hide if need be. Now, do as I say."

"Fine. And you will be back soon. Bastard took you to your grandparents' house."

"Futtenfarter," I grumble. *"I'm handing this back to Kai now,"* I say as I shake my head and give Kai back his earpiece.

Lindsey's giggle has me turning toward her and she pokes my cheek. "You curse funny."

This has all of us chuckling, breaking some of the tension around us.

"Let's get out of here," Timber says, and he leans down to kiss me.

I couldn't agree more.

Well, wait. I hold Liam back and gesture for Drae and the others to go ahead of us. When they're out of earshot, I let him know.

"When they pick up douche canoe, have them grab the barbed flogger in the cupboard. That was used on the three of us and I think it needs to be put in rotation when teaching them some manners."

Liam grins and relays my message to the others.

The sound of the gate opening has me jostling awake.

As soon as we got back to the van, Patch and Doc had cut the back of my dress away as much as possible so that the cloth wouldn't stick to my wounds. Where it already had, they decided to wait until we got to the clubhouse. They used bolt cutters to get our shackles off and Patch had looked at my wounds on my wrists and ankles with concern.

For the ride, I straddled Liam's lap while nestling my forehead in the crook of his neck and he held my thighs to keep me in place since some of the lashes are right above my behind.

The adrenaline rush crashed not too long after we left my grandparents and that's when the pain started setting in. With Liam's help, I was able to at least calm down enough to get a little sleep, but now that I'm awake, the pain is starting to increase again.

Sitting up, I hiss and try to contain my pain-filled groan as I feel the dried blood cracking and pulling. It's not going to be fun when they wash my back to prep it for stitches, but it needs to be done.

The door opens and I scowl at seeing Dad on the other side, my pain momentarily forgotten at the sight of him. "You didn't listen to me."

He sighs, and while I know he's trying to hide his own pain, I can see it written on his face and in his eyes. "Sorry, Baby Girl. I needed to put eyes on you first. We set Doc's stuff up in your guys' room upstairs and put a cot in there for me so I can still be near you. Once you're up there, then I'll take a pain pill and pass out."

Swallowing my retort, I nod. I had wanted to see him, too, but was so worried about him and losing all that blood that I needed to make sure he was okay.

I tighten my arms around Liam's neck as he gets out of the van and Dad makes a strangled sound when he sees the extent of my wounds. I was too scared to ask, so even though I felt it, I have no idea the extent of the damage other than my wrists and ankles.

Another car pulling up behind us has me turning and I grin when I see them park so that anyone from the road wouldn't be able to see what happens next. The door opens and Reaper kicks Bruce out and onto the ground, who's got his hands cuffed behind his back and his ankles zip-tied together.

"Pumpkin, I think I promised you two hits, didn't I?" Drae says, and Lindsey nods.

"Yes. Mae said I could have two instead of just one because she didn't want to unlock the door in case he was faking it."

Drae nods to me in thanks and I return it, fighting my tears at seeing them interacting together as well as fighting the rising pain.

"Well, then, little Miss Lindsey," Reaper says as he reaches back into the van. "I've got something here that I think would do a good job of that."

He holds out a small crowbar and Drae sets Lindsey down on the ground.

"Thank you, Uncle Reaper," she says as she hugs his leg. He does one better by lifting her up and squeezing her tight before letting her go.

She takes the crowbar but then furrows her brows and pulls on Reaper's pant leg. He leans down and she whispers in his ear.

The devilish grin on his face pretty much tells me what she's going to do.

Reaper grabs two other guys who turn Bruce onto his back. Cannon steps on Bruce's chest while Reaper and Devil cut the ties around his ankles and spread Bruce's legs.

He starts blubbering and begging. Atlas takes his handkerchief, wads it up, and stuffs it in Bruce's mouth.

"Stop?" Lindsey asks and then she lands a hard hit to his crotch with the crowbar. "Did you stop when Mama and Mae's mama begged you to stop? No, you didn't. You hit them harder. Hurt them more. Did things in front of me and in the room next to me that my mama said I shouldn't have seen until I was older," she snarls as she lands another brutal hit that has Bruce passing out.

Tears stream down my face and I know we're all wearing equally shocked looks on our faces. She drops the crowbar and runs into Drae's arms, sobbing. She had told me about seeing them hurt them both, but I hadn't realized the bastards had taken our moms where she was able to hear what they were doing.

Futtenfarter...

I pray they didn't actually rape our moms in front of her. No child should have to see that. Or hear that if they raped her in the next cell.

Drae takes her inside, but the look he gives me has me shrinking back in fear.

When the door slams shut, I turn to look at Liam, stunned. "I didn't know. I thought she just meant they hurt them in front of her. Those were her words. 'Can I hit him for what he did to Mama? For hurting her?' I swear, I didn't know."

He kisses my forehead. "I know, Sunshine. We all heard you both in the stairwell. I think it's just the shock of what he just learned about that's pissing him off."

Feeling numb all over, I can only nod.

Chapter 74
Timber

Doc and Patch just finished fixing Sunshine up. The damage this time around was worse than before. *Way* worse. It took some persuasion, but Doc convinced Mae to allow him to sedate her when she couldn't keep still.

It's a little after noon and I'm tired as fuck, but I can't sleep.

Pulling out my phone, I text Punisher, seeing if he'll come up here to sit with her for a few minutes so I can step out to get some coffee and maybe some food.

Seconds later, the door cracks open and he steps in. "I didn't want to knock in case she'd just gone to sleep."

I shake my head. "She couldn't stay still with the extent of the damage. Doc ended up sedating her."

His eyebrows raise in shock. "Wow, I'm surprised she let him after last time."

I nod and scrub a hand over my face. "Same, but he said they'd have a better chance of lessening the scaring if she didn't move, so she finally gave in." Sighing, I look back over at her. "Like before, don't rest your hand on top of hers. I'm just gonna grab a cup of coffee and I'll be back up."

"Can you grab me one, too?" Smoke asks from the cot.

"Yeah. Unless you need help getting up right now?"

He waves me off. "I need to take a pill before I attempt that. This shit didn't used to keep me down like this before."

"That's cause you're old, old man," Punisher teases him.

The fact that Smoke just flips him off is telling enough for both of us. Fucker's hurting big time.

"I'll get you a water and a coffee, just please don't do anything that will wake her up. Doc and Patch only just got done maybe fifteen minutes ago."

Smoke glances at his watch and then up at her on the bed.

"Fuck..." he hisses.

Yeah, it's been a long a fucking night, not to mention they didn't get started on Mae's back until around 7:30 this morning.

Closing the door behind me, I head downstairs, surprised to see Lindsey and Drae up. He looks up and then looks down, his face riddled with guilt.

Good.

Fucker messed with my woman's head with his shit.

Lindsey hops down out of her chair and I scoop her up as she comes running over to me. "Is Mae awake yet?"

I shake my head. "No, Honey. Doc and Patch just got done working on her back, wrists, and ankles not too long ago. He had to sedate her because of the damage, so she'll be sleeping for a while longer yet."

Drae stands and when she reaches for him, I pass her over.

Her face falls at my words. "Oh. Well, when she's feeling better, can I see her? I want to sing to her like she did for me this morning."

Drae gives a strangled noise and I cock an eyebrow at him. I won't glare at him in front of her or chew him out, but it will be happening.

"Pumpkin, how about you finish your lunch? I'm just going to talk to Timber for a moment."

She freezes in his arms and tightens her fists on his shirt. "I'll still be able to see you, though, right?"

Drae leans forward, kissing her forehead. "Absolutely. We're going to head into the kitchen for a bit of privacy, but you'll be able to see me through the pass-through."

"Is this about the mean look you gave Mae this morning?"

Drae freezes this time and I bite my cheek to keep from smirking as I see his cheeks and ears turn a little pink.

"Yes, Pumpkin, it is. I need to apologize. I'd just learned what all you'd witnessed and I thought she knew without saying something first."

Lindsey ducks her head. "I didn't mean to get her in trouble. I told her I saw them hurting our mama's."

Drae clears his throat. "Yes, and I know after our talk with Patch that none of that happened to you and that you didn't see any of that. I misunderstood part of what you said this morning. That's why I want to apologize. I'll talk to Mae once she's awake, but for right now, I need to talk to Timber. Okay?"

I narrow my eyes at him. He said *see*. He didn't mention anything about *hearing* it.

Drea gives me a slight nod when he looks over at me, and I bite my tongue hard to keep from cursing up a storm.

Mother-fucking assholes.

"Okay, Daddy."

He gives her a kiss on the cheek and sits her back down in her chair.

I turn on my heel, going into the kitchen and head straight for the coffeepot. "I can't be long because I have to get water up to Smoke so he can take his pills," I tell him as I fill a mug for both of us.

I take a quick peek in the fridge, but nothing's ready-made. I'll have to see if someone can whip something up for us later since I need to get upstairs to Sunshine and so Smoke can take his meds.

Drae sighs. "I really am sorry, Timber. I misunderstood part of what Lindsey said and thought Mae knew something she didn't tell me. Still, I shouldn't have acted like I had."

I level him a hard glare. "She really didn't know. Before she fell asleep, she said Lindsey had told her what they'd done to both of their moms in front of her. But I also realize you said 'see' earlier. She heard them raping them, didn't she?"

He nods and once again, I curb my need to curse. The fuckers will get their punishment soon enough.

Tucking a water bottle and straw into my back pocket, I grip both mugs of coffee.

Looking at Drae as he stares out the pass-through at Lindsey, I stop when I'm standing next to him, pitching my voice low.

"Mae said that when we decide to deal with our problems, she told me to make sure you got your own in, too. I want a few good licks in on Bruce for what he did to Mae. Though, just so you know, the damage on Mae's wrists and ankles is from her trying to break her chains free. Not from what Bruce did to her. We'll find out who hurt Jane the most, and you can take care of it if you want."

His head whips to face me, his face filled with shock. "Seriously?"

"Yeah, I mean it. Unless you already know who hurt Jane, Lillian, and of course Lindsey, the most."

His face hardens and he fists his hands at his sides. "Lindsey said Preston was the main one that hurt Jane, so I want him. I know you all want to beat on him for what he's done to Mae over the years, but if I could have him, I would appreciate it. As for Lillian, it was Bruce, X, and a few other guys with the same snake tattoo as X's."

"Lindsey?"

Drae frowns as he crosses his arms over his chest, looking out the window at Lindsey. "She was hit a few times, but mainly got starved, so I don't know who to punish for that."

"Okay. I'll see to it that you get yours and will let you know when it's okay to come up and see Mae. Now, I better get up there before the fool tries to move without taking his meds first."

I turn and head upstairs, gently knocking with my boot since my hands are full. Punisher opens the door and I pause when I see Mae shifting on the bed and whimpering.

"I think she's having nightmares. She's not responding to my voice, but maybe she will to you," he says.

Nodding, I set the coffee mugs down and look over at Smoke. "Let's get you situated quick."

Opening the water, I put the straw in and hand it to him before going over to his meds on the dresser. Grabbing his pill, I hold it out and he shifts slightly before putting it in his mouth and swallowing it.

"Do you want us to get you upright now, or wait for them to kick in?"

"Now. You took your sweet ass time and now I have to take a piss since Doc put the IV back in and hasn't taken it back out yet."

"Sorry. Drae caught me and we talked about shit." He raises his eyebrows in question, but I shake my head. "Vertical first, so you can take a piss. Good thing Levi got you sweats to wear last night cause I sure as fuck am not gonna hold your dick for you."

That earns me a strained chuckle out of him, but I'm fucking serious.

Punisher steps over onto the other side of the cot. Between the two of us, we manage to get Smoke up without too much swearing. We're steadying him when Mae's whimpers get worse.

"Fuck," I hiss, my chest tightening when I see her forehead creasing and her face scrunching up as her body jerks slightly.

"Go sit by her. I'll walk next to him with the IV pole," Punisher says as he tilts his head toward Mae.

"Thanks, man."

I snag my coffee and carefully crawl into bed after a couple of quick gulps so that I won't spill when I move. "Hey, Sunshine. It's okay. You're safe. You're at the clubhouse in our bed. It's okay," I say, my voice quiet as I run my hand along her forehead.

Immediately, she quiets down, and I breathe a sigh of relief. I hope we're able to get through this stretch with her not waking up from a nightmare and hurting herself when she jerks her body, trying to get up.

Four hours later, Mae starts to stir, and she opens her eyes, smiling when she sees me sitting next to her.

"Hey," she croaks.

I pull over the cooler chest that Doc brought up a little while ago. Grabbing a baggie of ice chips, I hold it up. "Ice chip?"

The way she is right now, I'm not going to be able to let her drink from a straw since she isn't near the edge of the bed.

She nods and I open the bag, grabbing one and slipping it into her mouth. A moment later, she reopens her mouth and I give her a few more.

"You've got an IV in, Sunshine. Do you need to use the bathroom?"

"God, yes, please. I feel like I'm going to burst."

"Just a second."

I crawl out of bed after putting the ice chips back in the cooler and walk around to her side of the bed. I move the IV pole out of our way, which Punisher takes for right now. Carefully, I wiggle my hand under her hips, trying not to press on her bladder, and the other right above her chest.

"Doc has pain meds going into your IV, so that should help with what you're feeling. Okay, Sunshine. Ready?

"No, but do it anyway. Just don't be surprised if I cry out or whimper."

Carefully I lift her and Punisher helps guide her feet to the floor. Slowly I help straighten her but stop when she hisses badly.

"Stop right there for now?" I ask her, even though she's mostly hunched over still. She nods.

I help guide her to the foot of the bed and she grimaces when she sees the walker.

"I know you probably hate it, but this should help you walk a little easier than using our arms. Neither Patch nor Doc want you to be constantly raising your shoulders to use our arms to get around, so they suggested the walker to help you heal better."

"Fine, but it doesn't mean that I have to like it," she grumbles, and we steer her toward it.

Biting my lip to keep from chuckling at her continued grumbling, I walk next to her in case I need to catch her. At least in here it's carpet, but I might need to get her some of those socks with those anti-slip things on the bottoms for at home.

When she gets closer to the bathroom, I walk around in front of her and she carefully passes the walker to Punisher, knowing my bathroom's a bit tight on space. I grasp her hands and lead her inside until she's able to put her hands on the sink. I take the IV pole from Punisher and he closes the door once I have it inside.

I reach around her to lift the toilet lid and she freezes when she sees the large hat to collect urine already sitting on the toilet seat. She shuffles around and it's only when she's facing me that she cocks an eyebrow in question.

"Patch wants to double check something, so he asked me to get a urine sample when you woke up. He figured this would be easier than holding the tiny cup you usually have to hold," I say, nodding to said cup on the counter.

She narrows her eyes at me but doesn't say anything else as I help her lower her panties and pants before gently lowering onto the seat. She releases a long breath when she finally rests all her weight on the seat. Her cheeks tinge pink and I turn around. She huffs but doesn't say anything.

A few moments later, she finishes up and I turn back around.

"What aren't you telling me, Liam?" she asks.

Clearing my throat, I ask her a question of my own instead. "Baby, have you had your period while you've been here?"

She freezes and when she slightly shakes her head no, I grin.

"Last night, I was helping Smoke get dressed to leave the hospital. He teased me about having to do the action soon when we have kids, since we're always fucking like rabbits. That got me remembering about when you thought your period would arrive. Patch asked me if you've had it since being her. I told them no. So, the other test he wants us to take is a home pregnancy test. He figured we'd want to know sooner than the bloodwork will show us."

Her hands hesitantly go to her stomach and tears well in her eyes. "He drugged me, Liam. I don't know what was in it. What if, whatever it was, hurt the baby if I really am pregnant?"

"Based on what you said, both Patch and Doc think it was a sedative again, but they did take your bloodwork in to see if they could find anything out about that as well."

"Holy shit," she whispers, then shakes herself.

I hold my hands out and she eyes them skeptically. "Baby, I've had my hands inside your body before. I'm not worried about a little pee on them."

Her cheeks tinge pink, but she places her hands in mine. I help get her started, but for the most part, she rises on her own.

When her hands are back on the counter, she nods. "Okay. Under the sink is a box of pregnancy tests. Open it and pull out the instructions," she says as she slowly bends at the knees and moves to pick up the urine hat.

"I can get that–"

She gives me a look, and I shut my mouth as I reach under the sink to get the box I'd found earlier but keep an eye on her as well.

Carefully, she pours the contents into the cup and washes her hands. Patting them dry, she clears her throat.

"What do the instructions say?"

"For the cup, dip the stick into it for ten seconds, making sure to keep the tip pointed downward for the duration of the testing. Replace the cap and lay flat for three minutes and the words 'pregnant' or 'not pregnant' will appear."

"Okay. Get a timer ready for ten seconds," she tells me, her hands shaking slightly as she opens the test.

Chapter 75

Mae

My hands shake as I place the test down on the counter. "Three minutes now."

Liam starts the timer and I turn, feeling exhaustion pulling at me again. Opening the door, my cheeks flame at seeing Kai right there.

"Well?" he asks, and my cheeks flame hotter.

"Does everyone know?" I ask as I give Timber a side-eyed look. He blushes slightly and ducks his head. Great. Just great.

"Levi and the club members do. You can thank your dad for that one, Lil' Bit. Though to be fair, it was probably more the pain meds. He came in last night after we got him back here, and the guys started giving him shit for being here. He said this was his daughter and grandbaby we're talking about. That he was going to be a part of the planning and be on the camera side of things. Not to mention, the front team ended up needing his help since the original entrance we wanted to use had been sealed tight."

"Sorry, Baby Girl," Dad replies from his spot in a comfy looking chair as he tries to hide a wince as he shifts, but I don't know if the wince is from his pain or about what he said last night.

Sighing, I decide to let it go. "Well, in three minutes, we'll find out if you're a liar or not."

Kai pushes the walker closer to me and I gingerly take my time crossing the room to our bed.

"I'm surprised my arms and legs didn't fall asleep earlier."

"Patch told us to make sure to move you periodically to help with that."

I lower myself back onto the bed and release a deep breath before giving him a small smile, grateful that they did that. "I'm glad they did, because this would have been hard if they had been numb. Or I might have freaked out because I couldn't move."

Liam's phone beeps, interrupting what Kai was going to say. Liam walks back into the bathroom, and I bite my lip as I wait for him to step out, anxious to see what the results say.

He appears in the doorway, but his face doesn't give anything away. Crossing the room, he kneels before me and cups my cheeks before kissing me. After a few moments, he leans down and kisses my belly. My eyes widen at the gesture and Kai whoops in excitement.

"We're having a baby?" I ask, my voice barely above a whisper.

"We're having a baby," he replies as he kisses me again. "You ready to break out of the room, get some food, and tell everyone the good news?"

I nod, more than ready, and my stomach takes the opportunity to make itself known. "Sorry. Other than the couple of snacks at the hospital last night, I haven't had anything to eat."

"Well, let's go get that rectified."

Liam's hands scoot under my butt, and I wrap my arms around his neck. He lifts me effortlessly and, in a few minutes, is carrying me down the stairs while Kai follows with my IV pole.

He sits me down at a table and I frown, wanting to get my own food, but the look he gives me has me snapping my mouth shut.

"Sunshine, you just woke up. I want to make sure you can get grub since it's after 4 pm, and then you need to head back up to rest."

Sighing, I nod, and he goes into the kitchen.

A combination of 'MaeMae' and 'Auntie MaeMae' ring out and I smile at seeing Lindsey, Jordan, and Sadie running toward me.

Kai steps in front of me, crouching down.

"Remember kiddos, no touching Mae's back and be careful around her wrists and ankles, right?"

"We remember, Uncle Punisher," they all say in unison.

He steps aside and they latch onto my legs and arm.

"I'm so glad you're awake," Lindsey says, with tears in her eyes.

I detach my arm from her grasp and wrap it around her shoulder, pulling her into my side. "Aww, I'm sorry if I worried you, Pumpkin. Patch and Doc were working on me a long time, and I needed to sleep off the sedation."

I lean down to kiss her forehead, but at my wince, Kai picks her up, setting her gently on my lap. Moments later, Drae follows Dad down the stairs with his IV pole. We sure are a pair.

Lindsey giggles and kisses my cheek before I kiss her forehead again.

The others want Kai to do the same for them, so I kiss Sadie's forehead, and then Jordan's.

Jordan turns in my lap and cocks his head to the side. "Is it true, Auntie MaeMae? Are you pregnant? I heard that Uncle Smoke thinks you are."

I look up at movement nearby and my gaze locks with Liam's as he brings me a plate of food and a water. He winks at me and I blush. Looking back down at Jordan, I smile.

"Dad was right. I'm pregnant."

Cheers go up from everyone and Jordan hugs my arm tight.

"I want another hug!" Sadie and Lindsey both cry and Liam and Kai both pick up one of them, letting them take turns hugging me again.

"Alright now, kiddos. I need to eat. We can hang out after I'm done, okay?"

All three of them cheer.

Ten minutes later, I've eaten all I can, and push my plate forward. Liam takes the cue and finishes my food as I sip a small cup of coffee.

Patch comes over and he sits down with me. A beat later, Doc sits down next to him.

"How are you feeling?" Patch asks me.

"Still tired, but I'm hoping that will be better after another night of sleep. It's really hard to sit or stand completely upright, but I'm guessing that's because the stitches are so fresh?" I ask them in question.

"It's natural for your stitches to pull a little as you move, but if it doesn't improve in a couple days, let us know," Doc tells me.

"If you haven't already figured out, your back is pretty much wrapped. The only parts that aren't are from your under arms and up, and those are covered with gauze and then taped down. You aren't going to be able to wear a bra for a week or so. Same rules you had last time apply now. No baths and keep your showers fairly quick. Pat dry the stitches and when they are dry, they can be wrapped again," Patch says.

"Thank you both for taking care of me again. Is it possible to get the IV out now?"

They both chuckle and Patch removes my IV. Doc passes me a bottle that Liam puts in his cut. "Take the next pill in six hours, otherwise follow the directions on the bottle."

I perk up when I see Thor and Phoenix coming out of Thor's office.

"Oh! That's right! I wanted to talk to both of you, Thor, Phoenix, Devil, and Reaper."

Doc turns and whistles before calling all four over. Liam comes back at that point after depositing our empty dishes in the kitchen. I can tell he wants to touch me, so I slowly get up. He quickly takes a seat and carefully pulls me back down on his lap.

Suddenly, my nerves get the best of me, and I'm not sure how to outright ask them about my idea.

"Just spit it out, Sunshine. It's okay."

Nodding, I take a deep breath. "After Bruce whipped me last night, I was remembering the first time Doc patched me up and was thinking about what all would be needed to patch me up this time around since I knew it was worse.

"I... I was wondering if it would be okay if I provided the funds for more supplies to be able to help anyone else in the future if they're hurt. That way, we wouldn't have to go to the hospital unless it was absolutely necessary. I know Doc's room is pretty set up, though I was going to suggest a bed you could incline. For here, I wasn't sure if there was a room set aside for something similar?"

The guys all share a look, and I worry I've overstepped.

Thor leans forward. "Are you sure, Mae? That's not a cheap endeavor."

"I'm sure. I'd rather we are able to do things here versus going to a hospital where a bunch of questions are involved. Not to mention police usually are, too. I really don't want heat coming down on the club because other people are stupid.

"Plus, you know exactly how much I inherited, and that's not counting the shares, what I'll get for selling my grandparents' house and cars, as well as the income from renting the cabins. I'll have a steady income that I can put toward this. I just want to make sure we're prepared when something like this happens again." I don't say 'if' because I know things will continue to come at us. Especially with this crazy group, cult, or whatever the heck they are called, in the mix now.

Slowly, Thor nods. "Okay. Patch and Doc, get some lists around for what you need and Mae can approve them."

"I can probably get them through my supplier guy and have them sent this way. Most of my stuff came from when I closed my clinic, but I kept my license active for the club. I wanted to splurge for the better bed years ago, but didn't have the means to get it, so I got the next best thing," Doc says.

"We should probably look into finding someone who'd be willing to be a doctor for us here," Patch says as he rubs his chin thoughtfully. "I can only do so much with my nursing degree, and no offense Doc, but being a doctor isn't what I want to do."

Doc sits back, stroking his beard. "I wonder if my niece would be willing? She's got a few years left in medical school and wants to go into private practice rather than a hospital. If she is interested, I could always come this way when needed in the meantime, so long as Patch can keep the person stable until I get here. If not, then we'd have to go to the ER."

Thor shares a look with Reaper and the others, and they all nod.

"I have a sneaky suspicion that things are only going to get messier in the future with these Oasis fuckers. Okay, Mae. We'll take you up on your offer," Thor says.

"What if we opened a clinic here in town?" Phoenix asks. "I mean, I know it's expensive, but if we're going to possibly have the doc on call for us, maybe the club could go in on it? That way, it's not just Mae shouldering the costs?"

"That will need to go up for vote and we should price things out first before we talk about opening a clinic outright. Also, we should still scout around for one or two other possible candidates so that your niece isn't the only doctor on call if we end up going the clinic route," Thor says as he knocks on the table. "For now, let's just focus on the supplies we'd need to patch someone up here. I know we'll need more here than Doc will, but maybe we can mirror Doc's setup with the exception of getting both of us new beds."

"It was really difficult to drink the soup last time since I couldn't really sit up well yet. I definitely want to get you guys the inclining beds," I insist.

"Alright. Now, how are you still feeling, Mae? Are you up for telling us what happened last night?" Thor asks me.

I nod. "I'm getting a little tired again, but yes, I'm still awake enough to be able to tell all of you."

"Thank you," he says, and then stands. "Church. Drae, you're coming, too," he bellows.

Looking up at Liam, I give him a small smile. "Can you carry me into Church?"

"My pleasure, Sunshine."

I grip his shoulder with one hand, and he stands. Kai grabs my coffee and we follow the others into Church.

"Wait," I say, looking around for Susie and waving her over. "When I'm done, how about a movie marathon up in our room? I'll probably need to rest some more, but the kids can pile around with a bunch of pillows and maybe we can even do popcorn?"

She smiles up at me, stepping forward to give me a half hug. "Sounds like a plan. I'll wrangle the kids for now. I know they'll be excited to cuddle you for a bit."

Liam carries me into Church and sits down in his chair.

I try not to squirm under everyone's gazes after retelling everything that happened since I woke up in my cell.

Drae clears his throat. "I'm sorry about that look after we got back here earlier this morning. I misunderstood some of what Lindsey said and thought you knew something you hadn't told me yet."

I shake my head. "She said they only hurt both our moms. She never mentioned anything else to me. I will admit, before she said that, I was worried since she said our moms were laying on beds in her cell. I wouldn't put it past those bastards to sink that low."

He winces. "She didn't see it, but she did hear it. She said that they would take Jane and Lillian into the room you were in, and from what she told me, she heard them raping them as well as beating them. At the cabins, they also held Jane and Lillian in the room next to where Lindsey was and the doors were left open on purpose so she'd know what to expect when she came of age."

Rage fills me, but I take deep breaths so that I don't explode. "Did Timber tell you what I said, Drae?"

He swallows thickly and nods.

"What?" Thor asks as he looks between the two of us.

"I asked him if he knew who had hurt Jane the most, Mom the most, and Lindsey the most. Whoever hurt and did the damage that killed Jane, I voted for Drae being the one to end them. Even if it's the same person who killed Mom. He deserves that vengeance more than I do." A look I can't decipher crosses Thor's face, but it's just as quickly gone. I hope I didn't overstep.

"Lindsey said Preston was the main one that hurt Jane, so I want him. I know you all want hits in for what he's done to Mae over the years, but if I could have him, I would appreciate it. As for Lillian, it was Bruce, X, and a few other guys with the same snake tattoo as X. But it was mostly Bruce and X. Judging by their descriptions, I think we have the snake guys," Drae tells me.

"What about Lindsey?" I ask, and he shakes his head.

"She mainly got starved, so I don't know who to punish for that. They all hit her a few times, but those were after the first escape attempt and when Jane or Lillian wouldn't 'behave'."

"I know you guys will want to talk about how to handle things, and since I'm not taking part, you probably want me to leave, but I have two questions before I step out. One, when will the funerals be for Jane and Mom? The second one is if it's okay that I see the pictures of the people who you brought back? I'm curious if I can identify any of them for you." I swallow thickly as I blink back tears. I hate that my mom and Jane died at their hands.

Thor nods slowly. "That we can do. For the funerals, we plan to have them tomorrow morning. An old buddy of ours is preparing them and he's trusted so we can control what the cops need for their records. As for the pictures, Smoke, can you pull them up?"

Dad pulls up the pictures and my eyes widen when I see who's all involved.

"Dad, can I have your stylus and laptop?"

He passes them to me, a question in his eyes, but he doesn't ask it.

Taking a deep breath, I start writing names by the ones I know, even if they already know them.

Bruce Martin, the man who was introduced to me as Michael Sawyer.

Preston Cole.

Christian Brown.

Derick Lede.

The other three, I don't know.

Passing the laptop back to him, I sigh. "Christian Brown is X's second-in-command from what I know. I've only met him once. Same with Derick Lede, but I think he was just a lackey. X isn't in this group. I have no idea where Phillip is if he wasn't with this group, but maybe he's with X?"

They all freeze and Dad circles one of the guys I had a question mark on. "This isn't X?"

I shake my head. "No, the neck tattoo is wrong. Also, I had no idea that voodoo tattoo was a group thing, but the lines around it are different. When I saw it before in the pictures I was texted, it was X. He has smooth, wavy, wispy lines around the voodoo doll. This guy has jagged tribal markings around it, almost like lightning bolts.

"X's neck tattoo is of a snake that winds up his torso and back with the head of the snake baring his fangs a little below and behind his right ear. This guy's snake head has its mouth closed with the tongue sticking out. I don't know who it is, but it must be some sort of underling of X's if his tattoos are so similar."

The guys all curse and I look to Dad. "Did anyone go back and check out the homestead? Is he there maybe?"

Dad tilts his head toward Bones and I turn toward him.

"I went out and flew a drone around. I only saw the men that we knew were there and they were acting like business as usual. Maybe we should plant some cameras around to see if we can capture anything? If X is hiding there, then he's somewhere where I can't see. We didn't go after them because we didn't want to tip our hand that we were onto them," Bones tells us and I groan.

Thor looks around the table and picks up his hammer. "Alright. I think it's time to make our guests sing," he says as he bangs it down on the table.

"Let me get Sunshine upstairs and I'll be down in a few," Timber tells Thor and I shift in his lap again so he can pick me up better.

Chapter 76

Timber

AFTER GETTING MAE SETTLED upstairs, I hurry down to the sticks. Susie and Nikki are getting a bunch of pillows to help prop Mae up and for the kids to use while they watch movies and eat popcorn. Lindsey latched onto Mae like a lifeline and is curled up in front of her right now. Sadie and Jordan are right there by her, too. Elvira went up there with them as well to help watch the kids and to help with anything Mae might need.

Earlier today, Drae asked if I could build him a house with a mother-in-law suite for Elvira. Thor approved it even though Drae's still a Prospect, so tomorrow, we'll pick out a spot and start working on the plans. In the meantime, I offered that they could stay with us if they wanted, since the clubhouse isn't a good place for kids right now. Depending on the house plan he chooses, and how weather holds up, it might not take us too long if I put our excess crews on it.

Punching in the code to the door that leads to the sticks, I make sure the door locks behind me and when I turn around, I can't help but smirk darkly at seeing our guests strung up.

A few months ago, when we were *entertaining* the fuckers who had kidnapped and tortured Levi and Reaper, Levi had made mention of having rails that we could move our guests around on.

Well, I had taken her suggestions to heart, and we installed them along with more hooks to restrain people with if necessary.

Right now, all eight of these assholes are strung up facing each other. All but Bruce and Gigi have their mouths taped shut since we want to start with those two first.

All of our guests' hands are connected to the rails in the ceiling and their toes barely touch the floor. Their feet are spread out shoulder width apart and chained to the floor. The most any of them will be able to move is an inch or two. We know, because we strung up each of the Prospects and had them move around as much as possible to test it.

Thor nods to me, letting me know the floor is mine. Smoke and I had already talked and since he's still healing from the gunshot wounds, I'll be leading things today.

Giving Thor a chin lift in return, I walk up to Bruce, gripping his face hard to cause the same bruises he'd put on Mae.

"Not such a tough guy now, are you? Got your ass kicked by my wife and we're going to finish the job."

"And my daughter," Drae says with a smirk that I return.

Bruce spits at me, but I sidestep it in time and backhand him for the action.

"Fuck you, biker scum. Mae will be mine soon enough, and I'll laugh as she cries over your dead body."

"You think so?" I ask, stroking my chin as I circle him.

"I know so. If you thought I was bad, wait until X gets his hands on all the women here. He'll be here soon. You can count on it. None of the women will be granted mercy for sticking your nose into our operation."

I quickly glance at Thor and then Smoke. Well, that confirms what Mae said earlier—that X isn't among these fuckers.

Walking over to the tool cabinet, I take the flogger that Bruce had used on Mae. "Strip them," I call out and several of my brothers walk out, cutting off their clothing and stuffing it in a bag.

Standing in front of Bruce, I'm about to say something when he looks over at Smoke, smirking.

"By the way, how's my daughter doing? My lovely Sadie?"

My gaze cuts to Smoke's in time to see his body tensing and then his gaze narrowing as he slowly looks Bruce over.

After a few moments, he walks over to him, putting on gloves, before taking the knife from Levi.

"She's not your daughter. She's Nikki's. You were nothing but a sperm donor who kidnapped my sister and raped her."

Fuck... I knew Nikki had been raped years ago, but Smoke couldn't find the guy after rescuing her. Fucker disappeared into the wind, and he's been looking for him ever since. I never knew it was Bruce that had done that to her. In fact, I'm not sure anyone knew it was Bruce.

"Yes, she was my first in the operation. I learned many things by making her scream. Things that we implemented over the years," he says with a smirk.

Smoke returns the smirk, reaches down and yanks on Bruce's balls before slicing them clean off.

"Something I've been wanting to do for years," Smoke spits out, and his smirk grows at hearing Bruce cry out in pain.

Needing to move this along before he bleeds out, I nod to Dragon and he gets out the torch, cauterizing Bruce's wounds.

He howls in pain even more, and I notice a few of our guests are looking a little green as they watch on.

Gigi's screams mix in with Bruce's as Sasha cuts into her. The volume and shrillness of Gigi's screams make me want to wince, but I don't.

Walking up to Gigi, I make a show of the flogger and her eyes track its movements for a few moments before snapping up to mine.

"So, you worked with ol' Brucey-boy there to try and trick Mae into thinking I'd annulled our marriage and proposed to you?"

She huffs. "That whore isn't good enough for you. She's scarred and ugly now. She'll probably never be able to conceive with what Bruce had me inject in her," she says as she laughs maniacally and the ice in my veins runs cold.

I hand the flogger to Sasha and fish out my phone, sending her a couple of pictures.

"Sasha, can you please inflict the same wounds on this bitch that Mae received? Both times."

Sasha grins darkly, as she steps in front of Gigi. "With pleasure," she purrs, and I relish in watching the color drain from Gigi's face.

Turning away from her, I walk over to Bruce, but Doc's already at his side, injecting him with something. Patch motions for me to go over to him and hands me a note.

> *It's a barbiturate drug that is loosely called the truth serum, but it isn't a fool-proof truth serum. Nothing is. There may be some deceit, but let's hope there's more truth than lies.*

Looking up at him, I nod. I'd rather try this and see what we get. He slips out of the room and I hope like fuck he's going to take another blood sample from Mae.

Turning around, I'm surprised to see Levi in front of Bruce, holding a wicked looking knife in her hands.

Her face is a cold mask, but I can tell she's beyond pissed off with what Gigi has shared. I'm surprised that Dragon and Thor are letting her step in since she was hurt yesterday, but honestly, I think Levi will be able to get answers out of Bruce better than Dragon, Thor, or me right now.

"What was it that you had Gigi inject Mae with?"

"N-nothing," he grits out through clenched teeth and beads of sweat start forming on his forehead.

"Are you sure?"

He presses his lips in a fine line and in response, Levi starts carving into him.

A few minutes later, his torso is covered with long, jagged, and deep cuts. He's sweating profusely now, but I notice his eyes are tracking her every move. Before he stared over her head. My guess is that the barbiturate drug is kicking in.

"How did you kidnap all those women before? What did you use?"

"G-grief. I hurt their l-loved ones. Then when they were too f-frazzled to pay attention, I gave them our s-special sedative to get them where I w-wanted them."

"And what was in the special sedative?" Levi asks him, her voice almost a purr, as she ignores the muffled cries of the others.

"I d-don't know. A-Andrew was the one that g-got it for us."

"Then what did you do?"

"C-chain them down and start to b-break them to fit the m-mold that was ordered."

"How do you know who wants what in a bride or pet?"

"C-carter handled that. He had a w-website. Listed all their r-requirements and wants."

"I've got the website. Next topic," an automated voice states in our earpieces and I'm guessing it came from Smoke.

Fuck, I didn't know we could do that with these devices. The corner of Levi's lips flick up slightly before she schools her expression.

"Tell me again what you use to get the women to go with you?"

He hesitates and, for a moment, I think he won't talk.

"It's a s-sedative. Some are mixed with a d-drug to prevent p-pregnancies. One t-temporary, and the other, p-permanent."

"Which one did you give your future bride?" she asks and I force my body not to react to her words.

He grins down at her wickedly, licking his lips as he leers at her. It's almost as if thinking about Mae and looking at Levi makes some of his pain go away.

"Neither. I gave my b-bride a sedative and a very special c-concoction of ours that would make her extra fertile. Every dose was extra strength. I gave her a dose when we n-nabbed her and before she w-woke up, she received another dose. However, neither d-dose was her first dose. She got her first dose when Carter k-kidnapped her. Mae was going to be my breeding machine."

Gigi shrieks in outrage over her cries of pain. "That's n-not what you told me, you asshole! You s-said she would n-never be able to c-conceive. That the drug would s-shrivel up her uterus like a r-raisin."

Bruce chuckles darkly as his gaze slides over to her. "No, that's what *you* received, Gigi. You might be tight, but you've also been used r-repeatedly by almost every one of these fucking bikers. I wasn't going to chance you already being p-pregnant and further sullying the well. Also, your mouth isn't worth it. You thought you were t-top bitch, but you were just a plaything for all the boys to sample."

Yeah, feeling like he's one of the top men in this room again is making him more confident. It's on the tip of my tongue to tell him Mae's pregnant with my baby, but I don't want to stilt the flow of conversation Levi's got going. We need all the information we can get on those Oasis bastards.

Gigi shrieks again, but it morphs into a cry of pain as Sasha whips her again. "Who's the mastermind behind Oasis?"

"X is. His o-operation stretches all across the states and into Mexico."

Levi pauses for a second in her cutting before continuing. "Who was the one who killed Jane?"

"Preston k-killed both Jane and Lillian. He and I mostly took Lillian. I could only stomach it if I took her from b-behind so I wouldn't have to see her brown r-roots. She looked like Mae that way.

"Preston used them both to w-within an inch of their lives as he beat them. He liked to force feed them date rape drugs, so they'd be more out of it w-when he took them. The others took them both, but Preston did the most."

I've heard enough.

Grabbing the tape, I tape Bruce's mouth shut and start to move onto the others. Along the way, I also tape Gigi's mouth shut because I'm sick and fucking tired of her ranting about how Bruce had lied to her. She's almost as dumb as Luscious was to think that these assholes would ever make her one of the first wives as they call them in Oasis.

Moving to the X-look-alike, I take note of his tattoos. Like Mae had said, the snake head on his neck has its mouth closed with the tongue sticking out.

Ripping the tape off his mouth, he grins a bloody grin at me.

"You aren't getting anything out of me, so you might as well kill me. I'm not as easy to break as that fuckwad over there."

Grinning darkly, I pat his cheek. "We'll see about that, Junior."

His eyes widen a fraction before he schools his looks. Hmmm... Maybe this is a family relation?

Six hours later, all eight of them are a bloody mess. All of us got in on beating the shit out of them when they stopped talking and didn't give us any new information. We knew they had more to give us and that's when things started getting messier.

However, Bruce and Preston got the worst of all of our torturing methods. Their wounds are deeper than the others and I took great pleasure in making them cry when it was my turn.

As for how they've been tortured, their fingers were all broken, nails torn off on their hands and their toes, kneecaps smashed, teeth pulled out and piercings pulled out. Ribs are cracked if not broken and each man, and I use that term very loosely, received multiple hits to the dick with a metal bar. Well, those that still have dicks. Both Preston and Bruce had their balls and dicks unceremoniously and painfully chopped off.

For Gigi, she got the same treatments as the men, though her hits with the metal bar were to her breasts and pussy. She also had the 'de-glorification treatment' as the girls call it, where Sasha chopped off all her hair as another strike to her vanity.

And on top of all of that, everyone's been cut and whipped to hell, though only Bruce and Preston got the acetylene torch treatment. Multiple burns are littered across both of their bodies.

As promised, after we all got a few licks in on Preston, Drae's the one that's handled most of his torture. And by the looks of it, the fucker is barely hanging onto life. In all honesty, Bruce is in the same boat. We all took great pleasure in hurting the sick fuckers.

Shaking my head, I rip off my soiled gloves and toss them down into the biohazardous bag. My gaze goes to Sasha who has just finished hooking up the metal bra to Gigi, which all of the fuckers are eyeing warily. As well they should. They'll be seeing something similar very soon themselves.

Levi had more of her 'toys' specially ordered and I was relieved when she said she now had enough for ten people. Something that is coming in especially handy right now since we have eight fuckers on our hands to deal with.

Pulling on a new pair of gloves, the guys follow suit and I start pulling out the boxes for her toys. Levi had asked if I could make or find little boxes so that we could keep all the paired devices together and not get them mixed up. There are numbers engraved into the boxes and I also made sure to engrave the corresponding number onto the remotes and devices. Since the cubbies will be getting messy as fuck, I went with thick, plastic ones that we can easily bleach and sanitize.

Setting a box down in front of each of the assholes, they all start blubbering when they see what's inside the boxes and they all start talking over each other. Ignoring them, we put the spiky cock rings on each of the men. We had left enough of the shafts of Bruce's and Preston's dicks to make sure they would still be able to receive this treatment. When we're done, I walk up and down the line, making sure to make eye contact with each one of them.

"Assholes and bitch, you've already been graced with one of our Queen's favorite toys for those who help in the hurting and raping of innocents. I'm sure by now you can feel just how *uncomfortable* things can get. But the icing on the cake is this baby," I say as I bend down and pick up one of the dildos.

I make a show of it, and holding it by the handle, I give the signal and Smoke makes the spikes protrude. All of them start squirming again.

"Now, you're all going to behave as we fit you with these because if you don't do exactly as we say, these little babies will be getting *very* acquainted with your insides. And if you *still* don't listen, you'll get an extra treatment."

I give Smoke another signal and the spiky dildo starts vibrating. After a few moments, he cuts the vibrating and retracts the spikes.

Without another word, I step behind Bruce as the others take their spots. Levi moves the chains so that our guests' arms are pulled toward the center of the room a foot or so.

Forcing Bruce's shoulders down, I start to ram the metal dildo into his ass. He pleads for me to stop repeatedly, but that just makes me push harder.

When it's in, I yank him upright as much as I can, and hiss in his ear. "All those women begged for you to stop raping them. To stop hurting them. But did you listen? No. Why the fuck would we stop when you beg?"

Out of the corner of my eye, I see Drae talking lowly into Preston's ear and I grin darkly as I watch Preston's face go white as a sheet before Drae thrusts the dildo into his ass.

Releasing Bruce, I step back and strip off my gloves, putting them in the bag as I wait for the others to be done.

Levi retracts the chains until they all are upright again and then raises them off the ground as much as their ankle chains will allow. The full weight of their bodies are now supported only by their wrists.

Stepping forward, I get ready to ask our round of questions again.

"Who is X? What's his real name?"

"K-Kristoff D-Davenport," the X-look alike stutters.

I step in front of him. "Where's he hiding? Where does he live?

"H-he has a house down in Louisiana. A p-plantation near the s-swamps. That's where h-he usually goes when he n-needs to escape or after p-procuring a new p-pet for himself."

"What's your name? Your real name. Don't lie to me, boy."

"Leon D-davenport. His s-son."

Fuck, I was right.

"Where's Phillip?"

"L-Last I saw, he was l-leaving with X a few hours b-before we l-left to grab M-Mae from the hospital."

"Why was X, Bruce, Phillip, and Preston targeting my wife?"

"They w-wanted her m-money. Not just w-what she'd inherited, but also w-what's under her dead n-name from the m-money laundering."

Fuck, I'd forgotten about that.

Turning slightly, I catch Smoke's eye and he gives me a chin lift. Spinning on my heel, I walk forward until I'm in front of Preston.

"What was your motive in targeting Lillian and Mae beside money?"

He grimaces slightly and then sneers at me. "I w-wanted her to p-pay. She r-ruined my life, so I w-wanted to r-ruin hers."

"How did she ruin your life?"

"She d-divorced me and t-took away my c-cover. The d-dealership b-blew up in smoke and t-then my house was r-ripped apart, d-destroyed to the p-point where it was almost c-caving in on itself. My c-cars were blown up. She r-ruined my life, so I m-made her p-pay." At the end of his rant, he's so worked up spittle's flying from his mouth.

Smoke chuckles darkly as he walks over by me. "None of that was her, you fucking idiot. I was the one that did that."

"She w-went to you b-before she left me. I know she d-did because I saw it."

"Then you didn't pay much attention then, because she told me you tricked her. That it was you who had cheated, not me. When she told me she wanted me back, I told her to get the fuck out of here and never talk to me again. That's it."

Preston stares at him in confusion, shaking my head. "N-No, she t-told you to d-do it all."

"What makes you think she did?" I ask.

"I had v-video proof sent to m-me that she did."

Tommy chuckles darkly from a few spots over. "All t-these years, you thought you w-were one of the top dogs, P-Preston, but you never r-realized you were l-led around by a c-carrot. That v-video was f-fake. You were led to b-believe she asked him to do everything, just like X wanted you to b-believe."

I walk over to him. "And why was that?" I'm surprised when the answer doesn't come from Tommy.

"D-Distraction. So that X could b-bleed more money from P-Preston without him r-realizing it so he c-could help fund his own g-goals. Also, if the h-heat got too hot with L-Lillian and M-Mae, X could easily dump him and escape himself. Just l-like he seems to have d-done," Leon says, smirking at Preston. "That f-fucker was so stupid and easy to p-play. It was like t-taking candy from a b-baby."

I frown at the part where he says X fled when we got too close. But then, that begs the question, why did X sacrifice his own son? Unless the bastard doesn't give two shits about him. Or he didn't think we'd take protecting our women to the extremes that we do.

Preston starts writhing in his chains, and both Smoke and I step back. I don't think we're going to get any other information out of these assholes.

Spinning back around on my heel, I stalk back up to Bruce. "Just so you know, Brucey-ol'-boy, not only will Mae remain my wife, but she's also pregnant with my baby."

His face reddens as he starts spewing curses at me.

Stepping up to the table by Smoke, I take the remote from him so that I can get in on a bit of this pain for Bruce, but ultimately, Smoke will be the one to end him. I may be Mae's husband, but Smoke is Mae's dad. It's his right.

"But I thought you said, if we told you what we knew, that we wouldn't be getting this treatment?" Leon asks in confusion and this time I smirk darkly at him.

"Now it's all of you that are the dumb ones. Our last order? The one you will obey? Is to die, you fucking rapists," I sneer as I flip the switch for both the cock ring and the dildo on Bruce. The others flip their switches as well, and the room fills with their screams of pain.

I up the intensity for a few moments and then hand the remote off to Smoke.

Ten minutes later, the only sounds are the dripping of blood onto the plastic tarps as all eight of them hang limp in their restraints.

Patch, who came back at some point, and Doc go around, checking pulses.

"They're all gone," Patch says and I pin him with a look.

"Did you get my text?"

He gives me a chin lift. "Allison's running the tests. We'll find out what was in them. I texted Mae to ask when her last period was, and she said it ended a week or so before she came here. Call and make an appointment with an OB-GYN to get in as soon as you can so you can get an ultrasound. Since Nikki works there, we might be able to get it arranged on the down low without Mae having to ask for the ultrasound over the phone. She needs to get one regardless of how far along she is. The less people that know about this drug, the better."

Thor's hand lands on my shoulder. "You and Smoke, go get cleaned up and see Mae. We'll take care of the cleanup."

Nodding, I head out toward the showers but stop when Smoke calls out to me.

"Guys cleared my boots and there's nothing else on me since I couldn't really partake. I'm gonna head up and get a coffee. I won't go up till you're ready in case they've all conked out. Give me your boots and I'll have them scrub them quick, so you don't have to do it."

I toe them off and hand them to him, giving him a chin lift in thanks. "I shouldn't be long."

Heading into the showers, I dump my clothes into a bag that Dragon will burn later. Once the water's warm, I hop in and wash myself quickly but thoroughly to make sure I don't miss anything and shut the water off.

By the time I'm out, my boots are already sitting on the floor. They're still slightly wet, but I know they're clean.

Dressing in my spare clothes, I make a note to bring more down here soon before heading upstairs to check on my Sunshine.

Chapter 77

Mae

IT's BEEN A WEEK since most of my demons were laid to rest. All of the guys are still on the lookout for Kristoff and Phillip, but time will tell when they pop back up on their radar.

Today it's Halloween and about an hour or so ago, we all got back from our Halloween drive. We dropped off all the donated clothing, coats, and boots at a few locations around town. They'll be handed out to families in need in the next couple of days.

In a few hours, we'll head into town to the park where we'll set up for Halloween. The club always has a couple of booths for trick-or-treating. There will also be candy, apple cider, and some games kids can play.

But first, it's time for my appointment.

Since a lot of people are worried about how my pregnancy is going thanks to those drugs, we have a whole crew going with us today. I'm finding that that's what comes with the territory when you have such a large chosen family in addition to my blood family. Everyone wants to support you however they can.

Timber, Dad, Sasha, Lex, Sadie, and I are in Timber's truck. Since Nikki is working today, we said we'd bring Sadie in with us. Levi, Dragon, Thor, Ethan, Drae, and Lindsey are in Thor's truck. And last but not least, Axe is driving Susie and Jordan, who recently announced that they'll be moving back to Forest Creek before the end of the year.

Obviously, not everyone will be able to watch the ultrasound, but the ladies, Dad, and Timber will. If we can all fit in the room, that is.

I've also been told that when we get back to the clubhouse, I'm to call the Junction Creek chapter. They weren't able to come out since they're getting ready for their own Halloween preparations, but I know I'll be seeing them for Thanksgiving, if not sooner.

"Ready, Sunshine?" Timber asks as he pulls up in front of Dr. Rowen's office, the doctor Levi's using.

"Nervous. Extremely nervous. Especially with what Bruce said he injected me with," I whisper and both him and Dad squeeze my hands.

"No matter what happens, you've got the club at your back," Dad tells me.

"Both clubs!" Sadie cheers from the backseat, which has all of us chuckling.

"Okay, let's see what we can find out about my jellybean," I say as I unbuckle my seatbelt.

The guys do a perimeter check, as always, and I step out of the truck. I've been able to move around easier now that about half of my stitches are either fully or mostly dissolved. The others are being rather stubborn.

Stepping up to the podium, I check in and Levi swings around me, hugging the lady behind the desk.

"Mae, this is Elaine, Dr. Rowen's wife. Elaine, this is Mae who is Timber's Old Lady and Smoke's daughter."

Elaine gets up and circles the desk, wrapping me in a hug that, thankfully, isn't too tight. Then again, I'm guessing she's used to not giving tight hugs with being around pregnant women all the time.

"Give us a few minutes and we'll have you back there to check on your little peanut."

I can't help but grin at her excitement and Levi loops her arm through mine as we go sit down.

Twenty minutes later, I've had my weight taken, which I'm glad has rebounded nicely as of late, and answered all of the doctor's questions. He was worried about my attacks when he saw my scars, but I'm guessing he knows a little about the club because of how he phrased his question. And apparently, he knows enough to not to say too much about it, either.

"Dealt with?" he asked as he cocks an eyebrow at Timber, who just smirked in return.

Dr. Rowen lowered my shirt and continued as if nothing was wrong or amiss.

Now, though, the nerves are back. Full force.

Nikki already warned me that they'd most likely do a transvaginal ultrasound, so I'm not surprised when they put a condom on the wand.

"Whoa, what's going on?" Timber asks as he steps forward.

Oops. Guess I forgot to tell Timber.

"Don't worry, big man. This is how you see the baby this early. It's completely normal," Nikki reassures him, and he takes a hesitant step back to my side.

Tears prick my eyes as I hear the rhythmic whooshing sound fill the room. Levi takes my hand and squeezes it, both of us sharing a grin.

Dr. Rowen and the technician's faces turn curious for a moment, and my stomach sinks.

The drug.

Did they lie about it?

"What's wrong?" I ask and I'm not able to keep my voice from cracking.

"Let me just adjust the wand slightly to make sure real quick," the technician says as she moves and then clicks some buttons.

Dr. Rowen straightens and grins down at me. "Seems the clubhouse is going to get busy really quickly."

The technician prints off a bunch of pictures and I stare at them, not able to believe the news. Dr. Rowen waits until the technician leaves before speaking again.

"It looks like you are right at eight weeks. I want to see you every two weeks for a while to make sure things are progressing correctly. Nikki brought me up to speed on everything already. Elaine can set you up at the front desk with your appointments. We'll leave you to get dressed." He tips his head at us, and then a moment later, the door closes behind him.

Looking up at everyone, I grin, even though I'm in shock. "I'll tell everyone at the clubhouse. I'm sorry for the guys waiting here in the lobby, but they're going to have to wait twenty minutes. Timber, text Mama Astrid to round the crew up and we'll call in as soon as we have everyone together."

He grins and does as I ask while the others all give me a hug, whispering congratulations in my ear, and then filing out so I can get dressed.

Timber hands me my pants, but I can't seem to tear my eyes off the pictures. "I can't believe it. It's a miracle."

Kneeling, he starts sliding my jeans up my legs, and I finally put the pictures down to get dressed and then slide on my boots.

He pulls me close to his side and kisses me.

"Best believe it, Baby. Now, come on. Mama Astrid's already blowing up my phone. Let's get home so we can tell everyone."

Bouncing with happiness, I do a little twirl before heading out to the hall where everyone's sulking.

"Why won't you tell us?" Jordan whines and I can't help but grin as I hold up the pictures but make sure they can't see them.

"I promise, it'll be worth the wait. Now, the sooner we get back home, the sooner we can call the Junction Creek crew and we can tell you about the baby."

Fifteen minutes later, because yes of course the guys went a little faster than the speed limit, I'm dialing Mama Astrid on speaker phone as the Forest Creek members all surround Timber and me in the main room of the clubhouse.

"We're all here, Mae! Tell us, is the baby healthy?"

"Yes, Mama Astrid, the baby is very healthy and we heard the heartbeats." I pause, chewing on my lips to see who would notice first. I glance up at Timber and his grin widens as he wraps an arm around my shoulders.

"Heartbeats? As in plural?" Dom asks.

I nod before I realize they can't see me. *"Yes, heartbeats, Dom. Plural. All very healthy heartbeats. We're having triplets!"*

Cheers erupt all around me and from everyone on the phone.

"When are you due? How early are triplets usually born?" Axe asks and I repeat his question for those that are on the phone.

"My due date is June 10th, but he said triplets can come as early as thirty-two weeks, which would be around April 16th. So, I guess time will tell."

Timber hands my phone off to someone else and pulls me into his arms, kissing me passionately.

I moan as I sink into him and laugh when we get catcalls.

Staring down at the pictures, I can't believe it, but I'm also relieved.

I've always wanted a big family, and it looks like I'll have one.

Bonus Content

Want more?
Read on to find out more a few more details
about Levi, Thor, and Dragon's wedding as well
as when their two little bundles of joy come
into the world <3

Epilogue: Chapter 1
Levi

WEDDING DAY

I can't believe it. Today is finally here. My wedding day.

We decided to have the wedding here at the clubhouse and the reception will be in the backyard. The guys laid out some white fabric as a runner in the main room and they set up a bunch of chairs for everyone. The ladies all helped me decorate a beautiful white trellis arch with flowers that will stand behind Andre, who's going to officiate our wedding. His whole club, minus a few that have to stay behind to protect their clubhouse, are here as well as my dad and a few of our close friends of the club.

Even some of our club bunnies are here, which still boggles my mind that I've become such good friends with six of them: Ashley, Ginger, Amy, Sarah, CJ, and Roxy. Technically CJ and Roxy aren't bunnies, but they're still on the books as t hat.

However, our two new bunnies, Crystal and Gigi, are most definitely *not* invited. Something that did not go over well with them, but they'll just have to suck it up. The others are here as our friends, not as club bunnies and my men made sure all of our club brothers knew there was to be no sex with the bunnies until later tonight. Though, I don't think they would have done that anyway out of respect for us until after we left.

Outside, there are more chairs set up as well as a few tents littered around for some shade. Bouquets of white and blue roses with silver ribbon are placed as centerpieces on all the tables. Later, the firepits will be lit.

My bridesmaids and I took over one of the unused bedrooms on the main floor to get ready. I smile when Mae's and my gazes lock. I still can't believe she's alive sometimes and that she's *here*. Not only here, but she's also getting married today.

I wasn't lying when I said I'd be honored to share our anniversaries with each other. She's already a close friend of mine and has proven in more ways than one that she's perfect for Timber.

As I watch my other friends get ready, my gaze cuts to a picture of my mom Sasha set up so she'd be here. Next to her is a picture for Mae's mom, Lillian, since we have no idea where those assholes are holding her. I quickly blink to prevent the tears from escaping, and soon Sasha's next to me and is fanning my face. God, I hate these pregnancy hormones.

"Nope! If you start crying, then I'll cry, and then Kristy will kick both our asses for messing up her amazing makeup job!"

I can't help but giggle at the image of Kristy kicking our asses. She's a short little thing right at five feet tall, but she's a feisty ball of craziness. I absolutely love the woman.

"Okay, all you fabulous and gorgeous ladies! Everyone's hair and makeup is done. Let's get Levi in her dress and then you all can slip into your dresses or finish getting ready," Kristy calls out as she claps her hands and immediately pivots on her heel, walking over to my dress that's hanging over the closet door.

For my dress, I ended choosing a simple spaghetti strap white dress that hugs my body like a stretchy glove, which is good because I wasn't sure how much I'd gain with my pregnancy. I think the saleslady called it a sheath stretch ruched dress and it has a small train. It cradles my eighteen-week baby bump perfectly. In fact, my belly is close to sticking further out than my boobs, which have also gotten bigger with my pregnancy. Something that my men really love.

There's a slit up my left leg to mid-thigh. The back is mostly bare except for where the fabric sort of twists and ties a couple times at my lower back. I've paired silver strappy sandals with the dress and for after our ceremony, I have a satin shawl for when the temperature dips.

I opted to not have a veil and instead chose to wear Mom's silver comb that she wore at her wedding. It's a gorgeous comb with diamonds and pearls on it that Kristy nestled in my half-updo at the back of my head.

For my jewelry, Dad gifted me beautiful teardrop diamond drop earrings with a matching necklace. Sasha gave me a diamond bracelet with emerald and sapphire gemstones peppered throughout it that perfectly matches the wedding bands my men gave me. Ryan's silver band has sapphires and diamonds in it, while Nick's silver band has emeralds and diamonds. On my thigh is my mom's blue garter, though Nick has one that we'll switch out for the garter toss later, so I don't have to lose my mom's garter.

When my dress and shoes are on, I turn toward the mirror and once again blink repeatedly to dry my eyes.

"Girl, your men aren't going to be able to keep their hands off you! I bet they'll be hauling you off within an hour of saying 'I do'," Sasha says as she laughs.

"Me? Colt is going to be dragging you to his room the first chance he gets!"

She's wearing a one-shoulder dark blue dress that wraps snugly around her waist and almost reaches the ground. There's a high slit up her thigh that I know Colt will appreciate.

When we were talking about dresses, I told all of them that I didn't care which style of dress they chose, as long as they were dark blue with silver shoes. I wanted them to be comfortable and, if possible, be able to wear the dress again for some other occasion.

All of them look gorgeous and even Erin seems comfortable in her dress, which is a little surprising. More than once we've heard her saying she'd look like a beached whale stuffed into a potato sack when she wears dresses, but she doesn't. Not by a longshot.

Her chocolate brown hair is half pulled back and lays in loose waves down her back. Her dress hugs her breasts beautifully without showing them off completely. The waist has a little rouching on it and it goes down to almost the floor with a slit that goes up to her knees. She doesn't believe she's beautiful and that her size doesn't matter. I'd like to beat whoever damaged her self-esteem and put those thoughts in her head of her being overweight and ugly. That she isn't worthy of being loved.

Phoenix has been trying to get to know her better, and he's also been trying to push those same thoughts out of her head. However, she keeps insisting she's not interested in anything other than friendship with him, even though I can tell she's attracted to him.

Kristy putters around, making sure everyone's hair still looks good after getting on their dresses. A few minutes later, there's a knock on our door.

"Everyone decent?" Phoenix calls through the door.

With a quick glance around, I answer. "Yes."

He opens the door and his gaze zeros in on Erin. "You look gorgeous, Sugar."

Her cheeks tinge pink. "Thank you," she says awkwardly, her gaze bouncing around to anyone and anything but Phoenix.

The rest of the groomsmen, my dad, and Jordan enter the room. Timber makes a beeline for Mae, and I can't help but smile at seeing them so in love with each other.

Jordan immediately goes over to Sadie and they start to giggle as they look at each other's biker boots, something they both insisted on wearing. I obviously didn't object because they both look freaking adorable in their boots.

"You sure you want to marry those two crazies out there, Sweetheart? We can still run and I'll get you out the back door in an instant," my dad says as he winks at me.

Instantly the guys all start to give him shit, which has me laughing.

"You know my men would hunt me down. Besides, I've already got them trained and I don't really want to start all over again." That comment starts another round of laughter and making jokes at my men's expense.

"Alright, you hooligans—settle your asses down! Line up with your partner," Kristy hollers.

When everyone's lined up, she bends down by Jordan and Sadie, who are up first. "Are you two ready for your big entrance?"

"Yes!" Sadie cries.

"Yes, Ma'am," Jordan says excitedly. Kristy gives them each a fist bump before heading out to make the announcement about there being two weddings instead of just one today.

As she talks, I watch Mae as she tries not to tear up at Kristy's kind words.

Seconds later, a little motorcycle starts up, and Jordan revs it along with the intro to the song, *'Born to be Wild'* by Steppenwolf. I hope like hell Bones is getting this all on camera since I can't see it.

Jordan and Sadie practiced so much to be able to ride down the aisle as she carefully threw petals out of her basket, trying not to shift too much and throw off their balance. Cheers from the crowd erupt when Jordan comes out of the hallway just as the singing starts.

I take a shuddery breath as I try to stamp down the butterflies in my stomach and get a grip on my hormones.

This is it.

I'm about to marry the men of my dreams.

"I can still get you out of here, Sweetheart," Dad teases me as he winks. I can't help the chuckle that escapes, and I squeeze his arm, knowing he asked that on purpose.

"Love you, Dad. I'd kiss you, but then you'd have lip gloss on your cheek." He chuckles and shakes his head.

"Love you, too." He leans down and kisses my forehead.

After Sasha and Phoenix walk forward, Dad steps forward and stops when Kristy gives us the signal so that I'm still out of sight. The song changes to *'I Cross My Heart'* by George Strait. I knew as soon as my men asked me to marry them that this was the song I wanted to walk down the aisle to because our love is definitely unconditional.

Dad leads me down the aisle and I feel all my nerves fade away at the sight of my men. Both of them left their long black hair down and they look so sexy in their dress shirts coupled with their cuts, black jeans and boots. Fuck, I'm not sure how long I'll last myself before I'm dragging them off for sexy times.

At the end of the aisle, Dad places my hand in Ryan's. The guys had decided I'd be legally married to Ryan, but after we say our vows and he kisses me, then I'll repeat the vows with Nick and then we'll share our kiss.

Twisting slightly, I pass my bouquet off to Sasha and then take Ryan's other hand. He winks at me and the heat in his eyes has me looking forward to later.

Epilogue: Chapter 2
Dragon

Wedding Day

Ryan and I anxiously wait for the wedding to start so we can finally lay eyes on Spitfire. We haven't been able to see her all day. Thank fuck she didn't make us wear a suit while we waited. I would not have been able to stand being in it for long.

Looking around, my chest swells at seeing everyone piled into the clubhouse for our wedding. Besides our club, everyone from Reaper's club except a small skeleton crew are here as well as a handful of our friends from town and some of our employees.

My mind goes to Mae, who is waiting in the hallway with Timber for their entrance.

Things are still a little rocky between her and her dad. I know Smoke is pissed as fuck at himself for what he said and did shortly after she arrived. He's been trying to mend that bridge, but Mae's understandably hesitant. Lillian wrecked Smoke in one of the worst ways, so I know he has trouble trusting women because of her. I just hope he can fully put it aside so that he doesn't lose Mae because of it.

In all honesty, I need to fucking apologize to Mae too, for all my bullshit that I added onto that dumpster fire. With them just getting in yesterday, I haven't had a chance to talk to her privately to apologize yet.

Thinking about what those assholes did to her while she was in Junction Creek has my anger rising, but I stomp it down. We had hoped to weed out where Preston, Phillip, Bruce, and that X fucker were while Mae was in Junction Creek, but so far, no luck.

Unfortunately, Mae not being in Forest Creek didn't deter the assholes and they somehow tracked her to Junction Creek. It's because of X and that fucker Carter that Mae was hurt.

However, I'm hella proud of her for not hiding the scars on her chest. Apparently, several of them will be on display, even though they aren't fully healed yet. Levi told me she chose a spaghetti strap dress that goes to the floor and shows a fair amount of cleavage. I hope some of the scars will fade eventually, but time will tell.

The sound of Jordan's little bike starting up has my attention going to the hallway and I can't help the grin that spreads across my face. Axe keeps a bike here for Jordan whenever he comes to visit, and we love seeing him tear around on it.

Future biker in the making.

When Mae saw pictures of Jordan riding it and giving Sadie a ride, she surprised us all by suggesting that we should have them ride the bike down the aisle instead of walking. Levi latched onto the idea right away and the kids immediately got to practicing. They've been at it all week. We're also doing things a little differently since normally the flower girl and ring bearer would walk before the bride, but we're starting with them because we love the idea of them riding the bike so much.

As '*Born to be Wild*' picks up, Jordan comes out of the hallway with the biggest grin on his face. Sadie has one arm around his waist and the other plucks little petals out of a small basket strapped in front of Jordan. Sadie's grin matches Jordan's as she tosses petals on the ground, switches arms around Jordan's waist, and then drops some more petals on the other side.

When Jordan gets to the end of the aisle, he stops and holds his hand out for Sadie to hold on to. She grabs it and I swear her grin gets even bigger.

Fuck, if these two stay close, I can definitely see them ending up together when they're older.

When Sadie's off to the side at her mark, Jordan pulls off to the side by us, shuts it off, and parks his bike. He unstraps the pillow with our rings from the bike and walks over by us. I give him a fist bump when he walks by me and Ryan does the same.

I fidget with the cuffs of my sleeves as Susie and Tripp make their entrance. When it comes time for them to part, I'm surprised when Tripp kisses Susie on the cheek. And honestly, I don't think I'm the only one surprised based on the look Susie quickly masked.

Next, it's Erin and Ethan, and then Ryder pulls the same thing with Allison, only it's not a kiss on the cheek, it's a kiss on her lips.

Mae and Timber follow them, and when he kisses her, a lot of awws fill the room from those that know theirs is the wedding that's after ours.

Nikki and Smoke are next down the aisle followed by Roxy and Alexei; and finally Sasha and Phoenix.

Next to me, I notice Phoenix inhale sharply as he looks over at Erin. I raise an eyebrow at him when he doesn't fully contain his growl, and I know he's thinking about Erin being on someone else's arm today.

"Easy there, Tiger. There won't be any blood drawn at our wedding, and if there is, I'm sure it'll be at Spitfire's blade."

He huffs and shakes his head. "I know Ethan or Punisher would never make a move on her since they know how I feel, but still, I'd rather she be on my arm."

The music changes and my response to Phoenix dies on my lips as my beautiful Spitfire walks out on Roy's arm.

Holy shit.

She's not beautiful, she's fucking gorgeous. A goddess.

I eagerly drink in the sight of her in her dress that seems to mold to her curves that have gotten even sexier with her pregnancy. My fingers itch to hold her, to touch her. When I see a flash of metal on her thigh, right where the slit starts on her dress, I damn near groan.

Fuck, her being armed and in that dress is going to slay me. I don't think I'll be able to wait long before needing to sink inside of her.

Roy slips her hand in Ryan's. She hands off her flowers to Sasha, turns back toward us and blows us each a small kiss, which I return. Fuck, I wish I could touch her right now, but it was my idea that she be legally married to Ryan, so I have to suck it up for now.

I barely pay attention to her and Ryan exchanging their vows, instead I continue to drink in the sight of her even more.

"Let me officially introduce, Mr. and Mrs. Ryan Gilbert," he calls out and everyone cheers as they kiss.

After a few moments, he pulls back and steps aside so I can step forward.

She sniffles slightly as I take her hands and I notice she's blinking rapidly to keep her tears from falling.

"Love you, Spitfire," I whisper to her and she says it in returns. I'm in a daze as I say my vows to her as I re-slide our ring onto her finger. We'd already had our wedding bands soldered to our mom's rings last week.

When she slides my ring on, I don't hesitate. I pull her flush to me and take her mouth in a searing kiss that has everyone cheering as cat calls ring out.

"I didn't say you could kiss her yet, asshole," Reaper grumbles as he tosses his hands in the air, which has more laughter ringing out.

Cocking an eyebrow at him, I smirk. "Since when do I need your permission to kiss my woman?"

He glares at me, but I see the corners of his lips twitching.

"Every fucking time," he mumbles and then looks out at the crowd. "Well, since this asshole jumped the gun, let me officially introduce, Mr., Mr., and Mrs. Ryan and Nick Gilbert."

Epilogue: Chapter 3
Thor

I swear, she's never going to let us touch her again. Levi's panting as she grips both Nick's and my hands when another contraction rips through her. I'm not sure if that's the right way to say it, but that's how it looks.

When it passes, she leans back against her pillow. I reach around for the ice chips and spoon a few into a cup. As soon as she sees it, she opens eagerly for them. Nick places a cool washcloth that Sasha wrung out for him back on her forehead as I give her the ice chips.

"Alright, Levi. I know it's hard, but on the next contraction, I need you to *not* push. The doctor's coming."

"You said that five minutes ago," I growl, but the woman isn't fazed by my tone in the least. She's about to say something when the door opens and in walks Dr. Rowen.

"I apologize for the wait. There are a lot of babies being born at the same time tonight, it seems," he says as he immediately starts scrubbing his hands and arms.

"She's fully dilated, Dr. Rowen, and the contractions are between two and three minutes apart."

"Alright Levi. On the next contraction, I want you to bear down and push. Let's meet your beautiful babies," Dr. Rowen tells her as he steps up to Wildcat's bed and in between her open legs. I'm pissed another man is seeing my woman like this, but I know Dr. Rowen is happily married and would never do anything to Wildcat.

Levi weakly waves and nods at him. She's been in labor for five hours already and looks exhausted.

Seconds later, Levi curses and crushes my hand.

"Fuck," I groan, and her steely gaze meets mine.

"Oh, I'm sorry for hurting you, Hun. How about you try to squeeze out two little watermelons and see how much pain you'd be in," she grits out before crying out in pain from the contraction.

When she slumps back against the pillow, I get her more ice chips as I try to discreetly shake out my hand. I notice Nick trying to do the same. As I put the cup to her mouth with more ice chips, a tear slides down her cheek and I brush it away.

"That was an excellent push, Levi. I can see the head so on this next one, it's going to hurt a bit more, but we're very close to meeting your first baby."

Refilling the cup, I give her some more ice chips and I know what she's going to say before her mouth even opens.

"I'm sorry, Ryan," she whispers, and I give her plump lips a quick kiss.

"Nothing to apologize for, Wildcat. You're right, this isn't something our bodies are equipped to do. You've grown our babies and are bringing them into the world. Something I'm very excited about."

She gives me a weak smile before her face screws up in pain and she shouts.

"That's it, Levi. Give me a big push."

A few moments later, I can see a smile on his face, but I don't budge. I made the mistake of looking earlier and I'm not going to do it again.

"The head is out. On your next push, you're going to meet baby A."

That's the jolt Wildcat needed, and a few moments later, the cry of a baby rings out.

"I need one of the dads to come over and cut the cord."

Nick eagerly steps forward and cuts the umbilical cord before a nurse whisks our baby girl away. Thank God Nikki warned us everything they'd do once the babies were born, otherwise I'd probably be chewing the nurse out right now. Both Nick and Nikki follow the nurse and help her clean up our baby. Sasha steps forward and takes Nick's place. I capture Wildcat's lips and when I pull back, both of us wearing huge smiles.

"You got this, Levi. In a few more minutes, you'll be meeting your other baby. Stay strong, girl," Sasha says as she grips Wildcat's hand.

Almost immediately, Levi cries out in pain again.

A few minutes later, another baby's cry rings out and I'm cutting the second umbilical cord before following the nurse to clean up the baby right as Nick steps toward Wildcat with our firstborn.

As I stare down at one of my baby girls, I choke back a sob as it fully sinks in that I'm a dad. When the nurse places our second daughter in my arms, I quickly walk back over to Wildcat and lay her down on Wildcat's chest.

"As much as I want you both in here, you both better go tell our motley bunch our good news. Nikki and Sasha will help me if I need it," Wildcat tells us with a wink.

Nick clasps my shoulder and grins at me. "Let's go give them the good news."

"Be back in a bit, Wildcat."

Fuck, I bet my grin is just as big as his is. We kiss both our babies and then Wildcat before making our way to the waiting room.

If I weren't so excited, I would have laughed at seeing the looks both our club and Reaper's club are drawing from the other families packed into the waiting room. Mae's the first to see us and her excited squeal draws everyone else's attention to us. She struggles to get up as she's four months pregnant herself with triplets.

"Are they here? What are their names? Everyone's healthy?"

Timber laughs as he pulls a darn near vibrating Mae into his arms. "Give him time to answer, Sunshine."

I look at Nick and we both grin.

"They're here, our twin girls. Adrianna Emily and Olivia Marie!"

Cheers erupt and Roy quickly brings us both in for a hug, his eyes brimming with tears.

"Thank you," he whispers as he pulls away and wipes his eyes.

I give him a chin lift. We knew right away that we wanted our daughters to have our mother's names as their middle names—Emily for Levi and our mom, Marie.

Author's Note

THANK YOU EVERYONE FOR reading *Steel Archangel's MC: Timber (SAFC2)!*

I hope you enjoyed Timber and Mae's story! Next up in the series is Patch's story as he finds and later saves his Siren <3

Reviews are very important for authors, and especially to new authors! Thank you to everyone that leaves a review, even if it is only a line or two or just leaving stars! Keep reading for info on how to contact me as well as other books by me. I'd love to hear from you!

About the Author

R. KNIGHT LOVES READING and writing romance novels, whether it be contemporary, MC, paranormal, reverse harem or menage. If you like strong women surrounded by the men who adore and worship them, then follow me to hear about current and upcoming books that will satisfy your craving!

When R. Knight isn't reading or writing, she's spending time with her amazing husband, two kiddos, two cats and a dog where they live in Eastern Wisconsin. The usual shenanigans involve watching movies, camping, playing board games and/or video games.

https://linktr.ee/Author_R_Knight